KINGDOMS FALL

THE COMPLETE TRILOGY

BY EDWARD PARR

2025

Edwardian Press

ISBN 979-8-9996446-0-2

Library of Congress Control Number 2025915972

Dedication

In memory of the soldiers and civilians
who fought and died during the Great War

In Flanders Fields by John McCrae

In Flanders fields the poppies blow
Between the crosses, row on row,
That mark our place; and in the sky
The larks, still bravely singing, fly
Scarce heard amid the guns below.

We are the Dead. Short days ago
We lived, felt dawn, saw sunset glow,
Loved and were loved, and now we lie,

In Flanders fields.
Take up our quarrel with the foe:
To you from failing hands we throw
The torch; be yours to hold it high.
If ye break faith with us who die
We shall not sleep, though poppies grow
In Flanders fields.

CONTENTS

Epigraph

Part I: The Laxenburg Message

Part II: The Korniloff Affair

Part III: The Wieringen Proposal

Epilogue

Map – Post-War Europe

Afterword

Nations are in uproar, kingdoms fall;
he lifts his voice, the earth melts.
Come and see what the Lord has done, the
desolations he has brought on the earth.
He makes wars cease to the ends of the earth.
He breaks the bow and shatters the spear;
he burns the shields with fire.

- Psalms 46:6-9

Part I:
THE LAXENBURG MESSAGE

Prologue

Gavrilo Princip sat at a small wooden table at the front window of Schiller's corner café looking out towards the Miljacka River as it flowed slowly through Sarajevo. The young man, sweating in his oversized trench coat, was exhausted. His eyes were bloodshot and circled by dark rings; his right hand shook slightly as he tapped a cigarette on the rim of his teacup and dropped ashes onto the spent leaves. His other hand was deep in the pocket of his dark overcoat, gently holding a small explosive device in his thin fingers. The fuse he kept separately in his right pocket. Outside the window, the late June morning was cool and cloudy, and finely dressed ladies and gentlemen chatted gaily as they strolled back from Town Hall and across the Ladina Bridge.

Princip pursed his lips together tightly: His plan had failed. No, that was not correct. It was Cabrinovich who had failed. Cabrinovich had thrown his bomb but it had glanced off the sedan's bonnet and detonated in the street, and then Cabrinovich had been captured alive. The fool had leapt into the river where it was now only two feet deep! The Sarajevo gendarmes would now be on high alert, and each of the conspirators was certain to be arrested at any moment. Princip knew it wasn't safe to return to their house. He doubted he could make his way back to Serbia on his own. But he had nowhere else to go.

Princip had been born in a poor region of Bosnia in 1894. His parents could not care for their large family, so he was sent to live with an older brother in Zagreb. At that time, the entire region was controlled and occupied by the Austro-Hungarian Empire. Emperor Franz Joseph had seized many of the southern Slav provinces in the Balkans after they had slipped from the grasp of the Ottoman Turks, and he was gradually incorporating them into his Pan-Germanic empire. Like many southern Slavs, Princip hoped that one day those provinces would be united with Serbia into an independent Slavic nation, a "Greater Serbia" aligned with their Slav brothers to the north and in Russia. But in 1908, when Franz Joseph formally annexed the whole of Bosnia into the Austro-Hungarian Empire, the hopes of the Slavs were dashed. During the Annexation Crisis, Serbia and its ally Russia came to the very brink of war with Austria-Hungary; Princip's brother left to join the Serbian army and Gavrilo was sent to school in Sarajevo. Although Russia ultimately failed the Slavs, Princip took part in many of the political demonstrations against Emperor Franz Joseph during the following years, until in 1912 he was arrested and expelled from school.

Princip next journeyed to Belgrade where he fell in with members of the Young Bosnia movement. In the parks and cafés in Serbia, he met other Slavs, including Cabrinovich, who were also striving for Bosnian independence. Princip tried to join the Serbian guerilla fighters living in the mountains, the notorious *Chetniks*, but the Serbian officer in charge flatly rejected him: Princip was too small and frail, he was told.

He returned to his friends in Belgrade desperate to prove his worth and to serve the cause of Greater Serbia. The Balkan Wars in 1912 and 1913 shifted the borders yet again, and the grip of Emperor Franz Joseph upon the southern Slav provinces became even tighter. He was clearly intent on annexing Serbia next and incorporating its territory into his sprawling empire. The Emperor was as dismissive as ever of the demands of the southern Slavs for independence, even though most Austrians, it seemed, despised the Slavs that already inhabited their territory. And there was no doubt that Franz Joseph's government was undermining the elected government of Serbia and its great Premier, Nikola Pashitch. The Austrian Emperor's fear of his neighbor Russia was the only thing that stayed his hand.

Princip and his comrades were determined to show the Emperor that the Slavs would not be ruled by an Austrian dictator. The Hapsburg autocrat had to see that it would be impossible to control the Slavs or dictate to the Serbian government. And how better to oppose an ailing 83-year-old Emperor, they thought, than to assassinate his heir-apparent – the merciless, war-mongering Archduke who despised the Slavs and their ambitions for self-rule? Who better to kill than the Crown Prince, and to do so at the very moment of his grand entrance onto the stage of Europe, a man whose sole qualification to become "All Highest" was centuries of aristocratic hegemony? Princip and his co-conspirators were determined to tear down the Hapsburg dynasty just as others had recently attacked the thrones of Italy and Greece when King Umberto and King George were assassinated. Only by disrupting the stability of the Hapsburg succession would the southern Slavs be able to secure their independence from the grip of the Emperor, he believed

Princip and his associates had then traveled back to Sarajevo in secret, carrying weapons they had obtained in Serbia, and with one desperate goal in mind: Assassination. But now their plan had come to ruin because of that fool Cabrinovich, and Princip was stuck on a path to arrest and speedy execution.

From the window of the noisy café, Princip saw the crowds outside abruptly halt and turn to face the Appel Quay Boulevard. He heard the grand *Gräf & Stift* automobiles as they rumbled up the street from Town Hall. Princip stood and hurried towards the door of the café. The Archduke's motorcade was speeding past, and Princip watched, frustrated and disgusted, a man who could do nothing as the Archduke was rushed from the city. The motorcade sped around the corner. The automobiles were already halfway down the block by the time

Princip reached the street. Then the motorcade stopped. It stopped! The automobiles were backing up, reversing slowly to where Princip was standing in the bustling crowd. His hand, shaking with sudden nervousness, tightly grasped the explosive device in his coat pocket. But there were too many people and no time to act. He could not possibly take out his bomb and attach the fuse in the midst of the crowd. The *Gräf & Stift* automobile bearing the Archduke quickly approached the corner.

Princip's right hand desperately lunged into his coat and gripped the handle of the pistol wedged into his belt. He pushed violently forward through the crowd, pulled the gun from his coat and immediately fired once, twice. The crowd screamed. People were running. Women were crying out. Princip was tackled to the ground and the gendarmes leapt on top of him, forcing the air from his lungs, kicking his sides, grasping his hands, and pushing his face down into the street.

Archduke Franz Ferdinand, heir to the thrones of Austria and Hungary, and his wife Sophie were assassinated by Gavrilo Princip in Sarajevo on June 28, 1914. Austrian investigators believed that the conspirators had been assisted by the *Black Hand*, a secret society of Serbian military officers. Mindful of the threat from Russia to the east, Emperor Franz Joseph first secured the support of Kaiser Wilhelm II, the Emperor of Germany and King of Prussia, before he demanded unconditional access to Serbia to investigate, capture and punish the perpetrators of the assassination as well as the members of all other anti-Austro-Hungarian political groups. Serbia flatly denied that it had been involved in the assassination and rejected the Emperor's demands which clearly infringed on Serbia's sovereignty.

Emperor Franz Joseph declared war on Serbia on July 28, 1914. Tsar Nicholas II immediately ordered the Russian armies to mobilize. In light of Kaiser Wilhelm's support for Austria-Hungary and the threat it posed on Russia's western border, the Russian Tsar also requested that his ally France mobilize its armies in the belief that the double threat against the Kaiser would keep Germany from commencing any military action. But the Kaiser had a long-prepared battle plan ready for just such a threat. He promptly declared war on France, and German troops immediately stormed through Belgium towards Paris expecting to quickly crush their ancient Gaul enemies before turning all their might on the ponderous Russian bear to the east. Great Britain, which had long promised to defend neutral Belgium and was allied with France and Russia, immediately declared war on Germany.

Before the end of August, war had spread throughout Europe. The Tsar's troops suffered a terrible defeat at the town of Tannenberg near its extensive border with Germany and retreated back into Russian territory. In early September, at the Marne River just to the east of Paris, the French army put an end to Germany's plan to quickly conquer France. The armies of France and Britain raced against the army of Germany to outflank one another, resulting in a line of trenches and defensive fortifications that spread over two hundred miles from Switzerland to the North Sea. In October, the Ottoman Turkish Empire, hoping to recover some of the territory it had previously lost in the Balkans, joined Germany and Austria-Hungary in attacking the Russian army. In November, Great Britain and France declared war on Turkey.

In the next four years, the war would spread around the globe. Battles would be fought by these great empires on the oceans and in their colonies in Asia and Africa and all along the Western and Eastern Fronts, six great nations who would become deadlocked in battle: Great Britain, whose navy had dominated the oceans since the Battle of Trafalgar and whose colonies spanned from Australia and New Zealand to India, Africa, the Caribbean and Canada; France, with vast colonies in Africa and Asia, and where legends of Napoleon's victories and vast empire still inspired its citizen-soldiers; Austria-Hungary, a nation of ethnic rivalries held together by an ancient and autocratic Hapsburg dynasty; Turkey, the last remnant of the Ottoman Empire that had dominated Asia Minor, the Near East and North Africa for centuries; Russia, a vast nation rich in raw materials and men yet still at heart a feudal society dominated by the Romanov's and the wealthy; and Germany, once torn apart by Protestantism and reunited only forty-five years earlier by the House of Hohenzollern, the rebirth of the Holy Roman Empire, the Second Reich, and perhaps the most powerful industrial nation on Earth.

Sixty-five million men would take up arms before the end of the war, more than thirty-eight million soldiers and civilians would be wounded or die, and of the great kingdoms that had ruled the world for centuries, some would disappear forever.

Suvla Bay

The British troops climbed over the railing of HMS *Grampus* in threes and fours, struggling in the dark to place their feet onto the cargo nets that led down to the "beetle boats" that would take them to shore. The men were quiet, excited, and nervous. Although the night was calm and a warm breeze was blowing, Turkish artillery was shelling the shoreline and beginning to extend their range to the British troop ships and destroyers in Suvla Bay. *Grampus* and the new battleships were bombarding the Turkish-held ridges in reply. This was no light arms fire, but the roar of huge guns disgorging fire, smoke, and iron.

The hatches of the beetle boat were open, but the light armor that covered the small landing ship made it more difficult for the men to board in the dark. Several of the troops fell into the warm Mediterranean water. Inside the boat, the men were packed shoulder-to-shoulder and remained steadfastly silent in total darkness. They were new recruits, trained but unsure how they would withstand the early morning landing under fire. They stood with their rucksacks and rifles and pith helmets, and stared out through the hatches at the starry night sky as the boat began to chug towards the shoreline. Before them, a curtain of artillery fire erupted up on the ridges surrounding the bay, flashing like lightning and sending red hot shards of metal soaring into the air.

No chains or mines or other obstructions in the bay slowed their approach. Slowing down would have only made them ready targets for the Turkish artillery on the ridges above. The light armor that covered the boat provided no protection against those larger shells. Several other companies had already landed and assembled on the narrow beach, and the *tak-tak-tak-tak-tak* of machine gun fire could be heard even farther off as the first British troops reached the enemy defenses. The sounds of battle grew louder as the boat approached the shore. "Speed is the key," their commander had told them. "Move forward; clear out the enemy positions." That was the plan to encircle the Turkish troops on the Gallipoli peninsula and cut all the way across the peninsula.

The troops, "Tommys" as the enlisted men called themselves, could also hear the booming artillery battle away to the south – a diversionary action intended to draw the Turkish forces away from the main landing at Suvla Bay on the northwest corner of the peninsula. Great fires were burning to the south and lit the sky like daylight, but the troops could not know if it was the Turkish-held trenches aflame or the British battleships or both. They tried not to see the flashes of light which erupted in their peripheral vision or hear the sharp whistling noises streaking through the sky in their own direction. Shell bursts, muffled under water, erupted around their landing ships like geysers, and the roar of the British artillery was deafening.

One very young, fair-haired man on the beetle boat wore the three diamond insignia of the rank of Captain on his perfectly tailored khaki uniform. Nervously, he rubbed the grip on his Webley service revolver and stole glances at the new Lieutenant who was pressed uncomfortably against his side.

"Did I understand correctly, Lieutenant, you were recently at Ypres, in Belgium?" he asked.

"Yes, that's right, Sir," said the dark and scowling Lieutenant, turning to the Captain beside him.

"I am awfully grateful to have an experienced man in the company," The Captain noticed that the Lieutenant, even though he was an officer, carried a rifle and field knife as well as a revolver, and he suddenly felt rather inadequate with his revolver alone – and his whistle. He had a whistle. Good Lord, what was he thinking? The Captain leaned in conspiratorially to the Lieutenant and added quietly: "Say, it wouldn't be improper for me to come to you for advice from time to time, would it?"

"If you like, Sir."

"I don't suppose old Abdul will be as difficult to manage as the Huns, eh?"

"He's done alright so far, hasn't he?"

Even the Captain had to agree that the Ottoman Turkish army had done a very competent job of stopping the three month old Allied offensive on the peninsula. After the Turks had closed the Dardanelles in October of 1914, Britain and France had begun naval operations to reopen the straights. Those efforts had ended in disaster in March after several British ships were sunk by mines and artillery fire. The British Admiralty, with British and French troops and the ANZACs, the Australian and New Zealand Army Corps, had then launched the offensive on the Gallipoli peninsula in late April. The offensive had not gone as expected. There had been no appreciable progress across the peninsula, especially when one considered that the Admiralty's master plan had the troops marching up the peninsula and into Constantinople by now. Just before they had left Egypt for Suvla Bay, the Captain and the other troops on the beetle boats had read the newspaper reports which had finally revealed how the campaign at Gallipoli had come to a dead standstill. The situation was eerily reminiscent of the entrenched stalemate on the Western Front in France and Belgium, and the number of allied casualties was a terrible embarrassment. The First Lord of the Admiralty, Winston Churchill, had already been removed from his post. But the new troops had joked that their Commander-in-Chief only needed a few really ruthless bastards to cut into the Turks.

The troops in the beetle boats that day had not received their orders from Sir Ian Hamilton, the Commander-in-Chief of the Mediterranean Expeditionary

Force. Instead, they were commanded by Lieutenant General Sir Frederick Stopford, an elderly commander with very little battle experience. Stopford had been selected by the legendary Earl Kitchener specifically for the Suvla Bay offensive. The surprise landing on the Turkish northern flank at Gallipoli was intended to bring the attack to the rear of the Turkish forces, thus encircling the enemy and leaving an undefended path to Constantinople before the Allied troops. Everyone knew that Constantinople was the key. Capturing the Ottoman capital would knock Turkey out of the war, clear the route through the Dardanelles to re-supply the flagging Russian Empire, and open a new front line against the Austro-Hungarian and German Empires that would draw troops away from the Eastern and Western Fronts. If they succeeded, the war would surely be over in the first months of 1916!

The Captain and the men in the beetle boat had trained for the landing ahead, but they were all new enlistments fresh from six months' training at Brackenber Moor near Kendal and four weeks more at Alexandria in Egypt. Still, many of them had combat experience of a different kind. Some of the men had come from cities in Ireland and some from the poorest streets of Manchester, and others were trade union men from the factories and were used to knocking heads. Every one of them was eager to kill the "Turks" on the ridges before them.

The company sergeants were experienced men, of a sort: Most had fought in the Boer Wars many years earlier. Conversely, their acting commanding officer, Captain James Wilkins, had only just celebrated his nineteenth birthday. He was the youngest British officer serving in the Mediterranean. Of course, it was obvious to the Tommys that Captain Wilkins must have achieved his rank through connections rather than merit since he was the youngest son of the Earl of Bartlett and a recent graduate of Eton (albeit the top student and a King's Scholar there). At least, they thought, Wilkins stood head and shoulders above his immediate subordinate, Lieutenant Charles Keeling. Keeling was nearly always tight and far too chummy, and it didn't make him a good officer. And finally there was the other Lieutenant, the new fellow called Gresham. True, he was the one man in the company who had previously fought in the front lines: He had been with the Lancashire Fusiliers in the trenches in France and had fought at Ypres; he'd been at Gravenstafel Ridge when the Germans had first used poison gas on the lines, and he'd even seen some action at the Suez Canal. But Gresham was surly and quiet, the other officers clearly didn't like him, and no one knew what to expect from him once the attack began.

Captain Wilkins was again shoved rudely against Lieutenant Gresham on the beetle boat, adding to his anxiety and dread over the landing now just seconds ahead. "Of course, I was disappointed when Major Davenport fell ill," Wilkins said, looking out the corner of his eye to see if Gresham was listening. "He should be here to command the company, not me. . . . I only just received our orders this evening and barely had a moment to glance at the maps, you see."

Gresham could not think of a gentlemanly response to these revelations, so he kept his mouth shut and focused his eyes on the shoreline. Gresham had served under a number of incompetent and inexperienced officers and knew how dangerous they could be. Gresham was also a young man, only twenty-two years old; he was shorter and stockier than most of the men in the company, and he generally avoided conversation. He knew the other officers distrusted him and criticized him constantly: Gresham's straggly coal black hair was too long, his chin was never freshly shaved, his mustache was grossly untrimmed and filthy; and, worst of all, he was the bastard son of a very wealthy Manchester industrialist. Wilkins beside him was by contrast the quintessential British officer: Fair-haired, perfectly clean cut, well-educated, and the cream of British nobility. It was surprising that Wilkins wasn't yet in charge of the whole damn regiment, Gresham thought.

The beetle boat chugged noisily on. Captain Wilkins nervously recited his orders in his head: Take the company north up the Kiretch Tepe ridge, capture the guns, proceed east along the ridge and then swing south to rendezvous with companies from the Ninth at the cemetery behind the village there. But now he couldn't remember the name of the village – if he had only spent more time with the maps! Colonel Banks had told him it was simply a matter of "overwhelming" the Turkish soldiers; the British Ninth and Tenth Divisions would easily encircle the enemy troops on the peninsula, and then it would be clear marching all the way to Constantinople. Wilkins prayed it would all be as easy as Colonel Banks had made it sound.

Gresham stood by a hatch and looked at the beach ahead; he felt slightly nauseous, but that was only due to the thick black smoke venting from the boat's engine. He knew what to expect ahead and was focused and at ease. The shore was beginning to turn grey in the pre-dawn light. Many beetle boats had already offloaded troops at the shoreline, and some were already headed back with the first casualties. A handful of troops lay dead on the rocks and bobbed in the water. As Gresham looked, an explosive shell landed in the midst of a pack of India mules that had been brought onto the narrow beachhead. As if in slow motion, the animals flew apart – their heads, vitals, and limbs flying outward in every direction. A few men standing nearby were knocked flat by the concussion and covered with bloody gore. Gresham had seen scenes of slaughter like those awaiting them on the peninsula. At Ypres, he had spent weeks rotating in and out of the trenches, scouting in No-Man's-Land, growing slowly accustomed to the stench and gore and wet. In the trenches he learned that although it was costly to advance, it was far, far worse to stand still. To stay in one location meant a slow but certain death from snipers, random artillery, gassing, disease, exposure, and, most of all, the ruthlessness of ignorant or ambitious officers. He had become inured to the sight of corpses and bloody wounds and the sweet, rancid smell of the dead. To stop moving and lay still among the dead drained the life and purpose from a soldier. It was a sensation that Gresham knew the Generals in their bunkers in the rear would never understand.

Suddenly a shell squarely hit one of the other beetle boats nearby. The explosion, blinding flash and flying chunks of steel panicked the men in Wilkins' boat. They all tried to duck down at once – an impossibility since the boat was so crowded. Even Gresham turned his head away. The men could hear the shouting and cries from the struck boat, and a murmur to get out of their boat swept through the troops. The struck boat then demonstrated another reason why the small lightly armored landing ships were known as "beetles" – it suddenly flipped over onto its heavy steel top and instantly silenced the dozens of men aboard in the warm, dark water.

The air was now filled with shells whining overhead. There was a constant but irregular *tink, tink, tonk* as shell fragments glanced off the boat's light armor. At last Wilkins' boat hit the rocks and ground to a stop a few yards from the shore. The entire front of the boat slammed down into the water.

"Get out!" Wilkins screamed. "Get out of the boat! Forward now, men. Get out!" He blew his whistle furiously. As a mass, the men pushed forward into the shallow water. Two troops in front suddenly exploded, hit by chunks of shrapnel from an artillery shell. A third man was wounded on the shoulder and he pushed back into the troops behind him. He fell, and the rest scrambled in panic right over him and into the red-stained water. Wilkins was still shouting, trying to contain the shrill anxiety in his own voice. The troops were eager to get up to the beach and away from the boat. Two more fell in the water and another on the rocky shore as shrapnel shells burst above them. The shore was littered with chunks of metal and wounded men and pockmarked by blackened shell craters.

Wilkins quickly glanced around to identify their position. "Goddamn it, we're in entirely the wrong place! We should be at the other end of the cove," he shouted to no one in particular. "Dunham, Hart, assemble the men and march them to the north end of the bay. Gresham, you stay with me; Keeling, you bring up the rear." The Sergeants immediately got to work shouting at the Tommys to form up. Gresham could see that the heaviest of the Turkish artillery fire was now directed at the ships, and since the Turkish snipers near the shore had mostly withdrawn to defensive positions, they were relatively sheltered for the moment. The sergeants screamed at the troops from several of the beetle boats to form up and march. It was less than a mile to Suvla Point at the northern end of the cove, but the ritual of forming lines and marching, which was all the raw troops really knew how to do, was reassuringly familiar.

Above them at Suvla Point were the smoking ruins of a small Turkish outpost that had been thoroughly battered by artillery bombardment. A dozen shattered and burnt Turkish corpses lay about the hill. Wilkins led his company up the hill and past the outpost to the scrub grass and sand above the beach. He crouched behind the only available shelter – the remains of a burnt-out shepherd's hut. He caught his breath and quickly checked himself for wounds while Lieutenant Gresham sat down and casually lit a cigarette. The troops amassed before Wilkins, Keeling, Gresham, and the sergeants. In the early morning light, Wilkins saw dozens of faces looking to him for their orders, for tasks that would put their minds and bodies to work and distract them from the carnage which surrounded them. Wilkins pointed up to the left of the bay.

"Gentlemen," he shouted, shaking the nervous stutter from his voice, "beyond this hut is the plain and beyond that are the hills leading up to the ridge. We are required to cross the plain and climb that ridge today. Undoubtedly, the Turks will give us strong resistance, but we must silence their artillery, for until we do, both the transport ships and every man coming ashore will be their target!" Wilkins paused before asking "where are Stickle and Black?" He pointed at the two smallest Privates in the company, one of whom was thought to be sixteen years of age and the other perhaps just fifteen. "You two will be my runners. Hold our position here on the shore and run any messages up to me. Lieutenant Keeling, take Sergeant Major Dunham and the second and third platoons; move down one hundred yards in support of our right. The rest of you will form the main advance with me and Lieutenant Gresham. Gentlemen, I want you to listen to our Lieutenant here. I realize that many of you consider yourselves experienced men, but the Lieutenant has been to the front – he's done this before, so keep close and follow his orders. I want to see every one of you at the top of the ridge. Am I understood?"

The men did understand, and were grateful that young Wilkins did not pretend to know how to lead the men into battle. There was a brief chorus of grunting acknowledgments. Wilkins turned and offered Gresham a pathetic grimace. Gresham suddenly realized that Wilkins was asking him to lead the men up the ridge.

"Yes, right," growled Gresham unhappily. "Only don't stay too close; I don't want your guts all over my only clean uniform." As Keeling marched his men off to the right, Gresham shouted: "Platoons will form up, twenty yards apart, just below the top of this hill. When the Captain blows the whistle, we will advance. You will *not* stick together in formation. You will fan out and run as fast as your f---ing legs can carry you. If you stop moving, you will probably be shot, so you *will* keep moving. Sergeant Hart will reform the platoons when we reach adequate cover. From there, we will continue forward in the same fashion, is that clear? Alright, get up now. Sergeant, fix bayonets."

Hart turned to the men and shouted: "F-i-i-i-i-x bayonets!" At once, more than a hundred men drew their bayonets from their belts and snapped them onto their rifles. The fresh, clean bayonets glittered dimly in the early morning light.

The company scrambled into their positions across the hillside just as the sun was rising over the ridges to the east. Gresham, in the middle of the line, looked both ways to ensure that the men were ready and then signaled to Wilkins. Crouched and alert, the Captain peered over the hilltop, took a deep breath, and blew the whistle with all his might. The men erupted over the hill, charged through the loose stone and dust and scrub, and leapt over the few low barbed wire obstructions and scattered bodies. They rushed forward barely able to see where they were going through the scrub brush and stunted oak trees.

The incoming Turkish sniper fire was light and sporadic compared to what Gresham had seen in Belgium, and the Turkish artillery was busy pounding the bay. It was obvious to Gresham that the Turks had been taken by complete surprise and had not had time to adequately fortify their positions around the bay. It appeared that the massive artillery bombardment to the south had thoroughly misled the Turkish commanders who had likely rushed reinforcements and supplies to precisely the wrong place. Ahead of Gresham, another company on the plains was taking machine gun fire from the ridge above them.

Wilkins stayed right beside Gresham. At least what Wilkins lacked in experience he made up for in courage, thought Gresham; it was probably wrong to criticize a man for admitting what he didn't know, and if Wilkins didn't know what to do in battle, then he was right to ask for help. But, damn, Gresham had no desire to lead these men against those machine guns.

Behind them, Sergeant Hart was screaming at the troops to keep up. "Fan out, boys!" "Keep you bloody heads down!" "Mind you don't stick your mate with that bayonet, Jenks!" "King an' country aren't paying you to look pretty there, my young Galahads!"

Bullets whistled past as the men scrambled through the scrub. Gresham looked back and shook his head in disbelief at the men clustering in tight groups. Yes, it was natural for men to seek safety by massing with others, but Gresham had learned that men in groups were more likely to suffer the wrath of the machine gunners. "Spread out! Spread out and hurry up, damn you!" he yelled.

Wilkins enthusiastically raised his pistol high and shouted: "Charge!"

The company still had far to go, and the Turkish troops held the high ground before them. The machine guns on the ridge were still out of range, but every shell hole, tree and bush could provide cover to a Turkish sniper who would harry the British troops as they advanced. Gresham believed that if the men rushed up the hill fast enough, they could reach the ridgeline and seize the Turkish guns before a significant number of the troops were killed. There was no way to win a battle like this without losing men. The only way to win was to win quickly. The one thing they must never do is stop moving.

"Old Gawain didn't get all that sweet cunny o' his by running off, lads," Sergeant Hart shouted at the troops. He had taken to calling the men by the names of King Arthur's knights, and every time he did the men would burst out in laughter, even as they advanced straight into the machine gun fire. To Gresham's satisfaction, the company was finally scrambling forward in a long, broken and uneven line spread across a hundred yards. The mortar fire and shrapnel shells fell constantly among them, but with the troops spread out, the artillery failed to inflict substantial damage to the company. As the troops passed through a line of trees, they saw a field strewn with wounded men. They advanced cautiously, and suddenly the ground exploded beneath the feet of a young Private. The Private's leg was sheared off as he was hurled into the air, and the shrapnel which flew up from the ground wounded the men who had

11

been walking beside him. In another part of the field, another explosion from below killed a second man.

"My God, the Turks have placed mines in the field," said Wilkins. "Have you seen anything like this before?"

"No, this is new," Gresham replied grimly. "Watch where you're walking!" he shouted to the troops. "Stay in another man's footsteps and don't step on anything metal!"

The company advanced carefully across the field without any further mines exploding, but it was not the last pocket of land mines they encountered. In each clearing, one or two men would simply explode and had to be left behind for the stretcher bearers as Sergeant Hart shouted at the company to continue onwards.

The sun was finally rising to the company's right and baking the rocks, dust and brush, and the day had only just begun. Gresham tried to count the machine gun emplacements ahead as they moved forward. The ridge was far more lightly defended than he could believe. The company ahead of them was already moving beyond the plain to the lower hills below the ridge. He saw a stray shrapnel shell burst fifteen feet above the ground, spraying iron fragments across the field like hail and a cluster of the men fell. The Turkish machine guns, however, were poorly directed. Men were falling, but there were too few defenders and they were too poorly equipped to handle the massive assault. More and more British and ANZAC troops were landing behind them every minute. It was still early in the day, but Gresham thought the offensive was progressing well and the casualties so far had been light.

With Wilkins still at his side, Gresham crawled over a spur and down into a shallow gully barely screened from the machine guns ahead. Any man who stood up would get shot in the head. They found a mass of nearly fifty troops from the forward company huddled together in the ditch, too inexperienced to know that a single well-placed artillery shell would blow the lot of them to pieces. A number of the troops were at the rim of the gully firing blindly up towards the machine guns, even though their Lee-Enfield rifles had nowhere near the range to inflict harm on the Turkish gunners. Gresham spied the thin, white-haired commanding officer from the forward company crouching in the shade of a tree deep in the gully.

"Major," Gresham shouted to him as he approached the officer, "are you wounded?"

The Major stood and eyed Gresham with distaste. "No."

"You must take your men up that hill, Sir."

"I will not."

Wilkins scrambled over to join them. "Major Sills, Sir, what have you discovered ahead?"

"It's a damned hot fight, Wilkins. Far more opposition than we expected, I'm sure of it. My scouts tell me there are at least two of those damned Maxim guns just in front of us."

The hill ahead was devoid of dead or wounded men, which indicated that Major Sills had stopped all forward progress here at the gully. The machine guns were a dangerous nuisance, certainly, but standing still even a moment longer in the gully would invite artillery fire, and Gresham was livid that the men were still clumped together. They reminded him of the mules on the beach, and he could easily imagine the same slow-motion disintegration occurring at any moment. A handful of lightly wounded men were scrambling over the spur behind him back to the beach. "Major," he tried, "take these wounded men back to the boats. Your remaining men can join Captain Wilkins' company for the attack on the machine guns ahead."

The understated threat to his command suddenly energized the Major. "Who are you to talk to me like that, Lieutenant? I'll have you shot for insubordination!" He raised the service revolver in his hand and waved it about vaguely.

Wilkins quickly stepped in front of Gresham, who clearly had no notion of tact. "Sir, the Lieutenant is merely fulfilling my orders. We have been instructed to advance up the ridge. We knew there would be opposition, but despite the potential casualties, you must give the order to your men to attack the machine guns."

"No, I will not. No. There is no chance of taking this ridge today, Captain. It simply cannot be done." Major Sills turned to his huddled company and addressed them: "Now see here, gentlemen, you've done a marvelous bit of work this morning. We've got a good foothold ashore, but we must secure our position. The Turks have been pushed well back today. You men march back down to the bay and await further orders. Another day or two of heavy artillery will soften up the Turks and destroy their defensive positions."

Even Wilkins understood that the Major was, in effect, ordering his men to retreat. "Please, Sir," he begged, "your orders are surely the same as mine. We must take the ridge and make our rendezvous with the Ninth Division."

"No, young man, it is readily apparent that this ridge is far more strongly defended than General Stopford was told. Our plans must adapt to circumstances. I expect you will follow along directly. Now get out of my way." The Major again began yelling at his men to get down the hill. But going down would be no easier than coming up as long as the machine guns on the ridge ahead were still in Turkish hands.

Wilkins fumed silently. "I suspect you will agree with me, Gresham, that the Major's expectation that we will follow behind him does not constitute an order to withdraw," he said quietly.

"Better let him go," Gresham whispered, "the old bastard might have decided to take over command of your company as well, and if he had, we probably would have all gotten killed."

Wilkins turned on Gresham sharply. "Lieutenant, you will please keep your opinions regarding our superior officers to yourself." He had nothing against the

Lieutenant and was equally disgusted with Major Sills, but he was not eager to be brought up on charges of insubordination.

The first few men of Major Sills' company to attempt the descent to the bay were shot down by Turkish snipers. Major Sills was crawling down slowly on his hands and knees, and the rest of the company slithered behind him. Meanwhile, more of Wilkins' company was coming up into the long narrow gully, and it was beginning to get crowded. Mortar shells were beginning to target them, and the men around the edges were beginning to panic, massing together like sheep.

Wilkins and Gresham were of like mind that progress up the ridge was the better path. They peered over the rim at the ridgeline ahead, trying to identify the next obstacles and determine the best route to proceed. Sergeant Hart from Wilkins' company was crouching nearby, also peering at the Turkish defenses ahead. The Sergeant, who was well over six feet and as thin as a rail, scrambled over to the officers. He had to kneel before them to keep his head out of harm's way.

"Sirs, it's not rightly my place to say, but it looks to me as though the two guns ahead of us are a bit misplaced, as there's no crossfire between 'em at all. We can dodge the right gun by going over to our left – the ridge there will cover our attack. Then we cut across and can dodge the left gun by going around to the right."

"Excellent spotting there, Sergeant Hart," said Wilkins.

"Right," said Gresham. "Captain Wilkins, get the men spread out at the other end of the gully. Hart and I will go out on our left and flank the first machine gun. You cover our attack, then take the company around the right to take out the gun on our left. You'll want to leave a few men here to hold our lines open.

"Agreed," said Wilkins.

"Come with me, Hart."

"Aye, Sir."

Gresham and Hart scrambled over the rim of the gully and rushed across to the left, keeping as best as they could under the cover from a low ridge. The machine guns opened fire from their embrasures, but couldn't swivel fast enough to where Gresham and Hart were scrambling through the rocks and scrub brush to the left. At the other end of the gully, Wilkins' men fired their rifles to keep the attention of the Turkish machine gunners. Sand and rock kicked up at Gresham's heels, but before long he and Hart were out of the line of fire. Suddenly, there was the crack of a rifle shot and dust kicked up in front of Gresham; his face was sprayed with pebbles and chips of rock. He fell flat behind a low rock and hugged the ground. Hart practically jumped on top of him.

"Hart, there's a sniper there on our left. Didn't spot him, now, did you?"

"Pardon me, Sir, but, yes, I did catch a glimpse of that fellow there. I thought we might catch old Abdul napping."

"What?"

"Every man needs a bit of sleep now and then, Sir."

"He's not asleep now, Hart. Any ideas?"

"Just the one, Sir, just the one, not altogether conventional, if you don't mind," said Hart. He reached into his kit and produced a small, modified milk tin with a fuse jutting out the top. "A little homemade item, Sir, might help in a situation like this. Quite a bit of steel and gunpowder in there, Sir. Have a lighter, do you?"

"Yes, but for God's sake keep your head down. How'd you know to make up that jam-tin there, Sergeant?"

"Why, Sir, I've been in the British army since before your ink was dry."

"How's your arm, it's quite a distance."

"Not bad, no, but I give you the honors, Sir. If it's all the same, I'd rather be killed by an officer's mistake than my own."

"You light it, and I'll toss it up, then."

Hart lit the fuse on the little tin, and Gresham lobbed it as close to the sniper as he could reach. The Turkish sniper mistook Gresham's upraised arm as a signal to the company to attack and began firing desperately all along the ridge in their direction, spraying both men with more pebbles and dust. Fortunately for Gresham and Hart, the fuse on the homemade grenade was very short, and the little bomb exploded in the air near enough to the sniper to spew shards of lead down upon him. He wasn't killed, but Hart and Gresham took advantage of the diversion to rush up on either side of the sniper. Hart landed on the man with both knees and thrust his bayonet through the man's throat. Twisting the blade, he withdrew the bayonet and the Turkish man's blood streamed out into the dust.

Now Gresham and Hart were too far up to the left of the ridge and nearly in range of the second machine gun. Shots poured down in their direction. They quickly scrambled to their right when suddenly a trench opened right before them. It was full of Turkish soldiers. The closest enemies began screaming at Gresham and Hart in Turkish, but many did not even seem to have rifles. Gresham felt almost relieved to finally have a target he could shoot and began firing his bolt-action rifle as fast as he could. He emptied his magazine before a handful of the enemy who had knives could charge into him and Sergeant Hart.

In hand-to-hand combat, Hart had the greater repertoire, but Gresham was an experienced knife fighter. While Hart bayonetted one Turkish trooper, Gresham drew out his field knife and began to work into the pack, laying several of the enemy out. His heart beat wildly as his arms became soaked in blood and clouds of small black flies rushed into the fight to drink their fill. The Turkish soldiers were compressed in the narrow trench and could not overpower the two British soldiers. As the dead began to pile, the remaining Turkish troops fled back up the trench towards the machine gun emplacement. Gresham and Hart charged up the trench after them. The Turkish soldiers leapt out at the far end of the trench and ran directly into Wilkins and the company flanking them on the right. "Fire!" Wilkins shouted, and the entire company fired at once, like a musket line of the old wars. The Turkish troops fell in a mass. But Wilkins was now taking fire from another Turkish-held trench down to the south of his position, and his men could only fall flat to the ground.

"Hart, help me move this gun around." Gresham and Hart lifted the Turks' heavy machine gun and wheeled it around towards the trench to the south. With Wilkins' company still prostrate on the ground, Gresham was in a perfect position to enfilade the enemy. As well-armed Turkish troops gathered below to charge up at Wilkins' company, the Lieutenant opened fire straight down the length of the trench, killing dozens of enemy soldiers. Lieutenant Keeling and his platoons then swarmed into the lower trench, putting down the rest of the Turkish troops and waving up to Wilkins that the right flank was secure.

Gresham and Hart next swiveled the heavy gun around towards the machine gun emplacement up the ridge to their left. Before they could get the machine gun into position, however, Wilkins gathered his men and charged into the trench from the right flank. The Turks were packed tightly into the narrow channel. Wilkins led the charge and, for the first time, fired his revolver at enemy troops. He could easily see his bullets, as if in slow motion, tear into the flesh and shatter the bones of the Turkish soldiers standing immediately before him, and at such close range, their blood splattered back upon him. The droplets of blood felt indistinguishable from the sweat that was already streaming down his face. His heart racing, Wilkins pressed forward, firing again and again until his pistol was empty and his men had swarmed over the machine gun and killed all the enemies in the trench. Then Wilkins climbed calmly up onto the firing step and looked for Gresham and Hart in the trench below and waved his still smoking revolver to them, even as he struggled to calm himself and swallow the bitter realization that he had become a killing soldier and no longer a mere King's Scholar at Eton.

"Send down a half dozen men!" Gresham shouted, and Wilkins promptly ordered a number of privates and a corporal to run down and along the trench to his Lieutenant's position.

"I have a new toy here for you fellows," said Gresham. "Keep this gun pointed down towards that trench there. If the Turks make a move to retake the lower trench from Lieutenant Keeling, you'll have no trouble with them. There will be more companies coming up behind us throughout the day, and you are then to move up and rejoin us."

Gresham and Hart scrambled up to Wilkins' position. "Well done, Captain," said Gresham encouragingly, after he saw the thirty or so dead Turkish soldiers in the trench. This far up on the ridge there were no more falling shells or shrapnel. The Turkish officers to the south and east were justifiably afraid to order fire on what they assumed, or at least hoped, was a position still held by their own men. Gresham took a hard look at Wilkins and was satisfied to see that the young officer was holding up well under the new stress of battle, even though the both of them were fairly covered in blood and had every reason to be exhausted. Wilkins, for his part, sought to emulate the steely determination and calm with which Gresham led the men and handled the battle; clearly, Gresham was well accustomed to killing.

Behind them, more British soldiers were climbing up the ridge, but far fewer than Gresham expected. "Captain, our company is getting a bit stretched out on this ridge," he said. "Do you know how many men are supposed to follow along in this direction?"

"The whole damned Division, Lieutenant. You and Sergeant Hart take half a dozen men and follow this trench along as far as it goes. Make sure the dugouts are cleared, but I'll have no unnecessary killing, Lieutenant."

Gresham and Hart took a handful of men and started down what proved to be a long and jagged trench. Gresham had seen a number of trenches in his military career, but in this one there was at least no mud and no dead and decaying bodies stacked against the walls. Instead, the firing step on the side of the trench had evidently been used for open air sleeping platforms by the Turkish troops seeking to escape the oven-like dugouts. The conditions were, in other respects, appalling: Every scrap of food and human waste and filth was covered with clouds of flies and maggots and the only water they found was foul and brown. And this was an area that hadn't even seen battle before now.

It was late morning and the sun was beating down into the trenches and heating them like a kiln. Gresham found only one Turkish soldier alive. The man was too weak from dysentery to be moved, which explained why he had been left behind when the rest of the troops in his company had retreated to the east. Hart and Gresham simply took his rifle away and gave him the last of their clean water. As they stopped to check one last dugout, the ridge behind them began erupting in a sudden series of huge explosions. Wilkins came running up the trench with another small group of the men to meet them. "Someone is shelling the ridge!"

"Is it the Turks or our destroyers intending to bomb the enemy?" Gresham asked.

Wilkins turned around and pulled his field glasses from his kit. He trained them first on the plains to the south and east, and then on the bay to the west.

"The Turks are still shelling the ships in the bay, it seems. These incoming shells must be our own. Why in the name of God are they shelling the very ridge we have just taken?" It was clear, in any event, that the line of shells was advancing up the ridge in the direction of Wilkins' company and so the need to move was paramount. Gresham, Hart, Wilkins and the three dozen remaining members of the company scrambled out of the trench and quick marched east along a path on top of the ridge. They soon encountered and easily captured two lightly guarded artillery guns and killed several dozen more Turkish soldiers. Many more Turkish soldiers could be seen pulling back to the east.

It was mid-afternoon when the company reached an abandoned Turkish command dugout overlooking the Gulf of Saros. A dry hot breeze was blowing over the ridge from the south and the sun was dazzlingly hot. Gresham, using Wilkins' field glasses, could see companies of Turkish soldiers amassing several miles to the east; it was unclear whether they were preparing a counter-attack. The ridge itself was eerily quiet as Wilkins ordered the men to stop for a drink from their canteens and to rest briefly out of the hot sun.

Then suddenly the front lines erupted and the enemy came back upon them from the south.

"Lord help us! The Turks are comin' on, hundreds of 'em!" howled a bull-like Private, pointing at the trenches below where Keeling and his men were guarding Wilkins' flank. Wilkins and his company leapt to their feet as Gresham climbed onto the top of the dugout with the field glasses. He could see many hundreds, perhaps more than a thousand Turkish soldiers rushing from the wide plains to the south back up into the very trenches on the ridge which Wilkins' company had just left behind. His company was parting like the Red Sea, with most of the troops desperately running down the ridge into the gullies below and Lieutenant Keeling and his men withdrawing quickly down the ridge towards the bay. The few troops attempting to run east along the ridgeline toward Wilkins were being shot by Turkish soldiers.

"My God!" shouted Wilkins. "Where is the rest of the Division? We just let the bloody Turks take back the ridge!"

"Not us," said Gresham with disgust. "But someone did." Gresham leapt down into the trench and examined his empty canteen. The rest of the company stood in front of the dugout staring with horror as they were cut off from the rest of their army.

"How could this happen!" Wilkins shouted.

"Someone halted the Division's advance up onto the ridge, otherwise the positions behind us would be filled with British troops defending the high ground," said Gresham.

Wilkins was beside himself with anger. "What do you mean, Lieutenant? I know what the day's orders are! The whole Division has been coming up this ridge behind us!"

"Where are they, then? There is only your company, Captain. Major Sills and the rest of our Division have apparently stayed safely down at the bay. We saw this sort of thing in Belgium again and again," Gresham said with a scoffing laugh.

"Major Sills could not have changed the entire Division's plans," Wilkins insisted.

"Clever men come up with those battle plans, Captain, men who look at maps and intelligence reports and make calculations with five– and six-digit numbers, and they tell the Generals what to do. But the Generals, they start to lose men on the battlefield and casualties look bad in the newspaper. It makes them look bad and makes Kitchener look bad, and they know the ones who embarrass Kitchener will be replaced. So when men start to die, the Generals play it safe. They halt the advance so the troops can dig in, bring up supplies, and 'prepare for the next big push.' It all sounds very reasonable and reduces casualties, but it doesn't win wars, because while we're digging in, so is the enemy, and that's why the stalemate continues."

Wilkins was furious with frustration and struggled to contain himself. "Regardless, Lieutenant, there are now Turkish troops between us and the bay," he said. "So do we stay here and await the Division? What would you suggest?"

"Those Turkish units back along the ridge will probably come along to clear this area as soon as they've secured the trenches, and there are many more Turks to the east who will head up here once they've reformed. We're back up against the sea here, so our only choice is to head south-east into those hills and try to get under cover as soon as we can. With any luck, we'll find a way back through the lines tonight, before things get locked up any tighter."

"We're behind the lines, then, eh?" asked a wounded Private. "I only ask as I am having a bit of trouble with my arm here." He was holding his left arm tightly up against his chest, but blood was dripping slowly from his elbow onto the dusty soil.

Gresham turned to the Private: "You know how to tie that up so it stops bleeding?"

"Can't do it one-handed," the Private growled.

"Let me help you with that, Dawkins," Wilkins offered and began preparing a tourniquet. "What about him," nodding at another man lying motionless on the ground with a bloody wound in his gut.

Dawkins sighed: "Sorry to say, Corporal Jenks is dead."

"I'm not dead, you stupid cod!" the man gasped.

"Will be soon enough, mate," said Dawkins.

"How bad is that gut wound, Jenks? Can you keep up?" Gresham asked.

"Don't rightly know, Sir. It hurts to bloody Hell. Don't suppose you've got a tot in your kit there, have you?"

Gresham pulled a flask from his back pocket and handed it to the corporal. "Just a bit of whisky left. Finish it."

"You don't mean to leave me, do you, Lieutenant?"

Gresham regarded the Corporal coldly for a moment, as if uncertain. In fact, he *was* uncertain. The badly wounded man would obviously not make it back to the lines, and if they dragged him along he would only slow the rest. But Gresham knew that the rest of the men would object if he suggested leaving the Corporal behind. "No. I suppose not." He took the man's rifle and rucksack and handed them to Wilkins. "Carry these." said Gresham. Wilkins was too stunned to object. "Let's move. No shooting if it can be avoided. We don't want to draw attention to ourselves."

Gresham led the remaining troops along the ridgeline. Sergeant Hart took up the rear. They stayed in a single line and were very quiet. The battle was still being waged behind them, but its intensity was slowing as the Ottoman Turks and Allied troops dug into their positions. Gresham brought the company east another mile and then they marched south a mile more; they encountered no Turkish troops or Turkish civilians. After two hours of cautious and quiet marching, the company halted for a rest in an area of dense brush. Gresham still had Hart with him, as well as Wilkins and more than two dozen more men. The sound of sporadic artillery fire was still audible off to the west, near the bay, but the day had grown mostly quiet and, if anything, hotter. Each of the men had sweat through their uniforms and no one had a drop of water left in their canteens. Every time they stopped moving, small black flies fell upon them in clouds.

"Lieutenant, how are we going to get back to our side of the line?" asked a young Private.

"No worries there, mate," replied his neighbor. "Like as not, we're all going to die of thirst before we ever get back."

Wilkins' face lifted. "We were supposed to take the ridge and move south to a rendezvous at the village cemetery to the south. The companies that were supposed to meet us there might have made it through. We must go see."

"It's possible," agreed Gresham. "There would be water there, too. But my guess is that we'll find a lot of Turks none too happy to find Tommy Atkins on their flank." He looked around at the remaining men of the company. Some men had thrown themselves down on the ground and gone right to sleep. Gresham had seen that in France too: Men who can't stomach war have a tendency to sleep through as much of it as possible. "Let's rest a bit and wait until dark to move on. Perhaps it will cool off."

"I wouldn't expect so, Lieutenant," said Sergeant Hart. "We had heat like this in India, and I can assure you it will not cool. Don't go gettin' the boys' hopes up, if you please."

"How long did you serve in India, Sergeant?" Wilkins asked.

"Can't give you a proper answer there, Sir, I'm sorry to say: Many years, and many years in Africa as well. Born and raised in the heat, you might say, Sir. I played with Mister Kipling when I was a lad in Bombay. Whereas he became a great author, I joined the army and became a great Sergeant. I like to think that I myself was the inspiration for Peachey Carnehan."

"But then you served in the Boer Wars?"

"Aye, in the second war, but that were different from this. We fought man-to-man, village to village, each man for himself. We'd spend days in the brush hunting those Boer bastards. The heat takes it out of a man; enough time in the brush can make a man feel like he's all alone in the world. Can't say I recognize any man as my superior any longer," then he winked and smiled, "but the Empire knows who I am."

"King and country, yes?".

Hart guffawed. "More country than King. King George is a navy man, and a German," he added.

"He most certainly is not. He is the grandson of Queen Victoria," Wilkins replied indignantly.

"Aye, but Prince Albert was a German, wasn't he?"

"Sergeant, those sorts of statements will confuse the men, that is, if it is not outright treason."

Gresham had been listening and could tell that Wilkins was getting angry. "You two, stuff it before the Turks end this argument."

To the south lay another ridge, one even taller than the Kiretch Tepe ridge they had just come down. Wilkins, incredibly, had not thought to bring a map, but Sergeant Hart seemed to carry maps in his head the way some people memorize poetry. The high ridge to their southwest, he said, was called Tekke Tepe, and the village Anafarta Sagir sat on its southern spurs. Wilkins thought that was the village where his company was intended to rendezvous with companies from the Ninth, so a plan was agreed to march there after dark.

They stayed in the shade as best they could but the sun beat down on them and the flies continued to fall on them in clouds. The flies especially liked Dawkins's blood-soaked arm and nearly covered him despite his best effort to swat them off. No man had any appetite for the hard biscuits and the few tin cans of greasy, flavorless "Bully Beef" which were their only food. As a hot breeze blew in, the men could smell only putrefaction and decay from the battlegrounds to the west. The company spent the rest of the early evening resting in the hot shade, and prepared to march as the sun set.

"My little sleepers," said Hart, kicking the sleeping men. "Get up, we're off again." Corporal Jenks, they found, had died, and a few minutes were taken to bury him in a shallow grave. The remains of the company continued east and south around the Tekke Tepe ridge, marching down shallow gullies and over gentle spurs, avoiding the Turkish troops and resting every mile or so among whatever trees they found. Finally, well after dark, the group walked through a pine tree grove and saw a number of low brick buildings a short way off. There was a vast array of troops and horses, carts and artillery pieces moving into the small crossroads village. All of them were Turkish.

"I don't think we can take the company in there," said Gresham, sitting with the men among the thickest grove of trees they could find. The air was cooler, but the ground still felt like a hot pan. Most of the men looked parched and woozy. Sergeant Hart seemed all right, and even Wilkins was holding up. The others grasped their rifles nervously. To get through that village would mean one hell of a fight. Ahead of them, on the road, Turkish soldiers were moving into the village by tens and twenties, while loaded horse-drawn carts traveled back from the front. Gresham knew carts like those had only one thing to bring back from the trenches – the dead. Hadn't Wilkins mentioned something about a cemetery near this village? Gresham turned to the Sergeant. "Hart, you're pretty good with your hands. Anyone else here a knife-fighter?"

"Aye, Sir," said a short, thin, and sleepy Private. "Got a little experience there, I'll admit."

"I have an idea, Cooper. Let's you, me and Hart go for a walk. Captain, these men and I will do a bit of foraging tonight. We'll meet you and the rest of the company in that gully over there on the west side of the village as soon as we can. Take your time and try to avoid any sentries. If we haven't met you by sunrise, you should continue back to the lines as best you can."

"As you say, Lieutenant," agreed Wilkins.

"Let's go then," said Gresham.

Gresham led Hart and Cooper back through the copse of pine trees and started a long, slow, crawl around the outside of the village to the east. He was in no hurry, as his plan had more chance of success in the darkest part of the night. Much of the village had been damaged by British artillery, but the artillery battle had ended for the time being. Beyond the eastern edge of the village, Gresham saw what he was looking for – the cemetery. What had once been a small village cemetery had become a dumping ground. Overwhelmed with the number of bodies at the front, the Turks had started carting the dead to the rear and burying them as an odd-job whenever men could be spared. Most of the bodies lay in a pit and were covered with a light dusting of lime. The flies and stench of death were overpowering, and Gresham could feel himself starting to swoon. He gathered Hart and Cooper close.

"Look, there will be another of those carts coming before long. They're bringing corpses to the cemetery. We're going to capture the next cart, steal enough Turkish uniforms for the lot of us, and take the cart all the way back through the lines. Go find someplace to hole up near the cemetery gate."

Gresham stepped into a small run-in shed where horses had been rested out of the sun. The smell of horse manure and urine was startlingly wholesome compared with the overall smell of rotting human flesh throughout the cemetery. Still, the flies were everywhere. Gresham pulled an old handkerchief from his back pocket and held it over his mouth. The flies could not tell a dead man from a live one, and they descended on Gresham, Hart and Cooper in clouds.

The waiting was horrendous, but they did not have to wait long. Within a half-hour, a cart slowly rambled into the cemetery: One driver, one passenger, one cart full of corpses. Gresham signaled to the others. Hart was the first. He leapt up and neatly garroted the driver with a piece of barbed wire. Cooper made short work of slitting the other man's throat. The suddenness of the violence spooked the two poor horses that were bound to the cart, and they were ready to bolt, but Gresham quickly grabbed their reins. His calm hand quieted the two cart horses quickly.

The dead men were stripped of their uniforms and thrown in the pit. Gresham was checking the bodies in the cart for more useable uniforms.

"Hurry up," he whispered, "before another cart arrives."

They found several more relatively unspoiled uniform jackets and dumped the remaining corpses from the cart quickly into the pit. Gresham tossed a Turkish jacket and helmet to Cooper.

"Put that on and take the cart around the back road to the other end of the village. Don't stop for anyone. Sergeant Hart and I will meet you on the other side. I want to see what they've got waiting for us in the village here."

Hart and Gresham started right off walking into the village. They carried a couple canteens and each wore an Turkish jacket and helmet. They still needed to avoid the troops on the road, but it was now very late and very dark and the number of troops moving on the road had dwindled. There were no sentries on the east side of the village to challenge them, as the Turks did not expect to be attacked from the rear. Hart and Gresham quietly and casually passed behind and around a number of burnt-out buildings until they could see into the village center, where they found several hundred Turkish troops sitting and lying about, resting.

"Look'ee there," said Hart, "old Abdul is bedded down for the night."

"There's the water supply," whispered Gresham, pointing to a metal cistern to one side. Just the sight of the water tank had caused his body to cramp up. It had been sixteen hours since his last drink. Gresham smeared some dust on his face, picked up his canteens, and walked boldly into the village square.

Hart laughed to himself, "what kind of bloody plan is this?"

Gresham walked calmly towards the cistern. He avoided the larger groups of men and stayed close to those who were lying down or asleep. The street was packed with Turkish soldiers. Gresham reached the cistern, quickly filled his canteens, and then simply walked off slowly down the road to the west. Hart followed him by a few minutes, likewise dressed in Turkish jacket and helmet (although, at nearly six and a half feet, Hart looked a great deal less like a Turkish infantryman). A Turkish Colonel stood up and approached Hart as he filled his canteens.

"*I-yak-sham-lar*," Hart growled at the officer, bowing slightly as he began walking briskly after Gresham. Fortunately, the Turkish officer was too confused and too tired to react.

"What the hell did you say to him?" Gresham asked, after they cleared the last group of sleeping Turkish troops.

"A Sergeant knows how to speak to officers, Sir; doesn't matter which army he's in."

Gresham and Hart were startled at the mass of German Maxim machine guns and Krupp field artillery that had been drawn up into the village to resist the British offensive, not to mention rolls of barbed wire and enormous stores of ammunition. They were glad the guns were quiet for now. In front of the village, the Turks had begun digging trenches and stringing wire. The village would be impregnable in a days' time. Gresham and Hart reached the west end of the village and located Cooper with the cart. "Here's some water," said Gresham, passing up a canteen. "Now, Sergeant, lie in the cart and pretend to be dead while the Corporal and I start up the road."

Hart jumped into the back of the cart, disturbing the thousands of flies feasting on the rancid liquids pooled on the cart's wooden slat bed. Gresham and Cooper whipped up the horses, and the cart began its slow trek west. Shortly after, they paused by a dark, narrow, gully long enough for Gresham to collect Wilkins and the rest of the company. Slowly and quietly, the men walked from the gully and climbed into the stack of "dead" men in the cart. After the last man was loaded, Gresham and Cooper continued westwards through one small Turkish encampment after another, across the Anafarta plain and back towards Suvla Bay. Given the smell of the cart, the load of "bodies" in the back and the dead of night, it was not surprising that no one challenged them or even came close enough to look at their faces. Soon the camps thinned out, and the cart simply continued into the empty plain beyond.

Gresham was exhausted. For the past twenty-four hours, he had focused solely on moving forward and keeping as many men alive to fight another day as he could, but his head hurt and his muscles ached and his sense of smell might have been permanently damaged by the odor of the cart. The road before him was dusty and dry. Too many men had died to take a ridge that no one seemed to want to keep. The ridge would have to be retaken. The war would go on and on and on. That was a mixed blessing, as far as Gresham was concerned. He thought back to his brief final conversation with his father, who had sent his bastard son away from Manchester with an ultimatum: Be gone for good; succeed or die, it made no matter.

Gresham's mother was a poor Irish kitchen servant who had died young, and Gresham had ended up an orphan in the streets of Manchester where he had fought to survive each day. He became such an embarrassment to his father that he had finally been abducted and sent away to public school. He had done so well there that his father had even arranged to send him, at great expense, to Oxford. That had not gone well at all. Now Gresham had been sent away from Manchester for good, and he had finally found something at which he genuinely excelled: He would be a cold-hearted ruthless bastard of an infantry officer, if only the British army would let him.

The cart approached a line of British infantrymen stationed a half-mile from the shoreline just as the night sky was beginning to turn light grey. Gresham, still dressed in a Turkish coat and helmet, pulled the cart off the road and leapt down to strip them off. "We've gone as far as we need to go by cart," he whispered. The men piled out and shook themselves, taking deep breaths of fresh air.

"I'll be damned," said Wilkins upon seeing the wary British sentries just fifty yards ahead. He and Hart stripped off their Turkish coats and walked with Gresham up to the picket line. The men there were also surprised.

"Ah, it's you, Captain Wilkins," said a fresh-faced Second Lieutenant cheerily. "Colonel Banks has been asking after you, Sir. He'll be delighted to see you well. You had better see him at his field quarters."

"And where the Devil *are* the Colonel's quarters?"

"There, Sir," pointing to a hill to the southwest, "at Lala Baba."

"Very well. I must freshen up first. Gresham, please accompany me."

"Yes, Sir" said Gresham. "Sergeant Hart, get the men squared away, and see if you can locate the rest of the company and Lieutenant Keeling."

"Aye, Sir."

As they passed the Second Lieutenant, Gresham stopped. "Say, Lieutenant, there's a Turkish Battalion two miles along this road. Do you have any idea why no one is shooting at them?"

"Orders, I s'pose, Sir?"

"Of course, that must be the reason." That response came as no surprise to Gresham, who continued his march with Wilkins back towards the bay where they had begun only twenty-four hours before.

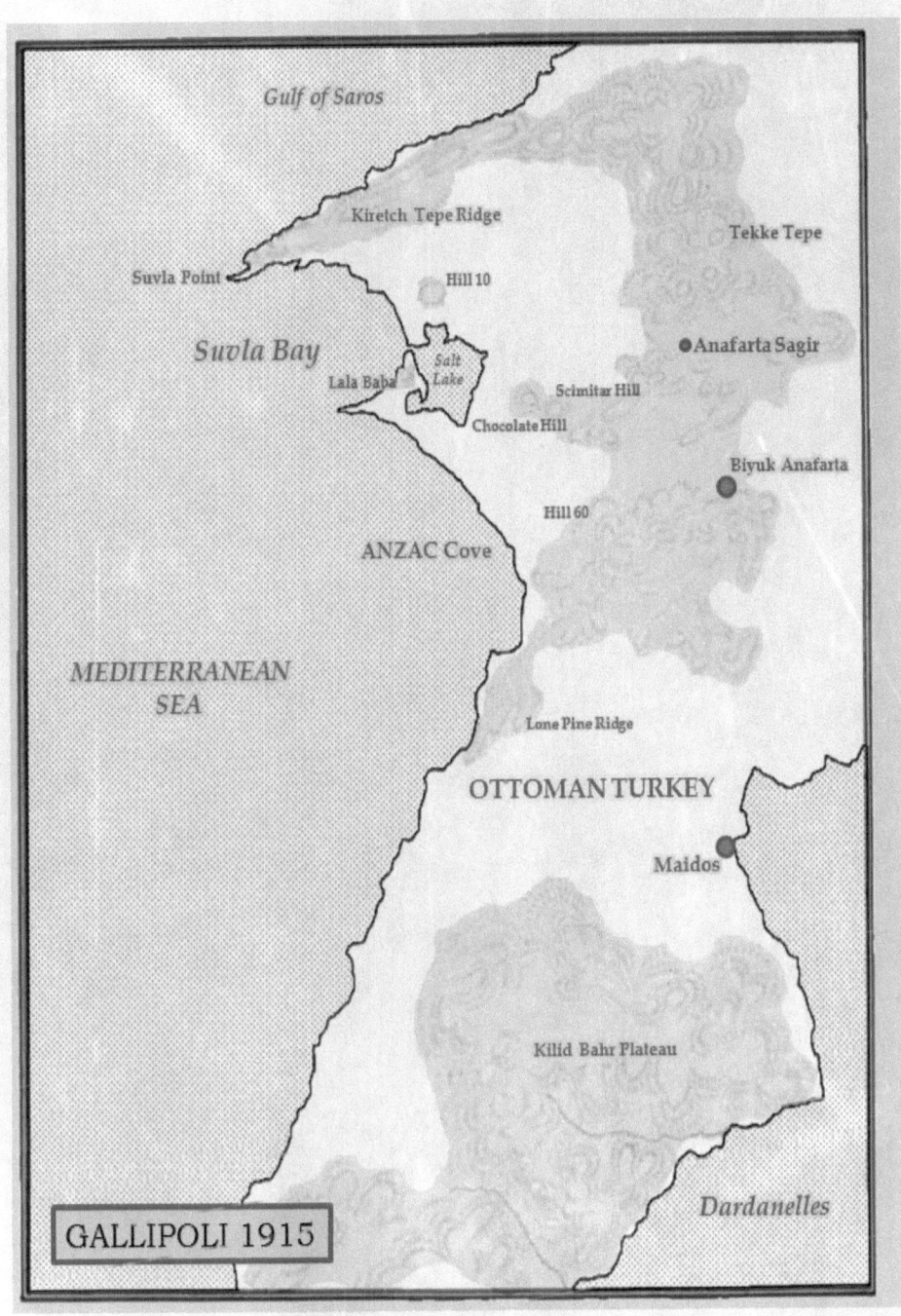

Gulf of Saros

Kiretch Tepe Ridge

Tekke Tepe

Suvla Point

Hill 10

Suvla Bay

Anafarta Sagir

Salt Lake

Lala Baba

Scimitar Hill

Chocolate Hill

Biyuk Anafarta

Hill 60

ANZAC Cove

MEDITERRANEAN SEA

Lone Pine Ridge

OTTOMAN TURKEY

Maidos

Kilid Bahr Plateau

Dardanelles

GALLIPOLI 1915

Imbros

Captain Wilkins and Lieutenant Gresham walked to shore and stopped long enough to rinse their faces and hands, smoke a cigarette, and drink a modest amount of rum. They still stank from the cart and were splattered with dried blood and the vast cloud of flies which it attracted as they hiked down to Colonel Banks' quarters. Banks was the Battalion commander, and he reported directly to General Mahon in command of the Division. Wilkins liked Banks; he was a difficult old man but was generally good at following orders, whilst Mahon was widely regarded as one of the finest Generals in the British army. The morning had started hot, and before Gresham and Wilkins reached Lala Baba, the sun had begun to bake the shoreline. It was still relatively quiet and the Turkish shells directed at the British position came only once every few minutes.

"I recommend you let me talk to the Colonel, Lieutenant," Wilkins said, as they walked through the amassed troops. "He can be quite difficult."

"As you wish, Sir. I find I rarely know the right thing to say to such men; they rather annoy me."

"That is all the more reason for you to remain silent. Officers like Banks want to know they are in charge, and it does no good to intimidate them. This old fellow's sure to rap your knuckles if you do."

"Yes, Sir," said Gresham. To the Captain, the world was just an extension of Eton, he thought, as he tried to sweep his filthy, disheveled black hair out of his eyes.

The shoreline was crowded with thousands of boxes, men and draft animals, and it was quite difficult to find a path through. It seemed an entire army had been forced into the fifty yards between the water and the top of the hill that surrounded the shore. At last they made it down to the hill called Lala Baba between the bay and the dry salt lake. Colonel Banks had the largest tent among those raised at the base of the hill. Wilkins wondered where General Mahon and General Stopford were located. Had they even come ashore yet? A guard went in to announce Wilkins as he and Gresham waited outside in the bright hot sunlight.

"Good God, you're a mess, Wilkins, but I am glad to see you alive," said the thin, grey-haired Colonel Banks as he stepped out of his tent and stood in its shade.

"Thank you, Sir," replied Wilkins.

"You reached the top of Kiretch Tepe, I hear. Is that right?"

"Yes, Sir, the Lieutenant and I reached the top of the ridge, but we had to leave men behind with Keeling to secure the trenches as we advanced. I thought those men would be reinforced by additional companies coming up behind us, but as those companies did not, and as my lines had become stretched, we and several dozen men in my company were cut off when the Turks began their counter-offensive in the afternoon."

"Of course, yes, I see. So you were stuck behind the lines."

"Yes, Sir."

"Well it was still a fine bit of work. The Manchesters advanced farther than any other British Regiment yesterday. Even if we couldn't hold the ridge, it was quite an achievement. How did you get back across the lines?"

"Thank you, Sir. We marched down to Anafarta Sagir to meet up with the Ninth per my orders, but we found the town overrun with Turkish infantry instead. We were able to sneak back across the lines during the night in a corpse wagon."

"Ha, Ha! A corpse wagon? How ingenious!"

"I must also report to you, Sir, that there are at least a thousand Turks in the village across the plain now, and many more appear to be coming up behind them. The Lieutenant reports that the Turks are digging in and are well supplied with artillery and machine guns."

"I see, yes . . . . Well, that's all General Stopford's doing. Mid-day yesterday he ordered us to keep to the shoreline until we could get both Divisions completely landed. There are still men and a vast amount of supplies ferrying across from the transports, and it seems to be taking much longer than the General anticipated. The Fifth Inniskillings moved up the ridge yesterday to join your men and, rather than advancing onwards, they simply dug in and relieved Keeling and sent him back down. General Mahon is furious."

"That's very disappointing, yes, Sir."

"Well, I don't want to hold you boys up chatting. You need to clean yourselves up a bit, and I expect you'd like a meal. We'll be meeting in the officer's mess at 16.00. Hopefully I will have our orders from General Mahon by then."

"Tea time. Yes, Sir."

"And you are Lieutenant Gresham, is that right?" the Colonel asked, turning to Wilkins' Lieutenant.

"Yes, I am, Sir."

The colonel eyed him stonily a moment. "I have been given orders for you to report to I-Branch at General Headquarters on Imbros as soon as possible."

"Imbros? You mean the island, Sir?"

"Yes of course the island. I don't know how you will get there, but I was instructed to send you and you are now sent. Wilkins, see you at tea, my boy," and with that the Colonel retreated into his tent.

Wilkins eyed Gresham warily as they walked up the shore line to where they had learned the Tenth Manchesters were encamped. "Do you have any idea what it's about?" he asked Gresham.

"No idea whatsoever. I've never even heard of I-Branch."

"I am sorry you won't be at tea. You deserve far more credit for taking that ridge than I do. Don't imagine I will forget it, really."

"It is your prerogative as commander to delegate, Captain. I simply attempted to fulfill your orders to the best of my ability."

"Now you are sounding rather toady, Gresham. I didn't have a clue what to do. Thank you for taking the lead. Ah, look, you can see Sergeant Hart there; we must be close to the camp."

The company encampment they found consisted of only two tents on a hill, a scattered pile of baggage, a small cook fire, and a large group of naked men either bathing in the warm bay water or sitting in the sun on the pebbly shore. A strong breeze of hot air wafted the scent of decomposing flesh and feces over the site, and there was no potable water to be found.

"You're alive, thank God!" said Lieutenant Keeling with a great smile as he rushed over to shake Wilkins' hand; his other hand held a sterling silver flask and he reeked of gin. "I was terribly afraid you'd died and left the company to me. How ever did you get back?"

"Gresham and Sergeant Hart played highwaymen and captured us a cart in which to sneak back across the lines. The Turks are so busy moving up reinforcements, they couldn't be bothered to pay much attention to us as we came back across the lines in the dark."

"Marvelous, really marvelous," said Keeling. "Dutton!" He shouted to Wilkins' batman, a personal servant assigned from the ranks. An older, rather dirty man with a long filthy mustache hustled over. "Get a lunch together and some decent uniforms out for the Captain and Lieutenant." Suddenly a shell burst some thirty yards away, but the men had already become so accustomed to the flying shrapnel that they barely flinched.

"The Colonel told us that the Innys relieved you," Wilkins said. "How many men did we lose?"

After hearing Keeling's report, Wilkins was relieved that the company had lost far fewer men during the landing and advance up the ridge than he had any right to expect, but the Manchesters as a whole had lost close to two hundred killed and wounded.

Half of Wilkins' company was off burying the corpses in their section. Gresham and Wilkins joined the men bathing in the warm Suvla Bay water, but soon found that they continued to be covered by the small, black flies even after rinsing off. Dutton prepared cold sandwiches of sliced Bully Beef and biscuit for them, and they ate grimacing as they accidentally swallowed some of the swarming flies as well. Then Dutton helped Wilkins dress, while Gresham dressed himself in his one remaining clean uniform, brushed his shaggy hair with his fingers, wiped some biscuit crumbs from his shaggy mustache and said a quick farewell to Wilkins and Keeling.

"See you anon, Gresham," Keeling said good naturedly.

"Come back as soon as you can, Lieutenant," said Wilkins, shaking hands warmly, "I don't wish to go back up that ridge without you."

"I shall. Thank you, Captain," said Gresham, and then Wilkins went into his tent to escape the hot mid-day sunshine.

Gresham marched back down the shore to where the lighters and beetle boats were still unloading cargo and men. Gresham saw wounded men being loaded onto one of the lighters and approached the crew. "I need to get to Imbros. Any ideas on how I can get there?" he asked.

"We're transporting wounded to hospital on HMH *Assaye*, Sir. We could take you over to the ship, and from there, some of the worst cases are being taken over to Imbros, so I'm sure you can find passage," suggested the crewman. The lighter was a mess, covered in blood (and flies) and full of severely wounded men. There was no alternative, however, so Gresham climbed aboard and sat in the cleanest corner he could find. Even in the hot sun and with shells bursting periodically nearby, the gentle rocking of the boat soon put him fast asleep.

Later in the afternoon, Wilkins had a shave from Dutton and dressed in a third clean uniform; he had already perspired through the second. It was terribly hot, and most of the men were with the Sergeants getting water from a large tank that had been cut loose and floated ashore from *Grampus*. Keeling had left earlier to oversee a crew laying telephone wire. Wilkins, alone in the tent, noticed the three exquisite, silver-handled shaving brushes Keeling had lined up on a crate of gin next to his camp bed and shook his head. Each of the brushes had been a gift from one of Keeling's three lovely fiancés. Keeling hadn't yet decided which one to marry.

Wilkins was partial to the chaste "Harrison Fisher girls." He tacked a couple of the portraits to the post beside his bed. They displayed the Edwardian ideal of womanhood that Wilkins much admired – beauty, gentility and zeal – but although Wilkins admired it, he had yet to find it. There was only one woman in Wilkins' life: His very intelligent and refined mother, the woman who had toured him through the marbled great halls of Europe during his holidays from Eton College, introduced him to kings and queens, and showed him, perhaps inadvertently, that being clever was as good as or even better than being wealthy (not that Wilkins father, Lord Bartlett, was not wealthy as well). Apart from his mother, Wilkins had only ever been close to his two older brothers, who were now in the Royal Navy, and his schoolmates at Eton.

He left his tent and walked down the shore to the officer's mess unsure of what he would say if pressed on how his company had taken the Kiretch Tepe ridge: He wanted to give Gresham credit, but he also knew that Gresham was a man that others would not want to congratulate. Could he not assist Gresham more if Wilkins himself were in a position to do so? He watched two British biplanes fly overhead, on their way to survey the Turkish forces. It was an astonishingly quiet day (notwithstanding the occasional shell burst) considering that a major offensive was supposed to be underway.

The officer's mess was up on the plain, next to the kitchens near Lala Baba. A hot dry wind was blowing, but at least it kept the flies off Wilkins' face. As he passed the stoves, he noticed the cooks had hung a couple of dozen privy seats on barbed wire to create a wind break to keep sand and dust out of the food. Large pots of chopped Bully Beef and root vegetables were boiling into a hot stew; nothing could have looked less appetizing on such a hot afternoon. As he rounded the corner of the tent, Wilkins discovered a dozen officers crowded together, sitting on crates and boxes around the end of a long table made of crates and wooden planks. "There you are, Wilkins," said Keeling. At once the large group turned to acknowledge Wilkins and burst into applause. "Well done, very well done," "wonderful work there, old man," and "bravo!" they cheered to Wilkins.

"Come have a seat," said Keeling.

"No room, no room," shouted another Lieutenant.

"Have some wine," shouted another, in an encouraging tone.

Wilkins looked around the table, but there was no wine. 'I don't see any,' he replied.

"No, there's only this bloody awful rum," said the first, sadly.

On the table there was a large silver platter of hard biscuits covered with flies and several tins of jam covered with flies. Instead of cups of tea, the officers were drinking rum from small Turkish coffee cups. Everyone was in a good mood, and they were all pleased to see Wilkins was well and to drink their rum, sometimes swallowing a fly or two as well.

"Take my seat, old man," said Keeling, who got up from the one real chair in the tent, a raggedy old upholstered wingback chair that had been found floating near the shore.

"Did you really ride back through the enemy lines on a corpse cart?" the Second Lieutenant asked.

"Yes, the poor horses – but I don't doubt someone will miss them when the Turks start to pile up," Wilkins jested.

"Herbert's trying to arrange a truce this afternoon so both sides have a chance to bury yesterday's dead," said a Lieutenant. "Apparently they do it all the time here."

"I would think a truce, at this moment, would advantage the Turks by giving them more time to move up their reinforcements."

"Where are *our* reinforcements?" asked the sad Lieutenant.

"You've been on reserve this whole time, Terry; you *are* the reinforcements," said another.

"I understood this landing was to be a surprise attack," Wilkins replied.

"Ah, but a surprise for whom? Ha, ha, ha!"

"Gentlemen," exclaimed an old Major, as he stood and raised his cup, "to King George." The other officers briefly stood, saluted "the King," drank, and sat back down. A couple officers had already had too much rum and were sleeping with their heads on the table. Others were chatting right over them.

Colonel Banks entered the tent and stood up at the head of the table as the men quieted. "Gentlemen, I have some fortunate news to share with you. I've just learned that Major Davenport is returning to the Regiment shortly; seems his enteritis passed quickly." A couple of the lieutenants spit out their drinks with laughter. "Now, now, I didn't mean it that way," the Colonel continued. "Of course, we all know the Major is a solid gentleman, so no surprise there. As happy as I am that he will be returning to us, I am honored to recognize Captain Wilkins' leadership of C Company's advance up the Kiretch Tepe ridge yesterday whilst in command of Davenport's company, and bollocks to the Innys who mucked it up. Captain Wilkins, my congratulations to you."

"Hurrah," "bravo," and "well done, James" came the shouts and applause from around the table. Wilkins smiled as best he could, but it was difficult not to be embarrassed for accepting credit for an attack he knew he did not actually command. He resolved to help Gresham along if he could – that is, if Gresham ever returned from Imbros.

The Colonel continued: "As you all know, we did not achieve all our objectives yesterday because of slow landings and changes in the timetable. I have no doubt we will advance again as soon as our commander decides to join us from his comfortable cabin on *Jonquil*. In the meantime, keep your men fed, watered, exercised, and healthy. Water is still in short supply, so trench digging details will be staggered, and please lay to rest any corpses or carcasses found in your sections. I'm afraid that's all I have for you today, and now I'll leave you younger gentlemen to your tea."

The officers sat stolidly as Colonel Banks left the tent. No one was excited to hear that they had been ordered to wait. Wilkins' blood rose and he became suddenly furious with frustration. Could no one here see that the element of surprise had been lost? He leaned towards Keeling: "I was in that damn village over there, and there should have been over two thousand British soldiers waiting for me, but instead there were a thousand Turks digging trenches and stringing wire. Doesn't anyone want to win this war?"

"Consider yourself the lucky one, James," said Keeling with a grin. "You're probably the only man here who will ever see that village."

Before long, there were a few card games in progress and the rum continued from tea straight into supper. Few had any appetite for hot "pontoon," as the stew was known. Wilkins, feeling rather sick, nibbled on a hard dry biscuit and excused himself at sunset. He walked unsteadily back to his tent alone; Keeling had disappeared again.

———————————

Gresham made his way from *Assaye* to the island of Imbros on a small Turkish caique, a grimy little fishing boat that was every bit as filthy as the lighter he had taken to *Assaye*. He arrived at Imbros well rested, at least, and had no trouble getting directions to the General Headquarters there. And everyone seemed to know where to find the "I-Branch," which Gresham quickly learned was the M.E.F.'s military intelligence office. "Intelligence – of course," he thought with a grimace. He was not especially surprised, nor was he in the least pleased.

In the small house where I-Branch was headquartered, a young Corporal grimaced at Gresham's filthy appearance but gave him a glass of cool tea with lemon and asked him to sit in a small breezy room in the back. The open windows had lace curtains and overlooked wild flowers, and for a moment Gresham almost felt like he was back at some cottage in the Cotswold. But he had a bad feeling in his stomach that wouldn't go away. The Intelligence fellows were trouble, and Gresham wasn't looking to make his life any more difficult than it already was. It was the Intelligence office which had sent him off "on holiday" to Arabia with that bookish fellow, Lawrence, and it was more luck than skill that they had escaped the ambush by a Turkish company near the Suez. By then, the Regiment had decided to ship Gresham off to Suvla Bay rather than return him to the front lines in Belgium where at least he could have made a name for himself; surely no one would remember the little part of the war fought on the Gallipoli peninsula. Gresham now had no other option than to do the best job he could for the Regiment and to pray for advancement.

Suddenly the door opened, and a smartly-uniformed officer with dark wavy brown hair entered the room. His eyes sparkled as he took a look at Gresham and chuckled. "Christ, you look awful, David," he said, sitting across the table from Gresham. "How are you?"

"As soon as I heard 'Intelligence,' I guessed it would be you, Mackenzie. I suppose you expect me to thank you for taking me off the peninsula, but I don't think I will."

"And here I believed you would be pleased to see me. You surely can't hold me responsible for what happened in Egypt. It was Archibald who asked you to escort Lawrence to Jidda; that was not my idea at all. But everything worked out well in the end – very well, I'm told."

"It's not that, as much as, you see, I can't just go running off from my regiment whenever you call. I have my duty and my career in the army to consider. How am I ever to get advanced if I run off on someone else's errands? It irritates my superiors." Not that they seem to have any fondness for me anyway, Gresham thought.

"Of course I understand, but officially you're here under General Mahon's orders to provide intelligence, so there shouldn't be any bother. Tell me, has Stopford mucked up the landing as badly as I hear?"

"It's a complete disaster," Gresham said bluntly.

"I *am* sorry to hear that. Bob Graves will be devastated – if you can believe it, he came all the way from London to be the British Administrator of Constantinople. That's assuming we ever capture the illustrious city, which seems more doubtful with every passing day. I daresay Graves will have to continue waiting. But you seem to have had some success with Lord Bartlett's son, is that right?"

"If you heard that I had something to do with it, then you're better informed than most."

"I'll take that as a compliment, but an unnecessary one. I know only what I am told. As I understand it, Mister Wilkins asked you to command the company onto the ridge and you brought the men back safely from behind enemy lines. Is that correct?"

"Yes, more or less."

"I applaud your foresight in saving Mister Wilkins' life. That was good in very many ways. Did you know that he is fluent in seven languages?"

"I had no idea."

"Captain of his class at Eton, too. Well, anyway, it's yet another instance in which you have shown both resourcefulness and insight. What is your opinion of Mister Wilkins?"

"He's young, but he will make a suitable officer eventually. I rather like him, to be honest with you."

"It seems to me that Mister Wilkins is not being used to his full potential. I'd love to have him in intelligence and out of the line of fire, but, with his connections, well, everyone seems to want him."

"What is the point of this interview, Mackenzie?"

"Ah, well, David, you have no need to be envious of James Wilkins. You have your own remarkable skills. You may rest assured they have been noted. And they are ones which my colleagues and I sorely lack."

"What are you talking about?"

"You are a damned clever soldier, for one. I am not a soldier. In fact, my sciatica is flaring up and I could barely walk here from my house today."

"We call it a billet."

"Yes, of course. It's all well and good for men like me to collect information and read reports, but we need men in the front lines to make decisions and to take action when an opportunity presents itself. Sometimes an opportunity arises which needs a man of your particular talents and skills to be properly completed."

"There's a whole bloody army right over there on the shore, Mackenzie. You can get any soldier you like."

"Perhaps, but I don't care for just any soldier, David. I am looking for a man of quality, and you happen to be here so, I thought, why not ask you?"

"Ask me what?"

"I would like to ask for your help on a small matter. But I can also see that you rushed to be here and perhaps I should let you clean up and we'll talk over supper. However, if you would rather go back to the Manchesters now, I can have those orders written for you instead."

"I suppose it would be ungracious of me to decline your hospitality, and as I have eaten nothing but hard biscuits for two days and am covered with blood and the stench of fish, you may talk to me as we eat."

"Excellent. Let me get my batman then." Mackenzie walked to the door and poked his head out. "John, please take the Lieutenant to my house and prepare him a bath and find him a fresh uniform. I'll be back in an hour for our supper."

"Yes, Sir," replied the orderly. Gresham rose and extended his hand to his former tutor, who shook it, and followed the orderly out the door.

Compton Mackenzie, formerly of Magdalen College at Oxford and an author of several popular novels, reviewed the coded telegrams on his desk again and scratched notes on a sheet of his personal stationary. There were so many problems to address that he could barely keep it all straight. He was accustomed to doing one thing at a time, and the rules of war were new to him. For example, he had just learned from an agent in Athens that a German officer was disguised as a Turkish woman and living in a house less than a mile from the British base on Imbros. The German would have to be arrested and questioned, of course. But then what? Should he be hanged as a spy? Exchanged? Turned? Why would the agent in Athens know about him at all? What was going on in Athens? How long would Greece remain neutral in this war? Would Greece be more beneficial to England as an ally or as an enemy? The politics were astonishingly new to him.

Lieutenant Gresham was another matter for consideration. Mackenzie liked David and always saw the young man's potential. His military record was strong and his background was fairly clean, notwithstanding the false last name of "Gresham." Apparently, the young man was no longer permitted to use his father's name and had elected not to keep his mother's controversial Irish name. He was, in effect, no one at all. He appeared to be completely apolitical and had no family and no connections whatsoever. He would survive by his own strength of will alone. Hadn't he done just that as a mere boy in Manchester? But what were his weaknesses? Could he be trusted?

Then there was the matter at hand. Mackenzie knew he would be of no personal use at all, and neither would any of the other I-Branch men. None of them could do what needed to be done – indeed, none of them had ever fired a weapon in combat or fought hand-to-hand with knives or hidden in dark places.

A new sort of man was needed; that's exactly what he had told intelligence director Cumming during their meeting in London. Now David had shown great resourcefulness and discretion during his recent adventure in Arabia, and the present matter would be a further test of his steadiness, certainly. But with any luck, David Gresham would prove to be just the man that Mackenzie and Cumming were seeking.

Night had fallen at Suvla Bay. Sergeant Hart kept the company entertained after their meal of tea and stewed Bully Beef and biscuits. Hart was telling bawdy jokes, pretending the officers could not hear. Lieutenant Keeling found the jokes hilarious, but he was so tight that he would have laughed at anything. Hart simply ignored him: He knew better than to muck around with officers, even an officer as affable as Keeling. Others played at cards, some were hiding from the flies under their oil sheets, and some were singing lustily:

> *When this lousy war is over,*
> *No more soldiering for me,*
> *When I get my civvy clothes on,*
> *Oh, how happy I shall be!*
> *No more church parades on Sunday,*
> *No more putting in for leave,*
> *I shall kiss the sergeant-major,*
> *How I'll miss him, how he'll grieve!*

Keeling soon became tired of being ignored and wandered into the tent to find Wilkins sitting on his camp bed beside a single candle, re-reading a letter from home.

"I rather like your girls, there, James," said Keeling when he saw the portraits by artist Harrison Fisher tacked to the post. "I don't suppose you could introduce me to any of them, could you? The one with the cap and the sergeant stripes there, she has quite a lovely mouth."

"Have you decided which of your three girls to marry, yet, Keeling?" Wilkins said with undisguised sarcasm.

"Hardly, no. One of them has money, one has land, and one is very pretty. I deeply fear she is the one that will win out, but I am mortally uneasy with the thought of poverty."

"Perhaps you could take her into India and earn your fortune there." Keeling came from a good family, but their money was all bound up in their estate. As a result, Keeling's personal prospects were fairly poor and he had no plans for after the war.

"Say, I was just chatting with a couple of the ANZACs up here looking for supplies. Perhaps the life of a sheep baron in the antipodes would fit me."

"What did the colonials have to say for themselves?"

Keeling collapsed on his camp bed. "Oh, James, those fellows have been sweating and eating flies here for months. They look rather far gone, to be honest with you." He got a serious look, which was unusual for Keeling. "They told me a very interesting story," he continued. "It seems they had six men out on patrol one night, checking to see if old Abdul had been cutting the wires between the trenches. The men got pinned down in a shell hole by two snipers. One of the bastards was on either side of them. So the men waited a while for the snipers to move on, and then tried to get out of the hole. But every time they tried to get out, the snipers chased them right back in. A full day went by, then another, then another. Their commanding officer didn't know where the men had gone and chalked them off as missing, but the men were actually still in that shell hole and the snipers were still there keeping the men pinned down, taking turns themselves to eat and rest.

"So anyway, a week later, another patrol was sent around to check the wires. Well, they found those six men still in the shell hole, every one of them, and they were all dead from dehydration. Do you see? Those two snipers, they sat there and waited, day after day, for those men in that shell hole to die. . . . So where do you think *we* are now, James? I think we're in the hole."

"It's not like you to get a wind up, Charlie," said Wilkins. "When we advance, we'll still have many more men than the Turks."

"I'm not afraid to advance, James. I just don't want to sit in this heat for months, eating bugs, drinking putrid water, and dying of the bloody flux."

Wilkins could not disagree.

On Imbros, Gresham and Mackenzie sat together on a breezy porch outside a small, freshly-whitewashed house; they were concluding a light supper of fresh tomatoes, onions and roast lamb. Gresham was wearing a clean uniform without insignia or rank or regiment; he brushed his long hair from his face and wiped the crumbs from his shaggy black mustache. "I am deeply indebted to you for the bath, the uniform, and the first decent meal I have had since Egypt, Mackenzie, so I suppose you have every right to expect me to listen to your proposal," he said happily.

"As for the proposal, I can be brief. There is an Ottoman officer from Damascus, an Arab, here on the peninsula, and he wishes to cross the lines. The Turks suspect this officer of being a traitor, so he has been sent to Gallipoli in the hope that he will die there. I would like you to assist him to our side before that happens. We would also like it to appear as though he has been captured against his will or possibly killed, if that can be managed."

"You're being obtuse again. Tell me why you want this fellow so badly."

"That is not relevant to you."

"It is bloody relevant to me. Now look, I know you can get my orders written however you like, but if you want me to be your errand boy, then I think I deserve to know why this officer is so important to you."

"I really don't see how that helps you. You're a clever young man, David. Surely you can put two and two together and see why we want this officer *from Damascus* brought over. Now you demand reasons, yet, earlier, you insisted that your sense of duty motivated you. Or was it your advancement in the ranks? Do you really place so much value in promotion?"

Mackenzie snapped his fingers.

"There, you are now a Captain in some regiment somewhere; I will have to check to see which one. As for duty, I'd like you to do some rather important work for our office. You can consider it fulfilling your duty, as it will significantly contribute to the war effort. To speak bluntly, the war has created tremendous opportunities which Great Britain must seize, but this particular task is an opportunity *for you*, David. I would like you to trust me as to the rest, as I am placing a very great deal of trust in you."

Gresham was silent for a minute as he smoked his cigarette. He knew very little about Mackenzie from their very brief time together at Magdalen College. Mackenzie was now in the "I-Branch," reporting directly to an important government office based somewhere that was doing something presumably to help win the war. And he wanted David's help.

"Did you really make me a Captain just then?" Gresham asked.

"Oh, yes, there are countless vacant captaincies; generalships are harder to come by, I'm afraid."

Gresham lit a cigarette and took a deep drag which he slowly exhaled as he sifted the information in his head. "This officer from Damascus, he would be an Arab, wouldn't he?"

"Most likely," said Mackenzie patiently.

"From what I saw, the Turks and the Arabs don't really get along well, do they?"

"I see you were paying attention when you escorted Mister Lawrence to Arabia and have drawn your own conclusions."

"Damascus is an important city. An Arab officer in the Turkish army, from Damascus, he probably knows a number of other Arab officers, doesn't he?"

"That's hard to say. One would have to ask him. Speaking of which, David, how would you suggest we retrieve this Arab officer from the other side of the lines so that we may question him?"

"It wasn't that difficult to get through yesterday, but the landing was still a surprise then. Today, there are probably ten thousand Turks digging trenches over there. Do you know where this fellow is now; can you even contact him?"

Mackenzie nodded. "We can get him a message."

"Then it's simple. He'll have to be in a specific location at a specific time. Our army advances to or past that point, pushing the Turks back, but your officer stays put. You reach his location at that time and bag your man before some Tommy finds him and shoots him dead."

"The army will undoubtedly advance, yes. Their gains, however, may be very temporary. It would be necessary to accompany the advance troops and act quickly both to retrieve the officer and to protect him. And where specifically would you suggest the officer 'stay put' so that we can 'bag' him."

"The Turks hold the village across the Anafarta plain. It's close by, so we should still be able to get into the area, at least for another few days. There's a small run-in shed off the east road, behind the cemetery. That would do nicely. He could hide there for a rendezvous."

"And will you collect and bring him to me, David?"

"I appreciate you asking this time instead of just having orders written for me. And you really did make me a Captain just now?"

"Yes, yes. I understand the Manchesters will be up the ridge again. I will have to get you attached to another company. Would you like anyone specifically to go with you?"

"Sergeant Hart, from Wilkins' company, I suppose. He knows his business."

"Then we are agreed. You will return to Suvla Bay tomorrow and stay with Mister Wilkins' company until it is time for the attack. If asked, you can say that G.H.Q. wanted you here to provide information about troop movements and defenses in that village. You can arrange the details of our operation with my staff in the morning, but look for confirmation to proceed from me directly." Mackenzie stood. "Thank you, Captain. Let us both pray that your adventure is the first success of many." He shook Gresham's hand and then said good night.

"By the way," Mackenzie added, "where does the name 'Gresham' come from?"

"He was a boy I knew in Manchester, a friend. He's dead now."

Mackenzie nodded. "Good night, then."

After Mackenzie retreated into the small house, Gresham lay down on the porch bench, closed his eyes, and continued to work on the puzzle of the Arab officer. Gresham knew the Ottoman – now the Ottoman Turkish – Empire had been around a long time, but it had also been getting much smaller over the past century. The Sultan had lost parts of Mesopotamia, Central and Eastern Europe, and North Africa. Ever since Napoleon's defeat, the great powers had fought over pieces of the Ottoman territory, especially in the Balkans and North Africa. Now, it seemed, the power of the Ottoman caliphate was crumbling for good. If the Arabs rebelled against the Sultan, the empire itself would likely fall – there'd be nothing left of it but the Turks in Asia Minor. Is that what Mackenzie and the intelligence office hoped to achieve? It was damned clever, but it would impact far more than the course of the war – it would set the whole Near East region in a new direction.

Anafarta Sagir

It took Gresham most of the next afternoon to return to Wilkins' company. On his trip back from Imbros, he visited Private Dawkins aboard *Assaye*. The ship was more a way-station than a hospital, as smaller ships continuously delivered more wounded men and other ships either took the lightly wounded back to the peninsula or transferred the badly wounded to the transports to Egypt. The doctors believed Dawkins' arm would heal and he was in fine spirits. "Don't know when I'll be back, Sir, but they say I'll be returning to the company."

"Look, Dawkins," Gresham told him, "between you and me, you stay on this ship as long as you possibly can, maybe even get on one of the ships to Egypt. There'll be a lot more useless dying on the peninsula before this is all over, and you don't need to be one of them. One wound like this should be all that's expected from any man."

"I agree with you there, Sir, have no doubt."

On shore, the landings appeared to have been mostly completed at last. There were troops swimming and sitting everywhere on the shore and in the sunshine, but still nothing was happening. It was extremely hot, and the stench of death had filled the air despite the best efforts of everyone to bury every deceased thing they could find. The regular shell bursts from Turkish artillery, one about every five minutes, were generally ignored even when shrapnel fell around the troops; for anyone wounded, it was just bad luck. Another huge water tank had been floated ashore to provide more water to the severely dehydrated troops, but water was still in short supply. Men were digging trenches up on the Anafarta plain, the Royal Engineers were constructing elaborate dugouts, wiring telephones and laying out latrines, and they were all being kept busy in other ways, as if making a permanent home on this narrow piece of shoreline. The business of actual fighting was on hold.

As Gresham approached the company encampment, Wilkins rushed up to greet him, "Lieutenant, I am glad to see you back. We've been very busy here, as you can see. How was Imbros?"

"Seems there's some interest at GHQ in the village we passed through; there were a lot of questions about the layout and defenses and so forth. But, I'm sorry to tell you, I also learned there was a mix-up with my orders in Egypt. It seems I may not be with the company very much longer."

"Oh, no," Wilkins exclaimed, genuinely disappointed as he felt he needed to rely on Gresham's experience as well as repay what he believed was a debt to his Lieutenant.

"It also appears I've been made a Captain," said Gresham casually.

"Really? That's such good news, congratulations," said Wilkins cheerfully, but feeling rather confused. Everything about Gresham was unorthodox, and yet he was the one being called to headquarters, and he had been promoted! Certainly Gresham was an excellent battle officer, but Wilkins thought he was the only one who knew it.

"I'll stay with you until my new orders arrive, if you don't mind," said Gresham.

"No, no, not at all. Keeling and I will make room for you in our tent. Keeling's gotten a bit shaken up, I'm afraid. He's gotten rather morose and gone tea-total."

"That's not unusual. I expect he'll come 'round. No news on our next advance, then?"

"Not a word, no. Everyone is waiting for orders, but nothing has come down. You didn't hear anything at headquarters, did you?"

"Nothing specific."

"It's damned frustrating. Even Colonel Banks is upset. He made a nasty comment at tea yesterday about General Stopford, and a few men nearly choked on their rum."

"Speaking of which, I've some bottles in my luggage. We may be waiting a long time."

"Do you play bridge, Captain Gresham?"

Gresham gave him a dirty look. "Can you play for money?"

"Ha, ha! Why don't you learn to play first," said Wilkins.

Two days later they were still waiting. A few men had become ill from the water and the food and the flies which went from feasting on dead mules and men to the rapidly accumulating piles of rancid Bully Beef tins to the men's food and onto the men themselves as they slept or sat by the shoreline. The overwhelming smell of death and decomposition was finally determined to be due, at least in part, to the workings of the hordes of rats and feral kitties that were digging up and devouring the poorly buried human corpses. Half of Wilkins' company had been detailed to scour their section for rodents and cats and to shoot as many as possible, so it seemed again as if they were in a war with guns constantly firing all around them. The other half of the company had been detailed to run barbed wire up to the front and to dig trenches. The two shepherd shacks found in their section were being torn down for firewood, and, in their free time, the men had been rounding up the few goats that had wandered near the camp. A debate was raging over whether to eat the goats or save them for milking.

Wilkins and most of the other junior officers were either a bit drunk or a bit hung over most of the time. As the shortage of water grew more severe, the officers had been wetting their mouths with rum, gin, whisky, brandy, and any other alternative liquids they could find. That afternoon, Wilkins was overseeing two platoons digging a communications trench. They had marched a short distance towards the Kiretch Tepe ridge (far enough away to avoid snipers), but

Sergeant Hart and Cooper, newly promoted to the rank of Corporal, were overseeing the actual work. As Wilkins stood beneath a tree nearby, fanning himself with a pastel-colored Japanese fan, a hefty Sergeant Major unknown to him approached.

"Captain Wilkins, Sir? Tenth Manchesters, Company C?" asked the Sergeant Major.

"Yes, who are you?"

"Sir, I'm sorry to tell you I have orders to take Sergeant Hart into custody, Sir. Is he here?"

"Yes. What's this all about?"

"I don't rightly know, Sir. I'm to bring Sergeant Hart to Division Headquarters."

"On what charge?"

"Don't know the charge, Sir, but he'll have to come along with me."

"Hart!" screamed Wilkins. "We'll have to ask the source."

Hart promptly came striding up to Wilkins and the Sergeant Major, placed his hands on his hips, and stared down at the two of them like Goliath. "Yes, Sir?" he said.

"Hart, the Sergeant Major here has come to arrest you. What have you done?"

"Couldn't say, Sir. Can't say I've had much of an opportunity to do anything. Would you be so kind as to make inquiry to the Colonel, Sir?"

"Indeed, I will."

"Then I suppose I had best go along and wait for you to do that, Sir."

"Yes, yes, you must. I will go to the Colonel directly."

Wilkins wasted no time leaving the company in the care of Lieutenant Keeling and ran off to see Colonel Banks in his tent. Wilkins may not have been sympathetic to Sergeant Hart's views on nobility, but he was a damn fine non-commissioned officer and Wilkins knew the company needed men like that if it was going to be commanded by someone with his own small experience in combat. Wilkins' past combat experience was limited to fox hunting and chess, and that, he knew, was worse than worthless.

"Colonel Banks, Sir, I regret to report that Sergeant Hart from my company has just been taken into custody. We are not aware of the charges leveled against him, and I fear there is a miscarriage of justice. Sergeant Hart is my most reliable and experienced non-commissioned officer."

"The Sergeant is merely being questioned about some matter. I have no more knowledge of it, but I have been assured that Hart will be returned to us in a few days."

"I would rather not do without him for a few days, Sir, especially if we're to go up onto the ridge again."

The Colonel's eyes narrowed and he regarded Wilkins coldly.

"Captain Wilkins, we all have to make do with what we have been given. The situation is not ideal, but I will not sit here and listen to complaints all day long. You will make do. That is, until Major Davenport returns to take command of the company."

"Of course, Sir. The men are looking forward to having Major Davenport back with us, but Sergeant Hart has done marvelous work with them. He does have battle experience in both Africa and India."

"Lack of experience is no excuse for poor performance, Wilkins. You are still very young, but you will learn from Major Davenport. Leadership is a quality of a gentleman, the sort of characteristic which you were bred and born to have. Trust me, I have no doubt you will grow into it. But you have been terribly rash. On the ridge, you were rash. Major Sills has been here to discuss your conduct with me; you and that Lieutenant of yours. You advanced too far and risked yourself and your men, Captain."

"But, Sir, I had orders," objected Wilkins.

"Yes, of course, we all had orders, Captain. Major Sills has told me that you ignored his instructions on the ridge and I am frankly astonished! Astonished, I tell you! Ignoring a respectable officer like Major Sills is a serious matter. Now, I have no desire to lay charges, but there must be repercussions."

"If you say so, Sir," said Wilkins dismally.

"Indeed I say so, Captain. I am your commanding officer, and I do say so. I will not tolerate impertinence. If Keeling had any brains in his head, I would make him the acting commander of Davenport's company. Do I make myself perfectly clear?"

"Yes, Sir," said Wilkins meekly.

"I do not mean to be too harsh with you, my boy. As I said, you will certainly grow into the work, I have no doubt. Mind yourself, and no more cheek, that's what I expect."

"Certainly. Thank you, Sir," stammered Wilkins.

"Very well. Return to your company and await your orders. Something is bound to happen before much longer."

Wilkins quickly left the Colonel's tent. He felt hot, overheated, and, for the first time in his life, bitter. Then his heart hardened. It was perfectly clear what needed to be done, and Wilkins was determined to prove his worth. Colonel Banks was an absolute idiot, and Major Sills was worse. Someone would need to fight the battles if the war was ever to be won, and it wouldn't be gentlemen from England with their noble countenances and aristocratic airs. No, it would be men who knew how to slit old Abdul's throat without making too much noise and aim a machine gun and target the artillery and get water and rations to the front lines. Wilkins hurried back to his company, justifiably concerned that he had left Keeling in charge.

The next morning, a messenger brought up a letter for Gresham as he, Keeling and Wilkins sat outside their tent trying to enjoy a fresh breeze that was coming in off the bay. Gresham scanned the note with surprising passivity:

All arrangements previously discussed are hereby confirmed. Proceed immediately to 1/5 Norfolk Regiment, Suvla Bay. M

"It seems I am to report for my new assignment, gentlemen," said Gresham. "Perhaps something is happening at last."

"It's about bleeding time," said Keeling, who had gone from morose to angry since he had quit drinking liquor. He was no longer enjoying himself and could see that war only sounded like a grand adventure to those who hadn't tried it. "Try not to get yourself killed, there, Gresham. It would be a bloody waste."

"Thanks, Keeling. Same to you."

"I should check with the Colonel," said Wilkins diligently and rising from his seat. "He may have orders for us. I am very sorry to see you go, David." He extended his hand. "It has been quite instructive. Good luck to you, and thank you for your service to the Manchesters," he said calmly.

"And to you, James," said Gresham, shaking hands. His one small duffle was already packed, but Wilkins' servant Dutton helped him carry the bag down the shore towards headquarters.

Colonel Banks did have orders for Wilkins: The Company was going back up the ridge, as they had expected. However, this time, instead of a handful of ill-prepared Turkish reserves, they would face a large number of reinforced and well-armed Turkish troops defending the ridge. It would be hot work, and the Colonel warned Wilkins that casualties would be high on both sides. Wilkins returned to the Company somber and shared the news with Keeling.

"The ridge again!" screamed Keeling. "The same God-damned ridge? The ridge we bloody well took four days ago? The same God-damned ridge we bloody well gave back to the bloody Turks?!" He swore murder up and down the encampment, until he finally busted out a reserved bottle of gin.

Wilkins was no happier, but then he did what he knew he truly needed to do: He asked his experienced company sergeants into his tent to plan the advance and get their advice about the best route of attack.

"This is damned unusual!" shouted Colonel Beauchamp, Commanding Officer of the Fifth Battalion of the "Royal" Norfolk Regiment. Captain Gresham and Sergeant Hart stood before him placidly in the hot dugout that had been prepared for the commander in the newly-completed trenches near Hill 10. Beauchamp was an older commander, portly and with huge sideburns that made his head look bulbous. He seemed uncomfortable and, perhaps, confused, and was quite agitated by the incursion into his dugout by Gresham and Hart. Moreover, Hart stooped over the Colonel threateningly. Standing with the shorter, darker and much hairier Gresham beside him, Hart and the Captain looked like some fairy tale nightmare come to life.

"Of course, Colonel," said Gresham. "I understand your orders are to clear the hills north of the Anafarta Sagir in advance of the main attack in the morning. Sergeant Hart and I are simply to accompany you and take custody of any prisoners located near the village."

"Prisoners?! I dare say there will be little occasion to take prisoners, Captain!"

"I understand, Sir, but there's a particular interest at headquarters in capturing and interrogating enemy officers, so I hope you will indulge my efforts to collect one or more to bring back."

"My men are perfectly capable of capturing officers! Why, may I ask, have you two been sent to me?!"

"Frankly, Sir, you may not ask."

The Colonel turned beet red, but had been struck dumb as well.

"As I said, we will not interfere with your command," continued Gresham, "but our orders are not your concern, nor am I permitted to tell you what they are. The Sergeant and I must reach that village this evening, and you must hold the lines open until midnight so that we can bring back a prisoner."

"I see," said Beauchamp. "Well I can see you're not regular infantry, Captain. We will do our best, that's all I can promise."

"Thank you, Sir."

The Colonel sat down and steadied himself. "The Turks have been busy the past few days drawing up reinforcements. The plains are fairly clear, but the hills are full of snipers. The Fourth Battalion infantry is moving up in reserve today, and our advance will be flanked by the Eighth Hant and the Fifth Suffolk. A naval bombardment will soften up the Turks shortly. I believe we will make an adequate force."

"I quite agree, Sir," Gresham replied. Beauchamp was a blustering old fool, he thought, but he did understand what he was supposed to do and seemed damned determined to do it.

"Then I suggest you stay with my adjutant," said Beauchamp.

"Thank you, Sir. That would be fine," Gresham and Hart saluted and stepped out of the dugout. The trench was packed with the Fifth Norfolks. The men had been standing in the sun with little water for more than a day already waiting for the order to advance. Like the men of the Tenth Manchesters, these troops were also new enlistees; many of them had worked at the King's house at Sandringham, and were therefore known in the lists as the Royal Norfolks. They looked nervous, as all untested troops do, but the company commanders could be seen standing upright and confident among the Tommys and the sergeants were screaming the men to a state of distraction. The trench bristled with raised, shining bayonets, dust swirled in the air, and the hot sun beat down on them all.

"Three battalions, another in reserve, and naval artillery," Hart chuckled, "you don't f--- around, do you?"

"None of that is my doing," said Gresham, rolling a cigarette. "This battalion just happens to be the one going where we need to go."

"Frankly, I'd rather be going up that ridge again with Wilkins tomorrow than back to that damned village with you. You saw how many machine guns were pulling in there the other night."

"Yes, but we shouldn't have to go into the village this time. We're going back around near the cemetery. There's an enemy officer there we need to capture, alive if you don't mind. He should be cooperative. The rest is the Norfolks' business. Then we're back here as fast as our legs can manage it, and you can rejoin the Manchesters whenever you like."

"As I said when you asked me along, I don't much care for subterfuge. I'll do what I can to protect you and keep your route open, but I prefer to do my fighting out in the open, so to speak."

"I appreciate your candor, Sergeant."

Suddenly the British destroyers in the bay opened fire and the familiar sound of the artillery barrage announced that battle would soon be joined. They could hear the massive shells whistling overhead toward the Turkish-held ridges to the east. From this distance, the boom of each shell exploding sounded like thunder. Gresham gripped his rifle and waited for the order to advance, and waited some more. The shelling continued minute after minute. The Turkish batteries opened fire on the bay in reply. Although the British shells were falling three, four and five miles to the east, Colonel Beauchamp had not yet been given the order to advance. Still the shelling continued.

After forty-five minutes, the order to advance was finally given and the battalion climbed out of the trench. Gresham and Hart could see long lines of troops to the south and north of them advancing as well. The Norfolks' path lay straight across the plain. A mile or more ahead of them, the scrub on the plain and hillside had caught fire from the artillery barrage. It would burn out quickly, but all that could be seen ahead was a dense smoke. It luckily screened the battalion's advance and they moved forward at a quick pace.

Gresham and Hart stayed close to Beauchamp's adjutant, Captain Ward. The Tommys were not quite marching in line, but still far more clustered and slower than Gresham would have liked. Large explosive shells were falling on the plain around them. The concussive wave of the explosive shells was simply blowing men over, many more than the steel fragments actually wounded, and those who were blown over more often than not popped right back up and continued as if nothing had happened. As the battalion neared the smoking edge of the plain and lightly wooded hillside, Turkish snipers began to fire blindly from behind the stunted oaks and pines. On their left, the Eighth Hants and the Fifth Suffolks were running into fierce machine gun fire from the ridges to the north. Line after line of British troops was falling there, and those battalions began to slow and dig in for a long hot fight.

Gresham and Hart found the adjutant at the edge of the thin woods. "Captain Ward," yelled Gresham over the noise of shells bursting on their right. "Ward, our left is tied up with those machine guns. The Battalion needs to turn half-right, into the smoke. The village is on our right. Please tell the Colonel."

"Yes, Sir," said the adjutant.

He scrambled to a small burnt and smoking copse of trees nearby and spoke to Beauchamp. Beauchamp evidently agreed with his adjutant, as he directed his company commanders to turn half-right. Three companies of the Norfolks' Fifth Battalion soon disappeared into the thick grey smoke.

Gresham and Hart moved with those companies into the hills north of the road leading to the village. The smoke obscured the view ahead, and each step revealed a new tree or bush, shell hole or shallow trench containing one or more Turkish snipers. Sergeant Hart stayed close to protect Gresham as the battalion advanced over the Turkish position yard by yard. It was hot work, and their progress was slow. Working together as a team, Hart and Gresham would pin down each Turkish sniper whilst one of them went around to fire from the flank. With the Norfolks, they were successfully clearing a wide swath through the hillside. Hart showed a particular talent for killing snipers and seemed to revel in the one-on-one contest of wills as he crouched and crawled through the light brush and smoke, found a position from which to fire, and took his shot.

As the sun set, the men of the battalion began to get worn down. The sense of excitement among the fresh recruits had worn off, and many men succumbed from smoke inhalation and the lack of water. A few men simply collapsed stone dead. The Turkish troops, at least, were faring no better. As the Norfolks slowly advanced, they found more than one burnt corpse of a Turkish soldier who had stayed at his post as the brush fire had swept across the dry hillside. Everything was enshrouded in smoke. Still, many Turkish snipers had stayed on the hillside and continued to shoot the enemy entering their field of fire.

The British sergeants were busy keeping the Norfolks quiet so as not to give away their positions as the companies continued to spread out across the hill. Each tree and bush was approached as a potential threat. Some of the platoon commanders were extremely methodical, like landscape men carefully pruning the verge. Gresham could see they were making slow but steady progress.

As the sun set, smoke made it more difficult to identify their position. Gresham and Hart stayed in the leading edge of the Norfolks as the battalion advanced east, but more and more of the Turkish sorties appeared to be attacking from the south and they were turning the Norfolks to their right flank in response. Gresham and Hart climbed onto a bluff and could see where the village lay to the south and east. A huge network of trenches, wire and barricades had been constructed in front of the well-defended village. A great many Turkish troops had amassed there in positions protected with multiple machine guns, mortars and trenches full of snipers. It appeared the Turks had elected to withdraw to a strong defensive position and send sorties up into the hills where they knew the British were spread out.

"That's a nest of hornets, and no mistake." said Hart.

"Yes, and let's hope the Norfolks don't stir them up too much before we retire. I fear that Beauchamp will take the men too close to the road and walk right into those guns. I need you to keep Beauchamp up in the woods so our line of retreat remains open. I think I can make it to the cemetery alright from here. Go find the Colonel and stay with him until I come find you."

Sergeant Hart found Colonel Beauchamp in the midst of the action, wet with sweat and very red in the face – he looked to be on the edge of collapse.

"Colonel, Sir, Captain Gresham wishes me to report that the village is close by to the south. He reports, Sir, that the Turks in the village are heavily entrenched and well-armed."

"I appreciate the information, Sergeant. We will hold the hillside here, have no doubt. The Turks have been sending sorties up to sweep through our lines, but we have no intention of entering the village. The Fourth Battalion will be coming up for that in just a few hours. Our task is to protect their left flank and dispose of these sorties as they emerge."

"Aye, Sir," said Hart. He was hesitant to say more about Gresham's whereabouts, but he kept close to the Colonel. Night had fallen fast and the smoke was beginning to dissipate. Finding a path through the partly wooded and partly burnt hillside to meet Gresham would be no easy task. Even as the Turkish snipers on the hillside continued to withdraw towards the town, sorties were still sent out to determine the Norfolks' position and test their line. Platoon after platoon of light infantry pushed relentlessly against the Fifth Norfolks, reducing their numbers and forcing the Battalion down from the hills, and, eventually, into the road directly in front of Anafarta Sagir.

Gresham quickly stripped off his jacket and stuffed it in his rucksack. He decided to leave his rifle on the hill and continued on as quietly and quickly as he could. The Turkish snipers had cleared out, however, and Gresham had only to hide quietly from the two small Turkish patrols he came across.

A couple hundred yards further east, Gresham spotted the cemetery again. As he suspected, the Turks saw no need to guard the dead and no one wanted to camp anywhere near the stinking trenches and piles of corpses. Behind the cemetery was the small run-in shed where, in better days, a horse or mule might have been kept. Gresham circled around to the north of the cemetery and approached the small shed slowly and quietly, his service revolver drawn. He stood at last beside the shed itself and listened, wondering not for the last time if he had been right to trust Mackenzie.

"*Salam alaykum*," said Gresham in as calm and normal a tone of voice as he could muster.

A tall, clean, well-groomed and smartly-dressed enemy officer stepped warily out of the shadow of the shed and held up his empty hands.

"*Wa alaykum e-salam*, Englishman," said the Arab officer.

"You speak English?"

"Yes, a little. I am Muhammed al-Faruqi. What is your name, please?"

"Woodrow Wilson."

"That is correct. Our friend gave me that name for you, very clever. You are not to shoot, please."

"No, I'm not going to shoot you," said Gresham, lowering his revolver. "But we need to be off quickly before someone else does."

"Yes. Begin then."

"Follow me and stay close."

Gresham retraced his steps as best he could up to the hillside and took a slightly higher path well out of sight of the village below. There was a lot of shooting by the heavily entrenched troops before the village, but higher up it appeared the hills were clear. There were Turkish and British bodies spread across the hillside.

"Where were you stationed tonight?" Gresham asked.

"Here, there," said the officer, pointing to the village, "I go where I choose."

"Where you choose?" Gresham remarked in surprise. "What is your rank?"

"I am what you would call a 'Major' in your British infantry."

"Do you have identification, papers?"

"Yes, of course I have papers."

Gresham was kneeling on the ground, examining a dead Turkish soldier whose face had been badly wounded; he began tearing off the man's jacket. "Let me have them, please, and your jacket, hat and boots. We need to leave your remains behind."

"Yes, I understand." The officer stripped off his jacket and hat and threw them to Gresham, who had the dead man sitting up to place the officer's jacket on him. The Major sat and Gresham helped to pull off his tall, well-polished and expensive black leather boots. They quickly finished switching clothes and papers with the dead man. Then, to make sure there could be no alternative identification, Gresham thoroughly smashed the dead man's face with the heel of his boot. It was past midnight when he and al-Faruqi returned to where Gresham had left the Fifth Norfolks.

The Norfolks were gone.

Then Gresham realized that Sergeant Hart had disappeared with them. He felt a knot in his stomach and swallowed hard. He wanted to find Hart, who was the only man at Suvla Bay who seemed to know what he was doing. Gresham hesitated.

"We must go," said al-Faruqi.

"I told them not to go near the village."

"If that is where your men have gone, then they will not survive. There is a young Lieutenant Colonel commanding our Nineteenth Division in that village. Mustafa Kemal is a very ambitious man and a ruthless commander. Your men will not take the village, and he does not take prisoners."

Gresham knew he could not leave the Major alone to go find Hart. They had gotten to the point where Gresham was more concerned about al-Faruqi being shot by the British than by the Turks. And if any man could take care of himself, he thought, it would be Sergeant Hart. Hopefully Hart knew enough to get the Hell out of the battle in front of the village.

Gresham clenched his fists, turned towards the bay and led al-Faruqi west.

They finally reached the end of the hills where the land flattened out and the wide open plains began. A couple miles easy march would take them to the British trenches. Behind them, the battle was being fought on the road leading into the village and Gresham felt sick, as he knew the Norfolks and Sergeant Hart were probably in that battle, perhaps even the cause of it. To the north, the Hants and Suffolks were fighting bitterly up onto the ridges around Kidney Hill, and another battle was raging on Scimitar Hill to the south.

"This would be a good time to put on my uniform jacket," said Gresham, holding his blood stained and dusty jacket out to the Arab Major. "We're more likely to run into British soldiers than Turks from here on out." Al-Faruqi silently put on Gresham's jacket, and the two men began a cautious hike across the plain. The pace of the gunfire behind them quickened, and Gresham began to worry that the Turks had broken out and were following them. Ahead, however, Gresham could suddenly see hundreds of fresh British troops with field artillery marching across the plain in their direction.

Gresham stopped and had al-Faruqi lie down. As the British troops approached, he hailed them. None stopped. Like a wave, the fresh battalion marched past Gresham and on towards the village. Some moved to the right and left, fanning out to push up the ridge in both directions to flank the village. Soon the battle behind them truly erupted into a firestorm of bullets, mortars and machine guns. A Colonel on a large black stallion suddenly emerged from the darkness and pulled up directly in front of Gresham and al-Faruqi.

"Who are you men; what battalion?"

"Aye, gov'ner, I'm with the Fifth Norfolks, Sir," said Gresham in the best Norfolk parlance he could manage. "The Captain here, he's a Royal Gurkha as you can plainly see from his skin, attached to my Company, and he's injured severely, Sir, and he looked to be bleedin' out so Colonel Beauchamp said I should take him back as fast as I can, but by the looks of 'im, I don't think he'll make it. I been carrying him the last mile or so, Sir."

"Where is Colonel Beauchamp?"

"I'm sorry to say the Fifth is in front of the village, Sir. Mighty hot up ahead, Sir, mighty hot: Machine guns, mortars, snipers, old Abdul in the trenches, and a lot of wire. The works, if you see my meaning, Sir. Perhaps you'd like me to take your fine horse to the rear, Sir, as I don't think he'll survive long up ahead? Makes a mighty big target with you on him, don't you think, Sir?"

"Yes, perhaps you're right. What's your name?" The Colonel dismounted quickly, although from fear or embarrassment was difficult to say.

"Corporal Pelt, Sir, Arthur Pelt, C Company."

"Very well, Corporal. Walk my horse back to the stables at Hill 10. The Gurkha Captain may ride."

"Thank you, Sir. I have every certainty that you have just saved this man's life, Sir."

Gresham helped the "wounded" al-Faruqi onto the horse's saddle. As the Fourth Norfolks rushed forward against the small village ahead, Gresham slowly led the horse and al-Faruqi towards the rear.

The Tenth Manchesters had finally begun their advance shortly after midnight. Wilkins and his company were on the hill leading back up to the Kiretch Tepe ridge. Ahead of the company, the artillery shells from the British destroyers were crashing all along the top of the ridge, creating a curtain of cinders, smoke, dust and iron. There was no sign of any living thing ahead but for the crackle of sniper and machine gun fire. The star shells and Verey flares could not cut through the dust and smoke, but the sky was filled with pockets of luminescence that lit the hills dimly. It was impossible to see if the shells had destroyed the barbed wire in front of the Turkish trenches. Colonel Banks had ordered Wilkins to advance straight through the British bombardment and to attack the Turkish machine gunners on the right. Time after time, Wilkins sent runners forward to locate the machine gun emplacements, but none of his men had returned. He shouted ahead to a deep shell hole in which several men sought cover. One man poked his head up to look and was instantly struck by a bullet. A second head came up, and a bullet struck off the man's pith helmet. He was bleeding heavily, but was not badly wounded. He became deliriously excited about his wound and called for stretcher-bearers to take him to the rear. When no stretcher arrived, he crawled from the hole in frustration and began running back. A bullet struck his leg, and he fell.

This battle was much different from the one Wilkins had fought with Gresham a few days before. This was brutal murder, and the cost of life was staggering: Wilkins had already seen many of his men die. He was no longer afraid for his own safety, as his expectation of survival was altogether gone. Now he just wanted to kill as many of the Turks as he possibly could.

Wilkins scrambled forwards to the shell hole and slid down below the rim. The hole was full of wounded men and dead men and parts of men. His whole company had gone to ground; the men were crouching in whatever shell holes could be found nearby. Suddenly with a roar the whole sky and every hill and tree were illuminated bright red – one of the British artillery shells had hit an ammunition cache. Wilkins could see a few men, including Sergeant Major Dunham, in shell holes around his own. By shouting, the order to advance was transmitted hole to hole. At last, Wilkins raised his whistle to his mouth and blew. More than a hundred men rose out of their pits and scrambled forward on their bellies. Wilkins and the first wave of troops reached the first, narrow trench only to find that the Turkish troops there had already been obliterated by the British shelling. Wilkins and his men slid into the first trench, seeking cover from the hail of shrapnel and machine gun fire overhead, gasping through the smoke and heat.

Only ten yards ahead, but on the other side of a thick barbed wire barricade, the second Turkish trench was heavily defended. Wilkins thought his company might be able to crawl under the wires, which he was angry to see the British shells had left untouched. He called to his men to prepare for the advance, and then raised his whistle to his lips again. He tried to wait for the flares to burn out, but there was no let up. The whistle blew, and the company scrambled up out of the trench. The Turkish machine guns were waiting, and dozens of men fell instantly. Some advanced to the wire. There was no way through. His men were being picked off one by one, so Wilkins ordered the men back into the narrow trench behind them. As he slipped back into the trench, he felt a sudden burning sensation across his left cheek and his left ear suddenly felt wet. Less than twenty men had made it back into the trench.

Wilkins soon realized that a bullet had scored his cheek to the bone and gone through his left ear. He was bathed in blood. He ordered his men to save their ammunition and to hold the trench against a counter-attack. He tore off part of his shirt and pressed it tightly against his cheek and ear to staunch the flow of blood, but he felt terribly light-headed and nauseous and his heart was beating wildly in his chest. He fell unconscious to the bottom of the trench.

———————

On the shore, a caique was waiting to take Gresham and al-Faruqi directly to Imbros. The Greek fisherman led them to the small enclosure on the deck where there were benches and tea with lemon to drink. As the sailboat drew away from shore, Gresham leaned his head against the wall to rest. Al-Faruqi finally appeared to relax and removed Gresham's ripped and bloody coat.

"Here is your coat, Mister Wilson, thank you." said al-Faruqi to Gresham. "You have been very helpful to me."

Gresham nodded, taking the coat.

"I have a question, Englishman: You referred earlier to 'the Turks.' Do you consider all your Ottoman enemies to be Turkish?"

"No more than I consider all British to be Englishmen."

"Are you not?" asked al-Faruqi abashedly.

"No, indeed. I'm half-Irish, by the way."

"I apologize for my rudeness."

"It's not my place to ask questions, but there's one thing I'm curious about. How many of the officers in the Ottoman army are not Turkish?"

"Hundreds, oh yes – there are many Arabs, some Kurds, Assyrians; there were also Ermeni, but they are all dead now."

"You mean Armenians? What happened to them?"

"Enver Pasha believes the Armenians fight for Russia, so they were executed."

"Enver Pasha – he's the man in command of the Ottoman Turkish armies, right?"

"Yes, correct. Last winter, he fought a great battle against the army of Russia at Sarikamish. The Russians were advancing through the Caucasus Mountains from Kars. Enver Pasha halted their advance, but then his counter-attack stretched his men and supplies too thin, and the Russians won a devastating victory. Very many of our soldiers were killed; it was a terrible defeat. Enver Pasha claims that his Armenian troops turned against him and fought for Russia. No one believes this to be true, but that is his justification."

"So then Enver Pasha ordered the execution of all the Armenian officers?"

"No. He ordered the death of all Armenian men. Also, the Armenian women, children and the elderly are being taken from their homes and cast out of Ottoman territory. Very many will die. Kurds will be next, I suspect. Then perhaps the Arabs? Who knows? Enver Pasha and his men have long hated these peoples."

"Wait a minute. You're telling me that Enver Pasha is killing *all* the Armenians in the Ottoman Empire?"

"It is happening, yes. A thousand thousand will die, more than man can count."

"Good God! That's outrageous!" Gresham was truly shocked. It was hard to imagine that any nation, even the Turks, would attempt to murder a whole portion of its people. Even the British bastards in Ireland had not yet tried to murder all the Irishmen. Gresham hadn't been to church in many years – his mother had been Catholic and often spoke with great passion about her devotion to the Pope, whom she called the Lion of Rome – but now, without thinking, Gresham crossed himself.

"Yes, it is haram, a very great sin. There are many officers in the army who wish to take no part in such evil. In Damascus, it is widely debated what to do."

"Is that why you are here?"

"I have said all I will say for now, my friend. You will forgive me if I rest now, please. I will have much to say when we arrive."

Al-Faruqi closed his eyes, but Gresham could no longer rest. The sun was beginning to rise as the little caique sailed gently past the British destroyers with their guns still blasting and left behind the tens of thousands of British, French and ANZAC soldiers who would go on hopelessly attacking the now deeply entrenched and heavily reinforced Turkish positions on the ridges around Suvla Bay.

Tenedos

Gresham waited beside the entrance to the medieval stone fortress on Tenedos, one of the islands off the coast of Asia Minor. The island was a Turkish territory, but since it was inhabited exclusively by Greeks, the dilapidated fortress had been taken over by the British and made into a field hospital for casualties brought off from the Gallipoli peninsula. Inside the curtain wall was a great assembly of tents and dugouts where some of the injured officers were being tended. At the entrance gate, there was a steady stream of stretchers being walked into the bailey where the tents had been erected, and Gresham didn't want to get in their way. It had been over a week since he had last been on the peninsula himself. While the fighting had abated since then, there were still casualties being taken off every day. As he feared, the Turkish commanders had been able to move up enough reserves and supplies to halt the Allied advance. Now both sides were deeply entrenched, in some places just a few yards from each other. The Allies were at a standstill, and the weather had only gotten hotter and the water shortage more severe. More and more of the casualties were sick rather than wounded. At last, Gresham was able to duck into the gate of the fortress. He quickly found a nurse who could take him to see Wilkins.

"Hello there, old man. What a surprise," said Wilkins with good cheer as Gresham was led to his bed. Wilkins was sitting up. The left side of his face was covered in thick white bandages that wrapped around his forehead and neck, but Gresham was pleased to see the bandages were clean and showed no sign of seeping blood.

"How are you, Wilkins?" replied Gresham.

"It's not too painful, although I'm told it's still rather ghastly to look under the bandages. Did you hear about it?"

"Yes, in general terms. How will it turn out?"

"The face will be alright – scarred, of course, but mostly on the side and thankfully no loss of vision – and I may end up with a rather mangled ear."

"I'll buy you a good hat."

"What about you? You're unharmed, it seems."

"Yes, actually I wasn't at the front very long; I got sent back with a prisoner – some high-ranking Turk officer. Had to keep him under guard for a few days and then never got sent back up."

"Whose company were you finally assigned to?"

"Well, I'm no longer with the Manchester Regiment, actually."

"You're not? Who, then?"

"Mostly I've been running errands for some people at GHQ. Not very exciting, really. I hear you did a damn good job on the ridge, though."

"Have you? I'm so glad to hear it. I really didn't want to muck it all up. We reached the top of the ridge again, but that's where the Turks had drawn their line in the sand. We tried desperately to penetrate their trenches, but their wires were completely untouched by our artillery barrage."

"It's not the first time I've heard that."

"The number of casualties was very high, I'm sorry to say. You know poor Keeling died not ten feet from me."

"Yes, I heard they got him. There were heavy casualties all along the lines."

"Eventually the Yorks came up to relieve us and found me unconscious in the trench with only eighteen men of my company still alive. Say, did you hear about the Fifth Norfolks?"

"Yes, I heard." Gresham didn't care to talk about the Norfolks or think about what might have happened to them and Sergeant Hart.

"An entire battalion gone – just gone, not even a wounded man left to be found," said Wilkins. "No one can believe it. They marched off into the smoke and haven't been seen since."

Gresham was silent a moment. He wanted to change the topic of conversation. "They say Italy has now declared war on the Turks, but then again the Italians have been at war with the Austrians since May," he said.

"You know," continued Wilkins, "I'm allowed to walk about outside if I'm accompanied. Do you have time for a stroll?"

"Certainly. In fact, I came to Tenedos just to see you."

"Did you? That's very kind, really. Give me a moment to change out of my pajamas and I'll meet you just outside."

Gresham wandered through the hospital tent, which was clean and orderly and breezy. There was a wide range of wounded men, from those who were destined to recover and return to the trenches like Wilkins to those whose fate was yet unclear, but generally the wounds seemed pretty bloodless. The men who had lost limbs or suffered other permanent disfigurements were taken right off to Egypt where the British hospital was more like a morgue.

Gresham saw a young R.C. priest sitting on a bed, talking grimly with an older officer who showed no obvious wounds at all. The priest reminded Gresham of the young, cheery vicars who took to the streets in Manchester to "save" the boys like Gresham who no longer had a home. Gresham had lived with his mother, of course, but she had died of a fever when Gresham was still quite young, so he lived in the streets with countless other homeless and abandoned boys. They slept in abandoned factories and warehouses and stole food. Of course, attempts were made to bring the boys to orphanages and foster homes, but nothing could make them stay and many ran away again and again. Sometimes the vicars or priests would come and talk to the boys about their salvation and serving God. Gresham had heard stories about some of those men and the other things they wanted from the boys, and he had learned to stay away from them altogether. Yet he accepted that for some, like Wilkins whom Gresham had seen praying quietly on more than one occasion, religion was a more respectable, reassuring and motivating power.

Wilkins and Gresham met in front of the fortress and walked to a quiet café down by the harbor. They sat in the sun, watched the lighters arrive with the wounded and small fishing boats come and go, and drank tea with a little whisky and lemon in it.

"Say, David, I heard a strange thing about the Norfolks. Apparently a very tall Sergeant joined their battalion immediately before the offensive began. You don't suppose that was Sergeant Hart, do you? It only struck me as interesting because, if you haven't heard, the Sergeant has gone missing." Gresham wondered if Wilkins was fishing for information. One thing about Wilkins, he was a damned clever bastard.

"James, is it true that you speak seven languages besides English?"

"What?" Said Wilkins, surprised. "Yes, yes, always had a thing for languages, since I was a lad."

"What languages do you speak fluently?"

"Well, speaking is far easier than writing, at least for me. Let's see – French, of course, Italian, German, Greek – both modern and classical, Russian, and a bit of the Slavic languages – Serbian and so forth. And I picked up a little of the Egyptian Arabic in Alexandria as well."

"That's remarkable. I learned quite a bit of the Irish language as a lad, but I struggled with Latin and Greek when someone finally tried to teach 'em to me. It's a wonder that you were placed in the lines when you would be so very helpful in other ways."

"Perhaps so. Between you and me, Father tried to get me placed in the Foreign Office, but I resisted."

"Would that have been so terrible?"

"Oh I don't mean it that way at all. It's difficult to explain."

Wilkins grew pensive, and Gresham let him alone for a while as they sipped their tea and watched the ships; there was a fresh breeze off the water and the sun was pleasant. Gresham was not the son of an English Lord, but he understood that Wilkins' situation was more complicated than his own: Gresham had no family and no future apart from what he made for himself. Wilkins had a family reputation to live up to.

"James, I'd like to ask a favor of you."

"Of course, please ask," said Wilkins, waking from his own reverie.

"I'm going to Salonika, and I'd very much like you to come with me."

Wilkins laughed loudly, then quickly raised his hand to his wounded face. "Ow–ow-ow. Good Lord, it hurts to laugh. Honestly, David, I can't fathom you at all. Salonika of all places, in Greece?"

"That's the one."

"You know that as a company commander my first duty must be to the men."

"You're not commanding anymore. Davenport has come in from Alexandria."

"Oh . . . I see. Of course I expected that," said Wilkins quite calmly despite his disappointment. Even though he knew Major Davenport would be returning to the regiment, Wilkins more than hoped that his leadership on the ridge had earned him a company of his own. It seemed he would instead resume his duties under Davenport.

Wilkins knew he had received a certain amount of deferential treatment due to his family connections, but he did not expect nor want promotion on that basis alone. On the other hand, he had worked hard to make himself a good officer, he had successfully led his men with courage into battle, and he had behaved with honor as a dutiful subject to King George on his family's behalf. None of those accomplishments, it would seem, counted for much any longer. He regarded Gresham for a moment with a mixture of curiosity and envy. Gresham was no one. Gresham was just a good soldier – a good soldier who did what he was told. "Why are you going to Salonika?" He asked finally.

"British troops will be landed there in a few weeks, and I've been asked to more or less clear the way for them. Part of that involves sweeping up the debris, which I can handle all right. The other part is more diplomatic. Of course, there are formal diplomatic discussions underway, but it was suggested to me that a little informal ground work could help grease the wheels. That's where I could really use your assistance. And when the Manchesters arrive in Salonika, you can rejoin them there, if you wish. Perhaps you would be given a company command then."

"Now you've told me something really important, David. The only Manchesters in the Mediterranean are at Suvla Bay. If they are to be redeployed to Greece, that means troops are to be drawn off the peninsula. Is it just the Manchester Regiment?"

"Well, no, I don't think so. Between us, it looks as though the offensive at Gallipoli is over. We've managed to tie down thousands of Turkish troops, but that wasn't our objective. We've also tied down thousands of Allied troops and the number of casualties is far too great. The Allied forces will almost surely be evacuated."

"Good Lord, what a terrible waste of men. A defeat like this will certainly bring down the government in London; it's already ended poor Churchill's career at the Admiralty. But why move the troops to Salonika rather than redeploy them to Egypt or send them to France?"

"We'll have to figure that out for ourselves."

"I would like to solve that riddle, and I also want to know who asked you to go to Salonika – was it Sir Ian?"

"General Hamilton will write our orders, but this is something else. Confidentially, it comes from our Intelligence branch."

"But the military intelligence office *would* report to Sir Ian, at least in the Mediterranean."

"So I understand. This is not a military intelligence office. It's a civilian intelligence office."

"I didn't know we had one."

"I believe they would like to keep it that way."

"And who controls this intelligence office, I wonder?"

"I haven't any idea, and if I did I'm quite sure they would not want me to tell you."

"I see. You have a way of putting things that make them sound distinctly unflattering."

"I don't mean it that way."

"Of course, otherwise you would not have asked me to join you. Well, I suppose I'd be no worse off if I go with you to Salonika, but I must have orders properly issued by my superiors. I'm all in favor of a little diplomacy or espionage or what-have-you, but I can't let down the Manchesters and I will not be party to any political intrigues that might embarrass Father."

"Of course; I'm sure it can be arranged as you like. Do you know when you'll be ready to travel?"

"Another week more or less, after the risk of infection has passed."

"Good. Let's skip the tea, then, and stick to straight whisky."

"Fine with me. Say, I did hear a good one the other day: Have you heard what the dragon said to the knight in shining armor?"

"What?"

"Oh, no! More Bully Beef!"

Gresham returned to headquarters on Imbros later that day to make his report to Mackenzie. After Gresham had delivered the Arab Major to the intelligence office, Mackenzie and al-Faruqi had held several long and secretive meetings, and Mackenzie told Gresham that he would prove to be extremely valuable in Arabia. In the meantime, Gresham assisted Mackenzie with the interrogation of several Turkish agents captured on Imbros. And then Mackenzie spoke to Gresham about the planned British landing at the Greek city of Salonika. Gresham knew only that Greece was still a neutral country and that Salonika was close to Serbia, a country which had thus far successfully prevented an invasion by the Austro-Hungarians. Mackenzie knew very little about the landing himself. Great Britain obviously wanted to stiffen the Serbian resolve and was hoping to bring Greece into the war on the side of the Entente. Mackenzie wanted Gresham to find out what was going on in Greece and make sure the Allies would be warmly received in Salonika by both the government and the local people. Gresham also knew that Mackenzie still wished to enlist Wilkins to the service and had proposed approaching his fellow officer in hospital about joining the trip to Greece. Mackenzie was delighted with the idea.

Gresham was taught a few simple codes and given a pad of special single-use code sheets so he could communicate with Mackenzie securely. The code sheets were supposedly impossible to decipher, he was told. Each sheet had a unique six-digit serial number and was printed with lines of random numbers in groups of five. One merely translated each letter (or empty space) of a given message into a number (A being one, B being two, and so forth) and added on the number in the corresponding place on the code sheet. One would then transmit the numbers with the sheet's serial number. The receiver of the message would reverse the process by using his copy of the same code sheet. Since each sheet was unique and the code numbers were entirely random, the code could not be decrypted. Gresham was instructed to name Mackenzie in his messages simply as *M* and sign each message with his three-digit code number, *006*.

For close work Gresham preferred to rely on the trench knife he kept strapped to the back of his belt. But for this operation, Gresham was especially determined to see that nothing bad happened to Wilkins, and the service be damned if they didn't like it, so he obtained a Browning M1911 magazine-fed .45-caliber handgun. The guns were made in America but were very popular in the British Navy for their moderate size, reliability and magazine loading. Lastly, for the trip to Greece, Gresham was given a fortune in British gold sovereigns and Greek drachmas, the better to buy the alliance of anyone who needed to be and could be persuaded in that manner.

In the evening following his return from Tenedos, Gresham met with Mackenzie for one last supper at the little white-washed house on Imbros. Mackenzie would be off early the next morning to escort al-Faruqi to the Foreign Office in Egypt, where plans vis-à-vis British support for an armed Arab uprising against the Turks were to be discussed.

"I wanted a final word before I leave for Cairo," Mackenzie began. They were sitting on the patio again drinking brandy. In the night sky above them, the moon was bright, but the air was still and heavy. "As you prepare to depart for Greece and leave your Manchesters behind on the peninsula, David, I imagine you have begun to wonder what you have gotten yourself in to."

"To be honest, Compton, I have tried very hard *not* to wonder."

"I really do appreciate the trust you have placed in me, to be certain, David, but you must understand that my purview is limited. For one thing, I work only in the Aegean arena; I may end up in Athens myself one day. But the intelligence service is a larger institution, albeit a fairly new and terribly disorganized one. Much of what our agents do involves counting railway cars, taking inventory of enemy ships, and questioning spies. We are gatherers of information and we pass that information on to those who will most benefit from its use, whether that is the army, the navy, our allies, or what have you. But I intend that you will be something far less passive than a mere information collector.

"I want to state plainly to you that I am not your superior officer. You shall keep in contact with me, and I will pass on your government's assignments to you, but in every other respect you will be your own man. Of course, you also hold the rank of Captain, in the Border Regiment as it turns out. But you will not be receiving orders or have any other contact with that regiment; they will not even know you exist except as a name on a list in a book that no one ever reads. You will be an independent instrument of our government, but, conversely, the British government will deny responsibility for anything that you do that may be embarrassing or even diplomatically uncomfortable. Is that clear?"

"Yes, I suppose so."

"It must be very clear, David, because I am saying to you now that you are charged with doing what you deem must be done to serve your country's best interests and fulfill your assignments, but even though you are an agent of your country's Intelligence Service, you may never admit it. If you are captured or arrested, you may not plead to us for assistance, as there will be none forthcoming. Do you understand?"

"For my part, I do. But what of Wilkins? I fear he would be very uncomfortable with such an arrangement, were I to explain it to him in those terms."

"Captain Wilkins shall remain a Captain in the Tenth Manchesters and, for a time, he can assist you in that capacity. After that, he will have to decide for himself whether he wishes to make a commitment to the service. Confidentially, I will tell you that Lord Bartlett would strongly approve of what James is doing. I am not naming any names, you understand. The Intelligence Service is not controlled by the War Office or the Admiralty, or by any Lord, Minister or King. It is run by the government, and by men who work anonymously in permanent offices set up by the government with the sole purpose to defend the people of the British Empire from harm."

Gresham felt a jolt of pride. He did not want to be judged for who he was. He wanted to be judged solely for what he did. Now he would serve his country doing what he did best, and his country would know him solely by his deeds and appreciate him solely for rewards it could perhaps not even clearly identify.

"I believe, Compton, that you have saved me," he said. "And not just by getting me out of Suvla Bay – that is obvious enough."

"I hope so, David, I truly do. Just be careful and use your head."

Gresham and Mackenzie parted that night with a handshake and a mutual understanding, yet neither knew when or if they would ever meet again.

Gresham, like Wilkins, wanted to know the reason Salonika had been chosen for a British landing, but he also felt it was important to understand the political situation in Greece and how that fit into the overall advancement of the war effort. He had been told there were already British diplomats in Greece seeking the King's consent to a British landing, but there were surely German and Austrian diplomats there as well and perhaps German intelligence agents, and most certainly a mysterious and complex political situation. While the British government had plans for Gresham, he knew his new role would require him to be more than a good soldier for his country. He would have to understand what his country was seeking to accomplish.

After losing Hart at Suvla Bay and learning about the murder of the Armenians in the Ottoman Turkish Empire, Gresham had become even more focused. More than that, he was fiercely angry. He already grasped that his government was developing a plan to destroy the Ottoman Empire by encouraging outright rebellion from within. It was an audacious way to win a war, and would likely prove to be more effective than killing men on a battlefield had been. But why Greece, why Salonika, and what was to come after that?

A few days later, Gresham and Wilkins stood on a pebbly beach up the coast from the fortress on Tenedos, a bottle of cheap rum that Gresham had purchased sat on the hot pebbles beside them; whisky was becoming hard to find. The sun was bright and warm, so the men had stripped down to their shorts and had been swimming in the cool blue water.

To look at them, both men had changed in the weeks since they had arrived at Suvla Bay. In preparation for the trip to Greece, Gresham was now cleanly shaved and his drooping black mustache and long greasy hair had been neatly trimmed, much more respectable looking and more suitable for the work he would be doing as an *agent provocateur*. He emerged a handsome young gentleman, no longer troll-like in appearance, sullen- or moody-looking. His blue eyes were sharp and bright, and he moved with a new-found sense of purpose. Wilkins, once a fair-haired boy, already had the gaunt and chiseled look of a war veteran. Across his left cheek lay a wide red scar which led to an ear that was noticeably smaller and more crinkled than his right. He had more confidence, which was justified by his experience under fire, and a more mature outlook on the war.

Side by side, Gresham and Wilkins bent over the M1911 handgun that Gresham had brought. He had purchased a second handgun for Wilkins and was showing him how the magazine was loaded. They planned to walk further up the coast and practice shooting. In two days, they would board the HMS *Fincher* and sail for Alexandria. From Alexandria, they would take a common passenger ferry to Athens as British soldiers on holiday and from there take a ship or train to Salonika. Wilkins had received unusually vague and open-ended orders signed personally by General Hamilton. Gresham no longer needed written orders at all. He would simply do whatever needed to be done.

Wilkins sat on the beach and poured some rum into his tin cup. "The choice of Salonika does make sense," he argued to Gresham. "British defeat on the Gallipoli peninsula will certainly embolden Bulgaria to join the war with Germany and Austria-Hungary. The Austrians have been trying to invade Serbia for more than a year so that the railway lines can be opened between Germany and Constantinople. With Bulgaria attacking from the east and Austria from the north, Serbia would stand no chance at all. And once Serbia is overrun, Greece itself would be threatened. The only thing that might dampen our enemy's ambitions is an Allied force backing up the Serbian Army, and the only place to land such a force is at Salonika."

"I follow that, but Salonika is in Greece, which is still a neutral country."

"Yes, and furthermore the Queen Regent is the Kaiser's sister, so we know how they will feel about British troops landing in their territory. But the Greek Prime Minister is very popular with the people and he favors the Entente – well, really, he just favors Great Britain, not so much France or Russia – which is how they've settled uncomfortably into a position of neutrality."

"Did you say the King's wife is the German Kaiser's sister?" Gresham asked, quite stunned.

"Yes, Queen Regent Sophie. She's Prussian, from the House of Hohenzollern. If I recall correctly, the Greek king's family is from Denmark, House of Oldenburg, I believe. Mother would know; she knows all the royal families."

"Why aren't the King and Queen Greek?"

"Greek? No, no. You don't understand how things are done at all, David. There was a Convention agreed upon by the great powers (I refer to Great Britain, France and Russia, of course), eighty or so years ago. Greece was in chaos after it had won independence from the Ottomans, and King Otto was enlisted from the nobility of Europe and undertook the responsibility to bring a stable government to the Greeks. Unfortunately, Otto proved to be a bit of rake and never had any legitimate children, so he was replaced in 1863 by King Constantine's father, George. He wasn't the Greeks' first choice, but they took him unanimously after Britain agreed to hand over the Ionian Islands to the Greek government as well. As you may also recall, King George was assassinated by an anarchist just two years ago, and that was when his son, Constantine, ascended to the throne. I was quite sorry, to be honest; I rather liked King George. We met at King Edward's funeral at St. George's Chapel."

"You were at King Edward's actual funeral? At Windsor Castle?"

"Well, yes," Wilkins replied modestly. "I was just across the river at Eton then, and my father asked me to join him. I wasn't in the procession in London, though. The service at Windsor was rather long and sad and hot, and the reception following was very subdued, but one rarely sees so many royals in one place at once anymore – apart from George the Fifth, there were eight other monarchs there, including the Kaiser, who is King Edward's nephew, of course. The Archduke Franz Ferdinand was there too; he was rather cold and pompous, to my thinking. President Roosevelt – he had just come from Africa, which sounded marvelous. But I especially enjoyed the King George from Greece. He knew a great deal about the ruins near Athens; I had a rather strong interest in archeology then.

"In any event, his son, King Constantine, has proven to be quite independent-minded and regrettably pro-German. But that is how things are done. Europe is run by the nobility. Privilege entails to responsibility, my friend, or so I have been taught."

"So you're saying he gets to be King because some blokes in England picked his name from a silk purse. I honestly don't see why the Greeks listen to a word he says."

"As the anointed monarch, his authority to govern flows from God Himself. The Divine Right of Kings, David – I would think you've heard of it."

"Yes, like King Arthur getting Excalibur from the Lady of the Lake." Gresham said sarcastically. He took the bottle of rum from Wilkins.

"Well, the theory rather went out of fashion in England when William and Mary took the throne from King James in 1689. Englishmen began to see the crown as a symbol of the power we grant to the monarchy, rather than the final arbiter of the rights granted to us. It doesn't hurt for the king to have the backing of the military either. In Constantine's case, for example -"

"I've heard enough, mate" he said, and gulped rum from bottle. "Let's go shoot something."

After they had each fired off a few rounds in the general direction of a stunted oak tree, scared away a trip of goats, and almost killed the shepherd, the two Captains decided they had perhaps drunk too much rum to practice shooting any longer. As they walked back to town, Wilkins was quiet and clearly thinking about something important. They stopped at the café to purchase another bottle of rum, and settled down against the sunny side of the building.

Wilkins finally spoke up: "David, I'm ashamed to say that I am rather grateful not to be going back to the front lines. I thought it would all be rather tactical, maneuvering the men about and so forth. I was rather stupid, I suppose."

"You're no different than most of the officers, James, and frankly steadier than most that I've seen."

"Is it the same on the Western Front?"

"In many ways it was worse on the Western Front, but at least there you can get away from the front lines from time to time. On the peninsula, there's nowhere for the men to pull back."

"When the Germans gassed the lines at Ypres, how bad was it?"

Gresham was silent a moment. It was an experience he didn't wish to remember. "Why do you wish to know?" he growled.

"It's just that I can't imagine how they could do it."

"The French used chemicals first – tear gas, they call it."

"Yes, but the gas they used wasn't intended to kill. It was used to force the Germans out of the trenches. To use a gas to purposefully kill men, it's horrifying."

"When the Germans gassed the trenches at Gravenstafel Ridge, the Frenchmen mostly just tried to get out of the trenches to get away from the gas and they were shot as they retreated. I was in a bunker, and we were sealed in tight when a shell collapsed the trench wall. We didn't even know the gas had come. When we finally dug our way out, we saw the bodies and knew at once what had happened. It was very bad. The gas tends to settle low in the trenches so I inhaled only a little, but it felt like my eyes were on fire and my lungs were full of boiling water. I didn't get it too bad, thankfully. The Regiment was already transferring some of the officers down to the new Divisions in Alexandria, and someone thought the warm, dry air would do me good."

"But I just think that to use gas that way, it can only mean the Germans don't want to simply win the war. It's as if they want to exterminate their enemies altogether."

Wilkins' comment reminded Gresham of the Armenians in Asia Minor. Is that what the Ottoman Turks wanted? To "exterminate" the Armenians? Not all the Turks, surely. Enver Pasha and his pals, they were another story. "Well, someone does, maybe," said Gresham. "Some believe the end justifies the means."

"No, that's not what I am saying. It's as if they believe they have the right to eradicate those men they consider to be inferior. There's been quite a fashion to talk about 'purifying' Europe of what are considered the 'inferior' races."

"You're not making me feel better; I'm half-Irish, remember." However, sitting in the sun with a bottle of rum inside them and another in hand made it difficult not to feel good. The café had wonderful grilled meat skewers, and before long Gresham and Wilkins were feasting on lamb, flat breads, fresh vegetables, and a simple local sauce made from goat's milk called *yoghurti*. Then they filled themselves with handfuls of rich, sweet pastries made from nuts and honey and drank Turkish coffee and a local liqueur flavored with anise until long after dark. At last, they staggered together back to the small tent they shared just outside the walls of the old fortress. Wilkins lit a candle. He was trying to teach Gresham how to play bridge, and they played late into the night.

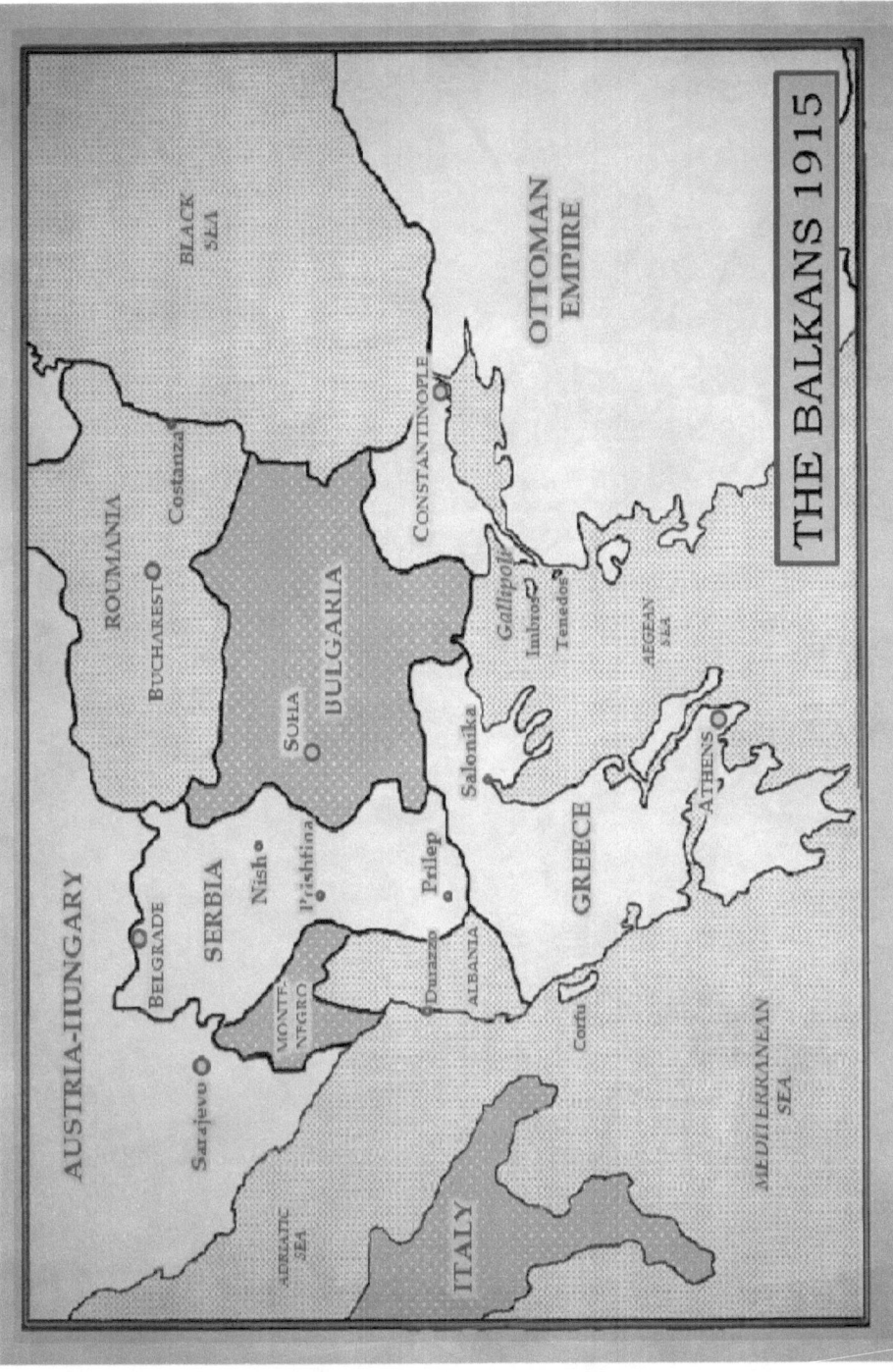

THE BALKANS 1915

AUSTRIA-HUNGARY

Sarajevo

ADRIATIC
SEA

SERBIA

BELGRADE

Nish
Prishtina

MONTE-
NEGRO

Durazzo

ALBANIA

Corfu

ROUMANIA

BUCHAREST

Costanza

BLACK
SEA

BULGARIA

SOFIA

Prilep

Salonika

GREECE

ATHENS

MEDITERRANEAN
SEA

ITALY

CONSTANTINOPLE

Gallipoli
Imbros
Tenedos

AEGEAN
SEA

OTTOMAN
EMPIRE

Athens

The Cambridge was the finest hotel in Athens that catered to British guests, and the men's lounge was particularly dark, stuffy and hot. Gresham and Wilkins were sitting, in uniform, at a small table drinking whisky, smoking cigarettes, and playing dominos with a British ex-patriot who had just returned from a trip to Barcelona. "Barcelona is wonderful," the gentleman said. "There was a lovely little senorita in the house across from *The Majestik*. I tell you the loveliest girls in Spain are in Barcelona. I do hope you fellows get a chance to visit. How long will you be staying in Athens?"

"Captain Wilkins here wishes to visit the archeological sites, Mister Penniworth, so we're leaving in a day or two to travel about the countryside," said Gresham.

"How terrible, terrible, when there's so much to do in Athens right now: Lovely ladies to be found for those who know where to look. Seems to me they would be of interest to you young officers, eh what? I'd be delighted to show you about. There are several excellent houses where I know the proprietors personally, and you may take your pick."

"You are most kind, sir," said Wilkins, who had gone quite red in the face. "I regret we have other plans for this evening."

"I am so sorry to hear that, really. Tell me of your trip from Egypt? Uneventful, I hope?"

"On the contrary, the trip from Egypt will likely prove to be the most exciting part of our journey," said Gresham. "Did Captain Wilkins not tell you about the underwater boat that followed us?"

"No, indeed, he did not."

"Let me just say that, for once, I was deeply grateful we were not aboard a British transport, for shortly after we departed Alexandria on the ferry, our trail was picked up by one of the German U-boats. At first, only its scope was in view, some two hundred yards astern. It was the middle of the evening, and Wilkins and I were playing cards with some Americans below decks. When the alarm was rung, we thought the ship was about to go down any moment and hurried to find our life vests and make our way onto the deck. Then the U-boat rose to the water's surface like a great whale, and old Fritz made no further disguise of himself. He followed us at two hundred yards or so throughout the voyage, all the way across the sea to Athens. We had to spend the entire journey on the deck in our life vests sitting beside the captain's gig as he expected any moment we would be torpedoed and sunk."

"Good heavens, in all my travels in the Mediterranean, I've never had the misfortune of seeing one of the German craft, much less to have it follow me, my word."

"The ship's captain was quite apologetic and became extremely generous with the whisky above-decks so we made quite a party of it," added Wilkins.

"Now, you boys must be equally careful traveling about the countryside in Greece," warned Penniworth. "As you know, it is still a neutral country, but only because the affections of its people are so deeply divided. In most places, yes, British officers will be received with favor, but in some pockets where the King still holds some gasp of approval, the sight of British officers may enrage the locals to acts of violence. If you feel in the least uncomforted, I advise you to retreat double-time."

"Your advice is most welcome, sir," said Wilkins.

"Now in Corfu, if you go to Corfu and you should because Corfu is a lovely place for Englishmen to visit, there is a house on Lemonia Square in the old town, a yellow house with green shutters. You must not miss it. Outside Athens, you will find there the most charming young ladies in Greece. There was a lovely girl I met there once, Sirena was her name then. Very enthusiastic, if you know what I mean."

"You are a font of wisdom, Mister Penniworth," said Gresham.

"Well, I must be off myself, gentlemen," said Penniworth with a wink, "but it's been a pleasure chatting with you boys. Hopefully I will see you about tomorrow."

"Perhaps," said Wilkins, obstinately keeping his seat as the gentleman rose to depart. Gresham stood.

"Thank you, Mister Penniworth," he said with a broad smile. "We shall see."

"Good God, I feared the man would not take 'no' for an answer," said Wilkins, when Mister Penniworth had departed the room.

"He's just a man of business, James."

"Nothing but whores on three continents!"

"I dearly hope the day will come when his sort of information is of greater interest to you, James. We have been at the front quite a while, you know."

"I won't be baited, David. The whole country is in an uproar and we have our duty."

"You weren't listening to Penniworth, then, James. The Greeks are more than unhappy about the war. They're damned afraid of what Bulgaria will do. They love this Prime Minister of theirs because they believe he will protect them. And who *won't* protect them? Their King! They hate him!"

"He would hardly be the first reigning monarch whose policies conflict with the whims of his subjects," said Wilkins, dismissively.

"No, of course, not. There's Louis the Sixteenth, for example-"

"You're exaggerating."

"And you are enamored of nobility because you owe your position and wealth to it."

"That is unfair. It is because of my family that I understand how the world really works, far more than the masses that cheer and wave at passing royal motorcades and hang portraits of the King in their windows. When I was a lad, we traveled through Europe several times and I met many of the noble families. My mother knows absolutely everyone. My very earliest memory, I shall never forget, I was playing in the sands on the shore at Nice. I saw a beautiful woman splashing in the waters. She emerged like Venus in her soaked bathing dress to towel her hair, and I clearly recall the look of simple pleasure on her face. My mother told me with some awe that she was the Empress Elisabeth of Austria, but it struck me even then how little the trappings of nobility truly distinguish an Empress from any commoner. She simply toweled her hair and sat under the shade to read her book. A few weeks after, she was assassinated in Geneva."

"So you're arguing that kings and queens are all kindly and compassionate because they're ordinary blokes on the inside."

"No, quite the contrary. They are ordinary, as you say, but they, or at least many of the nobility, are simply doing their best to manage the responsibilities thrust upon then by wealth and station. Perhaps the people expect too much."

"Perhaps the people would like to thrust those responsibilities on someone of their own choosing. Say, shall we have another whisky?"

"One more, perhaps."

"I have to raise the other issue again, James. Since we're going to meet the Athens agent, we can't let on that he has dealings with British officers, so we must change into civilian clothes. You can stay military on the inside, but we can't put this fellow at risk. And we are, technically, on holiday, you know."

"As I've said before, David, out of uniform we would be no better than spies."

"Must I force the issue?"

"I don't understand the secrecy. It's one thing to keep our military plans in confidence, obviously, but people pretending to be something they are not is ungentlemanly conduct."

"All I know is that lives are at stake, and we shall do what is required. The agent's identity must remain a secret or his life would be at risk. No further discussion is required."

"Very well. Since you are so insistent, I will comply with your wishes, but I shan't make a habit of it."

"Then we must change clothes and make our rendezvous."

Without a word in response, Wilkins rose and headed up to his rooms to change. He was somewhat uncomfortable with the clandestine aspect of the work he was to do with Gresham. Still, it promised to be more worthwhile to the war effort than dying in a trench at Gallipoli. He also had to admit to a slight thrill when he holstered his American M1911 handgun beneath his civilian walking jacket, knowing he would be walking through the streets of Athens armed and, in effect, authorized to undertake whatever actions he deemed necessary to complete their mission.

As to their mission, Gresham and Wilkins had stopped in Athens to obtain information, yet they could already see that the situation in Greece was far more complex than they had been told. The British diplomats who had come to meet with King Constantine had been sent away. The King was surrounded by pro-German advisors, German sympathizers, and actual Germans, including his Hohenzollern Queen Regent. Gresham and Wilkins would need to be creative if they were to be of any help to their country at all. With an American handgun under his jacket, however, Wilkins already could sense that there might be ways to accomplish their charge that were perhaps less than diplomatic. But Wilkins, who knew well how to bow to princes and princesses, was at rather a loss when considering whom to shoot.

It was early evening when Gresham and Wilkins, dressed in simple civilian suits, took to the streets of Athens from the kitchen door of their hotel. The city bustled with activity as the sun began to set and the streets cooled. There seemed a certain pride amongst the local populace in the ancient city as they busily swept and washed their stoops and storefronts in preparation for the active evening commerce. Narrow streets of white-washed storefronts and townhouses led to huge squares which surrounded the remnants of their once-great civilization. Gresham couldn't help but stare with awe at the Parthenon looming above the city, a reminder of Greece's place in the foundation of western civilization. How could anyone have believed that some Danish nobleman would be accepted as this ancient country's king?

Gresham and Wilkins stopped to sit at a café across the street from the Athens offices of Nash & Peters, Exports, Ltd. Wilkins' ability to speak Greek had already come in handy for obtaining directions through the maze of Athens' street, but even Gresham was able to order coffee as the men sat and watched.

"We'll just wait a few minutes," Gresham said. "I'd like to see if we've been followed, or if anyone comes in and out of the offices."

"You think we're being followed?"

"I'd just rather be certain we were not."

The street was quiet and, apart from locals coming and going from their homes, they saw no one. Neither did anyone enter or leave the offices of Nash & Peters. Finally, Gresham decided they had waited long enough, and they crossed the street and entered the small office quickly.

Inside the heavy front door was an extremely comfortable waiting room with leather chairs, mahogany tables and a small, cold fireplace. There were no windows, but several electrical light bulbs made the room very bright and hot. The heavy wood doors to the partners' offices in back were closed tightly. Suddenly one of the doors opened, and a modestly-dressed, older British woman entered.

"Good evening, gentlemen. Welcome to Nash & Peters. May I ask your business?" She asked politely.

"Thank you," replied Gresham. "We'd like to speak with Mister Nash or Mister Peters, on a business matter."

"Your name, sir?"

"Of course," said Gresham. "I am Sir Thomas Bruce."

"Ah, I see. And you wish to export marble statuary, I expect?"

"Indeed, from Salonika," replied Gresham.

"Then welcome, gentlemen. You are Misters *G* and *W*, yes?" She asked.

"I'm *G*; he's *W*."

"You may call me *K*. There are no names here, nor are there any Misters Peters or Nash, you should know. I am the individual *M* sent you to meet."

"You?" Wilkins asked incredulously.

"Yes, Mister *W*. There are a number of women in the service, I'm told. Please enter my office as we have much to discuss." She opened the door to her back office and welcomed both men in to sit; she bolted the door shut behind them and sat behind a large mahogany desk that was completely clear of papers of any kind. She had a lean appearance but well-tended and she looked very healthy considering her rather advanced age.

"Now, gentlemen, I received word from *M* that you would be coming to meet me – everything is coded, of course – and I have a general understanding of what you have been asked to do. My information on Salonika is quite limited, but I have an acquaintance there you may contact. He is a young man named Athos; he works at the spice shop at the docks, and you may tell him I sent you. Please pay him handsomely; he reports to me on all the comings and goings at the port in Salonika and should be most helpful to you."

"Thank you, that's very kind," said Wilkins. "Have you known this man, Athos, very long?"

"Athos is a very young man, little more than a boy, but I knew his father well. I've lived in Greece a very long time, Mister *W*. I came to Athens in 1882 with my husband, and he passed away many years ago now. But I am still an Englishwoman at heart. I travel throughout the country often and visit Salonika from time to time; it is rather dingy, but still the largest port and second largest city in Greece. Now, if I may get to business," she continued, "I must tell you that the political situation in Athens is changing quite rapidly and nearing a crisis."

"How do you mean?" Wilkins asked.

"Just today I have learned that orders have been issued in Bulgaria to begin the mobilization of their army. The Prime Minister of Greece, Eleftherios Venizelos is his name, will make a demand upon the King, who holds supreme authority over the military, to mobilize Greece's armies. But whether the King agrees to transfer soldiers north to protect Serbia remains to be determined."

"We understand the King will resist those requests," Wilkins said.

"That is regrettably correct. The King is most certainly enthralled by the Germans, but his hands are not entirely free to act as he wishes. You see, I have also learned from my little birds there is the treaty between Greece and Serbia that has a secret military rider, a mutual defense pact. Under the terms of this rider, each country is obligated to supply a specific number of troops in the event of an invasion by Bulgaria. Such an invasion now appears imminent and the King cannot completely disregard that treaty without disgracing his family name."

"So the King is obliged to draw up his armies for defense."

"In principle, yes. But, there's a twist of the screw. Serbia cannot provide the troops required by the treaty as they are all currently keeping the Austrian army at arm's length north of Belgrade and in western Serbia. King Constantine has been advised by his German members of court that since the Serbians cannot honor the treaty by producing the requisite defensive troops, he can assert that Serbia has violated the treaty and use that as his justification to keep Greece from defending its ally."

"And what is the opinion of the Prime Minister, Mister Venizelos?"

"Now the story gets even more interesting. The Prime Minister has cleverly and secretly arranged for the French and British militaries to supply troops *as a substitute for the troops which Serbia is obliged to supply* under the treaty. He will insist to the King that Greece honor its treaty obligations and enter the war as an ally of Serbia and, in effect, as an ally of the Entente. So you see, it is imperative from our point of view that the French and British troops land at Salonika as planned, or else we lose both Serbia and Greece and then the Balkans as a whole."

"We've been on the Turkish peninsula," said Gresham, "and it appears certain troops will be brought off to Salonika in the next weeks."

"British and French troops will also embark from Marseille and arrive at Salonika soon," said *K*, "but the real question is whether they will be allowed to disembark on Greek soil. Even if the Prime Minister is inclined to force the treaty issue, there is no possibility of landing them in Salonika until Bulgaria actually invades Serbia. Despite the mobilization, Bulgaria has stated publicly that it has no intent to invade Serbia or Greece. There will have to be an overt act of war before the landing can occur."

"Even then, Venizelos might still bow to the King's wishes and refuse the British and French landing, I take it?" Gresham asked.

"It's certainly possible, as much as he would regret it. The Prime Minister is not yet prepared to openly defy the King."

"And if the King rejects the allied troops, might the local officials in Salonika allow them to land regardless?" Wilkins asked.

"That is a very serious matter. My answer is possibly yes, but unless we have the consent of the Prime Minister at least, the political situation would be untenable: Any allied landing would be portrayed as an invasion of a neutral country. As to the Prime Minister, he has strong support from the people of Greece; moreover, he firmly controls the northern regions of Greece, including the Macedonian regions acquired during the Balkan Wars. So those facts are all in our favor."

"Then Venizelos is the key and we must have his cooperation," said Gresham.

"That is undoubtedly correct. Of course, he meets frequently with the British ambassador, but Venizelos has proven cautious absent proof that the moment of crisis is at hand."

"And if we could provide such proof?"

"I have no doubt he would do as his conscience dictates – he is a man of the people."

"Who protects him?" asked Gresham.

The room fell silent, and *K* frowned in confusion.

"Whatever do you mean, Mister *G*?"

"The Prime Minister is in a tenuous and politically-charged situation. He surely has personal protection. Is it the military, or the constabulary?"

"Yes, I understand now. The Gendarmerie – the civilian authorities – support him entirely; the military, however, answers only to the King and his German advisors," said *K*.

"The chief of the Gendarmerie, then, is an ally of the Prime Minister?"

"He certainly is. Vasilakos is his name."

"Have you identified any of the German agents in Athens?"

"Oh, yes, some. There are very many."

"How about anyone senior enough to know what is going on diplomatically between Germany and Bulgaria?" Gresham continued.

"There may be one or two 'undeclared' diplomatic subordinates who have that information. I try to track their numerous non-diplomatic activities, and some are much more active than others. But we have not been able to break their codes as yet, and of course they don't come out and tell us what they know."

"I need names, addresses of these men," said Gresham.

K stared at Gresham coldly. Wilkins lit a cigarette, and pulled out his flask, sending the message that he and Gresham were not leaving until the information Gresham requested was provided.

"We must play the cards we are dealt, Madam," said Gresham. "We will take that information, and then it would be best if we had no further contact with you."

"What do you mean to do, Mister *G*?"

"I would rather not say. My friend here and I are merely British soldiers on leave and apt to get into all kinds of trouble. It may turn out that the British government would want to apologize for our misconduct, but deny any prior knowledge of our intentions."

She stared at Gresham a moment longer, then sighed and produced a pen and paper from her desk. She jotted down a few brief notes. When she completed her list, Gresham took the paper and read it over.

"Thank you, Madam. You have been most helpful." said Gresham. He made eye contact with Wilkins, and the two rose and left the office.

"What *do* we mean to do, David?" asked Wilkins after they had walked a while through the busy evening streets.

"Civilians talk about armies mobilizing like it means nothing. For a country like Bulgaria, mobilizing hundreds of thousands of men, especially during the autumn harvest, is a serious commitment – it's expensive and costs the country food and therefore lives. If Bulgaria is truly mobilizing its army, then it can only mean that they have already signed a treaty with Germany and Austria – a treaty which undoubtedly makes all sorts of promises to Bulgaria, such as Serbian territory. The Prime Minister must have proof of the Bulgarian treaty with Germany when he goes to the King. It may make all the difference."

"If what you say is true, Venizelos will be forced to defy his King, David," Wilkins said with concern.

"That is exactly what we must make certain."

Wilkins stopped. Of course he knew they were doing the right thing for the British Empire, but it was a serious matter to prod the Prime Minister of Greece to defy his country's King. "Very well, but in that case we must obtain proof certain."

"Since you prefer to be in uniform, James, let's go to the hotel and change into those clothes. I think tonight we should be regular army officers on leave. Then I want you to find out where the Chief of the Gendarmerie, that fellow Vasilakos, resides. Make certain we can catch him at home tonight. He will be our avenue to the Prime Minister. I'll locate the Germans, and we'll meet in front of the archeology museum at midnight."

Wilkins eyed Gresham intently. Clearly Gresham was prepared to push the political situation to a crisis, and Wilkins surprised himself by finding that he was prepared to back up his friend and colleague. They rushed back to the hotel.

Gresham ducked out the back door quickly and walked to the district where the two most likely and most knowledgeable German agents were believed to reside. There was no lack of German-speaking customers at the public houses in that district, and Gresham entered one uncertain of the reception he would receive. In his British uniform, he immediately drew the attention of every eye. The Germans and Austrians, some of whom were in uniform themselves, looked at him with amusement and disdain. Gresham sat at a table and called for whisky.

"No, no, my friend," said a friendly and somewhat inebriated Austrian officer, in English. "You are in Greece now, so you must order the wine. If you cannot order correctly, we shall have to throw you out."

"The only wine I'll drink comes from France, and I don't expect you've got any," replied Gresham coldly.

"Not yet, perhaps, but it's just a matter of time. Then try the *uozo* – a local aperitif; it's quite delicious."

"No, thanks; I'll stick to whisky."

"Perhaps you should return to your dark dirty pubs, then, Englishman. You have no appreciation for the treasures of Greece."

"I'm looking for an old schoolmate who I'm told lives in this district."

"There is no other Englishman here."

"He's a German, from Berlin; his name is Ernst Muller. We spent a year at Oxford together, but he moved to Athens to work for the Ambassador. Do you know him?"

"No, but I might be convinced to ask my friends for you."

"You are very kind, and I shall repay your kindness by buying you and your friends a bottle of the Greek wine, if you will allow me." said Gresham, sipping his whisky.

"Most thoughtful, but the wine is cheap."

"Then gold, as I am most anxious to see my old friend and find out whether he intends to return to my sister and the child he left behind in England."

"Ah, now I see your intent most clearly. Money will do. Allow me to ask for you." The Austrian stepped to his friends and conferred with them a moment. There was some dispute as to whether to assist a British officer, but as Gresham placed five gold sovereigns on the table, the dissenters were quickly out voted.

At last the Austrian returned to Gresham's table and carefully lifted and pocketed the sovereigns. "There is a café three blocks from here, the *Piraikon*. You will find your friend there most evenings. Now you should leave, as some of my friends would like to take your money and cut your English throat."

Gresham rose and walked calmly to the street without another word.

The *Piraikon* was an almost identical pub nearby, bustling with Germans and Austrians who were drinking wine and steins of beer. Ducking into an alley, Gresham lowered his tie, dirtied his face and tousled his hair. He staggered out of the alley and approached the *Piraikon* drunkenly. At the door, he stopped.

"Where is Ernst Muller?!" he shouted.

A deathly silence fell, as Gresham scanned the room to see if his intended target could be identified. He staggered into the crowd, pushing through past the customers to the middle of the room.

"Ernst Muller!" he shouted again. A young man sitting by himself at the rear looked about nervously.

"Go back to Gallipoli, Englishmen, and die with the rest of your army," said a bald pot-bellied German businessman standing nearby.

"I'll be damned before you get away with it, Ernst," Gresham cried out drunkenly to the businessman. 'Where are you, Ernst?"

Suddenly two German officers tackled Gresham to the ground. He flailed helplessly as the Germans punched his face and side; Gresham was careful not to punch back. He scrambled to the street as the Germans' friends pulled them away, and he wandered off, staggering and muttering about his poor sister – at least, until he reached the alley.

There, Gresham stopped and watched the pub. The nervous young German man in fine civilian clothes soon left alone, and Gresham carefully followed him, staying in the shadows. One block, then two, to a fine townhouse, the very house believed to be occupied by one Ernst Muller. The young man looked both ways, and used his key to enter the house, quickly closing the door behind him.

The marble columns of the entrance to the new National Archeological Museum were impressive, but they lacked the aura of antiquity that permeated the rest of the city. At midnight, the museum was dark and quiet, and Wilkins waited in the park in front of the museum, still uncertain what Gresham planned to do. Wilkins was definitely more at ease standing alone in the dark in the eerily quiet city now that he was in uniform. Earlier in the evening, Wilkins had visited the nearest Gendarmerie and, after a bit of bribery, gotten the address of the Athens Chief, Vasilakos. The gendarmes were all vehemently anti-royalist, and Wilkins began to believe that Gresham's earlier reference to the unfortunate end of French King Louis XVI might not be far from the truth.

At last, Wilkins could see a British officer approaching, and indeed it was Gresham, more or less. Although in uniform, Gresham looked like he had been out drinking and brawling: His hair was wild and wet with perspiration, his uniform was disheveled and stained, his boots were covered with muck, and there were a few bruises on his face and some evidence of a bloodied nose.

"Where on earth have you been, David?" Wilkins asked with concern.

"Just playing my part in our little drama. I've been exploring the local pubs, especially those catering to the Huns. Afraid to say there's been a minor fisticuffs. That sort of thing is bound to happen when a British officer mistakenly walks into a nest of bloody Germans. I've found our prey, however. Let's go."

Gresham led Wilkins down a back alley, already having learned the back streets of the complex city. It was a short distance in the moonlight to the now-quiet public house where Gresham had made his public display. Two more blocks brought them to Ernst Muller's house.

At the door, Gresham pulled a neat set of iron picks from his pocket and easily unlocked the clumsy, ancient brass lock. He and Wilkins entered quietly and shut the door gently. In the dim light from the street, Gresham took out his handgun, and Wilkins did the same. They quickly searched the first floor of the house, which was empty, and started cautiously up the stairs.

The bedroom door was closed. Gresham cracked the door open enough for the two men to see Muller asleep in his bed. Gresham entered first, his handgun raised, and Wilkins followed. They surrounded the bed. "Muller, wake up," said Gresham. Muller wasn't asleep. He quickly twisted and raised his Mauser pistol. Gresham smashed his handgun down on Muller's hand, breaking the German's fingers and forcing the pistol from his hand. Gresham leapt onto Muller's chest and forced his M1911's muzzle against the young clean-cut German's throat. "Make a sound and I will blast your throat open."

"*Ich spreche kein Englisch,*" Muller growled.

"Well, we'll find out in a minute, because I'm going to cut off each of your fingers and toes until you learn how to speak English."

"*Ja*, alright, there is no need for such violence," said Muller. "I am no one; I am just a businessman."

"You work with diplomats and pass information for Germany. Those diplomats know the treaties with their country. And you know what they say." said Wilkins.

"When did Germany sign the treaty with Bulgaria?" asked Gresham.

"I have no idea if there is such a treaty."

"*Beginnen wir mit seinen schwanz,*" said Wilkins, drawing a short field knife from the back of his belt.

"*Ja, ja, ja*, the treaty, it was signed September 23," said Muller, now truly panicking.

"And how will your Kaiser reward his new ally?"

Muller shrieked, "of course I cannot tell you that!"

Gresham carefully positioned the muzzle of his handgun against Muller's left elbow.

"Listen to me, you English pig –"

Gresham fired. Muller's elbow shattered and his blood and bone splashed across the bedspread. Muller howled in agony and the smell of burnt flesh filled the room.

Gresham turned his head to see how Wilkins had reacted to the shooting of their prisoner. He was gratified to see only cold determination in his colleague's eyes, and turned back to Muller. "I would like to kill you, Muller. But since I cannot do so yet, I will have to enjoy hurting you some more."

"I cannot say!"

Gresham pressed the muzzle against Muller's left shoulder.

"Listen, Muller," said Wilkins. "Your secrets will not remain secrets long; it is just a matter of time before the terms are made known. Better to just tell us now, than to suffer needlessly."

"What was Bulgaria promised if they join Germany in the war!?" Gresham yelled.

"I cannot –"

Gresham fired again. This time his bullet entered the flesh of Muller's left shoulder and scored across the bone. There was a strong smell of flesh and droplets of blood sprayed across the bed and wall.

Muller groaned. "Lower Serbia," he gasped.

"What else?" Gresham asked, pressing the hot muzzle against Muller's right elbow.

"Macedonia – part in Serbia and part in Greece; it will all be split between Austria and Bulgaria. That is everything – I swear it," groaned the German.

"And when does the invasion of Serbia begin?" asked Gresham.

Muller spit at Gresham and laughed: "Next week."

Wilkins bound up Muller's shattered elbow and shoulder in strips of bloody bed sheets and the German was dragged through the dark city streets to the home of the Chief of the Athens Gendarmerie Vasilakos. Wilkins pounded on the door. A portly, older Greek man answered the door in an old, soiled robe and bare feet. His wild grey hair suggested he had been fast asleep.

"Αυτό είναι κατάσκοπος για τη Γερμανία. Έχει ζωτική σημασία πληροφορίες για τον πρωθυπουργό," Wilkins told him.

Vasilakos eyed the two British officers and the bleeding German man between them, and nervously ushered them into his kitchen. Wilkins told how he and Gresham had captured the German spy, and, more importantly, what the spy knew about the treaty and imminent invasion of Serbia. Vasilakos was clearly worried and upset, but he was finally convinced to run upstairs to dress and to fetch Prime Minister Venizelos to his home to hear from the German directly.

Gresham found a bottle of cheap Greek wine in the small dirty kitchen and poured a glass for himself and one for Muller. Then he went to the sink to wash the blood from his hands. He and Wilkins fed Muller wine through the night to keep him sedated and talkative. Near dawn, the back door opened, and Vasilakos at last returned, followed by an older man in a neat brown wool suit, the tails of his crisp white shirt hanging out and no necktie. His face was lined, but his pointed grey beard and mustache were elegant and neatly trimmed. He took his wire rim spectacles from his eyes and wiped them on the tail of his shirt. He looked at Gresham and Wilkins, and then looked grimly at Muller lying on the floor.

"Who are you men?" he demanded to know.

"Our names are not important," said Gresham. "We are British officers, as you can see. We discovered that this man is an undeclared agent of the German government, a spy in your country. We have questioned him, and have learned terrible news which we knew must be brought to your attention immediately. We have brought him to the Gendarmes so that your government can deal with him as you see fit."

The Prime Minister sat down on a stool by the door and scowled.

He spoke to Vasilakos in whispers for a few moments as Gresham and Wilkins looked on. The Prime Minister became angry and told Vasilakos to wait outside.

"This man is well known to us," he said at last to Gresham and Wilkins. "But we did not know he would have such information. Please tell me exactly what he told you."

Gresham knelt by Muller's side and propped him into a seating position, lightly grasping (and squeezing) the man's shattered elbow. "Muller, when did Germany and Bulgaria sign their treaty?"

"September 23," he said.

"When does the invasion of Serbia begin?"

"October 7."

"What will Bulgaria gain for its allegiance to Germany?"

"Half of Serbia and Macedonia."

The Prime Minister gasped and stood. "Germany has promised parts of Macedonia to Bulgaria? What parts?!" he demanded.

"Eastern Macedonia and most of the Central Macedonia."

"Kavala?"

"Yes."

"Vodena?"

"Yes."

"This is outrageous! How can this have been done without the King's knowledge?" said the Prime Minister with disgust.

"King Constantine knows the terms, *mein Herr*. Germany has promised Greece that the rest of your country will remain unmolested."

"Who is Germany to make such promises?! I see the King's perfidy all too clearly. He has sold off the most fertile parts of Greece to guarantee its security. There would be revolution if this news was made public."

"Your Excellency," said Wilkins, "As you know, British and French troops have already embarked for Salonika to come to the aid of Serbia. Will they be allowed to disembark in your homeland?"

Venizelos looked up at Wilkins, and his eyes narrowed. "I see. If you wish to know my response, return here this evening." He turned and stepped out the back door where the Gendarmes were waiting to escort the Prime Minister back to his home.

Wilkins turned to Chief of the Gendarmerie and pointed at Muller. "Θέλετε τον?" he asked.

The police chief shook his head and brushed his hand away.

"We'll take him with us," Wilkins said to Gresham.

They picked up Muller, who by now was deeply asleep, and carried him out the back door and down the alleyway.

"What do we do with him," Wilkins asked.

"I've made arrangements," said Gresham. "I will need to take ship to Salonika today. You must meet with Vasilakos tonight and follow me to Salonika tomorrow."

"Fine."

"I'll take Muller; you go back to the hotel and have a big breakfast where everyone can see you."

Gresham slapped the German to wake him and got him onto his feet.

"I'll take you home now, Ernst; you've been very helpful."

Muller grunted, half asleep, half drunk.

Gresham looked at Wilkins. "Go now," he said with a grim smile.

Wilkins walked briskly back to the street as Gresham dragged Muller down the alleyway.

That afternoon, Wilkins awoke from a deep sleep, dressed in a clean uniform and went down to the lobby for tea. The hotel was abuzz with news of a brutal murder that had been discovered that morning. An unknown British officer, understandably upset that his sister had been disgraced and left with child, had reportedly shot his sister's lover – a young German businessman. The body was found in the street in front of the German's townhouse, shot twice in the arm and once in the head. The Gendarmerie was asking after the British officer throughout the city, but he was believed to have already fled by ship. Opinions were divided, but most believed the murder was justified under the circumstances.

At dusk, Wilkins left the hotel and walked calmly through the back alleyways to the home of Vasilakos. In the alley behind the house, an older, burgundy-red Mercedes Phaeton sedan and its driver were waiting. Wilkins knocked on the kitchen door. Vasilakos greeted Wilkins and led him into the front sitting room, where Wilkins found Prime Minister Venizelos sipping a cup of tea at a small round table with a bright red and yellow check tablecloth.

"I have had a most unusual day, Mister British officer," said the Prime Minister. "Please sit."

"Thank you, your Excellency." Wilkins sat. The Prime Minister appeared exhausted and careworn, the lines on his face looked deeper, and he was clearly worried.

"Tell me, what is your name, British officer?"

"I am James Wilkins, sir."

"Are you related to Lord Bartlett, Thomas Wilkins?"

"He is my father."

"I met your father in Paris two years ago. Please give him my regards when you can – a most insightful man is your father; we enjoyed many long discussions together."

Wilkins was quite surprised to hear that his father had met the Prime Minister. "I am gratified to hear your good opinion of him, sir."

"In your country," Venizelos began, "King George has very little power; it is your Parliament that runs Great Britain. The recent Parliament Act took even more power away from your English Lords and gave it to the elected representatives of your people. In this country, however, the King still may do as he like, even when it opposes the will of his people."

"Then King Constantine will not allow the Allied troops to land, sir?"

"The King finally agreed to meet with me this afternoon after I had waited for five hours. While I waited, news arrived that Austria is once again bombarding Belgrade and Austrian troops are prepared to cross the western border of Serbia. At least 200,000 Bulgarian troops are amassed on the eastern border now. King Constantine admitted me only after he knew I had received this news. He stated to me plainly that he will not help Serbia because he expects the Central Powers to win; he does not wish 'to be beaten,' he said. So, no, the King will not honor his country's agreements. Perhaps he is correct that the treaty with Serbia is a dead letter, but to simply give away our lands rather than defend them with our lives? That is a choice that lacks honor. In my opinion the King no longer speaks for the Hellenes."

"How did you reply, sir?"

"It was my duty to resign from the office of Prime Minister; for the second time this year, I might add. I cannot serve both my country and its King. Now, I must go to Salonika. I ask you to go with me. When your ships arrive, we will find a way to land your troops. If the British wish to see a pro-Entente government in Greece, they must protect me and the men who oppose the King. The King will not like it, but he cannot prevent it."

"Very well," said Wilkins. "You have done what you needed to do for your people, your Excellency. I will convey this to my government."

"I have already spoken to your envoy, Sir Francis Eliot. I would prefer you to personally accompany me to Salonika. I will need someone there who can explain this situation to your military commanders. We will depart tomorrow morning on the 10.14 train." Venizelos stood wearily, "and your fellow officer, I hear, has already departed, yes?"

"Yes." Wilkins stood. "I will see you at the station in the morning, Your Excellency."

"Tomorrow, then," said Venizelos, as he rose slowly from his chair and shook Wilkins' hand, and then Vasilakos escorted the former Premier to his automobile in the alley behind the house.

Salonika

Gresham was staring out the window of his shabby little room on the second floor of the old hotel he had found in Salonika. The port city on the northern end of the Aegean Sea was busy with commercial shipping, and Gresham wondered what was carried in the many ships arriving from America each day. The ships were unloaded, and their cargos were re-loaded onto ships bound for Sevastopol, Constantinople, Varna, Alexandria, Genoa, and Marseille. It seemed the Americans were making a profit off everyone in the Mediterranean and on both sides of the war and no doubt reaping rich rewards at the expense of all Europe. The streets of Salonika were filed with another sort of cargo: Refugees from Serbia. Already the hint of invasion had spread through the Balkan country a mere sixty miles to the north, and Serbian families were moving south into Greece in large numbers, crowding the streets of Salonika with the hungry and homeless even as a cold autumn began to set in.

Gresham turned away from the window. His little room – an iron framed bed, a pine washstand, and a short stool – reminded him of the cheap boarding house he had lived in with his mother as a small child, even though his mother had kept their room much cleaner than this one. When Wilkins arrived in Salonika, he would have to share the room, as it had taken a huge amount of money just to secure this one. Out in the hall, groups of Serbian men were banging on doors and causing trouble. Gresham checked his handgun, and went to the door. He would wait in the public room a while and have a little whisky and perhaps something to eat; Wilkins was not likely to arrive for another day.

The hall and stairway were filthy with garbage and Gresham noticed evidence of rats as he made his way into the public room. With signs he asked the mistress of the house for food and drink. Nearby, a group of men sat around another table; one was actually a woman in man's clothing, it seemed. They were laughing quietly as they spoke to each other. After a moment, Gresham realized they were speaking English. He rose and approached them and was immediately beckoned to the table.

"Well hello there," said an older gentleman at the table to Gresham. "A British Captain, how wonderful. Please join us, Sir."

"Hello, my name is Gresham, David Gresham," he replied.

"Hello, hello," replied a younger gentleman. "I'm Peter Killington, and this is Delwyn Griffith and Geoffrey Smith-Davies. We're doctors come from England to join the Red Cross mission in Serbia. And this lady is Miss Flora Sandes, one of our nurses."

'It's a pleasure to meet you," said Gresham.

"We've just arrived in Salonika a few days ago and have been trying to find transportation to our station in Prilep," said the older man, Griffith. "No success so far. It's beginning to look like Serbia is cut off."

"But you, Sir, are the first British officer we've seen," said Killington. "If I may ask, are you the first of many? I only inquire as there are rumors of a mighty British force headed to Greece."

"Whether there is or is not such a force on its way to Salonika, I have no idea, I'm afraid. I'm simply in Greece on leave from Alexandria and was told the Ayia Sofia and the White Tower are landmarks in Salonika that I absolutely must visit. To be honest, I had no idea I was this close to the war. How far is it to your station in Prilep?"

"About 100 miles," said Griffith, "but no one is going in that direction."

"Surely the British are coming to Salonika," said Miss Sandes, "as the government has so frequently expressed its fellowship with the Serbian people and the desire to protect Serbia from the Austro-Hungarians. It would be a genuine disgrace for the Empire to abandon one of its most faithful friends in time of war. Don't you agree, Captain Gresham?"

Gresham had not really addressed Miss Sandes until she spoke, but as he looked at her he saw a woman by no means young but quite energetic and pretty in a rugged sort of way with her short hair and khaki pants. She was not old enough to be Gresham's mother, but her experiences with the Red Cross had clearly aged her. No, it was not age, he thought. Perhaps it was her bearing of seriousness and maturity. In any event, Gresham took a liking to her immediately.

"I quite agree with you, Miss Sandes. It is undoubtedly our duty to defend Serbia and most clearly in our own best interests to do so, as well. Were Serbia to fall, Germany would be able to readily reinforce and supply the Turks, and that would be bloody bad news to our men in the Dardanelles."

"It's because of Serbia that we are at war in the first place," said Killington crossly.

"That's unfair," objected Sandes. "There's no evidence that young anarchist fellow in Sarajevo had any connection to the Serbian government. One might as easily place the blame on the Kaiser for his rapaciousness or the Ottoman Sultan for losing control of the Balkans, or Napoleon, or Charlemagne. Regardless, British honor is at stake is seeing that Serbian independence is preserved. It is also clearly a matter of international security: Like Belgium in the west, Serbia is the gatekeeper in the east who protects European civilization from the Asiatic."

"Now, now, Miss Sandes. Let's not argue, especially as it appears you are far better informed than any of us," said Griffith sarcastically.

"I don't suppose you have been in the Dardanelles Campaign yourself, Captain?" asked young Killington.

"Yes, actually I was there last month, at the Suvla Bay landing. I'm sorry to say the campaign was still at something of a stalemate at the time I was sent down to Egypt."

"It's a terrible, terrible situation," said Griffith. "The papers at home are up in arms over it. It's a genuine disgrace that our lads have been held up by the Turks as they have."

"Perhaps they are simply better soldiers than we allowed," said Sandes.

"They are indeed fine soldiers, ma'am, and very well commanded," added Gresham. He was hesitant to say more about the situation at Gallipoli, however. "Have you been to Serbia before, Miss Sandes?"

"I previously served with the Serbian Red Cross in Valjevo. I don't believe I'll be able to get there directly this time, so I am waiting to see if we can at least all go up to Prilep together and then I can take the train north from there."

"How long do you plan to stay in Salonika, Captain?" asked Killington.

"That's difficult to say. A friend from Athens is coming to meet me here, so at least a few days."

"Days! Good Lord," said Griffith, "how can you possibly wish to stay on holiday in Salonika for days? It's a filthy little city and there's no end to the refugees at the moment."

"I, for one, would be happy to see the Ayia Sofia with you, Captain," said Sandes. "I'm told the iconography in the dome there is lovely. Shall we plan a tour for the morning?"

"It would be a pleasure to visit the church with you, Miss Sandes. I am certain we will all see each other again here in the morning, but, if you would be kind enough to excuse me for now, I did hope to take a walk along the docks and get a little fresh air before nightfall."

"Of course, of course," said Griffith. "Good night, Captain."

Gresham made his way out to the street. He had been somewhat uncomfortable talking with his fellow British subjects. Did he say he was on holiday in Salonika? How ridiculous! If only he was a better liar! Perhaps it didn't matter so much with a group of doctors, but others might wonder why he and, eventually, Wilkins were hanging about in Salonika for days or even weeks. But it was a wide open city in a neutral country, after all. Moreover, Salonika was truly a filthy little port city, and the crowd of refugees brought the nearness of war uncomfortably home to him. Although Gresham didn't understand the Greek or Serbian languages, he could hear the note of panic in the words spoken around him and see the desperation of the refugees, mostly merchants and middle class families so far, who had the means to travel but had found in Salonika nowhere to stay. The streets were quite crowded as Gresham made his way down to the docks. He strolled slowly, stopping at a variety of little store fronts that sold bread, cheese, and fish at prices that were already terribly inflated.

Before long, Gresham spotted the little spice shop mentioned by *K* in Athens. It reminded Gresham of his days in Alexandria – the smell of pepper, cinnamon, allspice, and frankincense filled the air. An older man sat on a stool out in front of the store, but since he was blind it was hard to believe he could stop any thieves. Inside, the store was overflowing with barrels and boxes of spices and jars of all sorts. On a counter set atop a stack of crates, an older boy, black-haired and dressed in filthy clothes, was filling small envelopes with his own mix of spices. Gresham watched a moment, and then the boy nodded at Gresham.

"Spice for souvenir?" the boy asked.

"Perhaps," Gresham replied. "A friend of mine in Athens told me that the spices here are the best in Salonika."

"This is the only spice in Salonika."

"Then your name must be Athos."

The boy squinted at Gresham and grimaced.

"Who tell you my name?"

"A lovely older lady from Athens. I believe you have done business with her."

"Yes, I know who you mean. Yes, in the past."

"You no longer do business with her?"

"Others pay now."

"Who?"

"People pay. They pay me not to say."

"I see, and if I pay you, will you keep my name and my questions secret too?"

"You pay, then yes."

"I only have one question for now, Athos," said Gresham, as he placed a small stack of gold sovereigns on the counter. The boy's eyes widened noticeably. "The others who pay you, do they speak English or German?"

The boy's eyes shot up to Gresham. He sneered again. "German. No more will I say."

"If that is all that money can buy, I will ask no more for now. But you are a Greek, so consider this: When the Austrians, Hungarians and Bulgarians come to Salonika, will you stay here or will you run like the Serbians out in the street have been forced to run from their homes?"

The boy looked at Gresham stoically.

"I will come see you in a day or two, Athos. Perhaps you will want to say more then. Good evening." Gresham took a small spice packet and walked out of the store. The cool breeze off the water was a relief after the heavily scented air of the shop. There were enemies in Salonika, it seemed, people asking questions, waiting to see how many British troops were coming, perhaps planning mischief. Finding them would be difficult and take time, but Gresham had nothing better to do, apart from visiting a church with Miss Sandes in the morning.

Wilkins sat in a comfortable and private first class cabin of the train that was taking him, the Prime Minister, several other government officials, and a large number of heavily armed gendarmes to Salonika. Their departure from Athens had been delayed after the Prime Minister had agreed to meet with some of the many supporters who wished to thank him for his stand against the King, and their passage was further slowed as crowds came out at each train station to cheer the Prime Minister. It was quite clear that the people of Greece strongly approved of the gentle old statesman. Moreover, Wilkins could easily imagine the hostile reception the King would receive at such stops, if the King even dared to travel in his own country.

It was difficult for Wilkins to imagine the same sort of disapprobation being directed at his own reserved King George or the same sort of admiration being bestowed upon his own abstemious Prime Minister Asquith. It was not, he thought, that the people of Great Britain were less engaged in political issues. It was more, in his estimation, that *King George* was less engaged. Surely some group of people must be discussing and establishing the policies of the British Empire – but most assuredly they did not include King George.

Late in the afternoon, the train was still hours from Salonika and Wilkins was asked to meet again with Venizelos. He was admitted to a large and crowded lounge car where Venizelos was concluding a meeting. Soon, all but Wilkins, Venizelos and three other men were ushered out of the room.

"Captain Wilkins, please meet my friends," said the former Prime Minister, beckoning to Wilkins by the door. "May I introduce to you Admiral Pavlos Kountouriotis, Minister of War Panagiotis Danglis, and my diplomatic colleague Nikolaos Politis. Gentlemen, this is Captain James Wilkins, the British officer I mentioned to you earlier."

The men stood and shook Wilkins' hand. Politis was a short, middle aged man with an educated look and calm demeanor; Danglis was an older man of severe military stature and bearing; and Kountouriotis was a tall and very elegant man of great nobility. When all five were seated, Venizelos continued:

"The Captain here is not a formal representative of the British military, but I have asked him to be our liaison to the British authorities whom we are soon to meet in Salonika. Captain, we have been having a rather robust dialogue on a significant issue that I think you should hear, namely, how many Allied troops should be landed at Salonika."

"Frankly, sir," said Wilkins, "I haven't any idea myself how many men are expected."

"Ah, well we can clarify that for you," said Politis. "Under the terms of the confidential Greek-Serbian defense pact, of which I understand you are aware, Greece and Serbia are both expected to provide 150,000 men for the defense against Bulgaria. Since Serbia is otherwise occupied with the Austro-Hungarians, we cannot expect the Serbian government to provide those troops. Therefore, the Prime Minister reached an accord with the Entente to provide 150,000 British and Frenchmen on Serbia's behalf."

"However," interrupted Venizelos, "the circumstances have changed. The King already considers the defense pact to be nullified; therefore, the number set forth in the pact is no longer of any consequence. We have been discussing the number of men that are actually *wanted* in light of the recent developments. That number, I can say with confidence, is substantially less than 150,000. You will help us to explain to the British and French, when they arrive, why fewer Entente troops will be permitted to disembark in Salonika."

"If our goal – I mean the goal of the Entente," said Wilkins, "is to prevent the fall of Serbia, it may take many more than 150,000 men."

"The invasion of Serbia is imminent. We do not believe there is enough time at this late date to prevent the country from being overrun," said War Minister Danglis. "There would need to be 150,000 men on Serbia's eastern border today to prevent it."

"The British and French commanders may disagree," said Wilkins.

"You must recall," said Politis, "that the Entente troops will be entering Greece without the King's permission and, in part, because the King has agreed to the annexation of Hellene territory by Bulgaria. The number of British and French troops cannot be so great as to constitute an invasion and occupation of Hellene territory, or even be perceived as such, or else the King will most certainly plead for assistance from Germany. No, it must be a modest number of troops, yet a number adequate to guarantee Greek sovereignty in eastern and central Macedonia."

"Why should the Entente wish to preserve the sovereignty of a pro-German nation?" asked Wilkins.

"The king may be pro-German, but Greece is not. The presence of an allied armed force will preserve the neutrality of Greece, as well as the pro-Entente faction of Greece's government."

"I see," said Wilkins. "Then you are asking the Entente to protect you from the King."

"That is merely consequential."

"And have you a number of British and French troops in mind?"

"Two Divisions" said Danglis.

"That's all?" Wilkins asked in shock.

"It will be adequate."

"And what will King Constantine do?"

"He will not send the army and provoke civil war. Otherwise there is little he can do," said Politis. "We will say the British and French have landed without consent on a humanitarian mission to assist the Serbian refugees. There will be many refugees before long."

"I understand what you are saying, and I will do my best to explain it to my superiors."

"There is another matter," said Venizelos. "Gentleman, please excuse me for a moment so I may speak to the Captain privately." He stood and walked with Wilkins into the next car and they entered Wilkins' compartment.

"Captain, I have not previously mentioned your British colleague whom I met in Athens to my associates, nor do I intend to do so. But there is another matter on which you and he may be of assistance to your government and to me."

"Yes, I would be pleased to hear it, sir," Wilkins agreed.

"We expect that very quickly the Austrians and Bulgarians will advance through Serbia and stand at the border with Greece. We have considered what must happen when such a disaster befalls the Serbian people. The government must flee the country before they are captured and forced to sign any treaties. The King and his son, the Prince Regent, must flee the country before they are captured and forced to abdicate. And if the Serbians are ever to recover their homeland, their army must not be captured and forced to surrender.

There are many among the King Constantine's retinue who hold great antipathy for the Slavs and who would see the Serbians utterly destroyed. Colonel Metaxas is such a man, and he is very ambitious. However, the men you just met and I can offer our personal assurance that both the Serbian government and its armies will have the friendship and support of Greece for as long as Serbia is occupied by hostile forces. We want the Serbian army to be able to fight in Serbia, and if it must retreat now, we want to ensure that it can return to fight another day. Now we know that Serbia's King Peter and Prime Minister Pashitch and his government are prepared to depart Belgrade, but they are resistant to all thoughts of retreat. I fear the country will soon be in chaos, and then someone will have to find them and convince them to evacuate along with the Serbian army and its commanders before any of them are captured."

"I see."

"We will find a place for them in Greece. I do not know where, but we will find a place for them where they will be outside of King Constantine's reach — one of our islands perhaps — and we will make arrangements with the British and French to transport and supply them there."

"Yes, sir. A dangerous game you are playing, if I may say so."

"On the contrary, I have every confidence that the Entente will win this war in the end, even if Greece loses its King in the process. But, Captain, we must be absolutely certain that King Peter and his government and his army are prepared to retreat. The army simply must be preserved to fight another day, perhaps when Great Britain and France have realized how much they have lost by foolishly sacrificing Serbia. I must ask you: Will you and your colleague go to Serbia and find them, speak with them and, if need be, convince them to retreat?"

"I understand your concerns, and if it is within our ability to do so, you may rest assured that my commanders will have us do as you ask."

Miss Sandes was waiting in the lobby when Gresham came down to meet her the next morning. As was usual for her, she wore rugged pants with high leather boots and a canvas motoring jacket. Gresham could easily imagine her in the trenches aiding the wounded, which she appeared prepared to do at any moment.

"Good morning, Captain," she said. "I have found two more of our delegation interested in joining our tour today, if you have no objection."

"Of course I have none, Miss Sandes. Were you able to sleep at all last night? There seemed to be a large number of drunken men wandering through the halls."

"Truthfully, I was rather frightened. I have my own revolver I brought from England, and I kept it rather close by my side last night. But at last sleep overcame my fears, and I am well-rested this morning. Shall we join our company in the lounge?"

Sandes led Gresham into the lounge where they found the older doctor, Griffith, drinking tea with a very pleasant-looking young woman.

"Ah, Captain, there you are," said Griffith, standing. "Allow me to introduce you to our other nurse volunteer, Miss Reta Häberlin."

"Miss Häberlin, a pleasure," said Gresham. As the nurse turned to greet Gresham, he saw a lovely young woman, close to his own age, with extremely short and ruffled blond hair, a charming smile and bright hazel eyes. Unlike Sandes, Häberlin wore a pleasingly tight tan dress that accented her slight curves and generous chest. She wore wool stockings and leather shoes that showed off her slim legs and small feet.

"For me as well, Captain Gresham," said Häberlin with a distinct German accent.

"Forgive me,' said Gresham, "but are you German?"

"Miss Häberlin is from Switzerland, Captain," said Griffith.

"Oh, of course," said Gresham. "Please forgive my ignorant question."

"I understand completely, Captain," said Häberlin. "I come from a small village called Zermatt, not far from Geneva. But I have been in Serbia for two years now with the Red Cross."

"How ever did you end up in the British Red Cross?"

"I have been with the Swiss Red Cross in Prishtina until two weeks ago. My delegation was recalled, but I have decided to stay and join the British delegation to continue my work."

"I must tell you how impressed I am with you and Miss Sandes for your dedication and courage," said Gresham.

"You have not been to Zermatt, Captain. It is a very small village far up in the Alps: Very boring."

"Shall we make our way to the Ayia Sofia," said Sandes with enthusiasm.

Sandes led the small party single file through the crowded streets of Salonika. Gresham took up the rear, which gave him the opportunity to speak further with Miss Häberlin. They walked side by side, and she had a way of looking David boldly in his eyes that he liked. She was direct, un-bashful, and self-confident.

"I have never seen the Alps, Miss Häberlin. Are they very beautiful?"

"Yes, indeed the mountains are truly majestic. In the summer, many people come to see. In the winter, it is terribly quiet. There is no train station in Zermatt so no one comes in the winter. As a little girl I had to learn to ski just to get to church."

"That must have been exciting. Do the skis go very fast?"

"As fast as you let them. Of course at first I was very nervous, but in time I learned you must go very fast to get away from all the bears."

"Bears?"

"No, no, I am teasing you. I doubt there are any bears still alive in *Die Schweiz*. But the skis, that is so. It is very exciting to go fast on the skis, and it is quite easy to learn. But Zermatt is a little place and there is no more to tell. Where are you from, Captain?"

"I'm from the city of Manchester, Miss."

"Ah, yes, very many factories I have heard. A very dirty place, yes?"

"Yes, I'm afraid it is; at least, the parts I knew."

"You are not a fancy rich snooty Englishman?"

"No, I rather think not."

"Good. I like you better then," said Häberlin. Her eyes sparkled and she smiled at Gresham in a way that caused his heart to pound and his tongue to stick in his mouth. He could only smile back. Fortunately, they arrived just then at the Ayia Sofia. It was a fairly square, squat church of yellow stone with a medium round dome on top. Gresham was at a loss to see why anyone would want to visit it, yet since he had suggested the tour he did his best to marvel at the design.

Inside, they met the sacristan who happily told them in broken English about the Byzantine history of the church, its use as a mosque by the Ottomans, and its recent renovations. In the center, they looked up at the millennium-old mosaics in the dome. "These show the Ascension," he said, "with Christ in center, Virgin Mary and Apostles." Gresham realized he had crossed himself again. Here in the church, more than a thousand years before, men had created the mosaics to show their devotion to Christ. Not even the Ottomans who for so long occupied Salonika had dared to desecrate their work; regardless of one's religion, the work stood as a memorial to those men and a marker of the power of faith.

But when those men made the mosaics, Gresham wondered skeptically, were they truly motivated by their love of God, or did they see their work only as their pathway to immortality, perhaps even to sainthood?

After a thorough examination of all the mosaics and frescoes in the church, Gresham and the others headed outside to find a café for lunch. Gresham was enjoying the company of Miss Häberlin, and even Griffith had proven to be good company. After a simple meal of bread, grapes and cheese, Miss Sandes next led the party to view the White Tower, the old Venetian fortress used by the Ottomans as a prison. It was in terrible condition, and there was little to see apart from some rusty old Ottoman cannons and some dingy cells where, in days past, the Ottomans had supposedly tortured their captives. The Greeks had painted the tower white, but one of the older locals said that it used to be called the "Red Tower" for all the blood that was shed there. The same locals pointed out the spot nearby where King Constantine's father, King George I, had been assassinated by a Greek anarchist in 1913.

Eventually they returned to the hotel. Griffith and Sandes excused themselves to rest and left Gresham and Häberlin in the lounge.

"Would you care for anything, Miss Häberlin?" asked Gresham, who saw no graceful way to leave her and frankly did not care to do so.

"What do you drink, Captain?"

"Whisky, if they have it."

"That would be fine for me, with a little water."

Gresham asked for a bottle of whisky and sat next to Häberlin. She had crossed her legs and was bouncing her sleek, muscular calf up and down nervously. Gresham found her hair to be really astonishingly short. She wore little or no cosmetics, yet her skin was so clean and healthy that she surely looked better without them. Her hazel eyes were intense, and she kept up almost constant and intense eye contact. Even in her tan uniform dress, she seemed so carefree and feminine, yet no one would ever mistake her for a lady.

Gresham was not used to pretty women taking such an interest in him. Although he was flattered, he also sensed that Häberlin was no ordinary woman. He couldn't imagine being a woman going off to a foreign country, perhaps to serve in a war zone like Miss Sandes and Miss Häberlin had done. He had never understood how a woman could bear to be treated like a pet or, like his own poor mother, a beleaguered victim, and therefore he viewed women as a mystery that he didn't especially care to solve. Miss Sandes and Miss Häberlin made him think of women in an entirely different way, and he liked it. And he very much liked the way Miss Häberlin bounced her leg while looking him quite frankly in eye. Now she produced a small tin from her hip pocket which proved to contain several pre-rolled cigarettes. She took one and held out the open tin to David. He took one himself and brought out his trench lighter, as she snapped the tin shut and put it away, tapped her cigarette on the table and placed it between her full, pink lips. He lit her cigarette and she sucked the smoke gently, and then blew it out through her mouth and nose.

"How long do you plan to stay in Salonika, Captain, now that you have seen everything that Salonika has to offer?" she asked with a slight smirk.

"I'm still waiting for my friend from Athens who is supposed to meet me here. I haven't gotten word that he's not coming, so I suppose I must wait a bit longer to see if he shows up. At least a few days, I should think. And have you any word yet on when your delegation will make the trip to Prilep?"

"I believe it will be a few more days also. To be honest, I am undecided about going. It seems to me that with so many Serbians refugees coming to Salonika, we might do more good by staying here. Perhaps the Hellenic Red Cross will come, so we shall see."

"That's quite sensible. There are rumors that the Bulgarians are ready to invade Serbia any moment now, and you would probably have to return to Salonika in any event. And, if I may say so, I would rather like you to stay awhile," he confessed feebly, looking in Häberlin's hazel eyes.

"You are very kind to say so; it is a pity there is so little worth seeing in Salonika. Perhaps you could tell me something of your time in Egypt. I have been told that the pyramids of Giza are among the greatest of mankind's achievements."

"I would be delighted to do so. And perhaps one day I could arrange a sedan to take us out for a ride in the country. Would you like that? It's rather crowded here in the city."

"And soon it will be more crowded still. There are rumors that many British and French soldiers are coming to reinforce the Serbians. I suspect you will be staying in Salonika more than a few days yourself, Captain." She looked at Gresham with upraised eyes as if she had asked a question, but it had sounded more like an accusation to Gresham. The hairs on his neck tickled.

A bottle of whisky was finally delivered to their table, and he poured them each a glass. Their eyes locked as they sipped the cheap, harsh whisky. "My station is in Alexandria, and I would prefer to stay there out of harm's way," he said.

"I find that hard to believe," she replied. "You do not seem like a man who would care to sit behind a desk. I believe you are meeting your army here; perhaps you arrived too early. Is this not closer to the truth?"

"Miss Häberlin, I believe you are interrogating me."

She blushed and looked away. "No, Captain, I am just curious. Or perhaps I do not wish you to leave."

Thoughts swirled though Gresham's mind and his heart raced. He was saved from making a fool of himself when Killington and Smyth-Davies came into the lounge for afternoon tea. Gresham excused himself and immediately made his way out the back of the hotel.

He walked slowly through a winding path of streets considering Miss Häberlin. She confused him, and that was a feeling he didn't especially enjoy. Was it simply her fine appearance upsetting him? No, there was something else. Whatever it was, he had to know immediately. He quickly retraced his steps and made his way down to the port.

Gresham went straight to the spice shop. The old, blind man still sat in front as though he hadn't moved in the past day, and Athos was inside dozing. Gresham grabbed the young man's arm and jerked him around.

"A woman?" he asked accusingly.

Athos' eyes lit up in surprise. Gresham drew a handful of coins from his pocket and slammed them down on the table.

"The German who paid you to keep quiet is a woman with short blonde hair, isn't she?" he demanded, his heart racing.

"One, yes," said Athos, eyeing the coins but more afraid of Gresham than eager to pocket the money.

"Who are the others?!" Gresham yelled, tightening his grasp on Athos' arms.

"Just one other; I cannot say," he pleaded, but then in a harsh whisper he added: "Venizelos is coming. He must be warned."

"The other, a man, means to kill the Prime Minister?" Gresham asked in a whisper.

Athos nodded.

Gresham let go of the boy and caught his breath, slowing his heartbeat. "You are a patriot after all," he said coldly and then turned and walked calmly out of the shop. The sun was just setting and the docks and cafes were strangely quiet. At the mouth of *Kólpos Thessaloníkis* Bay, a British Transport, HMT *Aeneas,* was lowering its anchor. Gresham watched the ship a moment. The British had come. Then he returned through the streets full of Serbian refugees to his hotel.

Even as the train pulled into the Salonika station, Wilkins could hear the cheers of the huge crowd waiting to greet the Prime Minister. There were thousands of Greek men and women standing around the station and the tracks hoping to catch a glimpse of the man they considered to be the true representative and protector of the Hellenic people. Between the sunset and the smoke and steam of the coal-fired train engine, the view was murky, yet a huge cheer arose from the front of the crowd as Venizelos stepped out onto the train platform. Those in the back could not hear his words as Venizelos briefly thanked the crowd and stepped quickly into a waiting automobile, followed by an entourage of important looking men, and was rushed away.

Wilkins got into the third car with several men he had not yet met, uncertain whether he ought to go with Venizelos or search for Gresham. First, he would see where Venizelos was staying, he decided. The car rushed through the streets of Salonika until the motorcade stopped on Aristotelous Street in a formal square of white stone townhouses reminiscent of Belgravia. The door of Wilkins' sedan suddenly flew open and a young Gendarme thrust his head into the automobile.

"Captain Wilkins, *το Premier επιθυμεί να μιλήσω μαζί σας αμέσως.*"

"Yes, yes, I am on my way," he replied in English, in his rush to get out of the sedan. Venizelos wanted him urgently. Something must have happened.

Wilkins was rushed across the street and into an elegant townhouse and up the staircase into a sitting room crowded with Gendarmes, soldiers, sailors and civilians. The diplomat, Politis, strode purposefully up to Wilkins.

"There you are, sir," he said. "It seems our arrival in Salonika coincides with that of your navy: A British troop transport has just anchored in the bay and a delegation is coming from the ship."

"They've arrived already?" asked Wilkins, surprised that his work as liaison would commence so suddenly.

"There's more. The Austrians are bombarding Belgrade again – a thousand guns – and there are skirmishes on the eastern border with infantry companies of the Bulgarian army. It appears the invasion is imminent."

"Clearly. I shall remain here at your disposal, sir, until relieved by my superiors."

"Excellent. We expect the delegation from the transport ship momentarily. Please excuse me," said Politis, and he disappeared into the crowd. Wilkins stepped to a nearby buffet and poured himself a glass of wine. More and more men were crowding into the small sitting room. Wilkins would have to stay and Gresham would have to wait.

There was only one innkeeper at Gresham's hotel who spoke any English, but she knew that Gresham was attached to the small Red Cross group and therefore had no objection to providing Gresham with their room numbers. There was only one number he truly cared to know.

Gresham bounded up the stairs to the third floor. The hotel guests were used to loud men charging through the hallways at night and banging on doors. At Häberlin's door, he stopped and drew his M1911 handgun, loaded the firing chamber and flipped off the safety. With a surge of adrenaline, he raised his boot and kicked the door as hard as he could. The door flew open. Häberlin was standing at the window, writing by candlelight in a small leather-bound notebook. Her eyes flew up in shock. "What are you doing?" She shouted.

Gresham saw she was unarmed, but he held his handgun pointed at her just to be certain as he entered the room and closed the door behind him.

"There is no need for these dramatics, Captain. I have no weapon. Do you intend to shoot an unarmed Swiss Red Cross nurse in her hotel room?"

"You're no nurse, fräulein" he spat back.

"You are certainly no tourist, but I am indeed a nurse and a citizen of Switzerland, Captain."

"Then why are you collecting information?"

"We are not in England. I remind you that I am a citizen of a neutral country, and we are in a neutral country."

"Are you working with another German agent in Salonika?"

"No, of course not! I have no idea if there are German agents in Salonika. I know nothing of such things."

"Then who are you spying for?"

"I think you have been too long in the war, Captain. Please sit down and put that pistol away. I fear you will be deeply disappointed in me."

As Häberlin stepped to the dresser, laid down her notebook and poured two short glasses of whisky, Gresham watched her closely and sat on the edge of the bed. She brought him a glass, and he lowered his gun and sipped. He realized only then that Häberlin was standing before him in only her skirt and a very thin, grey wool undershirt. Her arms and legs were bare. She was thin but looked very strong. Gresham's head was pounding and the whisky wasn't helping.

"I admit to you that I have sent personal letters to my uncle in Munich. Yes, he is in the German army, an artillery Colonel. What he does with my letters, I have no idea; perhaps he throws them in the fire. There has been nothing to tell. It is no secret at all that British troops are coming to Salonika. You are the first British officer I have seen since I arrived here from Prishtina two weeks ago. If there are, truly, Germans collecting information here as well, as you suspect, then I know nothing of it and my efforts to assist my uncle are all the more meaningless."

Gresham looked deeply into her sparkling hazel eyes. Did he believe her? He couldn't decide. If she was truly a Swiss Red Cross nurse, as she said – a claim that could perhaps be confirmed – it would strongly suggest she was harmless. He gulped the rest of his whisky, placed the glass on the bed, and stood. He stepped closer, his heart pounding harder.

She looked down at her glass and found she had already finished her drink.

With a grimace, Häberlin looked up at Gresham. "If I knew any more, I would tell you, I promise," she pleaded.

Gresham's left hand still held the Browning M1911, but his right moved around to the small of her back. His fingers touched the warm, soft skin beneath her thin undershirt. He pulled her forward and held her tightly, and they kissed.

Wilkins walked behind Venizelos down the stairs to the large dining room where the small British delegation was waiting to meet them. The room was crowded with representatives of the local Gendarmes, national and local Greek government officials including several cabinet ministers, and several Greek naval and military leaders, as well as the three British officers from the transport ship HMT *Aeneas*. When Venizelos entered, the room quieted instantly. The British officers stood, and Wilkins was startled to see his own commander from Suvla Bay standing at the head of the British delegation.

"My name," began the tall, efficient and clean-cut British commander, "is General Sir Bryan Mahon. I am here on behalf of His Majesty King George the Fifth."

"I have been asked to speak for the men in this room," said Venizelos humbly, "even though I am merely a former member of the government of Greece. My name is Eleftherios Venizelos."

General Mahon's eyebrows rose suddenly. "I was led to believe that you are the Prime Minister of Greece. Are you not, sir?"

"Not today, no, General."

"Then I must ask you plainly by what authority you speak for the King."

"We will get to that, General," said Venizelos. "Please, be seated."

Those around the wide mahogany dining table sat, but two dozen more of the many Greeks in the room had to remain standing stolidly for lack of chairs. Venizelos continued:

"First, General, allow me to share some recent news with you. Earlier today, soldiers of the Austro-Hungarian Empire entered Serbia, again. They are currently attempting to seize the capital city of Belgrade, and the Serbian government has withdrawn to the city of Prishtina. We have also learned that the armies of Bulgaria plan to enter Serbian territory within the next two days. Already small incursions are taking place all along the eastern border, testing Serbia's defenses."

"So the invasion has already begun, and we are too late," said Mahon grimly.

"Just so. In light of the threat to Greece's sovereignty, Major General Zymvrakakis," gesturing to a uniformed officer seated at the table, who nodded his acknowledgment of his name, "in his capacity as the regional commander of His Majesty King Constantine's armed forces, has declared martial law in the Macedonian provinces of Greece."

"Then I should be speaking directly with the General, as he is in charge in Salonika. Is that correct?" asked Mahon.

"Yes, that is precisely so. However, General Zymvrakakis has asked me to speak for him as he has no English," said Venizelos pleasantly, despite Mahon's brusque manner. "The armed forces of Greece are concerned with the security of Greece. The gendarmes, which are currently under the authority of Minister Zannas," gesturing to another man seated at the table, "are concerned with the Serbian refugee issue: As you may have noticed on your way here from the port, there are already several thousand civilian Serbian refugees in Salonika, and we anticipate there will be many thousands more before very long."

"Yes, I agree, sir" said Mahon. "And I have three thousand British soldiers who must be brought ashore, with the General's permission, sir."

"As you know, General Mahon, Greece is still a neutral country, and we cannot simply agree to provide your armies with safe harbor. A military landing by Great Britain and France in the territory of Greece – and we do expect such a landing to take place – must be made under formal protest. However, if a reasonable number of soldiers come ashore on a humanitarian mission for the purpose of assisting *and protecting* the Serbian refugees, as I expect you will agree they must, then General Zymvrakakis and Minister Zannas offer their assurances to you that neither the armed forces of Greece nor its gendarmes will interfere or obstruct you in any way. Their envoy Nikolaos Politis," who nodded to General Mahon, "will be available at your request to resolve the details as to the landing and accommodations and so forth. Is that clear?"

"It is not clear at all, sir," said Mahon impatiently.

"Very good then," said Venizelos, who stood without responding to Mahon, and every other man at the table followed his lead and stood as well. "I believe that will conclude our discussion. By the way, General, I recently had the opportunity to meet a very pleasant young British officer who I believe is standing over there against the wall," gesturing to where Wilkins stood by the door.

Mahon looked. "Good Lord, is that Wilkins?"

"Ah, then you know each other already," said Venizelos. "I am certain you would like to have an opportunity to speak together. We will leave the room to you. Good evening, General."

Venizelos and the forty or so other Greek officials filed slowly and silently out of the dining room, finally shutting the doors and leaving the dumbfounded British delegation alone with Wilkins.

"Captain Wilkins, what the devil are you doing here and what is going on?" demanded Mahon.

"Sir, General Hamilton sent me to Greece in advance of the landing, and it has been my honor to spend the past few days with Prime Minister Venizelos and several members of the Greek military. I believe I have a fairly good understanding of what is happening."

"Sir Ian is on *Aeneas* now with the Tenth Irish Division waiting to come ashore, Captain, so please explain very quickly."

"I believe you have just seen the beginning of a *coup d'état*, sir. Venizelos resigned as Prime Minister when he learned that King Constantine had traded Greek territory for a promise of security from Germany. However, Venizelos now controls the northern parts of Greece through his constitutionally-appointed colleagues. General Zymvrakakis has clear authority to declare martial law, and now that he has, he is evidently prepared to do whatever Venizelos requests. And, although Greece remains officially neutral, Venizelos needs a number of British troops here to protect him from the King, to aid the Serbians, and to keep the Bulgarians out of Greece. But I believe in the end the Prime Minister means to unseat the King, and that would be to Great Britain's great tactical advantage."

"I can't pretend to understand what you are getting at, Wilkins, so you had better come with me to *Aeneas* and discuss this with Sir Ian directly. This is entirely above my authority. My adjutants will stay here to discuss the details of the landing with that fellow Politis. That is, if we are still going to have a landing."

Gresham awoke early. Beside him, beneath the blankets, Reta Häberlin still slept, naked and warm. Gresham ran his hand through her short blonde hair, and she pressed back against him. He would have liked to awaken her to spend the day making love. But he needed to somehow find the German agent that threatened Great Britain's one indispensable ally in Greece. After considering the matter awhile, Gresham decided that Häberlin's own "intelligence" reporting was of no significant concern. She was right that anything the British did in Salonika was very much public knowledge anyway, and she had every right to do as she pleased in the neutral country as long as she was not working as an undeclared agent of the German government. Gresham dressed quietly and jotted a short note in Häberlin's notebook: "I will return tonight - David."

In the lobby, Gresham ran into Griffith. The old doctor was by himself, drinking tea and eating a soft boiled egg in the lounge.

"Good morning, Captain. I imagined you would be down early, what with the landing and all."

"So it has begun already? I saw the first transport ship enter the bay last night," said Gresham.

"Oh no; indeed no. But there's to be a formal landing and parade this morning, I'm told. The Greek Prime Minister has also arrived from Athens, and General Hamilton is on the transport ship himself. It's quite an event."

The mention of the Prime Minister raised Gresham's hopes that Wilkins had finally arrived from Athens. There were few hotels in Salonika, so Gresham knew he would be easy to find.

"Doctor, I apologize for prying, but while I have you alone, I have a question about Miss Häberlin. It's just because of her German accent, and perhaps I am being overly cautious, but are you quite certain she is a nurse from Switzerland?"

"Yes, yes, my boy. Have no worry there. She was working with the Swiss delegation here in Salonika when we arrived from England. It was our suggestion that she join us in Prilep."

"I'm happy to hear it. She mentioned yesterday that she might stay in Salonika and help with the Serbian refugees. Have you considered that yourself?"

"I fear that is exactly what we will have to do. Perhaps you have not heard, but the Austrians entered Serbia again yesterday. With the Bulgarians ready to invade as well, there will be no going into Serbia; only coming out. And there will be a great deal to do here."

"I am convinced, Doctor, that the Austrians and Bulgarians together will likely sweep through Serbia in a matter of weeks. If you stay here, I do not doubt the Serbian people will come to you."

"That is what we most fear, and what has kept us from pressing for passage north. Doctors Killington and Smith-Davies and I have no desire to practice medicine in a war zone, retreating every night, and losing more patients than we can save. As for Miss Sandes, however, I fear there will be no stopping her. She is determined to return to Serbia regardless."

"Perhaps if the British forces advance north, she could accompany them? I plan to visit the port this morning and see if anyone I know is around. Perhaps I can arrange something for Miss Sandes."

"That would be most kind, Captain. We would all be more comfortable knowing Miss Sandes would be safely in the hands of the British army if she insists on traveling to Serbia."

Gresham left the hotel and walked down to the port. The sailors at the one small tender from *Aeneas* gave him directions to the Prime Minister's residence, so Gresham decided to at least see if Wilkins was there. Gresham was standing in the front hall of the town house on Aristotelous Street, waiting for someone who could speak English, when a well-dressed and very anxious Greek gentleman came down the stairs and rushed up to meet him.

"My name is Zannas," he said quietly. "Please come with me." He led Gresham by the arm back through the house to the courtyard behind the kitchens. After checking to see that they would not be overhead, Zannas at last relaxed.

"Captain Gresham, I am in charge of the Gendarmes and a close associate of Mister Venizelos. I was advised by Captain Wilkins that you might come here."

Gresham nodded. "Is Captain Wilkins here? I wish to see him."

"No. He is aboard the *Aeneas* with General Hamilton now. They will be returning shortly for the landing. However, you will be of much more use to us if you remain away from this house. Do you understand?"

"Yes, I understand that. Will you inform Captain Wilkins that I am at the *Hotel Augoustos*."

"I will do as you ask."

"There is something else. There is a German agent here in Salonika whom I have been told will seek to assassinate Venizelos. I have not identified the agent yet. Do you have any information on this man?"

"No, I had not heard this until now," said Zannas, "but it is not unexpected. Germany is well aware that the fate of Greece, and perhaps the Balkans as a whole, depends on what Venizelos chooses to do next. Of that, I am uncertain myself."

"I trust you will keep the Prime Minister safe. I will do what I can to find this German agent."

"Thank you, Captain. I will send Captain Wilkins to you this evening. I fear it will be a very long day. You had best leave by the back gate."

Gresham still had no notion on how to locate the German agent and decided his only hope was to speak to Athos again. The boy apparently had some feelings for his country. Perhaps he could be convinced to provide a description or some other method of identifying the German. Gresham should not have left so quickly the night before, he now knew, but he had been upset about Miss Häberlin. Now that he knew that Reta was not a problem, he could only go back to the docks to appeal to the boy yet again.

This time, however, Gresham found a very different scene. The shop was open and unlocked but the old blind man was not on the stool outside. The shop was quiet, and Gresham entered slowly. No one was there. Some of the shelves had been smashed and many boxes overturned – evidence of a fight. There was fresh blood on the floor and splashed against the wall and the smell of smoke from gunfire and a great cloud of spice dust. There was no sign of Athos. Someone had come and taken the boy, perhaps killed him, perhaps for talking to Gresham. He left the shop immediately and strode as calmly as he could across the dock, then stopped to catch his breath. Behind him, a jet of flames and smoke suddenly erupted from the spice shop. Shards of wooden crates and barrels flew out, and the concussion from the blast knocked Gresham to the ground. The shop was on fire, and smoke and ash and spice powders floated through the air. Merchants nearby were already rushing to the fire, ordering buckets of water to be quickly carried up from the docks, as Gresham shook his head and wiped debris from his face.

Gresham realized he had only just escaped unharmed and decided he had better get away before someone realized he had come from the burning shop himself. Was the smoke he had smelled a fuse? Was the blast meant to kill him, or just disguise the evidence of foul play? Was Gresham being followed? He still had no leads at all. He pondered his next move as he ran up the street towards the hotel. In a few blocks, however, Gresham ran into Miss Sandes and the British doctors; Miss Häberlin was not with them. "Captain Gresham," Sandes called to him. "We're on our way to see the landing. Are you all right?"

Gresham realized he was covered with soot and bits of wood and spices.

"I'm sorry, there is a fire at a shop by the dock and I was trying to see if anyone was still inside. Fortunately, the shop was empty at the time. I was just on my way to the hotel to clean up."

"Here, here, young man. You're not as bad off as all that," said Sandes as she stepped up to Gresham and brushed the debris from his hair and jacket. "There, you are now perfectly respectable. Perhaps you will join us for the landing? We are going to the square on Lagkada Street."

"I would be honored, thank you. Is Miss Häberlin joining us there?"

"I am very sorry to disappoint you, Captain, but Miss Häberlin has gone out on some errand of her own this morning. Rest assured you may see her at the hotel later today."

They arrived at the square, which was a block away from the pier. The square was already full of locals who had turned out to see the British soldiers. An excited but quiet crowd of Greeks and Serbians lined the broad street. Near the pier at the bottom of the street, a small review stand had been constructed overnight and was crowded with dignitaries.

"Look there," said Gresham, pointing to the stands. "The short older man with the beard and spectacles, there in the middle, is the Prime Minister, Venizelos-"

"Former Prime Minister," interrupted Griffith. "I read in the newspapers that he has resigned again."

"Yes, of course," replied Gresham. "Anyway, on his right, that fellow is Zannas; he's chief of the Gendarmes. On the other side is our own General Sir Ian Hamilton and, next to him is General Sir Bryan Mahon, who was my commanding General at Suvla Bay." Next to Mahon, Gresham saw, was his own friend and colleague, Captain James Wilkins. He was extremely pleased to see Wilkins was well and that he had arrived, at last, in Salonika.

"Captain, there are a number of other military men there – do you recognize the uniforms?" asked Sandes.

"Some, yes," Gresham answered. "Most of them, I believe, are the uniforms of Greece, of course. And there, below Sir Ian, are several French officers. The others, beside Zannas, are Serbian officers."

There were another two dozen or so Greek and foreign civilians on the stands as well, and Gresham noted the many large, well-armed Gendarmes stationed around both Venizelos and the British Generals. He was pleased to see that his warning had been heeded, but it was still a risk for the Prime Minister to be standing outdoors in plain sight where any able rifleman could shoot.

In the bay, a second British transport ship had arrived that morning. Four tenders were carrying troops and supplies from the transport ships to the pier. Gresham recognized the colors of the Tenth Irish Division, which he knew had also been involved in the landing at Suvla Bay. So, he concluded, troops were already being taken off the peninsula. A full evacuation of the Gallipoli peninsula was certain to follow.

On the pier, the British troops were lining up and waiting for the order to march. Someone must have put the fear of God into the men, for they were deathly silent and still. In addition to the troops, another tender was unloading horses and crates of supplies onto the pier. Evidently the British had brought their own rations and were expecting no hospitality from the Greeks. At last the first companies were assembled and inspected, the officers had mounted their horses, and the parade march began.

The troops passed the reviewing stand and dipped their colors in salute, but the soldiers remained calm and serious. Their uniforms shone and their rifles were polished. Led by the mounted officers, the troops marched up Lagkada Street. Gresham learned that the troops would encamp on a farm a mile outside the city. There would be no troops allowed in the city itself, no fraternization, and no unpleasant incidents that might raise tensions with the Greek government. The crowd of Greeks and Serbian refugees remained quiet, in awe of the sight of the well-armed, battle-hardened troops who kept their eyes focused forward and ignored the occasional cheers and catcalls.

The formal part of the landing ended quickly, although there would clearly be more troops, more horses and more supplies arriving throughout the day. Wilkins left with the dignitaries in a long procession of sedans, but Gresham assumed he would see Wilkins later in the day and hear what had been going on with Venizelos.

As Gresham and his British Red Cross friends were preparing to return to the hotel, something caught his eye. Two men in military uniforms stood on the opposite side of the street, casually watching the parade and smoking cigarettes. Gresham had not seen the formal dress uniforms with the heavy gold braids before, but he knew what they were: German infantry. Right there on the street in Salonika, two German officers were watching the British landing. Gresham could only shake his head at their audacity, but he understood the two men had every right to stand and watch the parade. They made no pretense of being anything other than German soldiers and could see and say whatever they liked. And there was no reason Gresham could not watch them.

It seemed very unlikely that the uniformed Germans had anything to do with an assassination plot or the disappearance of Athos. Nevertheless, Gresham supposed they might be in contact with the German agent he was seeking, so he excused himself and followed the officers. He kept a fine distance, in case he himself was being watched and followed by spies. His task was not difficult, since the German officers walked only a few blocks before entering their own hotel. Gresham walked on and passed the hotel without a glance. While there was only a remote possibility the Germans would be of any use, he had nothing better to go on and decided to spend a day trailing the officers. A block further on he entered a restaurant and sat by the window. From there, he could see the entrance to the Germans' hotel. He ordered lunch, and waited. Six hours later, he was still waiting. The officers had not come out of the hotel (unless they had gone out through the back, he thought). He wanted to meet with Wilkins, however, so he headed back to his own hotel just as the sun was beginning to set and a light rain began to fall.

"David, there you are. I have finally caught up with you," said Wilkins, smiling, when Gresham entered his hotel lobby. Wilkins looked exhausted and stayed seated on the wooden chair.

"I am glad to see you, James. I saw you in the stands this morning; I thought perhaps you had made some new friends."

They shook hands warmly, and Gresham led Wilkins quickly up to his room so they could speak freely. Gresham's room was still dingy and filthy, and he couldn't help but wonder if Reta was in her room at that moment waiting for him. Gresham poured some rum for himself and offered his friend a glass as Wilkins told Gresham what he had been doing in the days since they had parted in Athens.

"I simply pray that, whatever the outcome, my name is not attached to it. To be perfectly honest, I have serious doubts that the son of an English Lord should be involved in overthrowing the ruling monarchy of a European nation. It's not that I have anything against Venizelos – I greatly admire him, in fact. But let he who is without sin cast the first stone, you know."

"Is that what you've been discussing with Hamilton?"

"Ha, ha! Certainly not. In fact, David, I must tell you that Sir Ian has been recalled to London, and he will go from here directly to Gibraltar. The Gallipoli campaign has ruined him, and General Monro is being sent from France to evacuate the peninsula."

"I'm not surprised, as you well know. But as for the troops there, will they be brought here to Salonika?"

"Some, but for a time far fewer than the 150,000 initially planned, I suspect. The British Salonika Force will have one mission for now: To keep central and eastern Macedonia in the hands of Greece. General Mahon's orders prohibit him from ranging farther north than Lake Doiran on the Serbia border."

"Then they have given up on Serbia altogether."

"Yes, I would say so, for now at least. However, we will preserve Venizelos, and that means we will save Greece. Venizelos intends to set up a Committee of National Defense with himself, Alexandros Zannas and General Zymvrakakis unofficially in control of the whole northern third of Greece. That brings me to the next matter. Venizelos has asked me privately if we will go to Serbia to find the Serbian Premier Pashitch and King Peter and arrange for the Serbian army to be brought safely into Greece. There is tremendous concern that the King and his government will be captured."

"Have you discussed that with Hamilton and Mahon?"

"I have, and they are convinced it is the only reasonable course of action. The Serbians resist, naturally; they hope that retreat will not be necessary. We receive regular dispatches from the Serbian government, and the ministers have already retreated to Prishtina. But it is unclear how long they will be able to stay there with the Austrians advancing. The Serbians will not reply as to the whereabouts of King Peter, and we believe he is in hiding. Time is of the essence, as the Bulgarians are expected to cross the border any hour. But it is most urgent that the Serbian forces be preserved, so that when Venizelos is ready, the armies of Greece and Serbia, together with British and French will be prepared to take back Serbia, or at least stand a reasonable chance of doing so."

"My orders, such as they are, certainly allow me to undertake the journey, but I don't feel I have completed my task here in Salonika yet."

"If you mean the German agent, I can assure you that Venizelos is quite protected now that you have warned Zannas. Zannas is also chief of Greece's intelligence service, you see, and he certainly knows his business."

"It's not simply a matter of what this one agent might attempt to do. We must send a message to the Germans to stay out of Salonika altogether. Our contact here is lost, I presume dead, and my only other lead is rather tenuous, but I would like to spend one more day following up."

"I can help you there, if I may. But then we must get to Serbia as quickly as possible."

"I would appreciate that. I plan to return to the German officers' hotel in the morning and track them if they ever emerge, in the hope that they will lead me to their agent. Could you spend a day watching the front of the hotel, so that I can watch the back?"

"Certainly, I can easily dodge Mahon for a day. The sheer complexity of the landing has everyone running around like rabbits. No one knows where anyone is located."

Before long, with a great quantity of rum inside him and a sleepless night preparing for the first British landing in Salonika, Wilkins fell asleep on

Gresham's bed. Gresham, however, was wide awake. After only a moment's hesitation, he stepped into the hallway and locked the door behind him.

Now that the British were in Salonika, the hotel had grown much quieter. Gresham stepped lightly down the hall and up the stairs to the third floor. It was astonishing how nervous he felt. His heart was racing, as he stood before Häberlin's door. He was genuinely afraid she would not wish to see him again. At last, he collected his courage enough to knock. He heard her stepping to the door.

"Who is it," said Häberlin quietly through the door.

"It's David. May I come in?"

He heard a bolt thrown back, and the door slowly opened on the darkened room. David stepped in, uncertain where she was standing. He shut the door and bolted it behind him. Then she reached out to him, and he found she was undressed. He took her in his arms and kissed her. Her mouth was moist, her thin body was firm, and her skin was soft and warm.

"Have you had a very busy day with all your British friends?" she asked, in a teasing voice that melted David's heart.

"Not very. I missed you at the landing. Didn't you wish to see the British come ashore with Miss Sandes and the doctors?"

"Of course, but the Hellenic Red Cross has sent a delegation to Salonika at last. I was at their headquarters this morning to arrange for my new assignment. I will be working in the refugee hospital as soon as the tents arrive."

"That's wonderful."

Then she kissed him, and neither had reason to speak again for a time.

Gresham spent the entire next day in a courtyard a block from the back door of the German officers' hotel; Wilkins was in the café overlooking the front door. As Gresham feared, there was no hint of the German officers, and he was becoming uncertain whether they even remained in Salonika. As the sun set, a light rain began to fall and the air was chilled. Gresham realized he would need to buy winter clothes before he left for Serbia.

At the end of the day, Wilkins was waiting for him in another café some blocks away. "Any luck?" Gresham asked.

"They did come out for a while just before noon. I followed them, but nothing seemed terribly out of place."

"I wonder why they are here in Salonika at all. Didn't they meet anyone or go anywhere? One would imagine they are at least counting the British ships in the bay or the troops who are landing."

"It may be a humanitarian mission," said Wilkins.

"How do you mean?"

"After they stopped to eat, the two Germans went to the Hellenic Red Cross offices for a time. It looked rather like they are in charge of it. The only other people in the office were a large civilian gentleman and a very pretty young nurse, and they were all speaking German together."

Gresham had turned very cold.

"Tell me about the nurse?" he asked.

"Thin, terribly short blonde hair, but quite lovely in every other respect."

"Tomorrow we will go to Serbia, James. Find out as much as you can about the Serbian King's location. We will need a horse cart at least, if you can get it. We will leave the city before mid-day. And I don't suppose your friends on *Aeneas* have some winter clothes to spare?"

That night at his hotel, Gresham went to Flora Sandes' room first.

"Excuse my intrusion, Miss Sandes. May I speak with you?"

"Of course, Captain. Please come in." She was dressed in her usual military-like attire including her heavy leather boots, and Gresham was surprised to find her room spotlessly clean. In addition, she had had her bed removed and had been sleeping on her own camp bed. It was quite obvious to Gresham that if Miss Sandes had been born a man, she would have enlisted in the infantry, as she was well suited to and coveted the lifestyle of a soldier.

"What can I do for you, Captain?" she asked pointedly, and Gresham could sense she had little patience for pleasantries at such a late hour.

"I am going to Serbia tomorrow, Miss Sandes. If you would like, I will take you to Prilep. I understand you are quite eager to go, even if your fellow delegates are not."

"Captain," she said with a great smile, "I am astonished and most grateful to you. I would very much like to go to Prilep and I happily accept your proposal."

"Are you quite certain you wish to go, Miss, even without the doctors?"

"Yes, I am. Doctor Killington and the others are actually seeking passage back to England now. The threat of war has terrified them. But I must confess, I also have personal reasons to return to Serbia."

"Of course, Miss Sandes, the decision is entirely yours. But Griffith told me he would seek to stay and work for the Red Cross here in Salonika. Have his plans changed?"

"There is no Red Cross in Salonika, Captain."

"I'd been told the Hellenic Red Cross opened an office here."

"We visited that office this afternoon. Whatever is going on in that office has nothing to do with the Red Cross, I assure you, and the gentleman running the office is most certainly not Greek. German war profiteer, perhaps. We were told our services are not desired."

"I am very sorry to hear that. And what of Miss Häberlin? Will she return to Switzerland?"

"Yes, she told me she intends to return to her home as soon as passage could be found to Genoa. It may take some days."

"Very well, then I will arrange our transportation to Serbia. Be prepared to depart for Serbia before mid-day tomorrow. And, Miss Sandes, please do not tell anyone that we are going. Can you do that for me?"

"Yes, if you wish, Captain. Thank you."

Gresham next went to Häberlin's room. He couldn't really see how he could explain not going to her room. It would only alarm her, and perhaps give her reason to warn her associate. He was also curious to see if she had any more tales to tell about the Red Cross. It was now all too plain to Gresham that she had misled him about her contacts with the Germans in Salonika, that the Hellenic Red Cross office was a false front, that there would be no refugee hospital, that Häberlin herself had conspired with the man running the false office, and that that man was likely the very German agent that Gresham was seeking.

He knocked on her door. "It's David," he said calmly.

She opened the door for him and kissed him passionately. Even knowing that she had been so duplicitous, Gresham nonetheless had to admit that he very much enjoyed kissing her. She was truly lovely, and interesting, and strong. He had never met a woman like her. Yes, he loved her, he admitted to himself. They made love passionately that night, and then he held her tightly to his chest as she fell asleep with her soft blonde hair against his cheek.

Gresham couldn't sleep at all. He rose when the sun was rising. As he dressed, Häberlin stirred.

"I must be off early today," he told her. "I am hoping to join one of the regiments here in Salonika, and I must meet with the General this morning. Will you be working at the hospital today?"

"Yes, at least, the Red Cross hospital will be set up and I will be working there all day," she said.

"Perhaps we will both be in Salonika a long time," he said. "We might find a house to live in together, if my duties permit. Would you like that?"

"Oh yes, yes, I would like that, my darling."

"I'll see you tonight, then," he said, and left the room. He went down the back stairs to the kitchens and out the back of the hotel. Gresham felt terrible, his chest was tight and he had difficulty swallowing. He didn't want to see or speak with anyone from the British Red Cross delegation. A block from his hotel, he hid in a doorway to wait and watch.

Häberlin came out a few minutes later.

She looked around carefully, but Gresham was well-hidden. He followed her as she walked several blocks to the north, then east, then north again, before turning south towards the port. There was no doubt she was seeking to avoid being followed. She finally entered an office with a sign in the front window. Gresham could not read the Greek letters, but he recognized the Red Cross. He waited, and before long, Gresham saw a man enter the office. He was young, tall, very strong, and certainly looked like a soldier but for his civilian clothes. He had deep scratches on his left hand

Gresham snuck into a doorway across the street and watched through the office window. The man was speaking to Häberlin without looking at her. She was very friendly. She touched the man's face affectionately. The man kept looking at his hands, examining the scratches, picking at them. One scratch began to bleed slightly. He licked the blood off the back of his hand, and then Häberlin took his hand in hers and held it. Gresham strode across the street enraged, drew his handgun, and entered the office.

"Hello, Fritz."

The man spun around and glared at Gresham with hatred and shook his head in disgust. Häberlin was in shock. Her face turned red and her eyes welled with tears.

"*Nein, nein,*" she said, collapsing into a chair.

"*Dreckige hure, schliessen sie den mund dismal,*" the man said bitterly to Häberlin. She was sobbing, her face in her hands. Gresham held his handgun tightly. He struggled to keep his hand still as he pointed the gun directly at the man's chest.

"Why did you kill the boy, Fritz? He wouldn't tell me a thing."

"He would have talked eventually, he was a Greek and they are all pigs. So, now you arrest us? Send us back to Germany, yes?"

"No."

Gresham fired. One round. The bullet entered the man's chest, pierced his heart, and blood sprayed out across the room. He choked and fell to his knees, then onto his back. Blood pooled on the wood floor around him. Häberlin's hands stifled her scream. She looked up at Gresham, her face wet with tears, splotchy red and sprinkled with drops of blood. She was shaking. "David, please," she pleaded.

He was furious, but he didn't want to hurt her. He stepped carefully around the man's body and drew a knife from his belt. Gresham reached down to the man's face and pulled out his tongue. With a grunt, Gresham viciously yanked and cut off the tongue with his knife, and threw the chunk of flesh into the corner. He glared at Häberlin. If he let her live, every enemy in Europe would know who he was. All hope of dissemblance would be lost and with it any further opportunity to serve his country.

"I'm so sorry, Reta," he said, and suddenly tears were racing down his own cheeks. "I'm so sorry."

He fired again. Her head snapped back, and her blood and bone and bits of her brain streaked across the wall.

Serbia

It was a cold day and a light rain had been falling for hours. The road to Prilep was rutted and muddy and choked with civilian refugees traveling south by foot, on horseback, and in carts and sedans loaded with their portable possessions: mirrors and chairs and books and Bibles. Atop the carts sat old women and little children unable to walk. Some led herds of oxen or goats. Wilkins and Gresham, however, were headed north, towards the city of Prilep.

Wilkins had commandeered a converted Rolls Royce ambulance from the Irish Regiment at Salonika; it was a significant improvement over the horse-drawn cart that Gresham expected, but on the terrible muddy roads they had been forced to proceed slowly. Gresham, lying on a stretcher in the back of the ambulance, had been very quiet since late that morning when they had met at the hotel in Salonika. And Wilkins, who had never driven anything larger than a sedan, was still trying to learn how to manage the unwieldy ambulance. Miss Sandes sat beside him. She was good company for Wilkins, who was pleased to have the energetic British nurse along with them on the journey to Prilep: She was enthusiastic to return to Serbia after waiting so long and chattered away about her experiences in Valjevo and Salonika (she even suggested that Gresham had become enamored of another of the nurses there). But as they traveled north and spoke to some of the refugees, Sandes had grown worried and quiet. Belgrade, they heard, had been captured by the Austrians with the help of two German Divisions, and together their armies were pushing south towards Kragujevac. There were rumors that Austrian troops had been ordered to kill Serbians on sight, both soldiers and civilians, and that whole towns were being put to death and forests of gallows had been erected in some villages. The Bulgarians had invaded across the eastern border of Serbia, one division advancing almost unopposed towards Nish in the north and a second division advancing quickly south towards Skoplje. There were *Comitadjes* – irregular Bulgarian soldiers who were no better than brigands – raiding farms, killing and raping, and robbing travelers at gunpoint. The Serbian army, which had been battered and its troops scattered across the north, was attempting to fall back to the west of Nish to organize for a counter-attack, and the Serbian *Chetniks* – guerilla fighters encamped in the mountains – were attacking the enemy wherever they could be found, so that fierce battles might break out anywhere at any time. Serbia had suddenly fallen into chaos, and there was little time to locate Premier Pashitch and King Peter and ensure their escape.

Wilkins, Gresham and Sandes reached a village just within the Serbian border late in the evening and were only able to find a loaf of stale bread for their supper, as food was becoming terribly scarce. Wilkins drove the ambulance to a relatively dry field, and they slept briefly on the stretchers in the back. The next morning, under skies grey and cloudy, they traveled on to Prilep and found the small city in a state of complete anarchy. The streets were flooded with starving refugees and wounded Serbian soldiers. They stopped at the small brick hospital near the ancient Roman walls.

The hospital was dark and smelled terribly. The administrators had evacuated; the wards were being run entirely by handful of Red Cross volunteers. Even the hallways were overcrowded with sick and wounded Serbian soldiers. Serbian women dressed in spare summer military uniforms brought around mugs of thin, meatless gruel and hard biscuits. Filthy linens had been thrown into the corners and the floors were wet and slippery. Soldiers, even some who had already died, lay wrapped in dirty blankets on the iron-framed beds. Many more lay on straw-filled mattresses on the floors and in the aisles. The ward was cold and very dark and smelled terribly of human waste. Sandes was visibly distressed. The only doctor, she was told, was an American named Costa, and he was at the Serbian army encampment just north of the city.

The ambulance was almost out of fuel, and there was none to be had in Prilep, so they walked the few miles to where the Serbian Second and Fourteenth Regiments were encamped to the north at Lake Prilep. Along the way, there was a steady stream of sick and wounded soldiers walking back past them into the city, and a chilly rain began to fall again. They could hear far to the east the sound of heavy artillery fire.

Gresham, Wilkins and Sandes were directed to a small farmhouse near the lake where the Serbian regimental commander was billeted. A few dozen soldiers camped beside it, some in uniform but most just in plain clothes. They had raised small canvass tents in the muddy field and were gathered around a handful of fires roasting wild goose and trying to keep warm. Some were attempting to shoot more birds with ancient rifles, and some were drinking liquor, shouting and singing. It seemed more a madhouse than an army camp. Gresham also noted there was no artillery of any kind, only a handful of horses, and no motorized vehicles at all. It was an army terribly ill-prepared to resist the Bulgarians, who were undoubtedly well equipped by Germany. At the farmhouse, a soldier in suspiciously expensive leather shoes ran off through the thick mud to fetch the commander.

The one-room farmhouse had a large fire in the hearth but the room was smoky and uncomfortably hot. A short, portly man in a stained brown overcoat, with a shock of wild grey hair and a large bald spot on top was quietly tending to a shrapnel shell wound on a Serbian soldier passed out on the dirty wooden plank floor.

"Are you Doctor Costa?" Sandes asked quietly.

"Yeah, that's me, what do you want?" he snapped back in a gravelly American voice, as he finished bandaging the soldier's wound.

"My name is Flora Sandes, sir. I'm a nurse with the British Red Cross, and I am returning to Valjevo, where I have served the past two years."

"You sure chose the wrong time to return, Miss."

"Be that as it may, have you had any word from the British delegation in Valjevo? Are they quite safe?"

"There's no British Red Cross delegation that far north anymore," said Costa as he turned at last to face Sandes and eyed the two British officers. "A couple of those folks passed through here on their way to Athens, but as for the rest of them, I don't know. They may have gone to Albania. The Austrians are very close to Valjevo already, so you can't go back there."

"Well, you see, it's just that I had really wanted to return to Valjevo as I know a number of people there," Sandes replied hopefully.

"Well, you'd better pray they're not there anymore: We've heard terrible reports from the north – attacks on civilians, executions, that sort of thing."

"Oh dear, we'd heard the rumors, but I had hoped ... I suppose I haven't any choice, then," Sandes said with determination. "If this is as far into Serbia as I can go, then I must stay to work in Prilep."

"I understand what you're saying, Miss, and you'd be very useful, believe me; but right now I can only ask the Serbian Red Cross volunteers to stay. The war is thirty-five miles east of us: The Serbians are trying to keep the Bulgarians from coming through the mountain passes, but I think it's just a matter of time before the Bulgarians push through."

"I've come such long way to return to Serbia, doctor, and I will stay and help," she said definitively.

"Are you quite certain you wish to stay here, Miss Sandes?" Gresham asked with concern. He had come to admire Miss Sandes and hated the idea of leaving her in Prilep. "It seems likely this area will be overrun before too long as well."

"Who are two – British?" Costa asked.

"Yes that's right, sir," said Gresham.

"We heard there were British troops landing at Salonika. There's not going to be a Serbia here much longer if you boys don't get up here. How many of you are there?"

"Just the two of us," Gresham replied.

"Sorry, what?"

"He means to say there are several British battalions at Salonika now," said Wilkins, "and a transport ship is overdue to arrive from France. However, it seems unlikely there will be enough men here soon enough to make a difference."

"Well, well, that's about what I'd expect from you damned Limeys," said Costa, shaking his head in disbelief. "A lot of promises about protecting Serbia and now you're just running off."

"I understand what you mean to say," Wilkins said. "My fellow Captain and I must discuss that with the Serbian commander. Will it be agreeable to you, however, if Miss Sandes stays to assist you at the hospital? Is that what you want, Miss Sandes?"

"Yes, certainly," said Miss Sandes. "I'm sure I will be fine, Captain. I do wish to stay, and if need be, I will evacuate with the Serbian army."

"If that's what you want, I'm not going to try and stop you. I'd be grateful for the help," said Costa as he gathered his supplies.

The door then opened suddenly and a tall, fierce-looking Serbian officer whipped into the room. He wore a field uniform with two bandoliers, a sword, and a traditional round black Serbian hat with a large brass shield emblem. "Captains, welcome," he said. "I am Colonel Jovan Dikovich. We are delighted to have British officers visit. I have many questions for you."

"We have questions for you as well, Colonel," said Gresham.

"You have no doubt had a long journey from Salonika. Please take some wine," he said, offering a bottle but no cups or glasses. "You must already know much of our terrible situation, but let me assure you it is far, far worse than you have heard."

"Is the situation deteriorating that rapidly?" Gresham asked.

"Doctor, Miss Sandes," said Wilkins, "I'm afraid we will bore you with the minutia of war when the sick and wounded are in need of your care. Perhaps you would excuse us."

"Of course," said Sandes. "Thank you so much for escorting me to Prilep, gentlemen. Perhaps you will stop back when you have completed your mission?"

"If you know how to use that revolver you brought from England, Miss Sandes," said Gresham, "keep it close."

She shook hands warmly with Gresham and Wilkins, and then followed Doctor Costa out into the rain.

"Now then," Dikovich continued, "the Bulgarian Second Division is right now attacking my regiments guarding the Babuna mountain passes. We desperately need the British and French to march north to attack the Bulgarian's left flank. Indeed, an allied attack into Bulgaria itself would undoubtedly bring their advance into Serbia to a complete halt. One division, advancing towards Plovdiv, is all we need. When can it be arranged?"

"Now that we are alone, Colonel Dikovich, let me speak plainly, as we are both soldiers," said Wilkins. "The Bulgarians have advanced far too quickly for the British and French to be of any assistance to you. Yes, the allied Salonika Force of twenty or perhaps thirty thousand will march north as soon as they are prepared to do so, but it will not be soon enough or in large enough numbers to stop the Bulgarians. At best, the allied forces can only draw away some part of the Bulgarian divisions from your heels. But you cannot expect more than that. You must be prepared to evacuate west to Albania."

"This is not good news. Not at all. We had assurances that our allies would come to our aid. Now you tell me there is no hope for Serbia?"

"It is not in our power to change that, Colonel, although, for my part, I wish it were otherwise. But as I'm sure you know, the political situation in Greece is unsettled and, after the campaign in Gallipoli, I fear the situation in Great Britain will be more difficult as well. It is these specific issues that we were sent to discuss with Premier Pashitch and King Peter. More to the point, there is tremendous concern abroad that either the King or his son or the Premier will be captured, and we are anxious to find them before it is too late. Beyond that, I'm afraid I can say no more."

The Colonel stared at Wilkins. The only sound was the crackle of the wet firewood in the hearth and a slow steady drip of rain outdoors. "So Britain has nothing to offer us," said Dikovich with great disappointment. "If we must fight to the bitter end then we will do so. My men will hold the mountain passes, and we will gather our army and march north to take back Belgrade."

"If that is what King Peter chooses to do, then I wish you the greatest success," said Gresham with mild sarcasm.

"We really must find the King at once," added Wilkins, "and I wonder if you have any notion of where he can be found."

"You must speak to Alexander, the Prince Regent. We are expecting him in Prilep today, perhaps tomorrow. I cannot say for certain when he will arrive."

"Then we must wait for him, of course. But what of the King?"

"I have no idea where King Peter is now. He is an old man and has been in the mountains with the *Chetniks*. But you must understand that Peter has already made his son Prince Alexander his Regent, so there is no longer any need for you to speak with him. You may wait for Alexander at the *Bella Kaphana* in the city and I will summon you when he arrives." The room grew silent again. At last, the Colonel walked to the door and opened it. "I need to ready these men for their next march to the Babuna Pass," he said, and then he simply walked off into the rain. Gresham and Wilkins understood well why he was disappointed: It was perfectly clear that Serbia had been abandoned by its allies. The Colonel slogged through the mud to the remnants of his regiments without even saying goodbye.

In Prilep, Gresham and Wilkins located the small public house called the *Bella Kaphana* and were able to secure rooms. Gresham was asleep on a bed of old, moldy straw at the small inn when someone began pounding on his door in the middle of the night, yelling at him in a language he didn't understand. He brought his gun with him to the door and, through signs and gestures, understood from the Serbian soldier there that he was being summoned. Together, they awakened Wilkins, who gathered that the Prince Regent had arrived and they were being asked to come immediately. To have awakened them and bid them come in the middle of the night could only mean bad news, they thought. Anxiously, Gresham and Wilkins left the hotel quickly and ran with the Serbian soldier through the darkened streets to a private townhouse nearby.

"Does this fellow have any idea what's going on?" Gresham asked Wilkins, as they approached the door.

"He only knows that we are wanted at once. The Prince Regent arrived this evening and is meeting with Colonel Dikovich now."

The house, a modest white-washed but muddy three story building with a red tile roof, had a large number of soldiers in battle-stained uniforms standing outside, and it appeared that every room in the house was brightly lit even though it was well after midnight. People and dogs walked in and out the front door at will. To Wilkins, who as a boy had visited the grandest palaces in Europe, it seemed an unusual way to meet a Prince, but he guessed that war had put an end to the usual protocols.

They were directed to a sitting room in the front of the house, but remained standing in expectation of being summoned to meet the Prince. There was some sort of a row upstairs; they could hear a man and woman screaming at each other, and a full banquet seemed to be underway in the kitchens as groups of soldiers streamed in and out with plates of food. One young soldier entered the room in a wet and muddy uniform; his riding boots had been removed and his feet were bare.

"Good evening, gentlemen" he said, in passable English, shaking Wilkins' and Gresham warmly by the hand. "Can I get you anything? Will you have some whisky?"

"Yes, thank you," said Gresham.

The soldier screamed in Serbian to the kitchen to bring liquor. "Please, be seated," he then said calmly. The soldier sat a high-backed wooden chair beside the fire and put his feet up on the warm bricks as he gestured with his glass to the two upholstered chairs beside him. A bottle of whisky and two glasses were brought into the room by another soldier and placed unceremoniously on the table. Gresham poured for himself and Wilkins.

As Wilkins sat uncertainly and waved off the glass offered by Gresham, he at last drew up the courage to ask: "Are you, in fact, the Prince Regent?"

"Yes, you have it," said the young man. "I am Alexander. Are you sure you won't have a whisky?"

"No, thank you, your majesty," said Wilkins.

"There is no need for such formalities, Captain. I understand you have come from Salonika with very bad news. Truly disappointing news, if I may say so. It seems we have been abandoned by our allies, as we have long feared: Russia is fighting its own battles, Greece is in turmoil, and the British and French send us a small fraction of the forces we were promised. Is this not the case?"

"You haven't actually been sent any forces so far," said Gresham bluntly, "unless you count the two of us."

"How many of the French and British troops are at Salonika?"

"For now," Wilkins continued, "there will be fewer than forty thousand arriving in stages over the next few weeks, and, of those, the British have been instructed not to advance north of Lake Doiran on your southern border. However, there may be many more men later if the circumstances warrant."

"When?" said the Prince grimly.

118

"We cannot make you any promises about when, sir, but Captain Gresham and I were sent to propose a plan of action to your government. More importantly, we were sent to ensure that you, your father and your government are secure."

"Our plan is to fight, Captain. This is our homeland, and we will fight until we prevail or die."

"Then you will die," said Gresham. "Only it won't be you doing the dying yourself, sir, of course. Your government will certainly flee to Albania and you will leave as well, before long. It will be the men and women of Serbia who die, the soldiers killed on the battlefield. Most civilians, it appears, are already fleeing because they do not expect your army to save them. From what I have seen, your army is ill prepared to fight the Bulgarians or, for that matter, anyone else."

"Who is to blame for that, Captain?! Have we not asked for artillery, guns, ammunition, soldiers? France has given us money to pay. When shall we have our supplies? When!?" demanded the Prince. "I am not a callous man, Captain. I am not nearly as callous as your government, I assure you. I do care for my people. My country has worked many years to force the Ottomans from the Balkans and maintain our independence from the Hapsburgs. Now the Austrians have come and they are killing my people, even the old women and children, they are killing us all, do you understand?"

"I cannot make excuses for my government, sir," said Gresham, "but you should know that Great Britain and France themselves have too few guns, too few shells, and too few soldiers. In London there is a great hue and cry over the inadequate supplies of ammunition. Everywhere it is lacking. No one expected this war to go on as long as it has."

"Then tell me of this plan you have been sent to offer us."

"Prime Minister Venizelos invites you, your government, and your army to retreat to the Greek island of Corfu," explained Wilkins, "over the mountains to Albania and then by sea on British and French transport ships. Your men will be supplied on Corfu by the French, and your security at Corfu will be guaranteed by the British Navy. Next year, I suspect, Greece will no longer be a neutral country. Then your allies will stand beside you to take back your homeland."

"This is not a plan, it is an ultimatum. The war will end, and we will be forgotten on an isolated Greek island in the middle of the sea. Most Serbians have never even seen the sea!"

"Sir," said Gresham, "I speak to you as a soldier who has seen this war from the trenches, not from an office in London or Paris, and I say you are wrong. This war will *not* end. It is fatally deadlocked. In France and Belgium, hundreds of thousands of men die in pitched battles over mere yards of territory, territory that was first made into a wasteland by millions of artillery shells. There are areas in Belgium where, for mile upon mile, not a house nor church nor even a tree remains standing. Believe me when I say to you that this war is nowhere near ending. Both sides will fight on until one no longer has the machinery to wage war or men who can die. You *will* have your opportunity to return to Serbia with your army."

"But your government must be kept safe," added Wilkins. "And at Corfu, you may bring your army with you. Otherwise they are certain to be forced into surrender in your homeland, and if you or your father is captured, you will be forced to abdicate. We cannot let our enemies lay hands on either of you. That is why we have been sent to assure your security. I know you will do what you must, but we must find your father, as well."

The Prince considered a moment. "You speak with passion, gentlemen, and I do know that you speak the truth. Perhaps this is the best plan for now. Regardless, it is not a decision I would make alone. Premier Pashitch speaks for the people and Marshal Putnik for the army; they must agree to this plan, but I tell you they will be more skeptical than I."

"And your father?" ask Wilkins.

"If my father were to approve of the plan, the rest would likely agree. I may be the Prince Regent, but my father still commands their respect."

"Then I must insist you tell us where we can find King Peter," said Wilkins.

"Well, truthfully, I do not know. He is with the *Chetniks*. They are perhaps in the mountains north of Prishtina. Since my father made me his Regent, he has often done as he pleases."

"Then with your permission," said Gresham, "Captain Wilkins and I would like to find your father and escort him to meet with you, Premier Pashitch and Marshal Putnik before it is too late."

"I understand. You wish to convince him that this plan of retreat has merit. Well, he must be found either way, as we cannot leave my father in Serbia while the rest of us escape to Greece, as you say. I will send you to him with a detachment of the Fourteenth Regiment. And I will send messengers to Putnik and Pashitch to meet us." The Prince stood, and Gresham and Wilkins quickly rose from their seats. He stepped to Gresham and shook his hand heartily. "Thank you, Captains, and I wish you good luck in finding my father."

Gresham and Wilkins departed the next morning in the company of twenty men from the Serbian Army's Fourteenth Regiment. The officers were traveling on horseback and searching in the mountains north of Prishtina for the *Chetnik* camp. Because they moved frequently, the *Chetniks* were difficult to locate. Gresham and Wilkins were growing anxious to find King Peter and running out of time before the date of the meeting that was to be held in the town of Petch, a few miles over the border into Montenegro. Each day the Austrians and Bulgarians advanced further into Serbia, and the noose was drawing tight. The Germans and Austrians were battering the Serbian army at Kraljevo, less than 100 miles to the north.

Gresham and Wilkins rose early each morning, shook the new snow or the frost from their tents and blankets, drank a cup of extremely strong tea with sugar, and rode through the plains, forests and villages questioning anyone they found. Although many Serbians had fled from the north and east towards the south and west, around the city of Prishtina there were still many small villages where the peasants remained. At times, Austrian aircraft flew overhead, and the sight of them put everyone in a bad mood. Once, a low flying aeroplane dropped bombs which exploded harmlessly fifty yards to the side or behind them, but after a few attempts the pilot ran out of ammunition and simply flew off. Later that day, from a bluff on the mountainside, they could see Austrian soldiers marching not far to the east.

The Serbian soldiers in the company were excellent foragers. They were careful not to loot from their own countrymen, but there were many stray pigs and goats wandering in barren fields. Something would be caught and roasted over a campfire each night, and that, together with stale bread and hard cheese, made up their only meal each day. Then they would drink by the fire to keep warm. "Do you know how this war started, Captain?" one of the Serbian soldiers asked Wilkins one night. "You don't? Well, then I will tell you. The Sultan of Turkey sent King Peter a sack of rice. King Peter looked at the sack, smiled, then took a very small bag and went into the garden and filled it with red peppers. He sent the bag of red peppers to the Sultan of Turkey. Now, my friend, you can see what that means. The Sultan of Turkey said to Peter, 'my army is as numerous as the grains of rice in this sack,' and by sending back the small bag of red peppers to the Sultan, the King replied, 'my army is not very numerous, but it is mighty hot stuff!' Ha, ha, ha, ha!"

Bad news also found them each day and increased their anxiety. There were reports from refugee families that the city of Nish was under siege by the Bulgarians and that huge battles were being fought in the plains of Ovche Pole and in the Morava River valley to the southeast of Nish. Time was quickly running out.

One afternoon, they were riding through a cold, grey forest when a band of Bulgarian *Comitadjes* found them. As usual, the company had spread out as they rode through the trees. Gresham and Wilkins were riding together over the light snow that had fallen during the night when they heard shots fired to their right. At once, the members of the company turned and rode to the sound of the small arms fire. A band of Bulgarian irregulars had ambushed one of the Serbians, mistakenly believing him to be alone. The Bulgarians chose to stand and fight, simply ducking into a thick copse of trees from which to fire. Gresham sent half the company with Wilkins around the right to attack the *Comitadjes* from the rear, as he and the remaining Serbian troops pinned down the Bulgarians. Within minutes, Wilkins had brought his men up behind and slaughtered the Bulgarians with no difficulty. Just then, another group of well-armed men on horseback, rifles drawn, emerged from the woods on their left.

"Који сте ви људи и ко је у команди овде?" said their leader, a tall, thin man with a large mustache and small eyes. He wore an unusual uniform with a bandolier, carried a rifle, and looked very angry.

"Јеси ли Српске?" Wilkins said, in reply.

"Ја сам мајор Танкосић, а ја понављам: Ко је главни?"

"This is Major Tankosich, the leader of the *Chetnik* fighters hereabouts," Wilkins said to Gresham, who nodded and lowered his rifle.

"Мој пријатељ и британски сам послао је кнез. Ми смо били замољени да пронађете свог оца и замолите га да дође на конференцију са премијером и маршала Путника," Wilkins told the Serbian Major.

Tankosich looked disdainful of the British officers. He spoke to one of the Serbian soldiers who had been traveling with Wilkins and Gresham, then dismounted and spoke to several more. His countenance remained dark but he at last walked over to speak to Wilkins directly.

"Ја сам уверавања да говорим истину. Краљ Петар је са нама на нашем кампу. Ја ћу вам донети тамо," Tankosich said coldly, and then returned to his horse and mounted.

"He means to take us to King Peter. The king is at the Major's camp and we are to go there directly."

"Excellent," Gresham said without enthusiasm as he turned to his own mount.

They followed Major Tankosich and his men for an hour through a maze of trees clearly intended to keep the visiting British officers confused. The forest was dense, dark and veiled in fog, and very soon Gresham and Wilkins were quite lost. They climbed down into a deep ravine, and then at last up onto a sheltered recess on the mountainside where tents were scattered about and a fair number of extremely large and sinister-looking men were tending to their dinner.

"Сачекајте овде. Ја ћу видети краља Петра," Tankosich said as he dismounted and walked into the largest tent. After only a moment, he emerged with an older man in a stained and dusty royal blue uniform, who strode quickly towards Gresham and Wilkins. The old soldier was a tall, wiry man with a great drooping grey mustache and very short grey hair. His eyes were serious, sad and clever at once, like a fox's eyes. He walked first to Wilkins and held out his hand.

"Gentlemen, it is very kind of you to come. I am Peter. Please tell me your names."

"I am Captain James Wilkins, your majesty, and this is my comrade Captain David Gresham,' he said, shaking the King's hand.

"I am honored, truly, gentlemen, to have you visit our camp. I understand you have been looking for us for many days. Please, come inside so we may talk comfortably." The King led them to his large tent and held the flap open for them to enter. King Peter had a small wood stove inside his tent and a camp bed, a few chairs and boxes, a phonograph and a fine buffet on which stood a large and gem-encrusted gold crucifix.

"You'll forgive an old man his comforts," the King continued. "The crucifix we rescued from a church that the Austrians had set ablaze. They did not think to steal the contents first. No doubt that is an error for which someone paid dearly. Please sit."

"Thank you, your majesty," said Wilkins.

"Please, call me Peter, or 'Pierre Kara.' That is the name everyone uses here; it's the name I was given when I served in the French Foreign Legion."

"When did you serve with the French, sir?" Gresham asked.

"I fought in the Franco-Prussian war, after attending university in Paris."

"You were raised in France, Sir?"

"No, no. In Romania mostly, and Geneva; in those days, my family was still in exile, you see. But, please, tell me why you are here, Captains. Is it true that my son sent you?"

"Yes, sir," said Wilkins. "You see, your allies and your son are quite anxious that your security be guaranteed and that there exist no possibility that you might be captured. In that regard, there's to be a meeting in the town of Petch in three days where your son the Prince Regent will discuss a proposal that Captain Gresham and I have presented on behalf of the Prime Minister of Greece and the British and French governments. Marshal Putnik and Premier Pashitch will also be there. However, your son thought it would be of tremendous value to have you attend as well."

"My son tends to be a bit imperious, and if he is discussing this proposal of yours with Putnik and Pashitch, it must be a very serious and delicate matter. So of course I am now anxious to hear it. Please, tell me why you are here."

"Sir, have you, in fact, been able to stay informed of the situation in Serbia now that you are living in the mountains with Major Tankosich?" Wilkins asked gently.

The king was chuckling as he went to pour a glass of brandy for himself and two more for Gresham and Wilkins. As he handed them the glasses, he replied: "You think perhaps I am a tin soldier playing in the mountains while my people are massacred and our country is taken from us by force. No, I am not that old, Captain. But you do not appreciate, perhaps, that I have already placed the powers of the throne into the hands of my son. He is my Regent, the one playing at being king now, just as I did for many years."

"Playing, sir?" Wilkins asked.

"A king may be very powerful indeed, but he only maintains that power if those who serve him are willing to obey. These days, no king in Serbia has much real authority over those he rules."

"But you, sir, you still have authority over those people who respect your judgment," said Wilkins diplomatically. "You may pass your power on to whomever you chose, but the Serbian people still view you as their ruler."

"No, no, you are very kind to say so, but this country is governed, as it should be, by our Premier, Nikola Pashitch. For that I am truly grateful, as Pashitch is a great man, a very great man. I am merely a king. In fact, Pashitch is the one who brought my family back from exile to rule Serbia – he himself made me a king. However, I must now admit that even as king, I was never more than a well-dressed soldier. I don't know whether you have had the pleasure to meet with Victor Emanuel, the King of Italy. He is a fragile little man, but he told me a very amusing story about his father Umberto. It seems Umberto once and only only gave his son advice about how to be a king. He told his son: 'To be a king, all you need to know is how to sign your name, read a newspaper, and mount a horse.' That, my friends, is about what it means to be king in Serbia as well, and that is why I am now with Major Tankosich, doing what I can to protect our people and our lands, like all good Serbians are doing throughout this country."

"Yet you are still the King, your majesty, and it would shake the very foundations of Serbia if you were to be captured, killed, or forced to abdicate. I have no doubt that what you are doing is admirable, Sir," said Wilkins, "and men like Major Tankosich and his company should stay in Serbia to aid those who will not flee. But in the meantime your army is on the verge of collapse and your government is on the verge of capture. Marshal Putnik's efforts to bar the Austrians from Belgrade were heroic, but Bulgaria has flanked him. Belgrade has fallen, and when Nish and Pristina and Kosovo are taken, there will no longer be any safe refuge in Serbia. It is of great concern to your allies what happens to you, your son, and your government. And if your army surrenders, they will be disarmed and unable to fight again. These dangers must be avoided at all costs."

"I know this only too well, but we cannot ignore the violence, the terrible massacres, being perpetrated against my people, Captain Wilkins. The whole of Serbia is at war. We shall never forget what is being done here. But I must ask you: Where are our allies now?"

"Regrettably, Great Britain and France have arrived too late, sir; there can be no argument about that. However, both governments vow to see Serbia returned to your people, and more. You will need your army, so we must shelter your arms today and fight when you and your allies are able to prevail. That is what we have come to propose. Greece will provide that shelter on the island of Corfu. That will give your army and your allies the time they need to equip and organize your men and prepare them for a counter-offensive. It will also give Venizelos time to consolidate his position in Greece, for without Greece on our side, you have no hope of regaining your country. This may not be the plan we all would have chosen a year ago, but today it is the very best offer you will have."

The king sighed and was silent a while, taking rather large sips of his brandy and staring up at the large gold crucifix. Suddenly he seemed a small and tired old man. "Major Tankosich has shared his own plan with me. Yes, he has a plan to win the war, did he tell you? No? He is plotting to assassinate the Austrian Emperor Franz Joseph, in Vienna. What do you say to that? We have many secret agents in Austria under the Major's control. Shall they undertake that mission? Will that save Serbia?"

"Killing the Emperor will not end the war," said Gresham. "There will only be another to take his place."

The King laughed gently. "Yes, I must agree with you there, Captain," he said. "I have learned from experience. You see, I have recently been informed myself that Tankosich's men were behind the assassination of the Archduke Franz Ferdinand. Yes, Tankosich is one of the leaders of the *Black Hand*. You have heard of them, I expect?"

"Indeed, sir," said Wilkins grimly. In fact, he was shocked to learn that the Major, their host, was involved in the very plot that ignited the war.

"It appears Tankosich met the boy Princip before the war when the poor young man tried to join the *Black Hand*." The King continued. "Tankosich turned him away, but the boy was so desperate to show his value that Tankosich finally agreed to supply the explosives and pistols used in Sarajevo. Well, they succeeded in killing the Archduke to everyone's surprise, and now we can see the result. My country is serving penance."

"Serbia did not start this war, sir," insisted Wilkins.

"Do you know," said the King, "I received a private letter from Rome, from Pope Benedict, telling me that this Austrian invasion is Serbia's punishment from God?"

"Another assassination will not remedy the first," said Gresham.

"Do not be overly concerned," the King continued. "I will not allow Tankosich to kill the Emperor. Franz Joseph is a very old man, even older than I am, and the new heir, the Archduke Charles, they say he is a mild and compassionate man. Some say he is weak, the sort easily manipulated by their army's Chief of Staff, Conrad – now that's a man who should be assassinated. Conrad despises the Slavs and would like to see us all exterminated. But killing any of them would solve nothing."

"I quite agree," Wilkins added quickly.

"Still, somehow, we must rid Europe of the whole Hapsburg dynasty one of these days, and the Hohenzollerns, and probably the Romanovs too." The King laughed. "My democratic idealism is perhaps too evident. As I said, I was educated in Paris."

"Would you spare our British monarchy then?" asked Wilkins with some sarcasm.

"I haven't met your King George," said the King diplomatically, "so I shall reserve judgment." He paused in thought a moment. "But I deeply respect him for doing so little. To be a king or an emperor, there is a great temptation to govern, but a wise king lets the people rule themselves and a learned people understand their king is little more than an emblem of their nation."

"Some kings seem rather to become emblems of despotism," said Gresham.

"The despot may be reviled by his people, young man, but still he rules with an iron fist. No, it is the foolish king, the one who loses the respect of his people, who truly has no power at all. Consider Louis the Sixteenth. It was not his despotism which made France despise him. No, it was allowing himself to be carted off from Versailles by a mob of angry washer-women. That is what truly killed him."

"According to your son, the people of Serbia deeply respect you, sir. So I must ask again: Will you come to Petch and help us save your people?" asked Gresham

The King rose. "Yes, of course we shall do whatever is required of us, gentlemen," he said with a wink.

Later that evening, Gresham and Wilkins found Major Tankosich in his smaller and much less comfortable tent making plans with several of his lieutenants for their campaign in the coming days.

"James, please ask the Major if we may confer with him privately for a moment," said Gresham.

"There is no need to translate; I understand enough. What do you want, Englishman?" Tankosich asked coldly.

"I see, then perhaps you should step out as well, James. I would like to speak with the Major alone."

Wilkins was somewhat surprised by the request. "Certainly, if you wish it. I will be outside," he said as he and the other Serbians left the tent.

Gresham was silent a moment and considered the Major before he continued. "King Peter has told us that you are not merely a military commander, Major, but that you are also a leader of the *Black Hand*. In light of this admission, I will tell you confidentially that I am not merely a British officer. I am a member of the British Secret Intelligence Service, and since we are both fighting the same enemy, it seemed appropriate to me that we should know each other. There are likely to be opportunities for us each to benefit from our association."

"That is a reasonable conclusion, Captain."

"I must tell you that I am opposed to any plan to assassinate the Emperor of Austria-Hungary; I believe it will end no better than catching a feral cat by the tail. However, I am certain there will be other, more effective means by which we may accomplish our mutual objectives."

"You need not concern yourself with the well-being of the Emperor. My men in Vienna say that the old man is very ill and likely to die a natural death at any time."

"And the heir, Archduke Charles, have you designs upon his life?"

"They say Charles is more Catholic than the Pope himself," said the Major with derision. "The new Pope, I mean, Benedict, the reformer."

"I must ask bluntly: Before anything happens to the Archduke, will you allow me to consider the matter and speak with my colleagues?"

"We have enough to do in Serbia for now, Captain Gresham. You may do as you like, and if my men or I may assist you in some fashion in the future, I assure you we will be most cooperative."

"Very well. You may count on the same cooperation on my part. Thank you," Gresham said and shook hands with the Major. Then he went out to continue drinking with Wilkins by the fire.

The next morning, Major Tankosich departed north with his company to join the Serbian army near Kraljevo, where the Austrians and Germans were advancing rapidly. King Peter rode south with Gresham and Wilkins and the men of the Fourteenth Regiment to Prishtina. As they reached the city that evening, news arrived that the Bulgarians had finally captured the city of Nish to the east. The Serbian defenders were fighting a rear-guard action as they retreated west, but they were heavily outnumbered. Prishtina was already crowded with refugees and many of the army's support units. Premier Pashitch and members of his government had recently been in the city but had already departed west for the town of Petch.

King Peter stayed at a fine hotel that night; Gresham and Wilkins slept in the kitchens, there being no other rooms available at any price. Before dawn the next morning, they were all bundled into automobiles that, to their surprise, headed east towards the fighting: King Peter had decided during the night to visit the front lines. The road was in terrible condition, however, and the route was especially slow as the entire population of Nish was fleeing west. The sides of the road were littered with dead men, dead livestock, abandoned sedans that had been set ablaze, abandoned children, and the detritus of the army and the fleeing civilians of Nish.

In a few hours, they reached the rear lines of the retreating Serbian army, and Gresham and Wilkins continued on to the front lines with King Peter in his sedan. Ahead, they could see the tremendous pounding of the shells from the Bulgarian army's heavy guns on the ridge hammering the Serbian front lines. The Serbian army had been forced to abandon most of its artillery during their retreat and could make no reply. As the Serbian position quickly became untenable, lines of grey-coated infantry began to wind their way back from the ridge into the woods, using ditches and an abandoned farm house to cover their retreat. Bulgarian assault troops appeared on the ridge, and a heavy skirmish erupted. Gresham and Wilkins, who had no rifles, pulled King Peter into a hastily dug trench, but the King, to the great pride of his Serbian soldiers, took a rifle from a young, wounded infantryman and began shooting at the Bulgarians himself. Wilkins was too anxious to let the King stay at the front for long, and very soon they were all packed back into the sedan and headed west again towards Prishtina, this time with half the Serbian army surrounding them and shrapnel shells falling about the road.

By the end of the day, Prishtina had been overwhelmed by panicked refugees and soldiers. The last trains south had passed through and the tracks to the north had been blown with explosives. Civilians crowded the streets, many with all their worldly possessions including herds of cattle and pigs. To make matters worse, a cold blinding rain had begun to fall, and thousands of men and women had to camp in the open with no cover at all and their miserable wagons filled with such furniture and household goods as they had been able to save parked in the thick mud. Masses of soldiers sat in dark doorways and crowded the public buildings, many weeping with rage and frustration and hunger. Crowds clamored at the bakeries for bread. Gresham and Wilkins followed the King to the army's headquarters, which were hastily installed in a village schoolhouse. Gresham and Wilkins sat for dinner with King Peter at a table with non-commissioned officers, their men acting as orderlies. Everyone ate the same fare – stale biscuits and a thin, hurriedly-prepared stew – the only difference being that at the officers' table wine was also served.

The Serbian casualties during the retreat from Nish, they learned, had been just under three hundred men killed that day, but the total for the past three days' fighting had been over two thousand. The Bulgarians outnumbered the Serbians by four to one. In spite of the crushing superiority of the enemy, the Serbians had fought with courage and confidence, defending their positions foot by foot. To the south, however, the Bulgarians were battering the Serbian units guarding the Babuna Pass and, to the north, the Serbians were retreating quickly from Kraljevo. It was thus clear to everyone that the Serbian army faced imminent annihilation or capture, making a forced retreat inevitable.

Early the next morning they learned that the Bulgarian army was only twenty miles from Prishtina. Orders were issued to fire the ammunition stores that could not be moved and to evacuate the town. On the routes leading south, there was a mass exodus of civilians and soldiers on cold and muddy roads. Gresham and Wilkins accompanied King Peter in his sedan again, only this time they drove as quickly as possible west towards Petch. There could be no further delay: The retreat into Albania must be ordered before the Bulgarians were able to capture the mountain passes to the south and encircle the Serbian army, forcing their surrender. Ever since the Austrian and German attack on Belgrade, the instructions of the Entente to the Serbian command had been to avoid risking everything on a pitched battle and to retreat slowly, delaying the advance of the enemy as much as possible until the French and British should be in a position to aid the Serbians. The Serbians had done so for several weeks, yet no help had come. The Serbians were now with their backs against the mountains of Albania. The one small force the French had sent from Salonika had been forced to retreat into Greece.

By the time King Peter, Gresham, and Wilkins reached Petch, a few miles over the border into Montenegro, Marshal Putnik was waiting to meet them. The collapse of the Serbian defenses and the imminent fall of Prilep had already forced Putnik to accept the plan to retreat over the mountains into Albania and ferry the army to Corfu. There was no need for discussion, and Pashitch and his government ministers had already proceeded to the city of Scutari that morning; they were to be evacuated by the British Navy. Crown Prince Alexander was on his way to Salonika to meet with Venizelos. King Peter, however, chose to accompany his army over the mountains to Albania, and Gresham and Wilkins stayed on to protect him.

The next morning they awoke to find the wide open plains of the Kosovo region were covered with a thick blanket of pure white snow. Over this, long lines of snow-clad soldiers could be seen marching west, the columns extending for miles into the distance. A deep silence filled the plains, except that overhead the sky was full of crows whirling and croaking over the heaps of dead oxen and horses left along the sides of the road. The soldiers looked exhausted and starving already, and the march over the mountains would be slow, with little provisions for them and no fodder at all for the horses and oxen.

Gresham and Wilkins were given the opportunity to ride in a lorry with a company of French munitions experts who had been destroying bridges and train tracks behind the Serbian army retreat. Eventually the lorries would have to be left behind, as the mountain passes in some places dwindled down to nothing more than foot paths, but Gresham and Wilkins were especially unlucky as their lorry's motor gave out rather quickly. They had to help push it off into a field, where it was doused with petrol and set ablaze. Nothing could be left for the Bulgarians. As they marched higher into the mountains, more and more vehicles were breaking down and were simply pushed over the edge into the ravines below. That night it began to snow again, and Gresham and Wilkins slept overnight in a dark munitions tent surrounded by explosives.

On more than one occasion, Wilkins remarked that the mountain crossing was reminiscent of Napoleon's expedition over the Alps prior to the battle of Marengo in 1800. Unlike Napoleon, the Serbians were not marching to victory in battle; rather, they marched in the last stages of defeat, their uniforms in rags and their boots held together with straps of leather or twine, with inadequate food and almost no means of transportation. The number of men freezing to death climbed with each passing night; some simply sat down on the side of the path to die.

As they traversed the plateau and began the long slow descent into Albania, Gresham and Wilkins stayed close to King Peter. Despite his seventy-six years he marched on foot with the vigor a younger man might have envied; some days, the King never once mounted his horse, which a soldier led behind them. Albania was a puppet state whose government had been installed by Serbia after the Second Balkan War, and the Albanian people were still, for the most part, hostile to the Serbians. They offered no hospitality except for payment in hard silver and refused to sell fodder for the animals at any price. The number of horses and pack animals was dwindling rapidly, and their carcasses had drawn the wolves out of the forests to harry the troops at night.

At long last, however, the Serbian army and Serbian citizens came down into the plains of Albania and forced themselves through the mud and snow for the final march to Scutari and temporary refuge. They would rest briefly there before the army would continue south to the port of Durazzo, and there board the British ships transporting them to Corfu.

Corfu

Wilkins and Gresham viewed their arrival on the island of Corfu off the western coast of Greece as a welcome opportunity to rest. In summer, Corfu was indeed a beautiful island that had been enjoyed by many British families on holiday, but in the winter the weather was cold and rainy and, apart from the comings and goings of the Serbian soldiers encamped in the countryside, the town was very quiet. Immediately after they arrived on the island, King Peter and Marshal Putnik left again for Salonika to meet with Venizelos, and the island was thereafter under the watchful eye and control of French soldiers and the British Navy, so there was little for Gresham and Wilkins to do.

Gresham had diligently wired Mackenzie in Cairo as to the major events of their mission in Athens, Salonika and Serbia; it took him several days to complete the process of translating his notes into code. He and Wilkins stayed at a comfortable little house in the heart of the old town where both food and wine were abundant – a great relief after the deprivations of Salonika and Serbia – and one charming young woman from the little yellow house on Lemonia Square helped to warm Gresham's bed, though not mend his damaged heart. (Wilkins professed a desire to remain above such debauchery.)

It was by sheer chance that Gresham and Wilkins, as they happened to duck into a little out-of-the-way church during a sudden rain storm, found Miss Flora Sandes standing in the small vestibule as well.

"Good heavens," said Wilkins. "David, look who it is! Miss Sandes, whatever are you doing here at Corfu?"

"Captain Wilkins, Captain Gresham, what a wonderful surprise. I am here with the Serbian army, of course; I came with them from Prilep, just as I told you I would."

"I am so pleased to see that you made the journey safely," said Wilkins.

"But, Miss Sandes, I see you are wearing a Serbian uniform," added Gresham. "Are you now a nurse with the Serbian Army?"

"Well, indeed, it began that way. However, my comrades on the journey felt it would be a bit safer for me to enlist in the Serbian army, as I would then be, at worst, taken as a prisoner of war rather than as a spy. But since then I have been promoted twice, first to Corporal, and just recently to the rank of Sergeant Major in the Serbian infantry."

"Kudos to you, Sergeant Major; well done," said Wilkins. "It is wonderful that you have had this opportunity to pursue your strengths to their greatest advantage. The loss is entirely the British army's. Will you give us the honor of toasting your success at supper? Captain Gresham and I were just on our way to a fish shop recommended by our host."

"Certainly, it would be a great pleasure to join you."

They ran through the rain to a small but comfortably warm little shop near the harbor, where they were served a hot fish stew made with rosemary, lemon and tomato, fresh warm bread and a white wine.

"I must thank you both," said Miss Sandes. "I can't remember having eaten so well in months."

"Are the Serbians not receiving better rations now that you have landed at Corfu? I thought the British and French were supplying full rations," said Wilkins.

"The quantity of food is adequate, but, unfortunately, the menu has consisted primarily of Bully Beef, and it doesn't sit well with men who have been on half rations for months. There are men dying still of dysentery, as well, although it's been reduced somewhat since the French began transporting the sick to the hospital on the little island of Vido out in the bay; my Company and I now work on the docks there. But I must say, on the whole, the French have behaved quite honorably towards the Serbian army, and I believe we will recover sufficiently to return to Serbia next year. Plans are already being drawn, I am told, but it will be a very long and costly battle."

"Do you plan to return to Serbia yourself?" asked Gresham.

"Indeed I do, Captain. I feel it is my duty, as an officer in the Serbian infantry, to do what I have promised to do. So, yes, I shall continue to fight with the men until the Serbian homeland has been returned to its people. Incidentally, were you gentlemen ever able to find King Peter, as you had hoped?"

"Yes, in fact we accompanied King Peter over the mountains to Albania," said Wilkins.

"Did you? Prince Alexander was with us in Prilep when we began our evacuation," said Sandes. "He accompanied us over the mountains as far as Durazzo, and I formed quite a favorable impression of that young man."

"In what regard?" asked Wilkins. "I ask quite seriously, as King Peter and Prince Alexander both seemed, to put it bluntly, the least 'royal' of the monarchs it has ever been my privilege to meet."

"Perhaps that is why I liked him," said Sandes. "He seemed to understand how the soldiers were suffering, and did not shirk from sharing their misery. I make no representations about their ability to govern, but the Prince and his father are leaders and the Serbians greatly respect them both. Will you gentlemen be returning to Serbia, or are you returning to Salonika? I believe you still have a friend there, do you not, Captain Gresham?" She asked.

"No, I'm sorry to tell you we are not," said Gresham vaguely. "Things did not end in Salonika as I would have wished, and I will not be going back."

"I am sorry to hear that. We have heard that Germany and Austria may now invade Greece," she added. "Do you think they will?"

"No, I think it unlikely," said Wilkins. "Germany has seriously overplayed its hand already. We have learned that the threat of invasion has forced King Constantine to mobilize at least one more division and the new Prime Minister – despite that he was hand-picked by the King – has forbidden Germany and Austria to enter Greek territory. And the number of French and British troops at Salonika is growing daily."

"That is a tremendous relief. Well, at least allow me to toast you both, sirs, and to thank you for all you have done for Serbia."

During their supper, the rain had stopped and a cold wind had begun to blow in from the north. Gresham and Wilkins walked silently back to their hotel. Compton Mackenzie was overdue to visit them on Corfu to discuss their next assignment, and Wilkins was still uncertain whether he would be traveling on with Gresham. Gresham, however, had begun to formulate a new plan in his own mind, and he was quite concerned what Wilkins would think of it.

Gresham and Wilkins were summoned to meet with Mackenzie at a villa on the hillside above the beach, and the three sat comfortably before the fireplace on a cold, wet day, sipping brandy and going over the events in Athens, Salonika, and Serbia.

"Well I repeat, gentlemen, you have done a spectacular bit of work, and I congratulate you," said Mackenzie. "You may have saved Greece and Serbia and you deserve medals. I haven't any to give you, but you may consider yourselves decorated. Have you enjoyed yourself, Mister Wilkins, or would you like to return to the front lines now?"

"Suppose you tell me what you have in mind for us next, and I will let you know whether I care to join in."

"Oh, well, I had supposed you fellows would wish to stay on Corfu and assist the Serbians. Someone must keep an eye out for trouble here for the time being," said Mackenzie. "There must be a huge reorganization before the army is prepared to return and fight their way back into Serbia next year."

"We're not needed here," said Gresham. "The Royal Navy has got this island sewn up tight, not that I mind a bit of relaxation."

"Since you wired me that you had a scheme of your own in mind, David, are you prepared to tell us what you have been plotting?" Mackenzie asked.

"Have you?" Wilkins asked. "Tell us."

"Mackenzie, do you recall when we were on Imbros that we once discussed whether there was some means or other to eventually knock the Austrians out of the war. I immediately began to consider whether there might be some method, not unlike what you have in mind for Arabia, to undermine the governance of the empire. I now have such a plan in mind, and by it I mean to destroy the Hapsburgs."

Wilkins laughed aloud. "Oh really, and how would you propose to do that?"

"When the Archduke Charles becomes the Emperor of Austria and Hungary, I would see to it that he makes a fool of himself, so the world will see him as a simpleton, the Germans will see him as an incompetent traitor, and his own people will demand his head."

"But how would you actually accomplished that worthy goal?" asked Mackenzie, skeptically.

"There was a time when I was a lad in Manchester, after my mother had passed away, when I lived in the streets with many other orphaned children. We waged our own bloody wars. We fought with knives and broken bottles mostly, because they were the only weapons we could get our hands on, but the killing was real enough. One day, my best mate got cut up pretty bad and he bled out alone in the back of an abandoned factory that was full of rats. I found him, what was left of him at least. Well, the next day, the dumb ruthless bastard that had killed him, he was all shook up about something; I'd rather not say what. But he came to me on the street and said we should call it *pax*, a no-harms-done sort of thing. I couldn't believe it. I mean, after finding my mate that way in that factory, all chewed up and all, well, you can't just pretend something like that didn't happen, can you? You see how what he was proposing was impossible.

"This war is like that one – only millions will be killed, lands and lives destroyed, innocent people exterminated. You have both seen the cruelty and hatred it has inspired. But even after all the killing and misery, you can be sure the kings and emperors, they're all going to want to pretend it didn't even happen. I don't think they really know what *is* happening. But the people have seen it, they do know, and they will not forget or forgive so easily. They'll be bloody angry that their sacrifices and misery and the deaths of their sons and husbands and fathers all amounted to nothing in the end. So when Charles becomes Emperor and says *pax* and suggests we all go back as if it didn't happen, what do you think his people will say about that?"

"Is that what Charles will do?"

"It is, once Wilkins and I plant the idea in his head, and I know just how to do it. Charles is still a young man and he knows nothing of war, he's inexperienced and sheltered. But when Franz Joseph dies any day now and Charles ascends the throne, he'll surround himself with advisors and ambitious generals. That is why we must reach out to him before the Emperor dies. We'll go to him in Austria, plant our seeds, and then get out fast. I want you to come with me, James."

Wilkins shook his head in disbelief. "So this is what it has come to, and I suppose I am not surprised. But quite frankly I am still shocked by your suggestion, David. The Hapsburgs have ruled in Europe for a thousand years, and you want to incite a rebellion against them? And what precisely do you believe will happen to Austria if you succeed, without an emperor able to maintain peace and order? It is an empire made up of many peoples who hate each other. I fear that anarchy will only beget more violence."

"I am no anarchist, James, but I could not care less what happens to the Austrians. Surely what happens to Austria and Hungary will be matters for their people to decide once this war has ended, and what they will want above all is peace and security."

"That is precisely what Napoleon promised to the French year after year, and all they got was more war."

"Perhaps, but now France is our ally and has a government that is answerable to its people, as do we in Great Britain, notwithstanding the crown."

"That will take time to achieve in Austria, even if it is inevitable. And as for the Hapsburgs, as I have said before, I will not become involved in anything that might become an embarrassment to my family, and to purposefully embarrass the future Austro-Hungarian Emperor? It is simply too much."

"Well, James,' Mackenzie said, "I must dispose of your objection, and I can do so without difficulty. I have brought you a letter from your father." He handed a sealed envelope to Wilkins. "Would you please read that now?"

"Yes, of course," said Wilkins, startled, as he broke open his family's wax seal on the envelope and recognized his father's handwriting. He read:

My Dear James,

I pray this letter finds you healthy and in good spirits. Your mother and I miss you and your brothers terribly, but we are very proud of your service to our country during these terrible days. Word of your injuries on the peninsula reached us quickly, but we are relieved to hear that you recovered without difficulty. You have always been the bravest of our children as well as the most clever and insightful. That is why it is a great delight to me that you have come to know my good friend and colleague, M., with whom I have shared many a long and thoughtful conversation as to our conduct of the war. I have no doubt he shall set you on the proper path, if you are so inclined. Of course, you may serve our nation in the manner you best see fit, but he and I agree that your talents predispose you to becoming an exceptional asset to the Service. I hope your experiences to date have swayed your own mind in that direction, for it is by your labour and that of your compatriots that the future of our civilization is to be determined. You must put aside your fondness for the past and look beyond the crystal palaces to the future which lies ahead. Nothing ever changes without loss, my boy, but it is your duty to ensure that the many upheavals which are now clearly upon us do not occur without true purpose and noble intent.

With loving affection,

Your Father

"You are a man of many surprises, Sir, to show up in Corfu with a letter like this," said Wilkins, with thick emotion. He took a large sip of his brandy and sighed.

"As you see, our objectives are those of Great Britain, and you are a young man who can do great things for his country, James. You should not be reduced to cannon fodder."

"Fine, I'll do it. I will go with you, David. We will do what we can."

"I am terribly relieved, James; I thought you might refuse to come along. You will see. Everything will work out in the end." Gresham turned to Mackenzie: "What do you think?" He asked.

"I see now why you asked for the false passports, but to enter Austria right now – they are a clever and cautious people, David, I must warn you."

"Surely you can help us think up a gaff to get us in from Switzerland, and we won't be doing anything besides talking, so they can watch us as much as they like. All the better, in fact – we'll make a big show of ourselves. We won't go near anything or anyone that would raise suspicions. James, you'll have to be a real spy this time, use a false identity and all. No more objections, I hope."

"No, I am with you. We must do what we can. Charles' wife Zita, has a brother in the Belgian army whom I met last year in Paris. I can contact him, as he is certain to be in Austria for the holidays and no doubt he can arrange an opportunity for us to speak with the Archduke."

"*M*?" Gresham asked Mackenzie again.

"I suppose it's worth a shot even though you're playing the long game. I know that *Control* would like it. I like it; it's a grand plan. If all you do is get in and out unharmed, news of that by itself would be a coup for the Service. The Austrians won't know what you've learned, and it will scare the hell out of them. And it will be a political nightmare for Austria if word of Charles making peace overtures was leaked, especially in their relationship with the Kaiser. We shall have to make sure it is made public. But I want the two of you getting out of Austria unharmed, and if you can't approach Charles, then you must escape as quickly as you can. Do you agree?"

"Absolutely," Gresham replied.

"You will need quite a lot of money, I expect. As you say, you will need to put on a show."

"All to the best, then," said Gresham, "but there is one thing I will want, and I'd better keep you out of it, too, *M*. James and I have developed our own connections among the Serbians. I'll speak to them."

"As you wish. I suggest you fellows make your way to Geneva as soon as possible; I'll arrange some aliases for you to use once you arrive there and you'll need an account to draw funds. And I do hope you'll have a very Happy Christmas, gentlemen. Please buy each other something wonderful at government expense. You deserve

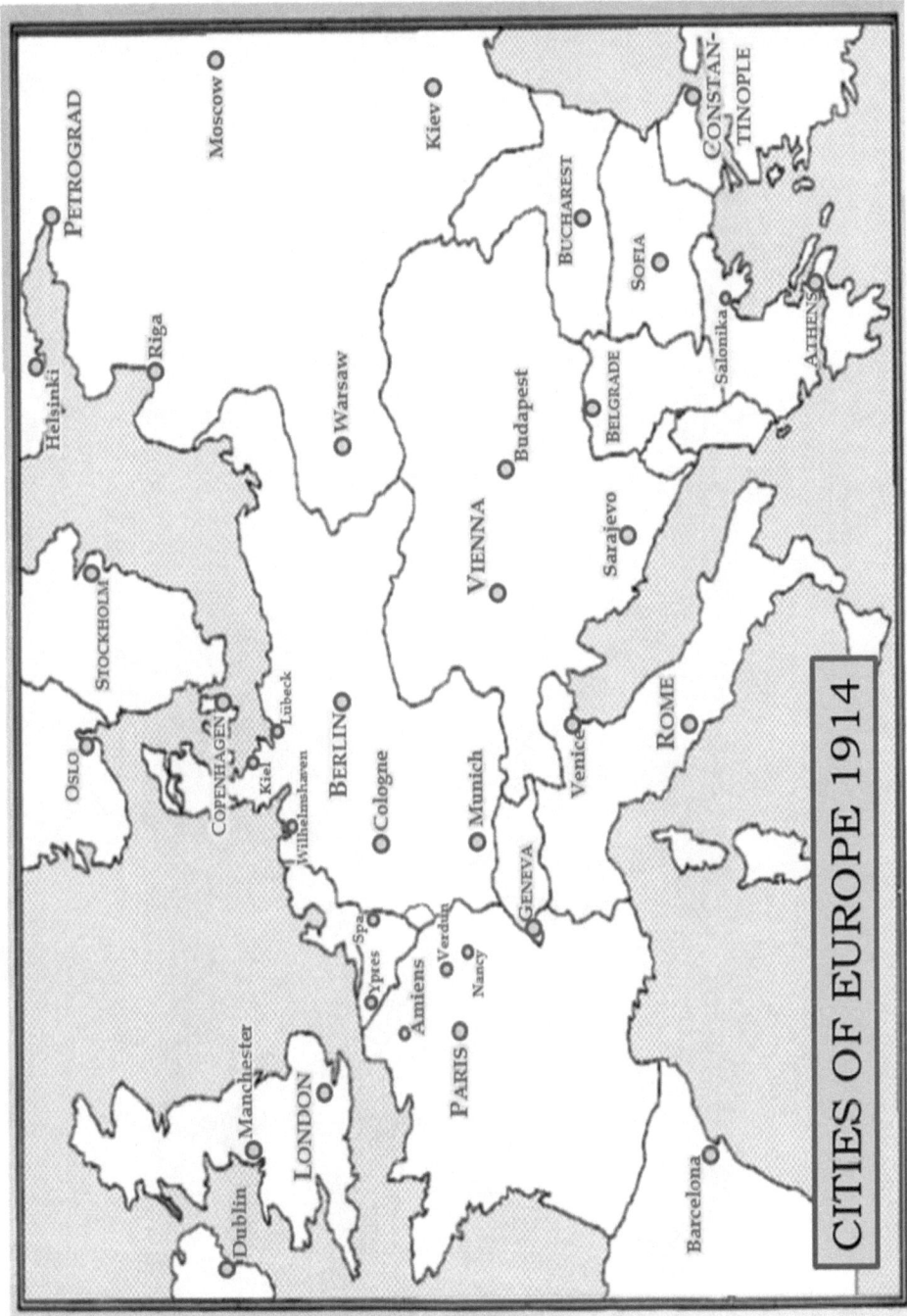

CITIES OF EUROPE 1914

Vienna

A light snow fell on the farms outside Vienna as the train neared the great capital of Austria. Gresham and Wilkins sat opposite each other at a table beside the lace-curtained windows, drinking tea from the fine Imperial State Railway porcelain and eating rich pastries that were replenished by the wait staff whenever their platter was half-emptied. Travel between Switzerland and Austria was inconvenient, and few people made the journey between the countries anymore unless they were certain to have no difficulties getting into or out of Austria. Since they had passed the border, Gresham and Wilkins had been politely questioned twice, their passports had been scrutinized, and their luggage and belongings had been examined to the extent of undressing and allowing the Austrian authorizes to check their clothing – pockets, seams and buttonholes. Most of the passengers remaining on the train either worked in the Austrian or Hungarian governments and had been to Switzerland on official state business or they were journalists. On this particular train, the journalists included one David "Kelly," formerly of Ireland, and one James "Kruger," born in German East Africa, who were collaborating together on a new biographical book about the Archduke Charles for the König Verlag publishing house in Geneva. Their credentials were entirely in order.

"Kelly" and "Kruger" (enjoying their tea and pastries) were quietly discussing the scar on Kruger's left cheek and his mangled left ear. Kelly was adamant that the injuries must have been caused by an attacking lion. Kruger, however, recalled that his injuries were caused by a misfiring elephant rifle, but he wasn't sure.

"You can't be unsure, James. You must remember the event vividly."

"I am unaccustomed to play acting."

"Just think it all out, every detail, until it feels true."

Wilkins had also grown a beard – albeit a rather short and sparse one – that helped to distract from the long red scar and better disguised his identity. There was a risk that Wilkins could be identified by someone he had met as a lad, unlikely though that might be. The beard also fit with the pretense that he was the son of a Boer from the West Cape Colony, one of Moritz's men who had fled to German East Africa during the wars with England, and that would imply an underlying enmity towards the British that would be reassuring to the Austrian authorities.

Gresham was finally embracing his Irish heritage: he had assumed the identity of David Kelly, a newspaper man from Ulster infamous for his anti-British writings, who had disappeared in 1913. The British knew that Kelly had actually gone to America, but for the sake of the ruse, Gresham was supposing that Kelly had fled to Switzerland. Gresham removed a slim silver case from his breast pocket, a recent Christmas gift from Wilkins, and withdrew a fancy pre-rolled cigarette for himself.

"Would you care for one?" He asked Wilkins.

"No, thank you."

Both "Kelly" and "Kruger" worked for König Verlag, one of the great old publishing houses of Geneva. König Verlag had recently been acquired by an American bank on behalf of a consortium of its depositors (all of whom were members of the British House of Lords). It was a highly respected publisher of fine books, and it would continue to be so. However, König Verlag had also recently "employed" a small number of individuals who were "writing books" on such arcane subjects as the German aviation industry, developments in Austrian agriculture, and the lesser-known political parties in Russia. As such, the publisher provided the necessary credentials and an adequate justification for Gresham and Wilkins to enter Austria and to make their way to Vienna first class.

The three-full-day trip (lengthy stops for baggage inspection and questioning included) had indeed been first class. Even the fine hotel they enjoyed in Geneva for the Christmas holiday was penurious compared to the Imperial State Railway. Wilkins, while not unaccustomed to excellent service, fine linens, sterling silver, and Dresden china, was quite impressed. For Gresham, it was an eye-opening experience: They had brought no servants, so the railway provided them; Gresham had forgotten his crate of Irish whisky, so the railway sent a car back to Geneva to fetch it; the sumptuous six-course meals were served with the finest wines; and even the border authorities were warned not to overly antagonize passengers traveling first class. It was almost assumed that if you could afford it, then of course you had every reason to be going to Vienna. But to Gresham, the opulence was disorienting and seemed antiquated.

From the train window, Vienna emerged before them like an ice-crystal fairyland. Throughout most of their journey in Austria, the authorities had required the window blinds to be kept down, presumably to obscure the war preparations being undertaken in various areas along the train's route. On the outskirts of Vienna, however, the blinds had been lifted and the city had presented itself gloriously: A light snow shroud and sheet of ice coated the magnificent buildings, parks, and streets of the city as the train arrived at the Westbahnhof at dusk. The Emperor, His Imperial and Royal Apostolic Majesty Franz Joseph, had invested many years into modernizing the city of Vienna. The bastions and glacis of the old city had been transformed into the modern Ringstrasse, an elegant boulevard that accommodated many of the fine *Gräf & Stift* automobiles as well as parks, palaces, concert halls and art houses. With the curtain walls removed, the towns surrounding Vienna had been absorbed into the metropolis and many areas renovated with running water and electricity as the city modernized for the Twentieth Century. Yet still the elegance of the old city remained as if preserved under glass.

Gresham and Wilkins prepared to disembark and make quite a show of themselves. Their strategy was to be blatantly ostentatious, in the belief that only spies would skitter about like rats in the dark. Everything they did and said would be completely out in the open, and anyone who chose to watch them was welcome to do so. This had worked perfectly well on the Imperial State Railway, but now, in Westbahnhof station as they disembarked, three uniformed Austrian officers were waiting to greet them. One, an extremely tall, muscular and cruel-looking Colonel, stepped forward. He did not offer his hand, but said bluntly, with no note of hospitality in his voice:

"*Guten Tag, Herr Kelly und Herr Kruger. Ich bin Oberst von Stumm. Ich bedauere, dass müssen wir sie bitten, mit uns in unser büro kommen, um den grund, warum sie nach Wien gekommen diskutieren und bestätigen sie ihre anmeldeinformationen. Es sollte eine kleine zeit. Bitte folgen sie mir.*"

"Can you tell him I don't speak German," Gresham said loudly to Wilkins.

"We have been invited to another interview, I'm afraid," Wilkins replied. Then to Colonel von Stumm he said imperiously: "*Wir freuen uns, ihnen unsere zusammenarbeit. Allerdings haben mein kollege und ich ein abendessen engagement bei Meissl und Schadn. Wir würden uns freuen, wenn Sie nicht halten uns wartet. Übrigens, mein kollege nicht Deutsch sprechen. Nur Englisch und Gälisch.*"

"*Und sprechen sie auch Englisch?*"

"*Natürlich. Wie sonst könnten wir zusammen arbeiten?*"

"Very well, then I will attempt the English. Come. We have questions for you." The Colonel led Wilkins and Gresham to a dim corridor and into a brightly lit windowless office. The two other Austrian soldiers followed and stood guard outside the door.

"Sit," the Colonel commanded. He towered above Gresham and Wilkins as they sat next to each other at the plain wooden table. The Colonel could barely fit in his uniform because of his massive muscles, but that raised a question in Gresham's mind as to why such a supreme physical specimen was not serving at the front. Gresham assumed the Colonel must be very smart or had been very brave to receive a comfortable job in Vienna away from the fighting.

"Why are you in Austria?" the Colonel asked.

"This is incredible," said Wilkins haughtily. "Simply incredible. How many times must we repeat ourselves? We are credentialed journalists, my dear Colonel. König Verlag has engaged Mister Kelly and myself to write a book about Archduke Charles. He *will* be the new Emperor 'ere long, and the whole world wants to learn something of his tastes, his interests, his family. We are in Vienna to conduct interviews, nothing more. We have several scheduled in the next few days, including our first this very evening at *Meissl & Schadn*, and you are perfectly welcome to attend, to follow us, to read our mail, and to listen to our telephone calls. We have nothing to hide."

"Who are you to write such a book? Two English-speaking men from Geneva?"

"*Wie kannst du es wagen?!*" Wilkins shouted back angrily. "*Ich bin ein bürger von Deutsch-Ostafrika. Mein vater gegen die Briten kämpfte.*"

"*Was ist mit ihm?*"

"Mister Kelly is an Irishman. Many of the Irish speak English, or did you not know? If you had a brain in your head you would give Mister Kelly ten thousand guns and send him back to Ulster to start a rebellion. But as we have already provided this information thrice, please either ask us something new or let us go on our way."

"We are familiar with your articles, Mister Kelly, and I am all the more surprised to learn that you are now writing books about Austria's Archduke. Does Irish independence no long interest you?"

"It is a matter of politics," Gresham replied. "Ireland needs allies, and I wish to see whether Charles is inclined to view Irish independence favorably. Of course, the money I am earning for the book is useful in purchasing arms in America, as well."

"And if money is so short, how do you come to travel first class, then?"

"That is my doing," Wilkins interjected. "I refuse to travel any other way. My father made quite a bit of money in the Transvaal gold mines, and I am afraid I am rather accustomed to it. I am paying for Mister Kelly."

"What is your father's name?"

Wilkins stared at Colonel von Stumm coldly. "Kruger, of course."

"I see. And you have comfortable accommodations arranged in Vienna, I suspect? Where are you staying? And for how long?"

"*The Grand.* We plan to stay for two weeks, but we may extend our stay if the interviews take longer than we have planned."

The Colonel stared at them a few moments and considered his two visitors. It was reassuring that neither seemed at all evasive. In fact, he was certain the buffoons would make quite a spectacle of themselves in the Vienna's social circles.

"I will need a list of the people you intend to interview," he said. "You will update me if anyone is to be added to the list. You will not interview anyone unless we know about it. You will not leave Vienna until it is time for you to depart Austria. And we will check to see that you are following these rules. If they are broken, you will be arrested, and either sent to a prison camp or simply shot as spies."

He handed Wilkins a sheet of paper and pen. Wilkins withdrew his own solid gold Montegrappa fountain pen from his jacket (a gift from Gresham) and wrote down five names, all people they had arranged to interview while in Geneva. Most of these were minor aristocracy, people who were unlikely to know any more about Archduke Charles than any member of the general public. The last name on the list, however, was Prince Xavier of Bourbon-Parma, the brother of Zita, wife of Charles, heir to the throne of the Austro-Hungarian Empire.

"Have you any idea how little money they are spending on the Balls this year?" Asked Count von Wilczek. "Why, it is only a fraction of the usual! They honestly believe that austerity will project sympathy for our soldiers at the front lines. Well, perhaps so, but it sends exactly the wrong message to our enemies. Opulence and splendor tell the world that Austria is at the zenith of its power and fears nothing. While our young men are fighting at the front, we should celebrate Fasching like the empire of old."

Count von Wilczek was a portly old gentleman who had an international reputation for talking too much. He had been willing to talk to Gresham and Wilkins if they agreed to meet him at the fine restaurant at *Meissl & Schadn*, one of Vienna's very best. Indeed, the Restaurant on the second floor was a marvel of snow-white Damask linens and fine, intricately etched crystal. "Gentlemen, at *Meissl & Schadn,* you may only have beef," the Count continued. "They serve a finer beef than anywhere else in the world. Perhaps, Mister Kelly, you would enjoy the boiled tenderloin with braised cabbage and potatoes. I assure you, it will far exceed anything you were ever tasted in Ireland."

"It sounds excellent," Gresham agreed.

"*Meissl & Schadn* raises its own livestock, gentlemen. They are kept inside a sugar refinery north of the city and fed on molasses and sugar-beet mash to give their meat its extraordinary sweetness. There are twenty-four variations of boiled beef, seventy-eight different cuts of beef (which can of course be prepared in any manner you request), and thirty-six accompaniments. Heinrich knows what I have, but please allow me to make a selection for you."

"That would be fine," said Wilkins. "We understand that the Archduke usually attends very few of the Fasching Balls even in time of peace. Is that correct?"

"Heinrich!" the Count shouted. The heavyset *maître d'hotel* with a thick, pink face and wide bushy sideburns after the fashion of the Emperor Franz Joseph himself strode promptly to their table. "My new Irish acquaintance Mister Kelly will have the *suppenfleisch mit meerrettich. Kruspelspitz für zwei, und Château Lafite Rothschild, '98.*"

"*Ausgezeichnet.*"

"*Und kaviar,*" said Wilkins.

"*Nein, wegen des krieges. Darf ich vorschlagen, die consommé?*"

"*Nein, nein,*" said Wilkins in disgust. "*Vein schnell, zwei flaschen.*"

Heinrich, flustered by the aggressive visitor from Geneva, hurried away.

"You must be kind to Heinrich; he is an institution in Vienna."

"You were telling us of the Fasching Balls," Gresham reminded the Count.

"Yes, the Balls," continued the Count eagerly. "Fasching is a very old tradition in Vienna, gentlemen, a very honorable and grand tradition. It is the quintessential celebration of Shrovetide. The main events are, of course, usually in February leading up to Lent. But the Balls begin in January, and this year the very first will be held at the Palais Auersperg. Yes, it's fortunate Auersperg has that distinction again this year, as I can assure you it will be anything *but* austere."

"And the Archduke – will he attend?" Gresham asked.

"Archduke Charles is likely to attend that one. He generally comes to the first Ball or two at most and then goes off to hunt in Laxenburg for a week or two until the main events. Of course, our young Archduke takes Lent very seriously. He is a deeply religious man."

"Has he had the privilege of meeting the new Pope, His Holiness Pope Benedict, yet?" Wilkins asked.

"No, no. Very difficult to travel to Italy nowadays, as I would think you would know, especially for an Austrian Archduke, and Pope Benedict was raised to his esteemed office last autumn, after the war had already commenced. But I do believe Charles had the honor of meeting with his predecessor, Pope Pius. He was a great admirer of His Holiness for his opposition to the modernists and reformers and so forth. The Princess Zita, if I recall correctly, met Pope Leo once or twice. But Charles likes the old church, the old way of doing things, *triumphans pompa nobile* and all that. He likes his Catholicism with a great deal of humility and a dash of suffering, just like his mother, Maria Josepha. Do you know, she has converted the Palais Augarten into a hospital! Heaven knows whether it will ever be fit to live in again."

"Does Princess Zita share her husband's devotion?" Wilkins asked.

"In the Princess, Charles has found the perfect counterpart. I fear Charles and Zita will be the most devout rulers Vienna has ever been forced to endure. Now mind you, I am myself a devout Catholic. Everyone in Vienna is Catholic. And we respect the Church. But we do not let the Church invade our politics."

"I fear we are again getting into matters of state that we had better avoid, my dear Count," said Wilkins.

Heinrich arrived to pour the Château Lafite. As he poured for the men, Gresham excused himself. He made his way through the dining room and down a short hallway to the lavatory. An attendant stood stoically just inside the door. Gresham began the laborious process of unbuttoning himself when another young gentleman entered the lavatory.

"*Wie geht es dir*, Otto?" the man asked the attendant, who smiled and nodded quietly.

Gresham was standing at the mirror, attempting to correct his cravat, when the young man came to stand beside him, placed a folded slip of paper on the counter before Gresham, adjusted his jacket, and departed.

Gresham picked up the paper and strode out into the hallway to read it. There was nothing to read: The paper was marked only with a large black cross.

It was not at all the message Gresham was hoping to receive, but at least it was contact.

Despite his assurances to Mackenzie and to Colonel Stumm to the contrary, Gresham *did* intend to hold an unapproved meeting in Vienna. He needed assistance to complete their mission, and Gresham had reached out to those who he believed would have no qualms about the task he needed done: The *Black Hand*. Mackenzie may not have had spies in Vienna, but the *Black Hand* did, and, on Corfu, Gresham found those who could assist him. Now in Vienna they had made contact, but the task Gresham had requested of them was still incomplete.

Shortly after Gresham returned to his seat at the table, a line of waiters arrived to deliver the silver-domed platters of beef. They were followed by a diminutive child, wearing a tiny tuxedo and cravat, who pushed a cart laden with the garniture: horseradish, *apfelkren*, mustard, pickles, potatoes, cabbage, spinach, onions, *sauerkraut*, and the rest, followed by Heinrich who inspected the table, refreshed the wine glasses, and nodded, thereby granting his waiters permission to uncover the platters and the guests permission to begin eating their meal.

"There, gentlemen, what did I tell you," said the Count with tremendous pride.

"Quite adequate, indeed," said Wilkins.

"My dear Count, Charles may be terribly Catholic, as you say," Gresham continued, "but is that not in accordance with the Hapsburg tradition?"

"Yes, of course, but the House of Hapsburg is so much more. Austria, Hungary, Bohemia, Switzerland, Spain, Portugal, Prussia, France, Belgium, Italy, England, Mexico, Russia, and even Brazil – their monarchies are all connected to the House of Hapsburg. From Count Radbot in the Herzogtum Schwaben a thousand years ago to the All-Highest Franz Joseph today, the Hapsburgs led Europe out from the Middle Ages to become the center of civilization it has become. Will Charles carry on that legacy, I ask you? Or shall he enthrall us to the Vatican?"

"But would he not then be inclined to view his fellow Catholic nations with great amity? Say, for example, if Ireland were to become an independent nation, would not the Archduke view such a nation as Austria's natural ally?"

Before the Count could answer, Wilkins cut him off: "With all due respect," Wilkins said icily to Gresham, "I believe our biography of Charles should be confined to personal matters, family, diversions, and so on. All this talk of empire and politics makes my neck tingle. My good Count, please tell us about the theater and the opera instead. What is the Archduke's favorite opera? Who is his favorite painter? Has he any pastimes? Have you visited his home in the Upper Belvedere?"

"Alas, I have not been to the Belvedere since Franz Ferdinand lived there. As you know, Charles has spent much of the war with the garrison at Teschen thus far, and the time he has been at home has mostly been spent with the Princess and their children in the country. Princess Zita has little interest in hosting galas at the Belvedere without him. It is generally known, by the way (and this is no state secret, Herr Kruger), that Charles will depart this spring to take command on the Italian front. It's long overdue, I say – good heavens, the man could become Emperor any moment and he has never held a command of any kind!"

"We've heard that Charles is a very kind and compassionate man," said Gresham. "Is he quite suited to the job of commanding troops in battle? Perhaps his skills shall prove to be more in the diplomatic line."

"You may be correct there," said the Count. "Charles has many friends, but a warrior must be fierce. That, I assure you, is not Charles. No, he stays in his country estate most of the time, he rides, he hunts, he collects coins, and he hikes in the country with Zita. He is a quiet man. Yet he is to be our next Emperor, so, somehow, he must discover his strengths."

After dinner, Gresham and Wilkins took a carriage through the brightly lit, shimmering white city to arrive at last at their hotel, the *Grand*, the finest accommodation in Vienna and one which Wilkins claimed was as good as the *Savoy*. He arranged for them to take an enormous, well-appointed suite: Each room even had its own telephone. At Wilkins' request, the hotel also provided servants to see to their needs; their luggage, which had preceded them, was already unpacked and stowed, and a bottle of Gresham's Irish whisky awaited him in their salon. Tempting though the whisky appeared, Gresham had drunk quite a great deal of wine with their dinner.

"I really am uncertain how many of these interviews I can bear," Wilkins said, flopping down on the divan and lighting a cigarette. "That inflated, billious Count, there's nothing he told us which the world does not already know. And tomorrow we must interview Baroness von Gutterburg, a woman with a reputation for scandal."

"I am rather partial to scandalous women. How old is she?"

"She is older than my grandmother."

"Oh. At least we are meeting with Prince Xavier in a few days," said Gresham, "and our colleagues know we are here."

"Did you make contact with them already? When?" asked Wilkins excitedly.

"Just a signal, in the lavatory, but no word as to whether or when they will respond to my request."

"And you did notice the gentlemen at the table near us at the restaurant, did you not?"

"Von Stumm's men, yes. They are keeping a close eye on us, as we expected. I am certain our colleagues were aware of them as well, or they would have approached more openly."

"Then we shall have to play our parts well. We are likely to have only one opportunity, my friend, and you had better be prepared," Wilkins said.

"Yes, I agree, at the Auersperg Ball."

Wilkins had arranged all of their interviews to take place at the most lavish and expensive public places he could devise lest someone accuse them of secrecy. Their interviews were conducted over enormous meals and innumerable bottles of the finest wines; expense was of no concern, and more than once Gresham and Wilkins had stayed out late drinking and making a terrible show of themselves. Gresham, in particular, spoke at length with anyone who understood English about Home Rule for Ireland and the fate of Ulster, he decried Irish participation in the war on the continent and spoke favorably of how Sir Roger Casement had rejected his British title to side with the Parnellites in favor of Irish nationalism, all to the delight of the Austrians. They were still followed occasionally by von Stumm's men, but within a few days' time the blanket of surveillance began to dissipate.

The interview with Prince Xavier would be the major exception to these public displays. In part, this was because Xavier requested to meet them at the *Grand*, and in part because no one in their right mind would accuse the Prince of treason. Indeed, even though he was an officer in the Belgium army and fought with the French army on the Western Front, he had *carte blanche* to enter or leave Austria even if men like von Stumm didn't like it. He was brother to Her Imperial Highness, Princess Zita of Bourbon-Parma, wife of Archduke Charles himself, and therefore above suspicion.

Although a "Prince" in name, Xavier's title, like that of his six brothers, was based on his father's claim to the Duchy of Parma, as descendant of Philip, Duke of Parma, the third son of King Philip V of Spain and Elizabeth Farnese. The Duchy was a fiefdom surrounding the city of Parma in northern Italy that had unfortunately been annexed during the Italian Unification and so it no longer existed. Xavier had been born in Italy, but was raised in Austria and Germany and attended university in Paris, where, in the months before the war, he had met the sons of Lord Bartlett. At the outbreak of the war, Xavier and his brother Sixtus enlisted in the Belgian Army; however, several of his older brothers were officers in the Austrian Army.

After Gresham and Wilkins conducted several minor interviews in their first days in Vienna (and indeed learned enough to write a very poor book about Archduke Charles) and had made quite a spectacle of themselves, the date of their "interview" with Prince Xavier at last arrived.

"James, how good to see you again, and how much older you look," said Xavier as he entered their suite at the *Grand*. He was a very tall, lanky man with dark, elegant Italian looks and a fine mustache. He moved fluidly, like a cat, even in his evening clothes. In Austria, he did not care to offend by wearing his Belgian uniform, and arrived at the hotel in his dinner jacket.

"How good to see you, Xavier, and thank you again for agreeing to meet with us. Please allow me to introduce my good friend and colleague, Mister

David Kelly, lately of Ireland. Would you care for an Irish whisky; I'm afraid it's all we're drinking nowadays."

"Perfect, I'd love one. Mister Kelly, I understand you are from Ulster. And now you and James are supposedly writing a book about my brother in-law, is that right?"

"Yes, exactly."

"Well, I shan't ask about that; perhaps you could send me a copy when it comes out in print," he said with a laugh.

"Of course we've formally requested an interview with the Archduke and your sister, but we've received no reply from Schönbrunn," Wilkins added. "I understand Charles is a very private person and has no wish to make a splash before his ascension to the throne."

"You can hardly blame him," said Xavier. "Just consider what happened to his predecessor."

"Where have you been serving, Xavier?" asked Wilkins.

"My brother Sixtus and I have been with the French Army in Champagne."

"It sounds as good a place as one could wish," said Gresham.

"Indeed, it's quite lovely. Things got fairly hot for a few weeks in the autumn, but otherwise we've simply been doing a great deal of drinking. It is Champagne, after all. James, you look like you've seen some action yourself. Whereabouts?"

"I was at Suvla Bay."

"Oh, I see, yes. I'm very sorry to hear it. Have you heard anything about the evacuation of the peninsula? It's all come out in the past few days, you know, about the evacuation that was ordered by General Monro. Most everyone should be taken off by now."

"It's been about three months since I left myself, so I can't speak to that. I am still recuperating in Egypt, or so my regiment believes."

Xavier laughed. "You don't look too badly off. And I can certainly understand why you would use an alias to enter Austria, James. Not many British officers come to Austria nowadays. On the other hand, I frankly have some misgivings about assisting you without knowing your true intentions. Why have you two come to Vienna?"

"Our intentions are entirely peaceful, I give you my word of honor as a gentleman," said Wilkins. "I speak for myself and for Mister Kelly. We are here only to preach peace, Xavier, and it is our sincere hope that Mister Kelly will be able to convey that message to the Archduke in person."

"You see," added Gresham, "you and James are not the only ones familiar with the war. I've seen battles just as you have, and James agrees with me that it will take a true leader to bring about an end to the war."

"And you think Charles will fill that role? I daresay you are thinking of another Archduke."

"But each of the nations involved now, well, you can easily imagine how entrenched their leaders have become, and how desperate they are to preserve their gains," said Gresham. "When the day comes that Charles becomes Emperor, it will mean a fresh start for Austria-Hungary. He will be in a unique position to do something about the war, to convey a message of peace. I have been empowered to assure him that there are some who will be very receptive. James and I are old friends, and he has helped me come to Vienna for the sole purpose of conveying that message to Charles."

"But who sent you, Mister Kelly?" Xavier asked pointedly.

"I cannot tell you that. I may only speak to Charles on that issue, if I am granted the opportunity."

"I see," said Xavier doubtfully. "Well, I'm afraid it won't do any good your coming to Vienna. Charles and my sister are in the country now with the children. And, anyway, I could hardly arrange a private audience for you without knowing more."

"But perhaps, Xavier," said Wilkins hopefully, "if you were to arrange an invitation for us to the Auersperg Ball? Charles will be there, will he not?"

"I suppose it's likely he and Zita will be returning for the Ball. But would you speak to him then, in public, on a matter of such delicacy? That will not do at all."

"No, of course not," said Gresham, "but I believe Charles will seek us out, if I give him reason."

"Well, I am willing to arrange invitations to the Ball for you both; that is no difficulty at all. And I will give the matter further thought, but more I cannot promise you."

Gresham and Wilkins arrived at the Palais Auersperg with hundreds of other sedans and carriages containing the most exquisitely dressed Counts and Countesses, Barons and Baronesses, and Dukes and Duchesses of Austria who had all come to Vienna for the Shrovetide celebrations. The ladies in their white gowns and bejeweled masks strode gracefully up the steps to the Palais. Snow lay thickly on the parks and statues, but an army of workers had been hired to clear the streets and steps. The men, the ones in black evening clothes and top hats, with their monocles and walking sticks, walked behind them. Many of the men, however, had instead dressed in their bright, pastel-colored and heavily decorated satin military uniforms with capes of bearskin and gleaming black leather boots. It was wartime, and each man who was able displayed his martial credentials.

Neither would anyone wish to miss the first Ball of the season, especially not the one given by the influential and wealthy Auersperg family at their historic Palais in Vienna. In their time, Mozart and Haydn had premiered operas at the Palais Auersperg, but now the most notable guests were Count Karl von Stürgkh, the Minister-President of Austria and the man who ensured that Austria stayed faithful to its Germanic roots; Count Stephan Burián von Rajecz, the Joint

Foreign Minister for Austria and Hungary and arguably the second most important man in the Empire after the Emperor himself; and Count Franz Conrad von Hötzendorf, the Chief of the General Staff of the Austro-Hungarian Army, the man who would destroy Serbia and the Slavs given the opportunity. These were the men who found themselves surrounded by throngs of the wealthiest and most powerful men of Austria and Germany seeking favor. His Imperial and Royal Apostolic Majesty Franz Joseph could not attend; it was said he was suffering a relapse of the pneumonia which had come and gone several times in the past year and would surely end his majesty's life before the new year was done.

Wilkins and Gresham passed into the Ball dumbfounded. Even Wilkins had never seen anything like it. The wealth on display in the form of tiaras, necklaces and bracelets, all crafted with each family's finest jewels especially for this event, was astronomical. The gold filigree, chains, and rope on dresses and uniforms must have weighed, collectively, hundreds of pounds. A full orchestra played waltzes by Johann Strauss, and lead crystal chandeliers brightly illuminated one ballroom after another, each containing invaluable paintings and other exquisite works of art, while gentlemen and ladies danced on the intricate parquet floors.

"I wish you hadn't given your word for me," Gresham hissed.

"What do you mean?"

"With a few of Sergeant Hart's old jam-tins, one man could take out the whole bloody Austro-Hungarian Empire here tonight."

"Don't talk like that; you don't know who might be listening," Wilkins chastised him.

"You sound like an old lady, James."

They walked casually from room to room, but it seemed Archduke Charles and his wife had not yet arrived at the Ball. As they came to a stop with their glasses of Champagne near the grand gleaming white marble staircase, many men and women who were interested in meeting the ostentation Irish revolutionary Kelly (who had been the talk of Vienna for days) soon surrounded Gresham to express their *Fraternität* with the Irish and support for those who would defy Great Britain. Among them, one gentleman walked right up to Gresham and took his hand. He shook it vigorously, saying "*meine Herren, ich bin Gotz. Sie schreiben ein buch. Rufen sie mich an. Ich habe viel zu erzählen.*"

The man then quickly walked away.

"What was he on about?" Wilkins asked.

In his palm, Gresham held a note that the man Gotz had transferred when he shook hands. Of all the places to give me a damned note, Gresham thought. He placed it in his pocket; he could not read it until he had some privacy.

"There you are, gentlemen," said Xavier, casually approaching with a half a dozen attractive young women swarming around him excitedly. "I am delighted you received your invitations to the Ball. These young ladies are extremely eager to meet the dashing young Irish revolutionary making the rounds in Vienna. It seems you are something of a sensation, Herr Kelly, and when these ladies found out that I knew you, nothing would prevent them from making your acquaintance."

"I certainly hoped they weren't all for you, Xavier," said Gresham. "Do any of them speak English?"

"We all do, Mister Kelly" said an excited, giggling young woman with large sparkling brown eyes.

"When are your sister and her husband arriving, Xavier," said Wilkins with impatience.

"Oh my dear James," said Xavier, "they have been here for ages already. Have you not spoken to them yet?"

"Good heavens, no. We had no idea. Where are they?"

"Charles is right there, speaking to the junior foreign minister."

Xavier pointed to the young Archduke, only a few years older than Gresham himself, wearing a formal Austrian military uniform without extensive decoration, speaking to an older man. He was of middling height and had wavy brown hair and a drooping mustache, and his eyes expressed a certain degree of boredom with the conversation. In fact, he appeared almost sleepy. He smiled slightly and laughed gently, perhaps merely out of politeness. Unlike the other dignitaries at the Ball, the Archduke had no throng of flatterers around him and no one seemed to be seeking him out.

"James, keep the ladies company for a moment while I introduce Herr Kelly to Charles." Xavier took Gresham by the arm and led him over to the Archduke, who looked at Gresham with only mild curiosity.

"*Entschuldigen sie, Eure Majestät, darf ich ihnen Herrn Kelly, ein Ire aus Ulster. Er schreibt ein sehr schmeichelhaft buch über Eure Majestät in der Schweiz veröffentlicht.*"

Gresham bowed.

"Herr Kelly," said Charles. "I have heard of this book you are writing."

"You do me great honor, Your Majesty. I pray that the book we are writing pleases you and will be a fitting introduction for you to the peoples of the world who are so anxious to learn of Your Majesty."

"Indeed," said Charles placidly.

"If I may, I have been told that Your Majesty is a collector of rare coins, and I have one here that I hoped would make a fine addition to that collection." From his pocket, Gresham withdrew a single shining brass coin, which he handed to Charles.

"Your gift is deeply appreciated. Best wishes on your book, Herr Kelly," said Charles, who then turned back to the junior foreign minister, slipping the coin in his pocket without a glance. Gresham bowed again slightly and was led away by Prince Xavier.

"I don't know what you're playing at, but I hope you took your best shot," Xavier said to Gresham.

"So do I," said Gresham. "I can't bear to think how James is treating those young ladies, Xavier. We had better return at once and rescue them."

"I find we are of like mind," said Xavier. He snatched a bottle of Champagne from a passing waiter as they returned to the party.

The rest of the evening was spent in show: Dancing, drinking, and flirting with the pretty young ladies. Gresham and Xavier struggled to keep the excited young ladies from making too much noise, and they ended up in a small lounge reciting obscene limericks that made the ladies squeal and blush. Wilkins found he was unable to escape one young woman, Edle von Weben, who was terribly infatuated with him; they spent most of the evening dancing waltzes in the grand ballroom.

Much later that night, Wilkins and Gresham returned to their suite at the *Grand* exhausted. As they entered the darkened rooms and headed off to their bedrooms, Gresham was first to notice that things were amiss. Before they had gone out, he had, with a bit of spittle and a few hairs, created a small unnoticeable seal on several of the closet doors and, when he inspected them upon their return, he could see that all the seals had been broken. While they had been out, their belongings had been thoroughly and professionally searched.

"James!" He called, and Wilkins rushed into Gresham's room. "It seems the Colonel is not done with us yet. Our rooms have been searched."

"What else would you expect? You shook hands with the Archduke, for pity's sake! You can't expect von Stumm to just ignore us after that."

"Good God! I completely forgot about the note!" exclaimed Gresham. He searched his pockets for the note he had been handed by Herr Gotz at the Ball. He found it at last deep inside his jacket and carefully unfolded the small paper. "There's an address and room number, and it says '*Mannerheim*'. What is that?"

"It's a hostel for vagrants. How terribly untimely: We might have been able to sneak over there yesterday, but now I fear we will be watched very closely again. I don't know how we can go there – it will be terribly suspicious."

"Then I must go at once and you will have to cover for me," said Gresham, pulling off his fine evening clothes. "Run the bath and order up some food and wine for me; put on a show. I will go to the *Mannerheim* and return as soon as I am able."

"You must be very careful, David. Make sure you are not followed."

Gresham finished dressing in his daytime clothes and put his overcoat back on. "After the food has arrived, contact Edle von Weben; I have her telephone exchange. Call her and go to her home tonight; leave through the back of the hotel. If they catch me out, they will come for you instantly and I don't want you sitting in the suite. Then call me here in the morning: If I am not back by dawn, James, you had better make a run for it."

"Good luck," Wilkins said, as he reached for the telephone.

Gresham was quickly out the door and took the service stairs down to the back of the hotel. He found a staff room and an old, dirty boiler-suit and cap there. He put them on quickly to better disguise himself and left his fine overcoat balled up in a waste bin.

Outdoors he moved slowly through the cold night, making as little show as possible, pretending he was just one of the many tired workers headed home at the end of their shifts. The *Mannerheim* was in the north part of the city, and it was a long walk, but many of the workers out that night were headed in the same direction. It was difficult to tell if anyone was following him. Gresham stopped several times to rest in warm doorways and watch the others in the street. It didn't appear anyone was after him.

After an hour more of quick walking, Gresham arrived at the tired and dingy men's hostel across from the china manufactory. He waited until he saw two men entering together, and then stepped quickly to join them. He grunted sleepily and shambled up the steps with them, continuing to the fifth floor where he found the room he was seeking. He knocked.

"*Was willst du?*" said a man behind the door after a brief pause.

"*Meine hände sind schwarz,*" said Gresham, repeating the simple German phrase he had been taught to identify himself to the *Black Hand* agent.

The door opened enough for a large, dirty man to look out. He looked Gresham up and down carefully, and opened the door to let him into the poor, shabby room. It was dark, and Gresham could not even see if they were alone.

"*Ist* for you?" the man asked with a heavy accent.

"Yes, do you have it?"

"Arrive today." The man pried up a loose floorboard and pulled out an envelope, which he handed to Gresham quickly.

"Is it real?"

"*Was?*"

"Is it genuine? Did he seal it?"

"I not understand. *Was ist?*"

"Thank you," Gresham said. He tucked the envelope into his boiler-suit and went to the door. He opened it slowly and looked out carefully. The hallway was clear. He went back down the steps and reached the street quickly and quietly. Suddenly, he saw that, although Colonel von Stumm was no longer watching authors Kelly and Kruger very closely, he was regularly watching the *Mannerheim*. Two men in military uniforms stood in the doorway of the China manufactory. They saw Gresham come out of the *Mannerheim* in the middle of the night and decided anyone going out at that hour was worth checking. Of course, Gresham would not even understand their questions, so there was no way he could bluff his way out. He started to walk quickly down the block and turned south when he reached the corner. The two uniforms were following close behind, their suspicions aroused.

As soon as Gresham was out of their direct line of sight, he bolted. Running as fast as he could, he went down several streets, turned and doubled back, doing his best to elude the uniformed men. He found himself in front of the general hospital and walked inside. He passed through the hallway towards the back, down the stairs to the boiler room, and then up to the staff entrance in the back of the hospital. Outside, two military sedans sped past the hospital. It seemed the uniforms had called in for assistance searching the neighborhood. Gresham would have preferred to hide in the hospital until the route was clear, but he absolutely had to return to the *Grand* before daylight. He exited the hospital carefully and continued his walk south, hiding in doorways and stairwells whenever he saw a sedan. He passed a theater, and as he turned the corner, he walked right into a very tall Austrian soldier. Gresham's cap fell back, and the soldier's face displayed the shock of recognition as he realized it was "Herr Kelly" standing right before him, out in the wrong neighborhood in the middle of the night.

"Was machst du, kleine ratte?" he said angrily, as he reached out and grabbed at Gresham's left shoulder with one massive hand and squeezed. Gresham gasped in pain, but the pain turned his shock and fear into a black rage. His eyes grew wide, and the Austrian laughed: *"Die kleine ratte möchten beißen?"*

Gresham growled and threw out his right fist, hitting the Austrian right between the eyes. For a moment, the Austrian didn't realize what had happened. He blinked twice, and then his face flushed red. *"Ich werde dich töten!"* The Austrian screamed and launched himself at Gresham. Gresham expected the attack and quickly dodged to the side. The Austrian had long arms, and Gresham knew he had to stay out of the man's reach. Gresham was lighter on his feet, but it would be difficult for him to keep from being cornered eventually. Now that he had been recognized, he could not run. He had to kill the soldier.

Back and forth they padded on the slippery walkway, and Gresham got in a few hard shots to the Austrian's sides. Without warning, the Austrian's heavy black boot suddenly came up across Gresham's thigh in a place where he had once been knifed in Manchester, and the pain fueled his rage still further. He dotted the Austrian's face with his right until the soldier's mouth and nose were streaming with blood. The Austrian was furious, and screamed at Gresham in perfect English: "I am going to kill you." He rushed at Gresham in mindless hate, but again Gresham's lighter size aided him, as he dodged out of the way and threw all his weight into propelling the Austrian into the brick wall head first. There was a loud crack, and the Austrian instantly slumped to the ground like a heavy sack. Gresham checked to see that the man was truly dead, scooped snow down over the soldier's corpse to hide it from plain sight, and ran down the street as fast as he could.

Gresham soon found himself again in front of the Palais Auersperg, dark and quiet after the enormous party had ended. He dashed through the park in front of the Palais, across the Ringstrasse, and safely into the city center. It was easier to walk unnoticed here - there were many men and women now on their way to their daily work. Gresham joined the shuffle of men until he reached the back of the *Grand*. He quickly recovered his coat from the staff room bin, put it on over the boiler-suit, and ran up the stairs. He removed and left the boiler-suit in a corner at the very top of the dark stairwell, and then went back down to his suite, just as the sun was beginning to rise.

A meal for two, untouched, sat on the table. "What happened, David? You were gone for hours!" Wilkins asked. He had been sitting in their salon awaiting Gresham's return.

"I was chased. Von Stumm's men had staked out the *Mannerheim*."

"Did they see you?"

"No, I ran and they didn't see my face, so there shouldn't be any trouble." He pulled the bottle of Champagne from the ice bucket and plunged his bruised and swollen right hand into the ice water.

Wilkins looked skeptical. "Just tell me you got it."

"Yes, I think so." Gresham took the envelope from inside his shirt and carefully laid it on the table. Wilkins took up the envelope gently and with a nod from Gresham tore it open. Inside was another envelope, one with a red wax seal embossed on the flap with the motif of a man in a boat.

"Is it genuine?"

"He didn't know. Perhaps it doesn't matter. So tell me why you aren't at Edle von Weben's as I instructed you?"

"It's simply not my custom to attend to women at their homes in the middle of the night, David," said Wilkins defensively.

"That's all right, my friend. I know the right one will come along. No word about the Archduke yet?"

"No, but it's very early. Let's get some sleep and we'll go out this afternoon to continue the show."

"What shall we do with this?" Gresham asked, holding up the sealed envelope.

"Keep it with you. If that doesn't get one out of a hangman's noose, I can't imagine what would."

The telephone awoke them later in the morning. It was Prince Xavier calling to invite Wilkins to tea that afternoon at *Café Sacher*.

Wilkins went to the hotel *Sacher* that afternoon uncertain what to expect. As he left the *Grand*, he checked carefully to see if von Stumm's men were following him, but to his surprise saw no one. Even if Gresham had not been identified outside the *Mannerheim*, Wilkins expected a certain general increase in security that would likely include himself and Gresham. Instead, the city seemed to bustle as usual. At the *Sacher*, he went to the famous cafe and was met promptly by the *maître d'hôtel*. The café was a Vienna institution, a brightly lit red and white room of fine china and charming white marble tabletops, crystal chandeliers and fine portraits on the walls. Wilkins said he was to meet Prince Xavier and was led to a table in a back corner at which sat Xavier, another gentleman who looked a great deal like Xavier only older and more sophisticated, and a cat-like young lady with thick, luxurious black hair and wide oval eyes.

"James, please take a seat," said Xavier quickly. Wilkins sat and said hello to the gentleman and lady.

"James Wilkins, may I introduce you to my brother, Prince Sixtus and my sister, Princess Zita," said Xavier.

Wilkins was terribly flustered. He clumsily attempted to stand and bow but the heavy table had pinned him to the wall as he stammered out "it's a great honor to meet you both, a great honor, Your Majesty."

"Please, sit down, James," said Xavier. "Let's not put on a show; this is an informal meeting."

"Yes, of course, as you wish," said Wilkins, regaining his composure and his seat.

"You must excuse my brother revealing your identity, Mister Wilkins," said Sixtus. "I pressed him to explain how he knows Mister Kelly and yourself, and he divulged your name, but only to me. My brother, my sister and I give you our word we will tell no one else, not even Charles."

"That is perfectly understandable, certainly, and I appreciate your discretion. I should add, that if I were here on behalf of Great Britain, I would have come under my own name rather than under an alias."

"That is precisely what we concluded," said Sixtus, who had a far more serious demeanor than his younger brother Xavier.

"I may be escorting Mister Kelly – that is also an alias, incidentally – but I am not at liberty to say whom Mister Kelly represents. Not Irish rebels, of course."

"Mister Wilkins," interrupted Princess Zita, "my husband was quite curious about the coin he received from Mister Kelly last night, and he has been asking questions, and those questions have raised concerns among those whose duty it is to protect the Archduke, especially as there are men running wild in the streets of Vienna. A great many people are now investigating you. You must tell me the real reason you have come to Austria. Please, does Mister Kelly indeed have more to say to my husband, as my brother has indicated?"

"Yes, Ma'am. All Mister Kelly wishes is to have an opportunity to speak privately with the Archduke for a few minutes. We have come to Austria under the guise of book writers in the hope that a brief interview could have been arranged and easily explained. Then, to be frank, Mister Kelly and I will leave Austria as fast as we possibly can do so."

"I am inclined to trust you, Mister Wilkins, because your family is so highly respected, and if you will vouch for Mister Kelly and assure me that he means no harm to Charles, I am willing to make the necessary arrangements for an interview."

"I can absolutely assure you that Mister Kelly only wishes to speak to Charles. I know Mister Kelly very well, and can attest to his honorable character."

"I am satisfied," said Xavier. "There's no reason why an interview should be of any concern. Do you agree, Sixtus?"

"Yes, it sounds fine. We are all in a difficult place with this war, and communication is one thing we should never oppose. It will be up to Charles to decide what it all means. That will be his business soon enough, and he must start somewhere."

"Very well, we are agreed" said Zita. "Mister Wilkins (or Kruger, I suppose we will say), my husband and I are returning to our country estate in Laxenburg tonight. I invite you and Mister Kelly to come for an interview tomorrow. A sedan will pick you up at the *Grand* at noon and bring you both to the New Castle in Laxenburg. Charles will probably want to show you through *Franzensburg* as well, and you had best plan to remain our guests until it is time for you to depart Austria."

"I am honored, Ma'am. Thank you. If you will allow me, I will leave you so that Mister Kelly and I can prepare for the interview."

Wilkins made his farewells and almost ran from the *Sacher* back to his suite at the *Grand*.

A luxurious black *Gräf & Stift* sedan brought Gresham, Wilkins and Xavier to the village of Laxenburg, a mere ten miles to the south of Vienna, the next afternoon. A light snow was falling. Gresham and Wilkins, anxious as they were to complete their mission, found that just leaving the city behind greatly relieved the fear of being unmasked that had hung over them for the previous two weeks, and each mile from the city put them more at ease.

Over the years, the village Laxenburg had been expanded and built up several times until it had finally become the perfect simulation of a rural idyll, that is, the sort of charming, affluent rural village that has never truly existed anywhere. The village was surrounded by woodlands used only for hunting, ponds used only for swimming and boating, and modern houses with running water, electricity and telephones lived in only by the Hapsburg family and its servants. It was a rural retreat for the Archduke and his family, as it had been for the Hapsburg family since the Fourteenth Century. This was where the Archduke Charles preferred to live and where he had mainly stayed with his wife and children since a minor wound had led to his withdrawal from his post at Teschen and his unnecessarily extended convalescence during the past year.

Gresham, Wilkins and Xavier were met at the New Castle by the head servant. The castle, which Charles and Zita preferred and where they stayed when they could escape the day-to-day demands of Vienna, was actually over 150 years old. It had been built for Holy Roman Emperor Franz I and Empress Maria Theresa and was more akin to a large, comfortable country estate house than what Gresham would consider a castle. Inside, the house was an explosion of Rococo creams and pastel colors and curves and ornamentation, every surface plastered with gilded stucco scrolls and pink-cheeked cherubs and mirrors and paintings in bright colors. It was bewildering to the eye and slightly nauseating.

157

To Gresham, it was incredible that Charles would prefer this sickly and effeminate house. The head servant, however, showed the men to their more austere rooms located in what Wilkins said was the servant's wing. The Archduke, they were told, wished to walk them about the grounds. Gresham and Wilkins (as Xavier had been on the tour many times) changed into clothes more appropriate for a tramp in the snow and then waited in the library. The library, at least, was a slightly more masculine domain with shelves constructed in dark hard woods and a dark parquet floor, but containing the same noisome stuccowork and paintings found elsewhere in the castle. The room smelled slightly of tobacco, and on that gently snowing day, a fire crackled lustily in the hearth.

At last, there was a loud double knock on the door, Gresham and Wilkins stood, a servant opened the door, and Charles entered. He had on the same formal Austrian military uniform that he had worn to the Ball, and his drooping eyes and mustache lent him the same appearance of boredom that he had worn at the Palais Auersperg, as his boots clicked across the parquet floor. As he approached Gresham and Wilkins, they bowed respectfully.

"Welcome to Laxenburg, gentlemen," said the Archduke calmly, in near perfect English and with only a slight accent. He did not hold out his hand, but stood fairly still and subdued.

"Thank you, Your Majesty," said Wilkins, still the one more comfortable with the protocols of royalty. "You have done us a great honor by allowing us to visit your home and meeting with us, sir."

"Come, come, I expect this to be a mutually enlightening visit. It is not often nowadays that we have visitors who are not members of the Austrian nobility, you see. I have planned to show you the *Franzensburg* Castle, and we may hunt this afternoon if you are interested in joining us."

"Indeed, sir."

"Come then, it is a short walk." He led them to a side, exterior door in the Library, where the servants helped the men into their overcoats, and they began the short walk on a shoveled path through the snow-covered gardens to the lake behind the New Castle. "You can see there the *Franzensburg* Castle. It looks very much like a castle of the Crusaders' time, does it not? It was built by my Great-Great-Grandfather, Emperor Franz II, and took over 30 years to complete. No one lives in it, however. It is a showpiece of a Crusader castle of the Middle Ages. Here, you can see it is built on an island in the pond, much like a moat. Both were constructed just for the castle."

The pond was iced over, and before them stood the towers and curtain wall and keep of a castle that looked like one built in a fantasy past. There was no real moat other than the pond, no glacis, the curtain walls were not terribly thick and the arrow slits impractically arranged. As a medieval castle, it would have been impossible to defend. Nor would the castle have been of any use during the Napoleonic Wars when it was actually built. Indeed, it was clear that the castle had no practical military use whatsoever in any time period.

"My Great Uncle, the Emperor, claims he has never been inside the *Franzensburg* Castle, but that is difficult to believe. I am certain that as a boy he must have played on the battlements, as I did myself. I would imagine the Ottomans besieging Vienna and wave my sword at them."

They walked across the ice to the gatehouse, followed by a small army of servants carrying urns of coffee and blankets in case anyone became cold. Inside the castle, fires had been lit. The interior was quite large and comfortable; a great many people could have lived there, but instead the castle was arranged like a showpiece, as the Archduke had indicated. In some rooms, mannikins had been staged to portray the castle as it would have been used in a fictional Middle Ages. Mannikin men in heavy chain-link armor sat at dining tables, and others shot arrows in the reception halls (perhaps they had only been brought indoors for the winter, Wilkins thought). In a medieval chapel, a mannikin priest was blessing a mannikin Baroness. The medieval armory displayed a variety of precious, gleaming, and impractically bejeweled swords under the coat of arms of the Austrian Empire embossed on the ceiling. Portraits of the Hapsburg emperors and empresses graced every wall. They visited the torture room in the basement, where mannikins were stretched on the rack and bled in iron maidens. On an ornate throne, a mannikin medieval king held his jewel encrusted sword aloft and ordered his mannikin knights into battle.

After an extensive tour, they returned to the first reception hall for coffee.

"Did you enjoy the Ball at the Palais Auersperg, sir?" asked Wilkins.

"The Ball, yes; yes I suppose so."

"And will you be returning to Vienna for Fasching?"

"Yes, the Archduchess and I plan to return for the premier of Strauss' opera. It is a comedy, though. I prefer the Germanic ones, Wagner and so forth. Have you seen *The Ring of the Nibelung*? It is a magnificent work. But Herr Director Gregor wished to have something light hearted in repertoire at the State Opera for Fasching. One could hardly object to Strauss."

"And then you will be traveling to the Italian front?"

"Yes, yes, I am very eager to take up my command. It is rather frustrating to be an Archduke in a country at war. Naturally, I wish to serve the Empire, yet I am required to stay out of harm's way. At the front lines, I will undoubtedly be expected to lead from the rear, but I believe I will be able to show the men my mettle. I am a crack shot, you know."

"Are you indeed, Sir? I imagine you hunt frequently here in Laxenburg," said Gresham

"Yes, exactly. I don't suppose you fellows would care to do some quail hunting this afternoon; I think we still have a little time before dark."

"Are they not difficult to find this late in the season, sir?" asked Gresham.

Charles stared at him a moment.

"They are released, of course," he said plainly. "*Erkundigen, ob Xavier und Sixtus sich uns anschließen wollen, um von der wachtel jagen,*" he added to the servant standing nearest. "I've sent for Xavier and Sixtus, if they care to join us."

It was only a very little while before the servants had prepared for the hunt. Charles was directing much of the preparation, and it appeared to Gresham and Wilkins that Charles was terribly uncomfortable talking with them. Xavier had come out to join the hunt, and Charles paired him with Wilkins, while the Archduke paired himself with Gresham to hunt.

Gresham and Wilkins glanced at each other: Charles was obviously orchestrating an opportunity to speak with Gresham privately. Gresham and Charles walked into the woods and spent a half hour shooting quail that the servants released from wicker baskets, and after Charles had capably shot two dozen and Gresham had managed to shoot three, Charles called his servants over and ordered them to fetch more ammunition. Obediently, the servants retired.

Charles opened the breech of his shotgun and laid it across his forearm. Off in the distance, they could hear Wilkins and Xavier shooting, but in the forest it was very still and quiet and the snow was still falling gently. Indeed, Gresham could not recall ever in his life being in a place so quiet and peaceful. Ancient pine trees surrounded them and in the distance the *Franzensburg* Castle towered like something from a Fairy story. Gresham took a deep breath of the sweet, clean, crisp air. There was a slight, pungent smell of pine and of the gunpowder residue from the shotguns. He closed his eyes and listened to the snow fall.

"Our intelligence people tell me you are a spy, Mister Kelly," said Charles. "Do you intend to shoot me?"

Gresham laughed aloud. Not because the idea was absurd. To the contrary, he laughed because he *could* shoot the Archduke as they stood alone together in the forest. What an astonishing opportunity to be given! Gresham looked down at his loaded shotgun. He was certainly not above shooting the Archduke, despite Wilkins' assurances. He had broken his own word too many times to be above breaking the word of another. The Archduke could simply die in a forest, just as Franz Joseph's only son, Prince Rudolph, had died so mysteriously at the nearby Mayerling estate so many years ago. Perhaps that death was the real end of the Hapsburg dynasty – the day Franz Joseph's only son had died and he had begun fishing in the pools of less reputable Hapsburgs for one pathetic heir after another, until, at last, this one, this poor fool of a young man so unprepared and so insulated from the world, became the forlorn hope of the once-great Austro-Hungarian Empire. How could Gresham shoot Charles and leave the empire in the hands of a dying old man and a cadre of the most belligerent fools in Europe, men like Count Conrad? No, he thought, murder was too blunt a tool.

"Yes, your majesty," Gresham replied, still laughing and wiping a tear from his eye, "I am a spy."

Charles looked at Gresham anxiously.

"Did you look at the coin I gave you?" Gresham asked.

"It is the first Vatican coin of His Holiness Pope Benedict, is it not?"

Gresham laid down his shot gun and reached into his jacket pocket. He withdrew the envelope with the red wax seal and handed the envelope to Charles.

"Do you recognize that seal?"

"Yes. Yes, I do," said Charles. "It's the seal of the Piscatory Ring, the seal of the Pope. This is a letter from His Holiness, isn't it?" Charles tore open the envelope like a child on Christmas, his face alight, laughing now himself. But he quickly discovered that the envelope was empty. "There is nothing inside. Where is the message?" he demanded crossly.

"I am here to deliver the message, Your Majesty. Yes, I am a spy, as von Stumm believes, but I do not serve your enemies. I am from the Vatican. His Holiness Pope Benedict has sent me with a confidential message for you and you alone. It is this:

"The Great War must end. The death and suffering of millions of Christians must end. His Holiness knows you will soon ascend the throne of the Hapsburgs, and you will then represent the greatest empire that Europe has ever known: the last true remnant of the Holy Roman Empire. The fate of many nations and of many men will then lie with you. His Holiness knows you will do your duty, not only because you are a good Catholic, but because the suffering of millions of Christians weakens Europe when our true enemies lie elsewhere: In Asia, in Africa, and in the Near East. Your Empire has nothing to gain from this war, some land in the Balkans ruling over a people who will never bow their necks to the Austrian yoke. No, the only nation which stands to gain is Germany, a nation which seeks to expand and dominate Europe, just as Napoleon did a century ago. Germany, a nation led by a Lutheran Protestant, a man who has steadfastly refused to defend Europe: When His Holiness Pope Leo asked the Kaiser to be the Sword of the Church, the German King laughed in derision. Germany's gains will not only weaken your Empire, they will weaken Europe and thereby strengthen our true enemies. You must end this Great War. That is your purpose and your strength. When you ascend the throne it will be Austria's opportunity to set the future course of Christendom. You will propose an immediate ceasefire. Each country will have gained and lost territory, and they may trade their gains and losses as they see fit, but the Alsace-Lorraine, which was wrongfully annexed by Germany after the Franco-Prussian War, shall be returned to France; the independence of Belgium shall be restored; and the kingdom of Serbia shall be independent. The Ottoman hegemony over Constantinople must be broken, and the city entrusted to Russia as the traditional seat of the Eastern Orthodox Church. This is the message you must convey throughout Europe. His Holiness knows you will fulfill this duty, and he guarantees that your message of peace will earn you accolades both on Earth and in Heaven. When you succeed in achieving a lasting peace in Europe, His Holiness will canonize you: You will be Saint Charles the Peacemaker, beloved of God. That will be your just reward for the great service you will have tendered unto Christendom.

"That is the message His Holiness bade me convey to you. *Benedictus est sermo Domini.*"

Charles was stunned. Gresham waited, motionless, watching as the words slowly burned into the Archduke's mind, the gleam of understanding, the spark of jealousy and betrayal, the ember of avarice and lust, and then, suddenly, panic, fear, and anguish: The shotgun slipped from Charles' arm and he fell to his knees, sobbing uncontrollably. "No, no, no," he cried. "No! It will be too late! I will become emperor too late to stop it!"

"Have you no faith in your destiny?" asked Gresham.

"I do, I do, of course," Charles insisted desperately. "But, you must see, I have only just learned of it myself. Germany is preparing an attack on France. It will be the largest military offensive the world has ever seen, a Final Judgment that will grind France to ashes. But I see clearly now that it cannot be permitted!"

"How have you learned of this terrible tragedy?" Gresham asked in a panic.

"I was briefed on the plans by the Emperor. He only learned of von Falkenhayn's plans himself at Christmas during a meeting with the Kaiser. Crown Prince William is preparing to land the deadly blow at Verdun, over a million men, and they will continue to smash Verdun until France has expended every last shell, every last bullet, and every last man. France is to be castrated, ruined. I tell you, countless men will die. You must tell His Holiness I will fulfill this duty he lays upon me, but I fear my opportunity will come too late."

"You may yet have that opportunity. Tell me of this attack. When will Germany strike?"

"February 12, two weeks from today," he said.

"You are truly blessed for your great faith and humility, Your Majesty. Together let us pray that you will have your chance." Gresham said, making the sign of the cross over Charles. "*Deus misericordiarum Pater, per mortem resurrectionemque Filii sui mundum Sibi reconciliavit et Spiritum Sanctum in nobis remissio peccatorum, per ministerium Ecclesiae indulgentiam tibi tribuat et pacem Dei et Pater peccata in nomine Patris et Filii et Spiritus Sancti.*" Then Gresham knelt beside Charles. They prayed and talked on until the sky grew dark.

"What happened?" Wilkins whispered, as he and Gresham strode quickly back to the New Castle, rushing to fetch their belongings and leave for Switzerland in the sedan that Charles had offered to Gresham.

"He believed every bloody word. He told me the Germans are about to attack Verdun. We must get to France immediately."

Wilkins laughed. "If there is a Hell, David, you will certainly be there, but you damn well won't deserve it."

Verdun

It was reassuring to be out of Austria but Gresham and Wilkins were anxious to return to France as quickly as possible. The Archduke's fine automobile and driver took them straight across Austria to the Swiss border in record time. Ordinarily, Austrian security officials made it almost impossible to leave Austria during wartime, but Gresham and Wilkins had papers from Archduke Charles that could not be questioned by anyone except the Emperor himself. After entering Switzerland, they boarded a train to Zurich where Gresham was at last able to wire Mackenzie about the Kaiser's plan to attack Verdun. Unwilling to even wait for a reply, he and Wilkins traveled quickly on to Basel.

In Basel, in the corner of Switzerland that intersected with both France and Germany, it seemed everyone was either a diplomat or a spy – German, French, Russian, British or American. Gresham was eager to avoid intrigue and so he insisted they promptly cross over the Rhine into France. Railway passage to Bar-Le-Duc, the closest stop to Verdun on the overnight train to Paris, was available, but once across the river it was none too easy for Gresham and Wilkins to convince the French authorities that they were truly British officers. Out of uniform, and with no papers apart from their false Swiss passports, they had to explain that they had urgent military intelligence for the French command and rely upon Wilkins' aristocratic sense of outrage and good French until they were finally permitted to enter France "provisionally".

A few hours into the train journey, the middle of the night, Wilkins and Gresham were sitting up in second class playing Picket when the train stopped at the station at Nancy. There, two gendarmes approached them with pistols raised.

"*Tu viens avec nous, on nous ordonne de vous amener à la station.*"

"*Qui a ordonné que?*" Asked Wilkins.

"*Le capitaine, bien sûr.*"

"Very well," he said, standing and getting his coat. "David we must see the local security officials here in Nancy."

"Perhaps we will find someone at last who can get us in contact with the French command," Gresham said skeptically. He had been unwilling to simply broadcast news of the impending German attack; it would benefit the French significantly if Germany's Crown Prince William did not know the French were aware of the Verdun plans, and so Gresham had resolved to tell no except the most senior French or British commander they could locate. Now they would have to suffer through more interviews and explanations for some regional constable. Gresham huffed in exasperation as he collected his case and overcoat.

They were escorted across the plaza to a nondescript two-story yellow stone building and asked to wait in a small office with no windows. They waited. In an hour, they went back to playing Picket. In two hours, Wilkins was napping in his chair. In three hours, Gresham discovered that the door was locked. And in four, the door finally opened.

One gendarme entered and stood beside the open door, followed by a short, thin, middle-aged Frenchman in a simple brown wool suit and spectacles who entered the office with a folder. His hair was straight and coal black, and his eyes twinkled maliciously. He closed the door behind him. Gresham kicked Wilkins to wake him up.

"Well, well, gentleman, good morning," said the Frenchman as he settled in at the table.

"If it is morning, sir, we would not know it," Gresham argued. "I must protest. We were taken off our train, have been up all night, and locked in this office for the past four hours. Is that any way to treat your allies? The Captain and I have important military business and must reach General Joffre's headquarters as soon as possible. You must allow us to proceed immediately."

"Now, now, now. I don't know what your business is and I don't know who you are. You wouldn't be the first gentlemen to enter France from Switzerland claiming to be British soldiers."

"I am Captain James Wilkins," he said, rousing at last, "with the Tenth Manchester Regiment."

"I am Captain Forest of the Border Regiment," Gresham added.

"Are you? Very good, that's very good. I will ask the questions, please. What were you doing in Switzerland?"

"We were passing through," said Wilkins.

"From where?"

"We are not at liberty to say, *Monsieur*; it is a matter of military security."

"I see, yes, yes." The Frenchman sighed and removed his spectacles to wipe them. "To whom do you report?"

"General Sir Bryan Mahon," said Wilkins quickly.

"Mahon? Where is he now?"

"Why, he is in France, Monsieur."

"No. No, Mahon is in Greece now," said the Frenchman sternly. "Were you with Mahon in Greece?"

"We are not at liberty to say," Gresham repeated.

A look of impatience, perhaps even anger, swept briefly across the Frenchman's face.

"Captain Wilkins, Would you be kind enough to wait for a moment in the next office and allow me to speak with Captain Forest alone?" The Frenchman turned to the gendarme: "*Emmenez-le à la salle suivante et d'envoyer Francois.*"

"*Avec moi, s'il vous plait,*" the gendarme said, gesturing to Wilkins.

"Really, this is intolerable," said Wilkins. "If you would only escort us to the French army headquarters near Bar-Le-Duc, I assure you your concerns will be eased."

"Please, Captain, allow me a moment with Captain Forest."

"Very well, but I insist that you allow me an opportunity to send a wire to my superiors."

"Yes, of course, in a moment. *Merci.*"

Wilkins left the room with the gendarme. A few seconds later, two others entered the room: A large, brutish man also dressed in a simple wool suit and a tall, austere woman in a simple dress, boots and dark leather trench coat. The brute stood behind Gresham, as the little Frenchman opened his papers again. Gresham sat patiently as the Frenchman reviewed his papers, minute after minute. The woman lit a cigarette and smoked impatiently. The room was quiet and hot, and Gresham could hear only the deep breathing of the brute standing behind him, the woman sucking on her cigarette, and the little Frenchman turning over his papers one by one. There seemed no reason for the delay, but Gresham was uncertain whether to antagonize the local official further. At last the Frenchman took a deep breath and exhaled slowly and looked up into Gresham's eyes with a slightly malicious smirk.

"Now, Captain, perhaps we can speak more openly, yes? Let us speak of Greece. Have you traveled in Greece under name of Gresham?"

"I am not at liberty to say, *Monsieur*; it is a matter of military security. You must deliver us to the French army immediately. I will not tolerate -"

"THAT IS ENOUGH!" the little Frenchman screamed. "Captain, I must inform you that you perfectly match the description of a gentleman sought for the murder of two Red Cross personnel in Salonika and a German envoy in Athens. So I must insist that you answer my questions. There shall be no more evasion. Were you or were you not in Salonika and Athens last autumn?"

"No," Gresham lied coldly.

Suddenly, the fist of the brute behind him smashed mercilessly into the right side of Gresham's head, knocking him from the chair. The brute instantly hauled Gresham up by the collar and threw him back into the chair. Gresham's head was swimming and he felt queasy. A slight trickle of blood dribbled from his right ear. He noticed the woman was now staring at him intently, her eyes like daggers. The little Frenchman pulled a small pistol from his coat pocket and held it aimed at Gresham.

"I must insist that you answer truthfully, Captain."

Again, the brute swung at Gresham, this time pounding his rib cage from the side. Gresham could hear a crack, and a jolt of lightning shot across his chest, forcing the air from his lungs.

"I would like to know who told you that Ernst Muller was a German agent?"

"F--- off."

Another blow to Gresham's rib cage knocked him from the chair, forced the air from his chest, then the brute's foot swung up into Gresham's gut and he retched.

"*Vous apprenez rien. Dépêchez-vous,*" the woman said sternly to the little Frenchman.

"What did Fräulein Häberlin tell you of her superiors, Captain Gresham?" The little Frenchman demanded.

Gresham remained silent, still gasping for breath.

"Did Fräulein Häberlin give you the names of her contacts in France or England?"

"No, but she squealed like a pig when I f---ed her."

The brute swung again for Gresham's ear, but the sudden sound of gun shots in the hallway outside the room threw off his aim and his fist glanced off the back of Gresham's head, knocking him to the floor.

"*Vois ce que c'est,*" the Frenchman said anxiously to the brute. The large man rushed to the door and opened it. As he opened the door, a bullet struck the brute square in the chest and he sank onto the floor with a choked scream. The Frenchman turned to see what had happened, and the woman swore angrily. Gresham summoned all his remaining strength to leap at the little Frenchman. He twisted easily away in his chair, but Gresham managed to knock the pistol from his hand. The brute, lying on the floor, was shot again, this time directly in the face, and his jaw exploded in a mist of bone and blood. The little Frenchman sized the moment to leap from the room and down the hallway. Gresham slumped onto the floor and seized the Frenchman's small pistol just as Wilkins rushed into the doorway.

"Good God! We've got to get out of here!" Wilkins screamed. Gresham was unable to get off the floor, barely able to move at all. Wilkins, noting the tall woman standing unconcerned against the wall, rushed to pull Gresham up by the arm. Wilkins held a French handgun and pointed it at the woman. "*Au revoir, mes amis,*" she said as Wilkins dragged the still-befuddled Gresham to the doorway. Wilkins fired twice down the passageway, and then pulled Gresham across into another office with windows looking out upon the train station. Gresham staggered to the window and pulled up the sash, then turned back to Wilkins. "Where is the little Frenchman!?" He gasped. The Frenchman had fled during the fight.

"Get out the bloody window, David," Wilkins barked. Gresham wanted to pursue the little Frenchman, but several men were firing at Wilkins from the end of the hallway. Gresham lowered himself gently onto the pavement and into the early morning light. Wilkins leapt out beside him, and helped Gresham across the train station plaza. There was a *Mors* sedan parked on the road in front, and Wilkins pushed Gresham into the passenger seat then climbed over to the driver's side, intent on stealing the automobile. Three gendarmes rushed out of the building behind and began firing their pistols. The glass windshield shattered as Wilkins swung the sedan into the road. Another bullet grazed Gresham's arm, and he clasped his hand over the dribble of blood on his sleeve. Wilkins turned again and they sped from the town.

"That little Frenchman was definitely not very French," Gresham groaned.

Wilkins pushed the sedan as fast as it would go. Even though it was a *Mors*, famous for their racing engines, it was an older model and could barely make a breeze.

"I became suspicious myself when they separated us," said Wilkins. "So I asked the gendarme guarding me for a cigarette – in German. Before he realized what he was doing, he had pulled out his tobacco. I immediately jumped and was able to overpower him. After I had gotten his revolver, I found there were already quite a few more men in the hall, and that's when the shooting began."

"Thank you, James, for getting me out," Gresham said quietly. "This handgun I took from the Frenchman, it's a German Mauser."

"And who was that woman?" Wilkins asked.

Before they could consider their escape further, two speeding sedans came into view behind them. Wilkins pushed the *Mors* to its top speed. The driving was treacherous with ice on the road and Wilkins struggled to keep the sedan under control.

The automobiles behind them struggled to keep up. It was a long, slow and constant pursuit. Every time Wilkins managed to get well ahead, the road would slow them down. They arrived in the town of Toul only to get stuck at the small bridge and barely made it across before their pursuers picked up their trail. But outside the little town of Saint-Aubin-sur-Aire their luck finally escaped them, as the sedan carrying Gresham and Wilkins hit a patch of ice and slid into a tree, cracking the front axle. Gresham was slumped in the front seat and Wilkins climbed out of the automobile as the two black sedans came to a stop only a few yards behind them.

Six men emerged from the sedans and approached, halting as they saw Wilkins raise his handgun. One older man in a French military uniform waved his hands. "*Écoutez!*" he yelled, "*nous ne sommes pas des bâtards de Nancy. Nous allons vous emmener au Général Dupont. Il vous attend. Nous avons eu des informations de Caire que vous viendriez à Verdun.*"

Wilkins laughed with relief. "*Dieu merci, mes amis,*" he said. "He says they are French officers, not with those men in Nancy," he called to Gresham. "Dupont had word of us from Cairo. We are to go with them to Verdun."

"Can you ask them if they have a medical kit?" Gresham called back. "My arm is still bleeding like a damned spigot."

Gresham, Wilkins and the French Colonel, Émile Driant, the man who had found Gresham and Wilkins as they fled from Nancy, strode through the cloister of the cathedral at Verdun. There was a cold light rain and heavy fog as their boots splashed on the ancient stones. Although a small city, Verdun had existed for nearly two thousand years and its cathedral nearly that long. The men passed out of the cloister and stopped at the building behind the cathedral and entered. Inside they found a comfortable sitting room with a fire, food, and wine. "Please make yourselves comfortable, gentlemen," said Colonel Driant. "I will tell the Générals you are here."

"Mercy," said Gresham, taxing the limit of his abilities with the French language. Gresham was still badly hurt and would have preferred to go to sleep, but he and Wilkins stepped to the table to pour themselves glasses of wine and gather some of the bread, cheese, and cured meat onto the plates that had been left for them. Even in war, the French ate well, thought Gresham. He sat gently down in a chair next to the hearth; Wilkins pulled up a stool to sit right beside him.

They were still gorging themselves when three older senior officers entered the room with Colonel Driant. Two were heavily decorated and appeared to be very serious and glum men. The third wore a uniform with almost no decoration, and he appeared to be in quite good humor. That officer came directly to shake hands with Gresham and Wilkins.

"Gentlemen, please remain seated; you have earned your refreshment," he said. "My name is Général Charles-Joseph Dupont. I command the external intelligence services of France. I received a wire from your colleague in Cairo stating that you would be entering France, and I apologize that it was too late to greet you when you entered the country. And I must further apologize for the unfortunate developments in Nancy. Needless to say, we very much wish to locate the gentleman who attempted to confine you there and I have a number of men out seeking him. But before we discuss that further, allow me to introduce you to Général Fernand de Langle de Cary, the commander of France's Central Army Group, and Général Adolphe Guillaumat, commander of the Second Army. They would like to hear from you, as well. Of course you have met Colonel Driant, who undertook the effort to locate you both."

"*Messieurs*," said Commander de Cary, "we are most anxious to know what you have learned about the German plans for Verdun. We have learned from our own spies that there are significant troop movements in the occupied sector opposite Verdun, but we believed those were simply normal troop rotations. Are they truly not?"

"Our information, Sir," began Gresham, "comes from the very highest level of the enemy's government. We have learned that the German offensive at Verdun will be commanded by Crown Prince William, but it was planned by von Falkenhayn. The Germans intend to batter Verdun until the city collapses, regardless of how long it takes. The attack is intended to bleed France white. You see, von Falkenhayn chose Verdun because he believes France will not surrender the city regardless of the price you must pay to keep it, yet it is a difficult location for you to re-supply and reinforce. Crown Prince William's headquarters at Damvillers, by contrast, is well and easily supplied by railway. The offensive was originally to begin in April, but the plans have been accelerated due to the dry winter. On February 12, over 1,200 artillery guns will open fire on Verdun and the defensive fortifications encircling the city, followed by an attack of 140,000 men from the elite Hessian and Brandenburger Corps. By the end of February, there will be 400,000 German troops under William's command at Damvillers, and over one million will be brought up before the end of spring."

"A million men, *mon Dieu*!" exclaimed Général Guillaumat. "The very life of France is at stake."

"You must understand," said de Cary to Gresham and Wilkins, "there are only 30,000 French troops in Verdun right now, *messieurs*. As for the fortifications that have saved this city so many times before, it was determined last year that they will crumble under the new German heavy artillery, so the decision was made to abandon them. They have been mostly stripped of their guns and are barely defended now. So you see, there is almost nothing we can do to prevent Crown Prince William from crossing the Meuse."

"If the weather continues like this," said Driant, "it will set the Crown Prince back a week or two.

"Yes," added Guillaumat. "In the meantime I must appeal to Minister Gallieni to send more men as quickly as possible. You know Joffre will not heed this warning; he is far too occupied developing his own plans to assail the Germans at the Somme this summer. But von Falkenhayn is correct: We cannot lose Verdun."

"I quite agree," said de Cary, "I will have Général Humbert bring up the Third Army, but I must meet with Minister Gallieni at once. Messieurs, might I ask you to remain in Verdun for a time, so that I can call upon you if there are further questions?"

"If you will permit me, gentlemen, I can answer that question for you," said Dupont. "The wire I received from Cairo also contained instructions for these gentlemen to remain in Verdun pending further orders. However, my friends, I assure you that we will make your stay as pleasant as possible. Colonel Driant will see to your needs; then he must return to his men in the Bois des Caures."

"I, for one, shall be quite content to stay in Verdun for now," said Wilkins.

"As you wish, Sir," said Gresham.

"Very good. Now, *mes généraux*, if you would allow me, I would like to discuss the Nancy matter with these gentlemen, as there appears to be a German agent loose in France and it is my responsibility to capture him."

As the city of Verdun was slowly and quietly evacuated, Colonel Driant arranged for Wilkins and Gresham to be billeted in a little house overlooking the Meuse River. The ancient stone structure was quite comfortable, and they hired a very pretty young Frenchwoman, whose husband had been killed at Artois, to tend to the house and prepare their meals. Wilkins took a rather protective attitude towards her and ate all his meals at the little house with her. After Gresham had recovered from his beating at the hands of the little Frenchman's brute, he preferred to eat out, usually with the French troops at the café. The *Poilus,* the French soldiers called themselves, the "hairy ones," because they were battle-hardened veterans with long hair and greasy mustaches and rarely shaved. They drank a cheap, raw red wine called Pinard and smoked cheap tobacco and woodbines late into the night. They had all seen fierce battles already, and the French Generals knew these men would stand their ground when the shells began to fall on the city.

As February 12 arrived, the weather worsened and so it seemed likely the German offensive would indeed be delayed. Commander de Cary had obtained the support of Minister Gallieni to reinforce Verdun, but General Joseph Joffre, Chief of the General Staff and the highest military authority in France, was being difficult – he wanted the extra men for his own offensive planned for the Somme. Still, a number of divisions from the French First and Fifth Army were quickly transferred to Verdun and in a few days the garrison was brought up to 200,000 men. General Humbert had been given acting command of the Verdun forces, and he immediately established a supply line to Bar-Le-Duc, where the nearest train line was located. The *Poilus* called the road the *Voie Sacrée,* the Sacred Way. As the city filled with small details of machine gun detachments, signaling parties, squads of stretcher bearers, artillery, miners, bombers and other army units, it was clear the army was preparing for imminent battle.

Gresham found Wilkins one dark, cold, raining morning in the cathedral.

"Have you started praying now, James? I don't think things are quite that bleak."

"I am not quite religious enough to believe that the fate of Verdun hinges upon my prayers, my friend."

"Are you personally troubled?"

"I must tell you, David, I have been playing spy now for four months, and it simply wears my nerves to tatters. This job is very tiring, and I sometimes doubt that I may buckle up. It seems there is a constant risk of some little thing going off, and I can't quite get adjusted to it."

"Well I wouldn't call our business a rest-cure at any time, but as far as things go, I think we've had it fairly easy compared to those who live in the trenches. Look at the *Poilu* here. The poor fellows know that soon the German guns will be raining shells down upon them for weeks, maybe months, and their job will be to bear it, to stand firm, and try not to be killed. Yet they drink and laugh today. Whereas, you and I, we've only got to act natural and play along."

"And you find it no difficulty at all?"

"Where I've found the job tight was when I had to act natural, the same as everybody else around, while all the time I knew I would have to do things that were unnatural. It isn't easy . . . it isn't easy to hold a woman in your arms knowing that in a few hours you will take her last breath from her."

"Yet somehow you keep a part of yourself clean, outside that daily life," Wilkins said.

"No. I have never tried that, James, to be honest. I've just tried to stay my ordinary self. And who that person is, well, perhaps he is not a person that most would admire, I admit. But I can see you have tried, James, and I guess you have found it wearing."

"Wearing is a mild word."

"Then perhaps you should give it up as a bad job, this attempt to keep a part of yourself lily-white. None of us will come out of this war without a little dirt and a few wounds, and I mean more than just scars to frighten the children."

"No, David, I disagree. Not about the wounds, I don't argue with you there. But you are different from me. You came into this war wounded."

"There's no cause for you to be cruel."

"That is not what I mean: You were already 'experienced,' damaged by a cruel and unjust world, you have already been forced to survive on your wits. It is plain to see that you are now quite flattered to be relied upon to do those tasks that you are able to perform so well. And now you are ready to act because you believe the result being sought is a just result. But I tell you plainly, you place too much faith in those who are deciding what constitutes a just result. The men in London who assign these tasks - who are they to make these decisions? How can they possibly know what will come of it? Is there not a small part of you deep down that wonders if those decisions are right or wrong?"

"Frankly, James, no one has ever asked me that before. I have never even considered it."

"Then listen to me, David. As your friend, I am asking that you consider it."

"Alright."

"And in fairness, I will attempt to put more faith in those who give us our orders."

"That is why I came to find you, actually. We just received a wire from Dupont. We are required to go to meet with him at Le Havre in two days' time to receive our next assignments from our superiors."

"And who are they, these superiors, I wonder?"

"I only know that the top man is called *Control*; at least, he is referred to as *C*, although I suppose that could be the first letter of his name."

The next morning, February 21, 1916, as the clouds broke and the Sun emerged for the first time in weeks, a sound like thunder could be heard coming from the east. The German bombardment of the French defensive forts around Verdun had begun. Soon high explosive shells began to fall on the ancient city of Verdun itself. For ten hours, the Germans shells fell without ceasing. That afternoon, the German ground assault began. Thousands of elite Brandenburg troops of the Germany army attacked the villages of Brabant and Beaumont to the north of Verdun.

In the Bois des Caures near Beaumont, Colonel Driant was in command of a network of trenches and bunkers that crossed the forest. After weeks of rain, the trenches were cold and muddy and, in places, flooded. Many of his soldiers had been killed and their bodies lay scattered like leaves. Many of the trees in the forest had been felled by the intense German bombardment and lay in jumbled heaps. By the time the German ground assault began, only one fifth of Driant's light infantry was left to defend his position, but the soldiers loved Driant and stayed by his side.

His soldiers fought desperately against the Germans with only rifles, bayonets and the new British "grenades," and at the end of the first day, they had held the Germans back from the French position in the woods. The next morning, Driant planned to counterattack, but the Germans renewed their assault before first light. The German infantry emerged from the morning mist, some carrying gleaming metal tanks on their backs. The French saw to their horror that from those metal tanks the Germans sprayed jets of flaming oil down into the French trenches. The oil set the men guarding Driant's right flank on fire, and the screams of pain and horror echoed through the forest. Less than eighty men were finally left to defend the Colonel's command bunker against the onrushing German battalions. With his revolver in hand, Colonel Driant joined his weary, bloodied men in the muddy trench. "*You know well they can never touch me!*" he shouted defiantly. But a moment later Driant was shot in the head and fell dead to the bottom of the trench. The *Poilus* looked on him in despair, their hatred for the "Boche" burning in their hearts as they vowed to have their revenge.

In Verdun, Gresham and Wilkins tossed their bags into the back of a French lorry and climbed in behind. The German artillery and infantry assaults on the forts north and east of Verdun continued as the lorry pulled away and began its long slow descent down the *Voie Sacrée* to the train station at Bar-Le-Duc, where Gresham and Wilkins would embark for Le Havre. Yet the months-long battle for Verdun had only just begun.

Gavrilo Princip

Archduke Franz
Ferdinand

Franz Josef I

Wilhelm II

Nicholas II

George V

Zita of
Bourbon-Parma

Archduke
Charles

Crown Prince
Wilhelm

Crown Prince
Rupprecht

Constantine I of
Greece

Pope Benedict
XV

Ferdinand I of
Romania

Marie of
Romania

Princess
Elisabeth

Peter I of Serbia

Crown Prince
Alexander

Crown Prince
Carol

Woodrow
Wilson

Raymond
Poincaré

Georges
Clemenceau

David Lloyd
George

Friedrich Ebert

Richard von
Kühlmann

Vladimir Lenin

Alexander
Kerensky

Leon Trotsky

Joseph Joffre

Mustafa Kemal

Douglas Haig

Alexsei Brusilov

Ferdinand Foch

Philippe Pétain

Denis Duchêne

Paul von
Hindenburg

Alexandru
Averescu

Part II:
THE KORNILOFF AFFAIR

First Interlude

As far as Oliver Locke was concerned, Princess Marina Petrovna was the homeliest young woman in the Tsar's royal family. However, she was also very well informed about the Russian Army's condition on the Eastern Front. It had become nearly impossible to get an honest appraisal from the Winter Palace nowadays; the Tsar's generals had become extremely close since the summer when public knowledge of the one million Russian casualties suffered during the offensive in Galicia had caused rioting in Petrograd, Kiev and Moscow. Certainly, Locke could have ventured to the front outposts to scout for himself, but he had no desire to leave Petrograd in winter, whereas the Princess had just returned from a tour of nursing duty near the front herself. Her observations of Russia's crumbling army would augment Locke's own reports to the British Foreign Office. Moreover, Locke had no reason to suspect the Princess of dissemblance; indeed, she seemed genuinely flattered to have been invited to dine with the tall, mature and dashing British attaché.

Donon's Brasserie was just steps from Locke's comfortable lodgings at the *Hotel Astoria* in Petrograd. The infamous restaurant consisted exclusively of dark and elegant private dining rooms - the perfect *milieu* for Locke to interrogate the Princess in some detail and privacy. Indeed, the young woman, who was dressed in a suffocating array of crinoline, velour and brown twill, was enthusiastic to share even the most embarrassing observations about the Russian Army: The striking railway workers, the rioting peasants, the rebellious soldiers, the inadequate munitions supply, the countless casualties and irregular medical care, the self-aggrandizing generals, and the afflictions of an early winter, all evidence that the Tsar's armies were struggling to maintain a defensive line against the Germans, the Austrians and the Ottoman Turks. Thankfully, Locke thought, Tsar Nicholas ruled his people with a firm hand and could be counted upon to continue pouring his nation's unimaginable resources of men and materials into the war. Everyone understood that 1916 had been a difficult year for the Russians, but it was almost the end of December now and Locke believed that 1917 would see the tide turn: Russia would attack with renewed vigour, the Germans and Austrians would be driven back, and the Tsar would have his righteous victory at long last.

Now that their heavy dinner was concluded, Locke was beginning to find Princess Marina's rambling monologue rather irritating. The private dining room, candle-lit and warm, that was so complementary to Locke's flirtatious questioning of the Princess earlier, now began to seem dark, smoky and stifling to him. There had been too much *Vodka*; the food had been too rich. Locke's mind was wandering and his stomach was on fire. Surely, he wondered, the more important of that evening's proceedings – those taking place at Yusupov's Palace nearby – had been concluded by now? But just then, something the Princess said pierced Locke's foggy mind.

"Did you say Rasputin, my dear?" He asked in astonishment.

"Yes, Rasputin himself came to the party!"

"I apologize, but whose party was this?"

"My dear sister's, Oliver. As I was saying, her party was to begin at ten, and shortly after I arrived it became clear that only a dozen or so ladies had been invited to attend, although some of them had the wildly mistaken notion that it would be quite clever to bring their innocent daughters along to meet the grand Fakir."

"Please, my dear, you'll burn my ears with such heresies. You know the Tsarina does not tolerate such epithets for her pet monster."

"As I was saying, Oliver, I had the distinct displeasure to be the one standing closest by the door when the evil genius – excuse me, I mean His Holiness the Great Rasputin – slipped through the door unannounced and seized my hand. If anything, he appeared more filthy and unkempt than usual. Then he pierced me with those glaring, glittering bloodshot eyes of his, like some hypnotist *manqué*. I was shocked that he even dared take my hand, but I somehow managed to conceal my revulsion."

"He is a powerful presence, truly," Locke replied sympathetically.

"His presence at this particular party was certainly overpowering. The ladies, of course, all tittered around him nervously like little birds while he scooped caviar and *zakusky* into his great, gaping mouth with his bare hands. They are all trying to curry favor with the Tsarina. Rasputin spoke in the most vulgar language and told only the most scandalous and debauched stories while he drank bottle after bottle of vodka, none of which seemed to have even the least inebriating effect upon him. More than once I saw him with his filthy hands buried beneath the skirts of one particular young lady whom I am too gracious to name."

"How terrible," Locke agreed, unimpressed.

"Oliver, really, it was repugnant. Simply no one can comprehend his profound influence over Tsarina Alexandra. She barely makes a move without him, and he meets day and night with the Tsar. Imagine it! A filthy peasant from Siberia, a pilgrim, no education, no credentials, no status at all! The man ought to be in a circus. Yet there it is: He is untouchable."

"If the rumors are true – that the young Tsarevich Alexei is deathly ill and only Rasputin can cure him – then it is hardly surprising that the Tsarina should grant Rasputin her favor," Locke passed off dispassionately.

"I have also heard it said that Rasputin himself poisons the child. He then withholds the poison from time to time to make his healing powers appear greater. But that is not why Rasputin is despised across the empire, of course. You of all people must be aware that he bends all his powers and all his will to convincing the Tsar to end the war against Germany. He claims that 'Germany is our beloved brother!' To have these rumors flow from the Winter Palace unchecked undermines the Tsar's authority and Russia's war effort. Some even say that Rasputin is in the pay of the Jewish bankers in Germany. *That* must surely concern your countrymen."

"Well it might, my dear. Anyone would reasonably deduce that Great Britain takes a dim view of Russia withdrawing from the Eastern Front and leaving France and Britain to fight the war alone – oh, and Italy, of course," he said with mild disdain. "But it is hardly of any concern to me. I am no soldier and, I admit, not a man of great substance when it comes to affairs of state."

"My poor Oliver," the Princess replied with sympathy, "are you really such a shallow fellow?"

She is the shallow one, Locke thought with disdain. Petrograd was a boiling stew of conspiracies. There must be fifty spies in Petrograd from Great Britain, France, and America alone, never mind the Germans or the multitude of caterwauling political factions in the State Duma. And just who in London had sent that dreadful boy, the one who had just moved into the *Astoria*? Locke wondered. What was his name again? Wilkins? Yes, that was it: James Wilkins – a tin soldier if Locke had ever seen one. It would take the boy several months just to learn how to pronounce the Russian names, he laughed to himself.

Locke at last delivered Princess Marina to her gleaming black lacquer *droshky* and was greatly relieved to be done with her as the horse trotted off through the snow amid a tinkling of silver bells. It had been a very long evening and Locke was eager to return to his rooms at the *Astoria* as soon as possible, but the frigid night air was remarkably refreshing after the hot, stuffy, smoke-filled dining room. He recalled that Yusupov's Palace was a mere three streets away, just over the *Moika* canal. Locke knew it was best to stay away from Yusupov's tonight, but he was terribly eager to know how the proceedings there had been concluded. Against his better judgment, Locke pulled his fur-lined coat up against the back of his neck, turned, and strolled over the canal.

From outside, the Yusupov residence looked much like all the other yellow townhouses that lined Petrograd's streets, that is, until one realized that every other house on that particular street was actually part of the Yusupov Palace. Theirs was one of the oldest and wealthiest families in Russia, and through their many industrial interests the Yusupova family had profited wildly from the war. Locke, as a frequent visitor, was promptly admitted into the grand Palace and shown into the brightly lit and gilded library where he was announced to Prince Felix Yusupov, Grand Duke Dimitri Pavlovich and the other young men assembled around the fireplace. Locke was angered to see the young Grand Duke in uniform: He and Yusupov had specifically agreed that the evening must be conducted as informally as possible.

"Thank God you have come," said Grand Duke Dimitri as he rushed to greet Locke. The look of panic on the Grand Duke's face surprised Locke, and a sudden chill stole down his spine.

"Why? What has happened?" He asked urgently.

"The poison didn't act! He ate cake after cake and drank all the wine, but the cyanide had no effect upon him! We couldn't believe it! At last, we convinced Felix to go downstairs and just shoot him. Three times he was shot in the back, and even then he rushed out the door to the side gardens before collapsing in the snow. It is incredible! We are all in a state of shock."

"But it is done, then? You have confirmed he is dead?"

"He is lying in the garden . . . ," Dimitri said before trailing off uncertainly.

Locke looked in fury from the agitated Grand Duke to the simpering Yusupov. The young men were in a state of panic still! The simplest possible assignment, Locke thought, and he had hoped to keep his hands altogether clear of the matter. "My God!" he exclaimed, as he strode past the young men, across the library, through the door, and down to Felix Yusupov's basement apartment. There, a shattered wine glass and an overturned table evidenced a struggle. Specks of blood on the marble floor led to the side door. Locke followed the trail of blood out to the snow-covered garden, and there, beside a statue of Pallas Athena, lay the body in the bloodied snow.

Locke approached cautiously. Incredibly, the monster was *still* not dead. His breathing was labored, his dark face, the sunken black eyes, the long shaggy black hair, the great hooked nose, all stared back at him as Locke shook his head in disbelief. "Oh for Christ's sake," he said in disgust, as he drew his pistol, aimed, and shot Rasputin cleanly between the eyes.

By the summer of 1916, after two years of combat, the Great War remained a bitter stalemate. Each day on the Western Front, on the Eastern Front, in the Balkans, and in the Near East, soldiers were ordered to advance. Countless men died as the front lines shifted back and forth by mere yards. More men and more materiel had been poured into the battles as the great empires amassed all their resources and strove to finally break through to open ground.

At Verdun, German Crown Prince William's elite Brandenburg forces surged against the French defenders, yet still the French troops held fast. To the north, at the Somme River, British and French troops amassed for their own attack, hoping to drive the German armies back from France and Belgium and relieve the French at Verdun. Italy struggled to break through the Alps into Austria, while defending their lines along the Isonzo River to the East. In Russia, General Alexsei Brusilov attacked the German and Austrian defenders along a hundred-mile front in Galicia. At Salonika, Serbian soldiers joined Allied forces preparing to challenge the Austrian and Bulgarian occupation of the Balkans. Ottoman forces captured the British garrison near Baghdad, advanced into the Sinai Peninsula and attacked Russia in the Caucasus. And Roumania debated endlessly whether to declare war at all, still uncertain whether the Central Powers or the Allies had made the more compelling territorial offer.

Behind the front lines, the battles also grew more desperate. The great empires struggled to survive the devastating losses of war. Great Britain enacted mandatory conscription, and its factories struggled to meet the demand for weapons and ammunition. Kaiser Wilhelm finally ceded unlimited authority to the Chief of his General Staff, Field Marshal Paul von Hindenburg, and his Deputy, Erich Ludendorff, and thereby turned Germany into a military dictatorship. In France and Russia, the troops on the front lines struggled bitterly to survive and spoke of revolution while behind the lines the elite attempted vainly to maintain the illusion of peace and prosperity.

Around the world, people began to wonder not only who would win the war, but who would survive it.

Munich

His boot heels echoed loudly on the white marble floor as James Wilkins, agent of His Majesty's Secret Intelligence Service, strode quickly down the sunny and immaculate hallway of the Royal Psychiatric Clinic in Munich. Despite Wilkins' German alias, his German uniform and his German military papers (taken from a captured officer and appropriately modified in London), the Director of the new hospital on Nussbaumstrasse had been extremely reluctant to allow Wilkins to visit his "Irish patient." The Director had only agreed to permit the interview when Wilkins asserted that he had been sent by Ludendorff personally. No one would rationally challenge the orders of the Army's Deputy Chief of Staff, at least not since the Kaiser had ceded absolute authority over Germany to his military leaders. Field Marshal von Hindenburg was the commander-in-chief of the German armed forces, but it was his deputy, Ludendorff, who was the unofficial leader of Germany's "silent dictatorship."

Wilkins' German papers had proved adequate at the military check points he had encountered since he first arrived in Germany. They had even been inspected by an officer from *Abteilung III-b*, the notorious German secret police force that had been growing exponentially in size and authority over the civilian population for the past months. However, the papers only gave Wilkins permission to "visit relatives" in Munich; he would need to obtain new papers to "return to the front" or otherwise make his escape from Germany, which would likely prove to be no easy task. So, despite his uniform and his capacity to speak German fluently, Wilkins was extremely anxious: He was deep inside the enemy's military dictatorship and the slightest misstep would result in his prompt capture and immediate execution. However, this time he had been told the very future of the British Empire was at stake.

Wilkins arrived at the door of the hospital room that was his intended destination and paused to remove his dark leather overcoat, straighten his fair, light brown hair, and collect his thoughts. He knew he was taking a risk by playing two different deceits during one mission, but there was no helping it. The persona of German Officer had gotten Wilkins into the hospital, but now he would need to play at being the patient's comrade – a comrade yet someone remote enough to be unverifiable. Wilkins had settled on playing a Russian revolutionary, sympathetic and perhaps helpful to the cause of Ireland's independence from Great Britain. He prayed that he could keep the languages straight, as he would need to speak Russian as well as English and German, both with a Russian accent.

In general, Wilkins still greatly disliked the dissemblance associated with spy work, but even he, the son of the Earl of Bartlett and accustomed as he was to the traditions and righteousness of nobility, could see that the war was changing the way things were done, for better or not. At the end of the day, Wilkins had a task to complete, and however it needed to be done, it must be done well to be done at all. He knocked sharply twice and opened the door.

Inside, the hospital room was dark and musty. No lamps had been lit and the shades were drawn. Only a dim hazy daylight filtered through the thick damask curtains. There was enough light that Wilkins could see a thin but elegant-looking middle-aged gentleman sitting on a painted wooden chair near the window. The man wore white pyjamas and a dark blue robe, but his feet were bare; his black hair, streaked with grey, was disheveled but his beard was neatly trimmed and came to a sharp point beneath his chin. He was looking down at the floor, and failed to raise his eyes as Wilkins stepped closer.

"Sir? Sir? My name is Belyaev, Aleksei Belyaev," Wilkins said in English using a slight Russian accent, in a soft and gentle tone. "Grigory Zinoviev sent me. Do you know the man of whom I speak?"

The gentleman slowly raised his head and looked at Wilkins. His noble face was gaunt, and his eyes were sunken. He nodded gently, without expression.

"You *are* Mister Casement, are you not?" Wilkins continued.

"Yes," the man stated quietly, in a voice that expressed no pleasure in admitting the fact.

'Sir, I – I am very sorry to disturb your convalescence, but when we learned that you were in Munich, I was sent to speak with you at once."

"Please, sit down," Casement said calmly.

Wilkins looked around confused. There were no other chairs in the small room, just a small dresser, a washstand, and an unmade bed. He stepped to the bed, sat on the edge, and looked across at the man he had been sent to interrogate: Sir Roger Casement, the revered British Consul from Ireland who had become a revolutionary, who had traveled to Germany in the midst of war, and who had somehow become a patient in this psychiatric hospital in Munich. Casement had been missing for more than a year. He had last been spotted in the city of New York where he was believed to have been raising funds for the Irish separatist group *Clan na Gael*. Then he had disappeared, and no one in London yet knew how or why Casement had come to Germany, or what Germany wanted with Casement. They sat silently a while.

"You are not a German officer, then?" Casement asked at last.

"Oh good Lord, no, sir, I am not. The uniform was just to help me get in the front door, you see. I'm not officially here, in Germany, if you understand me, sir."

"However did you get to Munich?"

"I was flown in an aeroplane from Switzerland most of the way and then deposited in a field not far outside Munich. I was met there by a comrade. It is he, my comrade here in Munich, who learned that you are staying in this hospital." It is always easier to stick with the truth, thought Wilkins, although in this case there was much he left out. He had in fact been flown into Germany,

186

but on a *French* Farman two-seater reconnaissance biplane and, even more frighteningly, in the middle of the night right over Lake Constance. Wilkins had never flown in an aeroplane before, and the rush of air past his face in the dark was terrifying – he felt he might fall out at any moment. He was greatly relieved when the aeroplane finally touched ground in the field outside Munich, but it stopped only long enough for Wilkins to leap out before it departed again. It was a *British* agent, an old gentleman living quietly with relatives in Munich and collecting information on German troop movements, who had sent word to London that Sir Roger Casement was a patient at the new psychiatric hospital. The shy, quiet agent had met Wilkins and led him into the city to a run-down and abandoned townhouse where Wilkins might safely hide. There, the agent had then left Wilkins entirely to his own devices.

"An aeroplane! How remarkable," said Casement weakly but with some enthusiasm. "I have never been in one. And you say Zinoviev sent you? I met him once or twice in Geneva, although that was some years ago. Is he still working with that fellow Vladimir Ulyanov and the other Marxists?"

"Yes, sir, as am I. I have been asked to report on the situation in Ireland and will be traveling to Dublin next to meet with the leader of the Irish Citizen Army there."

"You mean James Connolly," said Casement.

"Yes, sir, precisely."

"He is the Marxist. I am not, you understand," Casement said.

"That is not important."

"If you think it is not important, then you must be very young, Alexsei."

"Sir," said Wilkins in feigned outrage, "I may only be nineteen years old, but I am already a veteran of the war. I was at Tannenberg when the Second Army was destroyed. I witnessed the moral cowardice of Russia's generals, the ruthlessness with which they cast away the lives of Russia's youth. Before the war, I lived in Moscow. My father, a railway worker, was killed by the police during the strikes in 1904. My beloved mother and sister were garment workers in a bourgeois fashion house, but they were killed in a fire. So perhaps I am not as innocent as you believe. Let me tell you, comrade, the revolution is coming, and not just in Russia. British repression of the Irish proletariat is as much a concern to us as the repression of the peasants and workers in Russia. You are also seeking to free your countrymen, are you not? Are not our objectives complementary, sir?"

"Forgive me, Aleksei, I do not question your commitment to the revolution. And I have heard much the same, sad stories told by young men in Ireland and elsewhere. Was it at Tannenberg that you were wounded?" Casement asked, looking at the red scars on Wilkins' left cheek and ear, remnants of the wounds Wilkins had actually received during the British landings on the Gallipoli peninsula.

"Yes, sir, at Tannenberg."

"You are angry at those you deem responsible, then."

"No, sir. At first I was disillusioned and then I became angry. But now I am inspired by the revolution."

"Well, then, you had better tell me what has brought you all the way to Munich and what you wish of me."

"That is good, yes, I will get to the heart of the matter as you desire," Wilkins said quite sternly. He stood and held his hands behind his back formally. "We are frankly alarmed, sir, that you have sought the support of German imperialists to further the cause of independence for Ireland, and we wish to know, do you intend the Irish people to exchange one brutal slavemaster for another? What do you wish of Germany? Does James Connolly even know you are here?"

Casement's face instantly darkened and bristled with anger, but then, just as quickly, he visibly shrank and raised his hand to cover his anguished expression; Wilkins feared he was weeping. "I apologize, Mister Casement," Wilkins said, concerned that the Irishman's condition was far more delicate than he had expected. He had wished to bait Casement, not browbeat him. He stepped to Casement and placed a hand on the man's shoulder. "I did not mean to distress you."

"No, Aleksei, it is I who must apologize to you," Casement said quietly. "It seems you are correct to question my efforts here. It has not been at all as I had hoped. I will be leaving Germany very soon."

"Then you will return to America?"

"No. No, I must go back to Ireland," Casement said.

"I see. Am I to understand that the Germans have been uncooperative?"

Casement looked up at Wilkins and considered the young Russian standing before him before he spoke: "It is the Irish themselves who have failed me."

"Please explain."

"Alexsei, what is your plan to depart Germany? How will you get to Ireland from here?" Casement asked anxiously. "You know it is impossible to cross the border without written permission."

"Surely it will be less difficult than entering Germany," said Wilkins flippantly.

"I think not. The entire country is under strict martial law. You can expect to be examined by the police each day, and they act as if every man, woman and child is a foreign spy. And here you are, a Russian, an enemy, Alexsei, and unless you have the government's written permission to be in Munich then you are in fact a spy, and when you are captured you will be imprisoned for the duration of the war if not simply shot in the street. You are very foolish to think that your German uniform will protect you. The government tries very hard to make it seem that everything is normal in Germany, but it is not. The people here are suffering."

"How is it that you, a former British envoy, have no difficulty traveling, but I must hide in fear?" Wilkins asked.

"I have papers, but more importantly, I have the support of the Foreign Minister." Casement said. He looked at Wilkins and considered a moment. "At least, I believe I still do. Perhaps you should travel with me, Alexsei. I can take you with me to Ireland. I do not know James Connolly well, but I can at least introduce you in Dublin. I have that much authority still."

Wilkins was quite surprised by the offer. It was unclear to him what Casement was playing at with this show of generosity, but he did still wish to learn what Casement had been plotting in Germany and would need passage out of the country. Once they arrived in Ireland, well, that was British soil. "I would be most grateful to accompany you, sir. Thank you for your generous offer. I accept."

Wilkins had been sent to Munich with great urgency, but it certainly did not seem to him now that the future of the British Empire was at stake, as he had been told, at least not as far as Sir Roger Casement's intrigues were concerned. Still, he understood why the Secret Intelligence Service had sent him.

As Wilkins had himself only recently learned, there had been a very troubling incident that raised questions about Germany's intelligence activities, especially with respect to Great Britain's colonies. A few months earlier, the Americans had seized a three-masted schooner at a fishing village north of San Francisco; the schooner was loaded with small arms, rifles and ammunition. After intense questioning, it was revealed that her crew, which included several Punjabi Indians and German nationals, was *en route* to India and that the crew had hoped to incite an armed rebellion in support of India's independence from the British Crown.

Word of the plot had just seeped back to London, and both the India Office and the Colonial Office were in an uproar over the matter. The War Office was also concerned, inasmuch as hundreds of thousands of Indian soldiers were at that very moment fighting for the British Empire on the Western Front and in Mesopotamia.

The Secret Intelligence Service, still desperately holding its own sliver of independence from both the Foreign Office and the War Committee, was eager to show that it had the situation in hand, but in truth it did not. The S.I.S. had no idea what else the Germans might be planning. Thus, Wilkins and undoubtedly many other agents had been urgently sent to investigate the merest whispers of other German plots against the Empire.

Still, Casement hardly seemed a genuine threat or one worthy of the risks Wilkins had taken in coming to Munich. Although Wilkins had come to accept the nature of the covert work he was doing for his country, he was still uncertain about the wisdom of those holding his strings. Did the S.I.S. and its puppet master, a man Wilkins knew only by the initial "*C*", a man they called "*Control*", understand the impact that this war would have on the British Empire? Surely, uncovering these little German-backed plots would ultimately do little to quell the rising political unrest in parts of the British Empire such as India or Ireland. It would probably do far more good, Wilkins thought, to invest in India's railway system and thereby reduce the threat of famines, or to proceed with instituting Home Rule in Ireland and placating the Irish quest for self-determination, than it would be to send a nineteen year old spy to interview an unstable Irish revolutionary at a psychiatric hospital in Munich.

By the time he left Casement for the night, the sky had grown dark with storm clouds. Wilkins had to reach the abandoned townhouse where he could safely spend the night, but he was once again stopped and examined by the military authorities along the way. As he walked through the eerily subdued streets of Munich, he saw long and remarkably orderly lines for bread, for potatoes, and for tins of "beef." The beef, he was told, was actually fish with synthetic beef flavouring, a new German invention. A new artificial replacement for sugar called *saccharin* was also meted out by the cupful, if one had the correct coupon – everything was strictly rationed. It seemed that Germany was somehow manufacturing substitutes for the food and other necessities its people lacked. But Wilkins had also seen women and men dragged off the streets and deposited into military transports, their fates unclear but undoubtedly dark. Zealously patriotic soldiers were assembling for a meeting at the *Hotel Vier Jahreszeiten*. They were singing Haydn's popular melody *Deutschlandlied* and menacing passersby who failed to exhibit the proper nationalistic fervor:

> *Deutschland, Deutschland über alles,*
> *Über alles in der Welt,*
> *Wenn es stets zu Schutz und Trutze*
> *Brüderlich zusammenhält.*
> *Von der Maas bis an die Memel,*
> *Von der Etsch bis an den Belt,*
> *Deutschland, Deutschland über alles,*
> *Über alles in der Welt!*

The song, trumpeting Germany's global dominance, had become a popular tune with the soldiers after the first battle at Ypres in October 1914. Several regiments of spirited German youths had sung the song as they attacked the British trenches through a dense fog at the village of Langemark. Unfortunately, the enthusiastic singing also gave away the soldiers' positions and made them easy targets for the British machine guns. Tens of thousands of young German men had been killed or wounded that day. The song lived on, however, in the spirit of defiance as well as faith in Germany's eventual victory "over all."

From what Wilkins had seen, the people of Germany were extremely stoic, perhaps also afraid of their new military tyranny, but they were still dedicated to winning the war. The privations and rationing necessitated by the partial British blockade of shipping to Germany had been borne reasonably well. Still, how long could it go on? If Great Britain, which had ruled the seas ever since the Battle of Trafalgar in 1805, could finally contain the threat of the German U-boats, Germany would be cut off from the rest of the world. The wealthy, the aristocrats, and the military and government officials were not suffering now, and the few of the working class who complained were permanently removed from the streets, but how long could that go on when there was neither food to eat nor fuel to burn?

Wilkins safely reached the abandoned townhouse where he would spend the night, crept through the broken rear window, and then climbed down into the darkened cellar to eat the hard cheese and biscuits he had brought with him from Switzerland. It brought to mind his last dinner at home in the dining room of Grosmont Castle. His brothers had already gone to war. Lady Bartlett, his mother, struggled to maintain her calm demeanor as James, her youngest son, prepared to leave for the Mediterranean and Gallipoli. His father, Lord Bartlett, born Thomas Wilkins, was proud of his sons but already he was distracted by his work with the War Committee in London. Half the servants, including James' own valet, had already gone to fight in France, and several of them had died at Ypres. There had been an air of gloominess about his home that was shocking to James, and he wondered not for the last time whether his home would ever again exude the carefree splendour he knew from his childhood there. As Wilkins curled up alone in a cold and dusty corner of the forgotten cellar in Munich and wrapped his great coat around him, he admitted to himself that he was deeply grateful to be departing Germany so soon and under the protection of Sir Roger Casement.

The heat of the ship's engine room was insufferable. David Gresham, blackened with coal dust, sat on the floor exhausted and frustrated. His lanky black hair was saturated with perspiration mixed with coal dust which ran down into his eyes making them red and blurring his vision. With the ship finally arriving at port, he could at last put down his despised coal shovel and wipe his face with the tatters of his stained and sooty undershirt. Gresham was also an agent of the Secret Intelligence Service and had also been ordered to investigate a rumored enemy conspiracy, one involving a military ship in the German port of Lübeck that, according to a Danish informer, was being repainted to look like a Norwegian shipping vessel. Now that Gresham was arriving at Lübeck, he would finally get to look at the menacing German ship, the SMS *Libau*.

Although it had not taken him long to get to Germany, it was a journey Gresham would sooner forget. The French had provided him with transport to Copenhagen and there he had met the Danish informer, a drunken old captain named Erik Vinther. Gresham had stood on the bridge of Vinther's ancient steam cargo ship, the SS *Adolph Andersen*, just as the captain was preparing to embark on another illegal cargo run to the German port of Lübeck on the Baltic Sea coast.

"I don't like it," Vinther had told Gresham as he stroked his long and filthy white beard. "A ship like the *Libau* should not dress up to look like something it is not, like the ship of a neutral country, it is not wise. Once the Germans do it, the British will do it. Once the British do it, the German U-Boat captains will be ordered to torpedo every ship in the Baltic no matter the flag they fly. Your government does not wish me to trade with Germany, but Denmark is a neutral country and this is honest work. I have a right to trade."

"Your trade is not my concern, captain, but if I were to stop the German ship from completing its mission, would that please you?" Gresham had asked.

"Stop it? You are crazy! How would you ever get to Lübeck?"

"Are you not going there yourself?"

"Ha, ha, you are crazy. An Englishman in Germany! They would shoot you. You could not even get to shore before they would shoot you."

"I am not English, sir; I'm a half-Irish bastard, and I need to look at that German ship. If I must stowaway on your vessel to do so, then I will," Gresham insisted.

"And if I was caught with a British spy on my ship or even a British name listed in my manifest, the Germans would shoot me too." But then a malicious expression had slowly coalesced on the captain's face. "What I perhaps can do, for a crazy Irish bastard, is put you in irons and throw you in the engine room to shovel coal. That way I could say you are my captive if the Germans find you there. Would that satisfy you?"

"If that is the only way I can get passage to Lübeck, then I guess it must do," Gresham had admitted.

"Yes, you are crazy, ha, ha, ha!"

Gresham soon found himself in the blistering engine room of Vinther's ship shoveling coal into the ancient boiler. The voyage to Germany was mercifully short, however, and by midnight of the third day of their voyage from Copenhagen, the *Adolph Andersen* was finally moored to its berth in the port of Lübeck.

Vinther's regular Danish crew was busy unloading crates of fresh produce with the cargo derrick when Gresham, still covered in sweat and coal dust, risked a brief visit up on deck. The sun had just set and the sky was a pale, rosy grey and cloudy as Gresham reached the railing and caught his first glimpse of Germany, the country he had been fighting with all his strength and guile for nearly two years.

Gresham had entered the British Army when the war in Europe first began in 1914 – not by his own choice, but rather at the insistence of his father, a wealthy Manchester industrialist who was embarrassed by his violent and often unpredictable illegitimate son. Gresham, although disliked by his fellow officers in the British Army, had served competently in the trenches in France and Belgium before being wounded in a German gas attack east of Ypres. He had been sent to recuperate in Egypt where he was supposed to join the new Manchester Regiment being assembled there for a renewed offensive on the Gallipoli peninsula. It was in Alexandria that Gresham ran into his former tutor, Compton Mackenzie. Soon afterward, Gresham received unusual orders to accompany a young British officer named Lawrence on a journey in Arabia.

Lawrence had made a large impression on Gresham – not only because he was clever and thoughtful, but also because he maintained an aura of calmness about him: Lawrence was a warrior to his very core, he existed solely to defeat his enemy. Gresham admired his piercing clarity of purpose.

After Gresham returned to the Manchesters and joined the landing at Suvla Bay, he was sought out by Mackenzie once again, this time for a mission on the Turkish peninsula itself. Then everything had changed. Gresham was formally enrolled in the Secret Intelligence Service (there being nothing in the least formal about it) and given *carte blanche* by his country to lie, to scheme, to fight, and even to kill if circumstances required. Gresham, together with his former commanding officer and friend James Wilkins, had spent the autumn of 1915 in Greece preparing for the Allied landings at Salonika and in Serbia looking for its missing monarch Peter during the brutal invasion by Austria and Bulgaria. It was King Peter who had inspired Gresham to pursue his own mission next: A journey to Vienna and a fateful meeting with the Austrian Archduke Charles in the woods of Laxenburg. It was from the Archduke himself that Gresham learned of the imminent German attack on Verdun, and he and Wilkins had raced to France to warn the French generals of their enemy's plans.

Gresham and Wilkins had then been called away from Verdun to receive further instructions from their superiors in British intelligence. In Gresham's case, he was to go to Lübeck and investigate the SMS *Libau*. Still, Gresham recalled his friend's advice to consider the wisdom of these secret missions on which they were sent, and indeed this errand to investigate a German vessel that had been disguised to look Norwegian seemed a silly matter on its face: The ship might be doing nothing more ominous than sneaking food into Germany.

Now, on the deck of the SS *Adolph Andersen* in the port of Lübeck, Gresham looked across the dark bay to where electric lights blazed on the thousand-ton German cargo ship *Libau*. Its sides were painted black and emblazoned with the flag of Norway and boldly proclaimed the ship's false name and nationality in huge white letters:

AUD-NORGE

Gresham saw too that the ship was swarming with uniformed German soldiers who were loading (not unloading) unmarked wooden crates, and very carefully loading those crates in a manner, he noted, which suggested that their contents were either extremely fragile or highly explosive.

The port was brightly lit and countless German soldiers armed with rifles were watching all the ships closely. Machine guns had been placed around the port, and heavy artillery guns pointed toward the entrance of the bay in case any British warships sought to enter and destroy the German shipping. Only Captain Vinther had been allowed to disembark from the *Adolph Andersen*, and then only because he had been summoned to the harbormaster's office. Gresham thought it might be possible to swim across the bay to investigate the supposed *AUD*, but the Baltic Sea water, even in April, was certain to be deathly cold and Gresham had no idea what he could do even if he made it across the bay to the ship, considering the many soldiers swarming there.

Perplexed, Gresham returned below deck to consider the matter when he heard a sudden rush of soldiers coming across the gangway. They were shouting in German, and their heavy boots stomped as they spread out across the deck of the *Adolph Andersen*. Gresham rushed to the engine room to resume his feint as an enslaved Irish coal stoker, but just as he arrived at the boiler and raised his shovel, a dozen German soldiers streamed down the ladder and rushed to surround him, their rifles raised and pointed right at his chest. There was nothing to be done. Gresham sighed, raised his hands, and waited.

A tall, grey-haired German officer entered the engine room, followed by the filthy and unscrupulous Captain Vinther. The captain looked ashamed, and yet there was that familiar malicious glint in his eye. Gresham, appalled by his own stupidity, suspected that the captain had planned all along to surrender his secret British passenger to the Germans for some material reward.

"*Er ist derjenige, dass ich dir erzählt habe,*" Vinther said meekly to the German officer.

The officer approached Gresham, took away the coal shovel and threw it to the ground, and examined him closely.

"*Sind Sie sicher über ihn?*" The officer asked Vinther.

"*Ja.*"

"*Ein Weg, oder das andere,*" the officer said to Vinther. Then to his troops, he ordered: "*Nehmen Sie ihn zum Boot.*"

Gresham was furious. Although he could not understand more than a word or two of German, it was clear he had been betrayed. As the German soldiers took hold of Gresham and marched him to the stairs, he pushed back just long enough to spit in Vinther's face.

Captain Vinther laughed as he rubbed the spittle from his beard with his shirt sleeve. "*Ha, ha, Ich habe dir gesagt. Er ist verrückt!*" He told the German officer.

Gresham was marched up the stairs and onto deck and then pushed across the gangway. The soldiers roughly shoved him into the back of a German lorry. Three young soldiers sat surrounding him as the engine started up. The soldiers spoke to each other lightheartedly and, for the most part, ignored Gresham, but it was clear the soldiers were fully on guard: When Gresham so much as shifted in his seat, four hands restrained him and a rifle's muzzle was pressed hard against his chest. There was no hope of escape, and Gresham grew more and more disgusted with himself for falling into such an easy trap.

The lorry rumbled on for ten minutes and then came to a stop at another part of the port. The German soldiers climbed down and beckoned to Gresham. He stood and leapt down to the ground. The soldiers quickly laid hands on him and walked their prisoner around the lorry to a gangway leading up onto another ship, one that claimed to be a Norwegian cargo ship call the *AUD*.

Gresham's heart raced. Why was he being taken to the *AUD*? The deck was still crowded with soldiers moving crates below decks as he was quickly marched down the passageway and directly into the *AUD*'s engine room. One of the Germans thrust a coal shovel into Gresham's hands. The soldiers laughed amongst themselves as they turned and left Gresham there unguarded. There were two other filthy, coal-dust-stained men standing at the boiler staring at Gresham. "*Hvor har du kommer fra, bror?*" One of the men asked in Danish. Gresham laughed out loud. It may not have been in the manner a British secret agent would have wished, he thought, but, somehow, Captain Erik Vinther had gotten Gresham on board the SMS *Libau*.

Wilkins had no idea what to make of Roger Casement. The prestigious Irishman had German government papers that gave him permission to move freely inside Germany (and he was able to bring Wilkins along to the train station, under the alias Aleksei Belyaev, in plain clothes and with no further need of German papers), yet Casement somehow lacked adequate funds to purchase his own train ticket. Wilkins supplied enough German Marks for them both to ride first class, and Casement purchased tickets that would take the two men north from Munich. As they waited on the platform, Casement refused to tell Wilkins how or where they would leave Germany. Everyone on the platform was being inspected by military police, their papers and parcels examined in detail. Not Casement, however; no one seemed to pay Casement or Wilkins any attention at all. When they boarded the crowded train itself, Wilkins was thankful he had insisted on paying for a private compartment since second class was full of boisterous German troops.

During their first six hours alone together in their spartanly outfitted and dark train compartment, Casement gently and slowly questioned Wilkins about the situation in Russia and about "Alexei's" childhood in Moscow. Wilkins used all his guile to invent the most detailed and inspiring story he possibly could, desperately recalling details from his own childhood visit to Moscow with his mother in 1906 in the hope that such details would give his story some verisimilitude. Wilkins certainly recalled the grand palaces they visited and the many Grand Dukes and Duchesses of Russia that they met, but "Alexei" was unlikely to have been to such places. Wilkins also recalled the dark and dirty streets filled with factory workers and starving peasants. That's what they were, after all: A great mass of uneducated, poorly trained, penniless people, many that were sickly, an ill-fed rabble dressed in rags. Wilkins was in Moscow right before the new constitution was adopted, and although the streets of Moscow were eerily quiet while Wilkins and Lady Bartlett crossed the city, there had very recently been massive demonstrations that the Tsar had put down with brute force. The people were still angry and eager for change. Some, the Socialists, pushed for democratic political reforms and civil liberties that would give the workers and peasants a greater voice in government. Some among them were the more radical Maximalists who wished for social equality as well, to take the land away from the nobles and parse it out to the peasantry. Some of them did not even trust the people: They wanted the government to seize and control the land and factories and to dictate their utilization by an enslaved populace.

The demonstrators stared with barely disguised hatred at the *droshky* in which Wilkins traveled with his mother. It had scared the Devil out of the boy. Wilkins supposed that the new parliament, or "Duma" as they call it, created the year after his visit, must have assuaged the people to some extent, but even then he doubted it had quieted the Maximalists, or lessened the sense of looming danger, the terrorist violence, or the bloody vengeance that lurked just beneath the surface of the Tsar's grand Russian society.

Casement, who had never visited Russia, was mesmerized by Wilkins' stories. He seemed almost overwhelmingly sympathetic, at times patting Wilkins on the arm or placing a hand on Wilkins' shoulder. In response to Wilkins' own questions, however, Casement shared no meaningful information at all about his time in Germany or his objectives or what had happened to him there.

As they traveled further north, Casement became more and more agitated — at times shaking nervously, coughing uncontrollably, or viciously scratching his arms and legs like a madman. He would begin speaking and then trail off as his mind wandered. Then suddenly, he revealed with obvious distaste: "We'll be stopping off in Zossen soon." He was apparently unhappy to be making even such a small admission.

Wilkins eyed him for a moment. "Zossen is near Berlin, sir. Is that city on our route to Ireland?" He asked skeptically.

"Not Berlin, no. We would not want to go to Berlin, no, no."

"Then may I know why are we stopping in Zossen?"

"Two men are meeting us there."

"What men, sir?"

"They are coming with us to Ireland, and they are meeting us in Zossen."

"With respect, sir, and I do not mean to pry into your affairs, especially as you have been extremely generous to escort me to Ireland yourself, but may I be told who these two men are?"

Casement appeared to wince at the question and became even more agitated. Wilkins began to believe that Casement was close to tears.

"Mister Casement," Wilkins began gently, "I have entrusted myself to your care in this hostile and terribly dangerous country. I must ask that you tell me if you have become incapacitated in some way. Are you in fact well enough to undertake this journey?"

Rather than answering Wilkins' question, Casement stood and began to pace slowly back and forth from the window (which German law required to be shaded at all times) to the door (which was closed), a small enough space that Casement looked as though he was slowly spinning in circles.

"Mister Casement, please sit down!" Wilkins insisted crossly. Casement sat next to Wilkins, extremely close so that his arm and leg were pressed into Wilkins, which seemed to calm him a bit.

"The doctors in Munich," Casement said slowly, "they think my condition is related to the malaria I suffered in Africa many years ago. Perhaps that does play a part; I don't know. I am not well, and my experiences in Germany have not been at all encouraging."

"Now that you are leaving, sir, perhaps it would be no breach of confidence to tell me a little of what has happened here. You might feel better to tell it," Wilkins said with as much sympathy as he could muster.

"Well, well, what to tell? It is a very, very long and ugly story."

"If I may, sir, allow me to ask a few questions and perhaps I shall comprehend you better. It is my understanding that instead of advocating for Ireland's independence from Great Britain, you have long favored Home Rule for Ireland, is that not so?"

"Yes, yes, that is correct," said Casement.

"In fact, you spoke in favor of the Home Rule bill in the British Parliament in 1914, did you not? You believed it was enough for Ireland to govern itself without seeking independence from the British Crown, yes?"

"Yes, I did."

"And when the war began, and Home Rule was suspended indefinitely, I suspect that was rather a setback for your cause and an embarrassment to you personally, was it not?"

"Yes, certainly it was."

"So then you went to America seeking – let me see – money and guns, I assume, to advance the cause of Ireland's independence?"

Casement remained silent.

"And then you went to Germany seeking more of the same and perhaps diplomatic support from Great Britain's enemy. But they refused you, didn't they? Am I close to the truth?"

"No," Casement said with a scoff. "No, indeed, it was not the Germans who failed us. No, it was the Irish themselves."

"Which Irish? Here in Germany?" Wilkins asked, perplexed.

"The prisoners, Alexsei, it was the Irish prisoners who failed us."

The light at last dawned on Wilkins: "You came to Germany to recruit Irishmen, Irish prisoners of war, soldiers captured by the Germany armies, to fight against Great Britain, is that it?"

"Yes," Casement admitted, "but not just to fight, Alexei. We had great plans, you see, to create and train an army of Irishmen in Germany, an 'Irish Brigade.' But the men wouldn't have it! They wouldn't join up or agree to fight! Oh, they would listen, yes, and they were pleased to be granted whatever favors might relieve them from the monotony and privations of the prison camps. But to actually fight against Great Britain? No, they wouldn't have it!"

Wilkins, who had been on the front lines at Gallipoli, laughed inwardly at the absurdity of Casement's plan. Men who had fought together, who had lived together in the trenches and seen their friends destroyed by enemy gunfire, who had cowered together and prayed together and held each other as artillery fell around them like rain night and day, the officers and the enlisted men alike, these men formed a bond, a bond cemented by fear and by pride in their countrymen and by an absolute faith in their common, national endeavour. It was ridiculous to think these men could be convinced to attack their brothers on the field of battle. Casement's whole stratagem was absurd.

"Then who is joining us in Zossen?" Wilkins asked.

"Two of the men, two Irish officers who agreed to travel with us to Ireland, but I think, in my heart, I think it very likely they agreed to come along just so they could escape from Germany. I do not trust them."

"And so you will return to Ireland empty-handed. No wonder you are distressed. That is completely reasonable, sir. But you have tried, that much is clear. It was worth investigating, and you should be proud of your efforts here," Wilkins said reassuringly.

"As I said before, I think you are very young, Alexsei." Casement would say no more, but Wilkins could see that the admission of his failure in Germany had done little to calm Casement's nerves. Clearly there was more to the story that Casement had not yet revealed.

Wilkins knew only a little of Casement's personal history. He knew that Casement had been a noted British envoy in Africa for many years. He had documented abuse of the natives in the Congo Free State by Belgians operating under the direct authority of King Leopold. Later, Casement had gone to Peru and had documented abuses against the natives there by their British overseers. King George had knighted Casement then, but perhaps just to distance the Crown from the atrocities committed by his own people in South America. In 1914, Casement had backed the Government of Ireland Act passed in Parliament, which at last promised Home Rule, but the law was swiftly suspended due to the outbreak of the war with Germany. That had apparently pushed Casement to favor outright rebellion against Great Britain, to seek Ireland's independence by whatever means were necessary.

Wilkins had been sent to Germany in the fear that Casement was planning something big with the German military, but his mission, it seemed, had been for naught. Casement's "Irish Brigade" was an abject failure, and his mental condition was remarkably unstable. No wonder, Wilkins thought, the Germans had put Casement in the hospital in Munich. They were likely relieved that Casement was departing Germany of his own accord.

The two men sat side by side in their dark compartment, and after a time, Casement reached out and took Wilkins' hand in his own and held it tightly. Wilkins was eager to keep Casement as calm as possible and it seemed to steady him as they continued on in silence north to Zossen, sitting side by side, holding hands.

On the busy station platform in Zossen, the military police again searched and questioned all the passengers. After a momentary glance at Casement's papers, he and Wilkins were simply waved on. They then met Casement's Irish colleagues, and there were brief introductions: "Alexsei, these are Lieutenant Robert Monteith and Sergeant Daniel Bailey. Gentlemen, this young man is Alexsei Belyaev; he is a Russian coming to Ireland to assist our cause." Monteith, a slim, severe and mature gentleman, was quiet and disinterested in his colleagues; Bailey was a dashing and jovial younger man who seemed in high spirits. The four men boarded a second train to continue north, bypassing Berlin. Casement was still despondent and skittish as the four men sat in a now-cramped private compartment.

"So, you are Roger's new boy, eh?" Bailey asked Wilkins with a smirk.

"How do you mean, sir?"

"Even younger than that last fellow, that boy Christiansen," said Monteith with disgust.

"I liked Christiansen," Bailey said. "He was good for a laugh, at least."

"He was a filthy bugger, and no mistake," Monteith growled.

"Tell me again, Belyaev, why are you going to Ireland?" Bailey asked.

"I have been sent to meet with the leaders of the Irish Citizen Army and learn what support can be offered to the cause of Ireland's independence, sir."

"So you're one of them fellows too, eh, a Marxist or what-not?"

"I am a revolutionary, fighting for working men and women, men just like you, if that's what you mean. Are you not fighting for Ireland's freedom as well, to make a better life for yourself and your family?" Wilkins asked.

"Yeah, I s'pose so," said Bailey half-heartedly. "It's no surprise Roger took a liking to you; you're just his type," he suddenly cracked with a dark chuckle.

"Did you gentlemen both serve with the British Expeditionary Force in France?" Wilkins asked.

"I was at Ypres. That's where I was captured," Bailey said, "but me and the Lieutenant here," he said, indicating Monteith, "we was in India before that."

"You came to Germany from India, then, Lieutenant?"

"F--- off," Monteith replied.

"He came over from New York, isn't that right, Bob?" Bailey said.

Monteith remained silent.

"New York and India!" Wilkins said in astonishment, although confused by Monteith's hostility. "I have never been away from Russia until now. Tell me, I have always imagined Ireland to be a great, green country, is it truly?"

"I wouldn't know," Bailey snarled. "The green parts is the parts owned by Englishmen."

"Alexsei, I must ask you to please step outside the compartment a moment," Casement said. "I need to speak with the Lieutenant and Sergeant privately."

"As you wish, sir," said Wilkins. He went to the hallway and the door was shut behind him. A train employee passed by, and Wilkins was able to learn that the train was headed for the seacoast. Suddenly there was shouting in the compartment. Although the words were unclear (even with Wilkins resting his ear against the wooden door), Casement and Monteith were both terribly angry. After the shouting subsided and the room was quiet for a while, Wilkins was at last readmitted.

Casement, Monteith and Bailey remained deathly silent for the remainder of the journey. They seemed to not like each other at all, and Wilkins was pleased to leave them alone lest he be asked any more questions about himself; he wasn't sure he could remember half of what he told Casement about "Alexei's" past if he was ever forced to repeat it. Finally, the train arrived at the coast where they were to board a ship for Ireland. A new gleaming black *Mercedes-Knight* sedan was waiting for them at the station, they gathered their few pieces of luggage, and the automobile sped them across town to the port. German soldiers swarmed on the docks to keep track of all the vessels and their crews. Wilkins, tiring of the Russian charade, was relieved when at last they came to a stop at the gangway of a large Norwegian cargo vessel named *AUD*.

Wilkins and the Irishmen were led up the slim metal gangway by one of the Norwegian crew members and brought to the galley. Casement had suddenly grown more agitated than Wilkins had ever yet seen him. Casement stormed out of the galley and ran into the ship's captain in the passageway. Although German appeared to be the only common language on board, a language Wilkins spoke well, he could not make out the tense and angry whispering between Casement and the ship's captain. Then suddenly, Casement shouted in German: *"It is not acceptable! I cannot travel on board this ship! It is absolutely improper! I am a legitimate envoy. There must be another ship!"*

The captain tried to calmly argue with Casement, but it was obvious that his Irish passenger was close to losing control altogether and the captain wanted none of it. Casement finally returned to the galley in a sweat, shaking like a leaf in a breeze, and sat beside Wilkins – actually pressed rather uncomfortably against Wilkins and again took Wilkins' hand and held it tightly. The captain took one look, sighed, and stomped off. Sergeant Bailey just shook his head and chuckled, while Lieutenant Monteith looked away in disgust. Casement refused to say anything at all except to tell Monteith and Bailey to remain quiet. After an hour, the captain at last returned to the galley.

"*Sie gehen einen anderen Weg,*" he said. "*Ein deutsches Boot werden Sie von Wilhelmshaven zu nehmen. Wir werden Sie in Tralee Bay treffen sich auf der 20,*" the captain concluded with a sigh of relief and resignation.

"We will be taking another ship," Casement translated in a confident voice, much relieved. Wilkins also heard the rest of what the captain had said: His ship would *rendezvous* with Casement at Tralee Bay in Irish waters in ten days' time. Why? Wilkins wondered. What was this ship transporting other than a few Irishmen? He suddenly became extremely concerned about what Sir Roger Casement hadn't yet told him about his return to Ireland.

"What do you mean, another ship?" asked Monteith angrily. "What's wrong with this one, Casement? The sooner we are at sea, the better, and I'm bloody sick of delaying our return to Ireland for you."

"It makes no difference," Casement countered. "This ship is not departing for two days anyway. We'll likely be away sooner than that now."

"But, sir," said Wilkins, "if, as I understand the captain, we are to make *rendezvous* with this ship in ten days' time anyway, what then is the problem?"

"Don't you understand, gentlemen?" asked Casement anxiously. "This is a *German* ship disguised as a Norwegian one. If we are stopped at sea and discovered, the British will rightly conclude we are all spies. If we are instead captured on a ship bearing a German flag, however, we will at worst be taken as prisoners of war, if not simply repatriated."

"You think so little of our chances, then, do you?" Monteith asked. "You think we won't even make it to Ireland?"

Casement didn't answer.

"If this is a German ship, I would like to be told what cargo you intend to transport to Tralee Bay," Wilkins insisted.

"That's none of your business," Monteith replied vehemently, raising a finger at Wilkins. "You're just along for the ride, f---er. You're just Roger's boy, his dog, so let's not hear one more bloody word out o' your filthy mouth, you dirty c---sucker."

"That's enough, Lieutenant!" Casement shouted, as Wilkins stepped back in surprise at Monteith's hostility. Casement turned and made his way unsteadily up to the deck. Wilkins remained in the galley.

"*Der Wagen bringt Sie,*" the captain said to his crewmate.

Casement, Wilkins, Bailey and Monteith were led off the ship to the black sedan and driven directly to another port, one in the town of Wilhelmshaven on the North Sea coast of Germany. There, they discovered they would all be transported to Ireland aboard a German U-boat.

The *AUD* had been at sea for more than a week but Gresham, who had been laboring in the engine room, had still learned nothing of the ship's intended destination or cargo. The crewmembers of this "Norwegian" ship were obviously German military, and because none of them had the least interest in shoveling coal, Gresham and three fellows from Denmark had been press-ganged in Lübeck into serving hard labor on board. At the end of his first day at sea, Gresham was escorted to a small, dank cabin that he and the other stokers would share for their brief rests. The German crewman pointed to the top bunk, and then shut and locked Gresham into the darkened room. As he climbed, exhausted, up to his bunk, a quiet voice spoke out: "English?"

"Irish," Gresham whispered, seeing the huddled speaker on the bottom bunk. "Where are you from?"

"Odense."

"Any idea where this ship is headed?"

"No," the man replied, and then he rolled over and covered his head with his jacket.

Day after day, Gresham worked in the engine room and then was locked away for a small meal and a few hours of rest. Since Gresham didn't speak German, his efforts to listen to the crew's conversations had been unavailing. The captain, a German man named Spindler, had some English, but he never deigned to speak to Gresham. The one Danish laborer who spoke a little English translated the engineer's few commands. The mysterious cargo, whatever it was, was an enigma secured in the locked hold of the ship. The only thing Gresham learned was that four important passengers were to have joined the ship in Lübeck, but they had for some reason disembarked before the ship left port.

Gresham's days were long and hot and hard, and after many days in the sooty and stiflingly hot engine room, Gresham had begun to despair. Where in the world was the ship headed? At one point, the *AUD* had come within sight of land, but Gresham had no idea what land it was as they were still many miles from shore. However, soon after he learned that a British warship had come alongside the *AUD*, that officers from the British ship had actually boarded the *AUD*, they had spoken to the captain, tippled a bit of rum, and then departed. Gresham had missed perhaps his only chance to get off the *AUD*.

Gresham was sound asleep in his cabin when the alarms sounded early the next morning. He bolted upright, banging his head on the ceiling, as the door to the cabin suddenly burst open. A member of the crew shouted at the sleeping laborers to wake up. Men were running through the passageways and carrying heavy boxes up onto the deck. All order aboard the *AUD* had disintegrated. Some of the laborers feared the ship was sinking and tried to rush up on deck, but the chief engineer, holding a German *Mauser* pistol, collected his laborers and led them to the engine room. Another crewmember sat on a ladder above them holding a rifle. The engineer was talking to the men in German. The Danish laborers explained to Gresham that another ship that they were supposed to meet in these waters had not arrived and now a British warship had been sighted nearby. The German crew was very upset. Two of the Danish laborers were taken away to move crates from the cargo hold. The chief engineer, angry and drunk, yelled at the men to start stoking the boilers. As Gresham picked up his shovel, another crew member suddenly came to drag Gresham from the engine room.

In the passageway, Gresham saw more members of the crew carrying rifles and two were struggling to bring a heavy German machine gun up on deck. Gresham feared his identity had been uncovered as he was taken directly to the Captain's quarters. Still filthy, blackened by coal dust and sweat, Gresham stood silently while Captain Spindler worked feverishly at his desk. Finally the captain turned and looked at Gresham with an expression of disgust.

"Vinther said you are from Ireland, yes?" Captain Spindler asked in English, but with a strong German accent.

Gresham was half-Irish, but he had never actually been to Ireland. Still, on a German boat, it seemed wisest to be an Irishman rather than the citizen of just about any other English-speaking nation. "Yeah, that's right," he said.

"Were you in the British Army?"

"Yeah, well, that's the story there, you see, I'm supposed to be in France. It seems I got on the wrong boat."

"So you are a deserter. And do you prefer to be captured by the British or to stay on this ship until we return to Norway, at which time I will release you?"

"To speak truthfully, sir, I'm not likely to get much of a fair deal from the Brits. They tend to take a dim view of deserters, and they're apt to hang me first and conduct an inquiry after. I would prefer to go back to Norway with you, if that's all right."

"But are you willing to fight for your freedom, as many of your countrymen in Ireland are prepared to do?"

"Aye, captain," said Gresham warily. "Are we going to fight the Brits?" Gresham asked as casually as he could manage.

"We are in British waters now, off the coast of Ireland. We have arms to deliver to the Irish. Do you know Tralee Bay?"

Gresham's skin prickled. Arms! Of course! The Germans were planning to arm the Irish revolutionaries. Whatever arms were in the cargo hold, Gresham decided, they must never make it to shore.

"I know about Tralee, sir, but I'm from Ulster myself," he bluffed casually.

"Then I tell you, this ship has just been arrested by the British Royal Navy. My men and I intend to resist. We are not well armed for battle, but we can run. Will you fight if we are boarded?"

"Aye, captain," said Gresham confidently, "I damned well will fight, you can be sure o' that."

"*Geben Sie diesem Mann ein Gewehr,*" the captain said to his crewmate. "Then we understand each other. You will be given a rifle. Go on deck with the crew."

Gresham was pulled from the room by the crew member and rushed to the galley where a crate of small arms had been opened. Gresham took a rifle and several clips of ammunition and was led on deck. He saw that two machine guns and a partially assembled *Minenwerfer* short-range mortar had already been unpacked. The German crew members now wore German uniforms under their Norwegian outer-clothes and a German imperial flag was ready to be hoisted once the captain gave the order to resist. One hundred and fifty yards off the starboard side, the British minesweeper HMS *Bluebell* was escorting the German ship toward the coast of Ireland. The *Bluebell* was only slightly larger than the *AUD* herself, and Gresham saw that it was the same class of ship that had carried General Hamilton to Gallipoli – a ship with a very thick hull to protect against mines and torpedoes, but with very few guns on top. If the Germans did fight, and if they were able to loft a couple mortar shells onto the deck of the *Bluebell*, there was no doubt in Gresham's mind that the German ship would be able to make a clean escape. That could not be permitted.

Gresham approached the nearest crew member. The man was wiping grease from a machine gun, getting ready to fire a large crate of ammunition at the British sailors on *Bluebell.* "Got any potato mashers?" Gresham asked. The crew member looked at him uncomprehendingly. "Grenades?" he tried.

"*Ja,*" the German said brusquely as he pointed to a crate near the mortar.

Gresham loaded his rifle, checked the two extra clips of ammunition in his pants pocket, and strolled to the crate of grenades. They were the new British design, the Mills bomb – compact, four second fuse, plenty of explosive. Gresham shouldered his rifle and picked up two grenades. As he strolled to the mortar, he counted ten crew members on deck; that meant another ten or so below deck – too many. He pulled the pin from one of the grenades, casually dropped it into the mortar's barrel, and ran.

The crew members stared at Gresham and wondered why he was running on deck when suddenly the mortar exploded and shreds of steel flew into the Germans standing beside it. The men were screaming and others were shouting; several soldiers were shooting – some at Gresham, others toward the British ship. Gresham raised his rifle as he ran and shot the crew members who blocked his access to the passageway and the ladder leading below deck. As he descended, he screamed: "The attack has begun!" Captain Spindler emerged into the passageway. "There's been an explosion, captain. The British are firing on us," Gresham shouted. The captain ran to the ladder to see what was going on.

Gresham ran on to the cargo hold. As he expected, the doors were now open and he could at last look at the German shipment to Ireland.

It was a mind-boggling assortment of low-grade weaponry, an insult to Ireland and of very little use to anyone: Aging rifles from three or four different countries, crates of ammunition in an assortment of odd calibers, a few crates of grenades and dynamite, all intended for the Irish rebels and mostly useless. Germany had been proven an unfaithful friend to the Irish rebels, and Gresham sensed that the poor assortment of weapons was intended to cause more chaos and distraction to the British rulers than to win the Irish people their independence.

There was shouting in the passageway behind Gresham and he knew he had very little time. He grabbed a box of dynamite. The blasting caps were nowhere to be found. There was no other option, he thought. He kicked open the box of dynamite and laid the sticks against the hull, then ran back to the cargo bay door.

"Captain Spindler!" He shouted. Shots were fired toward the door, and Gresham fired back blindly to make it clear he was prepared to defend himself.

"*Aufhören zu schießen, idiot, sie schlägt den Sprengstoff!*" Captain Spindler shouted to his crew when he realized that the shooting could set off an explosion in the weapons-filled cargo hold. The shooting stopped instantly.

"In 30 seconds, this ship will explode!" Gresham yelled. "I have lit the dynamite already! Tell your men to abandon ship at once!"

"Will you blow yourself up, then?" The captain shouted.

"Only if you are blocking the passageway!" Gresham replied. "And you now have 20 seconds remaining!"

"*Verlassen Sie Schiff! Das Schiff wird explodieren! Verlassen Sie Schiff!*" Gresham heard Spindler shout in absolute panic. The crew members rushed to the ladders to escape. Gresham waited a few seconds and then pulled the safety pin on his one remaining grenade. He looked out; the passageway was clear. He tossed the grenade gently onto the stack of dynamite laid against the hull, and ran.

The explosion knocked Gresham to the floor, and by the time he regained his feet and his senses, sea water was already rushing down the passageway and smoke filled the air. In the cargo bay, there were more, smaller explosions as the ammunition began to pop. Gresham leapt to the ladder and climbed as fast as he could. The ship began to list to starboard, but he was able to pull himself safely to the deck. Smoke filled the air and the ship was listing hard. The German crew members were lowering the last life boats into the water, too busy to even notice Gresham on deck. The *AUD* was sinking rapidly. Gresham seized a white life jacket and calmly put it on. He saw that the German crew and Danish laborers were safely away. As water began to cover the deck aft, Gresham leapt into the frigid ocean waters and swam toward the rescue boats from *Bluebell* that were already approaching.

Wilkins lay exhausted in the hammock and tried to sleep, but all around him men were shouting and singing in German. The warm, moist air stank of diesel and human sweat and excrement. Traveling aboard the German U-boat was akin to being incarcerated in a watery prison. The diesel engines ran continuously when the ship was running on the surface and kept the air inside the submarine warm, but the cold ocean water surrounding the vessel caused condensation to form on the interior walls and everything inside the ship was wet. The U-boat was barely capable of handling the four additional passengers on top of its usual crew of thirty-five in the two-hundred foot long vessel. Wilkins, Casement, Monteith and Bailey were required to share one hammock, forcing them to limit their sleep to six hours each in turns. Every other recess in the ship was packed with men, metal, rotting fruit and meat and canned food supplies. When the ship submerged on occasion to avoid detection and ran on its electric battery motors, the sense of claustrophobia, being tightly packed inside the wet, cold, tin can, was overwhelming. Most of the journey, however, was made running on the surface, and Wilkins spent as much time as possible outside on the forward deck, standing or sitting beside the deck gun and staying away from the German crew and their captain, Kapitänleutnant Walther Schwieger.

The captain was a clever man and did not care for his cargo of four revolutionaries, but fortunately he had no more interest in Wilkins than he did in the three Irishmen aboard his ship. Wilkins, who now pretended he could not speak German at all, wanted nothing to do with the captain or his crew. He had heard of Kapitänleutnant Schwieger: He was the very man who had launched the torpedo that sank RMS *Lusitania* in May 1915 and had murdered more than a thousand innocent men, women and children traveling on board that tragic ocean liner.

Schwieger's U-boat had been ordered to avoid any contact with the British Royal Navy during its run to Ireland, so Wilkins was not overly concerned about making it safely into British territory, but with each passing day Roger Casement's condition became more and more fragile. Casement never slept, although he would sometimes lie in the hammock and quietly sob. He would often come and sit silently beside Wilkins on the deck when the weather was fair, sometimes taking Wilkins' hand to hold tightly.

Because of engine problems, they were due to arrive at Tralee Bay a day late, and no one knew whether the *AUD* would still be waiting for them. Although this had given Wilkins a little extra time with Casement and he had done his best to cultivate Casement's trust, the man was still reticent when it came to discussing his return to Ireland or the cargo that the *AUD* was bringing there. The day before their arrival in Ireland, sitting together on the forward deck of the U-boat in the weak spring sunlight, the ship rushing through a calm sea, Wilkins, desperate to get Casement to talk, hit upon a new strategy: "I have not read your famous report regarding the colonial abuses in Congo, although I have heard very much about it," Wilkins began. "I am wondering, have you had any opportunity to return and see whether the reforms you recommended have been implemented there?"

"No," Casement replied, quite stricken. "I could never go back there."

"No? Why is that, sir?"

"I will never go back," Casement insisted.

"You are being foolish, Roger," Wilkins told him. "Why ever not?"

Casement stared at Wilkins a moment before he replied: "I could not bear it, to be perfectly honest. I could not bear to see the atrocities inflicted on those poor, miserable people again, Alexsei. It would break me. The memories of my work there gnaw at me: Hardly a day goes by when I do not recall the miserable existence of the native people, the viciousness with which they mutilated their own women and children at the insistence of their Belgian masters, the cold calculation with which the white men goaded them to conduct such outrages."

"Tell me how they did so."

"When I was first posted to Congo, Alexsei, I thought it would be much like India. If one looks beneath the layers of British civilization atop India there lays a strong foundation of Hindu society, centuries of progress, the caste system, the Marathas, and so forth. The natives of Congo live in a far more natural state, and in a place far more barbaric. The Belgians used this to their advantage. The very governance of Congo was so structured in order to subjugate and abuse the natives so that the Belgians could seize Congo's one industrial resource – rubber. The people of the villages were required to produce a certain quota of rubber.

This was very difficult to do because of the time it took for the natives to locate suitable trees and vines, to tap them, collect and boil the sap, form it into blocks and return to their villages. The effort left no time at all to produce food, to farm, to hunt or to care for their elderly and children. I found some villages that had actually starved to death while attempting to meet their quota. The Belgians, limited as they were in number, appointed native men to oversee the local rubber production and gave those men greater status and rewards. Conversely, those overseers knew that if the village failed to meet its quota they themselves would very likely be beaten to death. The only way to meet the quota was for these men to inflict a punishment upon the supposed laggards, a punishment that usually involved cutting off of the hands or feet or in some instances the removal of an eye or an ear or the nose or the genitals; there are countless natives in Congo – old men, women, even very small children – who have been mutilated in these ways. Small brown children with no feet, no hands; women with no nose, ears or breasts – I recall those atrocities so clearly. I dream of them sometimes."

"The natives did this to their own people?"

"The Belgians contrived these punishments, but they rarely committed the greatest atrocities themselves. They forced the natives to inflict them upon their own people."

"But was it necessary to inflict such terrible and immoral punishments?" Wilkins asked in horror.

"Of course not, but at that time there were villages between Livingstone Falls and Stanley Pool where the natives still performed cannibalism, so the Belgians thought it necessary to devise punishments that would impress the people with their cruelty. Some of the Belgian soldiers were genuinely cruel and immoral men, certainly, but they were not alone in their depravity. At first it was difficult for me to comprehend a place where every man considered the life's breath of every other man to be of so little significance. It was not unusual for natives to disappear in the jungles, to be killed by wild animals or to suffer terrible diseases – it was a fact of life there. I spent many weeks abed with malaria myself, delirious, contemplating these horrors. I call them horrors still, but to the natives there was no question of right or wrong – it was simply a matter of survival. In the jungles of Congo, it was a struggle merely to survive day to day regardless of the rubber trade. The Belgians took advantage of these desperate people"

"Surely the natives fought back against the Belgians, where they could," Wilkins suggested.

"Not many and not often enough. For many Belgians in the Congo, these mutilations and the willingness of the native overseers to perform these terrible acts confirmed what they already believed, that the Congo natives were really not human at all. And it was all too easy to identify their supposed inferiors by virtue of their skin color. The natives, likewise, came to believe that they must be inferior otherwise it could not be happening. Thus the quotas, the arrests, the mutilations and the murders continued – a system that reinforced itself with each passing day. It would have continued on indefinitely, had I not sought to break the circle."

"I had no notion that the African people were so weak," Wilkins thought aloud.

"Weak? No, Alexsei, they are not weak, that is not what I am saying. They are people, Alexsei, ordinary people caught in a system of degradation. They are no weaker that the native people in the many other colonies that encompass the globe. Indeed, they are no weaker than the peasants who live in poverty across Europe even now. Is it not the same in Russia, Alexsei?"

"How do you mean?"

"I have come to believe it is similar in Ireland. Englishmen have governed Ireland for so many centuries. They've taken our property and our land, killed our people with impunity, relegated the native people to the most meager farmlands and placed us in indentured servitude, banned our language, our religion and our schools, destroyed our traditions. The British view themselves as superior to the Celtic people in every respect. Many of the Irish now believe it themselves, and this is reinforced by the simple fact that Great Britain continues to rule Ireland. And if the Irish people are inferior, does it not follow that Ireland *should be* ruled by the British? That is the circular logic that must be broken, Alexsei, just as it must be in Russia."

"You suppose the peasants, workers, and soldiers in Russia are suppressed by the factory-owners, landowners, and generals who support the Tsar."

"Are they not?"

"Yes, certainly, yes," Wilkins quickly agreed. "However, I had never considered Ireland in the light you now cast it, I admit. But the question remains, how is the circle best broken? Is it by violent or non-violent methods? By advocating for Home Rule in Ireland, you promoted revolution through peaceful means."

"We had Home Rule, but by suspending it the British have proven that Home Rule is not Self-Rule. It is not self-determination. It is worthless."

"And so you have turned to Germany now, have you? I believe the cargo ship meeting you in Tralee Bay is filed with German weapons and that you now mean to instigate a bloody revolution in Ireland. Am I wrong?"

"I cannot discuss that," said Casement meekly.

"Enough of that, Roger!" Wilkins seethed with anger and frustration. "If there is to be an armed revolution in Ireland, especially one sponsored by Imperial Germany, I would have you tell me now, and I must be told whether you have made any promises to the Kaiser in exchange for his support."

"Please, Alexsei, I do not want to discuss it."

"You still object, do you? You do not trust me because I am not an Irishman myself, is that it?" He insisted. "Even though I have held your hand and comforted you these past two weeks, and despite the insinuations of Monteith and Bailey that I am your lover as well? Shall I stand by and take it all as meekly as you do yourself?"

"It is not that at all, Alexsei. Please, I do not wish to discuss it because it is utterly hopeless!" Casement spat back. "No, no, the Germans received no promises from me, I guarantee it. Indeed, the Germans do not believe there is the even the slightest chance of a successful rebellion in Ireland, and so they have sent us only trinkets and toys, and they have sent those only to be rid of me. On top of that, as I told you, the Irish prisoners in the camps in Germany lack any will to fight the British, and it will be no different in Ireland, I am certain. So next week there will be a bloody revolution, Alexsei, and it will be a devastating failure. If I could stop it now, I would, but I have been away from Ireland too long, fooling myself into believing that Germany would offer us aid."

"Next week, so soon?" Wilkins asked in alarm.

"Patrick Pearse is in Dublin right now with James Connolly. Pearse will proclaim a republic in Ireland from the steps of the Dublin Post Office on Monday morning, as if just saying it will make it true. Then the shooting will undoubtedly begin. There is no plan, no strategy, and no soldiers. By the end of next week, Pearse and Connolly will have been captured and shot, and I – the tragic conclusion to my life of studied diplomacy. There it is, you now have the full and total truth!"

Wilkins was taken aback, and Casement was near collapse as he finished speaking and tears rushed down his face. It became clear to Wilkins why Casement had been so very anxious. There were too many disasters he had been contemplating for too long: The recurrence of his malaria, the atrocities of Congo and Peru, the failure of the Irish Brigade, the antipathy of the Germans and British, the personal disparagement of his colleagues, the imminent failure of the Irish rebellion and his probable execution all weighed upon him. Casement had no fight left in him, and no one to stand beside him except the handsome young Russian revolutionary "Alexsei."

"It will be alright, Roger," Wilkins said as he put his arm around Casement's shoulder.

"Once we are in Ireland, you must leave me, Alexsei," Casement said with deep concern. "I beg you to look out for yourself."

"We will see."

"You must not meet with Connolly under any circumstances. He is surely being watched already. Just observe and report, no more. Perhaps you will learn something from our failure here."

"Alright," Wilkins consoled him.

"And you must tell your people not to trust the Germans, especially the man they call Dunn."

"Who is that?"

"He works for Zimmerman. He is a Boer but he is Germany's man now. I do not know his real name, but he is known in Germany as Dunn."

"Did you meet this man in Germany?"

"He was one of my primary contacts, yes, although he arrives and departs the country frequently. His aim is to seek out and support those who lead rebellions against the Allied governments. But he is a violent man, and more interested in sowing unrest than achieving reforms. He is probably in Dublin now, drafting Pearse's absurd proclamation. Dunn is a *provocateur*. You would do well to keep him out of Russia altogether."

"Thank you, my friend. I will heed your advice."

Casement put his arms around Wilkins and hugged him tightly, and, for his part, Wilkins had never felt sorrier for anyone in all his life than for poor Sir Roger Casement.

At two o'clock the next morning, a small landing boat was prepared to deliver Casement, Monteith, Bailey and Wilkins to the shore of Ireland. The U-boat had not located the missing *AUD,* and Kapitänleutnant Schwieger had refused to remain exposed any longer in British waters. As the landing boat reached the shore at Banna Strand, a wide sandy beach north of Tralee, it overturned in the waves and threw the men into the cold salty water. Casement, almost immobilized by his illness and despair, nearly drowned before Monteith was able to pull him from the water. Then Monteith and Bailey set out for the town of Tralee, some miles to the south, to locate the revolutionaries that were supposed to collect the arms shipment from the *AUD.* Wilkins believed it unlikely that he would ever see either man again.

He led Casement up the dunes and past a darkened farmhouse until they reached a small, ancient, overgrown ringfort where they sheltered from the wind. Casement, wet and exhausted, could go no further. As the sun began to rise, Wilkins left Casement there to sleep and set off for the village nearby where he would summon the constables that would place Casement under arrest.

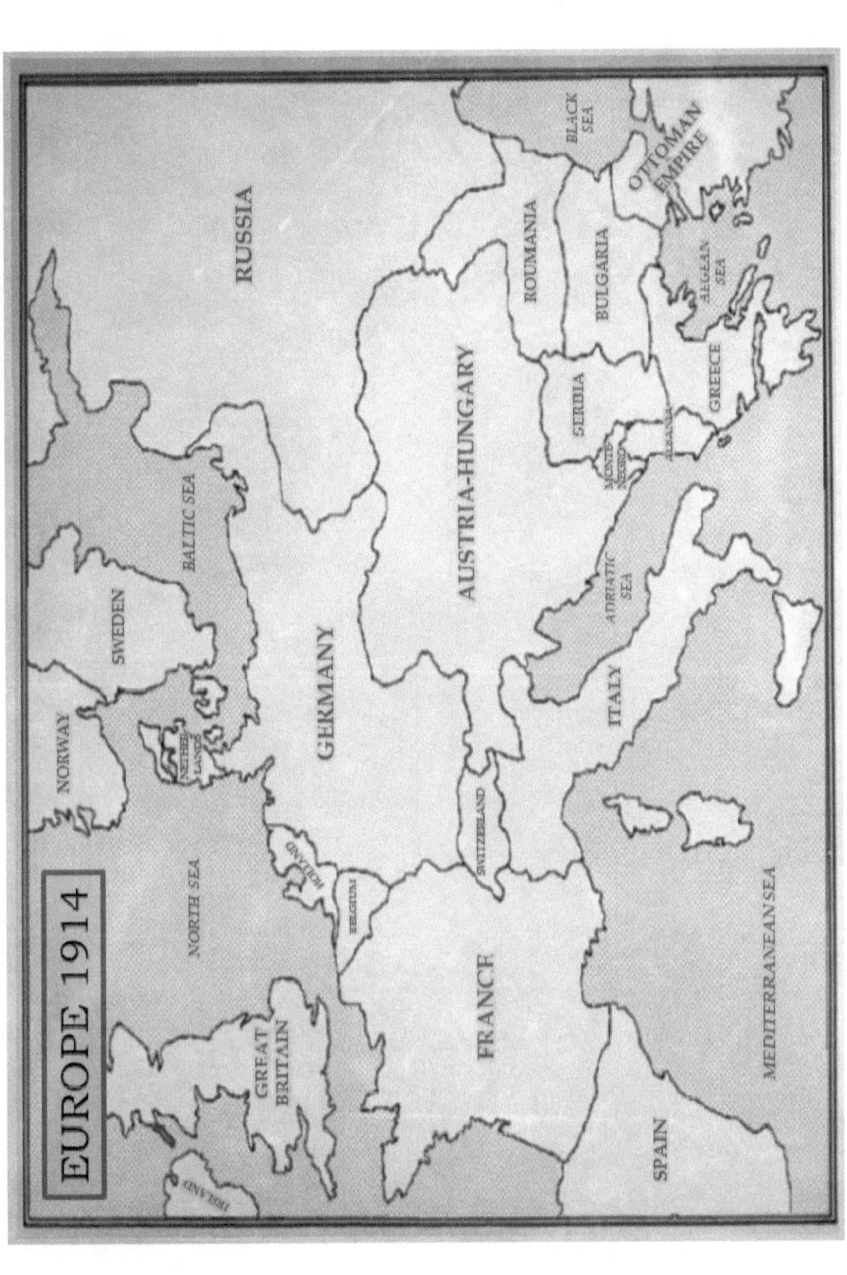

EUROPE 1914

IRELAND

GREAT BRITAIN

NORTH SEA

NORWAY

SWEDEN

BALTIC SEA

NETHER LANDS

BELGIUM

HOLLAND

GERMANY

FRANCE

SWITZERLAND

SPAIN

MEDITERRANEAN SEA

ITALY

ADRIATIC SEA

AUSTRIA-HUNGARY

RUSSIA

ROUMANIA

SERBIA

MONTE NEGRO

ALBANIA

BULGARIA

GREECE

AEGEAN SEA

BLACK SEA

OTTOMAN EMPIRE

The Irish Sea

Gresham reclined on a cold grey steel bench in the officer's lounge aboard HMS *Hampshire*, an armoured cruiser of the British Royal Navy at sea near the Isle of Man. His eyes were tightly shut, and he was sipping tea with brandy and milk from a thick white cup. The room was far too bright for his liking, and the uniform he was wearing was far too tight, and the ship was rocking far too much. It had been a very long week.

After Gresham had been rescued from the waters near Tralee and brought aboard HMS *Bluebell,* he asked for permission to interrogate Captain Spindler to learn the names of the rebels who were to take possession of the German arms shipment and of the passengers who had disembarked in Germany. Instead, *Bluebell*'s captain imprisoned Gresham on the ship for six days until his identity could be confirmed. Gresham spent the week eating, drinking heavily and playing cards with the other officers on board. Then one morning he was abruptly awakened and ferried to HMS *Hampshire* without a word of explanation. Still tipsy and nauseated, Gresham was led to the officer's galley where he discovered his friend and colleague James Wilkins. It was only then that the two men learned that they had briefly been aboard the *AUD* at the same time.

Gresham and Wilkins had not been brought to *Hampshire* merely to be reunited, however. They had been summoned. They were waiting, and soon they would meet the ship's renowned passenger, Field Marshal and Minister for War, The Earl Horatio Herbert Kitchener.

Wilkins was standing beside the billiards table, also in a new but in his case well-tailored uniform, recounting his adventures in Germany while the rough seas rolled the billiard balls gently across the table. He was patiently waiting for them to stop moving so he could take his next shot. The "Easter Uprising" in Dublin, he told Gresham, had been decisively put down. Pearse, Connolly, and the other leaders had been imprisoned; most would be hanged within days. Casement, because of his past service to the Crown, was to be given an actual trial, and Wilkins hoped that the Irishman's life would be spared – after all, Casement still had many friends in London. However, there were also rumors that Casement's private journals – ones containing explicit details about his affairs with several young men – would be used against him, and, if those rumors were true, it would surely mean a swift and bitter end to Sir Roger Casement.

"But I want details, James. I've always said you are a handsome young man. How warmly did Casement feel towards you?" Gresham teased.

"No more than appropriate," Wilkins replied with irritation. "Don't be vulgar. And straighten up a bit, will you? For pity's sake, it's not every day you meet the greatest living man in the British Empire."

"Excepting the King, you mean."

"Yes, of course," said Wilkins, blushing at his own misstatement.

"I wouldn't know if Kitchener is a great man, but he is, at least, a great poster," Gresham replied. Recruiting posters of Kitchener instructing Great Britain's young men to join the army had been plastered everywhere across the British Isles for nearly two years, and no one would dispute that the poster, and Kitchener's enlistment drive as a whole, had been essential to the British war effort (especially if one considered the extent of the casualties both dead and wounded already). Still, it wasn't enough, and already there were plans in the government to institute mandatory military service, or conscription, for all able-bodied men up to the age of forty-one. Even that might not prove to be enough, it was feared. Great Britain, like the other countries at war, had dramatically increased its production of war materials, but there was one resource no country could quickly enlarge: its manpower, specifically, the number of soldiers able to fight. Germany's recent attack on Verdun, which was allegedly designed to drain the material and human resources of France, showed that the scale of this war would surpass all prior wars. Nothing like it had been seen since Napoleon's time, and some already worried that the victors would prove to be the countries with the most men dead on the battlefield at the end.

"You need to stop drinking." Wilkins replied, as he leaned over the billiard table. "Leave off a moment. It's hard enough to make this shot without your meager wits distracting me."

"But why are we even here, James – you've always understood these things. We don't work for Kitchener, do we? Why should we even be aboard *Hampshire*?"

"For all we know, *Control* works for Kitchener. Indeed, for all we know, Kitchener *is Control*." *Control*, or just "*C*", was the man who ran His Majesty's Secret Intelligence Service. Gresham and Wilkins had never met the man who directed their movements and missions, and both wondered if he was some Lord or General or politician to have been given such an important position. "In any event, you can be certain that the Service has no desire to displease the Earl Kitchener, so just be on your best behavior."

"Of course, James, but you know I have been locked in a bloody stateroom for the past week and would like to get to dry land eventually."

"Perhaps we'll be sent back to Verdun. Would that please you?" Wilkins commented with sarcasm.

"The way thing are going, we're more likely to be sent to put down a rebellion in Canada. Have you ever been to Canada?"

"Been to Canada? Whatever for?" Wilkins replied.

There was a knock on the door and a young Midshipman poked his head into the room. "Captains, please come with me," he said. Gresham rose from his prone position with a groan and attempted to straighten his jacket and necktie. Wilkins dusted him off, and the two men followed the Midshipmen down the passageway to the large stateroom that had been prepared for Kitchener. The Midshipman knocked twice and opened the door to admit the officers.

Both men were immediately struck by the spaciousness of the stateroom and the many valuable furnishings that had been brought aboard. It was a cabin finer and larger than the best suite at the *Savoy* in London. Wilkins' eye roamed over the valuable paintings that hung on the walls and the fine Persian carpets on the floor, but Gresham narrowed in on the two gentlemen sitting in leather wingback chairs in front of a *faux* hearth. One, of course, was Kitchener, seated comfortably in his Field Marshal uniform; his distinctive face was easily recollected from the infamous recruiting posters that Gresham had seen all over Manchester in 1914, but Kitchener now looked older, greyer, bloated, and tired. The other gentleman was young, quite trim, with short dark brown hair, blue eyes, a neat beard and sharp features, wearing a somewhat shabby suit of clothes. He sat leisurely, his legs wide apart, one arm tossed carelessly behind his head, but his grey-blue eyes bore into Kitchener like steel bayonets.

Wilkins stepped beside Gresham and came to attention; he elbowed Gresham to do the same. Kitchener was speaking to the other gentleman but quickly completed his thought, then stood and turned his attention to the two officers standing before him.

"Captain Wilkins," Kitchener began, as he stepped forward and offered his hand. It seemed to Wilkins that time and politics had worn the great commander down. The infamous "Kitchener of Khartoum," the General known for his defense of the British Empire's territories in India and Africa, was now an old man. "Let me congratulate you, Captain, on the fine work you did in uncovering that plot in Dublin. It was a fine piece of work, really."

"Thank you, Sir," Wilkins replied, as he shook Kitchener's hand enthusiastically. Kitchener's grip was firm, and he wouldn't let go.

"Thanks to you, we were able to end the whole affair before it had a chance to catch on in the general populace, and without diverting our attention or our soldiers away from the real fighting at the front lines."

"I am very gratified to hear it, Sir. I fear that will not be the end of the matter in Ireland, however."

"As you say, yes, but it was damned improper of the Germans, to my way of thinking. War is evil enough without dragging civilians into it or trying to provoke rebellions and civil unrest and so forth. Your father and I don't see eye to eye in that regard; Lord Bartlett and I spoke on this very subject quite recently. But you and I are soldiers, are we not? We know where battles should be fought, eh?"

"Indeed, Sir," Wilkins replied.

"Do you know Duke Boris Zakrevsky from Petrograd," Kitchener said, turning to the gentleman who was still seated and releasing Wilkins' hand at last.

"No, I have not had the pleasure, Sir."

"Captain Wilkins," said the Duke, rising from his chair, "it is an honor." His Russian accent was so thick it was most difficult to understand him. "You look quite young to be a Captain, are you not?"

"Perhaps, sir, but I like to believe I have earned my rank."

"No doubt you have, no doubt," the Duke replied courteously.

"The Duke will be traveling with me to Russia in a few weeks," Kitchener said.

"Russia?" Wilkins repeated.

"Yes," Zakrevsky said, "we are looking to heat up the war in Galicia to take a little pressure off the French at Verdun."

"I'm certain that would be most appreciated, of course," Wilkins replied. "Are you in the Russian army yourself?"

"No, no," Zakrevsky replied modestly, "I am merely a politician, or, truthfully, even less than that, the advisor to a politician."

"Allow me to introduce -" Wilkins began, turning to Gresham, but Kitchener cut him off: "I need to see for myself what is going on over in Russia," Kitchener said. "We keep hearing about the strikes among the munitions and railway workers. My God! What does that rabble think they are doing? Do they think they'll fare any better if the Kaiser marches on Petrograd or Moscow? It isn't likely, I tell you. Prime Minister Asquith has asked me to look into the situation there personally."

For Wilkins, the irony of having recently pretended to be a Russian revolutionary was enough to bring a grin to his face. Fortunately, Kitchener mistook his expression as a sign of Wilkins' concurrence with his sentiments about Russia.

"Do you hold the same opinion of the situation in Russia, Duke Zakrevsky?" Wilkins asked.

"There is civil unrest, to be certain, but it is easily managed. It is only the war."

"Of course," Wilkins replied. He was actually becoming quite irritated. Firstly, he was very surprised to hear that the illustrious Secretary of State for War was being sent on such a mundane expedition to Russia when he surely should be strategizing with the War Committee in London. True, Kitchener had been held partly responsible for the inadequate supply of munitions on the Western Front early in the war and had also received his share of blame for the tragedy at Gallipoli, but he was still a vastly popular public figure and a great administrator of the rapidly-growing British army. With conscription soon to be imposed, the Army would be growing even more monstrous. Secondly, and more importantly, Wilkins was irritated that Kitchener had so far overlooked, indeed had pointedly ignored, his colleague David Gresham.

"Have you been to Russia recently, Captain Wilkins?" The Duke asked.

"No, sir, I have not been for many years," he replied. "How about you, David; have you been to Russia?" Wilkins asked awkwardly, trying to include Gresham in the conversation.

"No," Gresham answered simply, since, in his experience, it was often preferable to be overlooked.

Kitchener stepped over to Gresham, who was standing at ease and not smiling. "You must be the other fellow I was told about," he said in a cool even tone. "Captain Grimkins, is it?"

Gresham looked at Kitchener a moment. Did the old man not know his name or was he being purposefully thickheaded? "Yes, Sir," he replied simply.

"You're the one who sank the *AUD* or *Libau* or whatever it was called, is that right?"

"Yes, Sir, I did."

"Why?" Kitchener demanded sternly.

"The German sailors were preparing to fire machine guns and mortars onto *Bluebell*, Sir, and make off with a significant cache of arms and munitions bound for the Irish rebellion. I considered it my duty to stop them, Sir."

"And so you scuttled a perfectly serviceable thousand-ton cargo ship," Kitchener asked with remarkable coldness.

"Yes, Sir," Gresham said calmly.

"Where are you from, Grimkins?"

"Manchester, Sir. Cheetham Hill. You must know it," he said with some cheek. Kitchener had surely never been to that part of Manchester.

"Cheetham Hill? Where is that? Can't say that I've been there, no."

"I know it," Zakrevsky said, focusing his steely eyes on Gresham. "It's all factories up that way, isn't it? A very rough area, I believe."

"That's right," Gresham said, returning the Russian's cold gaze.

Kitchener smiled. "Well, my boy, that's just how I like my soldiers to be – rough and ready, eh? We're fighting to win this war, aren't we? Have you been on the front lines, Captain?"

"Yes, Sir, at both Ypres and Suvla Bay."

"Terrible what happened on the peninsula."

"Yes, Sir."

"I tell you boys, between the Dardanelles and Gallipoli and our failed attack on Baghdad last November, we may yet see a total collapse of British prestige in the Orient. It would be an utter catastrophe for the Empire and all the more reason we had damn well better get credit for relieving the French at Verdun, wouldn't you say?"

"Yes, Sir," Gresham repeated.

"Nevertheless, you should not have scuttled that ship," Kitchener added. The admonition was more than Wilkins could bear

"If I may say so, Sir," Wilkins interjected, "I know the Captain quite well and if there is any finer officer in the British Army, I haven't met him. From what he has told me of the circumstances on the *AUD*, I am quite certain he did what was both prudent and strictly necessary."

"Well, well, of course I am not going to second guess you now, but I have made my position clear." said Kitchener. "And your opinion is duly noted, as well, Captain Wilkins. However, I didn't bring you boys over to talk about Ireland. You are here so that I can give you new orders personally. I want you boys in France. Now is the time that your efforts are most critical to our success there. I would like you to report directly to General Haig and to no one else. Am I understood?"

Wilkins and Gresham looked at each other in exasperation. "Well, Sir, to be frank, … may the Captain and I speak with you privately regarding this matter?" Wilkins asked, eyeing the Russian Duke.

"I know what you would say, Captain, and there is no need. I know damn well who supersedes whom. You are to report to Haig for further instructions. Those are your orders."

"Very well, Sir," Wilkins sighed.

Gresham cast a glance at Duke Zakrevsky, who seemed greatly amused by the entire conversation.

"Thank you, gentlemen, and good luck to you both," Kitchener said dismissively. He shook Wilkins and Gresham both by the hand and waved them out.

Wilkins walked out of earshot before the tirade of expletives burst from his mouth. "Why the bloody Hell are we being sent to work for General Haig?" He asked as Gresham followed calmly down the passageway.

"It seems we've been press-ganged into the Army again, James. Since we are both still Captains in the British Army, we had better follow orders and let the Service figure it out. At least we're not likely to be sent to the front lines if we're working for Haig – he's the bloody Commander-in-Chief of the B.E.F., after all."

"I suppose you're right," Wilkins agreed glumly.

"Come then, would you rather we be sent to hunt for German spies in Canada?"

Wilkins laughed: "Dear God, no!"

"Then let's be thankful we're going to France and to dry, motionless land."

Amiens

It was a sunny morning in Amiens, but the lingering night air was cool and moist. Gresham stepped out of the charming and comfortable but inaptly named *Hôtel Ruin* to visit the café around the corner for his usual hot breakfast. He was relieved to see that the café, with its black lacquer woodwork and plate glass windows was intact, but then there had not been a successful German bombing run over Amiens in more than a week, not since Trenchard's Flying Corps had moved up behind Rawlinson's Fourth Army. Still, Amiens had been bombarded several times recently and the town was littered with brick, stone, dust and ash. Gresham and Wilkins had been in Amiens nearly two months, watching carefully as more and more troops moved up to the front lines, as well as support units, artillery, medical units, and now the aviators. It could only mean one thing: The British Army was preparing a massive offensive.

Everyone knew that a great battle was coming, yet another great battle far away was the main topic of conversation, one of the largest naval battles of all time, one involving over 250 combat ships, in the North Sea. Spirits had been running high among the British soldiers ever since the Royal Navy's "victory" over Imperial Germany in the engagement off Jutland at the end of May. Although the British lost many men and fourteen ships (including HMS *Invincible*, which broke in two and sank in ninety seconds with all but six of her crew aboard), the German ships had crawled back to their ports exhausted and mostly ruined. Great Britain now dominated the North Sea, and the merciless hunt for the dreaded German U-boats would soon ensure that the Allies' blockade of Germany was impregnable. Not even the Americans, who until now had made a fortune selling food and supplies to Germany as well as Great Britain and France, would challenge the blockade now.

Accounts of the great naval battle at Jutland spread quickly among the hundreds of thousands of British soldiers marching into the Picardy region of France. Every field and village north and south of the Somme River, between Amiens and Albert, to the east, where the British were currently entrenched opposite the German lines, was overflowing with weaponry and troops. New communications and reserve trenches were being excavated, and observation balloons and aeroplanes were mapping the enemy's defenses. As the fighting continued at Verdun and the French Army struggled bitterly to maintain its defense against the massive German onslaught, the Allies agreed that something had to be done. Russian General Alexsei Brusilov had commenced a summer offensive in the Galicia region, on the border between Hungary and Ukraine, to occupy the Germans and Austrians on the Eastern Front, but the Allied counterattack at the Somme River was the next phase. The great "Somme Offensive" would begin any day.

"Pierre!" Gresham called out as he sat at the chipped marble café table away from the many other British officers (and the plate glass front windows), and lit his first cigarette of the day. A tall, unshaven older man with long, lanky white hair, blue eyes, and a filthy apron entered from the kitchen, carrying a tray of fresh, warm bread.

"*Bonjour, Monsieur,*" he said in a growly voice, as he placed the tray on an empty table. He brought coffee and pastry to Gresham – the same thing the young man had every day. The fresh warm roll and thick black coffee each morning was an agreeable replacement for the weak tea and stale biscuits the troops were getting in the trenches. Many of the British troops were marching twenty or thirty miles each day on little more than a few hard biscuits.

Pierre was accustomed to the British officers simply pointing at what they wanted, and indeed Gresham, like many of the newly-arrived officers, spoke no French. After his frustrating days on the *Libau*, however, Gresham had finally come to accept that his difficulty learning languages would have to be overcome. In Amiens, given the surplus of time, Wilkins had begun to teach him to speak German. Still, Gresham knew enough French to thank Pierre for the bread and hot black coffee: "Mercy, Pierre."

Gresham ate and began reading his stack of correspondence. That was pretty much all he and Wilkins had been doing since they arrived in France. General Sir Douglas Haig, commander of the British Expeditionary Force in France, had never actually met with them. Instead, they had been sent to the military intelligence office in Montreuil where they were placed under the command of Cecil Cameron, known to some by the codename "Evelyn." He in turn had assigned Gresham and Wilkins each to a network of secret agents operating in German-occupied France and Belgium, and their task was to receive and analyze the correspondence from these agents. Based on the information they received, they were expected to coordinate responsive military action, if appropriate. This proved to be far less exciting than they expected. If Gresham was to learn that a German munitions train was headed to the front lines, for example, he would ride out to the Flying Corps and see if he could convince someone to fly over and drop a few bombs on it. Of course, the letters sometimes took many days to arrive and the information was often so stale that the target might never be found. It was precisely the sort of activity that Compton Mackenzie, the man who had recruited Gresham into the S.I.S., had said was standard for British intelligence, but it left both Gresham and Wilkins feeling restrained; they were accustomed to being in the field themselves and reacting when information warranted.

Gresham, however, was becoming extremely anxious that a number of his agents had gone missing. He and Wilkins were coming to believe that someone on the German side was doing a very effective job of capturing the Belgian and

French agents who reported to British intelligence, and there were even reports, perhaps only propaganda spread by the Germans, of an elaborate torture chamber where captured spies were interrogated by a demonic woman doctor. In several of the letters Gresham and Wilkins had recently received, their agents demanded to know whether the rumors about the "Fräulein Doktor" were true.

"David, do you know where Bill has gone?" Wilkins asked, as he strode furiously into the café. "Bill" was Wilkins' batman, a Lance-Corporal that had been assigned as his soldier-servant.

"I haven't seen him," Gresham replied, raising his eyes from a particularly old and useless letter. "Can't you do without a servant for one morning, James?"

"It's his profession and his duty, and he isn't very good at it."

"He really ought to be in the lines, James, or at least digging trenches with the other men. Besides, aren't you going out to the trench phone this morning?"

"Yes, I am. I need to find a signalman. We've had trouble with the telephone, and someone has to look at it." Before they arrived in France, someone had laid wires connecting a small church in the village of Acheux, currently on the British side of the front lines, with a small church in the village of Miraumont, which was on the German side. Each end had been equipped with a telephone, and one of Wilkins' agents was able to make reports to him over that telephone each week, or at least would do so until the wires or the agent were eventually discovered.

"*Que voulez-vous pour le petit déjeuner, Monsieur?*" Pierre asked as he approached Wilkins.

"*Une autre belle journée ensoleillée, n'est-ce pas? Thé, pain et confiture, s'il vous plait. Merci, Pierre.*"

"I'll go with you," Gresham said. "Nothing else to do today. We'll bring some wine and speak German. That should entertain the Tommys."

"Lord no, David, they'll shoot at us. You don't suppose the battle will start today, do you?" Wilkins asked wistfully.

"Artillery first, and there will be a lot of it, I would think. Several days at least." It was typical for the British to open an offensive with days and days of artillery bombardment of the enemy trenches, not that it would make any great difference. The Germans were expecting a massive artillery barrage from the British, and Gresham's agents had reported a great deal of digging on the German side of the lines – the "Huns" were readying their bunkers for the approaching storm.

"Say, Davis," Wilkins called to another British officer who was sitting near the café door, "I don't suppose we could borrow a couple of mounts from you today?"

"What, again?" The doughy and poorly dressed Lieutenant complained. "That's the second time this week, Captain."

"Would you prefer I not say 'please'?"

"Aww, come on then, they're the officers' horses, you know."

"Tell me, Davis, how accurate is our artillery nowadays?" Gresham asked. "When the barrage begins, will you be hitting specific targets or just laying a rug over old Fritz?"

"Why, that would depend entirely on what orders we are given, Sir, but I dare say General Haig prefers the scattershot method. He's not got what you'd call a delicate touch there, no respect for accuracy. Now, I don't want to brag, but if we had a good map and a decent spotter, and I'm talking about there being little or no wind, o' course, I'd wager we could accurately hit a specific building from twelve kilometers away on the second try."

"That's damn good, but not that Haig would care, as you say. And how do the horses fit into that, Davis?" Gresham asked.

"Yes, yes, alright, Gresham. I know you intelligence fellows are supposed to have 'em if you want 'em. Just come over when you're ready."

After breakfast, Gresham and Wilkins went to the officer's paddocks and borrowed two small draught horses from the artillery company. As they rode up the road towards Albert, it became warmer and a fine breeze blew away the morning mist. It was a lovely June day, and the poppies were beginning to bloom here and there where the ground had not been trampled, burnt or exploded by the passing war.

"The last time I was up this way," Gresham observed, "back at the start of the war, all I saw was winter and a bit of spring. Not to mention that I was in the reserve trenches or the front lines most of the time. This is much more pleasant."

The enlisted soldiers, "Tommys" or "Tommy Atkins" they were called, were enjoying the warm weather too. Many men were out of uniform, some were undressed and bathing in streams and ponds, some played football, and many were sitting out in the sunshine enjoying Tommy's favorite activity – picking "cooties" from the seams of his khaki uniform. Occasional shrapnel shells from the German artillery were entirely ignored as the men went about their work – mostly digging new trenches and dugouts or laying communications wires.

The road northeast to Albert was bustling with men and equipment moving up for the "Big Push." Huge fifteen inch guns were pulled slowly by steam tractors, followed by "four point five" batteries pulled by teams of six horses and "nine point two" howitzers pulled by engines with caterpillar tracks whose name plates proudly stated "Made in U.S.A." Gresham thought if someone put a bullet-proof shell over one of those engines, it could be driven straight across No Man's Land and right through the German lines.

Tommy, well-rested but covered with the fine white dust ubiquitous on the French roads, marched casually in lines four across – he relished the opportunity to chat with his mates, many of whom came from his own hometown, and to forget the tremendous ordeal awaiting him. He wore his wide-brimmed steel shrapnel helmet and his "Christmas tree" (the webbed straps to which were attached his gas respirator, water bottle, haversack, bayonet, spare ammunition clips and sundries) and carried a twenty kilo pack and Lee-Enfield rifle. Wilkins was struck by the great variety of men – they were all British men, certainly, but they were British men from England, Ireland, Scotland and Wales, Canada, Australia and New Zealand. There were dark-skinned British men from Africa and Egypt and others from India and the West Indies. The sight of the men evoked the vastness of the British Empire, and Wilkins felt a surge of pride in his great nation.

Most of the troops had been engaged in civilian trades before the war. In their ranks were every class and condition of man – miners, factory hands, clerks, shopboys, dock labourers, ploughmen, shepherds, college graduates and petty criminals, barristers and barbers, men from the wildest places of the earth who had faced danger each day and men whose chief adventures had been a Sunday stroll to church. They had collectively transformed the ghastly business of war into an everyday sort of work, sloughing off the need for hysterics or tremors or excitement of any kind. After two years of war, these well-tempered men from all four corners of the British Empire marched together as equals, and the more Wilkins saw of them, the more he came to believe in their fundamental decency and fairness.

"Say, Gov'ner," one young Corporal called up to Gresham, "any idea who's up ahead?"

"Fritz is up there, I'm pretty sure," he replied.

"No, I mean, are they Prussians, Bavarians or Saxons?"

"I don't know. Does it make a difference?"

"Oh, why, o' course it makes a difference, Sir," Tommy replied. "If it's Prussians, you've got to keep your napper below the parapet and bloody well out o' sight. It's bang-bang all the time and a war is on. If it's Bavarians, well, they're not much better really, but the Saxons, they're pretty good sports and behave as gentlemen, not that you can trust any of 'em overlong."

"I'm sure that Fritz is just as unhappy when the Scots are in our trenches," Wilkins said. "Where are you from, Corporal?"

"Yorkshire, Sir; Wakefield."

"Been out here long?"

"Came over with the first expeditionary forces back in '14, Sir, back when we all still thought we'd be home for a happy Christmas. I've had two Christmas dinners in the lines since then, and the way things are looking, I'm liable to have another couple before I see my wife again, that is, if Fritz doesn't drop a 'whizz-bang' on my head and send me back to 'Blighty'."

"At least now we can send back five shells for every one that Fritz sends our way," Gresham told the Corporal. "In the beginning, we had to take everything he sent over without reply, and he'd send twenty for every one of ours, you must recall."

"Lord, that's right. And the trenches, Sir, they were only five feet deep at best. You couldn't even stand upright. There was one we called the 'Suicide Ditch' 'cause Fritz had it taped to an inch, and when he opened fire, every man in that trench would come out on stretchers, if he'd come out at all, the bloody *boche*. The first time King George came up to the lines, our Colonel had us finally fill in that trench just in case His Majesty decided he wanted to poke 'is head in that particular one."

"So you've seen the King yourself?" Wilkins asked.

"Blimey, Sir, I've shaken the man's hand twice already."

"I see," Wilkins said, laughing. As a boy, he had traveled throughout Europe with his mother and been formally presented to select kings and queens. Each meeting had seemed a momentous occasion. Now Tommy Atkins could shake hands with George, the King of the United Kingdom of Great Britain and Ireland and Emperor of India, whenever the old fellow stopped by for tea and crumpets.

"Where is your Company headed now?" Gresham asked.

"Somewhere up by Fricourt, Sir. We'll be in the reserve trenches, until things heat up, that is."

"Well, good luck to you, Corporal. We're headed north from here," Wilkins said.

"Good luck to you both, Sirs," said Tommy, waving his hand to the departing officers. Wilkins and Gresham cut north across the shell-pocked fields before they reached Albert. In the skies to the north, two Fokker Eindecker fighter aeroplanes flew into view. They were approaching a line of the sausage-shaped observation balloons the British were using to map the enemy defenses. Suddenly, from the clouds above, a squadron of "Archies" dove down on the Germans. The "Allemands" turned quickly about to make their escape as the Archies fired down upon them. One of the Germans was trailing black smoke as it flew out of sight.

At Warloy, Gresham and Wilkins found the village was almost completely destroyed – not by recent shelling but from shelling perhaps a year or more earlier. The surrounding area was still littered with rubble, long dead horses, one badly burned aeroplane fuselage and more than a few unburied or half-buried human corpses whose skeletal appearance it was wisest to ignore. It was astonishing what artillery could do to the human body. By a grove of badly mangled fruit trees nearby, there were brown canvass huts erected for a British company. Many of the soldiers were drinking a bit of wine and chasing the "cooties" from their pants and shirts. Gresham and Wilkins dismounted and approached the huts, stopping along the way to speak with a Rifleman.

"Where can we find the commanding officer," Gresham asked.

"Isn't one anymore, Sir," the Rifleman replied, without a proper salute to his superior officers.

"He was killed, you mean?"

"Tha's what I mean, yeah."

"But who is your ranking officer?" Wilkins asked.

"There aren't any officers 'ere 'cept Ronald an' he's just visitin'," the man said, badly slurring his words.

"Well, where can we find him?" Wilkins demanded.

"Who? Ronald? He's o'er there," he said, pointing and then walking away without even a by-your-leave.

Gresham and Wilkins walked past the group of men who raised their wine bottles in greeting to the two officers. The officers saluted back, and then poked their head into a large hut pitched beside a badly burned apple tree. The hut was quite a mess inside, and one man, a Second Lieutenant, well-dressed with very fine brown hair and a neat mustache, sat at a table working on a dismantled trench phone. When he saw the officers, he stood quickly and came to attention.

"Good morning," the officer said guardedly.

"Good morning to you," Wilkins said cheerily. "The way you say it, I'm not sure whether you're happy to see us or not. I am Captain Wilkins; this is Captain Gresham. We're with the military intelligence office. Are you this fellow Ronald we were told about?"

"Yes, Sir. I am Second Lieutenant Ronald Tolkien."

"We're told you are the only officer here at the moment, is that right?"

"I am, yes, Sir, and I'm only here to repair the telephone. G.H.Q. is sending over a new batch of officers later today."

"You're a signalman, is that right?" Wilkins asked.

"Yes, I am, Sir."

"I need your help. Gather your equipment and come with us. We'll have you back in a couple of hours, I should think."

"But the men, Sir, I can't very well say what they'll do if there are no officers present."

"We won't be long," Wilkins assured him. "It'll be an adventure."

The young signalman hurriedly packed his rucksack and followed Gresham and Wilkins out of the tent. Since there was no third horse, the officers walked and led their mounts as the three men wandered through the rubble and found the road leading north. They walked quickly and in silence a while through the battered field, but the signalman seemed anxious. At last he asked: "May I know where we are going, Sir? We're not going to the front lines, are we?"

"Acheux," Wilkins said.

"God bless you," Gresham said. Wilkins shot him a dark look.

"You've just reminded me, I have forgotten my handkerchief," the signalman said.

"We're going to the village called Acheux. How long have you been in France, Ronald?" Gresham asked.

"Two weeks, Sir, and I've only just come down from Étaples today."

"And before the war?"

"Exeter College."

"Do they study telephones at Exeter?" Gresham asked.

"No, Sir, I just completed my degree in English language and literature this past March."

"Good Lord, you're a damned poet, aren't you?" Gresham exclaimed in feigned wrath.

Wilkins, who enjoyed a good poem from time to time, quickly changed the subject. "I'm having trouble with a trench phone, and I pray you can fix it," he said. "It's a huge secret, of course, so you mustn't tell anyone."

"Of course, Sir."

The little church on the outskirts of the village of Acheux, where the telephone was located, was in very poor condition. The building had been struck by several high explosive shells and mostly demolished, but its undercroft – really just a large storage cellar – was intact although very damp and dark, and that was where the telephone was located. The signalman quickly examined it and cleaned the contacts – the wires themselves were deeply buried and could not be repaired if that was where the trouble lay.

"Well it's almost time for my man to call," Wilkins said. "Let's just wait and we'll see if it's working." Gresham was at last able to bring out the bottles of wine and the bread and cheese he had brought along, and the three men sat down to drink. The signalman, it turned out, was indeed a poet of sorts and had just finished reciting a fanciful poem about Great Britain called *The Lonely Isle* when Wilkins was required to attend to the trench phone. He spoke to his agent for several minutes before returning to the party. "The connection was much better; thank you, Ronald. The report was all about Gommecourt this time," he said to Gresham. "Quite a lot of activity up that way – German troops moving in, new artillery, trench digging and all. That's the Third Army's territory, General Allenby's men."

"Shall we ride up and take a look?" Gresham asked.

"Certainly, but I would like to get back to Amiens in time for supper."

"You are getting terribly spoiled, James," Gresham said. "Ronald, would you care to join us?"

"You mean go to the front lines, Sir?"

"That's right."

"Thank you, but I shall see them soon enough, Sir. I must return to my Company."

After their farewells, the Second Lieutenant began his short walk back to Warloy as Gresham and Wilkins rode further north, soon reaching the woods of Hébuterne just to the south of Gommecourt. Again they found the burnt fields and forests crowded with British troops and artillery. Some men seemed to be doing nothing more than marching about in plain view of the German lines. Others were laying railroad track and telephone wires, while others were constructing roads. From a slight rise, Gresham and Wilkins could see the British trenches somewhat to the east, then four hundred yards or so of No Man's Land, and the German-held ruins of Gommecourt beyond. As far as the eye could see, mile upon mile, the ground was brown and grey; there was not a tree or bush or any green thing remaining. Instead, the ground was pockmarked with shell holes and littered with pieces of metal, corpses, and barbed wire. It was fairly quiet at the moment, but Gresham and Wilkins could sense that the area was tensed for battle. They approached the nearest encampment and quickly located the senior officer present, a tall, trim and serious fellow, Captain Henry Bassett of the 16th London Regiment, the Queen's Westminster Rifles.

"Henry, tell us what is going on up here? You seem to be putting on quite a show for the Huns," Gresham said, after he and Wilkins were seated in Bassett's airy hut with a glass of raw red wine.

"Surprising, I know," he said. "Our orders from Lieutenant-General Snow are to convince the Huns that our main attack will fall up here at Gommecourt, so we're trying to let them see our preparations. We have the men parading each day in great circles so it looks as though a steady stream of men is entering the area, and all this construction we're doing is to make it appear that Hébuterne is intended to be our new command center."

"Your diversion is working," Wilkins said. "We've just had word from one of our agents on the other side that Fritz is moving three Divisions to the area and an array of artillery – at least twenty of the heavy howitzers, the twenty-one centimeter *Mörsers*. It looks as if you fellows are in for plenty of the old whizz-bang. There are also new trenches and artillery dugouts. Have you a map? I can show you where."

"That would be most helpful. The Germans are constantly attacking our observation balloons and our maps are getting a bit stale, worthless really when it comes to making the attack itself."

"You don't mean to say you'll *actually* be attacking where the Huns are expecting it, do you?" Gresham asked, appalled. It was one thing to put on a diversionary show, but to then throw the men into battle where the Germans most expected it was suicidal.

"It seems we will, yes. And I know, you needn't say it." Bassett said, visibly distraught: His regiment would be destroyed, a blood sacrifice for the sake of the Fourth Army's main attack to the south. "It's all part of Haig's plan, you see. He simply insists that the main attack break through to open ground. He's even brought up the bloody cavalry, if you can believe it. But how he imagines that the Huns won't *also* be expecting an attack on their lines down by Albert, where our men and supplies have been amassing for weeks, is beyond me. The very idea of a diversion is absurd. Our Division is simply being thrown away."

"Rawlinson and Allenby agreed to this?" Gresham asked.

"Allenby has, but I believe Rawlinson is being difficult. He doesn't want one great break-through; he wants to continuously take little bites of the German lines here and there and gradually force the enemy back."

"A far more pragmatic approach, I'd agree," Wilkins said. "The very idea that we will break through the German lines adequately to allow a cavalry charge is simply preposterous. I sincerely doubt those men will ever see battle at all."

"But, as I understand you, your Division *is supposed* to take Gommecourt, is that right?" Gresham asked.

"Yes, once the artillery barrage ends and the German lines have been destroyed, we're to pack our kits and walk across to occupy the enemy lines."

"Diversion or not, it would be awfully nice to take the town," Wilkins said encouragingly. "But, I must ask, have you done this before, Henry?"

"Well," he hesitated, "no, not personally."

"It's just that, well, everything they tell you about the barbed wires being destroyed and the enemy being killed by the barrage," Wilkins said, "it's simply not true. You're to cross four hundred yards with no cover, and those trenches will be full of German soldiers long before your men make it across."

"And you say you're to 'walk across' as if all the Huns will be dead?" Gresham asked in astonishment.

"That's correct," Bassett said.

Gresham shook his head. "Then for God's sake, don't walk," he said. "When the time comes, Henry, tell your men to drop their packs, raise their rifles and run like Hell across that ground."

"You'll take that village, Henry." Wilkins added. "I just hope you'll be able to keep it."

That evening, Gresham and Wilkins returned to Amiens tired and hungry. Pierre had prepared an excellent meal for them of foraged foodstuffs: Fire roasted squab with wild leeks and mushrooms and a rich sauce made of red wine, butter and herbs. Wilkins was wondering where the squab had come from when Pierre came to their table holding a small, rolled note.

"*Pardon, Monsieur, mais, j'ai trouvé cette message. Il a été attaché pour le pigeonneau.*"

Wilkins snatched the note from Pierre's hand and spit out his mouthful of meat onto the floor. "*Tu veux dire que ce sont des pigeons voyageurs?*" He asked, incredulous. Gresham stopped chewing and waited to find out what was going on.

"*Oui, mai*" Pierre said defensively, "*J'ai acheter dans une ferme.*"

"These aren't squab, David. They're ordinary homing pigeons. One of them still had this damned note attached to its leg when Pierre brought it to the kitchen," Wilkins said, waving the note in Gresham's face.

"Tasty, though," Gresham said, continuing his meal undisturbed.

"*Lisez le message, monsieur,*" Pierre insisted anxiously.

Wilkins unrolled the message and looked it over. Inside, the note described in detail the movements of several British Divisions, the number, type and placement of many British artillery pieces, the location of ammunition stores, the exact location of Trenchard's Flying Corps, and more. It was obviously a message written by a spy – a German spy.

"Where did you get this?!" Wilkins demanded, as he leapt from his seat and grabbed Pierre by his jacket lapels. "*Où est-ce que vous avez obtenu ces oiseaux?! Dites-moi!*"

Pierre's reply was drowned out by the sudden eruption of a thousand canons: The massive British artillery barrage had begun. Two thousand guns firing ceaselessly upon fifteen miles of the German front lines. Hour after hour, the Tommys could hear the guns firing and the more distant 'booms' as the shells rained down on the Germans huddling in their trenches, dugouts and deep underground bunkers. Before long, the sky darkened perceptibly from the smoke, ash, and dust thrown into the air by the explosives. From high ground looking east, all one could see was a wall of darkness. The barrage continued day after day.

The little farm where Pierre had purchased the homing pigeons lay to the southwest of Amiens. Even miles from the front lines, the rumble of the British artillery barrage echoed across the fields as Wilkins and Gresham walked up to the farm's gate. The farm house itself was small and humble and the verge was terribly overgrown. There had clearly been significant damage done over the past two years as battle had raged over this countryside. The two officers walked up to the house, and, in the doorway, a small, thin, and very old peasant woman looked out at them, afraid.

"Good morning, Madame. *Parley vous* any English?" Wilkins asked.

"Some," she said coldly.

"Pierre sent us from town to see if you have any more pigeons for sale. We enjoyed them so much that we offered to fetch another kit."

The old woman stepped down gingerly to the dirt in front of her house. "No," she said. "No, they are the birds of my son. I only sell the ones who are dead already.'

"But if he has more birds, perhaps some he might sell alive if the price were right. May we speak with your son?"

"He is not here now. I do not know when he will return."

"You expect him, today?"

"I do not know. He will not sell you any birds."

"Surely it will do no harm to ask."

"He will not sell the birds, I say. Tell Pierre we have no more. Go now," the old lady insisted, then entered her little house and slammed the door.

"What an unfriendly person," Gresham said. He and Wilkins turned and returned to the road, walked a while, and then sat beneath a copse of oak trees from which they could surveil the farm house.

"Damn," Wilkins said as he read through a new letter from one of his agents, "here's another fellow who says one of his contacts has gone missing. It's that damned woman *Doktor* again. My fellow's afraid he will be given up and wants to come across."

"Does he imagine we have a secret tunnel somewhere?"

"How many agents have you lost?"

"Six since the start of the month," Gresham said.

"I've lost three. Do you think there's any truth to the rumors about the torture chamber, the crazy woman doctor, and all that?" Wilkins asked.

"Perhaps. It's bad either way as long as our people believe it. I'm not eager to go back to Evelyn to tell him I've lost all my agents."

The day wore on and the sun rose in the dusty sky. The officer's grew accustomed to the crash and boom of the British barrage. The artillery continued into the night, the flash of the explosions so frequent that the sky never fully darkened. No one knew how long the huge guns would go on firing, but everyone knew it would eventually end, and then the British soldiers would have to rise up from their trenches and attack whatever was left of the German lines. After dusk, as the barrage continued, Gresham and Wilkins decided to take turns watching the farm house.

The next afternoon, when Gresham returned to the copse of trees to relieve Wilkins, he could see in the distance that a dark blue *Peugeot* sedan was sitting in front of the little farm house.

"Who is it?" Gresham asked.

"You won't believe it," Wilkins said, smiling as he put down his field glasses. "Your timing is perfect. The sedan has only been here a short while. One man, probably armed. I think we had better take him now."

"After you," Gresham said, loading a bullet into the firing chamber of his Browning M1911 .45-caliber handgun.

The officers walked casually down the road towards the farm. They avoided the gate, and Wilkins approached the front of the house while Gresham went around the side. Suddenly a shot rang out from the house, and Wilkins dove to the ground, scrambling to take cover behind a burnt tree trunk. Gresham crouched down and continued to the back of the house.

"It's no use!" Wilkins called to the house. "We don't want to shoot you! Come on out now!"

The occupant of the house responded with more shots, none of which had any chance of hitting Wilkins behind the tree. Wilkins fired his handgun into the air both to tell the occupant that he was armed and to keep his attention. Gresham reached the back of the little house and peeked in through a window. The old woman was huddled in a corner, clearly terrified. There was one man with a pistol near the front door who was focused on Wilkins in front of the house. As Wilkins continued firing harmlessly in the air, Gresham pushed open the small window and took aim.

"My gun is pointed at your back," he yelled. "Drop your weapon!"

The man pivoted and shot at the window. The glass burst and shards fell harmlessly around Gresham.

"Look, I'm going to have to shoot you and your mother too if you don't stop it!" Gresham yelled.

There was a long moment of silence, and then Gresham heard the man's pistol hit the wood floor and the front door open. He looked in the window and saw the man standing outside the front door, his hands empty and raised above his head.

"Please, don't harm my mother," the man yelled. "She has done nothing!"

Wilkins saw that the man in the front was unarmed and quickly seized the spy and threw him to the ground as Gresham rushed to the front of the house. As Wilkins pointed his handgun at the prone little man, Gresham finally saw who it was: A short, thin, middle-aged Frenchman with straight, coal black hair and spectacles, the very man who earlier that year had kidnapped Gresham and

Wilkins off their train to Verdun, who held them overnight in a locked room in Nancy, who directed the brutal interrogation of Gresham about his mission in Greece, and who disappeared when Wilkins had come to the rescue.

"What a wonderful surprise to see you again," Gresham said maliciously.

"I said you wouldn't believe it," Wilkins told him, laughing, as he walked up.

"Is the old lady really your mother?" Gresham asked.

"Yes, she is," the little Frenchman said anxiously. "Please leave her in peace and I will tell you what you want. Please, she is not involved."

Gresham strode into the house and grabbed the old lady from the corner where she was still huddled, terrified. She screamed and began to cry as Gresham dragged her outdoors and she screamed again as Gresham held his handgun to her head.

"Please, please, don't hurt her," the Frenchman begged piteously.

"Then tell me, now, who is the 'Fräulein Doktor'?"

The little Frenchman laughed hysterically. "You saw her! Yes! Yes! You saw her, don't you remember? She was with me in Nancy. Please, let my mother go," he begged.

Gresham suddenly recalled the tall austere woman in boots and a dark leather trench coat that stood smoking impatiently while the little Frenchman's brutish henchman pounded Gresham's head and ribs. She had looked so cold and detached as she watched Gresham being beaten.

"So you work for her," Gresham realized.

"Yes, yes, exactly," the Frenchman cried.

"Where can we find her now?"

"She is in Bapaume, on the other side of the lines."

"Ah, of course, and that is where your homing pigeons fly?"

"Yes," he admitted.

"Does she ever come over to our side?"

"Not anymore."

"Then we will need to bait her. Where do you keep your pigeons?"

The next morning at 07.20, the British artillery barrage reached a crescendo with a massive explosion. A forty-thousand-pound mine beneath the German line at Hawthorne Ridge, three miles north and east of Albert, was detonated by the British Royal Engineers. A massive geyser of earth and corpses shot hundreds of feet into the air. Then other mines, months in the preparation, erupted, two to the east of Albert near La Boiselle, and seven more to the south near Tambour and Mametz. The roar of the explosions washed over the battlefields and announced to the British and German soldiers alike that the Allied infantry attack was imminent. At 07.30, the British artillery stopped firing and the world became silent again as the troops on both sides steeled themselves for the long-anticipated attack. More minutes passed as the Tommys awaited the signal, time enough for the Germans to climb from their bunkers and return to their guns. Then finally the whistles blew and the British soldiers went over the top. By the tens of thousands, thirteen Divisions in all, across the entire fifteen mile front from Gommecourt to the Somme River, the men advanced into No Man's Land. In some cases, lightly covered trenches called "saps" had been prepared to allow the Tommys to advance into the middle of the wasteland before drawing the fire of the German machine gunners. In other places, men rushed and crawled from cover to cover as the Germans clambered from their deep underground bunkers to defend their lines. In too many places, the men did as they had been told and simply marched calmly across No Man's Land and straight into the enemy's line of fire.

North of the road that connected Albert with the German-occupied town of Bapaume, the British fought all day with virtually no penetration into the German lines, with one notable exception. At Gommecourt, elements of the 56th Division (the Queens Westminster Rifles) immediately dropped their packs and rushed the enemy's trenches as soon as the barrage stopped, before the whistles were even blown; they handily seized the German trenches with few casualties, but the Division, unsupported and unreinforced, was forced back before the end of the day. At Serre, Beaumont Hamel and Ovillers, thousands of British soldiers were killed and no progress was made at all. At Thiepval, the British rushed uphill into enemy fire, took the German trenches, and resisted two counterattacks. They still held the Germans' first line at the end of the day. South of the Albert-to-Bapaume road, the Allies had more success, especially the eleven French Divisions south of the Somme River, and at Mametz and Montauban, where the British made modest gains despite massive casualties. Everywhere, the British encountered far stiffer resistance than General Haig had anticipated. The Germans were too well prepared, and the massive British artillery barrage had not destroyed enough of the Kaiser's defenses nor penetrated his dugouts nor emptied his trenches nor killed enough of his men. The British had not used enough high explosive shells to penetrate the Germans' deep, concrete dugouts, and nearly a third of the American-made shells the British used failed to explode at all. Still, the Tommys rushed forward toward the German lines as they were told. There would be no breakthrough, no cavalry charges, and no victory. Some 60,000 British and French soldiers and 12,000 Germans were killed or wounded that first day of July alone, and the battle would continue day after day after day until the end of the year.

To the north of Gommecourt, in a quiet sector of the British lines, lay the small village of Foncquevillers. Like most villages near the front lines, every building had been damaged or destroyed by the war. The elegant *Château de La Haye* was in ruins. Even the solid and stately church of *Notre Dame*, built in 1605, had been destroyed by German artillery in early 1915. The fields, pockmarked and muddy from repeated barrages, were now crisscrossed by barbed wire and trenches. The 37th Division, under the command of General Lord Edward Gleichen, was entrenched at the front lines there, and many of his men, mostly from the Midlands of England, were both relieved and regretted that they had been excluded from the great battle at Albert to the south. Gleichen, an experienced and ambitious General, maintained his headquarters with the British medical division at the *Château de Couin* five miles to the west, and it was there, on a hot and humid July day, in his sunny and comfortable library, that Wilkins and Gresham found him sulking.

"Thank you for meeting with us, General," Wilkins said.

"Nice to see you again, James; how long has it been? Two years, at least, it must be; since before the war."

"Yes, you're right, it was at Lady Feodora's art reception, I believe. How is your sister?"

"Very well, thank you, but there are regrettably few artistic commissions during times of war. She is rather bored."

"Sure to be plenty of work after the war, though. Father sends his regards, of course."

"How is Lord Bartlett?"

"Very well and very busy, thank you, as you must surely be yourself."

"Well, well, quite the contrary; not busy at all. It's dead quiet in this sector, and I can tell you it's a deep disappointment to me and the men that we were not included in the attack, not even the attack on Gommecourt."

"So I understand, Sir, and I am sorry to hear it. May I introduce to you my colleague, Captain David Gresham."

"My pleasure, Captain," said the General. "Please be seated, and tell me what I can do for you, James."

"Thank you," Wilkins said, as he and Gresham sat on the fine French chairs. "Well, General, I have heard from others of your deep disappointment at having been left out of the offensive to the south. I take it from what you have said that you wish to commit your men to battle?"

"Certainly, but Haig and I haven't always seen eye-to-eye, and I fear he has seen fit to brush me aside."

"That is very unfortunate, yes," Wilkins said. "As I indicated in my note, General, Captain Gresham and I are currently with the military intelligence office, and it came to our attention that your Division was in reserve in a relatively quiet sector of the front. We'd like to help you solve that 'problem.' To be blunt, we would like to borrow your men."

"Borrow my men? Whatever for?" The General laughed with good humor.

"There is an extremely dangerous and sadistic enemy intelligence agent that we absolutely must capture. Our network of intelligence agents is being decimated, and our ability to gather information has been severely compromised. It's not just that our men are being captured, General; those who are captured are also being severely interrogated, some have reportedly been mutilated, cut apart, and that has dissuaded others from assisting our side."

"Outrageous! This is appalling, gentlemen! Have the Germans no sense of decency?"

"We've recently had a bit of luck and captured the agent's accomplice here on our side of the lines, and with our persuasion he has arranged for us to have a *rendezvous* with the agent at a nearby farmhouse tomorrow morning."

"So you will capture him there. Very good. I would be happy to loan you some soldiers to help you take him into custody," the General said. Wilkins and Gresham had decided not to mention that the enemy agent was actually a woman.

"Well, there's more to it than that, sir," Wilkins continued. "You see, that farmhouse is three kilometers east of Foncquevillers – in *German* territory. So, in brief, we would like your men to break through the German lines long enough for us to capture the enemy agent."

Gleichen stared at them in shocked silence.

"Why, I believe you are quite serious, James," the General said in amazement. "Break through the lines? I've received no such orders; there is no fighting in this sector. It is simply impossible."

"You do indeed have general orders to cooperate with the intelligence office, General, and Captain Gresham and I are willing to lead the attack personally. We know how to do it. It is a risky gambit, I admit, but there can be little doubt that the Germans are not expecting an attack this far north, especially with the fighting at Gommecourt now abated. And we do not think our entire attack will last more than two hours," Wilkins said.

"Our plan is to punch a hole in the German lines with a creeping artillery barrage, then hold the trenches just long enough for two companies to reach the farmhouse," Gresham said. "You have 'saps' that run up to within *thirty yards* of the German front lines. Two Brigades can hold open the gap in the lines while the two companies race to the farmhouse and back. We do not believe the farm will be hotly defended. And, lastly, we can make it appear as though the Germans attacked you first."

"Very clever," the General said. "So you would deceive our superiors into thinking your little expedition is a 'defensive' action. And how do you know this German agent you're seeking won't bolt to safety as soon as the shooting begins? Why don't we just bomb the farm house and kill everyone in it?"

"The farmhouse is fairly isolated," Wilkins explained, "so our artillery will be able to cut off any retreat with a box barrage. We expect that when the shrapnel begins to fall, everyone in the house will simply take cover and wait out the storm."

"And we must take this agent alive if it is possible," Gresham added. "We must be able to damage the enemy's intelligence network as fully as they have damaged ours."

"I understand," Gleichen said seriously, "but still ...." He stood and walked slowly to the table which held his bottles of liquor. "I've known your family a good, long time, James, and we've been very great friends." He paused and considered the matter, then turned back. "It *has* been too damned quiet up here." With an avaricious grin, he concluded: "I give you my permission, gentlemen. You may proceed with your attack."

It was a quiet, warm and overcast morning in Foncquevillers. The birds were singing cheerily, although the sound of the ongoing battle miles to the south, beyond the Albert-Bapaume Road, could still be heard faintly. "Stafford Avenue" was a narrow, winding communications trench that ran up to the British front lines just north of the village. It was overflowing with men of the 110th Infantry Brigade, all standing very quietly and at ease, holding their rifles and bayonets, grenades, and ammunition, and nothing else. At the head of the trench, standing in the front line with the light infantry, David Gresham smoked a Woodbine as he waited for the signal. From the firing step, peering over the top, he could see the quiet German lines about three hundred yards to the east.

James Wilkins stood in the same British trench, but he was one hundred yards to the north at the head of another communications trench known as "Rotten Row" (named after the fashionable track in Hyde Park). Both in the Row and around Wilkins there stood a long line of men from the 111th Infantry Brigade, also prepared for battle. The men, in fact, seemed unusually chipper. Wilkins joked and chatted with the men as he checked his wrist watch, and then he raised a small red flag and waved it at the men around him.

The soldiers immediately began to toss grenades casually over the top into No Man's Land, dozens of them. Soon the mud, wire, and debris in front of the trench erupted, showering the men harmlessly with dirt. As the mock "barrage" continued, Wilkins picked up the trench phone: "By god, we're being shelled by the Germans!" He yelled. "For pity's sake, return fire!" A moment later, the long range guns of the 37th Division artillery opened fire. The shrapnel shells of the long range guns screamed overhead and, instead of falling on the German lines, disappeared several kilometers to the east.

"Hold on, fellows. Wait for the show to begin," Wilkins called out. "You'll get your chance at last!"

After a minute, British high explosive shells also began to fall like a curtain on a two hundred meter wide section of No Man's Land in front of the German front lines and on the barbed wire before it.

"Come on now, follow me!" Wilkins called to the men, as he entered one of the saps that ran close up to the German lines.

"Aren't we walking straight into our own artillery fire, Sir?" A worried young infantryman asked.

"We must trust our bombardiers to take their best aim," Wilkins replied, "but the closer we get to the German lines, the less chance old Fritz will have to fire back at us. You'll see."

Gresham led his Brigade into the saps as well. The men could only proceed in double file, but when the dam broke, the men would pour out upon the Germans. At the end of each of the saps, the men could feel the ground around them shaking as the high explosives burst on the wires in front of the German lines, and then the shells began to creep back slowly until they were falling like a curtain directly onto the first line trench itself. The surprised German soldiers ran for cover as the two British brigades waited and prayed that the artillerymen would keep their aim true. Gresham and Wilkins were silently counting each shell. When they reached two hundred, the barrage on the German trenches abruptly stopped.

The two officers burst from the head of the narrow saps followed by hundreds of men who immediately spread out into small groups and charged through No Man's Land at the German lines. Each group had designated wire cutters for where the barbed wires might remain intact, and the smoke and dust of the barrage obscured their approach. They rushed silently and quickly to get to the first German trench, knowing that once they had infiltrated the enemy's lines, the efficient German artillery would no longer be able to fire upon them. In a few places, the German soldiers regained their defensive positions quickly, well before Gresham's and Wilkins' men reached the front line, but still the enemy had few distinct targets in the silent smoke and dust upon which to fire. Some of the British attackers were forced to seek cover in shell holes, but far more reached the German outposts and cut viciously into the defenders, leaping down into the trenches, shooting the enemy even as they climbed out of their dugouts or ran to their posts. Using their rifles and grenades, Gresham and Wilkins led their men through the maze of trenches to silence the German machine guns.

"Where's my dynamite," Gresham yelled to the men behind him.

"Coming up behind me, Sir," said a small Corporal. Two very white-faced privates then ran up with rucksacks full of explosives.

"These are for the dugouts," Gresham said, as his distributed the sticks of dynamite to his troops. Soon the explosives and more grenades were being used to clear out each of the German dugouts and bunkers, and many of the survivors were shot as they tried to escape from the onrushing British advance. In the chaos of the sudden assault, few Germans attempted to surrender, but the few who did were collected in one deep bunker and placed under guard. Gresham and Wilkins then ordered their men to file back into the German trenches towards the rear to clear out any final defenders.

They next quickly created two strong defensive lines, one to the north and one to south of the one hundred yard breach they had made in the middle of the German lines using the enemy's own machine guns and mortars and a few Lewis guns that had been brought up. The enemy, realizing that their defensive line was badly breached, scrambled to move their machine guns about to enfilade the British invaders. But the Tommys were no longer attacking outwards – they were keeping low in the best defensive positions they could find. As the British men kept their heads down, the Germans to the north and south were soon firing across the breach upon each other.

Wilkins and Gresham led their men deeper and deeper into the German defenses, soon reaching the second line and the reserve lines as more men from the two British Brigades poured into the trenches behind them to reinforce the two defensive lines.

"Alpha Company, gather round!" Wilkins shouted, gathering his light infantrymen. Once collected, the men charged with Wilkins from the reserve trenches up onto solid ground and into the fields beyond, startling companies of German soldiers who believed they were safely behind the front lines and wondered what all the firing was about. To the south, they could hear the roar of Gresham's "Beta" Company as they charged into the German's forward artillery positions. Both light infantry companies advanced at a full run, firing their rifles only as needed to silence the artillery and clear the path before them.

Within minutes, they could see a small, heavily damaged farmhouse ahead. Wilkins approached from the north-west, Gresham from the south-west. All around and behind the house, shrapnel shells from the British artillery burst without ceasing – the box barrage from the 37th Division artillery. Anyone inside the house would be staying inside in supposed safety, but as the British light infantry came within range, a handful of German soldiers inside the farmhouse opened fire. In the muddy, smoke-filed fields, Gresham's and Wilkins' men crawled closer and closer, ignoring any risk posed by the falling shrapnel shells ahead of them. Suddenly a British shell mistakenly hit the house itself, and the roof was torn apart. The house caught fire.

"We've got to move now!" Gresham yelled to his men. Over the din of the shelling he stood and rushed to the side of the house followed by his men, while Wilkins and his Company continued their suppressing fire.

Wilkins led his men around toward the front of the house as the shooting from inside quickly intensified.

"Get down, Sir," a large, ploughman of a soldier yelled as he leapt up to pull Wilkins out of the line of fire. Suddenly the man twisted as a bullet hit his shoulder, spraying Wilkins's face with blood. The soldier fell with a grunt and dragged Wilkins down on top of him. Wilkins rolled off and quickly examined the man's shoulder which was drenched in blood.

"Oh s--t, damn it all," the soldier moaned. "I'm going to lose the arm, aren't I?" He asked Wilkins.

"No, no, absolutely not, Private. It's not that bad, really," Wilkins said to man encouragingly. "Cheer up – it's sure to get you sent home to Blighty."

"F--- Blighty. I'm not one of your damned Brits; I'm from f---ing Ontario."

"Canada?" Wilkins asked. He looked down at the huge bloody mess that was once the man's shoulder. Another Private pressed a wad of cotton bandages down onto the wound to staunch the flow of blood. "Well, I'm sure you'll be just fine, anyway," Wilkins said.

"Just doing my duty," he replied with a slight sneer.

Gresham reached the side of the house, then the window. The roof was fully aflame, and the shooting from the house itself had petered out. He climbed to the window and saw the floor was littered with dead and injured men. A tall, elegant-looking woman lay among them, and Gresham recognized her at once. As he smashed the window and climbed over the sill into the burning house, the woman lurched up and fired a pistol directly at him. Gresham heard the bullet whistle past his head, and then he lunged at her, knocking her hand on the floorboards and forcing the pistol from her grip. She kicked and screamed and scrambled, but Gresham seized her tightly by the throat.

"I've got you, you bloody bitch," he growled and yanked her up viciously from the floor by her neck. He brutally cast her out the window just as the burning roof began to collapse into the house. Then Gresham climbed out after her.

His men had already bound the woman tightly and one giant Sergeant hoisted her over his shoulder once Gresham made it safely out of the shattered window. Wilkins' Company led the way back to the German trenches, taking a route different from the one they had come and decimating the still astonished German troops in their path. Soon they were back in the German trenches where their northern and southern defensive lines continued to hold back the shocked German troops. Wilkins stopped to launch a signal flare, and as the incendiary climbed into the sky, the British artillery opened fire again, this time accurately placing their shells on the German positions to both the north and south of the British-held breach. Shrapnel fell like rain on the German troops. The two British Brigades began to quickly retreat back toward No Man's Land and into the safety of the saps even as the Germans to the north and south of the breach crouched down for cover. The German prisoners, who had been stripped of their weapons, were abandoned and the door to their bunker blocked with debris.

The British Brigades that had flowed into the German lines like a tidal wave now rapidly receded. Gresham was the last man out of the German trenches. He ignited another flare, and the British artillery switched to high explosive shells to cover the retreat. The German lines exploded, sending the German survivors deeper into their bunkers. The brutal pounding continued for ten minutes until the last of the British soldiers had retreated fully to their own outposts. Then the firing abruptly stopped. The fields grew deathly silent, covered with smoke and dust.

The raid at Foncquevillers was over exactly seventy-eight minutes after it had begun.

Gresham and Wilkins had issued orders that the enemy agent, the *"Fräulein Doktor"* whom they had risked so much to capture, be taken immediately to General Gleichen's *Château*, but she never arrived. As Gresham's men tied her, struggling and cursing, to a stretcher in the back of a medical lorry, two anonymous British intelligence agents quietly and quickly took command of the vehicle and drove her away. Gresham and Wilkins returned to Gleichen's headquarters only to learn that the enemy agent had been taken away by other British agents. The General in a state of extreme mental disturbance. As the two officers entered the mansion tired, dirty, and spattered with blood, the General rushed out to meet them.

"Gentlemen, yes, yes, extraordinary! I give you my heartfelt congratulations; it was an amazing show. However, it seems we have, perhaps, stirred the pot a bit too much. I've just finished speaking to a party sent down by General Haig, and it was made clear to me that *heads will roll.*"

"You told them that your men were attacked first, as we planned, yes?" Wilkins asked.

"Yes, yes, of course, not that anyone would believe it, but I told them."

"And the agent, she has been taken away?" Gresham asked anxiously.

"They have her, somewhere, but I fear it will go worse for you than for her. Haig knows I didn't dream up this scheme on my own."

Gresham led the two men into the library and promptly poured himself a tall glass of whisky. "All I can say is, it was worth it. Any old sod could do the work James and I have been doing. That woman, however . . . you don't know where she was taken, you say?"

"They wouldn't tell me," Gleichen said sadly. "You two are to stay here until they call for you. I'm to place you under arrest, if necessary."

"Well it's not," Wilkins said. "I'm going to have Bill prepare me a bath and afterwards I think a good dinner and some cards are in order. We'll simply have to see how this all shakes out."

The next morning, Gresham and Wilkins were summoned to General Sir Douglas Haig's headquarters. A sedan was sent to fetch them from General Gleichen's *Château* without delay. An armed guard sat beside them in the sedan and refused to speak a word.

Gresham and Wilkins were brought into Haig's headquarters near Montreuil and led by the armed guard downstairs to a dark, quiet corridor.

"Do you think we're going to be imprisoned?" Wilkins asked his friend.

"Very possibly," Gresham replied glumly.

A door was opened, and the two officers were directed at gun point into a small office. An officer sat behind a desk, gazing at them coldly as they entered the room. He was a tall, stout, clean shaven gentleman with short, grey hair, a square jaw and an aquiline nose. He wore a vaguely naval uniform and a monocle over his right eye. His hands were folded neatly atop an ominously empty desk. Gresham and Wilkins stood before the imposing man silently, waiting for the sword to fall.

"Let's see," the man signed in a deep, commanding voice. "You are 'O'-one-one," he said, pointing accusingly at Wilkins with one thick, ruddy finger.

"Yes, Sir," Wilkins said, surprised and alarmed that the man knew his confidential S.I.S. code number.

"You are "Double 'O'-six," the man said, looking at Gresham.

"Yes, that's right, Sir," Gresham replied, equally alarmed.

"Sit down," the officer commanded coldly.

Gresham and Wilkins sat as quietly and carefully as possible.

"I have been led to understand that you two men, on your own initiative, took command of Gleichen's Division, ordered up artillery, led an unauthorized incursion by seven thousand British soldiers into the German lines and penetrated three kilometers deep into enemy territory. You then seized one solitary enemy agent and retreated with her to the British lines. Is that correct?"

"Yes, yes, Sir," Wilkins and Gresham both admitted sheepishly.

"I have been told that well over one thousand German soldiers were killed or wounded in your little raid. There were twenty-two British casualties, none killed."

"My God, that's fantastic!" Wilkins said, beaming.

"That's not bad at all, I must say," Gresham agreed, turning to Wilkins with an uncharacteristic grin.

"I told you the flares would work, didn't I," Wilkins replied.

"The creeping barrage was my idea," Gresham boasted.

"Gentlemen, please, this is not the appropriate time or place to celebrate," the man continued tersely. "You have no idea how much trouble you are in."

"Trouble?!" Gresham asked incredulously.

"We have not had the opportunity to meet before now, Mister Gresham, Mister Wilkins, and it is long overdue. My name is Cumming, or "C". I am the man whom you know as *Control*. I am your commanding officer." He suddenly had Gresham's and Wilkins' complete attention. "You two have been extremely troublesome of late."

"But the raid was a smashing success, Sir," Wilkins insisted.

"Your raid is a terrible embarrassment to General Haig and he has every right to be furious!" *Control* said angrily. "But I am not talking about that. All mention of your raid is now classified 'Top Secret' and you may never speak of it again. *Never*. But before that, you did something far, far worse: You allowed yourselves to be commandeered by Kitchener," *Control* said menacingly.

Wilkins and Gresham were both confused.

"But, but, Sir," Wilkins said, "he is the Secretary for War, Sir, and he gave us a direct order."

"He *was* the Secretary for War, that is true, but now he is dead. HMS *Hampshire* sank in heavy seas near the Scapa Flow on the way to Russia and Kitchener was one of the casualties; we are still investigating what happened there."

"The Earl is dead?" Wilkins asked in shock.

"Do not be so saddened, Mister Wilkins. Even before he was a corporeal casualty, Kitchener was a political casualty. He was being sent to Russia to silence him so the War Committee could get on with its business in peace. Obviously, Kitchener thought commandeering a couple of my agents would do him some good politically. It did not. Now he is dead."

"I can't believe it," Wilkins said is genuine shock.

"What about that other fellow that was with him, that nasty Russian Duke?" Gresham asked. "I hope he's dead too."

Control looked at Gresham coldly a moment, then pulled a small notebook from his jacket. "I don't know, Mister Gresham. In any event, we must ensure that you are not commandeered again," *Control* said as he wrote a quick note. "Listen to me carefully: You two are responsible only to me and to the Prime Minister. If you receive an order that does not come directly from one of us, you may choose to disregard it entirely. Is that *quite* clear?" He said emphatically.

"Yes, Sir," the officers responded.

"To assist you fellows in that regard, I will have you both immediately raised to the rank of Colonel. Generals get far too much publicity, but anything below the rank of Colonel leaves you at the whim of too many others. You simply *must* retain your independence, gentlemen. Am I making myself perfectly clear?"

"Colonel?" Wilkins asked in surprise. "You're making me a Colonel, right now, just like that?"

"Yes, that's correct," *Control* replied calmly.

"Thank you very much, Sir," Wilkins gushed; it was all he could muster.

Gresham had previously been raised to the rank of Captain at the snap of Compton Mackenzie's fingers. However, he had since come to realize that his rank was entirely unimportant. Still, he was relieved to know that he and Wilkins weren't going to be sent to prison.

"I have your captive, of course; she's a nasty little creature, I must say – she likes to dissect people while they're still alive, it seems. She has become extremely cooperative in the past few hours, and it turns out she was well worth the risks associated with your, shall we say, labors, as she has a great deal of information to share with us. There is one name she has mentioned several times. Tell me, have either of you run across a man named 'Dunn'?"

"Dunn?" Wilkins recalled. "Roger Casement mentioned someone named Dunn, a German – no, a Boer, I think he said – but working for the Germans, for someone named Zimmerman. Who is Zimmerman, by the way?"

"Zimmerman is the Undersecretary in the German Foreign Office," *Control* said. "He is in line to become the next State Secretary for Foreign Affairs in Germany – a very important position, as you can surmise."

"Casement said that Dunn's mission is to support or incite rebellion in our colonies; he's an *agent provocateur*, an anarchist. Casement met him in Germany and greatly distrusted the man."

Control made another note in his little book. "Here's what I need you boys to do for me. Obviously, I want you to keep doing whatever you've been doing

– the two of you are among my most effective agents and I applaud the way you seize the initiative. Do *not* tell anyone I said so. Certainly you must keep an eye out for this man Dunn and if you find him put an end to him. But there is a most important mission I need you to complete at once: You must go to Roumania and do whatever is necessary to get that country into this war before the end of the summer, on our side of course."

"Roumania?" Gresham asked in astonishment. "Roumania doesn't bring anything to the Allied war effort, Sir. Its armed forces are far too small and ill-equipped, and the country is bordered by two of our enemies, Austria and Bulgaria. It will be like Serbia all over again."

"You are probably correct," *Control* replied. "But frankly I don't give a damn. We don't expect Roumania to win any battles, even if you must convince them that they can. I don't care if the whole bloody country is occupied by Austrian and German soldiers. It would take a great many men to occupy the whole of Roumania, and those are men who won't be able to fight us in France. We also need Roumania to offset the loss of Bulgaria. Its entrance into the war will influence other countries and provide us with at least a modest negotiating toehold in the Balkans after the fighting is done. And it will bolster the Russians, about whom we are now extremely concerned. So you can tell the Roumanian government anything you like, you can make any promises you can conceive – land, munitions, money – I don't care what you promise them, but we must have Roumania in this war before the end of the summer. Whether they succeed or fail is entirely unimportant."

"Yes, Sir," Gresham said.

"I suggest you travel via Italy. You can meet our man '*H*' in Venice and find out whether he knows anything about Dunn or if the man has been seen in Italy. We *cannot* let anything shake the Italian resolve, gentlemen. You should be able to obtain transportation to Roumania from Salonika."

"Not another aeroplane, I hope," Wilkins said quietly.

"Gentlemen, my secretary has your briefing materials, currency, code sheets, and so forth. Remember, absolutely no one is *ever* to hear about your raid at Foncquevillers. That is all, I think. You had best leave before Haig knows you are here." *Control* said as he stood stiffly and extended his hand. "Good luck to you, Colonel Wilkins, and to you, Colonel Gresham."

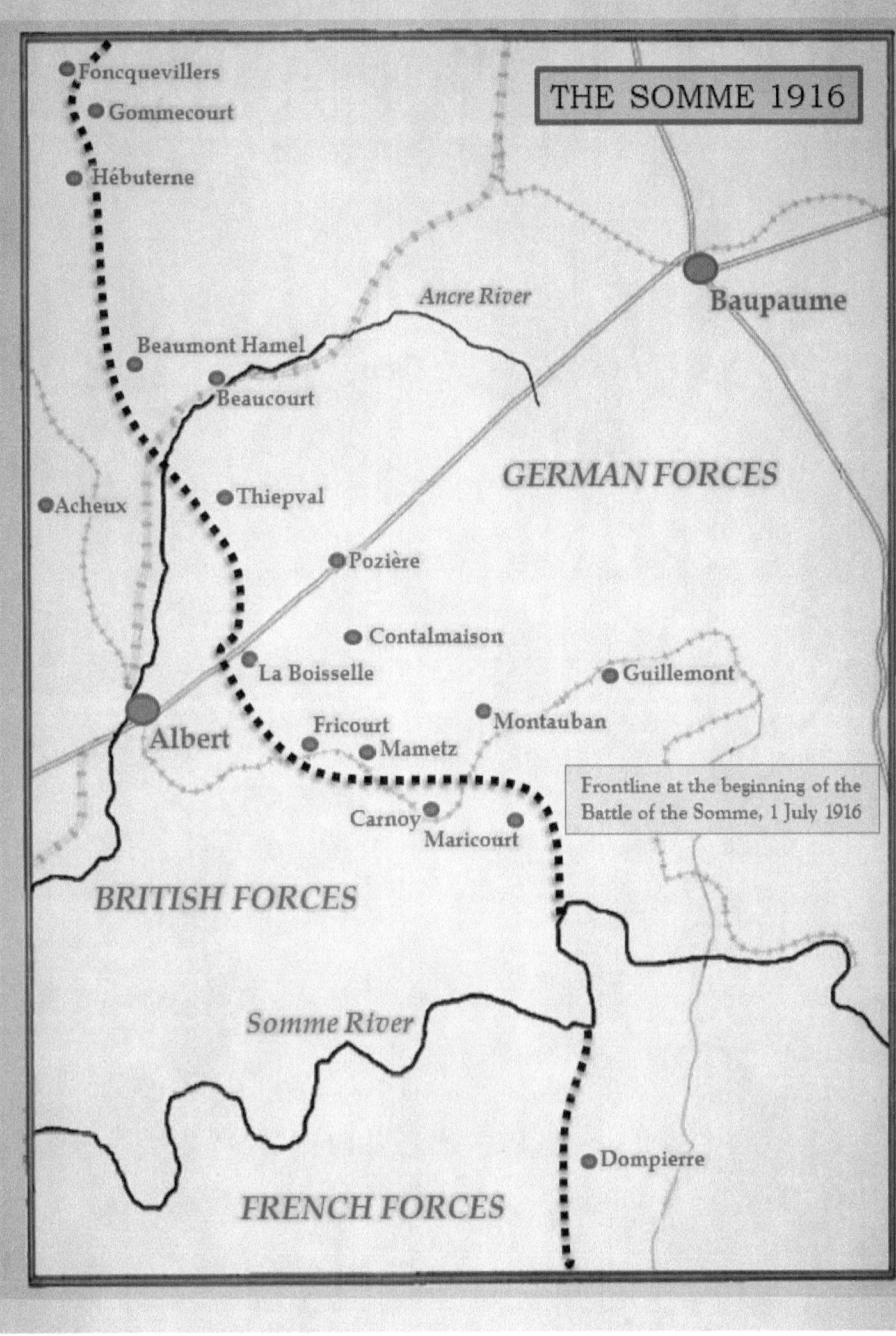

THE SOMME 1916

Foncquevillers
Gommecourt
Hébuterne
Ancre River
Baupaume
Beaumont Hamel
Beaucourt
GERMAN FORCES
Acheux
Thiepval
Pozière
Contalmaison
La Boisselle
Guillemont
Albert
Fricourt
Montauban
Mametz
Carnoy
Maricourt
Frontline at the beginning of the
Battle of the Somme, 1 July 1916
BRITISH FORCES
Somme River
Dompierre
FRENCH FORCES

Venice

The sun was rising over the *Rialto* as Gresham and Wilkins, rested and dressed in plain wool suits rather than their newly-tailored and as-yet-unworn Colonel uniforms, exited the *Santa Lucia* train station in Venice. The city was unusually quiet and seemingly empty – one could even hear the water lapping on the sides of the canal. While many residents had ignored the government's mandatory evacuation order and remained in the city (Venice was officially in the war zone), they tended to stay quietly in their homes or at work. The fighting was still many miles away, to the east of Udine in the Gorizia plain and to the north in the mountainous Trentino region. While there were no longer many successful bombing raids by the Austrian "*Taubes,*" at least not since the great French aviator André Beaumont had come to Italy with his squadron, still the churches and palaces of Venice, which had been carefully protected with sandbags and the priceless stained glass windows removed (even from the Doge's Palace) and the great works of art all safely stored away, were mostly empty.

Gresham and Wilkins had taken the overnight train from Paris since *Control* desired to remove the two men from General Haig's jurisdiction as quickly as possible. They had passed the border from France into Italy at Modane even as the fighting at the Somme continued day by day and the "Top Secret" raid at Foncquevillers became the subject of whispers and recriminations throughout France. Haig's staunch defense of antiquated methods of attack had made him the target of severe criticisms and his command of the British Expeditionary Force was in jeopardy. The new methods displayed at Foncquevillers (and elsewhere) were clearly the future of trench warfare. Before they left France, Gresham and Wilkins had even been shown the newest British super-weapon – a heavily armoured vehicle with caterpillar tracks for traversing rough terrain like that found typically in No Man's Land. That vehicle was the massive British Mark I "tank," and it was certain to revolutionize ground attacks for it would drive straight through the enemy's lines destroying or crushing everything its path.

But Venice, quiet empty Venice, seemed many worlds away from France, or perhaps what the world would be like after the great nations had finished exterminating each other once and for all. Gresham and Wilkins commandeered an empty gondola and made their way down the quiet Grand Canal, past the mostly empty St. Mark's Square, to the *Danieli Hotel*, where they were to meet "H," the man in charge of British intelligence in the Adriatic region.

Arriving at last inside the magnificent gilded lobby of the *Danieli*, Gresham and Wilkins were surprised to find it bustling with people – Italian, French, British, Russian and even Japanese officers and civilians, mostly men, were starting their day managing the war in Italy. Gresham and Wilkins registered at the front desk under false names and ordered coffee in the lounge while they waited to meet their contact, a man whom they knew only by his initial letter.

"Pardon my interruption," said a distinguished, clean shaven British gentleman walking past, "have either of you the time?"

"Mine has stopped, I'm afraid," Wilkins said.

"You should have it repaired. I know a man in the *Dorsoduro*, but he's quite dear."

"It's a family heirloom. Is he trustworthy?"

"Of course," the gentleman said and then sat. "I was waiting and saw you fellows come in. *Benvenuti a Venezia*. I hope you had a pleasant journey. My name is Sam."

"Thank you, sir. I'm James," said Wilkins, "and this is David. It's a pleasure to meet you."

"The honor's all mine; I've just been hearing about your wonderful raid at Foncquevillers – and from *Il Generale* Cadorna of all people, the commander of the Italian armies. That should tell you something about our ability to keep secrets. It was very well done, I must say."

"Thank you, Sir," Wilkins said sheepishly.

"Shall we continue our discussion with a bit more privacy? I have some rather good stuff upstairs."

"That sounds fine," said Gresham.

Once in the *H*'s small but comfortable suite, Gresham promptly removed his jacket as Wilkins poured the whisky. *H* sat on the love seat and crossed his legs as he lit a cigarette and offered them around.

"Why is the city so quiet?" Gresham asked. "It seems like the end of days around here."

"Well, this whole region is part of the war zone, you see," *H* said. "The authorities have cleared out all the civilians that would leave voluntarily. The Italians are fighting on two fronts, and there's a constant need to move troops from one to the other, depending on where General Cadorna and the Austrians decide to go at it next. The reserve forces are encamped throughout the villages north of Venice, among the few remaining civilians. I must tell you, Cadorna has some wonderful men, the *Bersaglieri* they're called, who can jump onto their motorbikes and rush from one battle to another in a matter of minutes. You simply must see them to believe it."

"Has it been very busy, then?" Wilkins asked.

"Oh yes indeed. The Austrians launched their spring offensive in the Trentino in May; the Italians counter-attacked in June, and then Austria responded with gas – terrible casualties, as I'm sure you've heard. It took a bit of the wind out of Cadorna's sails to be certain and the Prime Minister was thrown out of office. But now Cadorna's summer offensive in Gorizia has just begun. It's all coordinated, you see – the Somme, Galicia, Gorizia, and Salonika. We're attacking on every front at once."

"Will it do any good, do you think?" Gresham asked skeptically.

"We've been at war nearly two years already, and the current strategy I suppose is to see who can last the longest."

"And how long will that take?" Wilkins asked skeptically.

"No one knows," *H* replied with a shrug.

"How is the King?" Wilkins asked.

"Victor Emanuel? Yes, he comes to the front lines quite often. Charming little fellow, terribly short, you know. He's staying in Udine right now, not far from Gorizia. Italy is a constitutional monarchy so the King has very little power, but Victor Emanuel plays the part for show very well – out in all weather, cheering his men, rallying the troops on the front lines, and so forth. They adore him."

"Was it the King who decided that Italy should quit its alliance with Germany and Austria and join the Entente?" Wilkins asked.

"No, no, that was all Salandra's doing, the former Prime Minister. It was Salandra who negotiated with the Allies –a land deal, pure and simple. Italy was aligned with the Germany and Austria before the war, but they have been at odds with Austria over territory for years. The Italians are great irredentists – they believe they have the right to own any land on which Italians are residing, and they have been promised a great deal of land for joining our side in the war. Italy is still a very young country and they do not feel they have finished growing yet, I suppose. We shall see when this is all over."

"Is that so very unreasonable?" Gresham asked. "After all, the Serbians want a Southern Slav nation, the Arabs want Arabia, the French want the Alsace-Lorraine, do they not?"

"Ah, yes, and the British want India, Ireland and Egypt, as always." *H* said cryptically. "That is neither here nor there. It was Bismarck who observed: Italy has 'a large appetite and very poor teeth.' Unfortunately true. Now, I'm sorry to tell you I must be off soon. There has been a serious 'accident' on board one of the Italian dreadnoughts, the *Leonard Da Vinci* in the harbor at Taranto, and I must go down for the day to speak with the local officials."

"What sort of accident?" Wilkins asked.

"An explosion. The ship has foundered and it is deemed suspicious."

"Sabotage?" Wilkins asked.

"That seems the most likely explanation. The ship was undergoing repairs, yet the explosive used was Dunnite and the Italians had none aboard."

"That reminds me – have you learned anything new about the sinking of the *Hampshire*?" Gresham asked.

"*Hampshire*? You mean the ship that Kitchener was taking to Russia? No, not that I'm aware." *H* said. "Why do you ask?"

"This new incident simply reminded me of it, that's all."

"I would like to ask you about the matter for which we came to Venice," Wilkins said. "We are meant to learn whether you have any information about a German agent, a man who goes by the name of Dunn. He works for

Zimmerman in the German Foreign Office. Have you made any discoveries along those lines?"

"There are many German agents in Italy, certainly. I know of no one by the name of Dunn but it will take a few days to check. Do you have a description of this man?"

"No, nothing but a name," Wilkins replied.

"The best thing I can do is to send you to meet with a fellow who has been working for us here, an Italian who was formerly aligned with the Socialists. He may know of such a man. Mussolini is his name, Benito Mussolini."

"Is he trustworthy?"

"Not entirely, no. I have arranged to sponsor his newspaper, so he is friendly. We don't tell him what to write, of course, but he regularly denounces members of the Italian government who wish to end the war, a small but helpful bit of *propaganda*. He ought to know if the fellow you want is about anywhere," *H* said.

The next afternoon, Gresham and Wilkins, dressed in expensive black morning coats, vests and top hats, went to meet the Italian agitator Benito Mussolini in the *Ristorante Quadri* adjacent to St. Mark's Square. The usually busy restaurant was extremely quiet due to the evacuation of the city. The yellow and pale green stucco work that framed the pastoral frescoes on the walls made the sunny restaurant seem like picnicking on a serene country hillside. Gresham and Wilkins found one man sitting alone at an empty table covered in white damask, a gentleman with a severely receding hairline, a square jaw and a thin black mustache, whose bulging eyes suggested both intensity and a touch of madness.

"Are you Sam's friend?" Gresham asked, as he and Wilkins approached the table.

"Yes, yes, sit, gentlemen," he said without standing or shaking hands.

"I am Richard Starwell," said Gresham, sitting at the table. "And this is Mister Thomas Short. We want to thank you for coming from Milan to meet with us."

"Your government has been most generous, so of course."

"We are not sure how much Sam told you of our purpose here," Wilkins said. "This is merely a preliminary investigation – our superiors at the Bank of England are quite adamant that we obtain a complete understanding of the current political situation in Italy before any further investments are made in Italy's industrial infrastructure. That includes any threats to the stability of the government of course, and this being a time of war, we know there are many pockets of political dissent."

"Yes, there is always dissent," said Mussolini.

"You are a former leader of the Socialist *PSI*, the *Partito Socialista Italiano*," said Gresham, "is that correct?"

"Yes."

"But you are now the leader of the, the … what do you call it?"

"The *Fasci d'Azione Rivoluzionaria*."

"'*Fasci*'? What does that mean precisely?" Wilkins asked. "What are your political objectives?"

"No, you are not correct. The *Fascisti* are not a political party; we are a populist movement. You see, a '*fascio*' is a league of many strong organizations, be they labour unions, workers collectives, industrial syndicates, banking associations, farming collectives, and so forth. We are a league in which all the constituent organizations are dedicated to the advancement of Italian nationalism, both on the peninsula and abroad, using whatever methods are necessary, both the political and the non-political. We are not concerned with class conflict; we do not distinguish rich or poor, as long as each individual strives to advance Italian nationalism and the pure Italian spirit, and so we exert pressure on both private and public individuals equally."

"*Signore* Mussolini, please excuse my impertinent question, but what do you mean exactly by 'non-political' methods? And what do you mean by 'exert pressure'?" Wilkins demanded.

Mussolini's neck bulged in agitation. "I mean everything, of course, from propaganda and public demonstrations to intimidation and brute force if necessary, as your government well knows," he replied coolly.

"I see," said Wilkins. "So members of your organization physically threaten anyone who opposes your nationalist agenda, is that correct?"

"When necessary."

"And the government tolerates this?"

"There are many in the government who agree with our objectives," Mussolini replied confidently, "but even those who do not have found it difficult to speak against us. We are all Italian, after all."

"But what of your methods, *Signore*? How much of your 'non-political' methodology does the government condone?"

"We are at war and our methods are expedient. How is that your concern?" Mussolini insisted. "Italy is not a British colony. It is the stability of our economy that should interest you, not the methods used by the citizens to improve our government."

"Improve it?" asked Wilkins in disbelief. "And are you still a Socialist, as well? What is your opinion of industry, of Italians being employed to earn their livelihood in factories built on Italian soil? Who shall own those factories? Who shall own the farms – the peasants?"

"I am not a Socialist, no. The Socialists are opposed to the war and are obsessed with class conflict. Many of the *Fascisti* reject *bourgeois* liberalism; some, I admit, are Syndicalists, but none are Socialists. In my opinion, it is enough that the factories are owned by Italians, even when foreign investments of capital are required. However, the Italian economy must be controlled by the strongest and most capable of the Italian people with a view toward optimizing our capabilities. Thanks to the war, the industrialists in the north are now bound to the powerful landowners in the south, and it is they, together, that give purpose and direction to Italy's workers, farmers, and laborers. The war has brought the Italian people together."

"I see," Wilkins said with irritation, as he pretended to jot down a note in a blank notebook he withdrew from his pocket. "Funny," he said, "that not so many years ago, if you had said the word 'Italian', no one would have known to whom you were referring. It has only been fifty years since Garibaldi unified the Italian peninsula under one government."

"A nation is more than a name, *Signore*. It encompasses the history, the sentiments, the traditions, the language, and the culture of a race of people, and Italy's history reaches far into the past, much farther than that of England. You are correct that the unification of Italy as a nation is relatively recent, but this war is the essential process that will temper our nation like steel."

"What I want to know," said Gresham, "is whether there are any German or Austrian agents in Italy working to undermine your existing government. For example, we've heard rumors about an agent of Germany's Foreign Office, a Dutch-South African man, who has been trying to stir up trouble. Have you heard anything about that?"

"You mean the Boer, yes, I have heard of him," said Mussolini. "I have not met him myself, nor am I inclined to."

"So *his* methods are not acceptable to you?" Wilkins asked.

"His methods are absurd! He would set the people against each other like packs of vermin. You must understand – I am not in favor of dissent, not in any form; we must be united to remain strong. The Socialists, however, they are perhaps desperate enough to meet with him, but I cannot say."

"Well, I for one would like to know who he's meeting," said Gresham. "Can we see him?"

Mussolini laughed. "Why? He only wishes to bring about our humiliation! And if he truly is a Boer, then you can be certain he will not want to meet with two British bankers."

"Nevertheless, could you find him for us?" Gresham asked.

"I don't know that he is still in Italy, *Signore*, and I must return to Milan tonight – there is a pacifist rally there tomorrow and we must demonstrate against it. Perhaps you would allow me to give you the names of some of the *PSI* leaders who possibly know this man. That is all I can do for you."

The meeting with Mussolini had angered Wilkins. He did not care for Mussolini or his exploitative populist rhetoric, nor did he care for the radical politics sweeping through Europe in general. Of course he had studied Woodrow Wilson's treatise on government, *The State*, at Eton, and he knew the "Socialists" were intent on stripping power from the nobility and wealthy industrialists and land-owners and empowering the working classes; the more radical ones wanted to nationalize private property and espoused complete equality, even for women! But Wilkins had no idea how the goals of the "Syndicalists" differed; he had never even heard of them. The streets of Venice also irritated him as they walked back toward the *Danieli Hotel*. Venice – the most egalitarian of cities: There were no sedans or horses to be seen anywhere, so everyone, high and low, was required to walk, and as Wilkins and Gresham walked that evening it was getting extremely dark thanks to the strict blackout restrictions. The nights in Venice were black as pitch and it was virtually impossible to travel anywhere without risking a plunge into the canal. Their own footfalls, and those of one or two others following somewhere close behind them, echoed loudly through the dark, empty streets. Gresham was smoking a cigarette, quietly and calmly as ever, and Wilkins found Gresham's silence irritating as well. "Have you no sense of outrage?" he asked.

"If it is any consolation, James," Gresham replied jovially, "I am certain we will be sent back to Italy after the war to assassinate that man."

"That is not a satisfactory answer."

The walk to the hotel was brief, and Wilkins was in no mood to drink. He excused himself and headed to his suite. For his part, Gresham was grateful that he was still able to order a whisky in the dimly lit lounge where a few foreigners were chatting quietly. Unfortunately, he thought, there were no women to be seen anywhere. Out of the corner of his eye, however, Gresham caught sight of a trim young man with short dark hair and sharp features sitting alone in a dark corner. Gresham thought the man looked familiar and intended to introduce himself after his bottle arrived, but a moment later the young man was gone. After quickly finishing his first generous drink, Gresham began to feel distinctly ill at ease. The young man – he seemed too familiar, and Gresham had a bad feeling about it. He rose and walked quickly to the front desk.

"Do you have anyone named 'Dunn' registered at the hotel?" He asked.

"Good evening, *Signore*," replied the large but well-manicured middle-aged clerk. "I will check for you, *un momento per favore*."

As the clerk reviewed the register, Gresham glanced around the elegant lobby. There, exiting by the side door where the gondolas docked, he again spotted the young man from the lounge.

"No, *Signore*," said the clerk, "we have no guest by that name, I am very sorry."

"Thank you," Gresham said as he rushed off to the door. He quickly passed outside and looked around, but the dock was empty as far as Gresham could see into the black night. There were footfalls to the left and right, but to the right there was only an old *gondolier* near the San Marco Canal. Gresham strode quickly to the left, following the footfalls on the dock back into the deep darkness. Unable to see precisely where he was going, he walked into a stone step and nearly butted his head into the wall. He stopped to listen, and the footfalls were still there, slow and deliberate. He followed them around to an alley and then onto the street and deeper into the city. Suddenly ahead, on the left, he saw a door open and briefly spill a little light out onto the street. A trim, tall man seemed to look back at him, and then entered. Gresham ran to the door. He took his handgun from its holster beneath his jacket, loading a round into the chamber. He slowly pulled the door handle, and the thin, narrow door opened slowly on a small dimly lit antechamber. Standing before him was the young man.

"How kind of you to follow so diligently," said the man, whose intense grey-blue eyes bore into Gresham like steel bayonets. "It is a pleasure to see you again, Mister Larkin."

"How do you know my name?!" Gresham asked in shock. Compton Mackenzie, the man who had enlisted him into the intelligence service, knew his true name, the surname his unwed mother had given him, but no one in Italy could possibly have known it. And then he suddenly recognized the man in front of him. "You're Zakrevsky!" Gresham said. "You're the Russian Duke, the man who accompanied Kitchener aboard *Hampshire*!" And then "Zakrevsky" rapidly raised a small pistol and fired twice. At such close range, Gresham felt the full impact of the bullets hitting his chest, burning into his flesh. He returned fire, but his round went wild and then the "Russian" knocked Gresham's gun from his hand. There was shouting from the street and several men were rushing up as Gresham desperately pressed on his chest to keep his blood from seeping out. There was a lot of blood, he thought. He had difficulty breathing, he felt he was drowning and could not quite understand it, and then he collapsed into a sitting position against the door.

"I trust we will not meet again," the "Russian" said as he leapt over Gresham's legs and ran off. Someone on the street was shooting, and someone was rushing up to Gresham from the opposite direction, and then Gresham slumped over, and everything went black.

"There you are, at last," Wilkins said with great relief as he entered the small, white room and found Gresham lying on white sheets in an old, iron hospital bed. "They told me you had awakened at last." Wilkins's pale face and the dark circles around his eyes indicated that he had not slept at all. Gresham, beneath the crisp white bedding, was awake but still weak and foggy from the morphine and confused about what had happened to him.

"You were shot twice," Wilkins said seriously as he sat on the edge of the bed. "Do you remember it?"

Gresham tried to speak. "Just keep your mouth shut, please," Wilkins continued. Gresham nodded.

"Do you remember who did it?"

Gresham nodded again. "Zakrevsky," he whispered.

"That Russian fellow, the one we met on *Hampshire*?" Wilkins asked in astonishment. "Yes, of course, I see! The *Hampshire*, the *Leonardo Da Vinci*, now this. Is he Dunn, do you think?"

Gresham nodded.

"He must have been following *us*. By God, you were lucky, David. The bullets were a small caliber. One embedded in your rib and the other passed into your right lung – that's why you can't speak very well. You lost quite a lot of blood, but you're going to come around just fine, they say. You must rest and regain your strength."

Gresham looked at the very attractive brunette nurse who was standing on the other side of the bed in her crisp white uniform. Her porcelain skin offset her full pink lips and the luxurious chestnut hair, which was only partially hidden beneath her white nurse's cap. He smiled at her. Wilkins rolled his eyes. "That is Nurse Wolczak," he said. "She's been with you the past thirty hours. You've been unconscious a rather long time." Gresham looked back at Wilkins and winked.

"You need to get your rest, Mister Gresham," said the nurse with a distinctly hard American accent, and indeed Gresham drifted off again before she and Wilkins even left the room.

"You should get some sleep as well, Mister Wilkins," the nurse said in the dimly lit hallway. "There's an empty room there, if you want to stay close to your friend; no one will mind."

"Thank you, I will," he said gratefully. Wilkins was exhausted. He had been summoned to the American Red Cross hospital the previous night. Although Gresham's wounds were less serious than anyone could have expected, Wilkins sat and waited more than a day for Gresham to regain his consciousness. Nurse Wolczak, a remarkably bright and compassionate young woman whom he learned had come to Italy from Pittsburgh, Pennsylvania, had been in and out constantly to check on Gresham.

Wilkins went into the dark, empty hospital room and took off his shoes, then curled up on the immaculate white bed, closed his eyes, and fell instantly asleep. But he did not sleep well. He was tired, certainly, but Wilkins did not feel right; he did not feel like himself. It was a year ago, he recalled, that he had been in Egypt preparing for the landing at Suvla Bay – a new Captain in the Manchester Regiment, barely out of Eton, the youngest son of a wealthy and influential Earl. He should be at Oxford now, making trouble, drinking, gambling, and philandering. His future was secure regardless. His own townhouse in Belgravia already awaited him, as well as an enormous annual stipend. His oldest brother would one day take his father's place as the Earl of Bartlett, and his next older brother would soon to be made a Commodore in the His Majesty's Royal Navy. But what would become of James Wilkins? He did not yet know what he even expected of himself. Before the war, he had always envisaged a position somewhere in government since that had been of personal interest and his strongest subject at Eton. But what was James Wilkins fit for now – a killer, a torturer, a "Colonel" who could not wear a uniform, a spy who lied and murdered. He had let his ruthless partner do most of his thinking for him. In Vienna, he had falsely given his word of honor when he assured Princess Zita that he meant her husband the Archduke no harm. He had betrayed Sir Roger Casement, whom he sincerely respected. And now he was collaborating with vicious bastards like that fellow Mussolini.

As he lay wide awake but exhausted on the hard hospital bed in the dark of night and delved down into all the things that troubled him, Wilkins narrowed in on one incident that stung him more than any other. He recalled standing in the sunny, burnt-out field in France as he led a company of men towards a battered and abandoned farmhouse, shrapnel shells bursting like thunder around him, a feeling of recklessness, even elation, pure joy. And then a man, one of his *own* men, leapt up before him and frantically pulled down on Wilkins' jacket as the man's blood sprayed thickly across Wilkins' face. He could recall the salty taste and sickly sweet smell of the man's blood, the man falling, pulling Wilkins off balance and the sensation of dropping foolishly on top of the soldier who had just saved his life, a man he had never spoken to before, a man, it turned out, from Canada. Wilkins was ashamed of his folly, his stupidity, his imprudence to have stood out as an easy target for the German soldiers inside the farmhouse. And then Wilkins had lied to the man who had saved his life: Your arm will be fine, he told the Canadian, although it was obvious that the man's shoulder had utterly disintegrated and the arm would have to be removed. He had never gone to see that man in hospital; he had never thanked him at all; and he did not even know the man's name. Tears welled in his eyes as Wilkins wondered at how childishly, how selfishly he had behaved, until exhaustion at last overcame him and he slept.

Wilkins awoke late the next morning feeling rather humiliated – it was overly indulgent to worry about personal matters in the midst of a war, he thought. Someone, probably Nurse Wolczak, had come in and closed the curtains and left some bread and marmalade and tea for him. Now she was someone, he decided, and a woman his own age no less, who merited his high opinion. She had ventured far from home and half-way around the world to assist those suffering from this bloody miserable and endless war. When he felt low in the future, he would think of Nurse Wolczak and steel himself by emulating her.

Wilkins ate a few bites as he refreshed himself and then went next door to see Gresham, who was fully awake, sitting up in his bed, and reading a newspaper.

"Afternoon," Gresham said hoarsely.

"Why, you look so much better. How are you feeling?" Wilkins asked.

"Not bad," Gresham replied with an effort. "Sam was here. He was able to track down Dunn but the fellow escaped to Austria before he could be captured."

"Damn, that's disappointing," Wilkins said angrily. "We shall have a terrible time finding him again; at least it should be difficult for him to ever return to Italy. Has the doctor been in to see you?"

"Yes, and I'm not impressed," Gresham said with disgust. "I'm to stay in bed a month. Ridiculous – I feel well enough to stand and walk about now."

"I suppose I shall have to leave you and go on to Roumania alone."

"The Hell you will," Gresham said. "We'll both go, in a few days."

Wilkins laughed, but he knew he would have to leave for Roumania as soon as possible regardless of Gresham's condition. As he left Gresham's room, Wilkins was already considering miserably the many enormous falsehoods that he would have to tell the Roumanian government in order to secure that country's entry into the war. He passed the room where he had slept, and then Wilkins noticed Nurse Wolczak cleaning up after him. He watched her as she opened the curtains and began to change the sheets, moving in her graceful and authoritative way. She had a great deal of poise for a woman so young, he thought. And then, as she bent over the bed to smooth the new white top sheet, Wilkins noticed the curve of her back and the swell of her bosom and he thought something else, something that fairly startled him: He imagined what it would be like to press Miss Wolczak down onto those clean, white sheets, to press his lips against her full pink mouth, and to feel her arms confidently surround him. He stood silently watching her, his face flushed and his breathing deepened. Then she noticed him watching. Still bent over the bed provocatively, she looked up at him and returned his gaze silently as if daring him to speak. Then she smiled and winked at him.

Wilkins cleared his throat and forced himself to move. As casually as he could muster, he entered the sunny white room.

"Hello again, Mister Wilkins," she said, straightening up and looking him right in the eye. "Did you sleep okay?"

"Yes, Nurse," he said nervously. "Thank you for allowing me to stay here last night. I am just on my way out now."

"Mister Gresham is feeling much better today, isn't he?"

"Yes, he certainly is, yes. But may I …"

"Something you want to ask, Mister Wilkins?" she said with a delicate smirk.

"Well, I … I don't mean to be forward, but you, Miss Wolczak, by any chance, you wouldn't do me the honor of dining with me this evening, would you?"

"It's not really allowed, Mister Wilkins," she admonished him.

"I see," he said, his disappointment evident.

"We'll have to meet somewhere," she continued lightly, as if it were all a laughing matter.

"Well, very good, that's wonderful," he said as calmly as he could manage. "I'm staying at the *Danieli*. Could you, I mean, would it be alright for you to meet me there? At seven?"

"Okay," she said with a charming smile.

"Excellent," Wilkins said with a gasp of relief, "'til then, then," he said and stumbled out the door as quickly as decorum permitted. It was not until he reached the street that his heartbeat slowed at last and a huge grin broke out across his scarred young face.

Wilkins was a nervous wreck all afternoon, and when he saw Miss Wolczak standing by the door in the hotel's magnificent gilded lobby that evening, his heart nearly stopped altogether. She was astonishing in a diaphanous pale pink silk evening dress. Her neck and arms were bare, and her thick, wavy chestnut brown hair flowed over her shoulders.

"Thank you for coming, Miss Wolczak," Wilkins said as he took her hand and bowed. "You look truly lovely. There is a little place around the corner where I thought we could have a comfortable meal."

"That'd be fine," Wolczak replied with a smile. "Mister Wilkins," she said as they were walking side by side outdoors, her hip bumping frequently into his, "may I know your name?"

"I'm sorry," Wilkins said, embarrassed, "I'm James. And what shall I call you?"

"I suppose you can call me 'Emma'."

"Emma. How lovely. You really do look wonderful this evening, Emma."

"Thank you, James. The dress is borrowed, though, and I tend to let my hair down when I'm not on duty. I hope it doesn't look too childish."

"It's lovely. I should warn you, I'm rather an amateur when it comes to dining with young ladies."

She laughed. "I'm no lady, James, and I have no experience at all dining with fine gentleman so I think we're pretty even-Stephen."

Wilkins led Miss Wolczak into a little *osteria*, a small but elegant restaurant that served simple Venetian foods. They sat near the window at a little wood table, and Wilkins ordered their wine and dinner.

"So you've been in Italy nine months or so, I understand. How do you like it?" he asked.

"I haven't seen much of Italy yet," she said. "I spend most of my time in the hospital with the other nurses. We've been very busy because of the fighting up north this summer. I had to trade with my girlfriend just to get off duty this evening."

"I haven't caused you any trouble, I hope."

"No, no," she assured him. "I like Venice a lot, though. It's so much more interesting than Pittsburgh. I don't want you to have any illusions about me, James. I'm not a very fancy person. My father, he works in a steel mill; my grandfather was born in Poland; he's the one that brought my father over to America."

"What makes you think I am so high and mighty?" Wilkins asked defensively.

"I can tell," she said without accusation. "What are you, anyway – a Knight or something?"

It made Wilkins laugh to see he was so transparent. "No, no, I am not, my father is a nobleman, but not me. I *am* a Colonel in the British Army, if that's a consolation to you."

"A Colonel! You must be kidding me, right? You're so young! And why aren't you in uniform?"

"I've only come to Italy to gather some information. To be honest, I don't think I'll staying very long."

"Naturally," she said as if she'd heard it all before.

"Are you afraid I am simply trying to take advantage of you?"

"Good luck with that," she said defiantly. "I've beaten up boys bigger than you."

Wilkins smiled, "I don't doubt you for a moment. Do you like nursing, Emma?"

"Oh, yes, I love the work. I wish I could be a doctor someday."

"Why don't you?"

"Well, women don't do that kind of thing in Pittsburgh."

"But I admire your ambition," Wilkins said. "I watched you at your work; I could see how dedicated you are to your patients, and you seem to know a great deal more about medicine than some of the doctors. You traveled all the way to Italy to give these men your care. I know a great many highborn women who call themselves 'ladies' but who do almost nothing at all. I don't find that so admirable. But the world is changing, is it not?"

"Please, James, I'm just a nurse," said Miss Wolczak, although obviously flattered. "I thought it would be a great lark to come to Italy. I'm no Clara Barton, you know."

"Who?"

"She's the woman who founded the American Red Cross."

"Of course. Well, I would like to propose a toast to the American Red Cross, then," Wilkins said as he raised his cup of wine.

"*Na zdrowie*," Miss Wolczak replied happily in Polish. Wilkins found her captivating.

After their meal, Wilkins and Miss Wolczak walked about the quiet streets a while telling stories and laughing until the sun began to set, and then Wilkins walked her back to the hospital where she lived and worked.

"If it's not too presumptuous of me," said Wilkins nervously, "may I have the honor of kissing you 'good night', Emma?"

"Really, James, I'm not an innocent," Miss Wolczak said sternly. She stepped up to Wilkins and planted her lips firmly on his, and even Wilkins could tell she had done that before because she was so very good at it. Everything about her seemed perfect to Wilkins, and he felt he could have stood there in the street all night kissing her. "Thanks again for dinner," Wolczak said as she broke off the kiss and stepped back, leaving Wilkins in a warm daze.

"Shall I see you again? Wilkins asked.

"The day after tomorrow, if you like," she said. "I can get the day off. I'll come meet you in the morning and you can show me around the city." Without waiting for a reply, she skipped down the street to the door of the hospital, then turned to wave to Wilkins before disappearing inside.

Two days later, Wilkins was drinking coffee with Miss Wolczak in the lounge of the *Danieli Hotel*. They were dressed casually and prepared for a day exploring the old churches of Venice when Sam came over to speak with them.

"Hello there, James," he said. "Please introduce me to your charming friend."

Wilkins blushed and for a moment hesitated. "Hello, Sam, yes, of course," Wilkins said as he stood at last. "Allow me to introduce you to Miss Emma Wolczak. Miss Wolczak works at the American Red Cross Hospital where David is being treated. Emma, this is ... umm, this is Sam."

"I forgot, James," said *H.* "You don't even know my last name, do you. You see, Miss Wolczak, I work for the British government, but it's all rather hush-hush. We try not to use last names, but of course everyone in Italy knows who I am."

"It's nice to meet you, Sam," said Miss Wolczak as she confidently shook his hand.

"I hear David is doing just fine," *H* said to Wilkins, "and already anxious to leave the hospital, is he? I had planned to visit him today, but I've got to run up to Asiago."

"He's recovering well, yes," Wilkins replied.

"Mister Gresham is a terrible patient," said Wolczak. "The two of you should stress to him how important it is to fully recover from injuries like those before moving about too much."

"Indeed, we will," said Wilkins. "But you must understand that David and I have some rather important work to do, so he is anxious to depart. At some point soon, I'm afraid, I will need to proceed without him if he must remain abed."

"Not quite yet, I hope," said *H.* "Say, I don't suppose you and Miss Wolczak would like to tag along with me to Asiago, would you? Plenty of time to enjoy Venice when you return, and, I tell you, you've never seen anything like the battlefield in the Trentino. It's simply astonishing what the Italians are doing up there."

"The battlefield? Is it quite safe?" asked Wilkins.

"That sounds wonderful!" said Miss Wolczak. "The soldiers keep telling me I don't know what it's like up at the front; I'd like to be able to say I'd been there."

"Where I'm going it is absolutely safe, I assure you," said *H.* "It will just be us three and my driver," he assured them.

"It sounds fine, then, I suppose," Wilkins said uncertainly. "Are you sure you're up for it?" he asked Wolczak.

"Oh, yes, absolutely," she said excitedly. "When do we start?"

"Right away, if you don't mind," *H* replied, "so we can get back this afternoon. You see the large fellow over by the door?" Wilkins and Wolczak looked and saw a huge man in a British uniform, tall and muscled like an ox. "Follow him, and he'll lead you to our transport." *H* stood. "See you in a few minutes, then," he said and walked away.

The large British soldier stood still for several minutes after *H* had disappeared, then he went out the front door himself. Wilkins and Wolczak followed casually and were led to a launch that was docked a small distance from the hotel. *H* was already waiting for them there. It was a short trip to the mainland and they next boarded a comfortable *Fiat* sedan to travel at breakneck speed north to Asiago. In the back seat Wilkins and Wolczak sat stiffly as *H* pointed out a number of interesting sights along their journey.

As the *Fiat* continued through the richly green Italian farmlands, they saw many fields on which brigades of Italian soldiers were encamped. The row upon row of small white tents were quite orderly and disciplined, illustrating a respect for the officers that Wilkins had not seen in the more chummy British camps in France or at Suvla Bay. The elite Italian troops were often decorated with plumes attached to their helmets and other bright tokens of their bravery. In one field, they saw more than a hundred soldiers kneeling before a Catholic priest who was performing a Mass. The altar cloth (a soldier's blanket) had been laid on top of an ammunition crate, and a common soldier was ringing the bell as the priest raised the host. Miss Wolczak crossed herself (she described herself as Orthodox). Wilkins (Anglican) found it interesting that, even more than in England or in France, race and religion were deeply integrated with national identity in Italy. He thought again of Mussolini and his populist political agenda and could imagine bands of uniformed Catholic Italians racing around the country, enforcing some notion of national purity with the force of religious law, and God-only-knows what would happen to those who were not pure enough.

"Look there," said *H*, "you can see our destination."

The road was empty and lined with trees, but through the dusty windows of the sedan they could see across the sunny, green Asiago plateau and, in the distance, the chalky white and green mountain ranges of the Trentino rising up majestically to the sky. Miss Wolczak had never seen mountains so tall they looked impossible to climb, and, taken all together, seemed to create a solid wall of rock through which there was no apparent passage.

"That is where the Italians are fighting," *H* said.

"Good heavens!" Wolczak exclaimed.

By midday, they reached the remains of a small shelled-out village close to the mountain range, somewhat north of Asiago. They were not far from the front lines although it was unclear what passed for front lines in this area as there were no trenches. The village and all the land ascending to the mountains had been heavily shelled or burned and the rains had turned the ground to mud. Wilkins and Wolczak looked at the terribly thin young men marching quietly in their mud-splattered uniforms; they wore grey felt hats adorned with black feathers in lieu of shrapnel helmets. The sedan passed into the shattered village and came at last to a stop. A few hundred yards away, the white mountain-side rose straight up into the clouds. The jagged, dry and chalky rock ascended almost vertically for more than a thousand feet; small foot paths could be seen in some areas. At the moment, everything was quiet.

Emma Wolczak looked around at the terrible devastation – the damaged and burnt buildings, burst trees, shell-pocked landscape and bushes of mangled barbed wire. There were corpses here and there that no one had bothered to move. It was easy to imagine the unnatural forces required to cause such damage, night after night of shelling during which each man feared every moment that a yellowish-green cloud of toxic gas might roll down the mountainside and into his shelter. How long could a person withstand such conditions, she wondered? She had seen many men at the hospital who were crazed with grief or shocked into silence yet who had no visible injuries. They were often unfairly treated by their fellows, called cowardly or weak, but Wolczak now felt she knew better.

"If this is the front, where is the Austrian army?" Wilkins asked.

"Why, they're at the top, of course," *H* said. "You see, the Italians are attacking up the side of the mountain, climbing from one meager shelter to the next while the Austrians shoot down at them. Do you see the young men around us? They are the famous *Alpini*, the mountaineering soldiers who climb to reach the Austrian defenses."

"Good Lord! The Austrians could just throw stones down on them," Wolczak protested.

"Indeed, they do at times. On more than one occasion, I have even seen the Austrian officers come out and plead with the *Alpini* to descend – the Austrians are tired of killing these Italian boys and have made a decision not to target anyone who remains down here at the base of the mountain. Yet from time to time *Il Generale* Cadorna orders the *Alpini* to climb again, and each time it is the same – they cheer, they drink, they climb, and they die, all with a fervor that is almost incomprehensible."

Even as they watched, a small party of a dozen *Alpini* began climbing the mountainside to a shelter that had been dug into the rockface more than a hundred feet up. Ropes had been anchored to the wall, and the men showed their agility and skill as they climbed quickly. A handful of shots were fired down from high above them. One man, slightly injured, climbed back down. The others reached a small tunnel that had been excavated into the mountain side and waved to their comrades below.

"Why do they climb at all?" Wilkins asked.

"Ah, yes, that is the cleverest part," *H* said. "They are tunneling. They are digging a tunnel up beneath the feet of the Austrians, and when they are done, the Italians will detonate a mine and blow the entire top of the mountain off."

"That's terrible," Wolczak said.

"*C'est la guerre, mademoiselle,*" *H* replied. "Now you must excuse me for a few moments. I will meet you at the pub here shortly."

Wilkins and Wolczak watched until the remaining climbers reached the safety of the dugout. "It's terrible," Wolczak said as she looked around at the devastation. "Let's go inside, James," she said, and then they entered the small and heavily damaged stone tavern. Inside, a few junior officers of the Italian Army were drinking wine and listening to a phonograph recording of an opera. As the lovely Miss Wolczak entered, their eyes turned toward her and a hush fell upon the room.

"*Ciao, Signore*," said an attentive young, clean-shaven Italian officer who leapt up to greet Wilkins and Wolczak. His short, straight black hair gleamed with oil. "Allow me to introduce myself – I am *Tenente* Paolo Rinaldi. Please, would you and the *Signorina* care to join me?"

"*Grazie, sì, Tenente*," said Wilkins. "We are visiting with a colleague to see how you fight in the mountains. It is most impressive to see the men climb."

"*Sì*, they climb magnificently, but fight perhaps not so good," said Rinaldi gaily. "Please, sit with me," he said, gesturing to the battered and stained wooden table beside him.

"Before I drink, *Tenente*," Wolczak asked, "please tell me if there are any wounded men about who might need medical attention. I'm a nurse, you see."

"There are many men here who would like to receive your attention, *Signorina*, but I suggest you leave them to our own *medici*. You are my guest, and they are *bruti*."

"As you wish, *Tenente,* thank you. I'll take a wine, then," Wolczak said as Rinaldi poured wine for them from a very large old glass bottle that rested in a copper cradle nearby. He tipped the bottle to pour out the wine, dark red and thick as syrup, into tin cups.

"Do you like the Opera, *Signorina*?" he asked, returning to the table.

"You mean the phonograph?" Wolczak asked. "Yes, very much."

"I had the pleasure of hearing Caruso sing at Covent Garden a few years ago," Wilkins said. "He is wonderful."

"You are most fortunate, indeed," said Rinaldi, quite pleased that Wilkins recognized the famous tenor singing on the phonograph. "But he spends far too much time in America now. As soon as the war is finished, I will go to live in New York City and I will hear Caruso perform every night. How do you like the wine?"

"It's very fine, thank you," said Wilkins, who thought the wine was far too sweet and raw. "You expect the war will end soon then?"

"Of course," said Rinaldi, full of confidence. "Once we break through the Trentino and cross the Isonzo, the Austrians will stop fighting. Will we break through? Of course! We must! We are fighting for the Italian people! The Austrians, however, they have no need for war. If they came down from the mountains into *Italia*, they would tire of us very quickly and simply go away. That is why we will be victorious."

"Why do you wish to go to America, if you love Italy so much?" Wolczak asked. "I'm from America myself. My family came from Poland and I sometimes wonder whether things in the old country could have been much worse. We were poor there and we're still poor now."

"America is a land where anything can happen, is it not? Who can say, *Signorina*? I will go to America after the war, and then, God willing, I will return to Italy a rich man and build a magnificent factory in my home town and employ many people. I will be a great man then."

"That is an excellent plan," Wilkins said encouragingly.

"Now you tell me," Rinaldi continued, "what will you do when the war is over?"

"Hmmm, I suppose I will be expected to go to university," said Wilkins, "although I haven't any idea right now what I would like to study."

"You must be very wealthy, I think." Rinaldi said with a wink to Miss Wolczak.

"Well, my family is, I suppose," Wilkins said. "All that really means to me is that I must generally do as I am told."

"Ah, I see, so then your father must be a very powerful man. Has he done many great deeds?"

"I like to think so; I hope so," said Wilkins.

"In Italy, great men are granted titles of nobility to reward their great deeds, not the other way around. And you, *Signorina*," Rinaldi addressed to Wolczak, "what are your plans for after the war?"

"I don't know. I'll probably go back to Pittsburgh and get married, I guess," she said with bitter disappointment.

"You are too *pessimista, Signorina*. Who knows what the future will hold? Have more wine; we must put you in a better mood. So why are you really here? Are the British planning to wage war in the mountains, perhaps?"

"No, I'm afraid not," said Wilkins. "We are only here because my colleague asked us to come along and see your magnificent *Alpini*. All the same, I have found the journey quite informative. It is a pleasure to see men so disciplined and enthusiastic about fighting."

"We are a passionate people, *Signore*," Rinaldi said proudly, "and we have a great love for our country, but the fighting has taken a terrible toll. These men outside, they are not the original *Alpini*, you know. The original ones are all dead; these are just young men who can climb. The generals, they will no longer tell us how many are killed, and the newspapers are filled with *propaganda*."

Just then *H* entered the tavern and spotted Wilkins and Wolczak. "Hello there, I see you have met my good friend Rinaldi," he said. "Have you been taking good care of my friends, Paolo?"

"Sam! *Ciao*!" Rinaldi exclaimed as he stood to hug *H*. "*Si*, we are making plans for when the war is done."

"Excellent, keep your spirits up, I say, but unfortunately, there is still a great deal to do before the war will be over. You boys are going to have to keep the Austrians busy in the Alps a while longer, I'm afraid."

"We are, we will, *Signore*," Rinaldi said confidently.

"Now I'm afraid I must gather my friends here and depart; I must return to Venice this afternoon."

"Of course, you are a busy man, Sam."

"Please allow me to repay your courtesy the next time you come to the city, Paolo; you are always good company."

"*Grazie, signores, e arrivederci.* Thank you, *Signorina*," Rinaldi said as he took Wolczak's hand and bowed. "Thank you for taking wine with me; you have been a most refreshing sight, and you and your gentleman friend have been most entertaining."

"*Grazie, Tenente,*" she replied with a gentle smile.

That evening Wilkins walked with Wolczak around Venice, along the canals and through *piazzas* as the Sun sank, but Wolczak was quiet and seemed distant to Wilkins; she was consumed by her own dark thoughts. Eventually, they strolled back to the hospital, but this time there were too many of her colleagues around to afford them enough privacy for a kiss. Wilkins and Wolczak quietly bid each other a good night, and then Wolczak went to change into her uniform for her night shift.

As Wilkins watched her climb the white marble steps of the re-purposed municipal building, he was forced to wonder whether there was any reason to go on courting Emma. She was lovely, and intriguing, but he would have to leave in a day or two at the most. Wilkins decided he should at least go up to see Gresham, however, and he found his friend sitting in bed with a bottle of Asti and an enormous pile of newspapers.

"There you are, James," said Gresham spiritedly. "Thank God you're here. I'm almost out of my wits with boredom. I'll get a glass so you can have some wine. You haven't seen that pretty Nurse Wolczak about, have you?"

"I believe she's coming on duty now," Wilkins said plainly. "What's the latest news about your condition, David? Is there any chance you're getting out tomorrow or the next day?"

"Not bloody likely. I do feel well enough to travel, but the doctors insist I stay in bed another two or three weeks in case there's an infection."

"That won't do at all," Wilkins said. "Let's face facts, David: I shall have to go on to Roumania without you. Here it is August already and *Control* wanted us to finish the job before the end of summer."

"I suppose you're right, James, but I'll tell you honestly I don't think you're up to the job. You have misgivings about lying as it is, and we'll have to bloody perjure ourselves if we're going to get Roumania to declare war before the end of summer."

"Yes, it's true I am not happy with this assignment, but I will do what is required of me. Don't I always?"

Just then the door opened quickly and Nurse Wolczak, again wearing her crisp, white uniform, strode purposefully into the room. "Good evening, Mister Gresham. I'm afraid it's time to change your bandages."

"You remember Mister Wilkins?" Gresham asked, gesturing to Wilkins, who was standing in the corner.

"Yes, of course," said Wolczak, somewhat flustered as she turned about. "I'm sorry I didn't see you there, Mister Wilkins."

Wilkins knew it would be polite to greet the nurse, but somehow he just didn't feel like it. Wolczak looked at him during an awkward moment of silence, then went about her work removing the bandages from Gresham's chest.

"Tell me, Nurse," Gresham asked, "are these wounds really so bad that I must stay in bed another two weeks? I think you probably know better than the doctors, and they don't seem to understand how important it is that Mister Wilkins and I be off as soon as possible."

"Someone must change your bandages, Mister Gresham, and check for signs of infection."

"And what will they do if I become infected, please tell me?" Gresham sneered. "Dose me with opium until I die peacefully in my sleep? I'm certain there are doctors in Roumania who can do that," Gresham said with mild frustration, "and I've got a bloody handgun that will do the job a lot quicker."

"Roumania? Are you going to Roumania from here?" Wolczak asked.

"Yes, but I shouldn't have said that," Gresham replied quickly. "I must ask you not to repeat it."

"No, no, of course not. It's just that my mother is from Roumania," Wolczak said lightly, "that's why I asked. I've always wanted to visit. Bucharest is lovely in the summer, or so I've heard."

"Your mother is Roumanian?" asked Wilkins in astonishment. "Let me get this straight, then. You're saying that you are a Polish-Roumanian Orthodox Catholic from America? Good Lord."

"Yes, that's right," she said, turning angrily to Wilkins. "My mother and father met at the church and fell in love and got married and had five children, including me of course. I think it's a rather nice story. It happens all the time in America. And if the two of you are so eager to run off to Roumania on your secret spy business – that's right, anyone could tell you're spies the way you two plot and plan and walk around out of uniform and all – well," she said turning to Gresham, "well, why don't you just bring a nurse along with you, Mister Gresham? Then you'd have someone to dress your wounds and look after you while you go about your secret spy business." She turned to Wilkins: "Why didn't you think of that, Mister 'high and mighty' Wilkins?"

"She has a point, James," said Gresham.

"How dare you call me 'high and mighty'?" Wilkins asked Wolczak angrily. "If I really believed I was higher than you, I wouldn't have asked you to dinner in the first place."

"Ah, now I'm getting the full picture at last," Gresham admitted.

"I know what you really want," Wolczak spat at Wilkins.

"You can't honestly believe that!" Wilkins shouted. "Have I given you any indication?"

"You would never take a girl like me seriously, and you know it," she shouted back.

"Nurse Wolczak," Gresham said calmly, "please let me assure you that James had nothing of the sort in mind. He is as pure as new-fallen snow and, to my way of thinking, rather afraid of girls in general, especially when they are as pretty as you. I'd say he must be rather smitten with you to have spoken up at all. And listen, James, I rather like the idea of Nurse Wolczak accompanying us to Roumania. I think we should hire her. What do you say?"

"Emma's work is here at the hospital," Wilkins said vaguely, still embarrassed by Gresham's comments about him.

"That's for Nurse Wolczak to decide. Would you care to go on a little adventure, Miss?" Gresham asked her.

"Is it important? I mean, I'd love to visit Roumania, but they do need me at the hospital here," she said.

"Strictly between us, I can assure you there will be a great many young men in Roumania needing a good nurse as well," said Gresham darkly. "You know, there are certain to be Red Cross hospitals in Bucharest, and it is your home country. At least, it's one of them," he added.

"I … I don't know. Do *you* want me to come, James."

Wilkins hesitated a moment. *Did* he want Emma to come along? Certainly she was beautiful, and he was genuinely charmed by the way she spoke back to him, and he admired the way she cared for her patients. But there was something more. She was like an open window, an opportunity for Wilkins to be a different sort of man, perhaps the man he had always wanted to be rather than the one he was expected to be. Whatever the reason, he was not prepared to say farewell to Miss Wolczak just yet. He hesitated only a moment, but then desperately summoned all his courage and stepped toward Nurse Wolczak. Taking her hand, he looked in her beautiful dark brown eyes. "Yes," he said confidently, "yes, I do, Emma. I want you to come with us."

She snatched her hand away and turned from Wilkins. "Well I guess, Mister Gresham, if you would like to hire me as your private nurse, then, well, alright then," she said.

Salonika, again

Wilkins was excited. At long last, he was able to wear his newly tailored Colonel's uniform in public. He hoped it would impress Miss Wolczak, who thus far had been extremely cool to him since their argument in Gresham's hospital room. She remained aloof during their brief voyage across the Adriatic and by train to Salonika. Both Wilkins and Gresham were impressed at how Salonika had changed in the months since they were last in the old port city in northern Greece. Since the beginning of the year, more than 200,000 additional British and French troops had landed at Salonika under the command of French General Maurice Sarrail. Tens of thousands of Serbian troops had also come from Corfu, the island to which the Serbian Army had retreated following the occupation of Serbia by Austria and Bulgaria the previous autumn. Salonika had become a city brimming with soldiers, a city in the midst of war, and a city bracing for the opportunity to attack north to restore the Serbian homeland.

Wilkins and Gresham both looked terribly important in their Colonel's uniforms, and Wolczak was deeply impressed with the respect the two men were shown when they disembarked from the train in Salonika. "Colonel Gresham, Colonel Wilkins," said a British lieutenant who saluted them at the station. "I've been sent to bring you to headquarters, Sirs." The officer collected their luggage, and they boarded a black sedan waiting to bring them to the white stone townhouse on Aristotelous Street where Wilkins had, only a few months before, worked with Prime Minister Venizelos to organize the initial Allied landings in Greece. The house, which was now also the Allied headquarters, was still bustling with activity as Gresham, Wilkins and Wolczak were led to a small office on the second floor where Nikolaos Politis was waiting to greet them.

"James, what a great pleasure to see you again," said Politis, the short, middle aged diplomat, as he rounded his desk to shake their hands.

"Nikolaos, Ελπίζω να είστε καλά, και ο πρωθυπουργός καθώς και," Wilkins replied. "You remember David Gresham?"

"Yes, I do. Colonel, welcome. I hope this visit to Salonika will bring you more pleasure than your last."

"Thank you," Gresham replied quietly. He was tired from the journey and not altogether pleased to be in Salonika. It was here the previous year that he had murdered both a German assassin and a beautiful woman – yes, she was a German agent as well, he knew – but still a woman he had loved in his way.

"Allow me also to introduce Miss Emma Wolczak," said Wilkins. "She is an American nurse we have engaged to treat Colonel Gresham's recent injuries."

"Miss Wolczak," said Politis with a slight bow. "You are ill, Colonel Gresham?"

"I was slightly wounded, but I am recovering, thank you."

"How is Prime Minister Venizelos? What is happening with King Constantine now?" Wilkins asked as they all sat.

"Alas, we are at yet another moment of crisis, James," Politis said gravely, yet it was clear that he was also excited to share the news. "Venizelos is in Athens now. He is to make a public denouncement of the King's policies and call for a new national government. We are forming a provisional government here in Salonika. General Sarrail has been extremely supportive. The Macedonian region is still under martial law, of course, and threatened by the Bulgarian and Austrian armies, but General Sarrail has forced King Constantine's army to demobilize and is preparing his own offensive into Serbia soon. We have also received generous assistance from your colleague Mister Mackenzie, who is here in Salonika as well."

"Compton Mackenzie is here?" asked Gresham with obvious pleasure. It had been months since had last seen his former tutor, the man who had enlisted Gresham into the Secret Intelligence Service.

"Yes, and he has become a great supporter of the Prime Minister. But tell me now: Why have you come to Salonika? What can I do for you, gentlemen?"

"We are simply on our way to Roumania," Wilkins said.

"Of course, that is no problem at all. There are aeroplanes that travel to Roumania and back almost every day," Politis said. Seeing Wilkins look of displeasure, he added: "It is quite safe, James. Bulgaria has no antiaircraft guns and very few aeroplanes of their own. I will arrange it all with the General's staff for you."

"Thank you, Nikolaos," Wilkins said.

"In the meantime, I hope you will join me and Mister Mackenzie for dinner tonight. Perhaps we can discuss your mission to Roumania and offer our advice."

"That would be most generous, thank you," said Gresham.

Gresham had no desire to stay in Salonika for even one night, but even their short journey had left him too tired to travel any further that day. General Sarrail's staff had arranged lodgings for Wilkins, Gresham and Wolczak in an elegant townhouse nearby, and Wolczak was reassuring and confident that Gresham's exhaustion was normal and said there were no signs of further bleeding or infection. Gresham slept for an hour while Wolczak and Wilkins strolled down to the docks to view the British battleships anchored in the bay.

"Are you still quite angry with me, Emma," Wilkins asked, as they stood looking out over the bay and the sun set.

"No, James, but I *am* frustrated. All that talk about what will happen after the war – I haven't much to look forward to. My adventure will be over then."

268

"It is impossible for me to believe, Emma, that your future is as bleak as you seem to fear. I have seen you work. I know your spirit. You could go anywhere in the world. You'll see. Doors will be thrown open for you."

"Thank you, James, really. It is hard for me to imagine it, though."

Compton Mackenzie, tall, stocky, and with dark wavy brown hair, looked noticeably older when they all met at a small, private café that evening. "David, James, how good to see you both again. How are you feeling, David? I heard all about it from Sam," he said with warm enthusiasm.

"Tired, mostly, but not too bad," said Gresham. "I've had to bring along a private nurse. Let me introduce you to Emma Wolczak. She's an American."

"How lovely to meet you, Miss Wolczak," Mackenzie said as he took her hand and led her to her seat. "We love Americans. We can hardly wait for America to join the war."

"Provided they join on the right side, of course," Politis added.

"Nice to meet you too, Mister Mackenzie," Wolczak said, "but I wouldn't count on America joining the war any time soon."

"I fear you're correct there. Too many Americans are making too much money off the rest of us. How long have you been in Europe?"

"Almost ten months. I've been working for the American Red Cross in Venice."

"Ah. So you were treating Mister Gresham in Italy, I understand," Mackenzie said with a wink to Gresham.

"You're winking at the wrong one," Wolczak said playfully, and Mackenzie looked in surprise to Wilkins, who quickly turned a deep shade of red.

"You are a charming and beautiful young woman, Miss Wolczak," Mackenzie replied, "and we are honored to have you join us. And now you are all on your way to Roumania tomorrow, I hear. I must warn you, David, Roumania is a problem that has been worked almost to the point of exhaustion, I'm afraid."

"It is much the same as the situation here in Greece," Politis added. "The King of Roumania is German, from the House of Hohenzollern, but his wife Marie is the grand-daughter of Queen Victoria and of Tsar Alexander; she was born in Kent, actually. Neither King nor Queen has tremendous influence over the government's policies, so neither gets what they want and the country goes on steadfastly neutral. The Prime Minister, Ionel Brătianu, he is the one in charge – as ruthless as that fellow Salandra in Italy: He's got the Roumanian army fully mobilized and ready for war, but he's waiting to see who is the highest bidder."

"What is being bid?" Wolczak asked.

"Land," Gresham told her. "Roumania wants land, and they are perhaps willing to join the war if they are guaranteed enough territory when this is all over."

"But it's not going to end anytime soon, is it?" She asked.

"Certainly not," Mackenzie assured her. "But there will come a day when one or more of these great kingdoms simply cannot sacrifice any more – no more money, no more guns, no more men. That is what it has come to, I'm afraid. Then the victors will re-draw the maps of the world, and everything will change."

"The people will demand more than new maps," Wilkins said. "What more do the Roumanians want?"

"Who knows? We've done everything we can to influence public opinion. London has been spending huge amounts of money on oil and grains in Roumania," Mackenzie added. "Most of our purchases are just being stored right there in the countryside, so at least the Germans won't get any of it. However, the Roumanians are still upset about the territory in Bessarabia that they've lost to Russia in the past, so while the Roumanian people favor the British and French, they dislike our other ally."

"Are they able to put up a fight?" Gresham asked. "I mean, what sort of condition is the army in?"

"It's the old fashion, much like the Serbian army was until we trained and equipped them on Corfu," Mackenzie replied.

"That is not a promising situation, no," said Gresham. "Still, we have our instructions. We shall have to see what can be done."

"If I may say so, it would be most beneficial to have the Roumanians armies attack Bulgaria while we are engaging the Bulgarian Army in Serbia," Politis said. "Ah, here is the wine at last. If I am allowed, gentlemen, may I propose a toast to your most splendid and successful engagement at Foncquevillers?"

"Good Lord, have you heard about it, too?" asked Wilkins.

"Certainly, who has not?" Politis said.

"Will someone tell me what we're toasting?" Wolczak asked.

"I'll tell you later," Wilkins said, again turning a touch red in the face.

After a pleasant dinner of fish, Gresham and Mackenzie stepped outside for a breath of fresh air. As they looked down at the British warships in the bay, Gresham lit a cigarette.

"Nurse Wolczak doesn't want me to smoke," he explained. "Compton, I have to ask you about something."

"Certainly, David," Mackenzie replied.

"The man who shot me – Dunn, we call him – we know he works for Zimmerman in Germany's Foreign Office."

"Yes."

"He knew my name, my *real* name: Larkin."

"That *is* surprising," Mackenzie said with concern. "I'd have said you'd done a fairly thorough job of leaving that name behind you, David. Clearly there has been a great deal of research done on you: Your enemies know who you are."

"Dunn must have been following us. He intended to kill me, but there were too many people about."

"Yes, he failed, thankfully. Not for want of trying, of course. Let me tell you, David, you have lived an anonymous life until now: Your boyhood in Manchester, public schooling, all the way up to Suvla Bay, you were anonymous in part because you were not a threat to anyone. You have become a threat, a serious threat, and our enemies will now stop at nothing to eliminate you. The same goes for James, I'm afraid. And this business at Foncquevillers, the two of you put on quite a show. Everyone in Europe knows about it. They know it was the two of you. Now you are going to Roumania, which is rife with German agents. You will have to be very careful."

"I understand," Gresham replied calmly.

"We need Roumania to declare war, David. Do what you must."

"We will. But I doubt very much they will last out the year, especially if they try to take on the Germans or Austrians."

"They must not. To the east of Roumania lies the Transylvanian Mountains. Roumania holds the high ground, and as long as the Austrians are busy with Sarrail's offensive in Serbia and Cadorna's offensive in Italy, I doubt they will bother with Roumania at all. That is why Roumania should attack south into Bulgaria. That is the best contribution they can make."

"Yes, if they will do anything at all."

———

It was a hot, sunny morning and the field north of Salonika was dry and dusty. A warm breeze swirled the dust and rippled the red streamers on the struts of the two British biplanes. They were F.K.8's, the two-seater model known as the "Big Ack", and these two had ended up at Salonika with the 47th Squadron doing regular flights over Bulgaria and north to Bucharest. Two planes, two pilots, two passenger seats, and three passengers, but they were the only planes available.

"I'll take that one," Gresham said, and he walked over to the first plane to speak to the pilot.

"Are you quite sure?" Wilkins shouted. His first flight, when he traveled into Germany to find Sir Roger Casement, had been at night, and Wilkins had found it somewhat reassuring to travel in the dark and unable to see the ground so very far below him. This flight to Bucharest would be by day and, to complicate matters further, it appeared Miss Wolczak would have to sit on his lap the entire way. Wilkins could not decide which fact disturbed him more.

"You two," shouted the second pilot, "climb on up already. Major Wigram wants me back before sundown."

"You had better get in first," Wolczak said with a slight, knowing smile.

Wilkins mounted the ladder and climbed over the top and into the rear seat of the biplane. Wolczak climbed up next and settled comfortably in Wilkins' lap before he buckled the harness around them that he hoped would keep them from falling to their deaths. An airman lifted and then pushed down the propeller, the motor started with a cough, and the noise of the engine drowned out their voices as the plane began to roll unsteadily toward the flat patch of dirt from which it would rise aloft. The wind spat dust and pebbles back into their goggles, and Wolczak pulled her pink silk scarf up over her mouth and nose. Wilkins buried his face into the back of her dress.

They saw Gresham's plane rise into the air before them, and then their own plane was suddenly off the ground and all the shaking and rattling stopped as the plane glided smoothly up into the sky. Soon they were high in the air, the fresh air whipping across their faces, and Wilkins realized his arms were wrapped very tightly around Miss Wolczak. She didn't seem to mind, but then she shifted in his lap several times and turned to look into his face with an expression of astonishment.

"Why, Mister Wilkins!" She said in mock horror. Wilkins's face turned bright red, and then he pulled down her scarf to bare her soft pink lips and kiss her. After all, it was a very long flight and there was no point in denying the obvious.

Bucharest

The new *Athénée Palace* hotel on the Calea Victoriei was where the British diplomats stayed in Bucharest. The German diplomats stayed at *Capşa's* hotel a few blocks away, but both the British and Germans dined at *Capşa's* restaurant as it was widely considered one of the finest houses in Europe. It was there, the very evening Wilkins, Gresham and Wolczak arrived in Bucharest, that the Roumanian diners began spontaneously singing a popular British song:

> *It's a long way to Tipperary,*
> *It's a long way to go.*
> *It's a long way to Tipperary*
> *To the sweetest girl I know!*
> *Goodbye, Piccadilly,*
> *Farewell, Leicester Square!*
> *It's a long, long way to Tipperary,*
> *But my heart's right there.*

The Germans in the restaurant were incensed and walked out in protest. At that very moment, a group of idle factory workers were marching down the Calea Victoriei demonstrating in favor of war against Austria. They saw the mass of German officials and soldiers emerge from the restaurant. It was only moments before horse dung was being hurled through the air at the Germans and a riot erupted. The crowd swelled quickly and the night ended with the mob sacking and burning the German legation offices. The next morning, it was reported that sealed tubes of germ warfare agents (anthrax) had been found buried in the German emissary's garden. By noon, the hot summer streets of Bucharest were filled with people clamouring for a declaration of war. In short, it was perfectly clear which way the winds were blowing in Roumania, but from the *Cotroceni* Palace where King Ferdinand and his Queen Consort Marie resided, there was stubborn silence.

"You don't understand, Colonel Gresham, we have already made those exact promises," said Sir George Barclay, the British Ambassador in Roumania. The British offices in Bucharest were a madhouse of activity, but Barclay had agreed to meet with Gresham and Wilkins late that morning at his home nearby. "The government insists on recovering the territory in Transylvania that is now occupied by Austria and also the territory in Bessarabia taken by the Russians," he continued, "and we have promised them both once the war is over, although the Russians don't even know it. We have spent millions on Roumanian grain and petroleum and pay very handsomely to keep them stored securely on

Roumanian soil. We have promised their army weapons, forty thousand Russian troops, and a coordinated offensive into Bulgaria by General Sarrail. I have no idea what else to offer!"

"Is it, perhaps, that Prime Minister Brătianu is not in a position to accept any offer at all?" asked Wilkins. "Surely King Ferdinand is opposed to declaring war against Germany and Austria, and the Queen and her subjects are opposed to declaring war against Great Britain."

"You may very well be correct, Colonel, but the reasons for the stalemate are ultimately irrelevant," said the older British Ambassador. "Roumania wants to fight, its army is ready for war, but Brătianu will simply *not* sign the treaty."

Silence fell over the room as Gresham and Wilkins considered their options. "What else do you know about Brătianu?" Gresham asked.

"He's an admirable man, his family has been in politics for decades. He was educated in Paris. He's a liberal, a reformer; he pioneered agrarian reform and universal suffrage in Roumania -"

"No, no," said Gresham angrily, "what's wrong with the man? What are his weaknesses?"

Barclay looked at Gresham with disgust. "Colonel Gresham, I cannot say what you hope to accomplish, but I will tell you Brătianu is above reproach."

"Then the King?" Wilkins asked.

"No. There is some gossip about Prince Barbu Ştirbey, he's been having an affair, perhaps."

"With whom?"

Barclay was silent.

"It must be a very interesting name for you to hesitate so. Go on, then, tell us," Gresham said.

"They say he is having an affair with Queen Marie, but there are only rumors."

"That's no good. The Queen is already on our side. Who else?" Wilkins said.

"There's the heir apparent, Prince Karol. They say he's a ladies' man and a bit of a drunkard."

"Aren't we all?" Gresham asked rhetorically.

"I know Karol," Wilkins said. "I met him a few years ago – bit of a wild card."

"I suppose we'll have to start there," Gresham said. "We'll take care of the rest, Ambassador. That's why we were sent, after all."

"So I understand," Barclay sighed.

That evening, Gresham and Wilkins wore their dress uniforms. Wilkins looked splendid, or at least Miss Wolczak thought so. Gresham's bandages puffed up his chest and back in a way that made him look and feel something like a hunchback, and his hair, which had again grown rather too long, was somewhat shaggy and his untrimmed mustache was frightening. Miss Wolczak, by contrast, was dressed in a beautiful white satin gown that accented all her curves, and with her hair tied up tight, and wearing a few modest jewels borrowed from Barclay's wife, she looked terribly fetching.

"Are you certain you're comfortable with this plan, Emma?" asked Wilkins uncertainly. "Truly, if you are at all uneasy -"

"Really, James," she insisted, "I've told you before, I am quite capable of handling myself. I am not a china doll. Colonel Gresham, please put down that cigarette immediately."

"Yes, Nurse," Gresham said, flicking his cigarette out the window.

"It'll be a lark, James," she continued gleefully. "Imagine, me, Emma Wolczak of Pittsburgh, the pot of honey waiting for the mean old bear to pounce."

"When you put it that way, I really do have my doubts," Wilkins said. "Must you look so wonderful?"

The dinner party that evening at Barclay's house was by no means a discrete affair. There were already over thirty persons present when Wilkins and Gresham arrived, followed a few moments later by Miss Wolczak who was posing as an American journalist from the Pittsburgh *Gazette-Times*. To be safe, Barclay ensured she was the only American invited to dinner. Wilkins and Gresham were offered glasses of champagne by several guests who were eager to hear the details of the raid at Foncquevillers, and both men, who finally gave up any pretense of secrecy, were willing to share the story of their daring excursion into German-held territory while keeping their eyes on Miss Wolczak from across the brightly-lit room.

Miss Wolczak received her share of admirers as well, especially among the young British officers present. Wilkins had to bite his tongue when he saw her chatting gaily and laughing with the young men. There were several members of the Roumanian royal family in attendance as well, including the stunning Princess Eleanor and Prince Karol, a handsome young man who was the heir apparent to the throne and a member of the Senate. One of the last guests to arrive was Prime Minister Brătianu, a striking and serious man with a shock of grey hair, a thick, wiry grey mustache and beard, and large brown eyes both piercing and doleful.

Once called to dinner, Wilkins noted that Prince Karol was seated next to Miss Wolczak, and it was gut-wrenchingly obvious to Wilkins that there was an attraction shared between the two. Wolczak's hand seemed to rest constantly upon the Prince's arm as she smiled and batted her eyelashes at him, and more than once the Prince leaned over to whisper in her ear, his lips practically brushing Miss Wolczak's neck. At times, Wilkins noted anxiously, the Prince's hand would disappear under the table, and Wilkins wished he could somehow get on the floor to see what was happening.

"Tell me, Miss Wolczak, are there so many Roumanians in Pittsburgh that your paper would send a reporter all the way to Bucharest?" Karol asked her.

"Good heavens, no," Wolczak replied. "I paid my own travel expenses, out of personal interest. You see, my mother emigrated from Jassy with her family when she was a young girl. However, there are certainly many residents of Pittsburgh who come from Roumania and many other countries too, of course – it is a city full of immigrants."

"All of whom wish to learn how the war is affecting their homelands, no doubt."

"Precisely, my dear Prince."

"And how do you come to afford such travels. Surely not on a journalist's salary. You have a wealthy husband, perhaps?"

"Not married, no. Father's a steel tycoon. He was one of the first investors in Andrew Carnegie's company."

"I see. Steel is a lucrative business in time of war, is it not?"

"I suppose; I only know we're making simply *huge* amounts of money. I don't suppose *you'll* be doing any fighting in the war, will you?"

"Unfortunately, Roumania is still a neutral country, like America."

"It just seems *such* a pity that a handsome and dashing young man like you won't get the opportunity to wear a uniform. I rather like a uniform on a man."

"I do have a uniform, of course. Would you like to see me in it sometime?"

"I'm not sure …"

"No?"

"I only mean, I'm not sure whether I'd rather see you in your uniform, or out of it," she said with a mischievous grin.

Wilkins heard none of the conversation between the Prince and Wolczak, but more than he cared to hear of the conversation between Gresham and Princess Eleanor whose porcelain skin and silky blonde hair was certainly astonishing. How unfortunate, Wilkins thought, that David looks so much like the *Hunchback of Notre Dame* with his bandages and wild hair. Or perhaps it *was* fortunate, since Gresham had a habit of using women rather casually and a princess ought not to be one of his conquests. She certainly seemed taken with the daring and rugged young British Colonel. As soon as dinner was finished, Wilkins promptly dragged Gresham away from her so they could resume their surveillance of Wolczak.

They found Wolczak and Prince Karol whispering conspiratorially by the great marble hearth in the library, drinking yet more wine, and ignoring the other young men and women who sought their attention. Wilkins felt sick at the sight of them. The party soon began to break up, however, when the Prime Minister departed. Gresham began to complain that his wounds were itching, so Wilkins thanked Barclay and his wife for the fine entertainment and dragged Gresham back to the hotel.

Sometime much later that evening, Wilkins was playing cards with Gresham in his room when they heard Miss Wolczak returning to her room across the hall. From the whispers and giggles, it was clear she was not alone.

"I really don't like this plan," Wilkins announced to Gresham.

"Easy there, lad," Gresham said. "I had no idea you were so taken with Emma. Are you quite sure she's your type of girl?"

"Oh I know what you would say, David, and more importantly I know what my mother would say. But, truthfully, I *am* rather enamoured of her. She is wonderfully unique."

"She is very pretty, granted, but how does she feel about you?" Gresham asked skeptically.

Wilkins looked hurt. "It won't be much longer now," he said. Then suddenly there was a loud and violent coughing from across the hall, a woman's piercing scream, and the sound of a body collapsing to the floor. In a flash, Wilkins and Gresham burst through the door into Emma's room to find a horrifying sight: She was lying lifeless upon the floor, wearing only the thinnest white cotton chemise and knickers, her face and chest wet with dark red blood; Prince Karol, kneeling beside her, shirtless, his hands covered with blood, was shocked and very intoxicated.

"You've killed her," Wilkins hissed at him.

"No, no, I haven't touched her," the Prince protested. "She was coughing up blood. I didn't do it. I didn't."

"A likely story," Gresham said accusingly. "I think you had better sit down and tell us what —"

"Good God, you're Prince Karol, aren't you?" Wilkins asked. "Don't you remember me, old boy? I'm James Wilkins, Lord Bartlett's son. I suppose it's been a few years, but I came to visit your family with my mother. You and I went riding together. You threw a frog at me, I recall."

"Wilkins? Yes, I remember, of course. Oh, thank God it's you," the Prince said, standing and almost in tears. "What am I going to do, James? I really didn't touch her. She was coughing and suddenly there was blood everywhere and then she dropped. This is very bad; I'm the heir to the throne, for Christ's sake!"

Gresham went to check on Emma. She was a mess with blood smeared all over her face and chest. Gresham couldn't help but admire her fine shape as she lay in her thin, cotton underclothes that were plastered to her naked body. "Hmmm," he said as he checked her pulse.

"Well?" Wilkins asked impatiently.

"Yes, she's stone dead, alright," Gresham announced soberly as he tore himself away.

"Look, Karol, this is my close friend, David Gresham. We'll take care of this for you. You trust me, don't you?"

"Yes, of course," the Prince replied. "Will you do that for me? Really?" he pleaded.

"This won't come back to you, I swear it," Wilkins assured him. "David will get you cleaned up and take you to the Palace. You were never here, do you understand?"

"Yes, thank you, James, thank you," the Prince gasped, overwhelmed by emotion and alcohol.

"Will you do something for me, Karol, a favor in return?"

"Yes, of course, anything, James."

"Then listen to me carefully," Wilkins said, now deadly serious. "You know why I am here in Bucharest. It's time for Roumania to choose a side, Karol. I want you to go to your mother, Queen Marie, and you get her to talk to Prime Minister Brătianu first thing, tonight if possible. You and your mother start putting the pressure on Brătianu, just get him to meet us somewhere, somewhere private where we can finally hammer out a deal and get this God-damned country into the f---ing war. Do you understand me? Otherwise, so help me God, you will hang for killing this woman."

"Yes," said the Prince, now much more sober than he had been a minute earlier. "Yes, I understand, James, all too well. I will go to my mother tonight. I will do as you ask. Believe me, I want the war too."

"David will see to it that you make it home safely."

"I've got a clean shirt for you," Gresham said consolingly. "Come with me and we'll get you cleaned up." He put an arm around the Prince and helped him up. The Prince looked at the lifeless body on the floor one last time and shook his head. "She was so beautiful," he sobbed. Then Gresham led him out the door.

Wilkins followed and shut the door behind Gresham and the Prince, then turned to look at Wolczak. Her thin, blood-saturated underclothes stuck obscenely to her bosom and, from where he was standing, Wilkins could see straight up her bloomers. In his embarrassment he tried to look away, but found he could not.

"Let's get you cleaned up, my darling," he said quietly.

Wolczak spit out the blood-filled rubber condom she had pierced with her teeth. "That was so much fun! Was I good?" She asked gaily.

"Very. Very good, yes," he said, utterly failing to avert his eyes any longer.

"Just look at me, James. This cow's blood has made my underclothes all sticky," Wolczak said in a quiet, pouty voice. "Could you please help me take them off?"

"Um, yes, of course," he said nervously. He had helped her remove nearly all her blood-soaked clothing before she finally stopped him with a kiss.

The next evening, Wilkins, Gresham, Prince Karol, Barclay and Prime Minister Brătianu met at the home of the Prime Minister's brother far from the center of the city and away from prying German eyes.

"I hope we can finally reach an agreement, Prime Minister," said Barclay, "and I want to assure you that Great Britain is prepared to meet your demands to ensure that Roumania is fully compensated for its commitment to the war effort."

"You have always been prepared to do so," Brătianu replied, "and if Roumania were ever to declare war, I would have no choice but to come in on the side of the Entente. The Queen, the Prince, the people, the oil barons and the land-owners all plead Great Britain's cause. The King is simply silent on the matter, as he knows he is now hopelessly outnumbered. We are not simply waiting for a better offer from Germany and Austria."

"Certainly Emperor Franz Joseph will not part with Transylvania simply because Roumanians live there," Prince Karol said. "If we can't have that, then what can Austria or Germany really offer us, Prime Minister?"

"Yes, I agree, but I do not think Russia will willingly give up Bessarabia either," Brătianu replied.

"But they have already agreed to do so, Prime Minister," Barclay insisted.

"I am quite skeptical about that, Ambassador. Regardless, I will tell you quite candidly, gentlemen, the reason I do not wish to declare war is because I believe it is not possible for our country to win a military engagement against the Austrians or Germans. I have spoken to our fine generals, and, yes, they speak with the voice of eternal optimism, but I know that our armies are no match for our enemies. We will lose terribly, and many of my people will suffer or die as a result. That is not acceptable."

"I think you are wrong," Gresham spoke up confidently.

"May I know your name, sir?" Brătianu asked.

"I am Colonel David Gresham," he addressed the Prime Minister, "and this is Colonel James Wilkins, sir. Perhaps you have heard of us?"

"Yes, indeed I have. And if what I have heard is true, then it was a most impressive action in France, Colonel."

"Then allow me to suggest, Sir, that instead of discussing 'if' you will wage war, we instead discuss 'how' you will wage war. Specifically, how Great Britain will help you to win. Isn't that what you are really asking?"

"Is that a question you are qualified to answer?" Brătianu asked. "For all his eminence, Ambassador Barclay is not."

"I absolutely agree," Gresham replied, "and, yes, I believe I am qualified. I am not a diplomat; I am a soldier, and I tell you that Roumania can defeat its enemies. To begin with, you have been promised 40,000 Russian troops. I agree that number is wildly inadequate. Great Britain can now assure you that Russia will supply as many as *200,000* troops before the end of this year, and they and their officers will be placed under Roumanian command."

"Colonel Gresham!" Barclay objected.

"Shut your mouth, Barclay; it's time for a professional to do the talking," Gresham said. "In addition, Prime Minister, Colonel Wilkins and I have just come from Salonika, where General Sarrail has over 400,000 British and French troops ready to invade Bulgaria. If Roumania will attack across the Danube, I guarantee that you will conquer Bulgaria in a matter of weeks."

"Well, Bulgaria, Colonel, frankly, we do not want it," Brătianu said dismissively. "For one thing, it is full of Bulgars already. No, we want

Transylvania, which is predominantly occupied by the *români* people. But surely Austria and Germany will not let us simply take it."

"Austria's armies are occupied in Italy and Serbia. Germany's armies are occupied with the Russian offensive and at the Somme and Verdun in France, far away. Our intelligence office tells us there is simply no German or Austrian army capable of attacking you in Transylvania, Prime Minister. They are utterly taxed. For the past eight months, the Germans have not been able to create even one new Division. For them to send an army to Transylvania is totally inconceivable. Still, we must secure Bulgaria first – it is the more tactically vital target as you cannot fight on two fronts. Take Bulgaria, sir, and then Transylvania will be yours."

"Why should I trust what you say, Colonel," Brătianu objected.

"I can answer that question," Prince Karol argued forcefully. "My mother the Queen and I fully concur with this strategy, Prime Minister. I have known Colonel Wilkins and Colonel Gresham a very long time, and I trust them both completely. I will vouchsafe that they speak the truth."

Brătianu looked at the Prince a moment, and then stared blankly at the ceiling a moment longer. "This was to be a negotiation, was it not?" Brătianu asked. "So here is my position, Colonel. Roumania will declare war on Austria *only* and attack Transylvania first. We will support your Russians, who will have our permission to cross Roumanian territory in order to invade Bulgaria in coordination with General Sarrail. And one more thing, Colonel Gresham, I want you and Colonel Wilkins seconded to our army for the duration of our offensive. If the stories of your success at Foncquevillers are true, let us see whether you can bring the same expertise and experience to our armies."

Gresham extended his hand to the Prime Minister as he turned to Barclay. "Write it down, Ambassador," he said.

"What in the name of Christ have you done, Colonel Gresham?!" Barclay shouted angrily as their sedan pulled away from the meeting.

"Really, David, I think that was a bit much," Wilkins agreed.

"To begin with," Barclay continued, "there are perhaps only 200,000 men under General Sarrail's command at Salonika, not 400,000, and they are supposed to invade Serbia, not Bulgaria. And the Russians have certainly *not* agreed to send 200,000 troops to Roumania."

"Then it will be your job to see that they do, Barclay," Gresham said calmly. "Or at least there had better be enough of them to ensure that Bulgaria does not attack Roumania from the south."

"How could you say there are no German Divisions capable of reaching Transylvania? I was never told that," Wilkins insisted.

"Perhaps that's just wishful thinking on my part," Gresham admitted, "but the Huns must be spread pretty damn thin, you'd have to agree."

"And if they're not? What if they can throw together enough men to stage a counter-attack? What then, David?" Wilkins asked.

"In that case, James, I suggest you come up with a damn good evacuation strategy, because if the Germans come down out of the Transylvanian Alps into Roumania, it's going to be a bloody ugly mess."

"Rather worse than that," Barclay said. "We have tremendous stores of petrol and grains in Roumania which the Germans most certainly cannot be allowed to seize. Good God, this situation is simply intolerable! You have promised the Roumanians guns and artillery that don't even exist!"

"I have followed my instructions, Ambassador. 'A declaration of war is required, any promises may be made, Roumania's success or failure is irrelevant.' If that presents any difficulty for you, I suggest you take it up with the Prime Minister – our Prime Minister, Asquith, I mean."

Barclay at last quieted down at the mention of Asquith.

"Can we do it, though, David? Can we help Roumania win?" Wilkins asked.

"I am fairly certain we cannot. They can invade Transylvania, but whether they keep it will be Germany's decision. Does it truly matter, James? Wherever the armies go, whatever territories they occupy during this time of war, the right to draw the maps and place the borders will, at the bitter end, go to the victors. Right now, our side needs Roumania to declare war, but the outcome of the war will not be decided based upon who occupies Roumania or Transylvania or Bulgaria a year from now. Any battle, any new front, extends the German and Austrian armies that much further. They *will* reach a breaking point."

"And the Roumania people will suffer for it."

"Everyone else is suffering – why should the Roumanians be spared?" Gresham replied angrily. Roumania would get much of what it wanted once the war was won, he thought. Could the country expect to gain territory without any losses at all? And damn Wilkins, Gresham thought, must we question everything we are told to do? *Control* was insistent that Roumania be brought into the war by summer's end, and surely he and Asquith and the War Committee knew very well what would happen: Roumania would burn.

Early the next morning, Gresham and Wilkins went to meet the Chief of Operations for the Roumanian Army, a Lieutenant Colonel named Ioan Răşcanu, a clever and knowledgeable man who, by the default of the aged and incompetent Chief of Staff and First Deputy, had become the *de facto* leader of the entire Roumanian military. Răşcanu, with his sunken black eyes and his wild and wavy black hair and drooping French-style mustache, stared at Gresham and Wilkins with curiosity and surprise as they were shown into his small windowless office. The office was littered with maps and folders, and his desk was covered with papers and diagrams and even a few oily machine gun parts. "You are the two Englishmen the Prime Minister has sent us, are you not?" he asked. "How pleasant of you to visit. Welcome."

"Yes, I am Colonel James Wilkins, and this is Colonel David Gresham."

"An honor to meet you both," Rășcanu said as he stood to shake their hands. "Please, be seated, gentlemen. I was told you would be here at mid-day, but it is a fine morning for work, is it not? May I get you anything? How may I be of assistance?"

"I understand you were a liaison officer with the French at the start of the war, at the Marne, is that correct, Colonel?" Gresham asked.

"Yes, that is true, and before the war, I was Roumania's military attaché in Berlin."

"We have also been led to believe that you are the person who actually makes the decisions around here," Wilkins added.

"Well, I am the Chief of Operations –"

"Let's not mince words, Sir," Wilkins said, "Colonel Gresham and I are not diplomats; we are soldiers like you and we have been sent to help. We wish to speak to the person who actually makes the decisions, not the person with the finest uniform, and we have been told that when decisions need to be made, you make them and your superiors agree to whatever you recommend. So, if that is the situation, then I suggest you order in some coffee and pull out your maps, because there is a great deal to do. Roumania is going to war as soon as it can be arranged."

Rășcanu smiled. "As you wish, gentlemen, and you may call me Ioan."

The rest of the day was spent reviewing the many reports in Rășcanu's office and determining how many active duty troops were prepared and equipped to go to war. They discovered there were 146 active-duty Divisions comprised of less than 800,000 men; that meant the musters of many Divisions were short and a rapid reorganization was required. The reconstituted Divisions were then to be arranged in four Army Groups of 150,000 men each, with the remaining troops stationed in and around Bucharest in reserve. Rășcanu also admitted that few of the commanders in the Roumanian military had any modern warfare experience, and while there was a fair number of new machine guns and grenades sent by the French, no one had yet trained the Roumanian troops to use them. Their artillery was limited to some old French 105 millimeter mountain guns and some smaller, but newer, 75's; there were no big guns at all. The armies would be reasonably mobile, but on the offensive, it seemed, men would need to be sacrificed in lieu of artillery shells.

Next they looked at the maps. Gresham, who had never been to Roumania, had no idea where the much-debated Transylvania region was located. The western border of Roumania, he discovered, had been drawn along the line of the Carpathian mountain range. To the west of the mountains was the lush, green, and prosperous region called Transylvania, and although it was now a part of Hungary, it had in the past been Roumanian territory. Over seventy percent of the current inhabitants there were *români*. To the north lay the Moldova region and to the east an area called Bessarabia that had previously been taken from the Ottoman Empire by their new ally, Russia; the Russians now shared Roumania's northern and north-eastern borders. To the south-east lay the area called

Dobruja, a region of Roumania which sat on the shores of the Black Sea; and to the south, below the Danube River, was Bulgaria. Bucharest sat squarely in the middle.

As Gresham and Wilkins poured over the maps, it was at first obvious that any offensive into Transylvania would have to go over the mountains and through the limited natural mountain passes, a difficult feat in itself and of great concern, for if their communication or supply lines were cut, the Roumanian armies invading Hungary would be completely isolated. In addition, a substantial number of Divisions, perhaps an entire Army Group, would be needed to guard the southern border with Bulgaria even if the Roumanians did not invade there first, lest the Bulgarians mount even a limited attack directly on Bucharest. And finally, the Russians (however many were ultimately sent) would be asked to invade Bulgaria through Dobruja.

For several days, as the military reorganization was frantically completed, Gresham and Wilkins advocated that only one Army Group be sent into Transylvania while one Army would prepare defenses along the border in the mountains and two Army Groups would be stationed along the Danube River to prepare for the invasion into Bulgaria. In truth, they feared that the Transylvania offensive would end in a quick retreat. However, their recommendations were harshly overruled by the Prime Minister and the governing war committee: Three Army Groups (the First, Second, and Fourth), it was decided, would invade Transylvania, advancing as quickly as possible to the Mures River, which was the first easily defensible natural boundary after the mountains (that meant a wildly optimistic incursion of over 250 kilometers into Hungarian territory); the Third Army alone would guard the border with Bulgaria.

As the secretly anticipated date of the war declaration approached, Wolczak announced that Gresham's chest wounds were fully healed – a relief to Gresham in more ways than one. Certainly he was pleased to be safe from a fatal infection and able to move about normally, but he was also beginning to feel awkward about being examined by Nurse Wolczak when she was spending every free moment, day *and* night, with Wilkins. One morning, for example, as Wolczak was checking Gresham for fever using a rectal thermometer, she asked him: "You don't think James will mind that I am to start work again at the Red Cross Hospital, do you?"

"Must we discuss that now?" Gresham replied.

She eventually discovered that Wilkins, who was quite busy planning the offensive into Transylvania, was very pleased that Wolczak would be regularly occupied with the work she seemed to love so much. She had no trouble securing a position in the Roumanian Red Cross hospital in Bucharest. Indeed, the doctors there, who knew very little of war wounds, chemical weapons or shell shock, were grateful to have found a nurse familiar with managing such injuries. They promptly set Wolczak to teach the other nurses (and quite a few of the doctors) what she had learned in Italy, including the rudimentary steps in treating such patients. They knew full well that the hospital would soon be overflowing with the wounded.

It was immediately after one such class of instruction, that Wolczak was approached by another nurse, a beautiful and elegant middle-aged woman who had been most attentive during Wolczak's lecture on the treatment of mustard gas injuries.

"My dear, I just want to thank you for your remarkable efforts to educate us all. We are all so pleased that you are here, and you have come all the way from America. Was I informed correctly that your mother was born in Roumania?"

"Thank you; thank you so much! Yes, that's right," Wolczak said gaily, "but my grandfather took her to America when she was still just a little girl. My name is Emma, by the way," she added, holding out her hand.

"Emma, what a pretty name," the woman replied kindly as she took Wolczak's hand. "You may call me Missy, while we are at work. Again, thank you, my dear."

As the woman left the room, one of the other nurses approached Wolczak as well. "What did she say?" She asked Wolczak.

"Who are you talking about?"

"The Queen! The woman you were just speaking to, that was Queen Marie, you foolish girl! She's volunteered to work here at hospital with us!"

"Gosh! I had no idea," Wolczak remarked in astonishment.

Later that afternoon, Wilkins rode with Barclay east to Jassy to meet with General Andrei Zayonchkovski, commander of the Russian 30th Army Corps (the Russians had sent only the 40,000 men previously agreed upon); Gresham traveled north-west to the city of Ploiesti, where the Second Army was encamped, to review the Roumanian troops.

Gresham watched the men training on a cheery, bright summer morning. In the rugged fields and hills, there was a sense of excitement and elation among the troops. Many of the men wore ridiculously bright and garish ribbons and plumes as they shouted and whistled and blew horns announcing their advance. None wore shrapnel helmets and none had gas masks. Some were wearing shoes that appeared to be made of cardboard and were already disintegrating; many had antique rifles they had brought from their homes claiming they were more reliable than the old *Mannlicher* rifles issued by the army command. Although some troops were equipped with the old French *Chauchat* light machine guns, no one had yet learned to use the new Maxim guns. A chill stole down Gresham's spine since the fate of these poor soldiers was easy to foresee. These men would be stricken by disease, shoeless in rain-drenched shell holes, shells bursting around them as a sickly yellow-green toxic gas rolled across the fields to suffocate them. They were typical of the nearly half-million men who would invade Hungary and occupy Transylvania for – how long – a month, a week? Were the men fighting this war truly that valueless to their commanders, to the politicians and to the kings and emperors who had started this conflict? Gresham was furious and turned away to find the Second Army's commander.

He found General Alexandru Averescu, billeted in a large and comfortable suite in the *Central Hotel* in Ploiesti. Averescu was a tall, trim man with short hair and a small, pointed grey beard who had spent a long career in the military and politics. He had previously been both the Minister for War and the Chief of the General Staff, but the only military action he had ever commanded was when the army ruthlessly put down a peasant's revolt some years before the war. Gresham was shown into the large comfortable office that Averescu had established in the hotel's largest suite, and he stood before the large mahogany desk as the older general and statesman, in his finest dress uniform, reviewed Gresham's written report.

Aversecu's scowl showed his displeasure with Gresham's harsh assessment of the Second Army and of the whole plan of attack into Transylvania. The General's eyes would, from time to time, flash up toward the contemptful young British Colonel standing silent and expressionless before him. At last, Averescu threw the report violently onto his desk and stood, towering over Gresham.

"Colonel," he began tersely, "in the course of my long career, I have spent many years in Austria and Germany. I have seen their disciplined troops, their artillery, their elite units, everything. There is not one fact stated in your report of which I am unaware. You will please tell me, then, how am I to correct these deficiencies in two days' time?"

"What you mean to do in Transylvania, Sir, is far different from what the British and French are doing on the Western Front. Your men are simply not prepared or equipped to conduct trench warfare, therefore they must not dig in. Your Army is not encumbered with big artillery guns, it is not a mechanized army, but your men are fit – farmers and factory workers mostly, swift and passionate. They cannot stand still. They must constantly swarm upon our enemies, and then withdraw. If Transylvania is, as you contend, predominantly inhabited by Roumanians, then let the civilians occupy Transylvania and make your Army their strike force.

"I have spent time with the *Chetniks* in Serbia, Sir. They fight fiercely; they do not take prisoners. They move quickly so the Austrians do not know where they will be attacked next. That is your example, General. You should be with your men. You should lead them from one engagement to the next, and do not expect the fighting to end until this war is finally finished."

"The soldiers of Roumania are not brigands like the *Chetniks*. Nevertheless, I understand that what you are suggesting is common sense," Averescu said as he sat down. "Where have you fought, Gresham?"

"At Ypres in '14, Sir; I was at Gravenstafel Ridge when the Germans gassed the French lines there. I've fought at Sinai and Gallipoli and in the trenches at the Somme."

"Yes, I've heard about your action at the Somme," Averescu said dismissively. "Do you know *why* you and Colonel Wilkins succeeded there?"

Gresham did know, and it was something he had not discussed with anyone until now, yet Averescu seemed to know his secret as well. Perhaps, Gresham thought, Averescu was not the inept commander he had assumed. "We succeeded, Sir, because we did not attempt to hold the territory we seized. It was merely a raid. If we had held onto those trenches, the German's artillery and inevitable counter-attack would have destroyed us."

"Exactly. We are now being sent to hold Transylvania, though, are we not?"

"You must know as well as I, General, that it will not be possible to hold Transylvania. Our enemies cannot permit it. If you dig trenches, they will use gas. If you occupy a town, they will shell it to rubble. The fighting will continue until there is a peace treaty, and there will be no treaty until your allies overwhelm the Germans. This is, partly, why Colonel Wilkins and I have repeatedly recommended to the War Committee and Prime Minister Brătianu that Roumania stay out of Transylvania altogether."

"I happen to agree with you, Colonel, but I have my orders. I must take the Second Army into Transylvania, at least until I am directed otherwise. But I also understand what you are recommending and the strategy you propose. If I were to have you assigned to personally lead two of my Divisions, some 30,000 men, do you believe you would you be up to the task?"

Gresham's eyes opened wide in surprise. "I ... I think so, General; it would be an honor. But that is a decision for the Committee, isn't it?"

"Of course, but it can all be arranged if you agree. Just bear in mind, Colonel – if you take my soldiers into Hungary, you had better be able to get them out."

"Yes, Sir," Gresham replied.

After the meeting, Gresham began to immediately regret his quick decision. Yes, he had been soft-soaped into accepting the appointment, flattered that the General would consider him useful, but in his heart Gresham knew the entire offensive was going to be a disaster. The Transylvania offensive was certain to provoke both the Austrians and Germans, whereas the incursion into Bulgaria that he and Wilkins had proposed remained the safer course of action. The mountain passes into Transylvania should not be crossed; they should be barricaded. There should be fixed machine gun bunkers, and the artillery could be stationary and their targets fixed. There was every reason to believe that the Germans and Austrians could be kept at bay, but after they entered Hungary, would there be time left to fortify the mountain passes against the inevitable enemy counter-attack?

The next morning, the War Committee commissioned Gresham as an acting corps commander with the nominal rank of Brigade General with instructions to lead the Fifteenth and Sixteenth Infantry Divisions of the Second Army. He drove west with Averescu up into the Carpathian Mountains to the village of Sinaia for a meeting with the other Second Army commanders. The small village was surrounded by dark, dense forests, and the villagers were timid, afraid of what the presence of the elegantly uniformed officers signified for their homes and families.

There were a limited number of mountain passes through which the First, Second and Fourth Armies could enter Hungary, and from the village Gresham could see up the valley toward the Predeal Pass through which he would lead his Divisions. His first objective would be to seize the town of Brashov. Gresham's two divisions were to be the spearhead of the Second Army's attack.

In the afternoon when he returned to Ploiesti, Gresham was introduced to his new adjutant, Major Vasile Neascu, a short, clever young man who had studied engineering at Cambridge. Although a cool and calculating man, he was seemingly excited to be assigned to the controversial and aggressive young British commander. Gresham doubted his others officers would be as receptive, especially when they heard his plans. Together, Gresham and Neascu rode to the Fifteenth Infantry encampment outside of town, where the adjutant had collected the two Infantry Divisions' senior officers into a large, hot hut. The elegant officers (most had purchased their army commissions and came from the ruling class of Roumania) were uncomfortable and wary of the new, young, and foreign General.

I shall have to be gentle with them, Gresham thought, at least for a time.

"Good afternoon, gentlemen. Thank you for coming on short notice," Gresham began, allowing Neascu time to translate for him. "Major Neascu has brought me up to date regarding the muster: In the Fifteenth Division, there are close to 11,000 able men, and there are 13,000 in the Sixteenth; those numbers I'm told include the pioneers battalion and the artillery battalion of each Division. Is that right, Major?"

"Yes, Sir," Neascu replied.

"We have also been given two regiments of the new ranger units, the *Vânători de Munte*, 6,000 men. They are commanded by Major Lazar and Major Christea. And lastly, we have the 44th Cavalry Battalion under the command of Major Mirunescu, some 400 men and their mounts.

"It's been my pleasure to review these troops over the past few days and see the enthusiasm and discipline of the men; I congratulate you. I have no doubt that, in a traditional engagement, these Divisions would ably overcome your enemies. However, General Averescu has another strategy in mind, and that is why I have been assigned to command these soldiers. It will require some reorganization and reassignment, but I know you will appreciate that these changes are necessitated by the General's plans and the fact that these units are to be combined under a single commander.

"To begin with, the 1st and 2nd Battalions of the Fifteenth and Sixteenth Divisions are being reassigned to Majors Lazar and Christea, bringing their units up to 5,000 men each, and it will be their duty to prepare the new companies as quickly as possible. Major Mirunescu, due to your seniority and vast experience, I shall require you to take command of our artillery; the two battalions are to be combined into one artillery regiment." As Neascu translated, the officers could see that Mirunescu was pleased with what he deemed a promotion, which was precisely what Gresham had hoped. "The men of the cavalry battalion will also be divided and reassigned to Majors Lazar and Christea," he continued. This announcement was met with considerable grumbling. The cavalry was the last refuge of the wealthy, those who could afford to supply and tend to their own mounts. By splitting the cavalry and placing the men with the ranger units instead, Gresham was in effect saying that the cavalry were no better than common foot soldiers. To Gresham, they were in fact less valuable than foot soldiers as long as they pretended to be aristocrats. He expected his men to fight – and while men on horseback could move swiftly, he did not plan to move his cavalry on the battlefield *en masse* like Napoleon or Wellington had done. "That will leave a combined division of some 8,000 infantrymen under my personal command, and the pioneers battalions, which are being assigned to Major Neascu to oversee."

There was a considerable and somewhat hostile silence following these announcements.

"Gentlemen, you have three days. At the end of that time, I want your men to be able to advance silently and stealthily, to advance utilizing any available cover – there will be absolutely no charging of the enemy's defenses and no more ribbons or plumes allowed. Your men must learn how to use the new machine guns and throw grenades; and they must be able to hit a target at a hundred yards. When we advance, there will be no baggage train; the men must carry what they need. We will be quick, we will be agile, and our enemies will not know where they will be attacked next. We will not give them time to dig in, and when they counter-attack, we will give up the battlefield and attack their flanks and rear. We will drive into them and pursue them all the way to the Mures River. You have three days."

Averescu had already sent dozens of men over the mountains into Transylvania to secretly gather information about Austro-Hungarian troop locations, fortifications, and the allegiances of the local population, and later that evening Neascu presented the reports to Gresham, Mirunescu, Lazar and Christea. Lazer and Christea were older and more experienced than Gresham; they were men who had been promoted from the ranks and knew how to fight. They were exactly the men Gresham needed. Their rangers would be Gresham's agile strike force while the troops under his own command would be the cannon fodder, the ones to hold the center while Lazer and Christea attacked the enemy's flanks. Behind them, the local Roumanian people would need to secure their own towns and villages. The vast majority of Transylvanians, the scouts reported, were sympathetic and willing (although perhaps not eager) to help the Roumanian Army.

Wilkins, meanwhile, had been asked to serve as liaison between the War Committee and Russian General Andrei Zayonchkovski. The Russian forces (still far less than the 200,000 which Gresham had promised) were amassed in Dobruja, north of the city of Costanza on the Black Sea coast. The Russian General was unenthusiastic about the planned offensive into Bulgaria. There would be no more Russian troops, he told Wilkins definitely. There would only be enough men to deter an attack by the Bulgarians into Dobruja. For even that, there might not be enough.

On the afternoon of 27 August, a formal dispatch was delivered by the Roumanian ambassador to the Foreign Minister in Vienna: Roumania had declared war on Austria-Hungary. In Bucharest, there were celebrations. People drank champagne in the streets and celebrated as if the war had already been won, but at dusk a total blackout was ordered and the crowds were ushered indoors to store water and blankets due to the possibility of an aerial bombardment. Although many of the German diplomats left the city, others simply disappeared into the shadows; the city was full of spies.

Sometime after midnight, one company of Gresham's rangers slipped quietly into the Predeal Pass and surrounded the small Hungarian custom house. The Hungarian soldiers, awakened by the pounding on their door and still in their bedclothes, surrendered without a shot. The invasion of Transylvania had begun.

Brigade General David Gresham stood at a window on the upper floor of the custom house watching as his troops, loaded with heavy packs, rifles, grenades, and gas masks marched silently in long lines eight abreast, through the silvery moonlight and into Transylvania. It was not yet autumn and the air was still mild. The sky was perfectly clear, but a thick fog had begun to rise around the marching troops as they descended from the Pass into Hungary. The effect was ethereal and, in some respects, beautiful, Gresham thought. It was a good night for war. Gresham felt certain that the Roumanian soldiers would fight enthusiastically and that his officers understood his strategy. Lazer and Christea, in particular, knew just what was required of them. It was thrilling for Gresham to see the great mass of men and machinery of war advance under his command. Still, in his heart, Gresham believed the invasion would fail. He recalled the day he and Wilkins had left Verdun, how the city crumbled behind them under the German artillery bombardment. They knew that a million German soldiers were even then rushing to attack the stoic French defenders. Gresham wasn't worried about the Austrian or the Bulgarian armies. No, he was worried that the Germans would come to Transylvania. If they did, the brave and enthusiastic Roumanian men now marching into Transylvania under his command would be slaughtered.

"Lazer is downstairs, General," Neascu announced from the doorway.

"Send him up," Gresham replied.

Lazer was a large, rough fellow who had spent a lifetime in the Roumanian army. Even at his age, Gresham thought, Lazer could probably still kill a man with his bare hands.

"Sir," Lazer said simply as he entered the room. It was the only English word he knew.

"Neascu, ask the Major if he is ready to take his men north to Sacele. If so, he can proceed now that we are through the pass without trouble."

Neascu translated. Major Lazer simply nodded to Gresham with a menacing grin and promptly exited the room. Gresham had decided to split his rangers and to send Lazer north along the mountain ridge toward Sacele, a small village located to the east of the town of Brashov. Brashov would be Gresham's first true test as a commander. The town was heavily fortified and occupied by thousands of Austrian troops under the command of the experienced Austrian General Anton von Goldbach.

Gresham descended to the road and walked with Major Christea as their combined forces marched down the valley into Hungary toward the village of Predeal. In the dark of the night, the forward scouts identified one thin picket line of Hungarian frontier guards. Gresham ordered the troops to halt and sent his light infantry into the woods to shoot and kill the Hungarians soldiers from cover in the surrounding woods. Not one of the Hungarians escape.

At dawn, as the sky was beginning to lighten and a thick fog covered the roads and fields, Gresham and Christea marched down into the village. The Roumanian villagers awoke astonished and elated to find that Predeal was now occupied by thousands of their countrymen. The people celebrated and cried and hugged the troops. It took Gresham some hours to get his men under control. Major Christea and his troops, however, were promptly sent to capture and occupy another small village to the west.

Early in the afternoon, Gresham led his remaining forces northwest down the main road of the valley toward the city of Brashov. The sun had broken through the fog at last and the men sang as they marched. They reached the village of Timisu de Jos, just outside Brashov, by mid-afternoon.

As Gresham expected, General von Goldbach had sent two infantry divisions out to stop the Roumanian invaders. The Austrians had thrown barricades across the road and simply waited for the Roumanians to attack. But Gresham did not attack. He ordered his men take up positions in the woods across from the Austrians. The two enemies began to exchange sniper and artillery fire. After an hour, the Austrian commander became impatient and began to send companies out in an attempt to push the Roumanians back. Gresham pulled his men back and slowly retreated up the road, scrambling back toward Predeal but resisting foot by foot. The Austrians pursued eagerly as the Roumanians retreated. Then, suddenly, the Roumanian trumpets blared, Gresham's troops stopped and threw themselves into the Austrians, and Major Lazer and his rangers rushed down out of a narrow canyon and slammed into the Austrians' left flank. The Austrians were caught in the cross-fire between Gresham's men and Major Lazer's rangers and were nearly decimated before the order to withdraw was finally given. Yet even the Austrian retreat was too late, for Major Christea's regiment had quick-marched to attack Brashov from the rear. His men infiltrated the close, narrow streets of the town and fought door-to-door as the local population hid and waited anxiously. General Von Goldbach was forced to order his remaining troops to retreat from the city. By midnight, Gresham had successfully taken Brashov and captured more than 3,000 enemy soldiers. His men were ecstatic, chanting Gresham's name and cheering his passage to the city center as the citizens of Brashov wept in joy.

Gresham promptly advanced from Brashov the next day, leaving behind the crowds of joyful *români* civilians. Major Christea and Major Lazer spread out on Gresham's flanks, charging to attack Goldbach's Austrian troops, first on one side and then the other, as Gresham's men doggedly advanced. In two days, they pushed Goldbach back to the village of Feldioara, and in ten days they had pushed the Austrians back some sixty kilometers, all the way to the Olt River.

From all along the Transylvania front, trainloads of wounded soldiers returned to Bucharest each day. Many were sent to the Red Cross hospital where Emma Wolczak worked side by side with the Roumanian doctors. As a nurse, she was not able to perform surgery on the wounded troops, but the doctors had come to respect her skills so much that they allowed Wolczak to treat many patients for light wounds and illnesses with little supervision. Every day Emma saw Queen Marie, or "Missy" as Emma called her, in the patient wards and they often worked together.

Wilkins stayed with the War Committee and worked with Ioan Rășcanu to administrate the slowly advancing Roumanian armies. He was also the liaison between the War Committee and the Russians and frequently shuttled with Barclay between Bucharest, Jassy and Costanza seeking a diplomatic agreement for the invasion of Bulgaria. The Russians resisted such a step. They were busy dealing with the Germans far to the north, they argued, and, even worse, General Zayonchkovski confided to Wilkins that the Russian soldiers themselves had refused to invade Bulgaria. Wilkins could not comprehend the General's statement – how could the troops simply refuse?

Nearly every evening, however, Wilkins returned to Emma at the *Athénée Palace* hotel.

In Transylvania, the Roumanian armies were battering the Austrian defenders as Gresham's forces spearheaded the attack against their retreating enemy. General von Goldbach's troops scrambled across the shallow Olt River taking every boat with them and destroying the few remaining bridges; the Austrians, uncertain where Gresham's forces were encamped in the forests, were bombarding the opposite shore. In the village of Mateias, just across the river, shells were falling from time to time as Gresham, Neascu, Lazer, Christea and Mirunescu met to plan their own river crossing.

"We are not yet halfway to the Mures River, and we must cross the Olt," Gresham said. "I simply do not understand, gentlemen, why we cannot simply cross it. I have looked at the river, and with the lack of rain the water level is remarkably low. Can the men simply not walk across?"

"The men can cross, General, but the artillery cannot," Mirunescu complained. "We must have a bridge for the artillery, especially for the larger guns which we have captured from the Austrians."

"We cannot stop for the artillery. Every day we delay gives the Austrians more time to prepare defenses, to dig trenches and construct bunkers," Gresham replied. "We cannot hesitate."

"*Austriecii au deja retrase din orașul Racos. Dar nu știm ce fac în continuare vest,*" Lazer said.

"Lazer's scouts say that the town of Racos across the river is undefended, but further west, Goldbach is likely digging in already," Neascu translated. "He will not retreat much longer, and then we will need the artillery on the other side of the river."

"Yes," Lazer added.

"Then you shall have to get some of those bloody pioneers over here to build us a few bridges," Gresham said to Neascu curtly, "but you, Lazer and Christea, I want you both on the other side of this river tomorrow morning. You may pursue the Austrians for twenty kilometers, no more. Don't let them run away or dig in. We must keep them busy fighting, even thinking they can beat us back, as long as they do not have time to construct defenses."

The next morning, Gresham's men moved across the river into the town of Racos as Lazer's and Christea's rangers scoured the surrounding countryside killing or capturing every Austrian soldier they could find. The pioneers prepared pontoon boats to form the bridge that would allow the artillery to cross the river. After only three days, the bridge was completed and Mirunescu's artillery began to cross in the middle of the night.

But, to Gresham's consternation, neither Lazer nor Christea had been able to find the bulk of Goldbach's army – wherever they had gone, it was apparently many kilometers from the Olt River. To make matters even more difficult, Gresham received orders from General Averescu to send Major Lazer and his rangers south to aid in the First Army's siege of the city of Sibiu. While Gresham understood that the city was an important symbol to the Roumanian people, taking Sibiu served no tactical purpose and Gresham would have to advance from the Olt River without a third of his forces.

Gresham proceeded as quickly as possible up the road as Christea's rangers probed ahead to discover what defenses the Austrian had thrown in their way. They proceeded several kilometers without encountering the enemy, but it was not long before the Christea's scouts came back with unfortunate news. Outside the village of Homorod, the Austrians had dug trenches and placed machine guns. Major Christea took his men around to the north of the village, but the Austrians were well defended, and soon Gresham had no choice but to bring up his mortars and begin a slow and steady bombardment of the enemy's lines with his limited supply of shells. It was exactly the sort of protracted stalemate that Gresham had intended to avoid. Unbeknownst to him, General Goldbach had been given strict orders: There were to be no more retreats. Then the Austrian artillery and aeroplanes began to respond to the Roumanian attackers, and Gresham was finally forced to order his men to dig in as well.

That night, Christea's rangers captured an enemy scout. He was brought to the little white church outside Homorod where Gresham had established his command center. The rangers bound the scout's hands and feet and left him sitting against the white-washed wall inside the nave of the church. That was where Gresham found him later that evening, and as he looked down he saw everything that needed to be said written on the man's uniform – his German uniform. *"Willkommen in Transsylvanien,"* Gresham said. *"Wer ist Ihr Commander,"* he asked, *"Goldbach?"*

The scout smiled menacingly as he looked up at Gresham. *"Nein, mein Commander ist Falkenhayn,"* he said with a laugh, and Gresham knew in an instant that Roumania's spectacular offensive in Transylvania was finished. Somehow, in a mere fifteen days, the Germans had created an entire new army and delivered it to Hungary under the command of Erich von Falkenhayn, the very man who had planned the devastating German attack on Verdun.

The pounding on the door of his room at the *Athénée Palace* in Bucharest awoke Wilkins from a pleasant dream, and then he realized it had not been a dream at all because Emma still lay beside him, warm, naked, and very soft beneath the soft, crisp cotton sheets.

"Go see who it is, darling," Wolczak mumbled, still half-asleep. Against his better judgment, Wilkins climbed from the bed, put on his robe, and then stumbled in the half-light of the early morning to open the door.

"Colonel Wilkins, Sir," said the anxious young Roumanian soldier breathlessly, "the Chief of Operations would like to see you at once."

"What has happened?" Wilkins demanded, now suddenly wide awake.

"The enemy has invaded Dobruja, Sir. General von Mackensen, he has formed an army in Bulgaria and has invaded Dobruja."

"Good Lord," Wilkins exclaimed. "I will be right with you." He dressed hurriedly, kissed Wolczak goodbye, and ran out to the sedan in which the Roumanian soldier waited to drive Wilkins to the War Committee offices.

Wilkins had spent many fruitless hours attempting to convince the wary Russians to send more troops to Roumania, and although it was largely unspoken, it was apparent to Wilkins that the Russian commanders were anxious. Although the war was nowhere near ending, the Russian troops were tired, they said, and promises of aid from Great Britain would no longer placate them. The men had seen their friends and relatives massacred all along the massive Eastern Front and no longer wished to fight. Wilkins could accept that the Russian troops merely guarded the border with Bulgaria, but now German General Mackensen had disturbed the peace with a new invasion into Dobruja. As Wilkins rushed to the War Committee to meet with Rășcanu, a feeling of dread crept over him. He had believed all along that things would eventually go bad, but now it seemed to be happening and far too quickly for his liking.

"Where did Mackensen get an army?" Wilkins asked Rășcanu as they looked over the incoming wires from Russian General Zayonchkovski. The Russian and his 30th Army Corps had not bothered to construct defenses between the Roumanian territory and the neighboring Bulgaria, and now they were in full retreat.

"It seems they are mostly Bulgarians forces, with a few Turkish and Austrian Divisions thrown in for backbone."

"Has the Roumanian Third Army reached the Russians yet?"

"Not yet, no."

"Zayonchkovski must counter-attack and quickly," Wilkins said. "You see here on the map – the railway line to Costanza? The Russians must keep General Mackensen south of this line otherwise you will lose both the city and the swiftest route by which the Third Army can be moved into Dobruja."

"And then? You know the Russians will not allow 40,000 of their troops to be tied down in trenches along a front with Bulgaria simply to protect Roumanian territory."

"More to the point, the troops themselves will not permit it, from what I have been told. We shall have to smash Mackensen's forces," Wilkins argued, "as we should have done before the expedition into Transylvania."

"So you have lectured me many times, James. But tell me, where is General Sarrail now? Why has his Salonika force not attacked Bulgaria, as you promised? Shouldn't Mackensen be fighting the French and British troops from Salonika?"

Wilkins winced. "I am sorry to tell you, Ioan, but I only learned last night: Sarrail has been ordered north to Serbia instead. He is even now fighting his way toward Prilep. He will not be attacking Bulgaria."

"Prilep?! Serbia?! That is not what your government promised us!" Rășcanu shouted angrily.

"Yes, I know it," Wilkins admitted, "but it is out of our hands now."

"We are not so gullible that we believed every promise made to us by Great Britain, James, but this?! It is incredible!"

"Damn it, Ioan, that's all well and good, but we must still deal with Mackensen. Just look at the bloody map and tell me what you think we can do?"

Rășcanu turned and looked down at the maps. It took some time for him to regain his composure, but obviously the problem of Mackensen's advance in Dobruja was of paramount importance. If Mackensen could push the Russians back far enough, then even without defeating them the Bulgarians would be able to cross the Danube and attack Bucharest itself. "We have the reserves in Bucharest," he said at last.

"That will help, but there are not nearly enough men. You must keep many here to secure the capital."

"Then we have no choice but to draw men out of Hungary. It seems you will get what you wanted all along, Colonel – a battle in Bulgaria, and we shall be forced to abandon Transylvania," Rășcanu said with unconcealed bitterness.

"Look here, Ioan, I can't help that the Russians are in such a state. If Mackensen is advancing east to attack the Russians in Dobruja, even a relatively small Roumanian force could cross the Danube to the west and attack Mackensen's rear. It could be exactly what you require – his new army would be destroyed swiftly, Bulgaria would be left defenseless, and your armies and the Russians could then focus exclusively on the Transylvania territory."

"Perhaps. That may be our only hope. I will suggest it to the committee." Still, Wilkins could sense that Rășcanu was angry and felt betrayed by his allies, even though their new relationship was barely a month old.

Later that day, the members of the War Committee met to discuss the situation and agreed they had no choice but to address the threat posed by General Mackensen. The First, Second and Forth Armies in Transylvania would be ordered to stand fast and discontinue their advances toward the Mures River until the Bulgarian army had been dealt with in Dobruja. Following Wilkins' advice, they decided that several divisions would be withdrawn from Transylvania to prepare for an attack over the Danube River at the small village of Flămânda, while the Russians would push south to protect the city of Costanza and the crucial train lines. Within hours, General Averescu had been recalled from Hungary to personally lead the proposed offensive across the Danube.

However, no one in the War Committee yet knew what Gresham had only just discovered – that a new German Ninth Army led by Field Marshal Erich von Falkenhayn had been formed in Hungary to drive the Roumanians out of Transylvania. German railroads had rushed divisions and reserves to Hungary as fast as they could be assembled. Gresham knew already that his tactical situation at the Olt River could not be sustained. All his forward movement had been stalled, and he found that in every direction he turned there were now massive numbers of Austrian and German forces. His men were not trained nor equipped to build defenses or to hold off the advances of a well-equipped enemy. He pulled his men back closer the Olt River, should he need to retreat. Certainly the shallow river would not stop the enemy either; it had not stopped him, but from the river all the way back to Bucharest, the only natural obstruction was the mountains. Gresham immediately ordered Major Neascu back to Brashov to hurry the construction of new defenses across the Predeal Pass.

Within days, news of the new German army in Transylvania spread across Roumania and the citizens began to panic. Those who were able immediately left for Petrograd, London, and Rome. The news that Falkenhayn's troops had taken back the city of Sibiu from the Roumanian First Army in a single day was greeted with dismay. The Roumanian forces in Transylvania were all retreating towards the mountains.

With his left flank now completely undefended, Gresham was also forced to draw back. His weary troops consolidated at the town of Faragas and fought through the night to keep the German Ninth Army from crossing the Olt River, but by dawn the banks of the river were overwhelmed. Gresham was forced to order his men to fight a rearguard action as they were slowly pushed back day by day toward Brashov. Then Major Christea's rangers were recalled to Roumania by General Averescu for the planned offensive action across the Danube. The Russians in Dobruja were struggling to resist Mackensen's army there, and Averescu's crossing of the river at Flămânda had become Roumania's sole hope of averting total disaster.

Wilkins was sent down to review and report on the enormous pontoon bridge being constructed so that Averescu's forces could cross the great Danube River. Some 2,000 men had been ferried across by boat to secure the opposite shore, but it would take two full weeks to finish the bridge. Wilkins stood with Averescu on the banks of the Danube on a cold and rainy afternoon in early October as the Roumanian troops and artillery finally began to cross the river. "How long before the crossing will be completed, General?" Wilkins asked.

"Thirty-six hours, and then we will proceed immediately to attack the Bulgarians," Averescu replied. "If all goes as we plan, the Bulgarians will be crushed within a week."

"That is an optimistic projection, Sir, but I pray you are correct."

"I should like to tell you, Colonel, your colleague Gresham has been of tremendous value to me in Transylvania."

"I am pleased to hear it. He is a ruthless soldier and I have long believed he would make an excellent commander, indeed, ever since I first saw him in action at Gallipoli."

"And you, Colonel? Are you not ruthless as well?" Averescu asked with a good-natured smile.

Wilkins laughed. "No, I am more the calculating sort, Sir."

"That is an excellent trait in a commander as well, Colonel. In the morning, I shall cross the Danube. Perhaps you would care to accompany me to Dobruja for a few days. I would appreciate your thoughts on the campaign."

"It would be an honor, Sir."

The cold, wet rain drove the General and Wilkins back to Averescu's warm headquarters where they discussed the campaign and drank brandy well into the night. During the evening, however, the cold damp rain grew into a tempest. The darkness, wind and sheeting rain obscured the view across the Danube, and Averscu was forced to delay further troops or equipment crossing the river until the storm had passed. As the night wore on, the river rose steadily and suddenly, after midnight, Wilkins was awakened by the sound of massive explosions. From his window, he could see that the pontoon bridge was aflame. He threw on his overcoat and boots and rushed out to learn what had happened.

Two Bulgarian gunships had been able to come down the usually shallow river to bombard the wooden bridge. The fires were burning out of control and the waters of the Danube, now high and rapid due to the storm, were tearing the remnants of the bridge apart. As Wilkins watched, the pontoon boats supporting the bridge began to break apart. In minutes, the bridge was utterly destroyed and, with it, any chance of transporting the Roumanian forces across the Danube in large numbers. Wilkins stood on the shore – he could hear the sound of battle across the river. General Mackensen had sent two divisions back to clear the small force of Roumanians that had already crossed the Danube. Wilkins could hear the fierce firefight in the dark, wet night as the Roumanian troops on the opposite shore were captured or killed.

All hope for a surprise attack on the Bulgarian army in Dobruja was gone. Averescu was furious. Wilkins found him at headquarters screaming at the engineers. "They say it will be at least two weeks to complete another bridge!" Averescu shouted to Wilkins. "Two damned weeks!"

"By then, there will be no hope of stopping the Bulgarians, General," Wilkins said.

"None, indeed," Averescu growled. "I have no choice. The offensive will have to be called off."

Wilkins was appalled. If the Roumanians and Russians were unable to contain the Bulgarians in Dobruja, there could be no reasonable expectation that they would be able to resist the Germans in Transylvania. Wilkins returned to Bucharest that morning and rushed to meet with Ambassador Barclay.

"What can I do for you, Colonel?" Barclay asked as he ushered Wilkins into his warm and quiet library.

"I have just come from the Danube," Wilkins said. "Averescu's offensive has been called off. The bridge was destroyed by Bulgarian gunships last night."

"There is no hope then," Barclay said somberly.

"No, and the news from Transylvania is fairly grim as well. The Roumanian armies have withdrawn to the mountain passes to defend Roumania from the advancing German Ninth Army. I understand Gresham has even been forced out of Brashov. They resisted street by street, but in the end he has lost too many men to hold the city."

"And the mountain passes, are they at least secure?"

"I suspect they are not. Gresham is one of the few commanders prescient enough to order defenses built across the mountain pass."

"Then it is a matter of days before the Germans break through, is that it? Damn it, Colonel – what of our enormous stores of petrol and grain! We have spent millions buying and storing Roumania's resources specifically to keep them from the Germans. Are we now to surrender them to Germany, and the oil fields, too?" Barclay asked accusingly. "You know damn well that our only hope of winning this war is to starve Germany into surrender before we waste away ourselves. We cannot possibly allow the Germans to gain access to all our resources in Roumania."

"Yes, I completely agree. Let me assure you that I will address the matter," Wilkins said quietly but with determination. "It is still our primary objective to starve the Huns, and I will see to it that we are prepared in case the Germans break through into Roumania. Absolutely, sir."

"Let us still pray it will not come to that," Barclay said.

The Roumanians held on desperately day by day to keep the Germans from crossing over the mountain passes. Gresham remained with his men in the Predeal Pass holding the enemy at bay even as massive German shells fell on the Roumanian bunkers and snow fell in thick wet blankets upon the troops. There could be no fires, no smoke, and the men were miserable and cold, but Gresham and the other Roumanian commanders understood all too well that Falkenhayn's army could not be allowed to breach the mountain passes, not any of them.

In Dobruja, Mackensen's Bulgarian army was steadily forcing the Russians back. They captured the city of Costanza in late October and seized the train lines; the Roumanians were forced to destroy the railroad bridge over the Danube.

Then, in early November, a young German Lieutenant named Erwin Rommel and his division of elite German mountaineers broke through the Roumanian defenses at the Vulcan Pass. Soon after, the German Army raced down from the Carpathian Mountains and on to the plains of Roumania. They were headed for Bucharest, as the desperate and overwhelmed Roumanian forces collapsed.

"Darling," Wilkins said gently as he jostled Wolczak from her sleep, "wake up. Quickly please."

Wilkins had returned to the hotel to warn Emma that they would soon need to flee to Russia. The government and the city of Bucharest were in turmoil as the Germans advanced across the plains with little resistance from the retreating Roumanian armies.

"What is it, James?" Wolczak asked sleepily.

"Listen, my darling, we must give some thought to our departure from Bucharest. The whole city is evacuating. We cannot stay much longer."

"No, no, I understand. It was just a matter of time," she said.

"I shall take you with me to Russia, to Odessa. We cannot stay in Roumania when the Germans come. The Roumanian government will have to withdraw as well."

"That's not what Missy says, though," she said, still half asleep.

"Missy? Who is that?" Wilkins asked.

"My darling, 'Missy' is the Queen, Queen Marie! Didn't I tell you she has been working with me at the hospital?"

"Yes, of course, but what did she say?"

"She won't allow the government to abandon Roumania; she has is a plan to retreat only as far as Jassy."

"Jassy? Why there? Has she told you her reasons?"

"There are some sort of defenses along the Sereth River between here and Jassy. All sorts of cannons and concrete bunkers and that sort of thing; they were built years ago to keep the Russians from invading Roumania."

"But surely those defenses are pointed in the wrong direction, my dear. The Germans are coming from the west, not from Russia in the east," Wilkins said. "The guns and all will be pointed in the wrong direction."

"Well they'll just turn them around or something," Wolczak said. "Anyway, we're going to Jassy, James. I can continue working with the hospital staff there."

Wilkins was silent. He had already conceived a plan in his own mind, and Wolczak was seeking to change it. He was at rather a loss for words.

"But, you do wish to stay with me, my darling?" Wilkins asked.

"Of course. How can you even ask me that?"

"But we're supposed to go to Russia, you see, with Barclay. I can certainly postpone it, but eventually I will have to go. I ... I rather expected, or rather I hoped that you would wish to come with me."

"But my work, James – whatever would I do in Russia? I would have to start all over again at a whole new hospital, and I can hardly speak a word of Russian."

"I don't know. I don't, but I, well, I was thinking that maybe we would get back to England eventually."

"England?"

"Yes, of course, my dear; it's just that, well, I was rather expecting you and I would be married someday," he said bluntly.

"Married? Lord James Wilkins and some Polish-Roumanian American tramp he picked up in Italy! You've got to be kidding me, James. You've told me all about your mother and father. I can't for one minute imagine they would ever permit us to marry. And what would I be in England, with all the other lords and ladies staring at me all superior and what-not? Are you even using your head, James?"

"Damn it, Emma, this is my decision too, and I can ask you to marry me if I chose to. I am so very proud of you and, yes, I am terribly in love with you, darling, I am. Just come with me, please. I promise – I guarantee – we will find the perfect opportunity for you in Russia. And after that, we will go wherever you wish and live just as you like. Please, think about it. You must come with me."

"I'll think about it," she agreed, but there was already a hint of resignation in her voice.

Wilkins could see her disappointment. "I must go to Barclay's. I'm expected immediately," he said. "Just consider the matter, but for Heaven's sake please start packing now. We'll talk when I get back," he said as he rushed out the door. Wilkins had never been so flustered. All his plans, the bright future he had envisioned with Emma, were in doubt. He ran to Barclay's as fast as he could through the cold dark streets of Bucharest.

He found Ambassador Barclay in the foyer of his townhouse assembling bags for a quick evacuation to Russia.

"Come in, Colonel," Barclay said. "I apologize for summoning you so late, but there is a British officer just arrived from France and he has been asking for you."

"Thank you, sir. I think you had better leave him to me."

Wilkins entered the library to find another British Colonel seated by the mantle. He was a tall, muscular, middle aged man with piercing brown eyes and a bushy brown mustache; he was drinking a very large brandy.

"I am James Wilkins; I believe you sent for me?"

"Hallo, there, laddie! Yes, I did, indeed. I am Jack, Jack Norton-Griffiths is the name," the man said as he stood to shake Wilkins' hand. "It's damned good to meet you."

"Yes, of course, yes, I remember you. You're the man they call 'Empire Jack', aren't you?" Wilkins asked with pleasure. "You're the one who's been digging mines underneath the German lines all up and down France."

"Yes, that's me, lad. I understand you've quite a mess here and I've been sent to help. We're to blow up the Roumanian oil wells and what-not, is that right? Come have a seat and you can tell me what's going on." He poured a hearty tumbler of brandy for Wilkins as they sat.

"The one thing we don't have, Jack, is time. The German Ninth Army is already advancing toward Bucharest."

"Listen, laddie, I know what I've been sent to do. You and I are going to set this whole bloody country on fire. It'll be Hell for the bleeding Huns."

Wilkins spent the rest of the night going over the maps with Norton-Griffiths to identify the many oil wells, petroleum refineries, and massive stores of corn and other grains that would need to be destroyed within days. Together they came up with a plan to sabotage the entire oil industry in Roumania. In some cases, they would pour cement and nails into the oil wells and tear out the refinery pipes, but many sites would need to be detonated and the foodstuffs would all have to be burned. It was with this plan in mind that Wilkins and Norton-Griffiths drove west the next morning to the town of Piteshti some hundred kilometers from Bucharest to meet with Roumanian Brigade General David Gresham.

"Hello, James; you're a reassuring sight," Gresham said as Wilkins and Norton-Griffiths came into his office in the little inn overlooking the Argus River. He took Wilkins' hand and shook it warmly, then hugged his friend tightly. Gresham looked exhausted, battered, and more than a little sad, Wilkins thought.

"I'm glad to see you're all right, David. You've been out on the front lines quite a long time."

"It hasn't been all bad, until recently. You must remember, the Roumanians did make me a General, so I have been very well tended. But we had a terrible time up in the Predeal Pass, I admit, especially with the early snowfall and the German artillery. Who have you brought along with you, James?"

"David, I'd like you to meet Empire Jack."

"Old Empire Jack! Why I can certainly guess why you're here," Gresham said, shaking his hand as well. "I remember you used to ride around the front lines at Ypres in a *Rolls-Royce*."

Norton-Griffiths laughed. "Yes, I remember that one. She was a fine automobile. It got rather broken apart by all the shell holes in the road, though."

"Let me get the whisky, and then you can tell me what I can do for you," Gresham said.

"Tell me, David," Wilkins began, "how much longer can the Roumanians hold out?"

"Hold out?" he replied with a laugh. "James, we're not holding out at all! We're just fleeing very slowly. I'd say in a week we will be pushed back well past Bucharest."

"That soon? Good Lord," Wilkins said.

"It's every bit as bad as we feared. The Roumanian army does not have the equipment or training to beat back the Germans, and Falkenhayn is giving us no space to maneuver."

"Then we must act immediately," Norton-Griffiths said. "It will take time a fair time to destroy all the oil wells and refineries. I had hoped that we could simply disable them, but if time is so short we will have to explode many more than I would have liked."

"How long will that take?" Gresham asked.

"A full week, I should think, to do them all."

"We may be able to buy you some more time," Gresham said.

"How so?" Wilkins asked.

"I still have 17,000 men here, James, and if there's one thing they are good at, it is charging the enemy. If I send them up the river valley, even a few kilometers, the Germans will have to stop and deal with us before we split their army in two. It should buy you a couple days, at least."

"Ah, a diversion to keep old Fritz off our backs while we're burning the refineries. I like it," Norton-Griffiths said.

"How many men do you need?" Gresham added. "I could give you a company or two, and of course munitions. I should have everything you'll need by way of explosives."

"That would be most hospitable of you, thank'ee."

Early the next morning, Gresham's sole remaining Division broke out of Piteshti. They drove west straight up the Argus River valley and split the German lines. The startled Germans rushed to close the gap between their lines, not noticing that in and around Ploiesti the expansive Roumanian oil fields and refineries were suddenly bursting into flames. Across the country, stores of corn and other supplies that Great Britain had bought were doused with petrol and set on fire. Soon the entire country was covered in a haze of black smoke and flame.

As the country burned, Gresham's forces and the rest of the Roumanian armies finally collapsed. The German Ninth Army approached the outskirts of

Bucharest, and the few civilians who had not yet escaped from the city finished off all the wine and champagne that could not be carried away. The artworks and the treasures of the churches had been quietly removed and transported to Jassy. And one night the government loaded two dozen lorries with its entire gold bullion reserve and transported it east as well. On 6 December, the Germans marched into Bucharest. The city was virtually empty.

Gresham was officially relieved of duty as the Roumanian armies retreated east over the Sereth River. He had seized a magnificent black *Daimler* sedan from a German Colonel during the brief Argus River offensive and took it to collect Wilkins and Empire Jack from their final refinery demolition just to the east of Bucharest. Wilkins had already arranged to meet Wolczak in Jassy; she was helping to move the patients from Bucharest and open the new hospital there. She still had not decided whether to go with Wilkins to Russia.

Wilkins and Gresham and Empire Jack continued east ahead of the retreating Roumanian army. Empire Jack was exhausted and slept in the front seat. Gresham, too, was exhausted – he had been on the front lines for over three months and his nerves were in tatters. At least Roumania was at war, he thought. It was what he and Wilkins had been sent to accomplish. There would be hundreds of thousands of German and Austrian troops tied down in Roumania who would unable to fight on the Eastern or Western Fronts, and it would be years before Roumania could produce either oil or food again. Yet, as he looked out at the terrible smoke-filled wasteland that Roumania had become, neither he nor Wilkins was proud of their horrifying accomplishments.

"Have you heard any news, James?" Gresham asked. "I should like to know whether we are any closer to winning this God-damned war."

"Woodrow Wilson was elected President in America again, on an anti-war platform," Wilkins said.

Gresham shook his head. "Then there will be no help from the Americans after all."

"No, probably not. And there's some fellow in Russia, a priest or something by the name of Rasputin, who's been trying to convince the Tsar to enter into a separate peace agreement with Germany."

"Bloody Hell, James, haven't you got any good news to tell me?" Gresham barked.

"Well, yes, I was saving the good news for last. It seems that the Austrian Emperor Franz Joseph has died at long last. Archduke Charles has replaced him."

Gresham smiled: "That is something, I suppose." He recalled the forest outside Vienna where he had delivered a false message to Archduke Charles, a message that Gresham had dreamed up in a whorehouse in Corfu. Had he laid it on too thick? Or was the Archduke really so gullible that he genuinely believed he could be made a Saint by begging his enemies for peace? Perhaps they would find out soon. But the year since Vienna had been a disaster – Verdun, the Somme, being shot in Italy, and then Roumania. "All in all, my friend, I'd say it's been a very bad year," Gresham said, patting Wilkins on the hand, "a very, very bad year."

"Shall we spend our Christmastide in Jassy?"

"You will, James, with Emma," Gresham said sadly, "and I hope you will have a happy Christmas together. I have been thinking of going down to Salonika to see Mackenzie again. I'm planning to leave as soon as a flight can be arranged."

"And Roumania?"

Gresham looked out and saw the black soot, smoke and flame rising from the burning oil refineries and the long lines of exhausted and wounded Roumanian infantrymen retreating along the icy road to Jassy. "Our work here is finished," he replied.

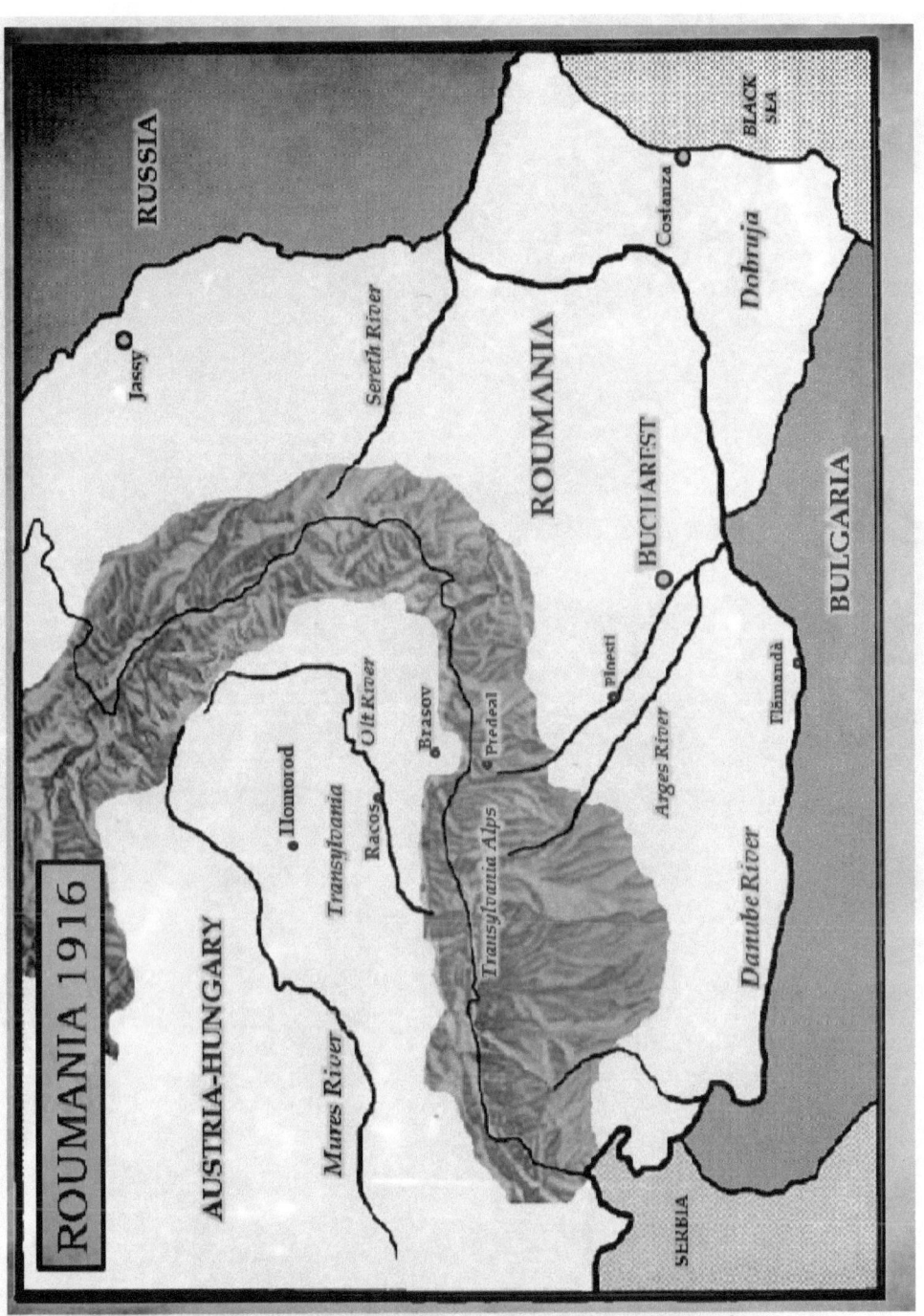

Wejh

Even this close to the equator, the nights were surprisingly cool. Gresham stood on the deck of HMS *Hardinge* as it cruised along the African coastline on the Red Sea and stared at the shore. The great moonlit expanse of shifting sands beyond the shoreline continued as far as the eye could see. There was no breeze, nor was the air particularly moist. Beneath him the warship's engines rumbled gently, but on deck all was quiet. Gresham was tired, but he could not sleep, not even the bottle of whisky he drank had helped. He scratched at his chest where his gunshot wounds still prickled from time to time, and tried very hard not to think about anything at all.

Gresham had joined Compton Mackenzie in Salonika, and his old tutor, sensing that Gresham was exhausted in spirit as well as body, had asked Gresham to join him on a quiet diplomatic journey to Jidda on the Arabian Peninsula. They were going to meet the newly proclaimed "King of the Hejaz," the Sharif of Mecca, Hussein bin Ali of the Hashemites. The Sharif was organizing the Arab tribes into a rebellion against the Turkish Ottoman Empire, and Great Britain was the first country to recognize the new ruler. The Foreign Office wanted a British delegation to congratulate the Sharif in person.

Gresham and Mackenzie had traveled by ship through the Suez Canal and were crossing the Red Sea to Jidda, the city where non-Muslims met dignitaries from Mecca (non-Muslims were not permitted to enter the city of Mecca itself). They were also delivering a large shipment of explosives, rifles, light artillery, and ammunition for the Arab rebels, weapons that were urgently needed to press the attack against the Ottoman Turks in Arabia.

Gresham had at first been hesitant to come along as a representative of the British Empire. He had come very far since he first joined the British Army in August 1914 and he had dutifully fought for Great Britain ever since, but after Roumania he was not certain that he cared any longer who won the war. He was certainly no great moralizer – he simply did what he thought needed to be done and never wholehcartedly regretted any of his actions – but Roumania had changed something within him. Even though he fully understood the logic behind enticing Roumania into the war, in hindsight it all seemed less black and white. To make matters even more confusing, when Gresham reached Salonika he received a rather unenthusiastic reception from Mackenzie who admitted he was not altogether pleased now that Roumania was in flames. Gresham was disappointed – for the first time, he had discovered that success could tarnish a man as thoroughly as failure.

However, Mackenzie had still asked Gresham to come along to Arabia, and the young Colonel decided to go along, not to represent his country but to visit the desert again and to speak with his friend and colleague, the Foreign Office's Liaison to the Arabs, T.E. Lawrence.

It was in the spring of 1915, when the Arab Revolt was still merely a suggestion in a memorandum in a drawer in the Arab Bureau in Cairo, when Gresham first traveled to Jidda with Lawrence. They had journeyed over land since Lawrence spoke the Arab's language well and wanted to make acquaintances across Sinai and down the coast of Arabia. They traveled quietly, *incognito*, and slept out under the wide desert sky. Gresham remembered how peaceful the desert was at night, and how piercingly clever and calm Lawrence had always seemed. It was something that Gresham felt he needed after Roumania.

"Are you alright, David?" Mackenzie asked as he came up to the railing where Gresham was staring out to sea.

"I couldn't sleep," Gresham said calmly.

"No? Perhaps another drink then?"

"I have had too much already."

"May I keep you company?"

"Of course."

They stood side by side awhile.

"This war isn't ever going to end, is it, Compton?" Gresham asked glumly.

"Well, the war may not end, but the fighting must eventually stop."

"Are we still going to win?" Gresham asked.

"I don't know," Mackenzie replied. "I thought so, of course, but now I am not certain. Another year like the last – another Verdun, another Somme – I'm not certain Great Britain, France, or Russia can take much more. However, I don't believe Austria and Germany are faring any better. We are all exhausted. Who can say what will be left when the fighting is over?"

"I know what will be left," Gresham said: "The dead, and a lot of very angry survivors."

"And they will have every right to be angry, I agree. Did you know that in Greece King Constantine has issued a warrant for the arrest of Prime Minister Venizelos on the charge of high treason – can you believe it? Has Venizelos committed treason, you might ask? Well, to be perfectly honest, perhaps so, yes. But the Greek people, David, they would charge the palace and hang the King before they would allow Venizelos to stand in the dock. They know Venizelos is their guardian and protector and has done more to serve Greece that their king or any of his predecessors. There is no possibility that Constantine can remain on the throne. I tell you, David, until the people have the final word they will never be satisfied, not anymore, not in Greece or anywhere else in Europe."

Gresham seriously doubted that empowering the Greek people would solve all Greece's problems, but he kept his mouth shut. Mackenzie, he knew, was an ardent supporter of Venizelos and his proposed democratic reforms.

"The real disaster is that Woodrow Wilson was re-elected," Mackenzie said. "The Americans are not selling war supplies to Germany any longer – they haven't since the naval battle at Jutland – but what we really need, if we're ever going to win this war, is American soldiers. Can you imagine the impact one or even two million armed American boys would have on the stalemate in France?"

"It would make all the difference, of course."

"Who knows whether the Americans will ever choose sides, though? They could not seem to care less what happens to the rest of the world."

"It's a damn bloody shame that the Irish Rebellion was put down with such a heavy hand," Gresham said.

"True," Mackenzie agreed. "There are a great many Irish immigrants in America, as well as Germans, and I fear we have not made many friends among them. As long as public opinion is against us there, President Wilson will not declare war."

"Perhaps if we stopped sinking the German U-boats, Germany would invade America next."

Mackenzie laughed, "I'm not sure the Americans would even notice. Did you know, last summer, two million pounds of munitions bound for England exploded in New York Harbor. People could hear the explosion as far away as Baltimore and their Statute of Liberty was nearly destroyed, yet no one even suspected that German agents might have caused the explosion until we suggested it to them!"

"It could have been an accident. The Americans are not known for subtlety. They need a more obvious inducement. Let's dress some of our Canadians in German uniforms and have *them* invade America," Gresham jested.

"Use real soldiers, you mean? No, that won't do – we don't know if the Americans can even fight: The only real war they have fought in decades was against Spain, and it wasn't much of a fight. Otherwise it's just skirmishes in Manila and bandits in Mexico. They don't even have a standing army. But keep thinking; I'm sure you'll fall upon something."

"Well, we could have one of our agents in Germany send a wire to Wilson just *saying* that Germany has declared war."

"No good - Germany would deny it," Mackenzie said.

"What about that other country, then, the one to the south."

"Switzerland? Declare war on America?"

"No, no. You know – the one to the south of the United States, Mexico."

"You're not thinking clearly, David. Why would Mexico declare war on America?"

"Land, of course; they'd want their land back – California or Texas or whatever it is they lost to the Americans."

"And how would that help us, exactly?"

"Well," Gresham thought a moment, "what if Germany asked Mexico to do it, you see, so the Americans would have to fight a war at home and stop sending us all their war supplies?"

Mackenzie looked at Gresham keenly. "That's not half bad," he laughed. "But again, Germany would deny that they had anything to do with it."

"True. It would have to be undeniable." Gresham fell silent, but his mind was racing. "Remember that German fellow that Dunn works for – Zimmerman?"

"Arthur Zimmerman, yes, he's just been appointed the new State Secretary for Foreign Affairs in Germany."

"Even better, and have we any agents in Mexico?"

"One, I believe. I'm afraid to ask . . . ."

"What if our fellow in Mexico sent a wire to Zimmerman – in code, of course, we've broken all the German codes, haven't we? – and in this wire, Mexico would formally ask Germany to support Mexico's claims to territory in America should Mexico decide to invade the United States. You see, something like that could provoke a response from Zimmerman. Zimmerman might just wire back and say something like 'Yes, Germany will support Mexico's territorial claims if Mexico invades America.' We could give it to the Americans, and Germany couldn't deny it was genuine."

"Holy Christ, David, you're quite serious, aren't you?" Mackenzie asked in surprise. "You want to trick the Americans into declaring war on Germany? How much have you had to drink tonight?"

Gresham laughed. "It's not funny unless it would actually work."

Mackenzie stared at Gresham. His young *protégé* had no scruples at all, he realized, and Mackenzie could not decide whether that was good or bad. Certainly it was dangerous, and he was grateful that Gresham was on Great Britain's side, at least for a moment: It was easy to believe that things might eventually get out of hand. "I've got to get some sleep, David," he said at last. "I'll be certain to mention your suggestions to *Control* – he might find them quite entertaining. For now, I'm going to bed."

"I was just joking, you know," Gresham said, sensing that he had gone over the edge of what Mackenzie could tolerate.

"Oh, yes, I know, David, but perhaps that is what I find so frightening."

———————

It was a great relief to be done with all the ceremonies in Jidda. Gresham had left Mackenzie behind and was riding through the Wadi Safra with a small party of the Sharif's men. They were traveling up the coast to Yenbo, a six-day ride on camelback. It was exceedingly dull but, to Gresham, a restorative journey. They rode silently mile after mile on hot hard-packed sand and dirt and camped each night under clear and silent skies. His companions spoke no English, so there was nothing to say. There was no liquor. And there was no chance of running into the Ottoman Turks. The Turks were now bottled up in the city of Medina, many miles to the north-east, at the southern end of the Hejaz railway. West of Medina on the Red Sea coast was the town of Yenbo.

Until recently, the Ottoman Turks had also occupied Yenbo and had threatened the Arab coalition, Jidda, and even the Holy City of Mecca itself. Yenbo had finally been captured by the Sharif's son, Faisal bin Hussein, with the assistance of the British Royal Navy and the Sharif's new special British liaison, Captain T.E. Lawrence. And, it was at Yenbo that Gresham hoped to find Lawrence.

Gresham had passed through the small town of Yenbo during his previous journey to Jidda. Arriving now, however, he found the town transformed into a sprawling encampment. There were countless tents both modest and grand, and camels and horses and Arab men wearing the traditional cotton tunics with long dark jackets and kufiya on their heads. Many carried old British rifles and most had well-used scimitars. Gresham arrived in the evening and his guides led him to the Hashemite camp, one set apart from the Bedouin tribesmen nearby. A palatial pavilion rose in the center of the camp, as large as a house but decorated with the finest wool rugs and silks, gold decorations, and countless candles. The tent was crowded with Arabs pledging their swords to Prince Faisal, the man who had become the popular leader of the revolt ever since his capture of Yenbo and the salvation of Mecca.

Gresham was brought to the rear of the assembly in the pavilion and simply left there. He was uncertain what to do or say when he reached the front of the crowd, but he knew he would have to pay his respects to the Prince. He could see him seated on the pillows in front, an elegant man with a thick black beard and piercing grey eyes. Just as Gresham reached the front of the crowd, another Arab man rushed over to stand beside him, a man his own height and age with unusual blue eyes who wore a pure white tunic and coat and a white headdress with gold filigree.

"Wa ismaḥū lī an uʿarriḍa lakum, Ṣāḥib as-Saʿādah zamīlī. Ismuhu Dāwīd Jirīsham, wa ḍābiṭ fī al-jaysh al-Briṭānī," the man said to Prince Faisal.

"Ah, yes, I am pleased you have come to Yenbo, Colonel Gresham," Faisal said formally, in reply. "You are most welcome. El Aurens will take you to your camp."

"It is a pleasure to meet you, your Excellency. Thank you," Gresham replied. He bowed and was dismissed with a wave of the Prince's hand.

As Gresham and his new companion left the tent, he asked: "Do you speak English, then?"

"Well of course, old man. You don't recognize me, do you?"

Gresham looked at his companion more closely. "Good Lord, it's you, Lawrence!" Gresham said with shock. "What the Hell are you wearing?"

Lawrence laughed. "It's a pleasure to see you too, Gresham," he replied. "The Arabs are distrustful of anyone in western uniform; they can't seem to tell the Ottoman and British uniforms apart, so I have started to wear this to gain their trust. You had a quiet journey, I hope?"

"Yes, absolutely, and how have you been faring in Arabia?"

"Very well, very well indeed, old man. Come, there are some others I must introduce to you. Our camp is right over here."

The small, informal British encampment was not nearly as grand as the tents of the Hashemites, and there were only a handful of Allied officers stationed with the Arabs at Yenbo. They were gathered around a small campfire drinking tea from tin cups, and that looked perfectly fine to Gresham.

"Colonel David Gresham, may I introduce to you Major Herbert Garland, a former chemistry tutor who is our munitions expert, and Captain Ali Raho, a Frenchman with an expertise in trains, and this, of course, is Miss Gertrude Bell."

Garland and Raho both stood and came to attention at once. "Please, fellows, I am a 'Colonel' in name only; call me 'David,'" Gresham said. "Miss Bell, it is an honor to meet you in particular. *M* mentioned that I might."

"Please, call me 'Trudy'," Bell said. "It's such a great pleasure to finally meet you, David. I've heard so much about you. Would you care for some tea – between us, I'll admit that it is almost pure whisky."

"That would be excellent, thank you," Gresham said. He did not know Garland or Raho, but Bell, a mature woman dressed in the dusty garb of a desert archaeologist, had studied at Oxford and traveled throughout the Near East for many years. She was reputed to be one of the main organizers of the Arab Revolt and had virtually selected Hussein bin Ali on her own to be the new "King of the Hejaz."

"We have been discussing our next offensive, Lawrence," Raho said. "Now that Yenbo is secure and the Turks have retreated to Medina, we don't believe they can threaten Mecca again – the roads are too poor and, if they ever left Medina, their men and their supply lines would be attacked by the Howeitat."

"So, instead of attacking the 10,000 Turks in Medina itself," Garland continued, "Ali and I think we should focus on destroying the Hejaz railway that supplies them. The railway is defended only by Arabs whose loyalty to the Turks is questionable, and once the railway is cut, the Turks in Medina will have to either retreat north or surrender. In any case, they will be contained."

"Yes, absolutely brilliant. The railway is the key to the whole problem in the south, and its cutting, or its dislocation, must be our priority, I agree," Lawrence said. "But we must also keep the Bedouin together and attract more of the Arabs to Faisal. To do so, we must go on the offensive. As time goes by, we run the increasing danger of the Arabs getting sick of the show and melting away. There must be military victories and spoils of war. We need a soft target. Wejh, I was thinking; it's the next major port up the coast and we've been told it is lightly defended. A victory there will also ensure the allegiance of the Billi tribe."

"You are quite right," Bell said. "The Arabs are not ready to take the Turks at Medina 'head on,' especially without British naval support. But is there any significant artillery in Wejh? Could the British gunships not assist us there?"

"The Royal Navy will assist us all the way up the coast, at least until we reach Aqaba where the big guns are located," Lawrence replied. "But I certainly agree that Garland and Raho should focus on the railway. I'll discuss it all with Faisal in the morning."

"Were you at Salonika, David?" Garland asked.

"Just briefly, only long enough to learn that General Sarrail is facing a tough fight into Serbia. Mostly I have been in Roumania the past few months," Gresham replied.

"A terrible loss, Roumania," Garland said gently, uncertain what Gresham's part had been in the catastrophe there.

"Yes, it was," Gresham said, "but a calculated loss, perhaps. We will see." Gresham was uncomfortable discussing his mission in Roumania.

"We cannot always foresee where our paths will lead us, David," Lawrence said. "Nine-tenths of tactics in war are certain and taught in books, but the irrational tenth is the true test of generals."

"It is not irrational, Lawrence," Bell admonished him, "but it is cruel. This is a *very* cruel war, and although you have not suffered overmuch yourself, many have and many more will. We have become so very good at inflicting injury, wouldn't you say? David, you'll find that the war in Arabia is fought much differently than the war in Europe. The Arabs are not an industrial people. They have no grenades or gas or flamethrowers, no aircraft or zeppelins. There are no tanks from America or canned beef from Argentina, and many of the Arabs fight with little more than a pint of water on their hip and a sharp sword. But we win hands down if we keep the Arab simple — to add luxuries will only wreck their show. I know that they will do what even the British could not do at Gallipoli. They will utterly destroy the Turks."

The next afternoon Prince Faisal summoned the Bedouin, the Harb, the Ateibah and the Jumeinah tribes to begin the long journey north along the coast to seize the port of Wejh. Garland and Raho went east with a contingent of the Howeitat to disrupt the Hejaz railway, but Gresham decided to go north with the Prince, riding a camel beside Lawrence. It was a long and uncomfortable journey that would take nearly three weeks in the hot sun. Around them, the Prince had amassed a crowd of nearly 4,000 Arabs mounted on camel and horse and another 4,000 infantrymen on foot (many were Arabs who had deserted the Turkish Ottoman army and still wore parts of their Turkish uniforms, particularly the fine German boots). The infantrymen were silent as they marched. Their feet kicked up far more dust than the camels, so they marched in a hazy white cloud under clear, hot skies.

"I imagine you've seen quite a bit of the war since our last journey through the desert, haven't you, David?" Lawrence asked as he and Gresham rode their camels a few hundred yards behind the infantry.

"More than I care to recount, to be honest," Gresham admitted.

"I have been rather fortunate in that the British Army has chosen to ignore me altogether."

"That will change with your successes here in Arabia. Tell me about Prince Faisal. He seems a very calm man and confident."

"He's a remarkable man. I met Faisal just last October," Lawrence explained. "I was sent over to see which of the Sharif's sons would be best able to lead the Arab rebels. Faisal had just then taken Rabegh from the Turks, so he was one possible choice. I was led to the inner courtyard there where I found him, tall and slender, robed all in white and framed between the uprights of a black doorway. I felt at first glance that this was the man I had come to Arabia to find – a leader who would bring the Arab Revolt to full glory. I was sent back in December to act as his liaison."

"And are the Arabs capable soldiers? I frankly expected to find a cadre of British Sergeants drilling them."

"That is a most delicate problem," Lawrence answered. "The Arabs do not trust the British or French, so if we assist Faisal too openly it will drive many of the Bedouin over to the Turks, who they say are at least Moslem. The thing you must understand, David, is that the Arabs may want to be free of Constantinople, they may want to liberate Damascus, they may slaughter their enemies with ruthless zeal, but they do not yearn to fight their fellow Moslems. The Arabs are a people well accustomed to warfare, and they welcome our advice on how to conduct an expedition in modern army-like fashion, but they do not trust us. We shall have to see how they fare at Wejh. I can see already that there has been inadequate attention paid to our supplies along the route, water in particular. This first stage of our two hundred mile journey takes us only as far as Um Lejj – we will need to speak to Prince Faisal then, once our deficiencies have shown themselves and become undeniable."

By the time they reached Um Lejj, Lawrence was proven correct. It was clear that the army was journeying north with inadequate intelligence to support such a large number of men. Prince Faisal readily accepted advice from Lawrence and Gresham and agreed to split his army, sending half by the shore road toward Wejh, while others would take a more inland road. This also separated the tribes whose ancient hostilities were on the cusp of spilling new blood. The least part of the Prince's army, some 550 men who were deemed too sick, too young or too lazy to be of any real service, were sent by Faisal to board the British ship HMS *Hardinge* that would meet the Prince's army in Wejh following the attack.

Gresham continued north with Lawrence and Prince Faisal on the inland road for the next week. Supplies were running perilously low, and the Arabs were forced to reduce their water and could give none to their mounts. Then one night, as Gresham sat beside a small fire watching the stars, Lawrence rushed from his evening meeting with the Prince into the penumbra of the campfire's light. "David, old man, will you like to come along for a skirmish?" He asked with the excitement of a schoolboy. "We have a problem that needs to be addressed immediately, and we are late for our *rendezvous* at Wejh already."

"Of course, Lawrence. What's the matter?"

"Come on, then," Lawrence said as he rushed off toward their camels, Gresham following behind. They mounted and rode quickly off to join a small band of the Jumeinah, and then galloped east *en masse*. Gresham was hard pressed to stay on his camel as it bounded along with the others of its own accord, but the cool night air racing over his face was very refreshing.

"We must find a caravan," Lawrence explained at last. "The Arabs are a great people, David, but they are still terribly divided. Our target, Wejh, is in a region controlled by the Billi tribe, and their chief is the Emir Suleiman Rufida. He is a cautious man who has declined to choose sides so far. Faisal knows him very well and predicts that the Emir will allow us to attack Wejh and destroy the Turkish garrison there, but will not help us until he knows we have already won."

"He is a very pragmatic man, I would say," Gresham gasped.

"So we assume. But if he were to resist us instead, it would mean disaster for Faisal and for the Arab Revolt."

"And the caravan we are to find?"

"Gold from Medina – every last bit of the Turk's gold, I am told – a huge sum meant to pay Suleiman Rufida to take the Turkish side and to resist our entry into Billi territory. We must make sure that the gold is not delivered to Rufida. Faisal will not proceed another mile north until we return with it."

The image of a fortune in gold appeared in Gresham's mind, and he felt something he had not felt in years – not since he was a boy living on the streets of Manchester – a sort of lust for independence. As a boy, Gresham had been a near-penniless orphan, but he also wanted for nothing, stole what he needed and slept where he liked. Now he was wealthy, but in a very limited sense: All his money came from the British Crown and there was no lack of funds to enable him to complete his missions, but that money had a great many obligations attached to it. Gresham felt a great yearning for independence and, indeed, he realized it was that which he reveled in most as he galloped through the desert and across the sands in a bare sliver of moonlight.

They rode through the night and finally reached the hills where Lawrence and the Jumeinah tribesmen had been told the courier from Medina would pass. However, there was no golden caravan in sight as they had hoped. They were either too early or too late.

"We will have to split up," Lawrence insisted. "Half of us will travel east toward Medina, as far as we are able. The others will head toward Wejh in the hope of catching up to the caravan if we are late for it. I myself must go toward Wejh to see what the Billi have prepared for us there. Which way will you go, David?"

"I'll ride to Medina, then," Gresham said. "You'll want a pair of British eyes on the caravan if it has yet to come up from Medina."

"Quite right," Lawrence said. "Best o' luck, old man." Lawrence immediately rode off with half the Jumeinah tribesmen, leaving Gresham with the other four, who immediately got off their camels to rest briefly.

"Any of you blokes speak English?" He asked them.

"Very well, yes," said one of the tall, dark warriors. "But it is entertaining to hear you speak with El Aurens," he laughed. "You may call me Hamza. We will wait here and see what comes. Later we will travel toward Medina."

"Fair enough," Gresham agreed.

"You have forgotten your rifle, Colonel, have you not?" Hamza asked.

"I might have brought it if I had known where we were going, but I have this," Gresham said, as he patted his American M1911 handgun. "And this," he said, pulling out his eight inch field knife.

"That little knife? No, no," Hamza said with disdain. He strode over to his camel and pulled a long, sharp scimitar from his pack. "You should have one like this," he said, throwing the sword on the sand at Gresham's feet. "Keep that; it has a very good blade."

Gresham sheathed his knife and picked up the sword respectfully. It was a surprisingly crude weapon, steel with a leather-wrapped handle, a weapon made for hacking at your enemy rather than running him through. "Thank you. *Shookrun.* I take it you know what the caravan is transporting, is that right?"

"Yes, we all know," Hamza said, "but the gold is not important. It is only important that the Billi not be bought by the Pasha in Medina. The Billi are dogs with no honor, no pride, who will work as slaves to the Turks, but they are very many. We cannot permit the Billi to resist us."

"Have we any idea how large this caravan might be? I mean, there are only five of us."

"We do not. The sun is rising now, Colonel. We must ride up to the hills to watch the road. We should not let them see us," he said.

The small group rode east onto the foothills of the Hijaz mountains. With the sun rising, they were able to keep in the shadows and watch the road below as they journeyed silently south-east toward Medina. The day wore on, and Gresham frequently unpacked his field glasses to survey the empty road ahead as the camels picked their way through the rocks.

It was well after dark on that moonless night when they sighted a small campfire off the road. Gresham and the Jumeinah warriors left their camels behind and carefully climbed down to assess the group below.

There were twenty-two men all in Turkish uniforms and heavily armed in the small camp. They surrounded a *Rolls Royce* ambulance that looked quite old, and there were two additional sedans as well. One of the sedans had a machine gun mounted in the back.

"What do you think, Colonel?" Hamza asked.

"We each pick two or three to shoot, then close in and finished the rest by hand. Just make sure the two on the machine gun go first."

"My brother is an excellent shot; he will dispose of them."

Without warning, the firing began. Gresham saw the machine gunners go down first as he himself aimed at the Turkish soldiers closest to the ambulance. Before he could take his shots, however, the other Jumeinah warriors had pulled out their swords and were already charging down to attack. The Turks were in a state of panic and uncertain where the attackers were located, nightblinded as they were by their bright campfire. Their shots went harmlessly off into the darkness.

Gresham pulled out his new sword and joined the melee. As he rushed forward, a Turkish officer raised his handgun. Gresham stepped to his side and swung the scimitar down hard, then was shocked to see that he had sliced cleanly through the Turkish officer's outstretched arm below the elbow. The handgun, hand and forearm lay on the ground as blood gushed from the man's grisly stump. Gresham raised his sword to pierce the man's gut when he recalled that the sharp-edged but blunt-tipped weapon would be less effective in that manner. Instead, he swung the sword at the Turk's chest. The sword buried itself deep, slashing into the man's ribcage, and Gresham had to forcefully yank it free. Blood followed in gushes. The scimitar was a thrilling weapon, and Gresham was grateful to have it on hand.

As the Turk dropped to the ground, Gresham quickly charged the next Turkish soldier who was attempting to retreat into the sedan. Gresham raised the sword over his head and then the blow fell cleanly on the Turk's neck, cutting his head off altogether as blood sprayed wildly from the stump. Gresham spun around to find his next victim, and again he slashed the sword down, this time onto the shoulder of another enemy. The blade cut inches deep as the man screamed in agony and blood poured down Gresham's blade and over his hands. Then there were no more Turks to kill; the Jumeinah had finished the rest.

Gresham was covered in blood, his clothes were sopping wet with it. He pulled off his shirt and wiped first his face and then his sword as he sought to catch his breath and slow his racing heartbeat. War was all well and good, he thought, but killing was purifying. The act was definitive. Afterward, the killer was either elated or distraught; there was no middle ground. And Gresham was definitely elated.

"Colonel," Hamza called, "you had better look here." Gresham walked calmly to the back of the ambulance. Inside were a dozen boxes. Hamza had already opened one, and it contained hundreds of gold Kurush coins. "An amazing sum to purchase the loyalty of a mere dog," Hamza observed.

"It looks like rather a lot to me," Gresham said. "I suppose the Prince gets it all, eh?"

"I fear so," Hamza said with a smile.

"Well, you won't mind if I drive back in the sedan, at least, will you?"

Prince Faisal's army was soon on the march again. Lawrence had returned to the camp to say that the Billi tribe, now left without payment from the Turks in Medina, had decided to go north and leave the road to Wejh undefended. Nothing stood between the Arabs and their victory over the small Turkish garrison in the port. The other half of Prince Faisal's forces rejoined them just to the south.

As they neared the town, HMS *Hardinge* could be seen sitting calmly at anchor in the bay. Gresham rode with Prince Faisal and Lawrence as the army entered Wejh three days late only to discover that the Turkish garrison had already been defeated. *Hardinge* had arrived on schedule and most of the Turkish garrison had fled at first sight of the British warship before it even opened fire. There was a small contingent of Turkish soldiers who had retreated into the town's central tower. Although the ship could have simply bombarded the tower to rubble, the captain had instead sent his contingent of 550 sick, lazy and youthful Arabs onto shore. Half of them had refused to leave the beach, and many others went to loot the town, but fifty men had stormed the tower and captured the remainder of the Turkish garrison. Wejh had fallen with barely a fight.

Within hours of Prince Faisal's victory, Suleiman Rufida arrived in Wejh to pledge the Billi tribe's support to the Arab Revolt. He was soon followed by the chiefs of the Aida and the Western Huweitat, tribes that had remained in the service of the Ottoman Turks in Medina but had learned that the Pasha had no more gold to pay.

In the following weeks, the Hejaz railway was disrupted to fully isolate and contain the Turkish garrison at Medina. To the northeast of Arabia, British troops in Mesopotamia recaptured the city of Kut and began their march north to conquer Baghdad. Lawrence and Prince Faisal were contemplating an attack on the port of Aqaba, the Turks' last major port south of Damascus. And, as Gertrude Bell had predicted, the Arabs were doing what the British had failed to do at Gallipoli: They were beating the Ottoman Turks.

Gresham decided to remain in Wejh a while, but he sometimes rode out with Hamza and the Jumeinah to attack the railway or harry the small Turkish garrisons remaining nearby. It was on a warm and cloudy morning in late February, as he sat in the peaceful courtyard of his little townhouse in Wejh drinking Turkish coffee, that Gresham finally had the opportunity to review some recent copies of *The Paris Herald*.

It seemed the war was still being fought in the places Gresham had left behind. In France and Belgium, the Germans had withdrawn some thirty miles to a line of virtually impenetrable trenches, concrete bunkers and defensive fortifications that had been months in the preparation. The English and French had followed on the German's heels all the way to the new "Hindenburg Line," as it was called. It now appeared the three armies would sit astride that line in perpetual stalemate yet again.

Then Gresham laughed out loud. There was news of an uproar in America. The newspapers there had made public an intercepted German cable whose content had roused the American people to unprecedented heights of rage: The cable at issue, one sent by German Foreign Minister Zimmerman to the German ambassador in Mexico that had been intercepted and decoded by the British, was published in the *Herald* in full:

We intend to begin unrestricted submarine warfare, [Zimmerman wrote]. We shall endeavor in spite of this to keep the United States neutral. In the event of this not succeeding, we make Mexico a proposal of alliance on the following basis: make war together, make peace together, generous financial support and an understanding on our part that Mexico is to reconquer the lost territory in Texas, New Mexico and Arizona. The settlement in detail is left to you. You will inform the President [of Mexico] of the above most secretly as soon as the outbreak of war with the United States is certain and add the suggestion that he should, on his own initiative, invite Japan to immediate adherence and at the same time mediate between Japan and ourselves. Zimmerman.

Zimmerman not only wanted Mexico to wage war on America, he hoped to entice Japan to do so as well! United States President Woodrow Wilson was expected to ask Congress for a declaration of war within days. Gresham laughed again – at least *someone* in London was every bit the ruthless bastard he was himself!

Gresham leapt to his feet. He would have to find Lawrence at once to tell him the fabulous, world-altering news that millions of Americans would soon be fighting with the British, French and Russians. Here there was hope at last, hope that they would stop the German Kaiser once and for all! Between the Russians on the Eastern Front and Allies on the Western, Germany could at last be crushed!

Gresham threw on his boots and prepared to depart when a clean, young British Lieutenant from Cairo suddenly arrived at his house.

"Are you Colonel David Gresham, Sir?" The young officer asked anxiously

"Yes, that's me. What is it?"

"A message from Cairo, Sir," the officer said as he held out a small envelope. "I was sent by H.Q. to deliver this to you most urgently. It must be very important, Sir."

"Thank you," Gresham said as he took the envelope and ripped it open. Inside, he found a simple un-coded message from Petrograd, a wire that stopped Gresham's heart and made his blood suddenly run cold. It said:

RUSSIA COLLAPSING COME AT ONCE JAMES

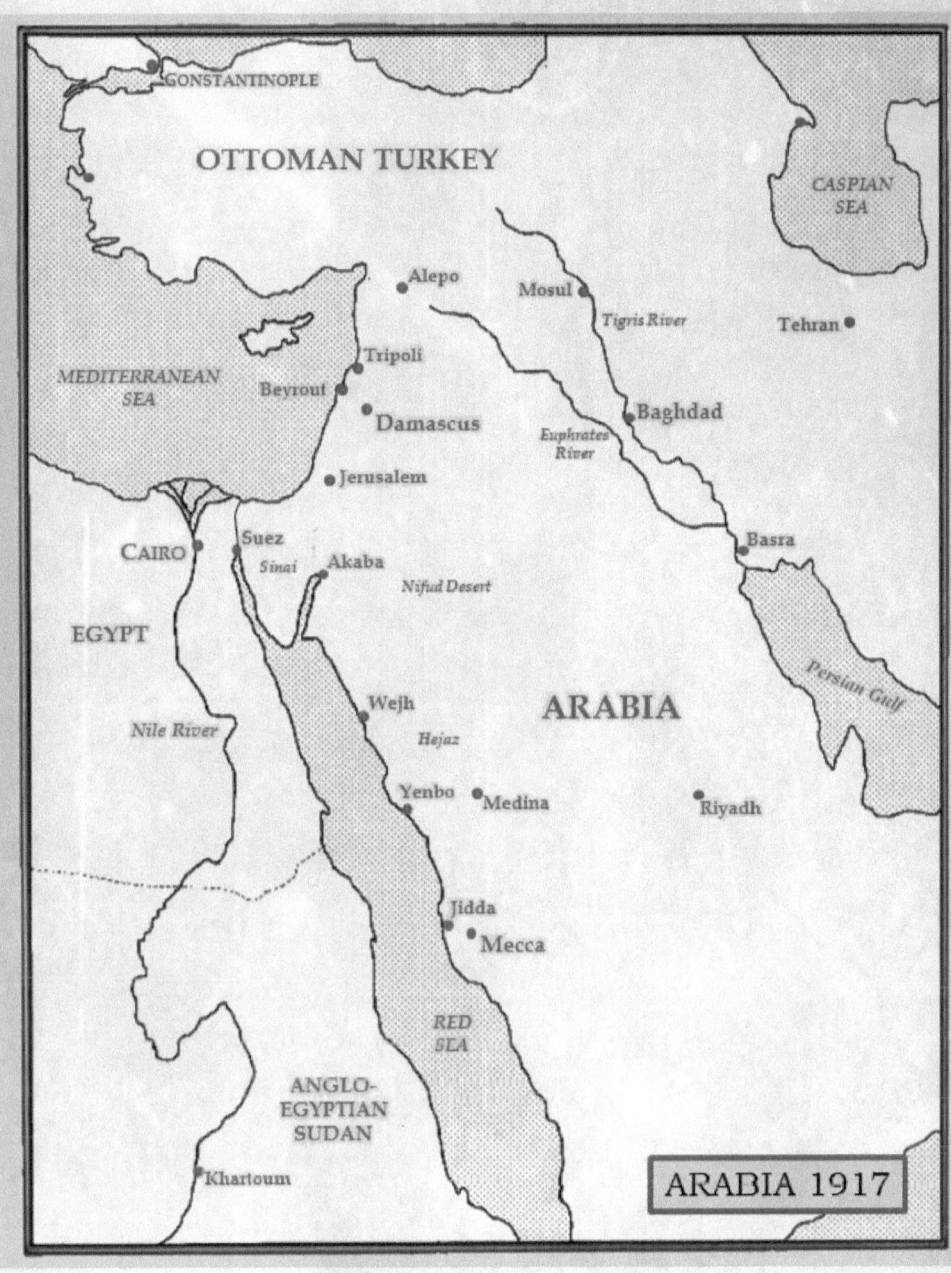

CONSTANTINOPLE

OTTOMAN TURKEY

CASPIAN
SEA

Alepo

Mosul

Tigris River

Tehran

MEDITERRANEAN
SEA

Tripoli

Beyrout

Damascus

Euphrates
River

Baghdad

Jerusalem

Basra

CAIRO

Suez

Sinai

Akaba

Nifud Desert

Persian Gulf

EGYPT

Wejh

ARABIA

Nile River

Hejaz

Yenbo

Medina

Riyadh

Jidda

Mecca

RED
SEA

ANGLO-
EGYPTIAN
SUDAN

Khartoum

ARABIA 1917

Petrograd

Three weeks! Wilkins had been in Petrograd three weeks and British Ambassador Buchanan *still* deferred meeting with him. Well, he must have his favorites, Wilkins thought. There was no shortage of British agents in Petrograd already – four or five from the Foreign Office and at least a dozen from Military Intelligence, not to mention the dozens who advised the Tsar and his ministers on everything from munitions supplies to railway maintenance and fertilizers. Wilkins guessed that he was not the only agent from the Secret Intelligence Service, but he had been given no contacts and no one had approached him. His only instruction from *Control* was to go to Petrograd as soon as he was able. What he was to do there, and how, was apparently left to his own discretion.

It hadn't taken Wilkins long to comprehend the magnitude of the problems in Russia. The city was tense and expectant as crowds of sailors, soldiers and factory workers roamed the streets at night shouting about revolution, breaking windows and plastering their slogans on the city walls. The prisons were overflowing, and the deserters from the army who were found in Petrograd were now summarily executed. The troops were on the verge of mutiny, but also the Generals were frustrated, the workers were striking, and the peasants were starving. Food, ammunition, coal, wood, and medicines were all in short supply.Tsar Nicholas II, Emperor of Russia, Grand Duke of Finland, and King of Poland was blamed for all of Russia's woes. Since the Tsar ruled Russia and its territories, principally Finland and Poland, with unlimited autocratic authority and had actively resisted any delegation of power to the elected representatives in the state Duma, it was perhaps just and reasonable to give him the fault. The people of Russia were suffering terribly, and the Tsar had left himself with no one else to blame. The only citizens who seemed to still support the Tsar and the Romanov dynasty were the wealthy land and factory owners who were getting richer day by day from the interminable war and the Tsar's bottomless coffers.

The war in Russia was itself suspended for the winter, more or less, inasmuch as the cold and snow made fighting virtually impossible. There were skirmishes, certainly, but the big offensives were saved for the spring and summer when troops and artillery could move over dry ground. Even so, it was widely rumored that the Russian army was in terrible condition, that the troops no longer wished to fight, and that some were actively petitioning for a peace treaty. Tsar Nicholas himself had been urged day and night by his closest confidant, the conniving monk Rasputin, to seek peace with Germany. That had been simply too much for some of Russia's elite. Rasputin had been found murdered, floating and frozen solid in the Neva River shortly after Wilkins arrived in Petrograd. The wealthy celebrated the murder; strangers on the street congratulated one another as word spread quickly through the capital. The Tsar, however, was distraught and had banned any mention of the murder in the newspapers.

Still, nothing could be more alarming to London than peace. If Russia entered a separate peace with the Kaiser, then millions of German soldiers and mountains of artillery and supplies could be transferred to the Western Front for use against Great Britain and France. It would be a catastrophic development, and one which Great Britain was certain to resist with every ounce of its strength.

Wilkins had come to Petrograd as ordered, but he had refused to leave Emma Wolczak behind in Roumania, not even in the secure temporary capital of Jassy. She had not wanted to come at first, and Wilkins supposed that, in the end, he had begged her so pathetically to come that she had simply surrendered to him. Now that they had been three weeks in Petrograd doing almost nothing, seeing no one, and learning very little, Wolczak was becoming more and more disappointed with Wilkins, and he was nervous that she might leave him.

Their accommodations at the *Hotel Astoria* were excellent, but none of the other guests, mostly from England, seemed to care who Wilkins was or what he was doing in Petrograd. The fact that he was (discretely) sharing rooms with Miss Wolczak was further reason that he should be disregarded. And he was ignored by all, all except for Oliver Locke, Wilkins thought. Locke was another British agent, a middle-aged man-about-town who Wilkins assumed was working for someone in London. Locke seemed to know everyone and liked to collect inside information that he rarely shared. Wilkins had no idea what Locke's instructions required of him as they had never been inclined to discuss the matter.

It was to Wilkins' great surprise, therefore, that Locke invited him (and guest, meaning Miss Wolczak) to Grand Duke Dimitri Pavlovich's party at the *Astoria* one evening in mid-January. Wilkins and Wolczak had not previously been invited anywhere and had not met anyone since they arrived in Petrograd, so Wilkins considered it a great kindness. Certainly, they had heard and even seen many other parties at the *Astoria*. The *Maître d'hôtel*, Joseph Vecchi, had worked at the *Savoy* in London and the *Kaiserhof Hotel* in Berlin, and he could arrange events that people would remember for years.

Wilkins, uncertain of his objectives in Russia, had decided to stay out of uniform for the party. He dressed in a fine black suit with a red velvet vest and black bow tie; Wolczak looked lovely in a dark red velour dress that accentuated her chest, and she wore some modest but quite valuable jewels that Wilkins had given her for Christmas.

The party that night in the bright and handsome private rooms at the *Astoria* was very well attended. There were several hundred guests including many members of the state Duma (the powerless Russian parliament), officers from the Russian Armies and Navy, foreign dignitaries from Great Britain, France and the United States, and countless Russian Dukes and Duchesses. Even the Princess Marina Petrovna from the royal family was there. Wilkins finally had a chance to meet (briefly) the British Ambassador, Sir George Buchanan, who looked exhausted from his constant efforts to prod the Tsar toward government reforms, as well as the American Ambassador David Francis and a member of his staff, a high-strung young man named Edgar Sisson whom Wilkins guessed was a spy.

The attendees cheerfully drank clear, ice-chilled *Vodka* and ate the heavy *hors d'oeuvres* that the Russians called *zakusky*. Goulesco, the popular "King of Gypsy Musicians," played lively *tzigane* music with his small orchestra. Roman Alexandrovitch Zalpius, a well-known practical joker, was accompanied by a dozen lovely ballerinas from the Imperial Theater; wealthy and important men rushed over to meet the beautiful young ladies and offer their deepest and most heartfelt admiration.

Wilkins considered Wolczak the most beautiful woman at the party, and a number of guests seemed to agree inasmuch as a small circle of gentlemen soon formed to speak with her. She was smiling and laughing for the first time in weeks so Wilkins left her briefly to seek out Locke and thank him for the invitation. He found Locke seated at a small table near the back speaking to a mature gentleman with a bald head and closely trimmed black beard. "Excuse me," Wilkins began, "I am sorry to interrupt."

"Of course, my boy," Locke said with mocking civility.

"I would just like to thank you for inviting us tonight. It's a fabulous party."

"No trouble at all," Locke replied. "I am a personal friend of the Grand Duke's, and I have no doubt he would have invited you," he said with an ironic chuckle. "All the same, you are an Englishman and we must hang together."

"Naturally, and thank you again," Wilkins replied icily. He was not accustomed to being treated so indifferently. If only Locke knew, he thought, that I twice escorted the Tsar's eldest daughter, the Grand Duchess Olga Nikolaevna, to the Opera in Paris. Yet neither Locke nor anyone else in Petrograd seemed to recognize the name Wilkins or care that James was the son of Lord and Lady Bartlett. Nor was Wilkins, who was still uncertain why he had been sent to Petrograd, yet convinced that he should try to elbow his way into Russian society and politics. Russia was no Roumania, no Greece, no Serbia, after all, and making the wrong acquaintances was worse than having none at all.

"I will do you another small courtesy," Locke continued, as he gestured to the other gentleman at the table. "Allow me to introduce you to a rising and influential member of the Duma, Vladimir Nikolayevich Lvov."

"My honor, sir," Wilkins said as he bowed deeply.

"Thank you," Lvov said as he nodded his head in reply.

"Lvov will be a very important member of the Duma, I am quite certain, and he is a great reformer. However, if you would please excuse us, Vladimir Nikolayevich and I have further business we must discuss before dinner."

"Of course," Wilkins said as he left the two men at the table. Clearly, Oliver Locke believed he was an important person dabbling in the center of Russian politics.

There was suddenly a great deal of excitement at the door at the arrival of General Aleksei Brusilov, the Commander-in-Chief of the Russian armies. Wilkins noted the man, the commander-in-chief who had led the Russian offensive against Germany the previous summer. Brusilov had been extremely successful, at least by the standards of this war, Wilkins thought cynically. He had pushed the German army back dozens of kilometres! Wilkins had also heard that Brusilov employed a number of novel strategies, some of which Wilkins and Gresham had themselves innovated during their raid at Foncquevillers – Brusilov attacked on a broad front so as to dissipate the enemy's reserve, he limited the duration of his bombardments and used a creeping artillery barrage so as to move his troops closer to the enemy trenches, and he sent his cavalry to the rear since they were useless in the face of machine guns.

Brusilov was soon embroiled in a heated conversation with several members of the Duma who were strong defenders of the Tsar. The Russian army was the largest in the world, they claimed, with 232 infantry divisions and 50 of cavalry, altogether some 13 million men who had been called to fight! More than 3 million of whom had deserted, Brusilov replied. Millions more had been taken prisoner or simply surrendered to Germany – men who were now farming the fields of Germany and working in its factories, thereby freeing German men to fight. The cavalry, Brusilov said, was good for little more than occupying space. The railways were completely inoperable, and in any event the factory owners refused to produce necessary supplies if they could not be sold at an exorbitant profit to the government. Brusilov had pleaded with Tsar Nicholas to take control of the munitions factories, but the Tsar had demurred, claiming that nationalization of the war industry sounded too much like socialism! How could war be waged under such conditions? Brusilov demanded.

Wilkins finally returned to Wolczak who, surrounded by handsome young Russian officers, was happy for the first time in weeks. "Oh there you are, James," she said gaily as she kissed his cheek and pressed her bosom against his arm suggestively. "I'm so pleased you've returned to save me from this overly-excited mob of Russian men."

"My dear, they are rightfully excited at the sight of such a beautiful and vivacious young woman," Wilkins replied enthusiastically.

She kissed him on the cheek and the Russian officers moved away. "But seriously, my darling, how much longer are we to stay in Petrograd? You are doing nothing here, and no one seems to want us. Shouldn't we go back to Roumania?"

"Must we discuss that now? I want you to have an enjoyable evening, darling."

"I am, James, I really am enjoying myself. Alright, just promise me we'll discuss it later, okay?"

"Yes, certainly. Just understand – you know that I was sent here by my government. I do not yet know what I am to do. But I am very pleased and deeply grateful that you agreed to come with me. I promise you, Emma, I will make certain that your journey to Russia is as much to your benefit as mine. Just, please, trust me a little longer."

Rather than answer, Wolczak kissed James passionately. He could taste the *Vodka* and caviar on her tongue, but that did not bother him at all.

The gathering was so cheerful that the *Maître d'hôtel* did not summon the guests to dinner in the adjoining room until nearly eleven that evening. Vecchi had arranged an astonishing meal of fine wines, *Truite de Gatchina*, *Polarde a la Broche*, and *Asperge* with *Sauce Hollandaise*. Wilkins and Wolczak sat at a second table far from the more notable guests with several junior members of the Duma. Most did not speak any English at all, and Wilkins was hesitant to speak Russian as that would leave Emma out of the conversation altogether. Fortunately, the gentleman next to Wolczak spoke English quite well. He was pale-faced but vibrant man in his thirties with short, flat-topped brown hair and large brown eyes.

"Are you enjoying yourself, sir?" Wolczak asked him.

"The dinner is fine, yes. Don't you agree?" He replied politely.

"Oh, yes, of course, this is wonderful," she said. "We're staying here at the *Astoria*, and Joseph is always so wonderful. Still, he has outdone himself this evening."

"Are you not accustomed to such rich foods then?"

"Heavens, no, my *fiancé* and I have been in the war – I'm a nurse, you see, and James, well, he was in the British army."

"You were?" The man asked Wilkins. "But you are not in uniform now, I see. Allow me to introduce myself. I am Aleksandr Fyodorovich Kerensky; I am a member of the Duma from Simbirsk."

"An honor to meet you, sir," Wilkins said as he pushed back his chair, stood, and shook Kerensky's hand. "No, I am not here with the British army," Wilkins added but declined to elaborate further. He was certain that, for a man as clever as Kerensky appeared to be, nothing more needed to be said.

"My pleasure," Kerensky said, and then he turned to Wolczak. "What are you doing with your days, young lady? If you are a nurse, you should be working at one of the hospitals here in Petrograd, no?"

"No, I haven't looked for a position yet. I don't speak much Russian, so I'm not sure what I can do."

"It's a shame," Wilkins added, "because Emma is a highly trained and experienced nurse from America who has treated all sorts of injuries at the front lines in Italy and Roumania. She knows more about battle wounds than many of the doctors themselves."

"Do you indeed?" Kerensky asked. "We have a great many such wounded men in Russia – far too many I regret to say. You would certainly be of great assistance."

"You are very kind to say so, Mister Kerensky," Wolczak replied somewhat sadly.

"For which political party do you stand, Mister Kerensky?" Wilkins asked.

"I am a Social Democrat – the 'Esers' they call us."

"There are Socialists in the Duma?" Wilkins asked in surprise.

Kerensky laughed. "Oh yes, quite a few, but it is owing to our lack of ability to do anything that we are permitted to be seated. You see, no one believes the Duma can do any harm to the Tsar. There are a wide range of reformers in the Duma from those who wish to impose constitutional limitations on the Tsar, to those seeking electoral reform, to those seeking agrarian reform, and so forth."

"Are there many Marxists?"

"That depends on what you mean when you say 'Marxist.' Many of the more radical reformers, I include myself in that coalition, agree with Marx on a philosophical level. However, I suspect you are referring to the *Bolsheviki,* the Maximalists, who wish to impose a Marxist state upon Russia by nationalizing both her farms and factories."

"Yes, exactly," Wilkins replied.

"There are very few who express such opinions openly anywhere in Russia now, but I suspect more than a few members of the Duma would fall into that category."

Just then the dessert arrived, and the magnificent pastries were too engrossing to allow any further polite conversation. Afterwards, Wilkins went off with Kerensky and the other men from their table to drink coffee and smoke cigars. (Wilkins intended to learn a great deal more about the workings of the state Duma.) He left Wolczak to speak with the women at the table, but in the end none of them spoke English. A thin young ballerina called over her dancing instructor, a tall, mature woman dressed extravagantly in ruffled silks and enormous diamonds. "Hello, my dear," she said to Wolczak, "Anna tells me you are all alone, and yet you are such a beautiful young woman. What a travesty! Do you dance, my dear?"

"Oh, no! No, I am not a dancer. I'm a nurse," Wolczak replied. "My name is Emma, Emma Wolczak."

"A nurse? And you are from America, am I correct, Emma?"

"Yes, that's right."

"I am Matilda Kshesinskaya – perhaps you have heard of me? No? How refreshing! I have something of a reputation, I'm afraid," she said in a conspiratorial whisper. "Tell me: Are you enjoying Petrograd?"

"I haven't seen very much of the city yet, but I am enjoying the party tonight very much."

"Yes, it's grand. Dimitri Pavlovich has wonderful parties. Have you attended the theater, my dear? Our ballet is the finest in the world. Anna here will be dancing *La Bayadère* in two days. May I send you tickets? Are you staying here at the *Astoria*?"

"Yes, I'm staying here with my *fiancé*. Would you really send us tickets? I would love to attend," she replied enthusiastically.

"Why of course! You must get out into the city, my dear. You are simply adorable and all the young men –" There was a sudden hush across the dining room as the sound of gunfire echoed through the street outdoors. The guests sat in stunned silence as a fierce gun battle erupted directly in front of the *Astoria*. A few of the women screamed.

"Excuse me," Wolczak said anxiously to Kshesinskaya as she got up and rushed to find Wilkins in the next room. The men there were also standing in shock, silently staring toward the front of the hotel as if the gunfire would suddenly burst into the party. Wolczak found Kerensky near the door.

"Mister Kerensky, where is James?" She asked him anxiously.

"He went to see what is happening," Kerensky said quietly. "I am certain he will be very careful, Miss Wolczak. Most likely, it is the police firing on the protesters."

"They are shooting the protesters?" She asked in horror as the sound of gunfire continued. "How can that be allowed? Have they no right to speak their minds?"

"This is not America," Kerensky said. "The Tsar has become quite intolerant of dissent."

"I must go find James," she said anxiously.

"No, stay with me; he will return safely in a moment," Kerensky said calmly. Then he leaned closer to Wolczak and whispered in her ear. "Tell me please: Your Mister Wilkins, why was he sent to Petrograd?"

A chill ran down Wolczak's neck and she turned to look at Kerensky in surprise. His deep brown eyes stared back at her placidly.

"He doesn't have any instructions, Mister Kerensky. None at all, I assure you."

"That is very unusual."

"So is James," she replied proudly.

Wilkins rushed back into the room as the sound of gunfire finally faded away. "Emma, come quickly," he said to Wolczak. She rushed with Wilkins to the front door of the hotel, followed by Kerensky and a number of other men. In front of the hotel there were five men shot and bleeding in the street. "It's quite safe now, darling. The police have moved away and the shooting has stopped. Can you help them?" Wilkins asked her.

"Yes," she said, rushing out to attend to the wounded men. Wilkins and Kerensky accompanied her to keep watch as a fresh mob of protesters marched down the street singing and waving banners. A light snowfall was already blanketing the wounded men as Wolczak found three already dead. She bound the leg wound of a fourth man with strips of cloth from the red banner she found in the snow beside him.

"How often does this happen, Mister Kerensky?" Wilkins demanded.

"Too often, Mister Wilkins, far too often," Kerensky said with revulsion. "There must be reforms; the people demand reforms. They are starving and cold, Mister Wilkins; they are desperate while the wealthy drink *Vodka* and eat caviar. Look at them," he said, pointing to the front of the hotel where dozens of the over-dressed elite, some with snifters of brandy, stared at the dead and wounded protesters with disdain. One man yelled at Wolczak to stop helping the wounded men; she stared back at him with pure rage in her eyes.

"Tsar Nicholas is intractable," Kerensky said. "That situation cannot last. Do you understand me clearly, Mister Wilkins? The Tsar *cannot* survive for long."

Wilkins looked at Kerensky searchingly. The Russian certainly knew far more than he would say. Yet, as the protesters passed down the street and around the corner toward the Tsar's Winter Palace, one thing was patently clear: Kerensky was correct. The Tsar would not survive. Everything Wilkins had learned of the Russian armies, the terrible conditions and their mutinous soldiers, and what he had seen in Roumania, the Russian soldiers who simply refused to fight, and now the violence in the streets of Petrograd, it alarmed Wilkins to his core. He now understood why he was sent to Petrograd. He was there to prevent a catastrophe for Russia's allies Great Britain and France, a disaster that would alter the course of the war and the future of Europe. He looked at Kerensky and nodded, and then went into the hotel to send a wire to Gresham via *M*.

True to her word, the *prima ballerina* Matilda Kshesinskaya sent tickets for the ballet, and Wolczak was delighted to escape from the hotel where she had been sitting for weeks. Her patience had begun to run thin. As much as she loved Wilkins and believed that he intended to marry her, it was deeply frustrating to be so idle. The ballet, at least, was diverting and the ethereal Russian ballerinas were astonishing in their grace and skill.

Even more surprising was the note she received from Kerensky that invited her and Wilkins to dine with him at *Donon's* restaurant the next evening. Wilkins was excited when he saw the invitation: Kerensky might be his *entré* to the shadowy world of Russian politics (despite the fact that the man was a Socialist), but Wilkins could not understand why the invitation had been sent to Emma. Was Kerensky just being cautious?

They arrived at *Donon's*, just steps from the *Astoria Hotel*, at nine o'clock and were shown to a small private room in the back where Kerensky was waiting. He was dressed more modestly than at the Grand Duke's party, in a plain brown wool suit, and he looked more like a hard-working lawyer than a man with political influence.

"Good evening, James. Emma, how pleasant to see you again," Kerensky said. "Please, be seated. I hope you don't mind, but my time is limited so I have gone ahead and ordered a simple meal for us."

"Thank you, Aleksandr Fyodorovich, we are both grateful – for the invitation and for your thoughtfully planning the menu," Wilkins said. "What an unusual restaurant, is it not? Are all the dining rooms private?"

"Yes, they are," Kerensky said. "That is why people come to *Donon's*, to tell you the truth. It provides the opportunity to speak privately over an excellent meal, and I knew it would be convenient for you. However, to get to the point, there's a reason why my invitation was sent to Emma, instead of to you."

"What is that, Mister Kerensky?" Wolczak asked.

"Please, Emma, call me 'Aleksandr', or even 'Comrade,' if you prefer," he said with a wink to Wilkins. "James told me a great deal about your nursing background the other night and asked me if I could help find you a position here in Petrograd."

"Did you, darling?"

Wilkins nodded, surprised that Kerensky had remembered the conversation. He had told Kerensky of Emma's high ambitions, and also that he was eager to keep her close to him in Petrograd.

"Well, I believe I have found a position for you at the Women's Medical Institute."

"Aleksandr, you are so kind, thank you," Wolczak said cautiously. "Is that a hospital for women or is it a clinic?"

"No, no, you do not understand, my dear," Kerensky said chuckling. "Yes, there is a hospital, but it is primarily a school, a medical school, where women are trained to become doctors. I have secured a position for you at the school, and they have confirmed to me that there are several English-speaking instructors who will oversee your education."

"What?" Wolczak asked in stunned disbelief.

"James told me that you have the desire to become a doctor, and after I saw you rush out to the street to help the injured men the other night, I was convinced that you are precisely the sort of person who should become a doctor. Someone who will look after the people. You may begin your training –"

"Oh, my gosh!" Wolczak exclaimed. "Are you serious? I am to become a doctor? A real doctor? Oh, my, James, did you know?"

"Not at all. Aleksandr, I have no words to express our gratitude," Wilkins said sincerely.

"It's a miracle!" Wolczak exclaimed. "Thank you; thank you so much. I've wanted to study medicine for so long, but it would be impossible in the United States. Women are simply not allowed." She leaned over and kissed Kerensky on the cheek, and then she kissed Wilkins.

"It is my pleasure, Emma," Kerensky continued, smiling. "As I say, I am confident that you should become a doctor, and you will be a very good one."

"Please, allow me to order some *champagne* to celebrate," Wilkins said.

"If you wish, of course," Kerensky said. "I haven't much time. There is a meeting of the Petrograd Worker's Council tonight that I must attend. Perhaps you would like to come along, James?"

"Tell me plainly, Aleksandr," Wilkins asked, "are there plans to overthrow the Tsar?"

"James, there have been plans to overthrow the Tsar for many years; plans come and go – that is nothing new. But you must understand that the war has now made the people desperate. You should get out of your hotel and walk the streets of Petrograd or go to the country to see for yourself. The people of Russia are suffering terribly."

"I *do* understand – the people of France and England and Italy are suffering just as much. I was in Serbia when the people, civilians I mean, were forced to flee their homeland, and when Roumania was set on fire. The world is full of injustice and suffering now. But ask yourself this: You may not like the Tsar, but will Russia fare any better under the Kaiser if it becomes a territory of Imperial Germany?"

"That outcome is improbable, as you must know. Germany cannot occupy the whole of Russia, and therefore Hindenburg could never defeat us. Napoleon himself tried to conquer Russia and it ruined him. Nevertheless, my preference is to remove the Tsar *after* the war is concluded. However, I invite you to come with me to the Worker's Council tonight and judge for yourself whether the Russian people will wait until the conclusion of the war. I doubt it very much."

"Why have I not heard these alarms before now? Can the British, French, and Americans all be wrong about the security of the Tsar's government?"

"Of course I do not know what you have been told, James. I am certain your government does not *want* to believe that the Romanov's, who have ruled Russia for three centuries, could be suddenly swept from power. Tsar Nicholas is the cousin of your own King George, after all."

"Then I must judge for myself." Wilkins turned to Wolczak. "I must go with Aleksandr this evening, my darling. I have a great deal to learn about what is happening in Russia."

"Of course, James. Just be sure to wake me when you come back to the hotel. We'll have a celebration of our own," she said with a sly grin.

The Petrograd Worker's Council meeting that night took place inside an old, hot, brightly lit gymnasium that was packed to overflowing with men and women from the factories and many soldiers and sailors. Wilkins' first impression was of barely restrained rage: Nearly every one of the hundreds attending the meeting was angry – first with the police for killing "peaceful" demonstrators, but also with the Generals for perpetuating the war, with the factory owners for mistreating the workers and the land owners for stealing the peasants' labor, and with the Duma for its inability to act. Most of all, they were angry with the Tsar as the leader of what the people considered a totalitarian regime.

Since the last demonstrations, a number of workers now openly carried handguns or rifles and were prepared to fight back should they be confronted by the police; hundreds of their "comrades" had been imprisoned. Soldiers who claimed to have been ordered to fire on the demonstrators and refused to do so said that that their officers had been cashiered and fifteen non-commissioned officers had been hanged.

Wilkins was the only one present in an evening coat, he noticed, and it made him feel terribly conspicuous. Many at the meeting wore nothing more than rags. These were the people employed in the factories and servants from the nearby farms, those who were unable to work because they must spend hours in line each day awaiting their meager ration of bread, who burned their furniture for lack of wood or coal, whose brothers and fathers and sons had died in the war or had come home crippled or mutilated. The rhetoric was revolutionary: Some advocated killing the factory owners and running the factories themselves; soldiers reported on whole battalions that were prepared to mutiny. There were some who advocated killing the Tsar, and a reverent eulogy was read for Grigory Rasputin, who they believed had almost convinced Tsar Nicholas to end the war. Several members of the Duma spoke in favor of political and economic reforms, and there were calls to repeat the glory of the French Revolution and the unfulfilled promise of the 1905 demonstrations in Russia itself.

At last Kerensky took a turn at the podium, and the crowd fell silent as he was considered a great speaker. He began by calling the people to create a new government in Russia and to achieve revolutionary change through the law, through the courts, and through the Duma. Some in the crowd grumbled. "You've been told of the French Revolution in 1792," he began gently. "I ask you: How did 1792 end in France? It ended with bloodshed, with the fall of the republic, and with the rise of the dictator Napoleon. How did 1905 end? With a triumph for the people of Russia!" There was a roar of approval. "The Russian Socialist parties must prevent such an end as there was in France," Kerensky demanded. "We must ensure that our comrades are freed from prison, that they have the opportunity to speak and not be obliged to flee to Switzerland." Now Kerensky chided the Marxists: "We have been told that we should not fight with words, but show by deeds that we are fighting for the revolution. What means are recommended for this fight?" Kerensky paused carefully, then gave an answer dripping with sarcasm: "To slaughter *Russians*!?" The crowd erupted in laughter. "Comrades, I have the highest respect for Marx, but Marx never taught such primitive and brutal means. Socialism nowhere recommends or requires that we slaughter our own people. The Marxists ask you to kill and destroy. I say we must build the Russia we wish to live in, not burn down the one we have." The crowd shouted its approval, and soon it was almost impossible to hear anyone speak due to the shouting and applause.

The meeting went on and on into the night. There was no agenda and it produced no result – it was simply a mass expression of frustration and pain that continued hour after hour until those present were exhausted. At the end, the crowd sang "the Internationale" and many broke down weeping:

Stand up, ones who are branded by the curse,
All the world's starving and enslaved!

Our outraged minds are boiling,
Ready to lead us to the deadly fight.
We will destroy this world of violence
Down to the very foundations, and then
We will build our new world.
He who was nothing will become everything!

This is our final and decisive battle;
With the Internationale humanity will rise up!

Enough of the will of kings
Stupefying us into the haze of war!
War to the tyrants! Peace to the people!
Go on strike, sons of the army!
And if the tyrants tell us
To fall heroically in battle for them -
Then, murderers, we will point
The muzzles of our cannons at you!

This is our final and decisive battle;
With the Internationale humanity will rise up!

Wilkins was stunned. He had not seen or heard of anything like it in Great Britain or France – not even in Ireland where there was a constant risk of rebellion. Most worrisome was the utter absence of direction or purpose to these people. Surely someone would eventually sway the crowds to action, and then anything at all could happen.

Wilkins felt compelled to determine whether Tsar Nicholas was at least aware of the imminent threat against him, and so the next morning he sent a note to Grand Duchess Olga Nikolaevna, the daughter of the Tsar that Wilkins had befriended in Paris, at the Winter Place. He asked if she would permit him an audience.

Wilkins walked through Palace Square, past the Alexander Column, and looked up at the ornate, pale green façade of the Winter Palace to deliver his letter in person. There were countless guards at each entrance and at the windows and some with machine guns on the roof. The very fact that the Tsar remained with his family in the Winter Palace evidenced his intransigence – surely any reasonable man would have moved his family out of the city or, in the Tsar's case, to the Catherine Palace at *Tsarskoye Selo* only fifteen miles from Petrograd.

Hours later, Wilkins received a brief reply from the Grand Duchess: She remembered her lovely evenings with James in Paris and thanked him for his kind words but she was ill, she said, and was unable to entertain visitors at that time.

Wilkins persisted in making acquaintances and learning the political landscape in Russia, and he was all too pleased to remain in the city as long as Emma continued her studies. However, by early March the situation in Petrograd had become far more difficult. Winter still held the city in its deathly cold grasp. Many people were reported to have frozen to death in their homes, and none but the wealthy had enough to eat. Russian troops were dying by the thousands from disease and starvation on the Eastern Front. Wilkins had heard nothing from Gresham and was uncertain if his friend had even received his message. Wolczak, at least, had begun her studies at the Women's Medical Institute and was exhilarated to cross the Neva River each morning for her anatomy instruction.

Then the strikes began. First, the workers at several munitions plants decided to walk out and refused to manufacture any further weapons, artillery shells, mortars, grenades, bullets or uniforms for the Russian war effort. That evening the munitions workers marched up the Nevsky Prospekt, many of them armed with rifles stolen from the factories at which they worked, led by students from the university who waved great red banners. One group of demonstrators split off with the intent to ransack the Artillery Museum across the Neva River, but a regiment of Cossacks, who were fiercely loyal to the Tsar, blocked access to the Troytskiy Bridge.

Emma Wolczak, returning to the *Astoria* from the hospital where she studied, walked right into the angry, well-armed crowd before she realized what was happening. The Cossacks, seated stoically on horseback, brandished both swords and rifles; they had a reputation for being merciless to their enemies and the Tsar increasingly relied upon them to keep order in the major Russian cities as the usefulness of the police fell into doubt.

Buried in her heavy wool coat, muffler and fur hat, Wolczak stared in fright at the assembled Cossacks as they yelled at her in a language she couldn't understand and pointed rifles at her. Scared and uncertain how best to return to her hotel, Wolczak turned to quickly retreat to her medical school, retreating up Kammennoostrovsky Prospekt as fast as possible. She was startled when a beautiful black and gold *droshky* came jangled to a stop beside her, and she cried out when a woman, wrapped entirely in luxurious sable furs, yelled at her: "*Мост закрыт!?*"

"I don't speak much Russian, I'm very sorry," Wolczak squeaked in fright.

The woman seated in the *droshky* quickly pulled the scarf from her face and climbed down as Wolczak shrank against the wall of the building. "You are Emma Wolczak, are you not? Emma, please accept my apology for frightening you. It is Matilda Kshesinskaya!"

Wolczak recognized the ballet instructor and began to cry: "Oh, Matilda, I am so very sorry. The Cossacks were so threatening, and I am just trying to get back to my hotel."

"Please, my dear, come have a seat in my sleigh and we will take you home. There are other bridges we can cross, and there is ample time before I must arrive at the theater. Tell me, why are you here in the Petrogradsky District so late?"

"I am studying medicine, to become a doctor, at the Women's Institute."

"The one on *Ulica Rentgena*?"

"Yes, exactly."

"I know it very well!" The ballerina replied gaily. "You see?" She asked pointing toward the corner. "My house is right there, the one with the solarium just before the bridge."

"Oh, it's a very beautiful house," Wolczak replied.

"Come now, we will take you home to your young man, my dear, and if you ever again find yourself alone or tired during your return to the hotel, I would like you to stop at my house; it would be my pleasure to entertain you any time."

"You are very kind, Matilda. Thank you so much."

As the driver turned the *droshky* about to attempt the Palace Bridge, Wolczak calmed her nerves considerably. "Thank you again for the ballet tickets, Matilda. James and I enjoyed the show very much. I must confess, I had never seen ballet before, although I have heard of it, of course."

Kshesinskaya laughed. "My dear, you are so innocent. If you were not so very beautiful, I might have nothing to do with you. We shall have to see how much longer the ballet can continue with all these demonstrations upsetting the city. We have not had a full audience in weeks! I love the ballet, my dear, but I must also be paid or else I shall have to move to Paris."

"Do you think the demonstrations will stop soon? James does not believe they will, not unless the weather turns warmer."

"Then we are for a great deal of trouble, because Petrograd never warms until June. Still, I am sympathetic to the wishes of the common people. It is impossible to deny that they have good reason to protest. And besides, as an artist myself, I am attracted to the *avant-garde*."

"Are you a Socialist, then?"

"I do not like to put names on things, my dear, but we must be open to radical new ideas. I frequently entertain members of the *Bolsheviki* at my home. You must come listen to them."

"I haven't heard of them. Who are they?"

"Why, they are the most radical of all! They seek not just political equality, but economic and social equality for all Russians. Those with great wealth would be forced to hand over their property to the government, who in turn would ensure that the poor have enough to survive. They say: 'From each according to his means; to each according to his needs.' A noble sentiment, don't you agree? And I must confess there is one gentleman, the one who edits their newsletter, that you simply must see to believe – a strikingly handsome young gentleman," she said almost giggling. "Now, here we are at the *Astoria* at last, my dear. I pray you are over your fright, and please give my regards to your young gentleman."

The horses were pulled up and the *droshky* came to a stop in front of the hotel.

"Thank you again, Matilda," Wolczak said. "I *will* come to visit you. You can count on it."

"Be well, my dear, *au revoir!*"

The next morning began with the largest demonstrations yet. It was "Women's Day" in Russia and the Petrograd Worker's Council had planned a series of events, marches, rallies and speeches. Workers at virtually every factory in Petrograd and many around the country went out on strike. On the Nevsky Prospect, where many of the rallies occurred, the cable cars sat vacant on the street as huge crowds sang and marched toward the Winter Palace. Nevsky Prospekt had a special significance because it was there that the attempted revolution in 1905 had begun and had been put down by a bloody massacre.

Wilkins went out to view the demonstrations and spent much of the day with Kerensky. Wilkins had come to understand that Kerensky, although not a leader of the workers *per se*, was among the most influential and important members of the state Duma to support the rights of workers and farm laborers and wanted to guarantee civil liberties for all Russians, even women and those of Jewish beliefs.

The demonstrations continued well into the night, and then continued the next morning without any pause at all. There was growing concern in the Winter Palace that the demonstrations had not ended as they normally had in the past, and the President of the Duma, Mikhail Rodzianko, pleaded with the Tsar to allow the workers to continue peacefully venting their frustration. As the demonstrations continued into the third day, however, there were signs that Tsar Nicholas was becoming impatient. The factories could not stay closed indefinitely, he told Rodzianko.

Wolczak was excited to pass through Palace Square that evening as the latest rally, one mostly of women, continued. However, the Tsar had at last heard enough. He ordered the mounted police and the Cossacks to clear the square. Wolczak saw the mounted police form a broad front and advanced in a close on-line formation. Suddenly shots were fired, and the police raised their rifles and began shooting into the crowd. The rally turned instantly into a panic as the police rode down or shot a number of the women. As Wolczak ran for cover, she noted that the Cossacks, by contrast, just sat and watched passively as the crowd fled the square and left the injured to be arrested, trampled or executed by the police. As the crowd finally began to disperse, the Cossacks suddenly decided they were unwilling to stand by and let the police execute injured women. The Cossacks rode swiftly against the police forces and drove them back out of the square, then took up positions that prevented the police from approaching the demonstrators again.

Wolczak hurried back to the *Astoria* to tell Wilkins what she had seen.

"You're certain? He asked excitedly. "The Cossacks were protecting the protesters?"

"Absolutely. The Cossacks have sided with the revolution, James. There can be no doubt."

"That changes everything. Without the Cossacks, only the police will be left to protect the Winter Palace. The Tsar will have to recall front line troops to Petrograd."

Indeed, they discovered the next morning, as the Women's Day demonstrations continued for a fourth straight day, that armed soldiers had been sent by General Brusilov to restore peace in the capital. Tsar Nicholas was rushing back from a tour of the front lines to join his family at the Winter Palace

Rumors soon spread that the police had sent officers in plain clothes into the demonstrating crowds to incite violence, to thus justify a massive and violent crackdown on the striking workers and rallies. The ploy was quickly uncovered. The state Duma repudiated the Tsar's tactics. Rodzianko insisted to the Tsar that the time had come to reform the government. The Tsar remained adamantly opposed.

Then to make matters worse, many of the armed soldiers sent to Petrograd, whole companies of men who had come from the front lines, refused to take up arms against their fellow citizens and joined the protesters. The Fortress of Peter and Paul was seized by the deserting troops and the arsenal was passed out to the mob. By the end of the day, the city was in chaos. Bands of soldiers and Cossacks roamed the city hunting down the police and either shooting or incarcerating them. Mobs stormed the prisons and released all the demonstrators who had been arrested over the previous weeks. Police stations and courts were set on fire.

The fighting and demonstrations continued day after day, completely out of anyone's control. The Worker's Council selected representatives to force their way into the Duma and demand a new government. Tsar Nicholas sought to return to Petrograd aboard his private train, but General Brusilov ordered that the train be stopped outside the city because it was not safe for the Tsar to enter the capital. President Rodzianko and General Brusilov, certain that mere political reforms could not quell the riots, pleaded with the Tsar to abdicate.

The growing violence in the city had forced many to seek shelter. Wilkins and Wolczak remained inside the *Astoria* for several days, happily nestled in their extravagant and comfortable suite. Sleep was almost impossible as the shooting continued through the night, but they had just drifted off when Wolczak awoke to a pounding on their door. She put on her robe and walked barefoot to see who it was. As she unlatched the door, a man with lanky black hair and a wild mustache and beard forced his way into the room.

"Pack your things at once. You must leave immediately," the man shouted with great urgency.

"But, but –" She began.

"Who is it, Emma?" Wilkins asked as he stepped sleepily from the bedroom in his undershorts. Then he saw the man standing in the doorway nearby. "Good Lord! Is that you, David? Have you just arrived in Petrograd?"

"David? David Gresham?" Wolczak asked, looking again.

"Yes. Yes, and it's lovely to see you Emma. You're as fetching as ever. Now go pack your bags, and be quick about it."

"David, what are you doing here? When did you get to Petrograd?" Wilkins demanded.

"The Bolsheviks are coming right now, James. Now. They plan to storm the *Astoria* and kill the foreigners that they believe forced Russia into the war, so get your damned clothes. We must leave immediately!"

"Certainly," Wilkins said without hesitation. He ran to the bedroom to pack his clothes and to dress. In a few minutes, Gresham was leading them down the service stairway to the kitchens. As they rushed through the back corridors, Wilkins yelled to stop.

"I must make a call," he said as he ran back to the kitchen. He found the house telephone and had the operator connect him to Oliver Locke, the only other Englishman that Wilkins knew in the hotel. "Mister Locke, it's James Wilkins," he spoke into the telephone. "Listen – the revolutionaries are coming now to sack the *Astoria* and kill the foreigners. . . . Yes, I am quite certain. You must leave at once. . . . Yes, Lvov's, I will see you there –" Wilkins heard gunfire in front of the hotel, perhaps in the lobby itself. "Go now," Wilkins said, and threw down the phone. He ran back to Wolczak and Gresham.

"Here," Gresham said, handing Wilkins a piece of paper. "Go to this address. You will be safe there. I will join you later."

"But why –" Wilkins began, but stopped when he saw Gresham draw his handgun.

"Later," Gresham barked as he ran back toward the kitchens.

Wilkins and Wolczak fled out the back door and put several blocks' distance between them and the hotel before they stopped to look at the paper. It gave the address of a flat quite close to Wolczak's hospital. As they hurried through the dark, smoke-filled streets of Petrograd to find it, they learned that the sailors from the nearby Kronstadt naval base had murdered their commanding officers and mutinied. The sailors were joining the revolution and bringing war ships down the Neva River to bombard the Winter Palace. No one knew what was happening in Petrograd, but it was perfectly clear that the Tsar had no way to stop it. Peace might be restored only if the Tsar stepped down.

Early the next morning, Tsar Nicholas II at last abdicated and gave the throne over to his younger brother, Grand Duke Michael Alexandrovich. However, the Grand Duke could see what was happening in Russia even if

Nicholas could not. He refused to take up the crown, and for the first time in five hundred years, Russia no longer had a king.

Stockholm

Wilkins woke alone in Gresham's cold, gloomy flat in the Petrogradsky District that afternoon. The bed he deemed comfortable enough, but it was the only remaining piece of furniture in the flat; a pile of broken hardwood chairs and tables to be used as firewood sat by the stove under the mantle. The windows were shuttered, and the sour odour of boiled cabbage permeated the dark, single room. Wilkins dressed and went to wash his face in the lavatory down the hallway. Then he went to the street to find out what was happening. The announcement of the Tsar's abdication had stunned the crowds to silence, for the moment at least. Eventually Wilkins returned to the flat and waited. It was fully dark when Gresham finally appeared.

"Where is Emma?" Gresham asked.

"At the hospital, studying," was Wilkins' surly response.

"That's just as well. You and I need to chat."

"How long have you been in Petrograd, David? Why didn't you tell me you were here? Where have you been?"

"Everyone knows you work for Great Britain, James. I thought it would be better for me to come in secret and make my own inquiries before speaking with you. I arrived in Petrograd about three weeks ago."

"And what have you been doing since you arrived here?"

'Working, writing for *Pravda*."

"*Pravda*? *Pravda*! You can't be serious! How did you come to be working for that dish-rag?"

"The Bolsheviks are a fringe party with an impossible political agenda, and people like that always want to know what everyone else is doing, so it seemed a sensible place to start."

"And they simply took you in with open arms?"

"They made inquiries."

"Had they heard of our work at Foncquevillers as well?"

"Thankfully no, but in any case I haven't used the name 'Gresham.' Have you ever learned my real name, James?"

"No, it's none of my concern what you call yourself, David."

"Well, my true name is not 'Gresham', it's 'Larkin,' as in 'Big Jim' Larkin. Do you recognize that name?"

"Yes, of course, the Irish revolutionary, you mean. Wasn't he forced to flee to America some years ago?"

"Yes, he did. He's my cousin, James; Big Jim and my mother grew up together in Liverpool. I've never actually met him, but the name was enough to get me into the Bolshevik's good graces, within limits of course. They sent me to work at *Pravda* correcting their English-language translations."

"I see. Well, I must give you credit – that's more than I have done. Clearly I could do nothing to stop the revolution," Wilkins said with self-loathing.

"No one could have stopped the revolution, James. The Tsar was too stubborn far too long. But you have done something very worthwhile. I know all about it."

"How do you know? And what have I done, for that matter?" Wilkins asked, perplexed.

"The Bolsheviks know everything that goes on in Russia, James. There are quite a few of them, it turns out, and they are very dangerous, but they keep wonderful records on everyone they consider a threat or otherwise of interest to them, including you. I've read your file. You've done something no one else from Great Britain has done."

"You're joking, surely."

"You've become friends with Kerensky," Gresham said seriously.

"Kerensky! He is no one, only a member of the Duma!"

"Kerensky is more important than you know. A new Provisional Government has been formed today to fill the void left by the Tsar's abdication, and Kerensky is the new Minister of Justice."

"A Minister? Is Kerensky a Bolshevik?"

"No, he is a moderate Socialist."

"What do you know about Oliver Locke? Did you read his file?"

"He's with the Foreign Office, probably involved in the assassination of Rasputin. He's particular friends with Vladimir Lvov who is also a new Minister of the Provisional Government and a member of the Duma. Lvov's a reformer whose politics are contradictory: He was a monarchist, then a constitutional monarchist who professed to be a Kadet, a member of the Constitutional Democratic Party. He's not well trusted by the Socialists, so he's been put in charge of reforming the Russian Orthodox Church. Thomas Cromwell is to be his model, I suppose."

"Alright then, David, I can see you know far more than I. What do you think we should do?"

"You shall have to help the Russians rebuild their government, James. That is your task, and what I believe you are better suited for."

"And you think Kerensky is our man?"

"I don't know that, but I think it will be your job to make him our man. Many of the Russians are distrustful of Great Britain; most of the Englishmen here, the ones who collaborated with the Tsar's government, are being sent away. We are fortunate you did not do so and that you befriended a man whose importance in the new regime is unquestionable. You must get closer to Kerensky."

"And what will you be doing?"

"To be honest with you, James, I came to Russia for only one reason. I would have been perfectly happy to stay and fight with Lawrence in Arabia – the Arabs are beating the Hell out of old Abdul and I was rather enjoying myself. When I got your message, though, I knew I had to come – for Dunn. He must be here somewhere; this is precisely his sort of thing."

"I agree, but I have heard nothing."

"The Bolsheviks say they do not know him, but I will find him, James. I assure you, I *will* find him and kill him."

Wilkins paced the room as Gresham fed the small fire in the woodstove.

"You and Emma must keep the flat, James," Gresham said. "I can make other arrangements. There are plenty of people I can stay with – perhaps the fellow I work for, some crazy bastard by the name of Josef Stalin. He's one of the people in charge at *Pravda*. And you mustn't contact me directly. Perhaps Emma could pass messages for us. We must have a signal. Would Emma be able to arrange that?"

Wilkins wasn't listening, and at last he stopped pacing. "I know what I must do next," he said and then grabbed his overcoat and rushed from the room, leaving Gresham behind.

Wilkins found Kerensky in his modest office in the old Tauride Palace, the building where the Duma held its meetings. Kerensky was busy with the other newly-appointed Provisional Government Ministers, but Wilkins did not have to wait long before he was shown to Kerensky's private office. Kerensky, seated at his desk in the large, mostly-empty room, rose at once to shake Wilkins' hand.

"Good evening, James." Kerensky said happily. "I wasn't sure I would see you again; we heard that the *Astoria* was set on fire and I was concerned for your well-being. I am very pleased to see you are unhurt. And Emma?"

"She is fine, thank you. Fortunately we were not at the hotel at the time."

'Very good. Now tell me what I can do for you." He asked warily.

"Minister Kerensky, first allow me to congratulate you – for your appointment to the Provisional Government, of course, but moreover for the astonishing changes that you and your comrades have brought about in your country. It is still almost impossible to believe that you have finally rid yourselves of Tsar Nicholas and the Romanovs. It is about the Tsar, in particular, that I have come to speak with you so urgently."

"Yes, the Tsar and his family. That is a difficult problem," Kerensky said.

"Aleksandr, you know of course that I am an Englishman, you may also know that my father is a member of the House of Lords, and you may even suspect that I am an agent of His Majesty's government, but I come to you today to discuss the issue of the Tsar without resorting to subterfuge."

"Your Ambassador Buchanan has already been here, James, and it is quite understandable that King George would offer sanctuary to Tsar Nicholas and his family. The issue is already under consideration."

"It is absolutely impossible, Aleksandr."

"Pardon me?" Kerensky asked in surprise.

"Of course King George *must* make the offer – Nicholas is his cousin, after all. However, the British Empire and our government want nothing to do with the tyrant Nicholas Alexandrovich Romanov. We do not want him on British soil. It would be an ineradicable stain on our country to harbor such a man, nor do we not want the former Tsar conspiring on British soil to return to Russia or to overthrow your new government. So I tell you quite candidly: You must not send him to England. England does not want him."

Wilkins had never felt so ill. His entire life had been spent in the service of nobility and respecting royalty. In one gasp, he had thrown the Tsar of Russia, the cousin of his own King, and the Tsar's lovely family, even his daughter Olga whom Wilkins had found so charming – down into a chasm from which they were unlikely to ever escape. If they could not leave Russia, the Romanovs would live in a prison the rest of their lives, if they were to live at all.

"I am stunned, James," Kerensky said in astonishment. "Naturally, we assumed that Ambassador Buchanan was sincere when he presented your government's request. *Are* you here on your government's behalf?"

Wilkins took a deep breath before continuing on what he deemed a reckless but logical path.

"I must request that what I tell you now, Aleksandr, not leave this room."

"I agree," Kerensky replied.

"As you undoubtedly suspect, I am an agent of Great Britain, and I am also a Colonel in His Majesty the King's Royal Army. However, I am accountable only to the new Prime Minister, David Lloyd George, and I was sent to Russia to assess the situation here for myself and to take whatever actions I deem necessary to preserve the strong alliance between our great nations. You will note that I have in no way sought to impede the long-awaited and remarkable developments that have taken place here over the past few weeks. I shall not in any way interfere with the formation of a new, more enlightened and democratic government in your country. In fact, I applaud it. When I tell you Nicholas must not be sent to England, you may be assured that I am speaking on behalf of His Majesty's government, if not His Majesty King George."

Wilkins could not believe he had just said those words. He had thrust his own King aside in the best interests of his country and his mission in Russia. Kerensky was equally surprised.

"Here is my address," Wilkins said as he wrote the address of the flat on his card and held it out to Kerensky. "I will remain here in Petrograd as long as your government will permit it, and you may call on me whenever I can be of service to you or to the Provisional Government. It is in Great Britain's long term interests to have a stable government in Petrograd, Aleksandr. I trust that you will one day recall that Great Britain stood by your country in this time of turmoil."

Kerensky took the card and sat down at his desk silently.

"How am I to know you are who you say, James? Shall I simply take you at your word?"

"A man is best judged by what he does rather than what he says, don't you agree? I suggest you contact Prime Minister Venizelos in Greece. He will tell you just what sort of man I am."

Kerensky nodded. "Very well, James. I would be pleased to have you remain in Petrograd, for now."

Wilkins approached the desk and held out his hand. "Again, I offer you my congratulations, comrade." Kerensky shook the extended hand, and then Wilkins turned and left the room.

In Petrograd, there was a quiet period of mourning for many days after the revolution as the casualties were solemnly buried, martyrs to the cause of the revolution and freedom. There was also an increasing tension about Russia's future in the war. Many of the members of the new Provisional Government insisted that Russia withdraw and seek a separate peace with Germany. However, the announcement that the United States had declared war against Germany had a profound effect around the world, including in Petrograd. The promise of American soldiers, American rifles, American artillery, and American gold gave new hope to the Allies who were exhausting their nations. But it would take months for the Americans to prepare for the journey across the Atlantic Ocean. Spring had already come and summer was fast approaching. That meant there would be new offensives and many more lives lost before a single American soldier would fire a rifle on the battlefield. News had already spread of the Allies' disastrous spring offensive in France.

French General Robert Nivelle, the man credited with saving Verdun in 1916 and subsequently appointed Commander-in-Chief of the French armed forces, had planned a massive attack across the *Chemin des Dames* with assistance from the British First, Third, and Fifth Armies at Arras. His optimistic plan called for the French and British to break through the German lines within 48 hours, and to then meet up and sweep into Belgium. Nivelle had even projected less than 10,000 Allied casualties. However, even before the offensive commenced, many noted that that the plan differed very little from past Allied offensives, particularly General Haig's plan for the Somme offensive in 1916. It was not surprising, therefore, when Nivelle's attack ran into difficulties almost at once. Although the French captured portions of the German front lines, there was no breakthrough or link-up of the French and British forces, and, in a little over two weeks, the Allies suffered over 180,000 fresh casualties.

Although Nivelle was promptly sacked and replaced with General Philippe Pétain, of greater concern was the number of new desertions in the French army. Tens of thousands of French soldiers walked out of the front lines and went to the rear refusing to fight any further. The French army was on the verge of total collapse. Thousands of deserters were arrested; hundreds were sentenced to death. General Pétain, an old soldier himself, would spend the rest of the summer pleading with the French troops to stay in the trenches until the Americans arrived.

The Russian armies were in a state of mutiny as well. In many parts of the army, the Russian soldiers arrested and in some cases executed their commanding officers. They formed Soldiers' Councils to administrate and issue orders. There was very little will to fight, and more often no ability to do so: Reports came back from the front lines that ammunition manufactured in the Russian factories failed to work or was manufactured to the wrong caliber, even when the Russian troops did agree to fight. Deserters had torn up train tracks that supplied the front lines. Germany freely distributed anti-war *propaganda* to Russians soldiers at the front lines. The situation grew even more grave when a Russian pamphlet was distributed that set forth new "General Orders of the Council of Soldiers Deputies." No one knew who had written the orders nor who was distributing them, nor did the troops question whether the "Council of Soldiers Deputies" had the authority to issue such orders. But they were wildly popular among the soldiers: The General Orders banned capital punishment in the army, banned the saluting of officers, required each military unit to elect a governing council, and in essence dispelled any remnant of discipline in the army.

Shortly after the General Orders were issued, Gresham was sitting at his desk one afternoon in the old cavernous loft used by the Bolsheviks for their *Pravda* printing office. He was reading the English translation of a *propaganda* piece by Stalin about the "Glorious Council of Soldiers Deputies," and Stalin was at the office himself that morning to rush publication of the article. As usual there was a vigorous debate about whether the Bolsheviks should support the Provisional Government. Stalin was in favor of the new government and spoke favorably of Kerensky, but Stalin was also a quiet man who seldom spoke at length and didn't care to arouse emotions. Gresham had been staying in Stalin's townhouse the past week and rarely saw or spoke with him, but he soon came to see that Stalin was also handling a great deal of money and Gresham wondered where all those funds came from. Suddenly a messenger arrived at the office and there were exclamations of excitement, cheering and applause: Lenin had returned to Russia!

Lenin, Vladimir Ilyich Ulyanov, was the leader of the Bolsheviks who had been exiled to Switzerland. He despised the war and had described the conflict as "one slave owner, Germany, fighting another slave owner, England, for a fairer distribution of the slaves." The messenger said Lenin was preparing to make a public announcement that day, and the *Pravda* staff leapt up to put on their coats and hats to attend the speech. Gresham joined the rest of the *Pravda* staff as they rushed across the Great Nevka River to where Lenin would speak from the balcony of the mansion owned by *prima ballerina* Matilda Kshesinskaya.

By the time the staff arrived at the ballerina's mansion on Kammennoostrovsky Prospekt, an enormous crowd had already assembled below the balcony. The day was cold and the weather dreary, yet thousands of factory workers and soldiers stood in the street waiting to hear Lenin speak.

Gresham was shocked by the level of excitement and size of the crowd. He was ushered with the rest of the *Pravda* staff into the mansion where they would best hear Lenin and report his words to the world.

Lenin, short, bald and extremely tired, stood near the doors to the balcony. He was speaking quietly to Stalin, Trotsky, Kshesinskaya, and a few others. Gresham briefly considered shooting Lenin on the spot, but then decided it would be premature. He moved closer in case he changed his mind as he checked to see that his handgun was accessible beneath his heavy trench coat. Then suddenly Gresham's heart skipped a beat: Who was that shaking Lenin's hand? He stared in disbelief. There, standing beside the ballerina Kshesinskaya, was Emma Wolczak! Before she could see him and, God forbid, blurt out that he was a British spy, Gresham quickly turned and retreated into the foyer.

The crowd was electrified by Lenin's speech: He demanded an end to the war! He demanded that political authority be given to the Workers Councils and Soldiers Deputies! He demanded that the Provisional Government stop collaborating with monarchists and others who would perpetuate the existing class divisions within Russia! He railed against England, France and America. He claimed that the abdication of the Tsar was only the beginning of a global revolution. The crowd shouted their acclaim.

Gresham was relieved that Lenin did not call for the crowd to take up arms on the spot: No one was really keeping the peace in Petrograd and the government was still uncertain whether the Cossacks could be relied upon. As the speech concluded and the crowds at last drifted away, Gresham spied Wolczak departing the mansion alone. He caught up and followed her as she returned toward the hospital where she studied, and then he called out her name: "Emma," he said softly. She turned in utter shock and recognized Gresham at once.

"David, you scared me!" She admonished him.

"Were you afraid it was James?"

"No! Why? Should I have been?" She asked.

"I can't say. What were you doing there at Kshesinskaya's mansion?"

"She is a friend, that's all," Wolczak said defensively. "I had no idea that the Bolsheviks would be there today. It was a complete accident. What were you doing? We've heard nothing from you since that night at the *Astoria.*"

"I've been working. Listen to me, Emma – did Kshesinskaya invite you to come meet Lenin? I must know the truth," he insisted. Wolczak hesitated. "I promise you, I will not discuss this with James," he assured her.

"Yes, she did," Wolczak admitted. "She thought I should meet him because he is famous and interesting and *avant-guard*, just as she fancies herself to be. I doubt she would be so intrigued if she realized he meant to take her mansion away and house a dozen families there. Not that her mansion isn't obscene the way it is now, of course, but I don't wish to criticize her: Matilda has been very kind to me."

"And Lenin? Tell me, what is your impression of him?"

"I think he means to end the war and correct centuries of injustice in Russia. It is difficult to argue with that."

"Have you heard that America has declared war on Germany?"

"Yes. So what?"

"You are an American, Emma. Your brothers, your family, they will be fighting the Germans in France. If Russia does not remain in the war, there will be a million more German soldiers fighting against the Americans. Don't you see, Russia must stay in the war!"

Wolczak was silent as she considered what Gresham had said.

"America!" She spat back at him quietly. "I will never go back there, David. I was told my entire life that women were only good for two things, f---ing and cooking, and then I met you and James and a whole new world has opened up to me. I don't care a fig for America."

Gresham stared back uncertain how to respond. 'Just tell me one thing, Emma," he said finally. "Lenin was in Switzerland a few days ago. Switzerland is a landlocked country surrounded by Germany, Austria, France, and Italy. Do you know how Lenin traveled to Russia?"

"He took a train through Germany and then a ship to Finland."

"I see," Gresham said calmly. "Tell James that I ran into you and that *I* told you that, would you?"

"If you want, okay," she said.

"I may run into you again sometime, is that alright?"

"Sure, David," she said, regaining her spirit. "Come by any time. James is able to get plenty of food."

"I will, and thank you," Gresham said as he turned and walked back toward the *Pravda* office.

Gresham understood what Lenin's travel arrangements signified, and so did Wilkins when Wolczak shared the information that evening. Wilkins had been to Germany and had traveled the railways with Roger Casement, and he knew full well that no one could travel through Germany without written authorization. It was obvious that Germany had facilitated Lenin's return to Russia, and that meant Germany supported the Bolsheviks. There was one man whom Gresham and Wilkins knew to be the likely connection between Germany and the Bolsheviks: Dunn.

Gresham redoubled his efforts to find evidence that the Germans were supporting the Bolsheviks and hoped that a paper trail would lead him back somehow to Dunn. But almost immediately, the country was again thrown into chaos. The Bolsheviks released a letter from Foreign Minister Milyukov to Great Britain and France assuring the allies of Russia's commitment to the war effort and the defeat of the Central Powers. The Russian people, who had believed the Tsar's abdication meant the end of the war, rushed to the streets to demonstrate again. Milyukov was forced to resign, and a number of the Kadets in the ministry, the constitutional monarchists who hoped to eventually return the Tsar to his throne, were replaced by Socialists so that the entire Provisional Government would not be abruptly brought down.

Wilkins had not heard from Kerensky in days, but shortly after the Milyukov incident, Kerensky sent a note to Wilkins asking that he come to the Tauride Palace at once. Wilkins was surprised to see that the Duma was now protected by a substantial number of regular army soldiers, and Kerensky's office itself was the most guarded of all. Wilkins was escorted into the office at once by an armed soldier.

"James, a pleasure to see you again," Kerensky said with uncharacteristic exuberance. "Please have a seat. We have much to discuss."

"Thank you," Wilkins replied as he sat on the old, brown leather arm chair. A single incandescent light lit the room from the high ceiling in a way which made the office seem more like a poor hospital room.

"I hope you have been well," Kerensky stated politely.

"Yes, although some intriguing information has come to light, Minister, which I have been pursuing."

"Indeed? We shall have to discuss it, but first, let me explain why –"

"May I inquire, since our last discussion, what has happened to the Tsar and the royal family?"

"They are in custody and closely guarded, but otherwise unharmed. They are not permitted visitors, especially none of the Kadets or Generals from the army. They will not be sent to England."

"Thank you."

"As I was saying, regarding the reason I asked you to come to my office today, there have been a number of developments since we last met. As you likely have heard, the Provisional Government has been entirely reformed and a number of the Ministers have been replaced. As of today, I am the Minister for War."

"Congratulations, Minister," Wilkins said with genuine pleasure. He also immediately recognized the possibilities implicit in having a relationship with the Minister for War, especially as his principal objective was to keep Russia fighting.

"I will be leaving to see General Brusilov at the front, in Mogdilev, tomorrow morning. The Russian armies are in a dreadful state, and there is increasing pressure to withdraw from the war. Of course, I appreciate that is not what Great Britain would wish to hear. Since you are an experienced British officer and the tactician behind the remarkable attack at Foncquevillers –"

"You heard about that, did you?" Wilkins asked in embarrassment.

"Certainly I did, James. Listen - I want you to come with me tomorrow to the front. I want you to see what is really happening there. I will listen to your honest advice. I understand from Prime Minister Venizelos that you are quite good at giving advice. You would, of course, be traveling with me in an unofficial capacity."

Well, well, Wilkins thought, Kerensky has finally completed his own investigation. "Don't worry; I left my uniform in Bucharest, Minister," he said.

Kerensky and Wilkins spent the long train ride to the Eastern Front preparing for the new War Minister's meeting with the Commander-in-Chief, General Alexsei Brusilov. It was a meeting that would be crucial to the future of Russia, and although Kerensky acknowledged the political pressure to end the war, Wilkins argued that such a goal could nonetheless be compatible with the goals of Russia's allies. After all, he said, Russia must have an army and must defend itself and the revolution. Germany had not surrendered, so Russia could not simply stop fighting. The soldiers must stay on the front lines and wage a different war, a defensive war. As for General Brusilov, he was at heart a soldier, he said, and a soldier knows his duty.

As the train arrived at Mogdilev the following evening, however, Wilkins was astonished by the terrible conditions at the front. Thousands of soldiers were sitting or lying about with no organization at all, most of them half-starved and in rags, many inebriated while the sick and wounded were left untended. The barracks and offices were filthy, spattered with mud and ice. There were no officers to be found anywhere. It was the most undisciplined mess that Wilkins had ever encountered. Kerensky was noticeably irritated, but the troops still cheered when they saw him pass by. *Kerensky!* They shouted. *Kerensky! At last, the war will end! At last, a man who will listen to the soldiers!*

Kerensky and Wilkins arrived at the elegant country house where Brusilov maintained his headquarters, and they were greeted by General Lavr Korniloff, a former senior officer of the Petrograd garrison who now commanded the Russian armies on the Northern Front. Korniloff was short and thin; he maintained a thin mustache which he believed was quite gallant, but his manner was imperious. He cared little for idle conversation and promptly led Kerensky and Wilkins to the library where Busilov was waiting to meet them.

"Minister Kerensky, greetings," said Brusilov tactfully as he shook Kerensky's hand. "I am relieved that you have come. There is a great deal to discuss." He looked at young Wilkins skeptically, but as there was no introduction forthcoming, Brusilov assumed he was merely an aide. "Allow me to offer you my congratulations, Minister. I trust that our concerns will now be addressed. As you have seen for yourself, the condition of our armies is a matter that must be addressed immediately."

"Yes, General, and I have prepared an agenda of the matters we will discuss, and these include discipline and supplies for the armies, but more importantly I wish to set forth the Provisional Government's diplomatic and political objectives which, with all due respect, it will be your duty as the Commander-in-Chief of Russia's armies, to implement."

"The Provisional Government is a *charade*, Minister," Korniloff interjected defiantly. "The Provisional Government has no more authority to dictate policy to the Commander-in-Chief than the 'Soldiers Deputies' have to issue orders to the troops. We are in the middle of a war, for God's sake. In Petrograd you are seeking to prevent anarchy, but here at the front lines were are defending our very lives."

"The purported 'General Orders' of the 'Council of Soldiers Deputies', for example," Brusilov began with barely restrained fury, "they have done enormous harm. The soldiers are now, in the main, unwilling to fight at all, they are deserting the lines, and a great many of my officers have been murdered by their men. One Colonel was executed for merely insisting that his men salute him. I demand to know: By what authority does this 'Council' purport to issue orders that countermand those of the Commander-in-Chief himself?"

"As of today, by *my* authority, General," Kerensky shot back angrily. "Those in the Duma were selected to represent the people of Russia, and I have been selected by the Duma. As for the 'General Orders,' I have today signed a 'Declaration of the Rights of Soldiers' that adopts a great many of the reforms proposed by the Council of Soldiers Deputies, and those rights shall be respected, General. The Ministry will appoint Commissaries to come to the front lines to ensure that those rights are respected. As for discipline, the Commissaries will also be responsible for ensuring that the order and duties of the troops are respected and your orders are obeyed."

"That is outrageous!" Brusilov raged. "The chain of command –"

"That chain begins with the Minister of War, General."

"I shall be forced to resign –" Brusilov shouted.

"Then I shall compel you to fight in the trenches as an ordinary soldier!" Kerensky shouted back. "You are the commander of our armies, General Brusilov, but it will be the responsibility of the Ministry to ensure that the soldiers do their duty."

"The soldiers will not fight if you do not reinstate the death penalty," Korniloff stated bluntly. "They will not fight!"

"They *will*, General Korniloff," Kerensky argued. "They will fight because it is the only way to preserve the revolution. Where our armies once fought to defeat Imperial Germany, now they will fight to preserve the freedoms that our enemies are desperate to destroy. Our enemies are terrified that the revolution will spread outside the borders of Russia. They will do everything in their power to destroy us before the revolutionary spirit of our workers and soldiers spreads into their own countries! Your duty, General Brusilov, is to defend Russia from those who would destroy the revolution."

"Shall I instruct our soldiers to build walls, Minister? Are we to sit and simply wait for the enemy to storm the lines?" Brusilov asked dismissively.

"On the contrary," Kerensky continued calmly, "it is my expectation that you will prepare and press an offensive upon our enemies this very summer to demonstrate that Russia is able to defend itself with deadly force."

"We have already committed to our allies to launch such an offensive this summer, Minister," Brusilov observed cautiously.

"Let me be perfectly clear: The fact that our offensive fulfills the expectations of France and Great Britain is irrelevant. Russia's summer offensive shall be conducted for our own aims. It shall be a demonstration, perhaps only a small one, of our determination and the strength of the revolution."

Brusilov silently contemplated Kerensky's words, but General Korniloff scoffed: "The soldiers still will not fight, Minister, and they *cannot* fight without munitions, food, clothes, reinforcements, and operating railways and factories."

"As I have said, General Korniloff, it shall be my duty and that of the Ministry to ensure discipline and instill the proper revolutionary fervor in our soldiers, and it shall be the duty of the Provisional Government to ensure that our armies are adequately supplied."

Wilkins observed the two Generals placidly. Their objections had been predictable, but he was pleased to see that Brusilov understood the main: The war would be continued almost as though the revolution had not occurred at all. Korniloff, however, was understandably skeptical that Kerensky could deliver either soldiers or supplies. Indeed, Wilkins was also uncertain of the fact. If Kerensky could not, then it would make no difference at all *why* Russia was fighting Germany. Russia was being defeated by Germany before the revolution, and if they continued to be defeated after the revolution, then surely no amount of political or social reforms could salvage the perilous situation on the Eastern Front.

As soon as the meeting was concluded, Brusilov escorted Kerensky and Wilkins to the railway station. Kerensky seemed confident that he had communicated his position to General Brusilov, but as they returned to the train, Kerensky suddenly strode down the platform to a great crowd of soldiers and called them together. He spoke to the soldiers for over an hour. He exhorted the troops to be faithful to the revolution and to preserve the freedoms they had struggled so long to achieve. He assured them that the Provisional Government, and he personally as the Minister of War, represented and respected the will of the people, and he demanded that the soldiers in turn prepare to defend the revolution against its enemies both foreign and domestic. The soldiers cheered Kerensky again and again and they vowed to fight for the new Russia. However, Wilkins noted, there were many who listened for a time but then wandered away unmoved and exhausted.

Kerensky's proposed offensive began in July with a broad and daring attack on German positions deemed by Brusilov to be the least adequately defended, and, indeed, the Russian armies made substantial headway on some fronts. But in Petrograd, there had been growing dissent and anger that the war was to be continued. The revolutionary message had taken hold, and the Bolsheviks argued that the ministers of the Provisional Government were merely puppets of the capitalists in France, England, and America. Thousands of copies of *Pravda* were printed each day containing details of the "tragic and unnecessary" deaths on the front lines and calling for the Provisional Government to be disbanded and replaced by a council of representatives from the workers, soldiers, and farming collectives.

Even as Kerensky's limited offensive was coming to a swift conclusion on the Eastern Front, a regiment of more than one thousand war-weary soldiers on reserve in the northern districts of Petrograd (a regiment specifically targeted by Bolshevik agitators) reached the boiling point and stormed into Petrograd. They crossed the Neva River, seized automobiles parked on Nevsky Prospekt, and equipped the motorcars with machine guns. They drove through the streets of the city shooting bystanders and bombing government offices. The Bolsheviks immediately called for a renewed revolution, and workers and soldiers flooded into Petrograd to join the rebellion. Kerensky directed the Cossacks, infamous for the ruthlessness and cruelty, to defend the Provisional Government, but the heavily-armed rebels effortlessly shot down hundreds of the Cossacks. Within two days, the streets of Petrograd were covered in fresh blood and effectively under the control of the Bolsheviks. The Provisional Government was uncertain how to respond. Most members of the Duma went into hiding as Kerensky wired Brusilov to suspend the offensive on the Eastern Front and send troops loyal to the government to restore order.

Gresham, and indeed everyone at the offices of *Pravda*, were stunned by the sudden and unexpected success of the Bolsheviks. Lenin spoke at length to enormous crowds assembled in front of Kshesinskaya's mansion. He hailed the revolution and again demanded an end to the war.

Gresham was sitting in the mansion's crowded glass solarium listening to the crowd cheer Lenin when Wolczak suddenly entered the warm, sunny room with Matilda Kshesinskaya. Wolczak was as usual in a plain dress and had undoubtedly just come from the hospital. The ballerina, however, was dressed entirely in silk and looked out of place among the serious Socialist intellectuals in her home.

"Mister Larkin," Wolczak called to Gresham as she pulled away from Kshesinskaya. "Comrade, welcome, I am very pleased to see you looking well," she said with a wink.

Gresham understood her conceit at once. "Yes, thank you, ma'am, I am feeling much better. It is very difficult to find fresh food, nowadays."

"But you have recovered from your illness," she replied as she held out her hand to Gresham. "May I ask you a few questions? It would be a great benefit to my education to hear more about your care at the hospital."

"Certainly, it would be my pleasure," Gresham replied.

Wolczak leaned in and whispered in Gresham's ear: "Kerensky has summoned 20,000 troops from the front; they will arrive any minute. James wanted me to tell you that the arrest of the Bolshevik leaders and everyone at Pravda is imminent; the paper is to be shut down." Then she continued aloud: "Yes, I must speak to the head nurse about that. It is certainly unfortunate that you had to wait so long unattended."

Gresham was furious. He had difficulty containing his disgust. He had spent months working his way closer to the Bolshevik leadership, to the people who were certain to know of the Bolsheviks' connection with Imperial Germany and, in particular, Dunn.

"You can tell the damned 'head nurse' for me that I have no intention of changing my plans. If I must go to the "hospital' with the others, then I will," he said to Wolczak as calmly as possible.

Wolczak looked distraught. "I really don't think …" she said before cutting herself off. "I'll pass that on," she said.

"Emma, my dear, are you alright?" Kshesinskaya asked as she suddenly appeared beside Wolczak.

"Yes, of course, Matilda. This is Mister Larkin, one of my patients at the hospital," Wolczak said.

"Mister Larkin, a pleasure to meet you," Kshesinskaya said as she placed her hand on Wolczak's shoulder, rather than offering it to Gresham.

"I work at *Pravda*," Gresham said.

"You speak English?" She asked in surprise.

"I'm from Ireland," he replied. "I work on the English translations of *Pravda* that we send abroad."

"Wonderful, it's a pleasure to meet you, Comrade Larkin. Emma, dear, I want to introduce you to some other people. Can you break free a moment? Please excuse us, comrade."

"Of course," Gresham said. "Thank you again, Doctor," he said to Emma. She gave him a small concerned smile in return and then was led away.

Gresham returned that afternoon to the *Pravda* office. The bare loft with its old wooden desks and tables and printing presses were bustling with activity and stank of the oily ink that had soaked into the floorboards. Gresham didn't wish to be arrested in Russia, but he could imagine no better way to get close to the Bolshevik leaders than to spend time in a prison cell with them. Perhaps he could then learn when and where they met Dunn.

Before midnight, messengers rushed into the office with dire news: Troops were arriving at Moscow station, thousands of them. There was already shooting on the Nevsky Prospekt, and many of the mutinous soldiers who had started the July revolt had already laid down their arms and fled the city.

Gresham was bent over his desk when Stalin rushed in. He and Kamenev had initially tried to co-opt the Socialists in the Provisional Government and had argued that the Bolsheviks should reunite with their more conservative Socialist brothers. It was Lenin who had rejected that argument and insisted that the Bolsheviks denounce the Socialist "collaborators" like Kerensky who, he claimed, only wanted half a revolution. Gresham shook his head. Despite the previous days' gains, the Bolsheviks were in a poor position. There was no hope in fighting the ones with the guns, and at the moment Kerensky had the guns.

"*товарищ!*" Stalin called out. "*Это мой несчастный обязанность рассказать вам, что временное правительство предал нас. Солдаты идут сейчас, чтобы поставить нас под арестом.*" There were shrieks of dismay from the staff.

The chief *Pravda* translator, an old Jewish man from America with great wrinkles and palsy, leaned over to Gresham and whispered: "The revolution is finished. We're all to be arrested." Gresham tried to appear properly surprised.

Stalin continued speaking intently for some time, even as some of the workers collected their coats and quickly fled the office. There was a growing air of panic. "Larkin!" Stalin suddenly shouted. "Where is Larkin?"

"Here," the old man shouted. "He wants you. Stand up," he told Gresham. Gresham stood and walked over to Stalin. "Yes, comrade?" He asked.

"David, you know Comrade Kayurov?" Stalin asked in broken English as he looked into Gresham's eyes as intently as Gresham had ever seen.

"Yes, of course," Gresham said.

"You go to Kayurov's, now," Stalin instructed him urgently.

"Yes, comrade," Gresham said. He grabbed his overcoat and immediately left the office. Benyamin Kayurov was a member of the Petrograd Worker's Council and an important member of the Bolshevik leadership. Gresham had been to his flat to collect papers on several occasions, and he assumed that he was to do the same again. He rushed through the streets as the sound of gunfire echoed through the city, but there was far less gunfire than Gresham expected to hear. The Bolshevik revolution, it seemed, had faded away in mere minutes at the sight of real soldiers. Kerensky had won back the capital.

It took Gresham only a minute to arrive at Kayurov's across the street from the Finland Station. The street was quiet and Gresham rushed up the stairs where he found one man with a rifle standing nervously beside Kayurov's door. At the sight of Gresham, he raised the rifle menacingly.

"I'm Larkin. Stalin sent me."

Although the man spoke no English, he heard the name Stalin and rapped on the door, shouting to the men inside. The door opened and Gresham was directed in. The flat was dark, but he could hear men arguing in the kitchen. As he entered, however, the conversation stopped suddenly and a dozen grim faces looked in his direction. "Don't stop on my account. I don't speak Russian," Gresham said.

"Wait in the bedroom," one angry man from the Worker's Council told him curtly.

Gresham waited alone for over an hour before the same man came to find him. "Your name is Larkin, is that right?"

"Yes."

"Big Jim is your uncle?"

"Cousin, on my mother's side."

The man nodded. He had heard it all before. "You will be going to Finland tonight, to Helsinki."

"As you wish, Comrade, but may I be told why I am going to Helsinki."

"That is not for me to say at this time. We are in very difficult circumstances. If the others believe that you can assist us, then you will be told."

"Yes, Comrade."

Once night had fallen, Gresham was summoned to join the other men as they crossed the street to Finland Station and hurried up the tracks to a freight train that was prepared to depart. They were bundled into an empty freight carriage and the door was quickly pulled shut. The carriage was pitch black and the men were silent. Almost immediately the car jerked into motion and the train proceeded north toward the Russian territory of Finland.

Two days later, Gresham was in a hotel on the Pohjoisesplanandi in Helsinki overlooking a quiet, sunny park. He had seen no one and spoken to no one, but he had learned one crucial fact: When they had finally arrived at the station in Helsinki and left the dark train car, he discovered that one of the men in the car was Vladimir Ulyanov. Lenin had apparently decided to leave Petrograd rather than risk being arrested. However, Finland and its capital Helsinki were still part of the Russian Empire, and so Gresham assumed that Lenin and the other Bolsheviks who had fled Petrograd were eager to maintain as low a profile as possible. They stayed in their rooms quietly, and Gresham was the only one who had gone outdoors (to buy cigarettes), and then only at night.

That evening the English-speaking man came to fetch Gresham. He was brought to a suite on the top floor, although a "suite" in the cheap hotel was hardly more than a bedroom and private bath. Gresham could tell at once by looking at the faces of the other men that the news was bad. The *Pravda* staff in Petrograd had all been arrested and the printing press destroyed. The Bolshevik leaders that had remained in Petrograd had at first retreated into the Peter and Paul Fortress, but they had been surrounded and eventually surrendered to the troops summoned to the city by Kerensky. Here in the cheap Helsinki hotel room with Gresham remained the last free leaders of the Bolshevik movement.

Lenin sat silently by the window. There was a tremendous argument underway among the other men, but as the argument was entirely spoken in Russian, Gresham decided to wait silently and lit a cigarette. He again considered pulling out his handgun and killing the lot of them. It might mean the end of the Bolsheviks, especially if he were able to kill Lenin. But that would interfere with his mission to find Dunn and furthermore, considering the situation, the Bolsheviks hardly seemed to matter anymore. They had already been defeated.

At last the argument concluded, and the grizzled, English-speaking man stood and approached Gresham. "There is something we need you to do," he said. "We must send someone to Stockholm, but if any of us were to leave Russia now, we would not be re-admitted at the border. We have decided to send you because you are Irish and will have no difficulty re-entering Russia."

Gresham stood. "I am prepared to do whatever the revolution requires of me, Comrade. Even if I am arrested at the border, at least the revolution will go on."

"Well spoken, Comrade," the man said with some satisfaction. "You will be given directions to a bank in Stockholm and a letter authorizing you to withdraw funds from our account there. You are to bring the funds to our bank here in Russia. We must have money to rebuild *Pravda* and free our comrades in prison, or else the revolution will end here and now. You understand the gravity of what we are asking and the trust we have placed in you, Larkin."

"It is an honor to be given such an important task for the revolution, Comrade. I will not disappoint you," Gresham said with appropriate fervor.

Gresham boarded a ship that afternoon and sailed directly to Stockholm. He arrived in Sweden the next morning and walked to the Nya Banken on Skomarkagatan, near the Royal Palace. He had shaved while aboard ship and trimmed his hair and he wore a fine black wool suit so that he would raise no alarm at the bank.

It was still early, so the bank was as silent as a library when Gresham entered the cavernous room. Light filtering in through the great windows showed the air was thick with dust. Clerks were busy scribbling, and far away in some remote office was the clacking of a typewriter. Gresham strode purposefully to the large mahogany front desk, his shoe heels clicking loudly on the grey marble floor. He stopped at the desk and looked down at the elderly banker in his antiquated suit and tie.

"Have you anyone here who can speak English?" Gresham asked politely.

"Yes, sir," the banker replied, looking up at Gresham skeptically. "How may I be of assistance?"

"I wish to arrange a transfer, from this account," he said as he passed over a paper which authorized him to withdraw funds from the bank.

The banker looked at the paper, examined the signature, and drew his conclusion: "Of course, sir. Please be seated. I'll just be a moment." The banker directed Gresham to a padded leather seat and stepped away with the account information. Gresham looked around the bank, seemingly unconcerned, and lit a cigarette while he waited. A moment later the elderly banker returned. "I'm very sorry, sir. There are of course funds in the account, but the courier has not yet arrived with your monthly deposit for this account."

Gresham's heart was suddenly racing. A courier! With funds!

He sighed dramatically in annoyance. "How unfortunate," he said. "I cannot stay in Stockholm more than a day or two. Do you have any idea when he is expected?"

"Well, I can't say sir, although he was expected yesterday evening. Would you be able to return tomorrow morning? Perhaps he will arrive tonight?"

"I have no choice, do I?" Gresham snapped back.

He stood and walked calmly from the bank. Outside, he found a café a few steps from the bank and waited and watched. The day passed slowly.

Gresham was eating dinner when he saw the courier. He recognized him at once – Count Zakrevsky, Dunn, whatever his real name, it made no matter. Gresham recognized the trim young man, his grey-blue eyes, his short dark brown hair, neat beard and sharp features, the man who had shot Gresham twice in Italy and instigated rebellions in Ireland and India. Gresham seethed with hatred for the man, Zimmerman's lackey, but he waited patiently. The sun had fully set when Dunn at last emerged from the bank, and Gresham followed him. He followed Dunn down the alleys and away from the gas lights that lit the streets around the Palace. Gresham cared not where Dunn went as long as it was night and dark. A few more streets – that was far enough.

Gresham stepped closer:

"*Haben Sie die Zeit?*" He asked.

"*Natürlich,*" Dunn replied as he paused to check his watch. Before his hand had raised the watch to his eyes, Gresham's field knife was buried deeply in his gut. Blood poured out over Dunn's shirt and Gresham's hand.

"If you try to kill someone," Gresham said icily, "you should always be certain to finish the job."

Blood was drooling from Dunn's mouth as he tried to reply, but the life was already draining from his eyes. Gresham pushed him back, and Dunn fell onto the cobblestones, the knife still buried deeply inside him. Gresham waited until he was certain Dunn was dead.

At the bank the next morning, the elderly banker had good news for Gresham: The courier had arrived with the substantial funds for the Bolshevik account. "Shall I prepare a bank draft made payable to your usual account in Petrograd, sir?" He asked.

"No," Gresham replied, "our account in Russia has been compromised. I will give you the number of another account, one in Switzerland. All the funds are to be sent on to the account there."

Petrograd, again

Kerensky had won. His extraordinary success in putting down the Bolshevik's coup and arresting its leaders was matched only by Brusilov's "extraordinary failure" on the Eastern Front. Not only had the summer offensive been bungled by Brusilov (or so Kerensky claimed in order to deflect criticism for the large number of casualties), but now the Germans had advanced deep into Russia and captured the city of Tarnopol. The panic caused by the German army's swift drive into Russian territory and the thwarted Bolshevik uprising in Petrograd had forced the Duma to coalesce behind a new leader: Kerensky was named the new President of the Duma and leader of the Provisional Government. His first act was to remove Brusilov as Commander-in-Chief; he had blamed Brusilov for the failures of the summer offensive. The new Commander-in-Chief would be General Korniloff. Kerensky also purged the few remaining Kadets from the Provisional Government. For the first time, the Russian people were hopeful that the country would move forward.

Wilkins understood that Kerensky was a Socialist, and he had shown himself to be far more liberal than Wilkins initially expected. However, Kerensky was also a pragmatist, and Wilkins suspected that he was simply attempting to placate the masses until a constitution could be drawn up and put to public referendum, thereby settling the issue of Russia's future governance. Wilkins was the only one who knew of Kerensky's plan to ultimately declare the country a republic and to hold the first free elections with universal suffrage in Russian history, but then it was Wilkins who met secretly with Kerensky day after day at an office not far from the Duma to begin drafting Russia's new constitution. Not British Ambassador Buchanan, nor even Emma Wolczak, knew that Wilkins had become Kerensky's most stalwart foreign ally or that Wilkins had promised Great Britain's full diplomatic and financial support for the proposed Russian republic.

It was, therefore, an unwelcome surprise to Wilkins when he received a note from Oliver Locke inviting him to tea at Vladimir Nikolayevich Lvov's house on Voznesenskiy Prospekt. He had assumed that Locke had forgotten about him, as Wilkins had not seen the Foreign Office agent for several months – indeed, not since the *Astoria Hotel* had been sacked. Locke, however, evidently knew that Wilkins was still in Petrograd and knew precisely where to find him.

Lvov's pale pink townhouse was in poor condition, but it still suggested a level of wealth that Wilkins found surprising. Gresham had said that Lvov was a constitutional monarchist and a Kadet, but as soon as the Tsar had abdicated, Lvov moved in the opposite direction by throwing his full support behind the Socialists. He had been made Ober-Procurator of the Holy Synod of the Russian

Orthodox Church and had been charged with purging the church's governing council of anyone who had supported the Tsar. Lvov had effectively gutted the Holy Synod and ensured that the Russian church stood behind the Provisional Government and its liberal reforms.

Wilkins was brought to Lvov's plainly decorated front room where he found Locke and Lvov waiting for him.

"James, what a pleasure to see you again," said Locke with mild geniality. "You remember Vladimir Nikolayevich, I expect?"

"Of course," Wilkins replied. "Thank you for the invitation."

"Yes, my pleasure," Lvov said, although he did not sound terribly pleased at all. "Be seated."

"I have not had an opportunity to thank you as I should have," Locke began. "It was very fortunate that you awoke me that evening at the *Astoria*, or else I might have died there. I owe you a great debt for your consideration, James."

"It was nothing, Oliver."

"Please, allow me to pour the tea," Locke continued. "It is in repayment of your kindness on that instance that I felt it important for us, Vladimir Nikolayevich and myself, to speak to you. Of course you are aware of the rumors about you?"

"To which rumors do you refer?" James asked innocently.

"He means your relationship with Kerensky," Lvov answered sharply.

"It is true that I have met Kerensky on a few occasions because of his kindness to my *fiancé*, Miss Wolczak, and I once joined a tour of the front lines at Mogdilev at which Kerensky was present, but I have no other 'relationship' with Aleksandr Kerensky," Wilkins replied.

Lvov and Locke looked at one another briefly.

"So you deny any further conspiracy with Kerensky or the Provisional Government?" Locke asked skeptically.

"Conspiracy?" Wilkins asked in feigned surprise. "No, of course not! Frankly, I am at a total loss as to why I am here in Petrograd at all. My father, Lord Bartlett, asked me to come and find out what was going on in Petrograd, but I have only stayed to appease Miss Wolczak. To think that I could be involved in any way with the Provisional Government is absurd."

"It is said that you meet with Kerensky regularly," Locke pressed him.

"As I have said, I meet Kerensky from time to time on non-political matters," Wilkins replied. "Perhaps he believes that I could be of use to him, that I might write to my father and tell him that Kerensky is a great leader or something, but I have not been asked to do so nor would I consider it my place to make such a recommendation."

"I see," Locke said, somewhat mollified. "We wish to impress upon you, James, just how dangerous Kerensky truly is. He has risen quickly and stands now at the pinnacle of the Russian government. We fear that he aspires to become a dictator and take the rule of Russia solely into his hands."

"I haven't any inkling of that," Wilkins replied. "In fact, if I can recall correctly, he said something about holding elections this autumn. Surely that does not sound like the actions of a dictator. Perhaps he intends to make Russia a democracy, a republic. Great Britain would support such a development, would it not?"

"What are you thinking, James?" Locke asked crossly. "Good God! Of course Great Britain would not support it! For Russia to remain our ally and remain in the war, it must be led with great strength by men who wish to destroy Germany and by those who, to be blunt, most stand to profit from the war."

"Yes, I see," Wilkins said. "Still, Kerensky this past month ordered an offensive against Germany, did he not?"

"But then he sacked Brusilov!" Locke said. "Listen, Wilkins, it's clear you have no idea how dangerous Kerensky has become. He is playing a game! He wants us to believe his intentions are reasonable, to beguile us. I have spoken to Ambassador Buchanan, and I tell you that Great Britain has one and only one policy regarding Russia, and that is in favor of the full restoration of the monarchy and of Tsar Nicholas."

Wilkins was astounded and could barely repress his laughter. If Great Britain (meaning who, exactly? King George, Ambassador Buchanan, or Oliver Locke himself?) believed that the Tsar could be restored in Russia, then it (or they) were foolishly mistaken.

"I am not as optimistic as your countryman that the Tsar can be restored," Lvov argued. "Nevertheless, it is quite clear that to maintain order and discipline, which in turn would ensure that Russia fulfills its commitments to its allies, Russia must be governed by a strong leader. The Russian people are not ready for democracy. Kerensky will not give Great Britain and France what they want. He is a very unstable man, and his loyalty to Russia is suspect."

"I'm confused, sir," Wilkins replied. "In what regard is Kerensky's loyalty at issue?"

Lvov stared at Wilkins stupefied: "Why, because he is a Jew, of course!" Lvov stated emphatically. "The Jews have been a plague in Russia that we have long sought to eradicate. Given the chance, he will destroy Russia; he will seek revenge for his people. How such a man could have ascended to a position of power in Russia is simply inconceivable."

Wilkins was at a loss for words. He was certainly aware of the animosity toward the Jewish people of Europe, but he had never heard such animosity so openly expressed. For that matter, only Kerensky's father was Jewish and he, himself, had never expressed any religious views. However, Wilkins shook his head slowly as if he had suddenly been shown the light. "I had no idea," he said at last. "I can see the peril. It is unfortunate that I have remained unenlightened for so long, but I can assure you, regardless, that I have been and will remain utterly uninvolved in matters relating to Russia's government."

"I am relieved to know that we understand one another at last, James," Locke said. The threatening undertone in his statement was all too clear.

Wilkins returned to his flat to discover another surprise. "James!" Wolczak shouted. "Come see who has returned!"

"Good Lord! David, you're back!" Wilkins said with pleasure when he found Gresham at the woodstove.

"Yes, I am," Gresham said with a grin.

"What have you brought?" Wilkins asked when he saw the small room was crowded with parcels.

"There's fresh beef and lamb, caviar, French wines, pastries, everything!" Wolczak said with glee as she gave Wilkins a kiss.

"How come you're kissing him?" Gresham chided her.

"Where did you get it all?" Wilkins asked.

"I was in Sweden and ran into a bit of good luck. I thought I'd bring you and Emma a few treats."

"Are we celebrating?"

"Oh yes, indeed," Gresham said. "For one thing, the gentleman we discussed is no longer a problem."

"Are you certain?"

"Pretty bloody certain," Gresham said with a laugh and a wink. "I can also tell you that Lenin is stuck in a hotel in Helsinki, but I don't think he can cause any more trouble after this," he said pointing to a stack of documents. "They're records from a bank in Sweden that prove the Bolsheviks have been funded by Germany. They should make quite a splash with any remaining Bolshevik sympathizers in Russia. As for the Bolsheviks themselves, I'm afraid they are out of funds altogether."

"Why?" Wolczak asked.

"I stole their money, my dear. All of it, and it was quite a lot of money."

Wilkins laughed. "That explains your miraculous generosity," he said. "Will you be staying in Petrograd? You cannot go back to *Pravda* or stay with Stalin."

"No, but I will stay here for now in case you need me for something. I haven't any orders, James, and I'm honestly not sure what I mean to do next. I feel such a sense of relief to be done with Dunn."

"Will you continue here with the name 'Larkin'?"

"No, I've gone back to using 'Kelly,' as I did in Vienna, and I mean to take a flat over by the Finland Station, in case I must leave quickly. But tell me, James, how are you getting along with Kerensky?"

"Very well, I think. I have made a great many promises, but none that are undeserved. We can discuss that later. But I *am* concerned about the German advances – they are pushing the Russian army back and General Korniloff seems incapable of mounting a strong defense."

"Is Kerensky still pandering to the Soldiers Deputies?"

"He has no choice. Without the backing of the army, there is no one to keep the Provisional Government in power."

"Napoleon could not conquer Russia, James, and neither will Hindenburg. Now, please have a seat and pour the wine because our chops are done," Gresham said as he lifted the smoking frying pan from the stove top.

The next day, Wilkins sent a note to Kerensky stating that their meetings would require greater discretion. They did meet that very evening at the little office where they and a handful of carefully chosen men had been discussing the proposed constitution. Kerensky had personally drafted a declaration of civil rights which went far beyond what Wilkins had proposed, but Kerensky seemed disinterested in arguing his position. Wilkins pulled him aside.

"What is the matter, Aleksandr? We are nearly done," Wilkins said.

"Korniloff was here today. He has made a number of demands that he says are absolutely necessary to prevent the Germans from marching all the way to Petrograd. He cannot abide the Declaration of Soldiers' Rights. He demands reinstatement of the death penalty for deserters, all the old demands, although he has been told many times that they are impossible. Yet I fear he is correct, and that Russia is at risk."

"Do the soldiers not understand the risk as well?"

"I'm certain they do, but the Soldier's Deputies are prepared to give up Poland, the Baltic States and Ukraine to Germany if it will mean an end to the war."

"That is a very heavy price to pay for peace."

"I shall be going to Moscow next week for the All-Russia Conference. I believe it will be the moment for me to announce our intent with respect to the republic and present the draft constitution. I would like to have you there. Will you speak for Great Britain?"

"I have no credentials to speak."

"You don't need credentials, James, only an introduction. Even if you speak as a private person about democracy and the rule of law, people will see that there are options better than surrender and anarchy. You are young, and the soldiers will listen to you."

"I will come and speak if you wish it, Aleksandr."

Wilkins and Gresham arrived in Moscow the following week along with thousands of others who had come for the national conference. There were representatives from the church, from factories and farms, from the army and navy, from the Cossacks, and many more from trade unions, councils of workers' and soldier's deputies, and municipalities across Russia. The conference was convened by the Provisional Government in order to consolidate all of Russia against further revolution and garner support for the establishment of a new national government, but as Wilkins and Gresham entered the enormous municipal hall, it was clear the meeting had already fallen into disarray. The hot and brightly lit room was so full that some factions were giving speeches in side rooms and in public houses nearby. At best, Wilkins thought, the conference would be the proper venue to spread the word that a national referendum was coming.

Suddenly a huge cheer arose from the crowd. Wilkins strained to see who had arrived. It was General Korniloff, Commander-in-Chief of the Russian Armies, a life-long military man who had come from the front lines at Mogdilev to speak. Korniloff was hugely popular with everyone except the soldiers who were aware of their commander's preference for corporal punishment and the death penalty. He was accompanied by Rodzianko, the former President of the Duma, and Guchkoff, the former Minister of War, both of whom had been Kadets before the Tsar had abdicated. At last the shouting died down and Korniloff spoke.

He began by praising the soldiers, the ones who fought each day to protect Russia from the enemies that were seeking to destroy her – the Germans and Austrians, and also the British, French and Americans. He called for unity in order to preserve Russia, and then spoke at length about the need to maintain a strong military. He described the failures of the Provisional Government's Commissaries to maintain order in the military, and then suggested he had seen the same lack of discipline throughout the cities of Russia. He spoke of the need to centralize Russia's civil and military authority in one body and warned that, even as he spoke, Germany was marching toward Petrograd to destroy Russia once and for all. Time was of the essence, he said, for the fall of Russia was imminent.

It was a disturbing speech and, when Korniloff left the room, the representatives were worried and quiet. By the time Kerensky came to speak, the conference was already held hostage by fear. Kerensky was forced to change his speech and spent an hour assuring the representatives that Petrograd was well-defended and that the army would not permit Germany to conquer Russia.

The next day, the news arrived that the city of Riga, only 300 miles from Petrograd along the Baltic Sea coast, had been captured by the German army.

A week had passed since the Moscow conference, and Kerensky was still attempting to subdue the panic caused by General Korniloff's unfortunate speech. To make matters worse, the German army had left Riga behind and was slowly marching almost unopposed toward Petrograd. Stores had closed and many of the wealthier residents had left for extended visits to Moscow. Wilkins learned that Kerensky had even made plans to evacuate the Provisional Government to Moscow.

Wilkins received an unexpected invitation from Oliver Locke to join him for dinner at *Donon's* and, not wanting to raise alarm, decided he must accept. He dressed and reached the restaurant just on time, and then was led through the dark restaurant to Locke's private room.

"Good evening, James," Locke said coldly. "I'm so pleased you found the time to join me. Be seated."

"Thank you for the invitation, Oliver. It is very kind of you," Wilkins said as he sat on the fine upholstered chair. He was always impressed by *Donon's* which, despite the revolution, still catered to the richest and most influential men of Petrograd.

"Whether it was kind or not, you shall have to decide later. We have a great deal to discuss," Locke said.

"Do we indeed?" Wilkins asked innocently.

"It is very unfortunate that you elected to pursue Kerensky's favor, James," Locke explained. "I thought at our last meeting my message was clear enough, but perhaps not. I was told that you are very intelligent, but I am forced to wonder. Your trip to Moscow, for example, your purpose could not have been more plain to see. And you have continued to meet with Kerensky despite my warnings. Your involvement with Kerensky must now come to an end."

Wilkins felt a cold chill as heard Locke speak. Perhaps he had not been very clever, Wilkins thought. He felt manipulated and on guard.

"Why is that?" He asked quietly as Locke's gaze rested calmly and icily upon him.

"With the German advances, Kerensky has been forced to request that troops be sent for the defense of Petrograd. General Korniloff has decided, upon my recommendation, to send Krymov's Cavalry Corps; they are due to arrive tomorrow. Do you know it? It is called the 'Savage Division.' Forty thousand well-armed men with artillery, mostly Moslems with no great love for Russians in general, but they are fiercely loyal to General Korniloff – did you know that Korniloff was born and raised in Turkestan?"

"I did not," Wilkins said simply.

"I can assure you that Petrograd will be most secure, but the same cannot be said for Kerensky. I fear his hours now are numbered. He is to be arrested for exceeding his authority, and a new government is to be established in Russia. Korniloff will take command; perhaps the Tsar will be eventually restored, or else Korniloff will become the new Tsar. In either case, this dalliance and pandering to the rabble of Russia will be over. Order will be restored and Russia's soldiers will fight with renewed purpose."

"Have you done this, Oliver?"

"Not me alone, no – Lvov has been instrumental. He has spoken privately with Korniloff on several occasions, and with Rodzianko and many of the Kadets and monarchists who have remained quiet the past few months while the Socialists and Bolsheviks have argued. It is Lvov who secured Korniloff's approval for our strategy. It is Korniloff who will rule Russia. The remaining Bolsheviks will be rounded up and executed in the next few days, and I am sorry to say that includes your pretty *fiancé*, Miss Wolczak."

"Emma?" Wilkins asked, his mouth now dry.

"Yes. I'm sorry, did you not know that Miss Wolczak is a Bolshevik, James? I assumed you would have known. She has spent hours in that dreadful ballerina's mansion meeting with Lenin and Trotsky and the rest. I am *truly* sorry to be the one tell you."

Wilkins stood and left the room at once. He knew he had to find Emma immediately, but first he had to warn Kerensky. Kerensky could perhaps fix everything by rescinding his request for troops, or something, anything! Something had to be done!

Wilkins rushed to the Tauride Palace and ran up the stairs to Kerensky's office. The guards there told Wilkins that Kerensky was in a meeting and could not be disturbed, but Wilkins pleaded that the matter was of the utmost urgency until, at last, one guard agreed to carry a note. It was met with an immediate response, and Wilkins was promptly escorted into the office, only to find that Kerensky was meeting with Vladimir Lvov.

"James," Lvov said graciously, "very pleasant to see you again. I expected that your dinner with Oliver would take longer."

Kerensky looked ashen and distraught. "Do you know?" He asked Wilkins.

"I have only just learned of this plot myself," he replied.

"Plot?" Lvov said. "No, no, I fear that Oliver has overstated the case yet again. It is not so dire as a 'plot,' no. Kerensky has no choice but to declare martial law if the capital is to be defended, and, therefore, complete and unlimited authority must be given to the Commander-in-Chief of the Russian armies. Since the Provisional Government was never intended to be anything more than temporary, it makes perfect sense that the Ministers should now resign, and it will then be General Korniloff's privilege to form a new government."

"And I?" Kerensky asked.

"You must go to Mogdilev and surrender to General Korniloff personally. But first you must sign the orders I have prepared with respect to martial law and the dissolution of the Provisional Government," Lvov stated icily.

"I find it difficult to believe that Korniloff is behind this," Wilkins said. "He is a soldier, not a statesman. Why would he want to assume the mantle of power this way? It makes no sense!"

"I agree," Kerensky said. "Korniloff is an excellent commander, but he is a military man and no more. I will not sign anything until he confirms to me that these are his wishes."

"Then you must go to Mogdilev. But you must sign the papers first," Lvov insisted.

Kerensky seethed. It was inconceivable that Korniloff would thrust himself forward as the new dictator of Russia.

"Where is the teletype?" Wilkins asked.

"Yes, of course!" Kerensky exclaimed. "We shall speak with Korniloff directly." He called for the guards and quickly proceeded with Lvov and Wilkins to the teletype room in the building next door. Kerensky was clearly shaken and worried. Was it truly possible that General Korniloff was attempting to overthrow the government?

Kerensky ordered the teletype room emptied except for one operator, an older woman. Lvov instructed her to send a teletype to Mogdilev requesting General Korniloff to come personally to the teletype there. Minutes passed as Kerensky and Wilkins waiting nervously.

Finally they received a response: *Yes*

Kerensky instructed the operator to reply: *Kerensky on the line. We are waiting for General Korniloff.*

General Korniloff on the line, came the immediate reply.

"Be careful what you say, Aleksandr," Wilkins said. "These lines are not secure."

Kerensky nodded and then dictated: *How do you do, General. V.N. Lvov and Kerensky are on the line. We ask you to confirm that Kerensky is to act in accordance with the information conveyed to him by Vladimir Nikolaevich.*

Kerensky and Wilkins waited impatiently for a response. At last the teletype chattered and the message came through:

> How do you do, Aleksandr Fedorovich. How do you do, Vladimir Nikolaevich. To confirm once again the outline of the situation I believe the country and army are in, an outline of which I sketched out to Vladimir Nikolaevich with the request that he should report it to you, let me declare once more that the events of the last few days and those already in the offing make it imperative to reach a completely definite decision in the shortest possible time.

"He is being cautious," Wilkins said. "He must confirm what Lvov has said."

"I agree," Kerensky said. He turned to the teletype operator. "Please type exactly what I tell you," he instructed her, and then he continued:

> I, Vladimir Nikolaevich, am enquiring about this definite decision which has to be taken, of which you asked me to inform Aleksandr Fedorovich strictly in private. Without such confirmation from you personally, Aleksandr Fedorovich hesitates to believe me completely.

Again, moments passed as they waited anxiously, and then the machine chattered as the next reply came through:

> Yes, I confirm that I asked you to transmit my urgent request to Aleksandr Fedorovich. He must come to Mogdilev.

Wilkins heart sank. It was true. Everything terrible threat Lvov and Locke had made was true. Korniloff was to become the new dictator of Russia. The nation was to become a military dictatorship. Kerensky replied:

I, Aleksandr Fedorovich, take your reply to confirm the words reported to me by Vladimir Nikolaevich.

Kerensky, white faced, turned and quickly left the room alone.

"You have no idea what you have done, Lvov," Wilkins said, "you and Locke both. This will be a disaster."

"You are very young, Mister Wilkins," Lvov said with a scoff. "You should not play games you cannot win."

Wilkins ran back to Kerensky's office. Kerensky was alone in the austere room, his hand on the telephone. He looked up and saw Wilkins standing in front of him and shook his head.

"I am sorry, James," he said with icy determination. Wilkins expected to find Kerensky in distress, but instead found him cold and dispassionate.

"Korniloff will at least protect Russia –" Wilkins began.

"Korniloff will not become the next dictator of Russia!" Kerensky said emphatically. "You have known all along that I am a Socialist, James. Russia cannot abandon the revolution. We will not replace one Tsar with another."

"What can you do?" Wilkins asked.

Kerensky shook his head. "It is very simple. I am releasing the Bolsheviks from prison and will give them weapons. The Red Guard will defend the government from General Korniloff. Korniloff's soldiers will turn against him, and I shall form a new coalition government with the Bolsheviks."

"Aleksandr! You will give up everything we have strived to create the past few months? The constitution we have crafted? All hope for a republic? You know what the Bolsheviks will demand! And will you sacrifice Poland, Latvia, Ukraine – just give them to the Kaiser as the Bolsheviks demand? Is that what you will condone?"

"Yes," Kerensky stated calmly as he stared into Wilkins' eyes angrily. Then he looked away. "I am sorry," he added.

Wilkins sank into a chair and his head fell into his hands.

"I must caution you, James, it will be necessary for me to purge the capital of any further foreign influences. The Bolsheviks will not tolerate it. You must leave Petrograd as soon as possible. Tonight. The Red Guard will be in the streets within the hour and I can no longer ensure your safety."

Wilkins looked up at Kerensky, then stood and left the office without another word.

There were already crowds in the street, tens of thousands of Russians, cheering and singing the *Internationale* as they marched to the prisons where the Bolsheviks were being released. Members of the Bolsheviks' Red Guard, now armed, were already departing to arrest General Korniloff. Wilkins pushed his way through the crowded, rowdy streets to his flat where he hoped to find Wolczak. He rushed up the stairs and burst through the door into the darkened room.

"Wake up!" Wilkins shouted.

"What is it?" Gresham asked from a chair near the window. "What is going on out there?"

"Where is Emma?" Wilkins demanded frantically.

"She's not here, James. I've just come from my flat to find you. What the Hell is going on?"

"It's the Bolsheviks: Kerensky has released them all and armed them. We must leave the city immediately." Wilkins grabbed a case and hastily thrust his and Emma's clothes inside. Gresham rushed from his seat to assist.

"Emma must still be at the hospital," Gresham said. "We will take the train to Finland, and then we can catch the boat there to Stockholm."

Wilkins stopped and turned to Gresham: "Is she a Bolshevik, David?" Wilkins asked desperately.

"Emma? No, I don't think —"

"But she has been to the ballerina's? Have you seen her there?"

"Once or twice, but she is very clever, James. She wouldn't —"

"Come! Now!" Wilkins ordered as he pulled open the door and rushed down the stairs.

The streets were overflowing with people, many with weapons and many with red banners. They had come out to celebrate the Bolsheviks' release and fire their guns into the air. It took Wilkins and Gresham many long minutes to reach the hospital and they rushed inside. Wilkins' boot heels echoed loudly on the white marble floor as he ran down the brightly lit and silent hallway of the Women's Medical Institute of Petrograd. He finally found Emma, alone, dozing in a waiting room. It was inconceivable that she could sleep so soundly as the citizens of Petrograd marched and sang by the thousands on the streets just outside. The city was riotous.

"Emma, Emma, my darling. There has been a disaster, and we must leave at once."

"What? What is all that noise?" she asked sleepily. Her eyes were circled with dark rings and her lovely chestnut brown hair was askew. She yawned and wiped her mouth. "I'm sorry, James, I have a patient in a delicate condition, and I decided to stay the night to see him through. I should have let you know."

"That's all right, my darling. But it is not safe for us to remain in Petrograd any longer. We must leave tonight. I have brought your clothes from the flat. We will go to England —"

"What? James, be reasonable. I can't leave Petrograd now!" She told him passionately.

"But I am telling you, we must go, my darling," Wilkins said frantically as he placed his arms around her and hugged her tightly. "We must go, right away."

"No, James. No. I must stay. My patients, my training – they are here in Russia. I am to become a doctor!"

"But we are to be married, my darling. We can go to England now and be married right away."

Wolczak was silent a moment, but then she gently pushed Wilkins away.

"I'm sorry, James. I can't leave. I will join you when I can. I know people here. I will be perfectly safe. Perhaps I can join you in England later."

Wilkins was shocked and tears began to run down his cheeks, but on Wolczak's face there were no tears, no anguish, and no distress whatsoever at their imminent separation. He wanted to reach out to her, but he knew his touch would no longer be welcome

John J. Pershing

Erich
Ludendorff

Max Hoffman

Erich von
Falkenhayn

Wilhelm Goener

James Harbord

Dennis Nolan

Robert Lee
Bullard

Herbert
Kitchener

Lavr Kornilov

Luigi Cadorna

Ian Hamilton

Bryan Mahon

James Robertson

Flora Sandes

Ronald Tolkien

Prince Sixtus of
Bourbon-Parma

James Webley

Mansfield
Cumming

Samuel Hoare

Compton
Mackenzie

T.E. Lawrence

Roger Casement

Bruce Lockhart

Eleftherios
Venizelos

Ionel Bratianu

Sidney Riley

Benito Mussolini

Despina Storch

Paul Bolo

Agnes von
Kurowsky

Harrison Fisher
Girl

Elsbeth
Schragmüller

Joseph Stalin

Mata Hari

Grigory
Rasputin

Part III:
THE WIERINGEN PROPOSAL

Second Interlude

Count Laszlo Szőgyény-Marich sat rigidly in the back of his dark red *Mercedes* touring sedan and scowled as he furiously drummed his knee with the fingers of his right hand. He would have ordinarily enjoyed the pleasant ride out to Potsdam; it was always a relief to leave behind the noise and confusion of Berlin. The weather that July was particularly fine; the passing farmlands were lush and green and the air smelled sweet. The Count had often visited *Sanssouci* palace, and after his many years as the Ambassador of Austria-Hungary to Imperial Germany, he now considered Kaiser Wilhelm II to be his personal friend. However, on this particular day, this very difficult day, the Count's duties as Ambassador brought him no pleasure at all.

It had only been one week since Archduke Franz Ferdinand had been murdered in Sarajevo – a terrible tragedy, perhaps. The Count privately considered the Archduke to have been among the most belligerent and dangerous men in Austria, a man whose future reign over the largest empire in Europe had been dreaded by many, including some in Austria itself. Franz Ferdinand's particular hostility toward Hungarians was infamous, and Count Laszlo was himself Hungarian. Still, the assassination was a terrible tragedy, no one would deny it.

However, since the assassination the Imperial Foreign Ministry in Vienna had placed Count Laszlo in a dreadful position. At issue was what should be done about the murder of the Archduke and his wife. Of course, the perpetrators had been captured quite quickly, and although they had confessed to having received some support from officers in the Serbian army (only a few pistols and explosives that might otherwise have been obtained anywhere), it was far from clear that the Serbian Premier and his government were complicit in the crime. Those in Vienna did not seem to care, as the calls for war grew louder each day. So, was it strictly necessary to hold the whole of Serbia responsible for the desperate and despicable act of a few violent men? That question had been ignored in Vienna. A handful of men in the Foreign Ministry led those clamouring for war: The "Young Rebels", they had named themselves. They were eager to end decades of confusion in the Balkans by seizing Serbia and placing it under the Austrian crown.

At the more statesman-like age of seventy-three, Count Laszlo was distrustful of rash solutions to intractable problems. The Balkans would never be secured with guns, he believed. Indeed, the recent hostilities of 1912 and 1913 had proven that war would resolve nothing. More importantly, an Austrian declaration of war against Serbia would undoubtedly re-ignite the long-standing dispute with Russia that had been so carefully avoided during the Bosnia Annexation Crisis in 1908. Russia had significant economic interests in the Balkans and wished to maintain her access to the Mediterranean Sea, and the Russian people viewed the southern Slavs as their natural allies. Thus, when Emperor Franz Joseph annexed Bosnia in 1908, Tsar Nicholas had loudly threatened to wage war, and it was only the sudden mobilization of Germany's massive armies that finally cooled the Tsar's fiery temper. Yet how many times could one bait the "Great Bear" that was Russia? Was there any reason to believe that the Tsar would tolerate yet another affront to his interests in the Balkans and to his allies in Serbia? How could one expect Russia to stand idle yet again if Austria were to declare war against Serbia? And how then would Russia's other allies, the notorious *Triple Entente* of Russia, France and Great Britain, react? Would war spread across Europe? Would any nation be spared? These were dangerous concerns to simply ignore, the Count concluded. It was all too easy to imagine the great armies of Europe marching to battle and the countless lives that could be lost. It is no foreign policy at all to constantly rely on your adversaries to back down, he thought.

Deep in his heart, Count Laszlo was even more perplexed that the aging Franz Joseph, the venerable Emperor of Austria and King of Hungary, would wish to rule over the Serbian people. After all, it was widely known that Austria-Hungary was having difficulty managing the many nationalities already found within its borders – the predominant German "Austrians" and Magyar "Hungarians" (who greatly disliked each other) were ruling unhappily over Poles, Czechs, Ruthenians, Roumanians, Slovaks, Tyroleans, Bohemians, Moravians, Croats, Bosnians, Moslems and Jews. The Empire had gone to great lengths to pacify these smaller nationalities, yet the Emperor had shown an intolerable lack of imagination when it came to handling the occasional strike, boycott, demonstration and political unrest, which were more often than not put down with police batons and mass arrests. The Hungarian parliament was torn apart by related issues – some sought to re-write the laws which prevented huge numbers of non-Hungarian citizens from voting, others wrote laws forcibly indoctrinating the lesser populations into the Magyar culture, religion, and language, while the Socialists sought to carefully pit the varied masses against those of wealth and noble birth. These were only a few of the troubles Austria-Hungary already faced without adding a rebellious Serbian population into the mixture.

Not that Count Laszlo had any great affection for the Serbian people, certainly not. But, as a Hungarian serving under a Hapsburg ruler, he sympathized with the Serbians' desire for self-determination. Hungary in the past century had gone through its own political upheavals in order to place limits on the "Dual Monarchy" of Austria and Hungary. The Count's father had been

378

one of the great advocates of Hungarian autonomy, and there were many respectable politicians who continued to press for limitations on the authority of the Hapsburg king.

No, it was ridiculous to think that Austria should occupy or annex Serbia. That is precisely what Count Laszlo would have counseled the Kaiser when he arrived at *Sanssouci* – would have counseled but for the arrival that very morning of an unexpected and greatly unwelcome envoy from Vienna. The Count had been awakened at dawn to attend to Alexander von Hoyos, a disagreeable young man who had just arrived from Vienna with letters from Austria's Foreign Minister. Hoyos was one of the more radical members of the Young Rebels, but he had doggedly worked his way up to become Chief of Staff to Foreign Minister Berchtold. Upon learning that Hoyos had arrived in Berlin, Count Laszlo knew at once that he had brought very dark news, and, indeed, as the Count settled in his study that morning and reviewed the letters that Hoyos had brought to be presented to the Kaiser, the Count's head pounded and a chill stole down his spine. Berchtold demanded to know whether Kaiser Wilhelm could be relied upon to confront his cousin Tsar Nicholas yet again if Emperor Franz Joseph chose to wage war against Serbia. Laszlo was directed to obtain confirmation from the Kaiser that very day. The decision to wage war, it seemed, was all but final. Only Kaiser Wilhelm could stop it now and only then if he had the good sense to put an end to the escalation. Otherwise, Europe stood on the brink of ruin.

The Count's sedan rushed past the Brandenburg gate on its way into Potsdam, a village that had belonged to the House of Hohenzollern, the Kaiser's family, for nearly five hundred years, and sped on to the grounds of the *Sanssouci* palace. The heavy green foliage and dark red brick and mustard yellow buildings felt stolid and cramped among the countless marble statues and terraced gardens, not at all like the graceful and airy *Versaille* or even *Schönbrunn* palaces. To his surprise, the Count saw that the New Palace was abuzz with activity. Several motorcars were being loaded in preparation for the Kaiser's forthcoming voyage to Norway. As the Count stepped from his Mercedes, his eye fell upon the heavy statuary that surrounded and crowned the huge Baroque building. Two gleaming black army sedans idled nearby. A footman in a vaguely military livery stepped forward to welcome the Count, and then an army officer stepped from the building. He was a man the Count had met once or twice in Berlin. The officer noticed the Count and strode purposefully down the wide granite stairs in his direction.

The Count recalled the officer as Colonel Karl von Metzger. He was a tall, thin man with a square jaw and greying brown hair, clean shaven, an ambitious man from a highly regarded naval family who, if the Count recalled correctly, hailed from the city of Kiel on the Baltic Sea coast. Now Metzger looked decidedly tired and careworn.

"A pleasure to see you again, Colonel," the Count said with a nod of his head.

"And you, Ambassador," Metzger replied grimly. "I must give you our apologies: The Kaiser has become quite agitated by our discussions this morning, and I expect you have serious and sober matters to discuss with His Highness."

"Yes, that is true. But I have only just arrived to lunch with His Highness, and I expect a glass of wine will temper his mood."

"You will only have to wait a moment longer, I assure you. The Kaiser is finishing his discussions with the Chief of Staff now."

So Field Marshal von Moltke was inside, the Count realized. He knew it would be improper to ask the Colonel why he and the Imperial Army's Chief of Staff were visiting *Sanssouci* or to share with them the purpose of his own journey to Potsdam, but the silence was awkward. He asked politely: "Will you be visiting your home on the coast this summer, Colonel?"

"I'm afraid I no longer have time for holidays, Ambassador," he replied coolly, but then he added: "I am expected to return to Aachen immediately."

"Aachen?" Count Laszlo was not aware that any of the German armies maintained headquarters in Aachen, the ancient city close to the western border of Germany near Belgium. And why would Colonel Metzger pointedly reveal that information? "Yes, quite an interesting city, quite," he said uncertainly. "And are you still serving in the Eighth Army Inspectorate?"

"Yes, precisely," Metzger replied somewhat ominously. Did this mean that the Eighth Army Inspectorate had moved to Aachen? The Count could make nothing of it, but he began to feel lightheaded, like he was falling very slowly down a rabbit hole. Suddenly Field Marshal von Moltke rushed red-faced and agitated from the doorway and struggled down the broad steps. He immediately stepped into his waiting black sedan with barely a nod to the Ambassador. Count Laszlo knew the Chief of Staff well and was astonished and confused by the perfunctory greeting.

"You must excuse me, Ambassador," Colonel von Metzger said abruptly. "There is a great deal to be done," and then he marched quickly to Moltke's sedan and they sped away. The Count looked on in astonishment.

"This way, sir," the footman said. He led the Count up the steps into the New Palace and through great empty ballrooms and up and down a confusing and narrowing succession of staircases and hallways until he at last reached the Kaiser's private residence deep within the palace. Inside the large, mahogany-paneled royal family dining room, a small square table had been set for lunch, only two place settings, and the wine was already being poured by the footman. It was apparently to be a very brief meeting. Near a side door, the tall, grimacing Kaiser, Wilhelm II, stood speaking in harsh whispers to Moltke's second-in-command, the Deputy Chief of Staff, General Quartermaster Hermann von Stein. The Kaiser was wearing his customary grey uniform draped in medals and his gleaming black boots, and his mustache was turned up as always into a sort of menacing grin. He spoke to Stein quietly, but in harshly arrogant tones. He turned briefly to acknowledge the Count's presence with a cursory nod. The Count had never seen the Kaiser quite so agitated. Wilhelm began sawing his huge right hand through the air demonstratively even as he held his withered left arm tightly against his chest. He was still speaking to the General Quartermaster when the luncheon was carried in on silver serving trays. The Count waited patiently as the meal cooled.

Finally, the Kaiser was heard to command Stein to depart. As he left the room, the General Quartermaster gave Count Laszlo a nod with an expression full of – of what, exactly? Malice? Concern? Fear? Excitement? Before the Count could comprehend the expression, the man turned on his heels and marched quickly out the doorway. Then the Kaiser was suddenly striding purposefully toward Count Laszlo with his right hand extended.

"Laszlo, how pleasant to see you again. Damned difficult business, don't you agree," Wilhelm asked rhetorically as he took Count Laszlo's hand and squeezed it very tightly.

"Your Highness, thank you for agreeing to see me today," the Count replied in some confusion. "It is always a great honor to visit *Sanssouci*."

"Now you have me all to yourself, Laszlo," Wilhelm said solicitously. "However, I haven't much time, so let us sit and we will speak while we are eating. I must still prepare for my voyage to Norway tomorrow."

"You are still going, then?" The Count asked as the footmen rushed to pull out their seats and the Count and the Kaiser sat at the meticulously-arrayed table.

"Yes, although I deeply regret it. My Foreign Secretary insists it would appear too belligerent if I was to cancel the journey at this point, but it is the damned worst moment to be traveling. There is far too much to be done."

"But I quite agree with von Jagow, Your Highness. If you were to stay in Potsdam, everyone would assume that Germany is preparing for war," the Count replied. Based on what Metzger had said and his haggard appearance, the Count suddenly wondered if the German armies were already quite busy in that regard.

"Have you any news about the investigation?" Wilhelm demanded.

"If you mean anything that would incriminate the Serbian Premier, then I regret not."

Wilhelm pounded his right fist on the table, badly startling the Count: "It is unconscionable! I am appalled that he would commit such crimes," the Kaiser spat back. "Assassination is a coward's act, a folly, a disgrace! There has been far too much of it. Twice the Socialists attempted to murder my own grandfather, you know. Now I am not even permitted to attend the Archduke's funeral out of concern that there will be an attempt on my own life. You cannot know how that distresses me."

Count Laszlo, his heart now beating too rapidly, was uncertain whether Wilhelm was referring to the risk of assassination or to his inability to attend the funeral. He felt it more polite to assume the latter. "The Emperor, and all of Austria-Hungary, appreciates your deep sympathy for the Archduke, Your Highness," he replied.

"The Serbians must pay a bitter price, Laszlo. I pray that Franz Joseph will not allow this criminal act to go unanswered. Serbia has consistently provoked violence throughout the Balkans, and it is time for her to answer for those crimes," Wilhelm stated emphatically.

It was not at all what the Count had hoped to hear. Suddenly the footman swooped in with trays of boiled beef and stewed cabbage, not even asking but simply depositing the food onto their plates, and then just as suddenly one of the footmen quickly took the Kaiser's plate away to carefully slice his meat for him.

"If I may, Your Highness," Laszlo continued, but then he paused, unable to collect his thoughts momentarily as his head throbbed. He felt faint. How could he follow his instructions from the Foreign Minister to seek the Kaiser's support for a war against Serbia and yet still suggest that such a war would be a grave error? It was an untenable situation, he thought miserably. "Of course," he began again, "indeed, yes, I quite agree with you. However, the larger issue is not Serbia, *per se*; we all agree that Serbia is an enduring problem, and one that must be resolved in one way or another. The more difficult issue before us now is of course the Tsar. It hardly seems likely that Nicholas will tolerate an Austrian invasion of yet another nation in the Balkans, especially if the goal is annexation through military conquest."

"We quite agree," Wilhelm stated simply as he began eating.

"Well, yes, in that circumstance, Your Highness, we cannot consider this as a simple matter of punishing Serbia. A war between Austria and Serbia would likely involve Russia, and then, if I am not too presumptuous to say so, it would involve Imperial Germany, and then perhaps Russia's allies France and Great Britain, and then our ally Italy. It is my duty to lay these cards on the table, lest there be any recriminations later, your Highness: A war with Serbia could soon spread into a conflagration across Europe and to the colonies abroad."

"Yes," Wilhelm replied with shocking passivity as he forked his meat into his mouth.

"Then I only wish to say, Your Highness," the Count observed cautiously, "that is to say, that in light of such a potentiality, no one would consider it unreasonable for you to withhold your support for Austrian military action against Serbia."

"Indeed, but why should I do so, Laszlo?" Wilhelm asked tersely. "Should I be afraid of war? Am I not prepared for war? Are my capabilities so underestimated?"

"That is not it at all, Your Highness," Count Laszlo assured him anxiously. "It is not simply a matter –"

"We have already discussed these issues at length with my General Staff. Over a decade ago, Marshal von Schlieffen made the first analyses of just such a situation. In sum, we believe it will take Tsar Nicholas a great many weeks to mobilize his armies, Laszlo, *many* weeks. In that time, my armies would not be idle, not at all. France presents us with no difficulty at all – in 1870, we defeated the French Army and captured Napoleon III in a mere six weeks. Great Britain is of no concern – King George may have his Royal Navy, but my Imperial Navy is undoubtedly greater. So I tell you, by the time Nicholas is able to field a single army in Russia, Serbia will be in ashes and my armies and Franz Joseph's will be entrenched in Prussia and Galicia. We shall see then whether my cousin the Tzar has the courage to wage war. I dare say he will not."

By "Prussia" and "Galicia", the Count understood the Kaiser to mean Poland, but why then had his armies been sent to Aachen on the border with Belgium? Why not place troops to secure the border with France? Laszlo's head was spinning.

"Let me assure you," the Kaiser continued, "my cousin Nicholas must draw the same conclusions and appreciate the complete futility of challenging any action that Franz Joseph may choose to take with regard to Serbia. But, regardless, it is our duty to urge Franz Joseph to act as the circumstances warrant."

"Then you accept that the war might spread, Your Highness?" The Count asked, now ashen-faced and feeling ill.

The Kaiser bristled. "I am not concerned with war, Ambassador, but with duty. It is my duty to increase the heritage bestowed upon me. It is that for which I shall be called to give account. With our victory, Germany will at last rank foremost among the great nations, and then and only then can Germany assert itself as a mighty champion of peace."

"Peace, yes," the Count replied with as little emotion as he could muster. "If I may, Your Highness, I must then present you with these letters from Vienna requesting that you state your position," he said as he produced the envelope from his jacket, "and I shall, of course, convey your unconditional support to the Emperor, with your consent, sir."

"Indeed," Wilhelm stated firmly.

Later that day, before returning to his townhouse in Berlin, Count Laszlo managed to wire the Foreign Minister in Vienna and convey the Kaiser's message. But the Count still felt perplexed and lightheaded and, more than anything else, old. Had the Hohenzollern dynasty of Prussia truly become so secure and powerful that they dared to take the whole of Europe into war? Were Austria and its Emperor, whom the Count had served so very long now, to be set aside so that Germany could ascend? That prospect made the Count feel his age acutely, and he returned to his townhouse that night utterly exhausted. He had long resisted retiring, but this new world order made Count Laszlo long to escape to his family's estate in Hungary. It seemed at last the proper time to do so. That night he began writing his letter of resignation.

As the guns began to fire on August 4, 1914, Count Laszlo Szőgyény-Marich resigned his post as Ambassador to Germany and returned to his native Hungary. In less than two years, he would be dead, along with millions of other men and women across Europe and in the colonies abroad.

Many of the assumptions made in July 1914 were proved false. Serbia did not collapse in mere days; the Serbians resisted the Austrian army for over a year, and it was not until the Austrians were joined by German and Bulgarian forces in 1915 that Serbia was finally overrun. France proved an indomitable foe after having learned the lessons of the Franco-Prussian War; Germany's long-prepared *Schlieffen Plan* for a pan-European war had the German armies bypass France's border fortifications by invading through neutral Belgium and sweeping through northern France to capture Paris in a few weeks. However, at the Marne River, France and Great Britain stopped the German advance. Field Marshal von Moltke was forced to resign in disgrace, and the Western Front became a bitter stalemate for the next four years. Great Britain proved itself far more than just a colonial and sea power; the British Empire sent nearly nine million men to fight on the ground, many in France and Belgium and many more in Greece, Turkey, Egypt and Mesopotamia. Rather than taking months to prepare for war as expected, Russian troops invaded Prussia and Austrian Galicia less than four weeks after the start of hostilities. Italy, aligned with the Central Power at the start of the war but long unhappy about the location of its borders with Austria, switched sides and joined the Allies. And the remote, isolationist United States, whose *Monroe Doctrine* had long been used as an excuse to stay aloof of matters outside the Western Hemisphere, eventually chose to send millions of men to fight in Europe and to assert itself as the global champion of democracy.

The war was not over by Christmas as originally expected, and as the ancient global powers crumbled year by year under the strain of war, soldiers and civilians, politicians and emperors, finally began to contemplate the new world order that would be left upon their ruins.

Ypres

Even deep inside the darkened bunker and down beneath his mouldy woolen blankets, David Gresham could still hear the cold rain fall and still feel the ground tremble from the never-ending barrage of British and German artillery. It had been more than two years since he had last been in Ypres, but the war had continued there in his absence and the town had been reduced to a ruined shadow of its former self. For nearly a thousand years, Ypres had been known for its fine lace and embroidery, as a pleasant town of wide cobbled streets and charming white townhouses. The Draper's Hall, across the Lille road from St. Martin's Church, had been a center of commerce in Belgium for hundreds of years. But after three years of war the foundations of the Draper's Hall were all that remained, and only part of the tower and a side of the church. The clean and comfortable Hotel de la Chatellenie (where Gresham had once billeted) had been shelled and burned to the ground, and the residents of the town had long ago moved away, and even the cobblestone streets were difficult to discern beneath the mud and dust and piles of debris. Even Gresham found the sight of Ypres disturbing. Yet, despite the terrible destruction inflicted upon it, Ypres had become a symbol to the British Army of their endurance just as Verdun had become for the French. To the east, throughout the wide Ypres salient, thousands of British guns roared without ceasing day or night, and further east, atop the ridgeline that overlooked the salient, the German guns replied.

Beyond the ridge lay the German Fourth Army, part of the Northern Army Group, and also the crucial Roulers Railway Centre that supplied it. The British commanders had initially hoped to flank the German U-Boat bases near Bruges and seize Roulers in the belief that its loss might force the Germans out of Belgium altogether. But that was something Gresham heard again and again: Small objectives expected to result in exaggerated gains and sudden victory. Now, after weeks of halting advances, the primary British objective was simply to capture the ridgeline itself. And atop that ridge, in a little village called Passchendaele, was David Gresham's own objective.

Gresham was an agent of the British Secret Intelligence Service, and somewhere in Passchendaele, in a bunker deep underground, he expected to find a German officer that he had been sent to capture. "Capture" was perhaps the wrong word, for a Belgian agent would detain the officer in Passchendaele and British soldiers taking part in the massive offensive were certain to seize him, but Gresham would then collect the officer and interrogate the man: the General Quartermaster, a position that ranked second-in-command, of the German Northern Army Group led by the Crown Prince of Bavaria.

Gresham was startled to have received explicit orders to do the General Quartermaster no harm. It was an unusual order in that regard, one that seemed to have resulted from Gresham's developing reputation within the Service as a violent and unpredictable young man, a yob from Manchester, a ruffian who killed for pleasure. Gresham could not have cared less for his reputation, but he believed the criticism was undeserved. In his opinion, he had killed only those who warranted death, and this was a time of war after all. He had learned that he had been roundly criticized by the Service's second-in-command in particular, a man he knew only by the code name "Z", for having assassinated a German Foreign Ministry agent in cold blood on the streets of Stockholm. The German, an *agent provocateur* named Dunn, had sought to provoke rebellions in the British territories of Ireland and India as well as in Italy and, with some success, in Russia. True, Gresham had been motivated to assassinate Dunn in part for revenge since the agent had tried to kill Gresham in Italy. However, the murder of Dunn had also been implicitly ordered by the man at the very top of Service, the man they called *Control*. There was nothing Gresham could do about policy disagreements among those in charge of the Service, but he had begun to wonder if it was all a bloody circus up there in Whitehall Court, where their headquarters were located. Gresham had been cautioned on several occasions to exercise his own judgment when it came to completing the missions he was given, and more than ever Gresham appreciated the wisdom of that advice. However, for a young man with few other opportunities, it had been difficult advice to follow - until now.

Gresham had recently obtained the one asset necessary for him act with total discretion – hard currency. After assassinating Dunn, Gresham had successfully stolen a fortune from the German government. Funds that Dunn had intended to support the Bolsheviks in Russia, Gresham had diverted to his own bank account in Switzerland. For the first time in his life Gresham was wealthy, extremely wealthy. He was still undecided what to do with his new-found assets. He had barely had time to consider the matter since fleeing from Russia, and immediately after arriving in Copenhagen he had received a wire from *Control* requesting that he go at once to Ypres. In the end, it was simply easier to go to Belgium for such a straightforward job than to decide quite suddenly what else he might do. But the question gnawed at him. The final assault on the village of Passchendaele was still a few days away, and Gresham had nothing to do in the meantime but to consider the matter and wait, wait in Ypres where his military career had begun some three years before.

It was in 1914, just after the war broke out, that Gresham's father, a wealthy industrialist eager to be rid of his illegitimate son, had arranged for Gresham's commission in the Manchester Regiment. Gresham, more from personal ambition than any sense of duty, first went to join the British Expeditionary Force in Belgium, but his background and poor pedigree had made him an outcast among the more noble-birthed British officers there. Although educated in a second-rate public school, Gresham had spent much of his early life on the streets of Manchester and the rough skills he had learned did not endear him to the other officers. Yet those same skills served him well as a soldier and tactician, one, he knew, who had proven himself to be a valuable agent in the Secret Intelligence Service.

Unable to sleep any longer, Gresham threw off his moist, mildewed blankets and wiped his lanky black hair from his eyes. He looked around the darkened bunker where he slept in Ypres. They called it a "bunker", but three years earlier it had been the large, deep, dry cellar of a fine townhouse. He remembered admiring the house before it was destroyed. Now, a row of close, charred timbers and a few sheets of tin and dirt were all that stood above the cellar's ceiling. The bunker itself was neither bomb-proof nor water-proof, but it was adequate for the time being, until Gresham could move up to Passchendaele and claim his prisoner.

So as not to disturb the other sleeping men, Gresham reached out one foot in the dark and gently rattled the camp bed beside his own.

"Christ, *that* was a big one, High Explosives, and damned close, don't you think?" Gresham whispered, hoping to rouse the fellow sleeping next to him.

"Leave me alone, f---er," replied a drunken and muffled voice from beneath the blanket.

"I'm in the mood for some cards; if you'll get up I'll make you some tea," Gresham pleaded.

"G' to Hell," his neighbor mumbled angrily.

"I've told you lay off the wine. It's no good having you come along if you're going to be tight all the time," Gresham replied tersely.

The blanket on the neighboring bed rolled back as its occupant, James Wilkins, sat up slowly. Wilkins had never felt so sickly and had never looked so pathetic. His damp light brown hair was matted to his forehead, and his pale pallour emphasized the long red scar on his left cheek. He was also an agent of the Secret Intelligence Service and a close comrade of Gresham's, but, unlike his colleague, Wilkins was the youngest son of an Earl and had lived all his life surrounded by wealth and nobility. Gresham was not surprised that Wilkins, who had recently been brought low when his first love affair had ended in disaster, by a woman who had refused to flee with him from Petrograd, would attempt to drink away his sorrow and disappointment, but it was rapidly becoming a tiresome spectacle. In fact, he had only invited Wilkins along to Ypres because he was wary of leaving his despondent friend alone in Copenhagen and hoped that a new mission might improve his mood. However, Wilkins had taken no interest in the mission, and he spent his days and nights in the ruins of Ypres drinking heavily and cursing his comrades.

"I don't *wish* to play at cards, David," he stated overdramatically.

"Then we won't," Gresham replied, attempting to be agreeable. "But will you tell me again about Munich? I like to hear about the breadlines."

"Oh, I've told you all that already – lines for food, lines for petrol, lines for bloody coal," Wilkins said wearily. He had been sent on a mission to Munich the previous year and had seen the results of the Allies' effort to blockade Germany from the rest of the world. After years of stalemate on the front lines, France and Great Britain now hoped to starve Germany into surrender. The tactic, although of uncertain effectiveness, had forced Kaiser Wilhelm to surrender his nation to the control of two men – the Chief of his General Staff, Marshal Paul von Hindenburg who was now in command of the German armies, and his Deputy Chief, General Quartermaster Erich Ludendorff who was responsible for supplying the war effort. This had in effect place Ludendorff in control of every man, woman, child, animal, place and thing in Germany, and under his "leadership," Germany had become a strict military dictatorship. "I don't remember ever telling you about the *Hotel Vier Jahreszeiten*, or did I?" Wilkins continued.

"No," Gresham said warily; Wilkins had a boorish habit of reminiscing about his affluent childhood tours of the Continent with his noble mother.

Wilkins sat up uncertainly and rubbed his bloodshot eyes. "Well, I'll tell you. It's the finest hotel in Munich, and I walked past it, just for old time's sake – I'd stayed there a few times before the war. O' course, I didn't expect to see anything, what with the breadlines and all that; I thought the hotel would be empty. Well, it surprisingly was not – there were well-dressed soldiers, quite a lot, hordes of them, going into the hotel for some event that evening. Grim, nasty men, they seemed, and the way they saluted each other, and the way they sang about Germany's domination over the whole bloody world with such certainty and passion, like they had come to a religious epiphany – I can tell you I found it damned disgusting."

"But you saw no sign of rebellion like in Russia?"

"No, none at all, and I must say, David, if there *are* any revolutionaries in Germany, they must stay bloody quiet, what with old men and women being arrested off the street for merely complaining about the breadlines. The secret police scare the people into submission. It's all that damned Ludendorff's doing. The only reason the Socialists aren't in prison is because they came out in favor of the f---ing war too."

"Can you keep it down, please," complained another officer sleeping nearby, "I have to go up to Vine Cottage in the morning."

"Now, Chris," Wilkins said, swinging around drunkenly to address the other officer, "you're Canadian, right?"

"Christ Almighty, Wilkins, we're all Canadians in here except for you and Gresham."

"So tell me, what's it like?"

"What's what like?" The officer asked angrily.

"Canada, of course!" Wilkins shouted.

"Oh, for Pete's ...," the man complained as he burrowed back beneath his blanket.

"Listen, James –" Gresham began, now sorry that he had awakened the still-inebriated Wilkins in the first place.

"A Canadian saved my life once, you know," Wilkins said.

"Yes, I remember," Gresham said soothingly.

"Promise me that you'll think about it?" Wilkins asked.

"What - the Canadian?"

"No, no," Wilkins said crossly, then he looked about exaggeratedly and whispered to Gresham: "The General Quartermaster, the fellow you're supposed to interrogate up in Passchendaele."

"Just go back to sleep, James. I'm sorry I woke you."

"That's a military intelligence job," Wilkins whispered, "interrogating a commanding field officer, isn't it? So *why* are they sending *you*?"

Wilkins glared at Gresham confrontationally, then abruptly lay down and pulled the blanket over his head.

Gresham thought he would perhaps leave Wilkins in Ypres when he went up to Passchendaele. It was certain to be very bad on the ridge, just as bad as the slow approaches made during the past few weeks.

Gresham still had no firm information about what he would find in Passchendaele when he was finally notified that the assault on the village would take place on the morning of 6 November. If the Canadians were able to overrun the village, the Germans would certainly counter-attack, so Gresham's opportunity to locate the General would be brief. Aerial reconnaissance had identified the location of several possible bunkers, part of the vast network of defenses that made up the indomitable Hindenburg Line. Gresham checked his handgun, the Browning M1911 that had served him so well, and clipped his field knife to the back of his belt. The day before the attempt on the village would be made, and well before the hopeless James Wilkins was yet awake, Gresham left the bunker in Ypres to work his way up to the front lines near Crest Farm, a quarter of a mile or so below Passchendaele.

It had taken several weeks for the British Army, predominantly the veteran Canadian Third and Fourth Divisions who had been sent to relieve the exhausted ANZACs, to push slowly forward a few hundred yards at a time using a new "bite and hold" tactic: Huge numbers of troops were set in to overrun small portions of the defender's front lines; the dense masses of men were often forced to resort to bayonets and hand-to-hand combat. Then the attackers would rush in reinforcements to resist the inevitable German counter-attacks. Once the new front was consolidated and the artillery was brought forward, the army would reach out to take another bite, thus taking one small step after another. The number of casualties had been appalling, the gains had been modest, but slowly and steadily the Canadians were pushing the Germans back from their well-prepared defenses.

As Gresham struck out and left Ypres behind, he found the Lille-Roulers road broken and almost impassable. Although the rain had trailed off for the past two days, it was still cold, grey and overcast, and the low lying country between Ypres and the ridge was muddy and badly flooded. Years of bombardment had churned the ground and broken the banks of the streams, and months of rain had left the low-lying country a fetid swamp of thick grey mud. Gresham, despite his newly-gained wealth, still wore his worn brown leather boots and his one old and badly-stained Colonel's uniform and wool overcoat, and he was soon covered in mud. There was rarely a straight path since High Explosive shells dropped by German artillery had left deep craters throughout the fields and roads. These craters had filled to the brim with putrid water, and, in some places, cemeteries where human remains had been buried following the many battles in the salient over the past three years had been up-turned by the constant bombardment. Decaying corpses and parts of bodies of those long dead floated and bobbed in the pools of black water. Horse and mule carcasses and the charred remains of carts and sedans and tanks lay strewn along the roadside, and the surrounding sodden plains were dotted with guns of all calibers placed in improvised breastworks made of sandbags and rubble. Filthy artillery crews worked in the open and slept between low parallel rows of sandbags with a bit of tin for a roof. Straining men and teams of exhausted draught horses worked incessantly to advance the artillery; guns of all shapes and sizes had to be forced forward through the deep, clinging mud.

By mid-day, Gresham reached the town of Gravenstafel. It was there that he had suffered through Germany's first poison gas attack, early in 1915. Now the village no longer existed at all, and not a single tree or structure or blade of grass remained as far as he could see. The once-rich farmland past the town had become a deathly bog, and from there to the ridgeline there were no longer any clear roads or firm ground. The only means to proceed to the British lines was atop rough wood duckboards. These, Gresham saw, were continuously being laid down in winding paths by countless soldiers from the engineering divisions. The duckboards were slippery and treacherous, and often choked with abandoned carts or cannon. Sometimes wounded soldiers returning from the front lines would slip from the duckboards into the fetid pools; some had drowned before they could be rescued. Gresham saw soldiers pulling a panicked horse from one such pool. In another, a tank had evidently slipped into the black water and, half submerged, a crew was attempting to salvage parts. Human corpses were stacked like spent shell casings alongside every path.

Even worse, German artillery had taped the duckboards to an inch and could drop a shell anywhere along the paths at any time, and they often did. High explosives would fall into the mud and shower the soldiers with dirt and stone. The German artillery never stopped firing, but then neither did the British.

There was never a single minute of silence day or night and the ground trembled continuously.

Here and there a passing wisp of fog or smoke would induce a sudden panic among the men, for sometimes these were clouds of poison gas, now delivered by artillery shells from the German guns. When these clouds were spotted, the soldiers would immediately scramble to put on their heavy, blinding respirators. The masks made seeing, breathing, and staying atop the slimy duckboards even more difficult. In the sky, dozens of German and British aeroplanes swarmed among the observation balloons. They flew rain or shine, day and night, dropping bombs and strafing their enemies, filling the air with bullets and bombs and smoke.

As his progress that afternoon continued, Gresham found the sights more and more overwhelming. He could not conceive that Belgium would ever be restored, that the scars of war could ever heal. The war had made a whole region of the world uninhabitable. But then again, it seemed the war would go on and on, and this is where young men would come for many years to die. Death was all that was expected of them. Something had to be done. There had to be a way to make it stop.

Gresham at last reached the bitter end of the world, his destination, where he found that all traces of humanity had been abolished. All that remained was a crumbling trench and a poorly hand-painted wooden sign that said "Crest Farm." The narrow, shallow trench was only a few feet deep and half filled with putrid water in which hundreds of quiet, filthy men now crouched, smoked, and waited stoically. They were experienced soldiers, at ease with the terrible conditions and their near-certain and imminent death. The falling German shells had ceased to concern them at all, although many wore their respirators continuously, it being thought preferable to be blown to bits by an explosive shell than to painfully drown in one's own bodily fluids because of the chlorine gas. These were hardened men who no longer cared why the war was being fought, but who carried on nonetheless because of their personal sense of duty and honor. A few of the men were quietly singing a fatalistic tune newly popular among the troops, sung to the tune of the old folk song *Auld Lang Syne*:

> *We're here because we're here*
> *Because we're here because we're here;*
> *We're here because we're here*
> *Because we're here because we're here.*

"Crest Farm" was on a wide shoulder of the ridge overlooking the "village" of Passchendaele. The enemy's trenches and grey cement pillboxes could be seen clearly in the distance, although little of the village itself remained. At the moment Gresham arrived, countless British artillery shells were falling heavily on the German lines, and the great cloud of dirt thrown up had made the air hazy and grey. The German soldiers must be equally hardened men to withstand such a barrage, Gresham thought, although there were also well-known incidents of German commanders ordering their artillery to fire on their own troops to prevent the men from retreating.

A large, muscular young Private in a well-worn brown and muddy uniform and shrapnel helmet, his face covered in dirt and dried blood, his eyes red and swollen, was crouching nearby in foot deep muck smoking a cigarette. He was the first to notice Gresham climbing into the soggy trench.

"Who are you, eh?" The man demanded in his Canadian accent as he raised a filthy and likely-unusable rifle.

"Intelligence," Gresham said bluntly. "Where's your commanding officer?"

"What do you mean 'Intelligence'?" The man asked angrily.

"I mean that I am a Colonel from the British Intelligence office, so take me to the man in command of the 27th Battalion."

"Uh, yeah, Sir, Lieutenant-Colonel Daly is down that-away, Sir," the Private said quickly. "I can show you where, okay?"

"At last," Gresham said as he followed the Private. They sloshed through the maze of trenches, past lines of stoic, exhausted men, with vacant expressions, until they finally reached the command bunker. It was not a traditional British bunker, the sort with which Gresham was most familiar. Rather than a dark, deep, moist earthen chamber with large wooden beams and packed dirt for a roof, this was a thick, dry box of concrete with a small steel door and narrow, slit windows. Of course, it had been built by the Germans and could withstand any kind of bombardment. The Private led Gresham into the dark room.

Gresham had expected to find yet another of England's old gentleman officers and was pleased to be disappointed. The commander, a solidly-built Lieutenant-Colonel with short black hair, only a few years older than Gresham himself, was speaking quietly with an clean-cut American Major who looked to be in his forties, thin and spectacled. Gresham had seen only a handful of Americans since he arrived in Belgium. It had been six months since the United States had declared war on Germany but barely more than 100,000 American troops had traveled across the Atlantic so far. Those who had made the voyage comprised the newly-constituted American Expeditionary Force or "A.E.F." under the command of General "Blackjack" Pershing. Although still in training, the Americans sometimes accompanied and observed French and British units in the field.

"That's the commander, there, Sir," the Private whispered.

"Is he any good?" Gresham asked quietly.

"Yeah," the Private said simply, and then he approached his commander.

"What is it?" The commander asked.

"There's a fellow here needs to see you; he's from the Intelligence office."

Gresham noted the lack of formality among the Canadian soldiers; they were focused on their task and seemed to have no time to worry about rank or protocol. Gresham said: "Don't let me interrupt you. We can speak when you're finished."

"That's alright," the Lieutenant-Colonel said as he stepped over to Gresham and extended his hand. "Tom Daly, 27th Battalion."

"David Gresham," he said as he shook the Canadian's hand firmly.

"This is Major Dennis Nolan from the A.E.F," Daly said.

"Colonel Gresham, a pleasure," Nolan said in a surprisingly firm, clear voice. "Do you work for Cecil Cameron?" Gresham hesitated before shaking the Major's hand. Cecil Cameron had been Gresham's commanding officer for a brief time, by accident, in 1916 before the battle at the Somme River, but Cameron was in the military intelligence branch. Gresham no longer answered to the military. More importantly, he was surprised that Nolan even knew Cameron's name.

"No, I work for another office," Gresham said evasively. He had been ordered not to disclose even the existence of the Secret Intelligence Service under any circumstances. "How do you know Cecil Cameron?"

"We met a few days ago," Nolan said. "General Pershing asked me to look into improving our own intelligence operations in the field, to bring it more in line with what you folks are doing here in Belgium and France; Field Marshal Haig sent me to Cameron, and he suggested I visit Ypres to see your boys in action."

"Cameron sent you *here*, to an active war zone, to learn how intelligence is handled?" Gresham asked in astonishment.

"I had the same reaction initially, but I can say truthfully that I've learned a great deal from speaking with Lieutenant-Colonel Daly here. Your aerial photographs are pretty grand, and it's how you use the information that is really impressive."

"Thank you for saying so, Major. And what brings *you* to Crest Farm, Colonel?" Daly asked.

"Oh, just task work - for some reason I've been given orders to tag along into Passchendaele tomorrow, to collect some information, interrogate a prisoner or two, all routine."

Daly squinted at him as if undecided, and then his eyes opened wide. "I believe I've heard your name before. 'Gresham', you said, is that right?"

"Yes," he replied cautiously.

"Ah, yes," Daly said slowly, nodding his head and scratching his cheek, "I believe I do know who you are, Colonel. Well, let's just say that I don't need to know any more. Frankly, I'd rather not hear any more about it."

"That's fine with me," Gresham said.

"I'd rather you didn't involve any of my men in your little information-gathering mission," Daly said. "You know how it is; I'm supposed to be looking after these boys."

"I don't intend to involve anyone if it can be avoided. I plan to just follow along behind."

"That'd be fine, of course. I'm sending two companies over to 'Tiber House', that's on our far right, just after nightfall. They'll be among those flanking the forward pillboxes in the morning and approaching the village from the south along the ridgeline in the first wave. You'd best join them, if that'll suit you."

"Yes, that's very good," Gresham said. He wondered what Daly had heard about him. Certainly Gresham had developed a reputation on the Western Front during the Battle of the Somme. His successful raid with Wilkins on an isolated farmhouse behind the enemy's lines to capture a German intelligence agent was the worst kept secret in British Intelligence.

"Okay then," Daly confirmed. "Roberts!" He roared and the Private immediately rushed back into the bunker. "Private, the Colonel is going to join your company as an observer. You're to bring him with you over to 'Tiber House' tonight. He'll be following your Company across the ridge tomorrow."

"Yes, Sir," Private Roberts said without emotion.

"It was a pleasure to meet you, Colonel," Major Nolan said as he shook Gresham's hand again. "Perhaps we'll have an opportunity to speak more after the action tomorrow."

"Perhaps," Gresham said, and then he followed Roberts outside into the muck of the trench.

"We'll be leaving right after dark, Colonel," Private Roberts said. "If you'll come with me, I'll introduce you to my company commander, Captain McKinley."

Gresham followed and received a warmer reception from the Captain who apparently had not heard of Gresham, or at least not by name. Then Gresham found a dry spot to sit upon the firing step of the trench and waited. He ate a hardened biscuit while the sun set and the sky grew dark but for the constant flash of the great guns and Verey lights. The noise and tremble of the earth were constant, and the smell of putrefaction was nearly overpowering. It wasn't long after dark that Private Roberts came to inform Gresham that the company would be setting out.

The distance from Crest Farm to Tiber House was only two or three hundred yards, but to avoid the front lines (and the shelling and snipers) as much as possible, the Sergeants led the company back toward "Deck Wood" (where long ago the trees had been shattered and burned) and then around toward the remnants of the Tiber farm house where the British front lines had recently been extended. The route lacked duckboards so it was slow going, and Gresham had his boots twice sucked off his feet by the mud as the company traveled through the deep, wet, putrid muck. The Company arrived well after midnight to find other companies of the 27th Battalion already waiting stoically for the morning assault. The men were quiet, not wanting to alert the Germans to the mass of British troops gathering so close to their front lines, but there were plenty of German shells coming nonetheless. The men kept their heads well covered. Because the ground was higher on the ridge, the trenches and shell craters were at least drier, and Gresham found a spot to sit against the shelter of a partial brick wall. As he wrapped his coat around him tightly, he discovered Private

Roberts sitting beside him. Roberts had removed his shrapnel helmet briefly and Gresham was surprised to see that Roberts was much older than he had first guessed, certainly in his thirties and not a boy at all. Roberts was tall and solid and had a face that was grim and sober and weary, but his face was still boyish due to its round shape and wide-set eyes.

"You've been over here long?" Gresham asked him.

"Year and a half, enlisted in '15," Roberts said. "And yourself, Sir?"

"I was in the front lines near here in '14, near Gravenstafel, but I've had to travel around a bit since then – Gallipoli, Salonika, Arabia."

"Oh, yeah? That's a long time."

"Seems like forever," Gresham replied.

"What's it like in Arabia?"

"Damned dry, for one thing, but there's plenty of decent food and it's mostly all hand-to-hand fighting. The Arabs fight with great huge scimitars in close combat, bloody sharp ones."

"Can't be any better than a good bayonet," Roberts opined confidently.

Suddenly the men heard a German shell whistling in their direction and everyone lowered their heads. The shell burst near the line and peppered the remains of the cottage with shrapnel. Someone injured was groaning in the dark. The shells would continue to come around toward the battalion every three or four minutes throughout the night.

"What did you do before the war?" Gresham asked.

"Oh, well, I was railroad engineer for the Alberta-Pacific line."

"The Pacific Ocean?"

Roberts laughed. "Yeah, that one. Doubt I'll ever see it again, 'though."

Gresham took a thoughtful swig of whisky from his hip flask and passed it to Roberts. "So, tell me, are we still going to shell the Huns all night, then sit here in silence for an hour at dawn before we finally get the order to go over the top?"

Roberts chuckled, "nope, we don't do that anymore," he said. "No, we've been using a creeping barrage nowadays, and we're supposed to follow along as close as we dare. Too bad we couldn't get more tanks up here, 'though. Too much mud, I guess."

"And the wires?"

"Oh, we've got these new shells. They're High Explosive with a fuse that detonates when it barely even touches the wires, blows 'em all to Hell."

"Good," Gresham said as he curled up against the bricks. "Keep the flask, if you like," he added. "You need it more than I do."

———————————

Gresham was ready in the early morning darkness when, at 0.600, Passchendaele suddenly exploded. Instead of a scattered barrage upon the

German lines, every one of the ten thousand British guns in the Ypres salient seemed to fire at once. Explosive shells fell all along the ridge with a thunderous blast sending men and mud and stone high into the air. Captain McKinley blew the whistle and ordered his company of the 27th Battalion to advance even as the barrage continued to roll back, and to Gresham's satisfaction the hundreds of men immediately fanned out in a scattered line to rush the village using every object and hollow for cover. Gresham had no intent to become embroiled in the fight, but he drew his handgun and followed behind the much larger Private Roberts. In a moment, the British artillery barrage came to an abrupt stop. The Canadians remained silent and business-like as they scrambled forward, using every dip and hole for cover, and quickly swarmed across the ridge. The German snipers were already busy. Among the attackers, men here and there would suddenly crumble like rag dolls – first their knees would go limp, and then their neck and their arms as they fell face forward into the mud. But there were simply too many men advancing to stop them all.

As they approached the outskirts of Passchendaele, the company became pinned down in a sunken cart path as they approached a German pillbox, this one a covered earthen dugout on a low hill. The German soldiers inside were firing a *Maschinengewehr* machine gun into the mass of attacking Canadians, and a great many men already lay dead or badly wounded and bleeding in the ruined barbed wires in front of the Germans' firing position. Captain McKinley called for volunteers, and Roberts was among five men who stepped forward. They leapt out of the sunken path and raced toward the pillbox as the rest of the company fired together on the Germans' position. The combined firepower of the Canadian attackers was enough to momentarily suppress the German machine gun and the five volunteers were able to scramble forward unscathed. Roberts was the first to reach the broken barbed wire barricades. He leapt over their remains easily and made his way to the rear of the machine gun next. Brandishing his rifle and bayonet, he charged heroically into the pillbox with a great yell. Shots were fired and the machine gun abruptly stopped. Several of the German soldiers suddenly bust out from the back to flee. Roberts emerged from the rear of the pillbox carrying the heavy machine gun in his bare hands. He began firing on the escaping Germans. At Captain McKinley's command, the rest of the Company leapt up and continued toward the village. Roberts led the way with the German machine gun still in his hands for as long as its ammunition lasted. Soon the Battalion, many hundreds of men, swarmed into the village like ants, and the hand-to-hand fighting began, all bayonets and knives, clubs with spikes driven through their heads, and even garrotes, although it was not unusual to see a British and German soldier fighting with bare fists. The Canadians scrambled yard by yard to clear the enemy and to push the defenders further back in order to open a buffer zone between the ridge and the German Fourth Army.

The final, business-like assault on the pile of rubble called Passchendaele only took a few hours.

As Gresham walked carefully amongst the ruined houses and countless Canadian and German corpses, thousands more Canadians climbed the ridge behind him and the preparations against the inevitable German counter-attacks began immediately. Taking ground was not difficult, but keeping it had proven to be the real trick. New trenches were being dug, new wires strung, Lewis guns and mortars put into position. There were a vast number of captured German prisoners, and Gresham scrambled through the village questioning as many as he could before they were taken to various points in the rear: "*Wo ist der Generalquartiermeister?*" He asked. "*Ich schickte ihn zu schützen. Sagen Sie mir, wenn Sie ihn gesehen haben.*" A few of the German soldiers believed that a General had indeed been in the village during the attack, but none knew where he was or if he had been killed.

Time was growing short. The German counter-attack was imminent and even the German artillery had paused to prepare for the vast bombardment that was certain to come. The Canadians, in a state of near panic, were digging in and repositioning both the captured German weapons and their own. The sun was rising high, vaguely visible through the overcast sky, and Gresham began to believe that the German General Quartermaster he sought must have either escaped or been killed in the attack. Suddenly Gresham ran into Private Roberts.

"Roberts, I need your help," he said, "and quickly before the Germans come back down on us. I am looking for a German officer, a General that we believed would be here in the village this morning. Can you help me?"

"I haven't heard of any Generals being captured," Roberts said warily.

"I know, but can you check the bunkers and see if you can find his body at least?"

"Yeah, I can do that," Roberts said. "I'll search south; you go north," he said as he set out to inspect the rubble nearby. Gresham likewise began to search the corpses that he found in the pillboxes and bunkers, but with growing pessimism. Roberts finally came back with nothing to report, and it was just then that they saw a group of men from Roberts' company attempting to dig out a collapsed cellar.

"Digging for gold there, boys?" Roberts shouted to them. "This ain't the damned Yukon, you know. You can't pan for gold in Belgian mud."

"For Christ's sake, Chris, there are men in here. Give us a hand," one of the men shouted back. Gresham and Roberts looked at each other and rushed over. In a few minutes they made a narrow opening into the dark bunker, the cellar of a long destroyed house. Gresham yelled down: "*Sie sind Gefangene der britischen Armee. Widersteht Sie oder kommt Sie heraus friedlich?*"

"*Wir ergeben. Helfen Sie uns raus? Wir haben hier seit letzter Nacht gefangen,*" came the plaintive reply from the dark bunker.

"*Ist der Generalquartiermeister mit dir?*" Gresham demanded.

This question was met with silence.

Finally another more-commanding voice spoke out: "*Ja, ich bin hier.*"

"Hold on, fellas," Gresham said to the digging men. Then he turned to Roberts. "Follow me."

"You got it," Roberts said confidently.

Gresham got down and pushed through the ragged hole into the bunker. He dropped onto the dusty floor of the cellar, and as he got to his feet, Roberts squeezed in behind him, rifle at the ready. In the dim light, Gresham found two German officers and a civilian standing in front of him. "Which of you is the General?" He asked.

A tall, thin man with a square jaw and short, greying brown hair stepped forward, his hands raised. "I am *Generalquartiermeister* Karl von Metzger."

Gresham stepped forward and extended his hand. "*Herr* General, I am Colonel David Gresham, and you are now a prisoner of the British Expeditionary Force." The General shook his hand and then withdrew his sidearm and passed it to Gresham. Gresham took the weapon and continued: "I would like to bring you away as soon as possible, Sir, to prevent the possibility of any harm coming to you during the counter-attack by your countrymen that we expect to come momentarily."

General von Metzger shook his head and laughed in derision. "There will be no counter-attack, Colonel. You see, I am not at my headquarters to order it."

Gresham suddenly realized that the utter silence outside was not a foreshadowing of a great storm to come – instead, the Germans were not coming at all, at least not that day. Beside him, Roberts' became noticeably relaxed. It was tremendous news. He could feel the expression on his face instantly soften.

"These other gentlemen, then? Who are they?" Gresham asked, still all business, as he nodded at the other German officer and the civilian, a short, old, balding gentleman who looked quite excited.

"This is my Aide, *Oberstleutnant* Schiller, and the other man is a former resident of this village whose name I do not know."

"I see,' Gresham said. "Roberts, please bring *Oberstleutnant* Schiller to Captain McKinley for safe-keeping, and then bring the General some food and something to drink, if you would."

"Yes, Sir," Roberts said.

"*Oberstleutnant Schiller, bitte gehen Sie mit dem Privat. Sie werden gut behandelt werden,*" Gresham said to the General's Aide. With some hesitance and the approval of his commanding officer, the Aide finally left with Roberts, allowing Gresham to speak alone to the General and the civilian.

"Do you speak English?" Gresham asked the old Belgian man.

"Yes, some," the man replied quietly as he sat down on a wooden crate.

"Tell me what you were doing here with the General?"

"I believe I can answer that question, Colonel," Metzger said with barely suppressed anger. "It is quite obvious that this man lured me to the village with the promise of tactical information for the sole purpose of entrapping me until your arrival. I have no doubt he is a spy, as you undoubtedly know."

"I regret," the old man replied stoically, "*Generalquartiermeister* von Metzger speaks the truth. My name is Julien Geerts. You will perhaps know me better as seven-naught-seven, *ja?*"

Gresham nodded. "And where were you born, Mister Geerts?"

"Why, in Ealing, Colonel Gresham, of course."

"Very good," Gresham said, accepting the pre-arranged password; Ealing was where the British Secret Intelligence Service headquarters were located. "In any case, I am sorry to tell you, Mister Geerts, that if the General has deduced the truth of his method of capture, then you must assume others will as well. It will not be safe for you to return to occupied-Belgium."

The old man shrugged indifferently. "Oh, that is all as well. I have no reason to stay, Colonel. My wife has been dead for three years, and I wish to join her brother in Paris."

"Then I will arrange for your transportation," Gresham said. "You have performed a tremendous feat in bringing the General to us, Mister Geerts, and I must thank you for that."

"Whether you will thank me or not will depend, I think, on what you do with *Herr Generalquartiermeister* Metzger. Please, sit down gentlemen, I beg. You must speak together. I believe you have a very great deal to discuss."

Gresham turned to consider the General Quartermaster. A General was quite a pleasant prize, and his capture was undoubtedly an accomplishment for the Service, one made possible because of the network of informants and *saboteurs* that the "Circus" (as Gresham had come to think of his superiors in Whitehall Court) had pieced together inside German-occupied Belgium. However, as Wilkins had suggested, Gresham still could not comprehend why he had been personally sent all the way from Copenhagen to interrogate the General. Surely there were others, Cecil Cameron over in Montreuil, for example, who could better interrogate a German General.

"Please sit while we are waiting for refreshments, General," Gresham offered. "After some nourishment, we will proceed to France. Mister Geerts, perhaps you can explain to me why I have been sent here? Although this gentleman is an important commander, it is very unlikely that he will voluntarily share any military or tactical information with us, isn't that right, General?"

"You are correct. I most certainly will not," said the General as he sat on a low stool in dimly-lit cellar.

"And I have been forbidden from beating anything out of him," Gresham continued. The General scoffed at the mere suggestion that he could be tortured for information.

"What is it, precisely, that you believe the General and I have to discuss?" Gresham asked.

Geerts chuckled. "No, no, Colonel, you speak. You decide. He is your prisoner now."

Gresham's curiosity peaked, he asked: "Are you a valuable hostage, General? Are you the bastard son of the Kaiser or something along those lines?"

"Certainly not," Metzger replied coldly, "although I am now as intrigued as you, Colonel, to discover what your Belgian spy believes would justify bringing me to this inglorious end. I have no family of any importance. I have served in the German army for many years, but I was promoted from a lowly rank. I am a mere soldier. I have long served under the direct command of Marshal von Hindenburg, here and on his staff. He is *Ratgeber,* my mentor, you might say. He personally ordered me to protect this sector of our defenses at all costs, but I am in possession of no plans or papers that would be of any use to you." He turned to the old man. "Do I not speak the truth?" He asked.

"Yes, you do, as far as I know," the old man said dismissively. "Tell us, *Herr General,* where were you born?"

"Kiel," he replied.

"Ah, yes, where the great German naval base is located," Geerts stated. "And your brother, he is in the Imperial Navy, is he not?"

"Yes. He is a *Flottillen-admiral,* but of no particular importance."

"So I have learned," Geerts agreed sadly. "But you, you were raised near the naval base, your father was in the navy, and your brother, quite naturally, entered the navy as well. I am certain a great many of your friends and family members have served in the Kaiser's great navy also, *ja?* But why did *you* not enter the Imperial Navy, *Herr General?* Why did you not join them?" Greets asked excitedly.

"I ...," he began, but then a dark scowl spread across his face. "How do you know this?" Metzger demanded.

"What is it?" Gresham asked eagerly. "Why did you not enter the Imperial Navy, General?" He asked.

Metzger glared at Gresham. "It was not permitted. At one time I had been a member of the *SAPD,* the Socialist Worker's Party – that was many years ago, a youthful indiscretion – and for a time the party was banned in Germany. Even after the ban was lifted, the Imperial Navy continued to refuse Socialist party members as officer candidates for many years."

"And in your youth, you were acquainted with Friedrich Ebert, were you not? You are particular friends with the leader of the Social Democratic Party still?" The old man asked.

"Yes, I know *Herr* Ebert very well, we are good friends. He is now a leader of the *Reichstag* and a highly respected member of the government," Metzger replied defensively. "There is no shame in being acquainted with such a man."

Geerts turned and looked at Gresham and raised his eyebrows questioningly.

Gresham had been in Russia earlier that year when Tsar Nicholas II had been removed from the throne and the Socialists and moderates created a Provisional Government in Petrograd. He and Wilkins had conceived of a new alliance between Russia and Great Britain, and Wilkins had nearly perfected a relationship between the British government and a new, democratic Russian government that was to be led by Alexandr Kerensky, a moderate Socialist like Germany's Friedrich Ebert. However, their plans had been undone by an unexpected alliance between Russia's top military leader, Larv Korniloff, and the old monarchists. In order to save Russia from turning into a military dictatorship under General Korniloff, Kerensky had turned in desperation to the even more radical Bolsheviks. Unfortunately for the Allies, the Bolsheviks also viewed France and Great Britain as enemies, enemies for perpetuating the war, and indeed the Bolsheviks were vastly popular among the soldiers of Russia specifically because of their pledge to end the war with Germany. And that, despite the harsh fact that Germany continued to advance further and further into Russian territory and any Russian-German peace accord would come at a very great cost for Russia.

Gresham now wondered how Germany compared. Considering what Wilkins had told him of the state of Imperial Germany, Gresham believed there would be few if any Bolshevik-type radicals in Germany and none in the military. The Deputy Chief of Staff, Ludendorff, and his secret police were surely imprisoning anyone who spoke out against the war. Although Gresham was certain that Germany's soldiers were as fatigued as the Russians (who had utterly refused to fight any longer) and the French (who had mutinied throughout the past summer), there was no indication that the German armies would suddenly cease fighting – at least not unless they were ordered to lay down their arms by their beloved commander-in-chief, Marshal Paul von Hindenburg. But how long would Hindenburg stand by his Kaiser? Was he perhaps another Korniloff in the making? How differently the outcome in Russia would have been if Korniloff had allied himself with Kerensky rather than the Monarchists, Gresham thought.

"General, I have a question," he said at last. "We have now been at war for more than three years. You may reach a peace accord with the new Russian government, but it is becoming quite apparent that you will not conquer France, especially not with the Americans now coming, and your war with Russia is over. So why are the German people still fighting? I'm not talking about the Kaiser, you understand, but the people of Germany. Why do they fight? Is it simply to preserve your Kaiser from disgrace?"

For a moment, General Metzger appeared perplexed by the question. "Why, of course, we are fighting to preserve Germany herself," he said confidently. But Metzger suddenly recalled the day in July three years earlier, before the war, when he and then-Chief of Staff Moltke had met with the Kaiser at *Sanssouci* palace in Potsdam. On that particular day it was most certainly not Germany's (or more specifically the Kaiser's) intention to merely survive the imminent war. What *had been* the Kaiser's intent? And, crucially, was his intent even relevant now that Ludendorff all but ruled over a German empire that had been three years at war?

For Gresham, the General's response was both enlightening and reassuring. Unlike Russia, Germany would not barter land for peace, but then again, why would France or Great Britain want German land or to govern over German people. Regardless of the war's outcome, there would always be a Germany because there would always be a German people, and were those people any less deserving of a self-representative government than the Russians, French, Serbians, Greeks or Arabs? If three years of military stalemate had proven anything to him, Gresham decided, it was that peace would not come from bloody warfare but instead from bloody politics. Peace with Germany was achievable – but not with the German government that currently existed, and of course someone would have to be held responsible for the war.

"If that is Germany's true aim," Gresham continued carefully, "then I believe it is an outcome to which Great Britain and France will eventually agree, under the correct circumstances. By that, I mean, if the German nation was unified under a new government, one that represented the true interests of the German people as you describe them."

"You are speaking hypothetically, Colonel Gresham," Metzger replied dismissively.

"Not so, *Herr General*. You must understand – I am here not as a mere Colonel, but rather as a representative of His Majesty the King's government, and more specifically of the Prime Minister, David Lloyd George. Therefore I will state Great Britain's position to you quite clearly, and as someone who has seen the remarkable developments in Russia during this past year firsthand," Gresham said confidently. "Germany is on a path to ruin; you cannot deny it. Your nation will barely survive this war. But to survive at all, Germany must do so without Kaiser Wilhelm II, as I believe you are all beginning to realize. If he were gone, and if there is to ever be peace, it will be a peace negotiated by your superior, Marshal von Hindenburg, in collaboration with a government leader that represents the people of Germany. But as you must see, it cannot be Ludendorff and it will never be Kaiser Wilhelm. It must be Ebert. Do you understand now why I have been summoned to speak with *you*, General, in particular?"

The old Belgian laughed. "Yes, yes," he cackled.

Metzger felt as if he had been struck by lightning. This young British Colonel had just laid out a narrow pathway to an end of the war, an end to the death and misery, an end with dignity that would preserve the General's beloved Germany. He, *Generalquartiermeister* Karl von Metzger himself, could put Germany on that path because he stood at the intersection of two essential men – his immediate superior, Marshal Paul von Hindenburg, the Army Chief of Staff, and Friedrich Ebert, the leader of the Social Democratic Party and representative of the people of Germany. The mere conception in his own mind of such an alliance made the General's heart race with sudden optimism.

"I understand you quite clearly, Colonel Gresham," he said calmly. "An alliance such as you suggest might be possible, but it would take time and great skill."

"Naturally," Gresham agreed, "but for a man prepared to facilitate such an alliance and with assurances made on behalf of the British Prime Minister, perhaps quite achievable," and then he called for Private Roberts who had been waiting at the entrance to the cellar with food and water. Roberts lowered flasks and packages of food into Gresham's hand, and Gresham offered Geerts and Metzger a simple soldier's meal of biscuits, jam, cheese and tepid water.

"So what shall I do with you, General?" Gresham asked at last. "What would you have me do?"

"If you wish to see an end to the war, Colonel, as I do, then perhaps I am indeed the man who can do what you propose," Metzger replied, "but only if I return to Germany."

"Return to Germany? Perhaps you misunderstand your situation," Gresham said somewhat cruelly. "No, I would have to get you back across these lines into German territory, General, and I am not inclined to do that. At least, not until you and I look each other in the eye and give our personal guarantees, one man to another, that you and I will work to end this bloody nightmare and seek a just peace between our nations. It shall be your duty to forge a relationship between Ebert and Hindenburg that excludes both the Kaiser and Ludendorff, and it will be mine to ensure that your enemies are prepared to negotiate an end to the war with those men. Do you agree?"

Gresham held out his hand. Something about his demeanor made a deep impression upon Metzger – not Gresham's earnestness nor that he would wager his honor upon such a grave matter. No, it was the sense that any deal made with Gresham would be one made with the Devil himself. Metzger knew that if he failed to live up to his agreement, the Devil would exact his revenge.

"I agree," the General said gravely as he reached out and shook Gresham's hand.

Was he mad to return an important German General to Great Britain's enemies, Gresham wondered? Or was that why he was sent to Passchendaele? He had seen something in the General's expression – not honesty or honor, but hope. Would it be so terrible, Gresham wondered, to return a man who wished for peace, someone who could possibly connect two men that could change the path of Germany's destiny? More importantly, Gresham could not think of any other material benefit to imprisoning General Metzger. He would only be replaced by another General, and perhaps by a competent commander who could have succeeded in keeping the Canadians out of Passchendaele.

Of more pragmatic concern, Gresham had twice before crossed the front lines to abduct his enemies, but he had never before helped an enemy to cross back. Although seemingly less difficult, it was essential that General Metzger cross the German front lines without raising suspicion. Most of all, it must be done very quickly, and Gresham nearly wished the Huns would counter-attack and re-take Passchendaele that day so he could simply leave the General there in hiding. With Metzger's knowledge of the German defenses, however, a plan was promptly decided.

"Roberts, get down here," Gresham called out, and then he turned to the old man. "Mister Geerts, I will have you escorted back to Ypres where you will find my colleague, Colonel James Wilkins. He will look after you and arrange your transportation to Paris." He then turned to Roberts, who had squeezed back down into the cellar. "Private, arrange for one of your mates to bring this gentleman back to Ypres. He is not a prisoner and must be well looked after. Then I would appreciate your assistance this evening, if you're willing, but you must keep it strictly off the books."

"I've got no problem with that," Roberts readily agreed.

"Do you know the railway line on our extreme right, the line from Ypres to Roulers?" Gresham asked.

"I know where that is on the maps, yeah, near 'Vienna Cottage' about a mile south of here."

"We must get there as soon as possible."

Geerts was soon on his way back to Ypres, and as the sky darkened into night, Gresham and Roberts escorted General Metzger south along the ridgeline past Tiber House, staying well outside the range of German snipers. It was unclear where the German infantry was now entrenched after their withdrawal from Passchendaele. However, the railway on the British right flank offered a wide path from the British side of the lines to the German, and Metzger knew precisely where the German pillboxes were located.

Gresham and Roberts found the well-defended British trench in view of the shattered railway tracks, and, some hundred yards beyond, was the German-occupied trenches.

"Are you still prepared to release me, Colonel?" Metzger asked.

"I suppose so," Gresham said, and again he wondered if he was making the right decision. "Before I do, though, General, I must make one more thing clear. I realize that you must do your duty, you must return to your command, and I won't ask you to do any less than your position dictates on the field of battle. I trust that you will also seek to develop the alliance we discussed. However, you must also trust me. If you see me or if I contact you in German territory, you must accept that I will be there with our mutual goal in mind, that and only that."

"I accept, because I am quite certain you would not wish to do anything that would undermine me or jeopardize our endeavor," Metzger stated. Gresham understood that the General's statement was also a caution.

"Of course," Gresham replied. "Remember these words: *'The Temple at Heaton Park'*. They are my signature, and whether written by me or spoken by a messenger, you will know that I stand behind them. I *will* be in contact with you."

"Very well," Metzger said shaking Gresham's hand again. "Now tell me what you propose. I cannot very well walk across to the German lines."

"No," Gresham said smiling. "Assume for a moment that you remained hidden in the collapsed bunker in Passchendaele throughout the attack as the

Canadians overran the village. As night came, your Aide informed you that a path was clear, so you both escaped back into the darkness, but well behind enemy lines. You had to avoid the British troops coming up to the ridge, so you were forced to turn south, toward the railway, to find a gap in the lines."

"That is all very well, until I am shot by your soldiers or by my own between our front lines."

"Well, you won't be shot by our side, I assure you. Are there any pillboxes over there?"

"You see there, on the right, that low hill. That is a bunker there."

"Good. Let's find Roberts a costume and pass the word through the lines."

A half hour later, Gresham was ready. As he patiently waited with General Metzger in the deep trench near Vienna Cottage, a sudden cry arose from within the rows of British barb wires in the No Man's Land between them and the Germans. "*Schiessen Sie nicht den Quartiermeister! Nicht Schiessen!*"

A large German officer was struggling left to right, straight toward the German pillbox. "*Schiessen Sie nicht den Quartiermeister!*" He yelled in panic.

The British troops in the trench began shooting at him, and Verey flares were shot into the sky. "*Nicht Schiessen! Schiessen Sie nicht den Quartiermeister!*" The officer yelled to his comrades. Some of the German soldiers stood up on the edge of their trench to see what was happening, and realizing that a German officer was attempting to escape from the British lines began to cheer him on.

Gresham and Metzger immediately set off in another direction over the top of the trench and deep into No Man's Land. They remained low and quiet and made straight for the tracks far to the left of the pillbox and the struggling, shouting German officer. Gresham worked at cutting a path through the British wires while the General crouched behind him. "*Schiessen Sie nicht den Quartiermeister!*" Screamed the German officer. Somehow the British troops were unable to get a decent shot at the man and kept missing.

At last Gresham finished cutting a passage through the wires and clapped Metzger on the shoulder. With a final nod, the General made his way into No Man's Land and carefully worked his way across to the German trenches, as the British continued to shoot at, and consistently miss, the other officer who was pleading with the Germans not to shoot.

"*Bitte, nicht Schiessen!*" The trapped German officer cried one last time, and then suddenly he groaned in agony and collapsed into a shell hole. It seemed the British had finally succeeded in shooting him, and the field grew deathly silent even as Metzger was welcomed back and congratulated by his own troops for his daring escape from the British. Gresham made his way safely back to his own lines and slipped into the trench unseen. Soon the flares would subside, he thought, and then Roberts, in the German uniform, could make his way safely back as well. Thankfully, their comrades in the British trenches had done a very convincing job of barely missing him with every shot.

"There you are at last," Wilkins said. Gresham could not miss the bitterness in his friend's voice. "I am very sorry you felt it necessary to go up the line without me."

Gresham, exhausted and muddy, found Wilkins sitting alone in the bunker in Ypres. He had not been drinking, fortunately, but he still looked dreadful. Gresham was uncertain whether Wilkins was offering an apology or making an accusation, but in either case Gresham had no desire to enflame the situation. "You were in no condition to go, and I believed it was better to let you rest," he said.

"And the General you were sent to fetch, where is he? You sent me a pleasant old Belgian gentleman to entertain, as if I was your social secretary, but now you have returned with no General, I see."

"No. I sent him back to Germany," Gresham explained.

"You did what?" Wilkins asked in utter disbelief. "Are you running your own intelligence service now?"

"Do you really mean to sound so peevish? Listen, James, I understand very well why you have been so upset. It was very unfortunate how things worked out for you and Emma, but in any case, you will have to decide what to do next. Harping on me is not one of your options."

Wilkins looked at Gresham with some embarrassment. His friend had been very tolerant of his drinking, and perhaps that *had* been overdone, but to go up to Passchendaele without him felt like a rejection. "Why did you ask me to come to Belgium and then leave me to sit alone in this bunker with the Canadians?" He asked. "Am I not fit for duty in your opinion?"

"Your fitness is for you to decide, James. I would not have you simply disappear in the meantime, before you are ready. You are needed urgently. The war has gone on too long, and everything is beginning to fall apart. Russia was only the beginning. The war must be finished, and a new world must be built. Whose duty is it to make that happen if not yours and mine?" Gresham asked.

To their surprise, a tall, portly officer in dress uniform and a large handlebar mustache suddenly came down the steps into the dimly-lit bunker. The man seemed out of place, even humorous, until Gresham and Wilkins noticed the man's black and red armband with the letters "APM." He was an Assistant Provost Marshal, and that always meant trouble.

"Can I help you?" Wilkins asked innocently. "You look quite lost."

"Yes, thank you," the Marshall said calmly in a deep voice. "I am looking for two Colonels, one by the name of Gresham and one by the name of Wilkins. You mightn't by any good fortune happen to be those two gentlemen, are you?"

"That depends on who is asking," Gresham said.

"Yes, I see, of course," the Marshall said knowingly. They would not be the first men to try to avoid the military police. "You gentlemen must come with me at once, and if you resist I am to place you under arrest."

"Good heavens, whatever for?" Wilkins demanded.

"That I do not know, but you must come with me immediately. Those are my orders, and yours."

Gresham and Wilkins found themselves swiftly headed back to France in the back of an American-made Oakland sedan. The Assistant Provost Marshall sat silently between them and one Red-Cap, a military policeman, sat with a rifle in the front seat while another drove. They would neither answer questions nor permit Gresham and Wilkins to speak together. Although ominous, it seemed likely the two agents were again being summoned to meet secretly with *Control*, just as they had following their successful raid at the Somme.

After nearly two hours of driving, the sedan pulled into a dark forest outside the village of Saint-Omer in France, and came to a stop before a hidden railroad siding at which a fine private passenger carriage sat waiting alone. Its curtains were drawn tight, and as Wilkins and Gresham exited the sedan they saw dozens of well-armed British soldiers patrolling outside the carriage. Mounting the steps, the Assistant Provost Marshall led the two Colonels to the door and motioned for them to enter.

As they passed through the doorway, other men, important-looking officers, one looked like Field Marshal Haig, were simultaneously departing from the other end of the carriage. Inside, the coach was brightly lit and fine tables and chairs and rugs decorated the open space. There was one man seated upon a richly upholstered leather armchair, an older man with thin, wavy white hair and a thick, bushy grey mustache. Gresham had no idea who the man might be, but Wilkins knew very well and drew himself up rigidly, quickly smoothing his hair and wiping his mouth. "Good evening, Prime Minister," he said.

Gresham quickly looked to Wilkins, who nodded, and then at the old man, their Prime Minister, David Lloyd George.

"Sit down," the P.M. commanded is a voice neither pleasant nor angry.

Gresham and Wilkins sat on the firm wooden seats placed in front of Lloyd George's armchair as he watched them without expression.

"I know you, Mister Wilkins," he said, "but I have not had the pleasure of meeting you, Mister Gresham."

"No, Sir," Gresham said. He and Wilkins, as agents of the Secret Intelligence Service, had been told they were answerable only to their commander, Mansfield Cumming, the man they called *"Control"*, and to the Prime Minister himself. Now they had been brought from Belgium to meet directly with their Prime Minister, and it could only be a very serious and troubling development.

"General Smuts and I are returning from an Allied war council at Rapallo, in Italy; General Foch was there, and Prime Minister Orlando for Italy," Lloyd George began pleasantly enough. "In light of the unfortunate success that the Austro-Hungarians have had at Caporetto, Premier Orlando has been forced to demand General Cadorna's resignation. The Americans also sent a representative, their Chief of Staff, a fellow with the astonishing name of 'Tasker Bliss'." He paused and looked over the two agents seated in front of him.

"Are the Americans being cooperative, Sir?" Wilkins asked to fill the silence.

"Cooperative, yes, I suppose you could say so. However, there are still far too few American soldiers in France. They are under the command of a General named Pershing, who I believe has some experience chasing criminals in Mexico and marching through the Philippine rainforests. We are told that the number of American soldiers will not substantially increase until the spring, and then there will be further training. Unfortunately, President Wilson insists that the American Expeditionary Forces be kept solely under American command, so they will not be placed them directly into our own armies."

"But when will the Americans be prepared to fight?" Wilkins asked.

"It does not appear that the Americans will be prepared to take the offensive until early 1919."

"1919!? Another year!? Good God! What do they think is happening over here?" Wilkins replied.

"Well, a year, yes, that is a very serious problem, more so in light of certain recent events than ever before," Lloyd George said, and then he leaned forward dramatically. *"Have you heard the news from Russia, gentlemen."* To Wilkins and Gresham, this came across clearly as a rather sneering and malicious statement rather than as a question, and they both realized the axe was about to fall.

"No, we have not," Wilkins said quietly as he looked at the carpet.

"There has been another *coup*," Lloyd George said with barely-concealed malice. "The Bolsheviks have taken over Petrograd and Moscow. Kerensky has fled." The Prime Minister pointed down to the coffee table, upon which Wilkins and Gresham saw the New York Times and read:

REVOLUTIONISTS SEIZE PETROGRAD; KERENSKY FLEES; PLEDGE IS GIVEN TO SEEK "AN IMMEDIATE PEACE"

MINISTERS UNDER ARREST
WINTER PALACE IS TAKEN AFTER FIERCE DEFENSE

GIVING LAND TO THE PEASANTS AND CALLING OF CONSTITUENT ASSEMBLY PROMISED.

Petrograd, Nov. 8. - With the aid of the capital's garrison, complete control of Petrograd has been seized by the Bolsheviks headed by Vladimir Lenin, the Radical Socialist leader, and Leon Trotzsky, President of the Central Executive Committee of the Petrograd Council of Workers' and Soldiers' Delegates. Their action has been indorsed by the All-Russia Congress of Worker's Councils. A proclamation has been issued declaring that the Revolutionary Government purposes to negotiate an "immediate democratic peace," to turn the land over to the peasantry, and to convoke the Constituent Assembly. Premier Kerensky has fled....

Wilkins turned white. "Where has Kerensky –?"

"He has fled Petrograd. We have no idea where he is," Lloyd George spat back.

"He must be found –"

"HOW COULD THIS HAVE HAPPENED!?" The Prime Minister demanded angrily. "*Control* assured me that you two had the situation in Petrograd well in hand, that Russia would honor her commitment to Great Britain and France. You said Kerensky was our man and that you, particularly you, Mister Wilkins, had forged an unbreakable alliance with his Provisional Government. You, Mister Gresham, I was told that you had dismantled the Bolshevik's organization, but as of yesterday they have taken over Russia and, by God, they are going to reach terms with Germany and cease fighting on the Eastern Front! Do you appreciate what that means?! Millions more German and Austrian soldiers will take the field in Belgium and France!"

Lloyd George, his face now red, stopped to catch his breath. Wilkins and Gresham had no reply.

"France is exhausted, gentlemen," Lloyd George continued. "Her spirit is broken, and now it appears that we, I mean the British Empire alone, must hold the enemy at bay for at least another twelve months!? Field Marshal Haig has done wonders in the past, but I cannot, with any confidence, tell you it is possible to last another year! France is on the verge of collapse, and the Italians are nearly in a state of rebellion! Good God, gentlemen! What the bloody Hell have you done!?"

"We did all that could be done, Prime Minister," Wilkins replied weakly. "Perhaps if we had not been undermined by the *cabal* of other British agents in Russia, Oliver Locke, for instance, who was pursuing his own agenda at our expense –"

"Locke!?" Lloyd George asked in disbelief. "Do not speak ill of Oliver Locke to me! At least Locke was attempting to restore the Tsar, not pacify vicious radicals. At least we know whose side Tsar Nicholas is on."

Gresham was astonished. "Do you really mean to say that you would have returned the Tsar to power in Russia?" He asked accusingly. "Have you no clue what is going on in Europe, Prime Minister? Have you really no conception of the reasons this war is being fought?"

"Mister Gresham, what Germany has –"

"Germany is not our enemy!" Gresham shouted back furiously. Both Lloyd George and Wilkins were shocked. "For Christ's sake, Prime Minister, men are dying by the millions, people have lost their lives, families, homes, they have made enormous sacrifices, and they are bloody well entitled to know what they are fighting for. You would speak to me of German aggression? No, sir! No! That is what we are fighting *against*! It does not answer what we are fighting *for*, and I tell you only the most just of causes can damn well justify, for even one more day, the unspeakable agony that is being inflicted upon these people. If you cannot tell us clearly and more definitely the *ideals* for which we are fighting, and even more concretely how those ideals are served in each and every theater of war and by each and every military action taken, then God damn you and God damn your fellow Ministers!"

"Colonel Gresham, you are insubordinate!" Lloyd George replied angrily.

"There has never been a more critical moment in this war, Prime Minister, and before any decision is made to fight on or to reach some sort of armistice, before any treaties are signed or further military offenses commenced, you, you personally, had better be damned bloody certain that our nation is behind you. Go to Asquith; go to the Labor Party and the unions. Reach some agreement. We must be clear and unified in our aims, now more than ever. Our people must be certain in our own minds about what we wish to achieve. But I assure you there are things we are *not* fighting for. We are not fighting to annihilate the German people; this is not a war of aggression against Germany. I know Ludendorff and the Kaiser have convinced the German people that we are bent on the destruction of Germany, but you must assure them, and Austria and Turkey as well, that we have no such intent. It is not Germany we wish to destroy, no, but the Kaiser's schemes for military domination, the threat of military domination over any part of Europe. Those are the childish dreams of a handful of men like Kaiser Wilhelm, men who have been handed their limitless powers by remote aristocrats, because of primogeniture and wealth. But this is no longer the medieval era, sir. No, those days are past, and although we did not enter the war with the intent to destroy the imperial dynasties of Germany or Austria-Hungary or any other country, how can we not do so now? You must agree that they are a dangerous anachronism. Would not the adoption of a democratic constitution by Germany and expulsion of the Kaiser be the most convincing evidence that her antiquated, militaristic spirit is dead? Would such an action not make it easier for us, indeed necessitate, that we conclude a peace agreement with Germany?

"Of course we joined this war as a matter of self-defense, in defense of the principles of justice, in defense of the independence of countries like Belgium, Serbia, Roumania and Greece. How could we *not* have joined this fight and stood idly by as military might and brute force overwhelmed the rights of these people, these nations, to exist. But now we must give these people their nationhood. That is what rallied our people to war, Prime Minister. We have all seen Lord Lansdowne's demand in the newspapers that you spell out our true intentions, to at least state why we are fighting. It is about time that you offered a reply. I ask you, Prime Minister, will Belgium, Serbia, and Roumania be restored? Will those people be given the chance to determine their own destinies, their own governments and to maintain their own borders without foreign interference? What about the Germans and Austrians? And what shall you say for the smaller nationalities within their borders: Will the Armenians, Poles, Czechs, Slovaks, and Slavs be given the opportunity for self-rule, or are we to continue writing their maps and laws for them? Shall Arabia be a free and independent nation as you have promised the Arabs, or will Great Britain and France divvy up their lands as mere spoils of war? I tell you, it is only by the consent of all these people, in every one of these nations, that any kind of peace will found, and once the maps are drawn, there must be a concrete expectation that their governments and their borders will be respected. Those are the things we are fighting for."

Wilkins had always thought of Gresham as a poorly educated albeit clever brute, yet his friend and colleague had just placed his finger upon the very great matter that must finally be addressed – the purpose and eventual outcome of the war.

Lloyd George was stunned to silence for he was not accustomed to being so roundly challenged by any subordinate, and his immediate reaction bent toward outrage. His face had become bright red and he was preparing to explode when, suddenly, Wilkin withdrew a printed pamphlet from his jacket pocket and held it out to the Prime Minister. Startled, Lloyd George looked down at the pamphlet and took it in his hand. It was the printed text of a speech, one given by General Smuts at a banquet in London the previous summer. It was a troublesome speech the Prime Minister had heard a very great deal about from Smuts himself during their recent trip to Rapallo and from many members of Parliament. It was a speech entitled "The British Commonwealth of Nations", and in it, Smuts had foretold the fate of the British Empire itself.

"These same questions loom large with respect to our own Empire, Prime Minister," Wilkins stated accusingly. "This speech is all the Canadian officers at Ypres were talking about. Europe is not so large as it once was. When the time comes for peace, these ideals for which we fight will not apply to Europe alone, but to the whole world and to the British Empire herself. Of course, to even call us an 'Empire' anymore is misleading because it makes people think we are one single entity, but we are truly an Empire no longer; we are a community of nations with a common flag. The Crown Colonies and Protectorates and Dominions are almost sovereign, they are almost independent, they govern themselves and they are growing to become great nations in their own right. The British Empire is as near extinction as the Romanovs, Ottomans and Hapsburgs."

Lloyd George was extraordinarily angry, yet he kept his mouth shut. He stood and approached a table to pour a whiskey and found his hands were trembling. After a great long pause, he at last turned to face the young agents.

"I will not have you peddling your Socialist philosophies around Europe any further or speaking in my name to any foreign officials. You, Mister Gresham, will go to Paris and you will remain there to report on any matters that might tend to undermine the security of the French government, until I say otherwise. You, Mister Wilkins will go to Rome and report on matters pertaining to the Italian government there. That is *all* you will do. You are dismissed, and I very much hope to see neither of you ever again." He turned his back and put his glass down heavily on the table with a bang, as Gresham and Wilkins stood and exited the carriage silently.

Outside, Gresham and Wilkins sat and waited for the transports that would take them away to Paris and Rome. Then they shook hands and patted each other on the back and said farewell with deep regret, for it seemed they were unlikely to see each other again before the bitter end of an endless war.

Rome

The café overlooking the bustling *Piazza della Rotonda* was warm and quiet, and Wilkins had a stack of Italian newspapers to keep him occupied for at least another hour. There was little otherwise for him to do in Rome. The intelligence chief of the Adriatic region, "*H*", was in Venice, but British Ambassador Rodd and a host of Foreign Service men in Rome already reported regularly to Prime Minister Lloyd George on the state of Italy's government. Wilkins merely read the newspapers and attempted to peel away the dense layers of propaganda, often finding, as with an onion, that there lay no kernel of truth within. It was a monumentally pointless task, and Wilkins had already begun to consider whether he should contact his father to request a transfer to the Foreign Service or just return to England to attend university, although neither option held much interest for him. Either way, Wilkins' active participation in the war appeared to have concluded, and he wore his Colonel's uniform only to avoid questions from the locals.

After arriving in Rome, Wilkins had decided to forego the usual hotels and took a private apartment in the *Piazza di Spagna*, near the "Spanish Steps." He lay off drinking at last and spent a significant part of each day walking briskly through the gardens of the *Villa Borghese* to clear his mind. He had begun to feel decidedly sober and ached to rejoin the fight. Most days, however, the winter rains limited his activities and kept him in his flat. Then, for a change of scenery, he would walk to the Pantheon and sit at one of the cafes for several hours at a time. He made no attempt to reach out to friends or colleagues in the city. This was, he admitted, due to his embarrassment at having been sent to Italy for no good reason at all, quite obviously as a punishment. More importantly, he had begun to sense that he was no longer the boy he had been before the war, although who or what he was becoming, he still did not know.

Away from Rome, the war continued, but since Italy's stunning defeat at Caporetto, the Italian populace had become grave about their prospects and began to question whether Italy should continue to fight in the war at all. Roumania had recently signed an armistice with the Central Power that ceded vast territories to Austria and permitted the German Army to continue occupying the country. Hostilities on the Eastern Front had completely ceased as the Russians prepared to discuss peace terms with Germany. The only bright news as far as Wilkins could see was the British Army's capture of Jerusalem, but then General Allenby's ultimate objective, Damascus, still remained many hundreds of miles away.

After his luncheon, when the rains had abated, Wilkins collected his newspapers and strolled across the *Piazza*. He entered a small, dim and cluttered shop on the *Via del Seminario*. Gleaming clocks and mechanical toys filled the crowded shelves and floor, and an old, short, and very well-rounded shopkeeper sat on a stool at the counter busily examining the interior of a gold pocket watch with his loupe.

"*Signore* Abato, how are you today?" Wilkins asked.

The old man put down his eyepiece and looked up at his visitor. "Ah, *Colonello* Wilkins, good day to you, sir."

"I wonder whether you have finished the repairs to my trench watch."

"Yes, of course, it was only a little moisture inside. You must try to keep it dry," he said as he brought the heavy wristwatch and new leather wrist strap for Wilkins to examine. The Zenith gleamed.

"I say, you are a marvel, *Signore* Abato. I was certain it was destroyed, but it looks as good as new. You are a splendid craftsman."

"Not at all, not at all, *Colonello*, the watch, it is nothing. But if you will allow me, I can show you some very interesting items, *sì?* This music box, for example," he said as he reached onto a shelf and handed Wilkins a very small black lacquered box. As Wilkins opened the lid, not one but three miniature dancers began to waltz to the music of Strauss.

"I have never heard such beautiful sound from a music box, *Signore* Abato," Wilkins said in genuine amazement. "Nor have I seen a music box with three such distinct figures moving so independently, even their arms and fingers and their facial expressions. The mechanism is astonishing, and in such miniature. You made it?"

"Yes, a trinket, I make many such little things." Abato replied modestly.

"Please, may I purchase it as a Christmas gift for my mother?"

"Certainly, yes, and thank you, sir," the craftsman replied happily. "Here is something else. As an officer, you must carry very important papers, yes? Take a look at this," he said as he handed Wilkins a lovely, etched-silver cigarette case. Wilkins examined it but could see nothing especially interesting about the case.

"I don't understand," he said at last.

"Exactly," Abato said as he took the case back. "But see here," he said demonstrating, "if I press on the hinges just so, the back of the case opens to reveal the secret compartment."

"*Meravigliosa,*" Wilkins replied. "How very clever. I'm sorry to tell you that I have no important papers to carry, but I shall keep it in mind. Thank you for showing it to me, *Signore* Abato. As to the music box, though, how much do you ask?"

As Wilkins exited the shop with his wristwatch and the new music box to return to his flat, the ground suddenly shook and the noise of a huge explosion echoed down the narrow street. The sound was confusing – Wilkins felt he had been somehow transported back to Ypres. Then all at once the incongruity of the explosion in the midst of central Rome struck him, and he ran excitedly toward the sound, past the *Trevi* fountain, and soon discovered the smoking carcass of a sedan just outside the fashionable *Hôtel Regina*.

"Qualcuno è stato ucciso? Cui automobile era quello?" He asked of those watching nearby. One man, the apparent bomber, had been killed, and his charred and shattered corpse lay in pieces on the street beside the burning automobile. The sedan appeared to be empty, the intended passengers having perhaps not yet exited the hotel. Wilkins could also smell the distinctive residue of the unusual explosive used within the bomb. It was Dunnite, a high explosive used in older naval artillery shells.

Wilkins circumnavigated the debris and entered the hotel lobby uncertain what he would discover there. Broken glass had showered the marble parquet floor and the grand front doors had been badly damaged. The hotel staff was already sweeping up the debris; the guests, including any possible targets, had long been evacuated. Who could the target have been? Wilkins wondered.

"Chi era l'obiettivo? Sapete?" He asked a young porter.

"No, no, ma forse era per il signor Beneš? Egli è il politico ungherese, che ha ordinato l'automobile," was the reply.

So the target was a Hungarian, a politician named Benesh, it seemed. But why would a bomb, one loaded with Dunnite of all things, be needed to kill a Hungarian politician in Italy? Wilkins wondered. If Benesh was a threat to Italy, a spy, the Italian authorities would simply arrest him. And if the assassin was not Italian, who else would want to kill the Hungarian? Wilkins went to the front desk. He wrote a brief note to Mister Benesh on his card and left his address. Unfortunately, there was nothing else to be done, and so Wilkins returned to his flat unsatisfied.

The rest of his day was equally unproductive, but Wilkins' modest home was quite comfortable, bright and warm, and very quiet. He had been desperately seeking a new Victrola, but they were difficult to find. With a small glass of wine, he spent the evening reading Somerset Maugham's latest novel. Then, near midnight, he heard a gentle knock upon his door. Wilkins tied his robe and went to see who was there.

"Good Lord!" He exclaimed. "Alexander, what a surprise!" On his doorstep, all alone, was the Prince Regent of Serbia, Alexander, whom Wilkins had assisted two years earlier during his mission there. Wilkins had gotten on well with the modest Prince, but they had not seen each other since Wilkins and Gresham had left the island of Corfu.

"So it *is* you, after all," Alexander replied with a broad smile. "I am delighted to find you in Rome, James," he said extending his hand.

"Please, do come in, your majesty," Wilkins said, shaking the Prince's hand. "May I offer you something, a whiskey perhaps?"

"Yes, thank you," Alexander said as he entered, "whiskey would be most welcome." Alexander removed his overcoat. He was dressed in a simple brown wool suit rather than his customary Serbian uniform, but he looked quite spruce. He wore a *pince-nez* and kept his mustache neat and thin. "What has brought you to Rome, James?" He inquired casually as he sat.

"Not very much, to be honest," Wilkins replied. "It seems I am to be stationed here for the duration, but I am doing very little. How are you and your father, and what is going on in Serbia, if I may ask?"

"We are well, and we are making some progress, yes, thank you, although it is very, very slow. Perhaps you heard: The French General at Salonika has been replaced. I am not at all disappointed to see him go, although I do not blame him alone for allowing Serbia to remain in the hands of the Austrians and Bulgars for so long. And as for the new French commander, well, we shall see."

"However did you find me?" Wilkins asked as he passed a glass and sat across from Alexander.

"I did not know you were here until just today, James. You left your card for my colleague, Edvard Benesh."

"Oh, of course," Wilkins remarked with surprise. "You got my address from Benesh. Strictly speaking, this business with the bombing is quite outside my jurisdiction, but I was so astonished that anyone would attempt to bomb a Hungarian politician in Rome that my curiosity got the better of me. Is Mister Benesh a spy?"

Alexander laughed. "No, no, not at all, he is among a great many Hungarian politicians who have gone into exile. Benesh is Czech; he is among those working for the eventual partition of Austria-Hungary after the war and is seeking support for the creation of a new Czech and Slovak nation, one independent of the Hapsburg crown."

"With all due respect, are not such plans premature?"

"Oh, no, I hardly think so, James. It is certainly possible that our plans will come to naught, but is it not better to be prepared should the Austrian empire suddenly crumble? Emperor Franz Joseph is dead, and Charles has proven himself unprepared for the crown. Many factions are beginning to voice their discontent and to make their alliances."

"That includes you and King Peter?"

"Certainly, as it must. This summer we reached an agreement with the Croats regarding the formation of a new nation to encompass the current states of Serbia, Bosnia, and Croatia; "*Yugoslavia,*" it shall be called. We are also meeting with a Slovene politician from Trieste. Indeed, that is one of the reasons I am here in Rome: The Italian government has its own intentions regarding Trieste and our "Yugoslavia Declaration" last July has been met with stiff resistance by the Italian government."

"Yes, I understand that Italy has long desired to possess Trieste. However, I would think that the Italian Prime Minister, Orlando, would be more agreeable to your Slavic federation now, after Italy's great loss at Caporetto, than he would have been from a more victorious position."

"We do hope so, yes, but the Italians are as always apprehensive about where their borders will lie. That is why we have invited Edvard Benesh and his colleague, General Milan Shtefanik to meet. Shtefanik is a Slovak currently serving in the French army. The *Yugoslav Committee* intends to express its support for the formation of a Czech-Slovak nation as well our own, and we hope to show Prime Minister Orlando that all these confederations, these plans for a final, mutually-agreed disposition of the Balkan and Austrian territories, are in Italy's best military and diplomatic interests."

"Very clever," Wilkins agreed.

"However, the bombing today, it has made us very apprehensive."

"I dare say so. You have no idea, then, who might have done it?"

"None at all. The assassin could not be identified, as you no doubt could see for yourself. We fear he will never be identified."

"But you believe the bomber might have been an Italian?"

"Precisely, although whether he was sent by the Italian government or some nationalist faction, I could not begin to speculate. Politics in Italy are difficult to unravel nowadays. There is a new group, the *Fascisti*, is well known to use violence and strong arm diplomacies. If the assassin was sent by the Italian government, however, then our situation in Rome is made far more difficult."

"Of course," Wilkins replied thoughtfully. "Unfortunately, as I mentioned, such matters are well beyond my purview."

Alexander stood and walked to the window slowly. "The British government has been extremely supportive of our plans for a unified *Yugoslavia*, James," he said, "but we do not yet know their opinion regarding the proposed Czech-Slovak state. We have had meetings with Wickham Steed, he is a British journalist who claims to represent your government, and with another gentleman from your War Cabinet. But we do not yet know who our allies are, who we can trust, especially within Italy. Unfortunately, that makes it impossible for us conduct our own inquiries concerning today's assassination attempt. Still, we must have an answer, do you see?" He asked, turning to look Wilkins in the eye.

"Of course," Wilkins replied. How revealing, Wilkins thought, that no one had bothered to tell him about the meetings involving the British representatives. Clearly his superiors had decided to brush him off to the margins for good.

"However, I do trust *you*, James," Alexander said questioningly.

Wilkins finally understood why the Prince had come to his flat. "Do you have any reason to suspect that the assassin was British?" He asked bluntly.

"None at all."

"If I was to investigate this matter for you and discover that the assassin was British, or was sent by the Italian government, you understand it would place me in a very difficult position, since Italy is Great Britain's ally. However, I don't mind asking a few questions, and I have plenty of time on my hands. You must understand that I cannot guarantee I will provide you with an answer to your query, even if I do find out who was behind it."

"Should it come to that," Alexander replied. "But I understand and agree with your conditions."

"Very well," Wilkins agreed. "Have you any clues?"

"No."

"I believe that Dunnite was used as the explosive, and that is very curious because it is a rare compound and difficult to obtain."

"The corpse and debris were removed quite quickly, so there is no way to confirm that Dunnite was used."

"Who was sent to investigate – the Carabinieri?"

"No, the Polizia di Stato."

"Then it would seem the Italians are not serious about finding whoever is responsible. The Carabinieri are the only ones who genuinely investigate crimes. However, I will go to the police station in the morning and see what they have learned. May I speak with Mr. Steed, as well, if you can arrange it?"

"Certainly; I can arrange a luncheon tomorrow."

"Don't give him my real name, though. Tell him my name is something else. 'Bell', maybe, 'James Bell'. Can you do that?"

"Indeed, I would be most happy to do so," Alexander said gratefully. "Thank you, James. I am very pleased to have found you in Rome."

The next morning, Wilkins went to the office of the *Polizia*, but there was little to be learned. The police lieutenant informed him that the body of the assassin had already been released to the sanitation department for burial. "And his personal effects – clothes and so forth, where are they?" Wilkins asked in Italian.

"*Signore*, those were collected last night by a high official from the Polizia di Stato."

"Did that official have credentials, papers?"

"I am quite certain he must have, yes, but I was not here at the time."

"Can you tell me anything about the personal effects? Were there any identifying papers?"

"No, *Signore*. The man had no papers and was badly burned; his clothes were tailored and his shoes were hand-made; there were no labels. He did wear a silver pin on his lapel that I noticed – it was a broadsword, pointed downward, and on top of that was a cross, but the arms of the cross were bent clockwise in order to form a circle – no one could identify it."

"Draw me a picture of that pin, please, if you would. Will the police be conducting any further investigation?"

"Why should we do so? The perpetrator is dead."

Wilkins took his policeman's drawing and then went to the telex office to wire "*H*" in Venice. He asked only about the Dunnite used in the bombing. Dunnite was a very stable explosive, but one that Wilkins knew was now rarely available. It was still utilized to some extent by the American navy but had mostly been replaced by other compounds. Still, there were sure to be caches of old Dunnite armaments stored in various places around the world, even in Rome, and many had likely been forgotten and plundered. Such old munitions would lack stability, and that would explain the untimely explosion that had killed the would-be assassin.

Wilkins had to rush to get to his luncheon with Wickham Steed at the *Café Colonna*. Wilkins knew something of Steed: He was a liberal (some thought Socialist) journalist and a notorious anti-Semite who despised Germany and had long called for the dissolution of Hungary. He had clearly not been sent to implement policy so much as to report on any developments among the Hungarian exiles meeting in Rome.   Currently Steed worked for Lord Northcliffe at *The Times* in London, and he was surely acquainted with Wilkins' father, Lord Bartlett, so Wilkins had decided it would be safer to conduct his investigation henceforth under the assumed name of "Bell."

Wilkins found Steed seated at a small table in the back of the café when he arrived. "A pleasure to meet you, Mister Steed. I am Colonel James Bell," he introduced himself.

Steed stood to shake his hand. He was tall and lanky with a neatly trimmed grey beard and mustache. "Certainly, Colonel Bell," he replied in a deep, authoritative voice. "The Prince Regent explained to me that our meeting was most urgent. May we order first? I haven't much time, I'm afraid."

After they had done so, Wilkins returned to the matter of the attempted assassination. "Have you any thoughts about who the bomber might have been?" He asked.

"If I may inquire, Colonel, why are you conducting this investigation?" Steed asked haughtily. "Would it not be more prudent to let the question go unanswered? The bomber was either an enemy or an ally, and if the latter, then surely it would not be in our interest, I mean in Great Britain's interest, to uncover that fact, and so the matter should be left alone. Indeed, those were the very instructions I received this morning."

"I understand completely. However, my concern is not with the identity of the bomber. The military intelligence office has asked me to determine the source of the munitions used in the bomb, the Dunnite that was used, to be precise," Wilkins lied. "I know it seems a small matter, but I must do my job, sir, and it is my responsibility to see to it that all such explosives are confiscated. We must do everything we can to prevent further bombings in Rome, you understand."

"I see," Steed replied uncertainly. "I know very little about explosives, Colonel, but our negotiations are at a very delicate stage, and I believe it would be preferable if your inquiries could be postponed for a time."

"But imagine if the bomber's accomplices were to strike again, Mister Steed! Your negotiations would be most seriously affected then, wouldn't you agree? You will recall that the first attempt on Archduke Franz Ferdinand's life was also unsuccessful. Why do you not simply tell me what you know, and then we will determine how best to handle that information in light of the delicacies of the situation."

"As you wish, Colonel," said Steed relenting. "You see, all of the current discussions regarding the eventual disposition of Eastern Europe and the Balkans are bound together. I am meeting with Serbian officials as well as pro-

Serbian and Slovene factions from the Croatian and Bosnian territories of Austria, Bulgaria, Macedonia, and Albania. I am meeting with representatives from Roumania and the Czech and Slovak territories of Hungary, and Hungarians now in exile. These representatives, who call their confederation the 'Congress of Oppressed Nations', are currently cultivating a mutual recognition of their proposed nation-states, and they hope by such *bona fides* to also obtain recognition from the Western European nations and Americans."

"It is easy to imagine that such a coalition would have many enemies, including Austria, Italy, Russia, and the Turks. But why was Edvard Benesh the target of this particular assassination attempt, do you think?"

"Apparently Benesh called for the sedan but he was expected to depart with three other men, so it is not clear that he was the intended target," Steed said. "These are the names of the other men," he said jotting them down and handing Wilkins a sheet of note paper.

Wilkins read the names of a Roumanian politician he did not know, the Czech General Shtefanik, and Robert Seton-Watson. "Who is Seton-Watson?" He asked.

"He was sent by one of our intelligence services to produce *propaganda* news articles in Italy. The Austrians are publishing dozens of newspapers here, and they have all condemned the *Yugoslav* declaration of this past July. Seton-Watson will be publishing our own version of those events to the Italians in order to sway them in favor of the proposal."

Wilkins didn't know Seton-Watson but was glad he had chosen to provide the false name "Bell" to Steed lest word get back to Wilkins' own superiors that he was conducting an unauthorized investigation. He withdrew from his jacket pocket the drawing he had obtained from the police – a rough sketch of a broadsword, point down, beneath a cross with arms bent clockwise to form a circle. "Incidentally, have you ever seen this sort of an emblem?" He asked as he showed the paper to Steed.

"That is familiar, yes. Now where have I seen that?" Steed wondered aloud. "Ah yes, a fellow at the Vatican I met some weeks ago, I believe, wore something like this. I meant to ask him about it, but I suppose I forgot to do so."

"Is it a Vatican emblem, then?" Wilkins asked with concern.

"Oh no, I don't believe so. A Monsignor that I met in the papal libraries was wearing it, but I have not seen it anywhere else. I'm afraid I don't recall his name. But you can't believe this has anything to do with the bombing, can you? The Vatican has been extremely circumspect since the incident with Monsignor Gerlach."

"Gerlach? I know nothing of that. Who is he?"

"Gerlach was Pope Benedict's chamberlain and confidant, a Monsignor originally from Germany, serving in the Vatican. He was caught red-handed transferring cash payments from Germany to various Italian journalists in order to influence their politics – they were paid to advocate Italian neutrality at the beginning of the war. The whole lot of them was rounded up, and after their conviction on charges of treason and espionage this past summer, most of Gerlach's accomplices were executed. Gerlach himself fled to Switzerland before the trial, some say with the Pope's assistance, and there was another fellow by the name of Ambrogetti, an art dealer for the Vatican, who was caught up in the scheme somehow, but I don't believe he ever served a day in prison. It was all terribly embarrassing for the Pope, and he has strived ever since to maintain the Vatican's neutrality on the conduct of the war."

Wilkins perked up at the mention of Ambrogetti. Before he had travelled through Italy a year earlier, Wilkins' superiors had given him the name of Giuseppe Ambrogetti, ostensibly a purchaser of fine art for the Vatican, who was in fact an agent of the "Holy Alliance," the Vatican's own spy agency based in Rome.

That evening, Wilkins stopped by the office of the popular daily newspaper *Il Messaggero* to learn more about the Gerlach affair. Ambrogetti, it seemed, was being protected by the Vatican. He claimed he had also been investigating Gerlach before the Italians arrested him.

The next morning, Wilkins returned to the shop of *Signore* Abato, the watchmaker.

"*Buongiorno, Colonello,* how are you today," said the cherubic old man. "Your watch is still operating perfectly, I hope?"

"Yes, both the watch and I are well, thank you, sir. I am wondering whether it would be possible for you to fabricate a lapel pin for me, something of my own design."

"Of course, I would be delighted," Abato said. "I often manufacture the *gingillo* of this kind."

"Have you ever seen a pin like this?" Wilkins asked as he produced the drawing. Looking at it again, Wilkins had to admit that it did seem familiar, and he scratched his memory to think where he had perhaps seen it before – not in Italy, surely.

"No, I have not, *Colonello,* but it would be no trouble at all for me to make this for you."

"I am delighted to hear it. Please make it in silver, and as soon as possible. I was also considering your wonderful cigarette case, and please forgive my question, *Signore,* if it offends you, but suppose I wished to conceal a weapon on my person, so that by all accounts I appeared unarmed; I have of course seen a sword disguised in a walking stick, but I am not in need of a cane. Have you any other thoughts along those lines?"

"Oh, *sì, sì, Colonello,* wait and I will show you something," Abato replied excitedly as he shot into the back of his shop for a moment. He returned promptly with a rather long, silver-plated box-frame belt buckle. "What do you think that is?" Abato asked gleefully.

"It appears to be a belt buckle, *Signore,*" Wilkins said, playing along.

"Ah, *sì*, but look," Abato said. As he pressed on the top and bottom of the buckle, one end popped out slightly, just enough for Abato's delicate fingers to withdraw from the buckle a short but wide and extremely sharp steel knife.

"Good Lord!" Wilkins exclaimed. "*Signore* Abato, you are a magician."

"Yes, in the evenings, I perform for the children. How did you know, *Colonello*?"

"Have you done any work with pistols, *Signore*?"

"Oh, *sì*, many repairs," Abato replied, trying to sound modest.

"I was thinking, could you perhaps build a pistol into a cigarette case, something discrete and hidden? And what could you do with this?" Wilkins asked excitedly as he placed his gold Montegrappa fountain pen on the counter. "And maybe a garrotte of some kind, and luggage with secret compartments?"

Abatto laughed and winked at Wilkins. "Come back tomorrow, my friend. I will give this all some thought. Give me some time to work and I will show you something tomorrow."

By the time Wilkins returned home that afternoon a wire had arrived from "*H*" in Venice. It seemed that Dunnite was indeed extremely rare in Italy, so rare that he could only recall one other instance in which it had been used in a bombing: Dunnite had been the explosive used to sink the Italian dreadnought *Leonardo de Vinci* at anchor in Taranto the previous year. At the time, Wilkins' colleagues (Gresham in particular) thought that the German Foreign Ministry agent Dunn had been responsible for that act of *sabotage*, but perhaps it was someone else, someone still at large? The only other suspect thus far, *H* reported, was a Trentino adventuress named "Ida Clementi" who was believed to have Austrian sympathies. Clementi had inexplicably been in the captain's quarters aboard the *Leonardo de Vinci* and had disembarked just seconds before the dreadnought exploded. Furthermore, once she discovered that she was under investigation, Clementi had fled from Italy, *H* reported. Was she perhaps a member of an organization of *saboteurs*?

The next morning Wilkins dressed in civilian clothes and went out to collect his new lapel pin from *Signore* Abato as well as the ingenious belt buckle, a new silver cigar case (complete with cigars), a steel flask, and his subtly modified Montegrappa pen; the luggage, it seemed, would take a few additional days. Thus "armed" and adorned with the provocative lapel pin, Wilkins walked across the river to the Vatican. He hoped to wander through St. Peter's and the art galleries of the Papal palace to see whether anyone would take note of the unusual lapel pin. However, after a full day browsing the galleries, no one remarked upon it, nor did he see anywhere a lapel pin even remotely like it.

At the end of the long day, Wilkins removed the reproduced lapel pin and stopped off at the nearby *Caffe Greco*. He had sent a message to *Signore* Ambrogetti asking to meet there about the potential sale of a very precious work of art to the Vatican and was gratified to find the respectable, well-dress young gentleman eagerly awaiting Wilkins at a small, empty table.

"Mister Ambrogetti, thank you for coming," Wilkins said in Italian as he sat.

"The pleasure is all mine, sir. Naturally, I was made very curious by your note. May I ask who it is that you represent?"

"I represent myself, Mister Ambrogetti, only myself. As for the painting I wish to sell, it is by Giambattista Tiepol." Ambrogetti sat up sharply and his smile disappeared instantly once he heard the British agent's passphrase.

"I understand," he said unhappily. "From the Udine period, is it?"

"Indeed, *'Death of the Hyacinth'*."

"Very well," he replied gravely. "What do you wish of me?"

"Mister Ambrogetti, I understand your role in the 'Gerlach' matter quite clearly. It is very unfortunate that you became embroiled in the affair; it was truly unlucky and you have my most sincere sympathy. Indeed, I suspect you are no longer an active agent, am I right? However, it is only about Monsignor Gerlach that I wish to obtain information. Specifically, were you ever able to discover the identity of the person for whom Gerlach worked and have you any idea of Gerlach's current whereabouts?" Wilkins asked.

Ambrogetti sat up stiffly. "Thank you for your sympathy, Mister ...."

"Bell."

"Certainly, Mister Bell, I have no idea of Monsignor Gerlach's current whereabouts. I only know that he was taken to Geneva by members of the Swiss Guard at Pope Benedict's personal request. They were friends, you see, and I believe the Pope felt it would be a sufficient punishment for Gerlach to be cast out from God's grace and from the Church for his crimes. Prior to his departure, however, we had learned that Gerlach had been working for a German spymaster named Koertiger who lives in Geneva."

"Was Gerlach ever implicated in the sinking of the battleship Leonardo Da Vinci last year?"

"No, not at all, to my knowledge."

"And did you ever see *Signore* Gerlach, or anyone else for that matter, wear a lapel pin like this one?" Wilkins asked as he produced the reproduction from his pocket.

"Not Gerlach, no, but I have seen this pin before. Monsignor Lerbingen, who now works in the Vatican library, wears one like it. But I can tell you he did not arrive in Rome until well after Gerlach had already gone."

"I see," Wilkins replied in disappointment.

"But I believe Lerbingen and Gerlach are both from Bavaria. Lerbingen, I am certain, is from Munich."

Wilkins heart leapt suddenly as he recalled where he had seen the assassin's lapel pin before. He had seen it in Munich, outside the *Hotel Vier Jahreszeiten*. Wilkins recalled his brief sojourn in Munich early the previous year. His first evening he had seen a mass of well dressed, passionate German soldiers entering the hotel for an event of some sort; the soldiers were singing about Germany's great supremacy and generally abusing passersby. The soldiers all wore lapel pins just like this one, Wilkins now recalled. Perhaps it was the emblem of an elite German fraternity in Munich. If the bomber who had sought to kill Benesh wore this pin, then surely that man was himself a German from Munich, there could be no doubt of that, and perhaps he worked for Monsignor Lerbingen, who had been sent to replace Gerlach.

"I thank you most heartily for the information, Mister Ambrogetti. And if I may add, I suggest the Vatican keep a very close watch on Monsignor Lerbingen."

"Oh but we have, *Signore* Bell," Ambrogetti insisted, "a very close watch and a very thorough examination of his background, I assure you. Monsignor Lerbingen is the most innocent of men. He has met with no one. He has not even gone outside the Leonine walls since he arrived at the Vatican from Spain seven months ago."

If that was true, then perhaps the bomber did not work for Lerbingen after all, Wilkins concluded. But who, then, did he work for? Germany surely had more than one spy in Italy. There must be someone else, someone who had access to Dunnite explosives and who also reported to *Herr* Koertiger, the German spymaster in Geneva.

Wilkins sent a brief note to Prince Regent Alexander that evening to assure him that the deceased assassin was most likely a German spy. To continue his investigation, however, Wilkins decided he had no other option than to travel to Geneva to investigate Koertiger, and since Wilkins had no particular duties in Rome, he believed there would be no difficulty in his departing for a week, two at the most.

Dressed elegantly in white tie and tails, cleanly shaven, his fine light brown hair lightly oiled, Wilkins rose from his chair at the *Baccarat* table. A vast horde of gleaming mother-of-pearl gambling chips obscured the dark green felt before him. He bowed quite formally to the beautiful woman who had come to stand beside *Herr* Koertiger. The alleged German spymaster was seated at the other end of the *Baccarat* table. The woman now standing beside him was very beautiful, a number of years older than Wilkins, but with clear olive skin, long, black hair, high cheek bones, and a wide, inviting mouth; her pale blue evening gown complemented her blue oval eyes. She stood in stark contrast to Koertiger himself, a severe, older gentleman with a neatly groomed white beard and small, beady eyes.

Koertiger, it had turned out, was well known in Geneva, and Wilkins remained in that city only long enough to learn that the German "diplomat" had recently traveled to Lausanne for an extended holiday. Wilkins followed and soon found Koertiger staying over at the *Alexandra Hotel* in Lausanne, although he spent most evenings either at the *Kursaal Theatre* or in the garish new municipal casino, which is where Wilkins had found him.

"Good evening, *mademoiselle*," Wilkins said to the young woman standing beside Koertiger. "Would you care to join us? Surely there is room at the table for one more."

"Thank you, *monsieur*, no. I will simply watch," she replied. Wilkins could not discern any sort of accent to her speech. She stood beside Koertiger but did not touch him, Wilkins noted. They were merely acquaintances, or colleagues, perhaps.

Wilkins nodded to her again, "as you wish, *mademoiselle*," and sat. He had done very well at the *Baccarat* table, whereas Koertiger had lost a little. The German was a very cautious gambler and rarely made large bets, nor was he a conversationalist. As Wilkins passed the cards, the young woman leaned over and whispered something in Koertiger's ear, in the process giving Wilkins a pointedly provocative view of her bosom. Then she looked up, smiled, and winked right at Wilkins.

"Will you deal next, *Herr* Koertiger?" Wilkins asked, blushing slightly.

"Unfortunately, I have reached my limit for the evening," Koertiger replied to all in a heavy German accent, "and since you have most of my money, I must wish you continued good luck."

"You are most courteous, thank you," Wilkins replied. "However, I believe I will take a rest myself. Would you care to join me in the lounge for a brandy?"

"No, thank you," Koertiger replied with a slight grimace as he turned away. The young woman walked away with him, but she glanced briefly over her shoulder at Wilkins and smiled before passing from the room.

Wilkins found a table in the fine, oak lounge and ordered a brandy. The lounge was quiet, nearly empty, and quite dark, but there was a very satisfactory selection of liquor. Wilkins lit a cigarette and waited. He was not terribly surprised to see Koertiger's young woman enter the room a few minutes later. She looked around casually and made a great show of "accidentally" discovering Wilkins seated at the table, and then walked up to greet him.

Wilkins stood: "What a wonderful surprise to see you again, *mademoiselle*. I suppose your companion has returned to his hotel, but would you care to join me for an *aperitif*?"

"Why, yes, I suppose I will, Mister ...."

"Bell, James Bell. And may I know your name, *mademoiselle*?"

"It's Hesketh, Josephina Hesketh," she said as Wilkins pulled out a chair for her and they sat.

"'Hesketh'," Wilkins considered, "I once knew a gentleman from London named 'Hesketh'," he said, "a Mister Charles Hesketh. Are you of any relation?"

"I don't believe so. Hesketh is my late husband's name, but I knew very few members of his family. Are you from London yourself?"

"Singapore, actually."

"And you are not in the war?"

"Not now. I was, very briefly," he replied, gesturing to the red scar on his left cheek. "I didn't care for it. Now I kick about Switzerland and Spain a great deal. I'm thinking of a journey to Brazil after the New Year."

"You seem to have won a great deal of money tonight, more than enough to pay for the crossing."

"More than enough for two, all told, I believe," Wilkins said cheerily. "If I may ask, *Madame,* was it very recently that Mister Hesketh, your late husband, passed away?"

"On no, it was some years ago now," she said pleasantly.

"I see, but then he must have left you in very good stead. I wonder, in what sort of business was the late Mister Hesketh engaged? Agriculture, perhaps?"

"You are close to the mark. It was the import and export of fruit, actually."

"A very perishable sort of business, I would think."

"Not so much as you would guess, and the demand is very great since so many people want fresh fruit nowadays. I myself still own and operate the business in Naples."

"But are you now traveling with *Herr* Koertiger?"

Hesketh blushed very prettily. "Oh, no, not at all. He was a business associate of my late husband. We have not spoken for years, and we were quite surprised to run into one another here. I of course reside in Naples, and he in Geneva, I believe. Do you spend any time in Geneva, Mister Bell?"

Perhaps they were associates and perhaps she does live in Naples, Wilkins thought, but Koertiger was most certainly not in the fruit business. "Myself, not at all, and to be brutally honest, I am quite relieved to hear that you are not associated with *Herr* Koertiger," Wilkins replied with a grin. "You are a very attractive woman, *Madame*, and I would have been quite disappointed to learn that you were traveling with that shriveled old fellow."

"Mister Bell, you are very forward," she replied in feigned shock, yet smiling.

"Please, call me James, and you *are* very beautiful, Josephina. May I call you that?"

"I suppose you may," she answered coquettishly.

"Are you from Naples originally?"

"No, I was raised in Bozen," she replied.

"You mean 'Bolzano', the city in the Trentino region? Only the Austrians call it 'Bozen'."

She blushed again, from embarrassment at her mistake this time. "Exactly," she said icily.

Ida Clementi was said to be from the Trentino, and here was *Madame* Hesketh, also from the Trentino. Wilkins regarded Hesketh admiringly. He believed it very likely that her true name was 'Clementi' and that her late husband, if any, was actually in the business of importing and exporting explosives such as Dunnite. She could easily have supplied the material for both the *Leonardo da Vinci* and Benesh bombings.

"And how do you like Lausanne?" He asked.

426

"It is dreary in winter, don't you agree?"

"I do, yes. And this lounge is so dreary, not even a proper fire to warm a fellow. Fortunately, I have a very comfortable suite at the *Cecil* next door. It has a marvelously large hearth. By any chance, would you care to join me in my suite for another brandy by the fire, Josephina?"

She smiled. "Why, James," she said with a hint of irony, "indeed, I would enjoy that very much."

Wilkins escorted *Madame* Hesketh across the street to his hotel. She was quite tall, he noted, and, as he put his arm around her, he also discovered she was quite slender, not at all as "well rounded" as his former fiancé, Emma Wolczak, had been. Wilkins further discovered that evening that Josephina knew a great many things Emma did not, and she kept Wilkins up very late that night displaying that knowledge in exquisite detail.

Late the next morning, long after they had called for breakfast to be brought to Wilkins' room, Hesketh announced that she had to depart for a luncheon engagement with *Herr* Koertiger.

"Won't you invite me along?" Wilkins asked jovially.

"I can't," she said sadly. "*Herr* Koertiger is a very private man and especially ill-at-ease with British gentlemen nowadays."

"Yes, that's certainly understandable. But perhaps I shall see you later?"

She smiled. "I expect so."

The instant after she left, Wilkins threw on his overcoat to follow her. Hesketh was tall enough to be easily spotted on the street, and Wilkins trailed her to the tramway where she boarded the N° 1 to the summit. Wilkins had to wait briefly for the next tram, but he knew there was only one restaurant at the top, the *Pavillion-Signal*, and surely he would find Hesketh and Koertiger there. He boarded the next tram when it arrived and squeezed in between two tall, heavyset men who had declined to disembark. The twenty minute ride was uncomfortable, and became more so when Wilkins suddenly realized there was a pistol pressed sharply into his ribs. One of the heavyset gentlemen whispered in his ear: "*Sie bleiben ruhig. Sie werden mit uns kommen.*" There was nothing Wilkins could do, and he felt a fool for having been so easily entrapped.

When the tram finally arrived at the top, the two men pushed Wilkins silently to the end of the platform where a black *Mercedes* sedan awaited them. One of the men reached into Wilkins' overcoat pocket and confiscated his Browning M1911 handgun, and then he pushed him roughly into the back of the sedan behind the driver. There, he found *Madame* Josephina Hesketh waiting for him.

"Josephina, what a pleasant surprise to see you again so soon," he said.

"I am very sorry, James. We did have such fun, but I'm afraid *Herr* Koertiger has insisted. He doesn't care for British spies following him about."

"Just Austrian ones, Miss Clementi?" Wilkins asked.

"No, you have it all wrong, James," she replied gaily, "'Clementi' is the alias. My name, my married name, is Hesketh."

"Was it you that supplied the bomb that was to kill Edvard Benesh, then?"

"Of course it was me, James, but Benesh was not the target; it was Seton-Watson we were supposed to assassinate."

"And now you intend to murder me."

"Oh, perhaps later, after Koertiger finds out who you are and what you know. *Holen Sie sich bewegen, ihr Narren!*" She said to the two large men in the front of the sedan. The automobile immediately set off on the road that led to the forest through fields lightly dusted with snow.

"Don't get me wrong, James," she continued. "I did have a very pleasant time with you last night. Young men are so very energetic."

"Delighted to have been of service," Wilkins said as he drew his cigar case from his jacket. "Would you mind terribly?"

"Later," she replied brusquely. She pulled the cigar case from his grasp and threw it forward to the brute riding in the front passenger seat.

"How long until we arrive?" Wilkins asked, but the sedan was already coming to a stop just inside the tree line of the forest. Another black *Mercedes* sedan was waiting for them there. A shriveled older man, Koertiger, got out of it and stood alongside. The driver of Wilkins's sedan pulled him from the back as Hesketh exited the sedan on the other side, and then she and the driver marched Wilkins up to Koertiger as the second brute advanced to stand guard beside the aged German spymaster. He tendered to Koertiger the M1911 handgun that he had confiscated from Wilkins' coat pocket.

"A Browning," Koertiger said as he examined the handgun carefully, "but this is an American weapon. You are not an American, are you, *Herr* Bell? No, of course not – you are British, and I sincerely doubt that 'Bell' is your real name. Would you like to tell me who you are and what you sought to accomplish by following me?"

"Not especially, no," Wilkins replied casually. The brute standing beside him instantly swung his fist into Wilkins' stomach and knocked the air from his lungs. Wilkins dropped to his knees and hugged his gut, gasping for air. Then suddenly Wilkins' silver cigar case, now resting in the jacket pocket of the man standing next to Koertiger, exploded. *Signore* Abato in Rome had not turned the cigar case into a gun, but rather into a bomb. And as the brute's chest instantly disintegrated in a burst of blood and bone, shards of steel were cast outward in every direction. One shard pierced Koertiger's head and killed him instantly. Wilkins had used the brief moment on his knees to retrieve the hidden dagger from his belt buckle, and as Koertiger and the brute beside him collapsed dead, Wilkins pivoted and plunged his knife deeply into the leg of the large man standing beside him, slashing down and slicing through the man's femoral artery. Before the brute could even draw his gun, he began convulsing and fell backward onto the ground. Blood flowed in a river down his pants leg. Wilkins immediately turned to Hesketh, who he found to be in shock and unable to speak or move. A two inch shard of steel was jutting out of her left shoulder.

Wilkins ran to retrieve his handgun as Koertiger's driver jumped out from his sedan. He began shooting as Wilkins dragged Hesketh back to her own motorcar. Opening the rear door for cover, he shoved her inside as a bullet shattered the window. Wilkins crouched behind the door, then raised his own handgun, aimed carefully, and fired twice, one shot a glancing blow that forced the other shooter to leap back. Wilkins then stood and marched forward, firing with each stride, until his handgun's magazine was empty and the driver lay dead, a bullet through his forehead. Four bodies lay sprawled and bloody on the white snow.

Wilkins returned and sat in the driver's seat of Hesketh's sedan. The lady was huddled on the floor in the back in shock, neither crying nor hysterical but deathly silent. Wilkins looked at her with sympathy. Even then he could not help but admire her beauty. "I believe, *Madame* Hesketh, it would be best if we were to depart Switzerland immediately," he said.

"I tell you again, James, it is not possible for either of us to stay here," Hesketh cried. "Where are we to go?"

She rolled over and took the bottle of sherry from the bed-side table and poured it into the cordial glass resting on her bare chest. Wilkins, exhausted, lay on the bed beside her. After crossing Lake Geneva, Wilkins had checked them into a small hotel where Hesketh had at last regained her senses. She immediately cautioned Wilkins that they could not remain in Italy: "Koertiger was only a broker," she warned him anxiously. "He worked for another man, a high-ranking German officer named Von Trauth who commands the espionage services of Crown Prince Rupprecht."

"Rupprecht, the Crown Prince of Bavaria? Are you quite certain? Is he truly the one overseeing this network of spies?" Wilkins asked in great surprise.

"So I have been told. It is Von Trauth who paid me and my late husband to smuggle explosives into Italy. He controls dozens of agents in France and Italy, and I tell you he will have every one of them hunting for you now. Since I survived this debacle, I have no doubt those agents will have instructions to murder me as well. We must flee at once," she insisted.

For Wilkins, another issue had begun to gnaw at his mind, and as always his thoughts quickly ran away from him, placing one card upon the next faster than he himself could often understand. It suddenly dawned on him that he could not now return to Rome. Alas, he had imprudently left his post there to pursue his own investigation in Switzerland, and now it appeared he could not stay in Italy either. To his surprise, he felt greatly relieved. It was not the relief of a weighty burden lifted, but that of a rigid constraint removed. He could finally put the disaster in Petrograd behind him and move forward. It was unfortunate that the British Secret Intelligence Service, at Prime Minister Lloyd George's command, no longer cared to utilize his talents, but he could still go to Athens to work again for Prime Minister Venizelos (now that King Constantine had abdicated) or to Salonika to work with the Prince Regent Alexander of Serbia.

There was *so much* that needed to be done. Alas, if only he knew where to find Alexandr Kerensky, who was undoubtedly in hiding, then Wilkins could perhaps still steer Russia away from its path toward Bolshevik dictatorship.

Having seen the Russian radicals in action himself, Wilkins could see that there was no greater peril to Europe than the Bolsheviks. When he worked with Kerensky in Petrograd, Wilkins had unexpectedly come to respect the Socialist aspiration for civil liberty, universal suffrage, and social justice, but Wilkins had also learned of the more extreme Bolsheviks' mendacity and ruthlessness. Everything that had happened in Russia since the revolution had proven that Lenin and the Bolsheviks were blatant liars and violent radicals to whom the vast majority of Russians were passionately opposed. Indeed, the Russians had recently held elections to appoint a constitutional assembly, and to the Bolsheviks' great embarrassment, it was Kerensky's party, the "Esers", who had ended up winning an absolute majority of the assembly seats; the Bolsheviks won only a handful! So desperate were Lenin and the Bolsheviks to preserve their rigid hold over the revolutionary government, however, that they had sent their Red Guard to violently disband the constitutional assembly and arrest or murder many of the elected representatives. The world now knew there would be no democracy in Russia – it would be a military dictatorship and nothing more, and the Bolsheviks' ultimate success depended upon their continuing effort to spread their social revolution across Europe through *propaganda* and the infiltration of labor unions and soldiers' councils. True, there were ruthless men with dictatorial ambitions everywhere, but Wilkins particularly detested the Bolsheviks' deceitful claim to have the interests of the common people at heart. However the Great War ended, surely the Bolsheviks would also need to be stopped.

Wilkins stretched and opened his eyes to look at the lovely Madame Hesketh, long and lithe, her long black hair draped over her shoulders, lying naked beside him in their small hotel room. Since returning to Italy, Wilkins continued to maintain his false identity and the name 'Bell', but after a day in the hotel together, Josephina had revealed something of her own history. It may have all been lies, but she said her late husband had been a wealthy older Englishman from India who owned the import-export business in Naples. She said her parents were probably still in Bolzano; they were of Austrian descent and had raised her to speak German first and Italian not at all. She also had relatives in Vienna, she claimed, and had grown to hate the British Empire. However, she also hated the Hapsburgs and thought the young Emperor Charles was a fool. She said the bomber in Rome had been her lover, and claimed to have no idea why Seton-Watson was targeted for assassination; she knew only that he was British. She claimed to know nothing of the Czechs or Slovaks or Slavs or Slovenes or Croats or ….

"My dear," Wilkins asked with an excited burst of inspiration, "might you be able to arrange passage for us to Poland?"

Paris

The *Tuileries* garden, its barren tree branches frosted with a thin film of ice, was quiet on Christmas morning. David Gresham, in an unusually clean uniform, cap and greatcoat, freshly shaved and hair neatly oiled and combed, was making his way through the garden and across the Seine to the hotel *Palais d'Orsay*. The morning was grey and overcast and a light snow drifted in the air. Eiffel's tower was illuminated for the first time that year, but there were confusingly few other indications of the holiday in the city. Not a single church bell was ringing. Not a single carol was sung. Few Parisians had anything to celebrate, and those that Gresham passed in the garden were mostly rushing silently to their homes. Many were women dressed in black, mourning their sons and husbands and fathers who had all been lost in the war. There were also French soldiers in uniform, some of whom had suffered terrible facial disfigurements or lacked one or more of their extremities, and there were British and Italian soldiers who were unhappy to be away from their homes for yet another year. But there were also a few excited newcomers: The American soldiers, the "Doughboys" as they were called, tried to be considerate of the suffering Parisians and to keep their high spirits in check. But, of course, the Americans had not yet seen much of the war, a war that was now entering its fourth dread-filled winter.

In 1914, the French had rallied desperately to halt the German armies before the Marne River only thirty miles from Paris and then counterattacked in Lorraine and the Ardennes; in 1915, they fought bitterly at Loos and Artois and Champagne; in 1916, they struggled and suffered for nine months to beat the Germans back at Verdun and joined the deadly British offensive at the Somme River. Through all those terrible long years, life in Paris had continued almost undisturbed: There was good food and wine for those who could pay, and music and theater and art exhibitions; it was still *La Belle Époque*. Then, in 1917, after the misguided Nivelle Offensive and the months-long battles at Arras and the Aisne, the French soldiers mutinied, labor strikes in the factories became commonplace, bread suddenly became scarce. The Republic reached the limit of its public debt, and even the editorials in *Le Journal* began to entreat France to seek a separate peace with Germany. The lights of *La Ville-Lumière* dimmed even as the meticulously crafted street-by-street replica of Paris, built on the northern outskirts of the city to mislead the German aerial bombers, blazed with light.

Although he was troubled by these difficulties, the diminished spirit of Paris had not prevented David Gresham from making the most of his posting there or enjoying the newly-gained wealth he had stolen from the Bolsheviks. He had taken a fine suite of well-appointed rooms at the aristocratic *Hôtel Brighton* and dined every night at the *Café Anglais* or at *Larue* or at *Henry's*, always with a different young lady – he had discovered the hundreds of pretty, young American women who had been sent to Paris to operate the switchboards for the American Expeditionary Force (a "force" that still numbered well under 200,000 men, smaller even than the army of Belgium). Conversely, Gresham did very little in the way of intelligence work. He received no instructions from the Circus and submitted no reports. It seemed that Gresham had been written off, disavowed.

Gresham had taken to attending the theater at night, and one evening, while dining alone at *Paillard's*, he was quite unexpectedly greeted by a former acquaintance: A tall and very beautiful young woman with long, luxurious blond hair and porcelain skin, wearing a very expensive silk dress and modest but obviously expensive jewels. She casually approached Gresham at his table, and there was a moment of discomfort as he wondered where he'd met her before. Then suddenly he recalled her name and leapt to his feet: She was the Princess Eleanor of Romania, with whom Gresham had dined at the home of the British Ambassador in Bucharest! The Princess was delighted to see Gresham again and even addressed him respectfully as "General" (since he had been briefly commissioned a Brigade General in the Roumanian army). She was spending the winter in Paris, she told him, and wanted to express her deep appreciation to General Gresham for his valiant efforts on behalf of her country. She told him that there was now an overwhelming consensus in Roumania that the government had been wrong to insist upon an invasion of Transylvania (an adventure that Gresham himself had strongly opposed) and that General Averescu continued to speak highly of Gresham, his one-time Brigade General from Great Britain.

Gresham was astonished that the Princess remembered him at all, and even more perplexed when a handwritten note from her was delivered to him at the *Brighton* the next morning. Princess Eleanor invited him to join her party at the *Opera* that evening. Feeling rather out of place, Gresham nonetheless dressed and attended the musical event with her that night. Afterward, he dined with the Princess and her *coterie* of young female aristocrats and their Belgian and French officer friends. He learned to his surprise and delight that the Princess preferred *absinthe* to wine and bawdy musical halls to opera. That was merely the first of many nights he spent in Paris with the Princess and her *entourage*, and how Gresham came to be the Princess' escort at one event after another throughout the following weeks. He and Princess Eleanor were seen often at art galleries and restaurants, parks and museums, and almost every night at the theater or music halls (although of course always in the company of other aristocrats and officers). They became close companions.

Although Gresham enjoyed her company immensely, he was nevertheless troubled. It dawned on him at long last that Princess Eleanor might actually be courting him, albeit in the cool, calm manner typical of aristocrats. Could that possibly be the case, he wondered? Certainly he had been on his best behavior:

He had not killed anyone for months nor had he visited any of the magnificent Parisian brothels. Still, for an actual Princess to express a romantic interest toward him was deeply confusing: Who did she think he was?

Each morning as Gresham shaved and looked at his face in the mirror he began to wonder more and more: Who was this fellow named David Gresham? Who was he really? Was there any trace of his old self, his childhood self, the desperate and angry boy named David Larkin who had once lived on the streets of Manchester, or had that boy disappeared forever? If so, what part of him remained?

After weeks of confusion, Christmas Day arrived and Gresham strode across the *Tuileries* and over the Seine to reach the *Palais d'Orsay* where Princess Eleanor resided. He entered the elegant marble lobby and shook the snow from his cap and stamped his gleaming new Cordova leather boots on the rug. Then he folded his coat over his arm and crossed to the lift. "Third floor," he told the lift man. He quickly reached the Royal Suite and knocked gently. A young lady's maid dressed in black opened the door. He said: "Good morning, Andra, and a Happy Christmas to you."

"Thank you, sir. Princess Eleanor will join you in a moment," the maid replied. "May I get you anything?"

"I'll help myself, thank you." Gresham walked to the table near the window that held the liquor and poured a scotch whiskey as the maid returned to the bedroom to assist the Princess. He saw outside the window that the snow was falling heavier now. The Royal Suite at the *Palais d'Orsay* was enormous and finely decorated, and Princess Eleanor had arranged for Christmas garlands to be brought in. A small fire crackled in the hearth, and Gresham sat on the rich red velour settee beside it with his drink, putting aside his nervousness to consider the troubles in France and the sad spirit of her people. A moment later, the bedroom door opened and Princess Eleanor entered the room. She was stunning in a simple, white lace dress with a dark green belt. It was a light summer dress, a dress that fit her very well and showed off her narrow waist. Her hair was loose and flowed like a wave of yellow silk over her shoulders. Gresham was quite astonished.

"David, I am so pleased you have come to spend the day with me," she said. "I find it is so very lonely to be away from home at Christmastide."

"I am grateful for the invitation," Gresham said, "although I have rarely celebrated Christmas in the past." He stood to kiss her hand. She instead ignored him and sat down on the narrow settee. Gresham sat again, beside her.

"No? Have you no family in England?" She asked with concern. "You never speak of it."

"No, I have no family to speak of."

"I am sorry to hear it," she said, "but then families are not always a blessing, are they? Perhaps that is why people get married; they come to think they can make a better family than the one they came from."

Gresham laughed. "Oh, so is that why *you* came to Paris: To find a suitable husband?"

"Oh, no; alas, if only I had that liberty. You know, I must eventually wed whomever my father and mother choose for me. I wouldn't say that their expectation in that regard is unusual, nor unreasonable, but I do intend to enjoy myself until that fateful day."

"Do you?" He asked with a grin.

"Now you are being rude," she chastised him playfully. "Are you not a gentleman?"

"That is the last thing anyone would ever accuse me of being, I'm afraid," Gresham confessed.

"Well, you shall have to at least *pretend* to be a gentleman, for my sake. Andra is off with the other servants for the rest of the day, so I am relying upon you to behave yourself."

"If that is what you desire, then of course I will. Even if I am not a gentleman, I would like to believe I am an ethical man."

"I am relieved to hear it. But what is your *ethos*, if I may ask – 'an eye for an eye', I suspect?"

"We *are* at war."

"Well, we are for now, yes, but we will not *always* be at war, will we?" She asked. "You are a soldier now, but afterward? Tell me, what do you think you will become after the war is over?"

"I honestly don't know," Gresham admitted. Even with his new wealth, it was a topic that he preferred not to consider.

"Oh, but you must become *something*, I insist. I feel I've begun to know you now, David, at least a little," she said teasingly, and then she grew serious. "You are very blunt, that is true, and that makes people uncomfortable. But you are also witty and clever and handsome. I think you will become a very great man, General Gresham."

He laughed skeptically. "You know I am no *real* General, and I must admit to you, Princess, that my birth name is not even really 'Gresham'."

Suddenly the Princess leaned over and kissed Gresham motherly upon the cheek. "Believe me. I know what I am saying," she whispered in his ear, and then she laid her head upon his shoulder. Gresham felt his face glow red. He placed his arm around the Princess and held her delicately. Her silky hair brushed his cheek. His chest suddenly felt as if it was bound tightly as his heart beat rapidly within.

"I have something for you," the Princess said gaily. "Would you like to see your present now?" She raised her head and looked him in the eye.

"I have a gift for you, as well," Gresham replied.

"Mine first," she said as she bounded up excitedly from the settee. She took a parcel wrapped in red tissue paper from the mantle and handed it to Gresham. He unwrapped the gift and found that it was a book: *The Romance of King Arthur and His Knights of the Round Table*. "This edition has the newest illustrations by

Arthur Rackham," she told him, "I just love him. It's all about King Arthur and his brave and noble knights, just like you."

There was not a hint of sarcasm in her voice, and Gresham looked at her in some confusion. Very few times in his life had anyone ever expressed such confidence in him, nor had anyone ever called him 'brave' or 'noble'. However, the book also reminded him of Sergeant Hart, the old, lanky Sergeant who was his brief companion at Gallipoli, who had disappeared in the fighting near Suvla Bay. Gresham recalled how Hart would call the British soldiers by the names of King Arthur's knights to boost their spirits, and suddenly Gresham felt very sad, sad at the loss of Hart, sad for all that had been lost in the war.

"I told you not to be rude, and now you are pouting," the Princess said, noting his gloomy expression. "Don't you like it?"

"I like it very much," he protested. "It just brought to mind an old friend, a man who died at Gallipoli, that I held in great esteem."

"Oh I am so sorry," she said in dismay. "I didn't know."

"No, no, please, it is a wonderful gift," he assured her. "I know I have your gift here somewhere," he teased, checking all his pockets as she smiled at him. "Ah, here it is." He handed her a small parcel in plain brown paper.

"What is it?" She asked excitedly.

"Go on then and open it," he chided her.

Princess Eleanor untied the parcel to find a simple silver box within. On its top was the silhouette of a woman's head and the words "Christmas 1914."

"Whatever could this be?" She asked with genuine curiosity.

"Well, you see, in 1914 at the start of the war, Princess Mary, the youngest daughter of King George, she wanted to arrange a gift for all the British troops serving abroad," Gresham explained. "She solicited donations to a charity that produced these little brass boxes and sent them to the troops. This is the one I received myself while I was in the trenches in Belgium, only I have had it silver-plated for you. The original boxes contained tobacco, pencils, and other small items that any soldier at the front lines might enjoy, but yours is filled with sweets. I hope it's appropriate. It seemed just the sort of thing a soldier could give to a Princess."

Princess Eleanor looked down at Gresham very seriously. "It's wonderful, David," she said. Then she sat right down on his lap and placed her arms around his neck. She looked at him meaningfully. "There's one more gift I'd like to give you, David, if you will accept it."

Gresham could feel his hands shaking and his heart racing as he slowly wrapped his arms around her and held her tightly to his chest, and then she kissed him. "Did I mention that you are also *very* handsome?" She asked breathlessly.

"Colonel Gresham, it is a pleasure to see you again. Thank you for coming in to speak with us." Gresham was summoned the next day to meet with *Général* Charles-Joseph Dupont, the man in charge of the French intelligence agency, the *Duexième Bureau*, at his small office in an apartment on the Boulevard Saint-Germain. Gresham had first met Dupont in the city of Verdun in early 1916 on the eve of the massive German assault upon the ancient French stronghold. Dupont's small office in the *Hôtel de Ville* was sparingly appointed, and another gentleman, a plump, square-faced man with heavily oiled dark hair and wearing a French Captain's uniform, sat silently near the window smoking a pipe. He did not bother to look up. "That is *Commandant* Ladoux," Dupont clarified, "my chief of counter-espionage."

"I was surprised to receive your note, General, but if I may be of any assistance to you, –" Gresham began.

"Information, Colonel, that is all we seek," Dupont said solicitously. "Please be seated."

"May I congratulate you on the fitting end you arranged for *Madame* MacLeod – a firing squad, is that right?" Gresham asked. "I read about it in the papers."

"Ah, yes. Ladoux is the one who sniffed her out at last. *Mata Hari* was her stage name, you know, and she was beloved by all Paris, well, by many men of Paris, at least. *Mais, voilà* – she has given us the name of her German spymaster Major von Trauth and identified six other German agents in France whom we have already rounded up."

"Well done, *Commandant*," Gresham said. Ladoux nodded.

"I understand you have spent the better part of the past year in Russia, Colonel Gresham," Dupont said. "Considering the events in Petrograd, we are naturally concerned about what could happen in France. You know of our difficulties with the troops this past summer. Those who instigated the mutinies were hanged, of course, but we are concerned nonetheless, and especially about what the Bolsheviks may be up to."

"*Are* there Bolsheviks in France?" Gresham asked.

"That is difficult to assess," Dupont admitted. "There are a great many Socialists in France, of course, and there are some who speak of Lenin with great admiration. Certain members of the Radical Party, in their rhetoric, have consistently opposed the war; indeed, one of their leaders is Joseph Caillaux, who was the Prime Minister until 1912. The French are an intellectual and a vocal people, Colonel Gresham, but the chorus is growing increasingly dissonant. Nevertheless, we cannot arrest everyone who differs from the government on matters of policy – foreigners, perhaps, but not the French themselves."

"So you simply do not know if there are French extremists privately advocating revolution within France," Gresham replied.

"Precisely," Dupont said. "I asked you here because we simply wish to know whether, during your time in Petrograd, you became aware of any correspondence between revolutionaries in Russia and anyone in France."

"No," Gresham said flatly, insulted by the insinuation that he would not have disclosed such a serious matter. "I am not aware of any such threat, and if I had been, you should damn well know I would have reported it at once."

"Good, very good, that is reassuring."

"Ideas, however, are not so easily confined, *General*," Gresham went on. "There may be men in France who have read reports of the revolution in Russia and are inspired now to act. I've noticed that you barely censor your newspapers."

"No, no, we do not. President Poincaré absolutely forbids it. France is a republic, after all, and therefore we must suffer a certain amount of *libertè*."

"Yet every day in the newspapers I see calls for France to negotiate a peace agreement with the Kaiser."

"Yes, there is public discourse in that regard, but I can assure you that the government has no intention of negotiating with Germany."

"But such talk is disheartening to the soldiers and will embolden those who wish to change the government itself. The promise of an end to the war was the central message that drew the Russian masses to the Bolsheviks; it was the central message of their newspaper, *Pravda*. It greatly influenced the Russian soldiers in particular, and they are the ones who generally tend to have rifles," Gresham said. "Have you investigated the newspapers? *Le Journal*, for example, is one of the worst. Who owns it? Who writes the editorials?"

"Ah, perhaps if you cited another example, *mon ami*, but *Le Journal* is under the direction of Charles Humbert, a Senator of the Republic and an army veteran himself. He has no sympathy for the *Bolsheviki*, I assure you. Your point about the newspapers is well taken, however. What do you say about that, Ladoux?"

"*Le Bonnet Rouges* is under investigation," the *Commandant* replied. "There are a few others we know have had some contact with Staub or Nezie."

"Who?" Gresham asked.

"*Mesdames* Staub and Nezie," Depont replied, "they are German agents. Irma Staub travels frequently from Switzerland. *Madame* Nezie is also known by the name 'Hesketh' but we believe she spends most of her time in Italy. Do you know these names? No? Well, in any case, you see we are investigating," he concluded dismissively.

Gresham left Dupont's office dissatisfied. Certainly Dupont and Ladoux were competent men. Their investigations within France had been quite successful, and yet it seemed to Gresham that they were blinded to certain risks because of their faith in the Republic and the fortitude of the Gauls. Senator Humbert, for example, why should he not be investigated? Perhaps Humbert stood to gain financially from some private dealings with the Russians? Gresham quickly decided to perform an experiment of his own. He returned to his hotel to change out of his uniform and took a taxi to the offices of *Le Journal* where, using a false name, he requested to meet with Senator Humbert.

Humbert was a large gentleman, tall and round, with a large mustache like a warehouse broom; his immaculate office suggested he did little hard work for the newspaper. "*Bonjour, Monsieur*, how may I assist you?" He asked jovially when Gresham was shown into his office.

"My name is Maclean, David Maclean," Gresham began. "You have heard of my father, Richard Thomas Maclean, the Manchester industrial magnate?"

"Ah, *oui*, of course I am familiar with that name, *Monsieur* Maclean."

Of course, Gresham thought, although I have just invented it.

"My father sent me to France in the expectation that my family's substantial wealth could be of some assistance to the French people in this time of terrible conflict," Gresham went on rather flippantly. "He directed me to identify and secure opportunities for the investment of substantial capital in various enterprises that might benefit the French war effort. Our opportunities to invest in Great Britain, you see, are already quite limited, and we wish to avoid unnecessary conflicts with certain colleagues."

"How very wise, of course," Humbert replied. "So, you would like my advice, *oui*?"

"Well, sir, to be blunt, *Le Journal* serves such a valuable role in educating the French people about this unfortunate war, and I have been so impressed with your own political commentaries in that regard, that we would like to make an investment in *Le Journal* itself. No doubt an investment of this sort would enable you to substantially increase your distribution to the parts of France outside Paris where your message must also be heard. All we would request in exchange is a modest security interest in the business."

"Well, hmm, that is a very generous offer, *Monsieur* Maclean, but foreign investments?"

"But this would be a strictly private matter, Senator, and of course we would not dream of asking you to change your editorial policies. On the contrary, we quite agree with your positions regarding the war."

Gresham could see that Humbert was terribly eager to accept the proposal and that he was quite excited at the thought of making *Le Journal* the preeminent newspaper in all of France, yet at the same time felt compelled to turn away funds from an unknown foreign source. Gresham almost hoped that he would. In a state of agitation, however, Humbert finally took a sheet of notepaper from his drawer and wrote down a name and address. He passed the note to Gresham. The name written upon it was 'Paul Bolo'.

"*Le Journal* has previously expanded its distribution with similar investments, but I am not familiar with how those transactions were conducted," Humbert said. "*Monsieur* Bolo has arranged everything for us in the past. He is a financial genius, an entrepreneur, a particular friend of the former *Khedive* of Egypt, and therefore a reputable man, *Monsieur* Maclean. You may speak with him about your proposal. It is beyond my expertise." Humbert, it appeared, did not wish to accept responsibility for the decision or for the other investments he had previously accepted.

"As you wish," Gresham said. "Thank you for your time, Senator, and I hope we will meet again."

Gresham soon found that Bolo was not an easy man to reach, and he nearly gave up on his experiment during the days that followed. Gresham continued to spend his evenings in the company of Princess Eleanor, and that was a far more enjoyable pastime.

Then, one afternoon, he was close to Bolo's residence near the *Gare du Nord* and decided to stop in one last time, only this time to find that *Monsieur* Bolo was unexpectedly at home. Gresham was escorted into a modest library of the small townhouse where Bolo came to meet him. A dapper gentleman with short, wavy black hair, a twirled mustache and monocle, Paul Bolo was gracious but exceedingly cool: "*Monsieur* Maclean, I have been away," he said. "Senator Humbert told me of your visit to *Le Journal* and explained your interest, but I had no way to reach you."

"I do apologize; I am staying at the *Brighton* but do not care to have my whereabouts discussed in public. Still, I am glad to hear that the Senator spoke to you, *Monsieur* Bolo, as we remain interested in making the investment I discussed with him."

"Yes, yes, I am pleased to hear it. However, sir, with all due respect, I do not know who you are. On the other hand, I do not particularly care. I can easily arrange for you to make an investment in *Le Journal*, but you will have to pay my fee to negotiate the transaction, and I must warn you it will be substantial. To entertain further discussions, I require an exhibition of your earnestness in the way of depositing the sum of 10,000 Pounds into an account at *Credit Suisse* that I can verify. Until that time, there is nothing further to discuss."

Gresham quickly surmised that Bolo's interest in the proposed transaction was limited to his own financial gain. Such a man, however, could easily be indiscriminate when it came to the source of such funds. Gresham quickly arranged the next day for 10,000 Pounds from his own funds to be placed into an account at *Credit Suisse* in the name of "David Maclean" and secured a second room at the *Brighton* under that pseudonym. Within a day, Gresham received an invitation to call on Bolo again. Gresham returned to the man's townhouse and got straight to the point.

"*Monsieur* Bolo, I expect you will now take our investment more seriously. I have learned that *Le Journal* is actually owned by one Henri Letellier and that Senator Humbert is his appointed Director. However, the Senator stated plainly that there have been other recent investments, and I must know who else has an ownership interest in the newspaper."

"The others are not equity investments, *Monsieur* Maclean, and need not concern you. You are correct that Letellier is the sole owner, and I must tell you that he does not care to dilute his ownership interest."

"I see, but you still want our money to expand production and distribution?"

"Yes, of course. You must comprehend that these things are easily arranged, so please allow me to suggest an alternative: You will buy printing facilities in France and lease them to *Le Journal.* That is an expense that Humbert, as the Director, is authorized to approve, and your profit and my transaction fee, of course, would be written into the lease, while you retain full ownership of your capital investment."

"That is quite feasible, *Monsieur,* but we must also have assurances that *Le Journal* will indeed use the facilities to increase its production. We would like to have Senator Humbert's words read in every household in France. Printing machinery is no difficulty at all. We can arrange to have them shipped from Manchester and ink from India, as well. Paper, however, is a substantial difficulty, and I very much doubt that you have an adequate supply of paper to print upon. Therefore, I will make you this proposal: If you can obtain a commitment in writing for the purchase of an adequate supply of newsprint, our company is prepared to invest up to one million Pounds Sterling in printing equipment in France."

Bolo's eyes grew large at the sum mentioned by Gresham. "That is a very large sum, far greater than I anticipated, *Monsieur* Maclean."

"*Le Journal* will need a very great amount of newsprint. I don't know where you are going to get it. You might inquire in America, or perhaps Canada? And, of course, you will need funds from your other investors to obtain such a commitment, if they are willing. I cannot buy paper for you."

"Indeed, I shall endeavor to obtain those funds promptly, as I foresee a potentially great profit for us both, *Monsieur,*" Bolo replied greedily.

Gresham returned to the *Brighton* that afternoon uncertain what would come of his experiment. He knew that Bolo would now have him investigated, and Gresham already suspected that he was being watched. He did not especially want to keep up an assumed name or live in Paris under the alias 'Maclean'; no, he wanted to be out with Princess Eleanor, dining or at the music halls with her. There had been far too few opportunities for them to be alone together, and he was uncertain how long she would even remain in Paris. Paris was exhausted. There had been no New Year's revelries, as no one was particularly excited to be entering a fifth year of war or wished to celebrate another year of casualties, famine and destruction. There was no telling when the fighting would resume, but it was clear that there were still far too few Americans in France to break the stalemate. On the Eastern Front, the fighting with Russia had ceased, and everyone assumed that Germany was already transporting hundreds of thousands of veteran troops to Belgium and France to break the Allies' resolve. Every day the newspapers and politicians in Paris clamoured for peace despite the heavy price that would be paid in lives already lost and the land in Belgium, Alsace-Lorraine, and Picardy to be surrendered, to name a few of the areas already occupied by the German armies.

After a few days of silence from Bolo, Gresham wrote off his experiment as a bad job and decided to dine out with Princess Eleanor again. They were joined by a collection of Belgian officers and their lady friends at *Larue*. The elegant restaurant was subdued, but for one elderly French General, Denis Auguste Duchêne, who was seated with a young lady nearby. The mean little man had a reputation for arrogance and was extremely dissatisfied with his meal. He finally marched red faced to the kitchen to yell at the chef, and Gresham's dinner companions erupted gaily in laughter as he left the restaurant in a foul temper. At Gresham's table the wine poured freely and there seemed a great abundance of fish soup, fish stew, fish and fresh oysters – all in all a very fine meal given the circumstances. Eleanor, dressed in a voluptuous blue silk dress, was caressing Gresham's knee beneath the white linen tablecloth in a most promising expression of affection.

Gresham then saw *Commandant* Ladoux and three uniformed soldiers suddenly enter the restaurant and begin to make their way toward Gresham's table. As usual, Ladoux's expression was grim. Gresham, decidedly ill at ease, removed the hand that rested upon his knee and stood to intercept the *Commandant* before he arrived at the table.

"Are you looking for me?" Gresham asked Ladoux.

"Colonel Gresham, it is my duty to place you under arrest. Will you come peaceably?" The *Commandant* asked in rather too loud a voice. The patrons at the tables beside them were now watching, and soon the entire restaurant went silent. Princess Eleanor rose and rushed to Gresham's side.

"Is everything alright?" She asked him with great concern.

"No trouble, my dear. I must go and speak with these gentlemen a while," Gresham replied. "I will see you tomorrow, I expect."

The expression of concern on Eleanor's face wrenched his heart as Gresham was led to the sedan waiting outdoors. He was driven through the darkened, damp streets of Paris to an abandoned townhouse near the *Champs-Élysées*. The windows of the house were blinded with heavy curtains. Gresham was led down a set of iron stairs to the servant's entrance and brought to an empty back room where General Dupont stood waiting.

"Good evening, Colonel," Dupont said icily.

"Dupont," Gresham acknowledged.

"I am afraid you have put us in a very uncomfortable position, Colonel. I will tell you up front that I may need to put you in prison. *Je regrette, mais* it is not my decision."

"May I at least know why?"

"Had you simply come to us in the beginning, this could have all been arranged in advance, but now both the Americans and your superiors in Whitehall Court have become involved, and there is the political impact here in France to consider. I cannot say what President Poincaré will do; he is quite livid."

"Good God, man, just tell me what has happened?" Gresham insisted.

"Earlier today, the respected French financier Paul Bolo was placed under arrest after we received a portfolio of telegrams, some intercepted by the British and some by the Americans, which indicated that *Monsieur* Bolo, known also as Bolo Pasha, received a very large transfer of funds at an account at the J.P. Morgan bank in New York. The purpose of this transfer, it seems, was to secure the purchase of newsprint from Canada for *Le Journal*. The transfer of these funds, as the documents clearly show, originated in Germany."

"Dear God," Gresham shook his head. He had suspected that the funds would come from Russia, but of course it now seemed all too clear that Bolo had been dealing with the Germans instead.

"Yes, our allies are now aware that one of the most prestigious newspapers in France, one which has been loudly denouncing our government for perpetuating the war with Germany, one that is run by a prominent member of the *Sénat* and a close ally of the President, is in fact a mere pawn of the German intelligence *bureau*. That, at least, is what everyone in Paris will say when the story is made public tomorrow morning. You must appreciate what an enormous embarrassment this will be for the President."

"Tell me, Colonel Gresham," Ladoux said, "what do you know of a gentleman by the name of 'Maclean'? He is also wanted for questioning in connection with the German scheme."

Gresham looked up swiftly and found Ladoux's expression menacing.

"You know damn well what I was doing, *Commandant*, or else you are not very good at your job, and my purpose was all too obvious after our last meeting. You are the ones who refused to investigate Humbert."

"Nevertheless, the British government has long agreed to leave matters impacting the internal security of France to our own discretion," Dupont said emphatically. "This is not your jurisdiction, Colonel, and you have done tremendous damage to France. Now we must determine whether you will stay in Paris in prison or be sent back to England."

Dupont finally allowed Gresham to return to his rooms for that evening as the matter was discussed in the President's office. Gresham entered his hotel in a foul mood and decided he must immediately pack his bags. But where would he go? Spain, perhaps. Barcelona? As Gresham entered his suite, however, he unexpectedly found Princess Eleanor waiting for him. She was distraught and had evidently been crying as she sat alone waiting for Gresham's return. When he entered, she threw her arms around him at once and hugged him tightly. "What has happened, David, you must tell me," she insisted. "Everyone heard that you were to be arrested."

"My dear, there is no cause for concern," he assured her; Gresham was quite touched by her discomfiture. "There was a little political indiscretion on my part, that is all, and the French are quite insulted. At worst, I shall be forced to leave France, I think."

"Oh no! I don't want you to go, David! You must allow me to help you, my darling. I can't bear for you to be sent away. I won't have it!" She buried his face in Gresham's neck, and he could feel her warm tears on his skin. He stroked her fine hair and kissed her forehead.

"But, my dear, what can be done?" He asked. "The President is quite upset; I have uncovered some difficulty with one of his close allies, and if Poincaré insists that I leave France, then who can disagree?"

"Who? But darling, there it is!" She said excitedly, lifting her head and wiping away a tear from her blue eyes. "You cannot appeal to President Poincaré; you must speak to Clemenceau, immediately. He is the only one who can help you now."

"The new Prime Minister? But surely —"

"Listen to me, David. Clemenceau is the very heart of France, he controls the National Assembly. I will introduce you to him."

"My dear, I can't allow you to barter your reputation to rescue me."

Eleanor pulled back and held Gresham's face in her hands. "Darling, just listen to you — you are far more of a gentleman than you will ever admit. But this is my decision to make. Perhaps it is the only decent thing I will have the opportunity to do for you. I will arrange for you to meet Clemenceau in the morning, and that's an end to it." She went straight to the telephone and asked the operator to connect her to the Prime Minister's office.

Georges Clemenceau, the Radical Party leader and recently-appointed Prime Minister of France, was well into his seventies, balding, with shaggy white eyebrows and a great, white, walrus mustache. He was a portly man, yet he bounded from his desk with tremendous energy, as would a man half his age. His eyes burned with excitement as he approached the Princess and her escort when they met in his office at seven o'clock the next morning.

"Your Highness, it is a great honor to welcome you," Clemenceau said graciously as he took her hand and bowed to kiss her glove. The old man was a great bear beside the thin young woman.

"The honor is truly mine, Prime Minister," she said. "Thank you for making yourself available so early this morning. There is a matter of great urgency I must to bring to your immediate attention."

"Yes, certainly," Clemenceau replied cheerily. He clearly expected this royal visit to involve some trivial diplomatic matter.

"Allow me to introduce my dear friend," Princess Eleanor said as she stepped aside. "This is Colonel David Gresham."

"Colonel," Clemenceau said with little enthusiasm as he shook Gresham's hand. "Please sit down, your Highness. I will have some coffee brought in."

"Thank you, that is not necessary," she said sitting. "I only request that you give Colonel Gresham a moment of your attention, sir."

Clemenceau scowled and stood stiffly before the Princess. "Since you wish it, *Mademoiselle*, but I must warn you I have very little time for conversation this morning. Of course, I am familiar with your name, Colonel. The President has explained to me the situation with respect to Senator Humbert. What do you wish to say to the Prime Minister of France on this matter?"

Gresham had carefully considered what he would say. Indeed, he had spent all night contemplating the new Prime Minister and the troubles of France and all that must yet occur before the war could be finished. It was the proper moment, he decided, to make a desperate appeal and lay his cards on the table: "Prime Minister, has President Poincaré received a confidential letter from Emperor Charles of Austria, perhaps through his brother-in-law Prince Xavier or Prince Sixtus, proposing terms to end the war?"

Clemenceau's expression changed instantly. His scowl disappeared and his eyes grew wide. He coughed nervously and slowly circled and sat down behind his desk to consider the question. "I can neither confirm nor deny the existence of such a letter, Colonel. If there were a letter, how is it you would come to know of it? Is Great Britain now spying on France?"

"No, at least not to my own knowledge, sir, I assure you. No, I know about the Emperor's letter because two years ago I myself went to Vienna disguised as an agent of Pope Benedict and presented a make-believe offer to canonize Charles, then the Archduke, if he sought to end the war and propose specific peace terms which I then dictated to him. Would you care to hear me repeat them?"

"David, I can't believe you would do such a thing," the Princess said with mock horror, shaking her head and laughing.

"Then the letter that Poincaré received from Charles is not in earnest?" Clemenceau asked.

"Well, sir, actually it is quite earnest, but it was never meant to be accepted. As you undoubtedly know, there are terms proposed in that letter that Kaiser Wilhelm would never accept, terms such as the evacuation of Belgium and Alsace-Lorraine. No, the letter was meant to become an embarrassment to the Emperor, and it was my intent that it would be made public. The mere suggestion of such peace terms is certain to undermine the Emperor's government and demoralize his soldiers, it will threaten the very existence of the Hapsburg monarchy, and the Kaiser will consider it a great betrayal. That is why you must publish the letter publicly, Prime Minister."

"That is an outrageously deceitful ploy, Colonel. It is a disgrace!" Clemenceau shouted. "Did your government, the British government, send you to Vienna for that purpose, to mislead and embarrass our enemy in that manner?"

"The British government?" Gresham scoffed. "Of course not. How could you even imagine that the British government, Asquith or Lloyd George, would ever be so unscrupulous? No, it was my own plan, Prime Minister, just as it was my own inclination to learn how Senator Humbert could so widely and successfully implore the French people to sue for peace from Germany. Frankly, I do not believe even Senator Humbert was aware that *Le Journal* had received funds from Germany; he certainly did not wish to know anything about it. Neither was he likely the only one to receive such assistance. That is the sort of war we are fighting, and regrettably the damage to France has already been done. You must understand, sir, Germany no longer wishes to simply win this war. Now the Kaiser must seek to destroy us. In Russia, the Germans have by and large succeeded, as I can well attest for I was in Russia much of last year. Germany supported the Bolshevik revolution; they sent Lenin back from Switzerland. Now France is at a difficult stage. I have been in Paris long enough to see that your fighting spirit is dimmed, the people are afraid, the soldiers no longer possess the will to fight, and yet the Americans have not yet arrived in sufficient numbers to turn the tide. Your people believe it may be better to sue for peace than to fight until France is destroyed. Peace or ruin – those are the only options they can see. They are the only choices they have been told. That is why France needs a new voice, right now, and another choice: Victory. Tell me, sir, will France fight?"

"There is no man in my country more determined than I, Colonel," Clemenceau replied.

"Then it rests entirely upon you, sir, the future of your country. You are the Prime Minister. You are the one they call 'the Tiger'. You were made Prime Minister because *France must fight*. There can be no more dissension, no more discussion of terms. You have read President Wilson's new message they call the 'Fourteen Points' and Lloyd-George's address to the Trade Unions regarding his proposed peace terms. They are quite reasonable, I believe, but there is no hope for reasonableness until Kaiser Wilhelm is utterly destroyed. I tell you France and Great Britain must wage war until he is gone."

"I do not disagree, Colonel, truly, but you must also accept that we are far from marching into Berlin."

"Berlin? Of course you will not march to Berlin, Prime Minister. Why would you ever wish it? France is not fighting to conquer Germany, and you are no Napoleon Bonaparte. But when it is time for peace, I can tell you it will be a different Germany negotiating the terms. You must trust that I know what I am saying; you now know of what I am capable."

Clemenceau brooded silently a moment. "Yes, I understand what you are suggesting, Colonel."

"Humbert should be charged with treason and kept in prison until the end of the war. It will send a message to the world that France is no longer willing to entertain thoughts of peace. You surely expect Germany to attack this spring, which it will do as early as possible before the Americans arrive in any greater number. You must withstand that assault. You must ready your country to hold fast. Every man, woman and child must be your soldier; they must be committed to victory. You must lead them, Prime Minister. You are the only man who can do it. Will you?"

As soon as Gresham and Princess Eleanor entered the motor taxi on the street, she leapt onto Gresham's lap, embraced him, and kissed him passionately. "My God, David, I have never seen anything like it," she gasped. "You were magnificent. We must return to the hotel at once. I will send Andra out shopping for the rest of the afternoon." Gresham was consumed with desire for the beautiful young woman. He pulled Eleanor close and caressed her as they kissed and the taxi sped back to her hotel. Their meeting with Clemenceau had indeed gone very well indeed. Before it was concluded, Clemenceau had personally telephoned Dupont to order that Gresham be given his liberty to remain in France, he was not to be touched, but Humbert was to be placed under arrest that very day and certain newspapers were to be shut down.

The arrest of Humbert produced a flood of criticism. The National Assembly was outraged. The newspapers condemned Clemenceau as a dictator and claimed there was to be a new Reign of Terror in France. A No-Confidence vote was brought before the Assembly, and Clemenceau was forced to enter the *Palais Bourbon* to answer the motion. Accompanied by an unknown British Colonel with a beautiful young Roumanian Princess at his side, Clemenceau reached the steps and, alone, mounted the dais to jeering and catcalls. He stood alone, an old man, to plead his case:

"I have been accused of political crimes, I have been attacked, and I have come here today to explain the policies of my ministry so that you will all continue to be assured of our freedoms and of our great Republic," Clemenceau began modestly, but the *députés* continued to shout and jeer at him.

"Of course, we should never be afraid of freedom, of freedom of speech or freedom of the press, nor should we ever be afraid that those freedoms might be taken to excess. That is why there are laws against defamation, and laws that protect citizens against the overindulgence of freedom. I do not prevent you from using your freedom. You can write, you can speak, and you, the *deputes*, have freedom to speak in this forum. But bear one fact in mind: We must be able to defend the Republic of France. We must acknowledge that we are in a state of war. We must wage war. We must think only of war. All our thoughts must turn to making war. We must sacrifice to ensure our victory, for we wage war to preserve the rights of our citizens, to save not one freedom, but *all* our freedoms!" At last the *députés* quieted, lest they be accused of desiring France's defeat.

"Despite this, I have come today to defend myself. You say that I have done wrong, but you also know that we are now preparing for the coming months of war, months that we must face together. It is on these matters that my mind is bent every hour of the day and night. I ask you to help me. To say that my actions are a threat to the nation is merely dogmatic opposition. It is not justified by the circumstances we now face. As the war has progressed, you have seen develop in this nation a crisis of morale, a crisis which is the result of war. The price paid by our armed forces, the abuses, the violence, the robberies, the murders, and the massacres, they heap upon each other and weigh on our minds. Yet it has long been said: 'The winner is he who believes, for even a moment longer than his opponent, that he is not defeated.' That is the maxim of my ministry. I do not have another.

"I entered this government with the knowledge that we must address the morale of our nation. Gentlemen, my whole policy tends to this end, to sustain the French people through the greatest crisis in our history. Among our actions, I challenge you to find one that is not inspired by this one thought: To safeguard the heroic spirit of the French people. That is what we want, that is what we have done, and that is what we will continue to do." At last, a few of the *députés* applauded.

"The morale of our soldiers is exemplary. They are steadfast and serene, and when it comes to fighting the enemy they show no hesitance to exhaust all their efforts and their very lives upon the field of battle. The parents of our soldiers, their fathers and mothers, they too have been steadfast; there are no complaints, no complaints at all. The public peace has been maintained for four years, and we must give all the credit to the previous ministries and to the French people themselves. This attitude, it must continue. Nevertheless, there will be situations where it will become more difficult than ever before. There are excuses. There is fatigue. There have been harsh words and scandals orchestrated by enemy agents and an onslaught of German propaganda. Despite all this, the citizens of France have shown themselves to be no less courageous than our soldiers at the front lines. We must maintain that fine spirit if we can help to do so.

"For those who oppose me, have the courage of your opinions. If you insist upon an immediate peace, then say what you will give up for peace, what land, what lives, what part of France would you surrender? Of course, I also have the desire for peace; everyone desires it. It would be a great criminal that would have any other thought. But know what it is you ask, for it is not the bleating of sheep that will silence the German guns. Our great Republic must wage war. And my policies? I say they are all one. Domestic policy? I make war. Foreign policy? I make war. I always make war!"

As Clemenceau stepped away from the podium, the *députés* rose from their seats to shout their acclaim for the 77-year-old Prime Minister. The motion of No-Confidence was easily defeated.

In the newspapers the very next day, Clemenceau published the text of letters that President Poincaré had received from Emperor Charles via his brother-in-law Prince Sixtus:

> *My Dear Sixtus:*
>
> *The end of the third year of this war, which has brought so much mourning and grief into the world, approaches. All the peoples of my empire are more closely united than ever in the common determination to safeguard the integrity of the monarchy at the cost even of the heaviest sacrifices.*
>
> *Thanks to their union, with the generous co-operation of all nationalities, my empire and monarchy have succeeded in resisting the gravest assaults for nearly three years. Nobody can question the military advantages secured by my troops, particularly in the Balkans.*

France, on her side, has shown force, resistance, and dashing courage which are magnificent. We all unreservedly admire the admirable bravery, which is traditional to her army, and the spirit of sacrifice of the entire French people.

Therefore it is a special pleasure to me to note that, although for the moment adversaries, no real divergence of views or aspirations separates many of my empire from France, joined to that which prevails in the whole monarchy, will forever avoid a return of the state of war, for which no responsibility can fall on me.

With this in mind, and to show in a definite manner the reality of these feelings, I beg you to convey privately and unofficially to President Poincaré that I will support by every means, and by exerting all my personal influence with my allies, France's just claims regarding Alsace-Lorraine. Belgium should be re-established in her sovereignty, [and] Serbia should be re-established . . . .

Having thus laid my ideas clearly before you, I would ask you in turn, after consulting with these two powers, to lay before me the opinion first of France and of England, with a view thus to preparing the ground for an understanding on the basis of which official preliminary negotiations could be taken up and reach a result satisfactory to all.

Hoping that thus we will soon be able together to put a limit to the sufferings of so many millions of men and families now plunged in sadness and anxiety, I beg to assure you of my warmest and most brotherly affection.

CHARLES

The publication of the letter had an immediate impact. As France steeled itself for another year of war, the government in Austria was thrown into chaos; the Kaiser railed against his old ally; but in France the soldiers and civilians readied themselves for Germany's latest crushing blow.

Irma Staub, like "Mata Hari," was known to have bedded any number of British and French officers in the service of Germany, yet she had never been caught in an act of espionage. Her sporty yellow *Peugeot "BéBé"* was stopped just outside her Parisian townhouse. She was undoubtedly on the telephone indoors already, arranging a *rendezvous* with her German contact about the new British tank designs which she had just stolen from her most recent conquest, an unhappily-married British General. It was a sunny morning, but the air was cold and crisp, and Gresham sat in a warm café across the street watching carefully.

The beautiful, young *Mademoiselle* Staub, like Mata Hari, was well known in Paris; many of Princess Eleanor's friends in Paris were familiar with her. There had been no proof of Staub's complicity with German intelligence: None of the men she had seduced were willing to reveal their own foolishness by testifying against her. However, Gresham had had no difficulty at all in locating an eager volunteer from within the Princess' own coterie, a British Captain whom he dressed in a General's uniform and supplied with a portfolio of imaginary tank

448

designs, to be seduced by the German agent. Once Princess Eleanor introduced the *faux* General to Miss Staub, it had taken merely a few hours and one bottle of absinthe before the false tank designs had been taken.

As Gresham sweetened his coffee, an idea suddenly came to mind. Taking the sugar bowl outside the café, he casually crossed the street to the yellow *Peugeot* and dropped several lumps of sugar into its gasoline tank. Then he returned to the café. He had a very short wait. Miss Staub, wrapped in expensive furs, soon emerged from her townhouse, started her *Peugeot* and sped away. Gresham stepped outdoors to his own motorcar, a blue Cadillac *Landaulet* that he had recently had shipped over from America, and with a simple press of a button, its engine roared to life.

Gresham easily spotted Staub's yellow motorcar well ahead of him, but he followed at a respectable distance. She passed through the *Bois de Boulogne* and continued west, away from Paris. The sugar that Gresham had dumped in the *Peugeot*'s tank soon began to take its toll on the engine. The motorcar smoked and sputtered until Staub was forced to pull over to the side of the road. She leapt out in a state of great agitation and flagged the next motorcar to come along: Gresham's.

"Good morning, *Mademoiselle*. May I be of any assistance?" He asked innocently after he stopped beside her. She was a very attractive young woman, and it was no wonder she had made so many notable acquaintances in Paris since the start of the war.

"*Oui, merci monsieur*, the motor, she is not running, you see," she replied.

"Well, I can't help you with that. I'm afraid I don't know anything about how these things work. I could give you a lift, though," he offered charmingly. "I'm on my way to Le Havre. Are you headed in that direction?"

"Yes, well, I'm going to Rouen," she said hesitantly.

"Why, that's on my way, I think. Please, allow me to take you there."

In the end, Staub, extremely anxious to make her *rendezvous*, had no choice but to accept Gresham's offer. Gresham did most of the talking, mostly about the theatre, to put Staub's mind at ease, and they soon arrived in Rouen. She thanked Gresham heartily when he left her at a small pastry shop in the city. Gresham pulled over and entered the hotel next door. He borrowed the telephone at the front desk to call General Dupont.

"Hello, General, this is Gresham. I have a peace offering for you. I am in Rouen if you can make it here quickly," he said before explaining what he had done.

Dupont's men in Rouen quickly arrived to raid the pastry shop. However, as Gresham entered in their wake he learned that Staub had eluded them. She had already fled through the back door. The French agents found only the shop owner and a pleasant old gentleman, a language professor with a Swiss passport. Gresham followed along as the professor was taken to the police station for further questioning.

Dupont was quite cool when he arrived at the station later that day. "*Bonjour,* Colonel," Dupont said. "You must know that I was under the impression our paths would not cross again, despite the Prime Minister's intervention on your behalf."

"I don't expect our paths shall cross, General, and of course I am pleased to leave the internal security of France in your capable hands. However, by way of making amends, I wanted to offer you a gift."

"A gift? But *Mademoiselle* Staub has escaped yet again and we still have no evidence to arrest her!"

"We shall see. The professor is still in custody. May I join you in questioning him?"

"Very well," Dupont agreed reluctantly, "but you may not speak, Colonel."

In a small, brightly lit office, the old professor sat calmly sipping a cup of tea with the police captain and a secretary.

"Good evening, *Monsieur,*" Dupont began. "*Captain, has this gentleman any identification papers?*"

"*Yes, sir.*"

"*Will you show them to me?*"

"*With pleasure.*" The captain took out a pocket-book bulging with papers and produced a passport made out in the name of "Hans Widenau", 72 years old, professor of foreign languages, born in Zurich of German parents. "*These are in perfect order,*" the captain remarked.

"It seems that you do a lot of traveling, Professor Widenau!" Dupont exclaimed. "You cross borders with remarkable ease. By the visas on your passport I see that within the last year you have been in France three times, in Germany twice, and in Italy five times. What reason have you to do so much traveling?"

"Oh, I love to travel," the professor replied calmly.

"Evidently. Yet your love for traveling does not quite explain why *this* document is in your possession." Dupont held out an Italian military map of the Gothard region that was among the professor's papers; Dupont handed the remaining papers to Gresham.

"Oh, that is only a map I used for mountain climbing; an Italian officer gave it to me. I love to climb mountains."

"Please explain why you are in Rouen, then."

"I am traveling to Paris to visit a former student of mine. I only stopped for tea."

"And the woman who entered the *boulangerie?* Do you know her?"

"Woman? Oh, yes, of course. There *was* a woman who entered the shop shortly before your men arrived. She went right out the door to the alley without making a purchase. Very curious, indeed."

Gresham saw only student essays and newspaper clippings among the professor's papers, along with an assortment of photographs. One photograph in particular caught his eye, and he handed it to Dupont.

Dupont looked at the photo of a man and woman standing beside an alpine lake curiously for a moment, and then passed it to the professor.

"Will you tell me, who is the man in this photograph?"

The professor looked at the photograph intensely and hesitated for a long moment before answering: "I do not recall his name."

"Then the woman?"

"That is my dear friend the Countess de Louvain."

Dupont shook his head, then turned to smiled at Gresham. He winked, clapped Gresham warmly on the back as if they were old friends, and then nodded as he turned back to face the old man.

"I am quite familiar with the Countess de Louvain, *Monsieur*," Dupont said. "That is the name by which *Mademoiselle* Irma Staub is known in Bavaria, and if you know her by that name it means you are Bavarian yourself. If I am correct, then I must conclude that you yourself are Major von Trauth, the commander of Crown Prince Rupprecht's espionage bureau. *Je suis désolé, Monsieur*," he said with a broad smile, "but it is my humble duty to place you under arrest.

Brest-Litovsk

You said your contact would meet us here at dusk," Wilkins complained to Josephina Hesketh. A freezing cold rain whipped across the dock and night had come early. One of Hesketh's many smuggling associates had transported them across the Adriatic on his small fishing vessel to a small harbor just north of the Austrian naval base at Trieste. The sedan that was intended to meet them there was long overdue. Wilkins, already drenched and frozen from the long journey, turned away from the choppy sea and icy rain and looked up at the dark, deserted castle behind them. It was quiet and still, like the ruins of an ancient civilization.

"That is Miramare Castle," Hesketh said. "Archduke Franz Ferdinand lived there at one time."

"Yes, it is one of the Hapsburg castles. Perhaps we should break in." Wilkins pulled his cap down tight over his brow and climbed the stairs to the castle. Hesketh followed behind him.

"It isn't very old, is it?" She asked as she admired the castle's stonework and large windows.

"No, it is not. This one was built by Franz Joseph's brother, Maximilian, as a present for his wife Carlota."

"Maximilian? Wasn't he the one who declared himself Emperor of Mexico?"

"Yes, he is the one," Wilkins said. "He was later executed and Carlota went insane; she still calls herself an Empress but she lives in Belgium now." He peered inside the etched glass French doors. All the furnishings and valuables inside the castle had been taken away for safekeeping at the start of the war. Wilkins could see nothing inside, but at least it was dry. He smashed the window pane with his elbow and unlocked the door. "We can't go anywhere tonight. Come inside and we'll wait until dawn."

The magnificent rooms were lavishly wallpapered and decorated with elaborately gilded plaster trim, but now the rooms stood empty and silent. Wilkins dared not turn on the lights, but he and Hesketh wandered from room to room admiring the fine workmanship and imagining the days when the young lovers Maximillian and Carlotta had spent carefree summer days here on the shore of the Adriatic. At last, in the dry cellars, Wilkins found some dusty canvas tarps and an old mattress. He and Hesketh stripped off their wet clothes and lay beneath the tarps to keep each other warm and share the brandy in Wilkins' flask.

"Are you ready yet to tell me why we are going to Warsaw?" Hesketh asked as she nestled provocatively against Wilkins. "If we have become the targets of Major von Trauth, I can't understand why you would choose to go to Warsaw. We are virtually entering the lion's den."

"As I told you already," Wilkins insisted. "I know a man who can get us out of this difficulty."

"So you say. Some 'man.' But in *Warsaw*? That is German territory, James," she objected.

"It is Russian territory presently occupied by the German army, and the man I must speak to is in the German army, my dear. He is a close contact, you might say."

"Yes, so you have told me, but who is he?"

"You must trust me and wait, Josephina. I insist."

By morning the rain had tapered off but the wind still blew hard and cold. Shortly after daybreak a motorcar arrived, an older *Gräf & Stift* model driven by an old, bald Austrian man. Wilkins and Hesketh climbed into the back of the sedan.

"Christoph, what took you so long? We have been waiting all night. Was it so very difficult to come down from Vienna?" Hesketh, in German, angrily asked the old man.

"It is very difficult to find petrol, Madame," the old man pleaded. "Who is this man you have brought with you?" He asked with concern.

"My name is Kruger," Wilkins said quickly, recalling his previous mission to Vienna with Gresham in 1916. "I am a German East African traveling to Poland to confer with my superiors in the German army. That is all you need to know. How long will it take for us to reach Warsaw?"

"That will take many days, sir, and I cannot tell you whether we will be able to find petrol along the way. There are so many shortages."

"James, listen to me, perhaps you could simply send a telegram to your contact now that we are in Austria," Hesketh suggested. "Must we drive all the way to Warsaw? I really must have this resolved."

"Unfortunately I must go there myself," Wilkins said firmly. "This is a very delicate matter and I must speak with the fellow face to face. If you do not wish to accompany me, then you may stay here in Trieste."

Hesketh was clearly perturbed, but she finally agreed to accompany Wilkins.

Since they avoided the larger cities, the trip took far longer than Wilkins anticipated, nearly two whole weeks, yet as they rambled northward each day and scrounged for food and petrol across the countryside, Wilkins was shocked by what he discovered: In one town after another, the Austrian people were starving. The farm workers had almost all been conscripted into the army and the harvest that autumn had been very poor. In most villages there was almost nothing to eat. It had been months since some Austrians had seen bread, and even in the more affluent towns, scurvy and starvation were rampant.

Outside the cities, Austria was in chaos. There were no roadblocks or checkpoints like those Wilkins had seen in Germany, and the bedraggled soldiers they met, especially the Hungarians, were utterly disinterested in war; they only wanted to return to their homes. More and more Austrian troops were being sent to fight on the Western Front under German commanders, which was widely regarded as a betrayal of his people by the new young Emperor Charles. Indeed, there had even been recent railway shutdowns and labor strikes at several of the major armament factories. Surprisingly, few Austrians were impressed or pleased that their country had won a major victory against the Italians at Caporetto, in part because that victory was due largely to the assistance of specially-trained German "Stormtroopers" and the very liberal use of poison chlorine gas. Even though Italy's reserves were now utterly depleted, its army reeling and unable to mount any kind of offensive, the French, British and Serbian forces at Salonika were still checked by the Bulgarian and German forces, and an armistice had ended the threat of invasion from Roumania or Russia, still the Caporetto offensive had seemingly expended the very last of Austria's will to wage war. Come what may, Austria's part in the Great War was near its end, and increasingly the people began to consider whether there should be major changes to their government and monarchy and greater independence for Hungary and the other ethnic enclaves within the old Austro-Hungarian Empire. Wilkins had plenty of opportunities to speak with villagers and former soldiers and learned a great deal about the growing tensions in the Baltic regions, and Ukraine and, in particular, Poland.

Wilkins and Hesketh at last passed quietly from Austrian Galicia into German-occupied Poland, a country that had been in turmoil for a century. After the Congress of Vienna in 1815, the Tsar of Russia had ruled over most of Poland's territory as its king, although parts of Poland had also been traded to the Prussians and Austrians. At the start of the war, many Poles aligned with Germany to fight against Russia. But with the Russian Tsar now gone, everything would change. As they neared Warsaw, the roads became more congested, the city lively, and Wilkins soon discovered that the German occupiers were viewed with widespread approval, particularly by the merchants who appreciated the opportunity to conduct business peacefully with Germany. To the vast number of Jews in Warsaw who had long suffered under the harsh Russian rulers, and from the *pogroms* and rampant Anti-Semitism, the Germans were viewed as liberators.

Afraid of receiving too much attention, Wilkins and Hesketh took a single room at a very modest boarding house on the outskirts of the city. There were many German officers in Warsaw, and it was better to avoid questions at the more respectable hotels. As they ascended the dark, narrow stairs of the boarding house to their small room on the second floor, made their way down the dingy, unlit corridor, and entered their miserable room, neither spoke. Hesketh sat on the old, iron bed waiting anxiously as Wilkins looked out the second story window at the snowy, darkened street below and sipped the last of his brandy. For over two weeks, Hesketh had barely let Wilkins out of her sight, and particularly now that they were in Warsaw, she had become truly anxious to learn the name of Wilkins' contact in the German army.

"When shall we meet him?" She demanded. "Will you make contact? Shall we send him a note? I cannot bear any longer to be considered an enemy of my own country, James; you owe it to me to clear my name."

"My dear, you must calm yourself. Everything will be fine. I will go speak to the gentleman tomorrow, and then I have no doubt that all suspicion will be cast away from you."

"You have no idea how this situation disturbs me; sometimes I feel I am suffocating, James. He must be a very powerful and important man, your contact?" She asked hopefully.

"Indeed, he is. I promise you, there will be no trouble at all when we return to Italy; everything will be settled at last."

"And we will return to Italy together?"

"Yes, certainly, but you must understand that I cannot allow you to go on importing explosives. That part of your life must come to an end."

"Of course, James, you have nothing to fear in that regard. I am done with the whole business. From now on I shall only be your lover."

"I rather like the sound of that," Wilkins said with a grin.

"And *I* promise to *you* that I will make you very happy." She went to Wilkins and kissed him passionately. She unbuckled his belt and opened his pants. "Very happy," she said again with a devious smile as she looked into his astonished face.

Wilkins woke in the morning to find that Hesketh had arisen long before him. She was waiting, and more impatiently than ever.

"Josephina, I see you are already dressed," Wilkins said as he wiped his eyes. "Go find us some bread, if you are already awake. And we will need a motorcar, I think. Could you at least ask the innkeeper about that?" He yawned dramatically. "I really don't think I can get out of bed just yet."

"Of course, James," she said nervously. "You just stay there and I will make inquiries." She locked the door behind her and ran down the stairs. By the time she returned to their room a minute later, Wilkins had disappeared.

Wilkins was convinced that Hesketh had only accompanied him to Warsaw in order to learn the name of his contact in the German army, and he realized that it would be necessary to shake her off long enough to first conduct another, secret meeting. Indeed, it was for that meeting that he had bothered come to Warsaw at all, and it was one he preferred that Hesketh knew nothing about.

He expected he would only have a moment to make his escape as she spoke to the innkeeper. Wilkins leapt from the bed and grabbed his clothes, threw open the window and lowered himself ungracefully into the snow drift on the street below. He stopped only long enough to pull on his pants and overcoat and, still barefoot, rushed around the corner out of sight of the boarding house. There were only a few vehicles on the street early that morning, but Wilkins leapt out to stop a passing motorist, drew his handgun, and made off with the stolen vehicle, leaving an astonished German officer shouting after him in the street. Surely the Germans would now be hunting him down, so Wilkins raced across the Vistula River and into the dense industrial sector where he had learned the Polish Legions were headquartered. He would have to find them quickly.

The Polish Legions had been founded early in the war. Thousands of Polish patriots had agreed to help Germany defeat the Russian army in the hope of winning independence for Poland. Their commander, Marshal Józef Pilsudski, had even forced Germany to acknowledge the independence of Poland, or at least to make that acknowledgment on paper. However, since the German invasion, the members of the "interim" government in Poland had been handpicked by the German Foreign Secretary, Baron Richard von Kühlmann, and now that the Russians had for all accounts and purposes been defeated, it was not clear whether Germany would honor its pledge of independence. No one yet knew how the potential peace treaty with the new Russian government would address the issue of Polish nationality, but the German envoys had portentously forced the Polish representatives to leave the nascent peace negotiations with Russia taking place at Brest-Litovsk.

Wilkins had learned that the leader of the Polish Legions had recently returned from the front lines in Galicia to make his headquarters in the industrial Targówek district on the outskirts of Warsaw. Wilkins barely knew enough Polish to ask directions to the unit's headquarters, but he was soon able to abandon his stolen motorcar and knocked on the door of their modest brick house. A young man in Polish uniform answered.

"*Co to jest?*" He asked coldly.

"*Nie mówię po polsku dobrze. Czy mówisz po angielsku? Chcę porozmawiać z Piłsudski,*" Wilkins replied.

The soldier glared at Wilkins a moment, then without implying his approval replied: "*Wejdź.*"

Wilkins entered the dark, run-down house and followed the soldier to a bright and sparsely furnished room in the back of the house. Wilkins sat on the bare wood floor wondering if Hesketh and the Germans were yet on his trail, but no one came to arrest him as he waited hour after hour.

Finally, the Legion's commander, Józef Pilsudski, arrived. A middle-aged man with fierce, narrow-set and dark eyes and a broad, pointed mustache, Pilsudski looked decidedly angry. "Who are you?" He demanded at once.

Wilkins stood. "I am James Wilkins; I am from England, and I wish to speak to you about the future of Poland."

"Good God, an Englishman? What the Hell are you doing in Poland? Did you come here to surrender?"

Wilkins laughed. "No, sir."

"Tell me what you want, then. We cannot have Englishmen sitting here at their leisure."

"Well, sir, I understand you have been fighting the Russian army in Galicia the past three years."

"Yes, until the Russians stopped fighting."

"I myself have spent much of the past year in Petrograd. I attempted to help Alexandre Kerensky establish a new government in Russia. And I suppose you know that Kerensky has now been overthrown by the Bolsheviks."

"Of course," Pilsudski said with undisguised animosity.

"Yes, I am pleased to hear that you have no affection for Lenin and his crew. Perhaps you have also heard that my own Prime Minister, David Lloyd George, made a speech recently at the Trade Union Conference in London where he pledged Great Britain's support for an independent Poland. And the American President made the same pledge in his address; it was one of his 'Fourteen Points'."

"That is what Dmowski and the National Committee have been doing in Paris while I have been fighting the Russians," Pilsudski said bitterly.

"Yes, you and Dmowski have had a difference of opinion in that regard: He felt Poland should side with the Entente, and you chose to align with Germany. I won't say I disagree with your decision – victory over Russia was clearly necessary for Poland to achieve independence. However, you must acknowledge that Russia has now been defeated. Your dispute with Dmovski is just water under the bridge."

Pilsudski stared at Wilkins a moment uncertainly. "I suppose that it true," he agreed at last.

"If I see him, may I tell him you said so? That you are prepared to work together now to achieve Polish independence?"

"If you see him," Pilsudski said with a chuckle.

"You are still dedicated to achieving statehood for Poland. Of course you must be. So tell me of the promises you have received from Germany. Now that the Kaiser's armies have occupied the whole of Poland and his Foreign Secretary has appointed your government, is Poland now free? Or do Germany's promises seem less genuine with each passing day."

Pilsudski glared at Wilkins angrily. "I suppose you have heard that Germany now demands we swear allegiance to the German crown?"

"Of course they do. Germany seeks to make Poland a vassal state or suzerain, and once you have taken their oath they will send your men to fight on the Western Front against the British and Americans, far from your homeland, against two great nations that have sworn to make Poland independent."

"So you would ask us to fight against Germany now, is that it?"

"No, sir, I do not. I come merely to learn whether you will continue to fight for Poland."

"We will always fight for our motherland," Pilsudski replied.

"In the past two weeks I have traveled through Austria, Galicia and Poland, and it is beginning to look as though this war is nearly over. Austria has all but stopped fighting. It is much the same on the Western Front, Great Britain,

France and Germany cannot bear to go on much longer. Hindenburg knows he cannot advance once the Americans arrive in force, so further stalemate is inevitable; it is now merely a matter of time before the belligerents acknowledge as much and the peace treaties are written. Then they will redraw the borders of the European nations. I do not know where those borders will fall on the Western Front, sir, but I intend to see that on the Eastern Front those borders fall as far within Russian territory as humanly possible. Europe will need a strong and independent Poland.

"I came to speak with you because there is another great struggle about to begin, and we must anticipate and prepare for it. When that conflict comes, I regret to say that Poland will be on the front lines yet again, and you will be required to fight for Poland against your enemy and the enemy of Great Britain, France *and* Germany. You and your men should not be resting in Flanders Fields when the Russians seek to return to Poland. This is where you belong."

"You believe the new Russian government will seek to reclaim Poland?"

"Certainly they will: For Lenin's 'revolution' to succeed, it must spread, and his fledgling 'Red Army' will prove far more effective at achieving that than *propaganda* alone. They will secure their government in Russia and then they will turn west to recapture Poland. That will only be the beginning.

"I cannot tell you when the Russians will come, Marshal, or whether Germany will seek to make Poland a puppet state, or in truth whether Great Britain or France would do likewise. You will have to wait and make that assessment for yourself. But I do know that you must be here, in Poland, when the time comes. You are a great leader, and the Poles will see how you have served your country. I came to tell you that France and Great Britain (and likely Germany, as well) will be your allies in the fight against Bolshevism. The day will come when you will want our help. My name is James Wilkins, and you may contact me whenever you wish Great Britain's assistance."

Wilkins looked Marshal Pilsudski in the eye and shook his hand and then walked calmly from the room without even waiting for a response. Outside, the afternoon was overcast and cold. A light snow was falling as Wilkins trudged back by foot over the Vistula River.

Wilkins was walking alongside Górnośląska Boulevard when he realized that a black motorcar was following him. He arrived at the boarding house soon afterward, and although nothing looked out of place, as he entered the building a large man suddenly grabbed his arm and forced Wilkins face down onto the damp and filthy wooden floorboards, his arms held tightly behind his back. His wrists were manacled, and then he was hauled back up onto his feet and led into an adjoining guestroom where Hesketh, seething with hatred, awaited him.

"Where have you been!?" She shrieked at him.

"Out for a stroll, my dear," Wilkins answered flippantly. It was a mistake. The man behind Wilkins held his arms tightly as Hesketh leapt forward and slapped Wilkins sharply across the cheek. Her rage had turned her face bright red.

"I want to know who your contact is, who you have been meeting. What is your real name, 'James Bell'? You will tell me now or I will have your damned eyes out!" She screamed.

"I'll tell you my name if you tell me yours first. Fair is fair."

"Hesketh, Clementi, Nezie, Davidovitch, Baroness de Bellville, take your pick," she spat at him.

"No, your true name, my dear. After all we've shared, don't you think I deserve to know who you truly are?"

She looked in him with bitter hatred but then stepped close and brought her mouth close to his ear and whispered: "My name is Derya Storch."

"You are very lovely Miss Storch, I must admit it, and I've enjoyed our time together immensely. A pity it must end. Come closer, and I will give you my name and the name of my contact in the German army. It is time we fully cleared the air between us."

She leaned in. Wilkins whispered in her ear, and her face suddenly turned white.

It was a long and unpleasant journey to Germany. Even though the railway was quite comfortable, Wilkins' captors kept him manacled and under constant guard. If his claims were true, and they had yet to be confirmed, then perhaps it would be better not to harm him impulsively. Certainly they could not simply execute him. However, the Germans in Poland were not quite sure whether to take their prisoner at his word – after all, he had admitted to being a wanted spy, notorious and long sought after by German Intelligence. In the end, the German military commandant in Warsaw decided to simply place Wilkins under arrest. Then the wire had come demanding that Wilkins be brought to Germany at once.

His train at last arrived at Cologne. At the railway station, Wilkins was blindfolded and taken by sedan out of the city. His hands were still manacled and the German officers sitting beside him were heavily armed. It was a quick ride over a river, presumably the Rhine, and another half hour before the sedan came to its final stop. Wilkins was led from the sedan and his blindfold finally removed. As he looked around, he shook his head and laughed: They had brought him to Stammheim, an estate he had visited several times as a boy. He knew exactly where he was, and there had been no purpose at all in blindfolding him during the short journey.

Wilkins followed the German officers calmly into the grand estate house and was led into the bright and airy library. A fire crackled in the hearth, and before it a trim, middle-aged German commander was seated on a simple wooden chair. His hair was grey and short in the military fashion, his mustache was full but modestly trimmed, and his eyes were alert and deadly serious. His uniform, however, was heavily decorated with both military and royal medals, stars and emblems, and his shoulders were adorned with gold epaulets as befit this Field Marshal, the Commander of Germany's Northern Army Group consisting of the 1st, 2nd, 6th and 7th Armies. He was His Royal Highness, Rupprecht, the Crown Prince of Bavaria.

Wilkins stood silent. The Crown Prince looked up and nodded almost imperceptibly. Wilkins' heavy steel manacles were removed and the German officers swiftly left the room. Wilkins rubbed his red, chafed wrists as Crown Prince Rupprecht stood and approached Wilkins. He circled around and examined the captured British spy carefully, and then came to a stop to face his prisoner.

"Tell me, James, how is my sister?" Rupprecht asked calmly.

"Mother was very well the last time she wrote to me, Sir, and she will be very pleased to learn that you have asked after her," Wilkins said.

The Crown Prince sighed heavily. "Sit down, James, and tell me what you are doing here," he said as he returned to the hearth and sank down upon the wooden chair.

"I came to see *you*, of course," Wilkins said as he sat down across from his uncle, the Crown Prince of Bavaria. Germany was a confederation of territories, the largest being Prussia. Bavaria was the second largest. Although the Prussian House of Hohenzollern held the title of Emperor, the King of Bavaria was among the most powerful men in Germany. His eldest son, Rupprecht, the Crown Prince, was one of Kaiser Wilhelm's top military commanders, but his youngest daughter, Elsa, had been married to an English nobleman, the Earl of Bartlett, James Wilkins' father. Wilkins continued: "You can't imagine I was captured by accident."

"Were you sent by your Secret Intelligence Service?"

"No. I don't suppose I work for the Service anymore; the Prime Minister was rather upset about Petrograd."

"Then David Lloyd George is an idiot. We were very concerned that you would reach an agreement with Premier Kerensky. We are even more concerned now that you did not."

"As well you should be."

"So am I to assume this is a social visit?"

Wilkins laughed a bit nervously. "No, Sir. Actually, I've come to make you an offer of service."

Rupprecht chuckled. "You wish to spy on England now? I certainly do not believe that."

"That's not quite what I had in mind."

"And would you have me take no notice of that terrible business in Switzerland?" Rupprecht asked with muted anger.

"I heartily apologize for *Herr* Koertiger's unfortunate demise. It was entirely accidental, a simple matter of self-defense gone awry."

"I might accept that explanation but for the fact that the director of my espionage bureau, Major von Trauth, has also been arrested in France. Did you have any involvement in that?"

"None at all, I assure you."

"So you were not in France?"

"No, certainly not. I have been in Italy reading newspapers for some time, and before that I was in Ypres, but only briefly."

"You were at Passchendaele?"

"No, only in Ypres, but I did hear something about your General Quartermaster – von Metzger, is that his name? – that he was almost captured by the Canadians, is that right?"

"Yes, something like that. *Herr* General Quartermaster von Metzger was in Passchendaele at the time of the British assault and became trapped briefly behind your lines; his aide gave his life to create a diversion so Metzger could escape."

"Very heroic."

"Yes. Tell me about the scar there on your cheek."

"Gallipoli," Wilkins replied.

"It's not so bad."

"It's nothing."

"I see. So, you have been tossed aside by your British spymasters, eh? You have some other proposal to make or else you would not have surrendered to our men in Poland."

"Yes, I do."

"Very well, then, tell me."

"Well, it is simply, as you mentioned, very unfortunate that Kerensky's government was overthrown. It will be especially unfortunate for Germany since you now share a border with Russia."

"Yes, I understand you very well."

"Have you already experienced difficulties?"

"You would be dumbfounded by what is going on at the front."

"Revolutionary propaganda coming across the lines?"

"A million copies of *Pravda* every week, and radio transmissions too."

"Radio – really? How very clever of them. And I suppose the Bolsheviks are beseeching your soldiers to overthrow the *Reichstag* and rebel against the Kaiser?"

"It has gotten so severe that Marshall Hoffman was forced to break up a few of our less reliable battalions. Even the German prisoners of war returned to us from Russia must be quarantined because they have been indoctrinated with revolutionary propaganda."

"It is no surprise to learn of such treachery. In Petrograd, the hazard posed by these new Russian dictators was quite clear. Their objectives lie far beyond the borders of Russia; their doctrine demands that they spread their revolution across Europe; if you can believe it, they even aspire to overthrow the American government! Certainly the propaganda is bad, but I understand they have now assembled a 'Red Army' as well."

"Yes, I have heard a great deal about this new army," the Crown Prince said with obvious concern. "My agents say that many of the former Tsar's best commanders are joining the Bolshevik forces, and the majority of those soldiers are volunteers."

"I will tell you how they obtain these volunteers, Uncle, for I have heard the stories myself from those who have fled to Galicia. The 'Reds' go to a man's home and ask him to volunteer. If he refuses, he is shot dead on the spot. It is especially revealing that just six months ago Kerensky was unable to impose the death penalty in the military system, not even upon soldiers who murdered their commanding officers and abandoned their posts. But now it has come to this. Things are changing in Russia very rapidly."

"There is a great deal of concern internationally, so much so in fact that the British and Americans have actually asked us to participate in a counter-revolutionary invasion at Murmansk this summer. Still, the Red Army seems but a small threat to Imperial Germany."

"Perhaps for now, but the Red Army will continue to grow. What condition will your armies be in at the end of this war? Would you have combat resume on the Eastern Front next year, or the year after? This is where the on-going peace treaty negotiations at Brest-Litovsk are so significant," Wilkins said. "First, there is the propaganda. Consider Poland. Everyone believes that Germany will annex the Kingdom of Poland. But what is Russia's intent there? Lenin rails against Germany's annexationist policies, but he surely wants to take Poland for himself so he can forcibly impose his revolution upon the Polish people. The Brest-Litovsk negotiations are an opportunity for you to draw out the new Russian government's agenda. The world must learn that 'Bolshevism' means no more than 'dictatorship'."

"And what if Germany *does* choose to annex Poland?" Rupprecht asked.

"My dear Uncle, it is perfectly clear to everyone that you intend to annex Poland, and of course the Kaiser believes he must come out of this dreadful war with something gained. However, it was my thinking that Germany must take advantage of the peace negotiations to lay an unsound foundation for the Bolsheviks build upon, to undermine both their government and their aspirations. I also recommend that you use your present military superiority in the region to establish a line of independent, allied nations, as a buffer to separate you physically from Russia. It hardly matters whether their governments are controlled by Germany or not, as long as they are your allies and not those of the Bolsheviks. I tell you: It is merely a matter of time before Great Britain, France and Germany will be waging war against Russia."

"These are very interesting suggestions, indeed. And I agree, James, these are crucial negotiations; I would be pleased to discuss your thoughts with the Foreign Secretary. However, it does not answer what I shall do with you."

"But you see, sir, I am here to ask that you send me to Brest-Litovsk as your personal representative," Wilkins said.

"What?" The Crown Prince asked incredulously.

"That is why I have come to see you, Uncle."

"That is not possible, James," the Crown Prince replied. "Would you take an oath of allegiance to the Kaiser?"

"That might be a bit much, I agree, but I will take an oath not to serve my country at the expense of Germany or her allies, and I give you my word of honor, as the son of Thomas Wilkins, Earl of Bartlett, and your own sister, that I will do no harm to anyone in Germany. I do so freely and without reservation, for as you seem to agree Great Britain and Germany share a mutual interest here. We must both know what is happening in Brest-Litovsk, and if you will send me, I will report back to you personally on the progress of the negotiations. You know that I can serve you very well in that capacity, and perhaps your Foreign Secretary would benefit as well."

Crown Prince Rupprecht laughed out loud. "James, you were always a surprising boy, too damned clever by half, but still you have caught me off guard. You are quite in earnest, I can see. You have already finished with this war and are preparing for the next. But will your government not consider you a traitor? Your mother would never forgive me if I were to ruin your reputation."

"I don't see that they need ever know of it, Sir."

"True, true. Well, since you are my nephew, James, I will consider it and discuss your proposal with my aides. However, in the meantime you must remain here at Stammheim and give me your parole: Will you swear not take up arms against Germany or make any attempt to leave this estate until I release you from this oath?"

"Certainly, I do, on my honor," Wilkins replied. "There is one other matter, Sir," he added. He produced from his jacket pocket the small silver lapel pin from Rome, the broadsword beneath a cross whose arms were bent clockwise to form a broken circle. "Just from nagging curiosity, I must ask you whether you recognize this pin."

Rupprecht stood and took the pin from Wilkins' hand. His face grew dark. "Yes, I do. That is the symbol of the *German Walvater Order of the Holy Grail,* a secret society in Bavaria. It is akin to 'Freemasonry', I suppose, but these fellows in Bavaria are Teutonic occultists: The broken circle on that pin, you see, is based on a symbol called the 'swastika'; I believe it's some sort of ancient good luck charm. I was invited to join their society but had to decline; many of the members are extreme ultranationalists affiliated with the Fatherland Party begun by Admiral Tirpitz and Colonel Nicholai, the director of Ludendorff's own intelligence service." Then the Crown Prince of Bavaria stepped suddenly to the hearth and cast the pin into the fire.

Before the week was done, Wilkins was on his way to Brest-Litovsk. As he well knew, Crown Prince Rupprecht would have to take him at his word. Such promises as Wilkins had made were deemed sacred, and he could never act in a manner that would bring disrepute to his family name. Yet there was still a long journey before Wilkins would reach Brest-Litovsk, a small city that lay far to the east in territory that, before the war, had been part of Russia. During his lengthy train travels, passing through checkpoints with papers specially prepared for him by the Crown Prince, Wilkins saw a great deal of Germany and could see that circumstances in that great industrial nation were also nearing the crisis point. The people he met, and the soldiers he traveled with, were rapidly losing hope in any kind of victory, and Wilkins could see that Germany would soon become fertile ground for the Bolshevik's revolutionary rhetoric.

Brest-Litovsk itself was everything that Wilkins expected. During three years of combat on the Eastern Front, the city had been almost completely destroyed. Now the region was occupied by the German armies under the command of General Max von Hoffman, and all that remained of the city was the Nineteenth Century fortress whose cold, uncomfortable concrete bunkers and brick barracks now housed the four hundred dignitaries who had come to negotiate the treaty that would end the war between Russia and the Central Powers. Wilkins had given his oath to do no more than observe the proceedings as an informal representative of the State of Bavaria and report to Crown Prince Rupprecht directly. His attendance at the negotiations and permission to speak to any of the other representatives was left entirely to the discretion of the German Foreign Secretary, Baron Richard von Kühlmann.

It was Wilkins' duty to present himself to Kühlmann upon his arrival, and he spent the better part of a day waiting in a dark, frigid hallway in the company of three young men from the Russian region of Ukraine. The excited but timid trio had brought several bottles of *Vodka* to drink as they waited to meet the Foreign Secretary. The *Vodka* they were happy to share with Wilkins in exchange for a few cigarettes. After hours of drinking, the three Ukrainians became slowly more garrulous. Wilkins could hear them talking angrily about Lenin and the Bolsheviks in Petrograd. At last he was compelled to ask after their business at the proceedings: "Have you merely come to watch?" He suggested.

"No, no, we have come to negotiate," the Ukrainian leader replied. "We were sent by the Central *Rada* in Kiev. Ukraine has declared its independence and established a republic; we cannot stand the Bolsheviks and we will have nothing more to do with Russia."

"Have you, indeed? My congratulations to you all," Wilkins replied cheerily. "How do the Russians feel about that?"

"F--- the Russians," one of the young men drunkenly replied, in Russian.

"I am the new Foreign Minister," said the third man. He appeared to be even younger than his two countrymen. Indeed all three men looked barely old enough to serve as soldiers. "I am the only one in our committee who has traveled outside Ukraine."

"Have you?"

"Oh yes, I have been to Roumania many times, and to Serbia once, when I was a boy."

"Do you know anything about the German Foreign Secretary?" Wilkins asked.

"Kühlmann? They say he was born and raised in Constantinople," the young Ukrainian "Foreign Minister" replied. "And he was at The Hague before the war."

"I hear the Germans are providing food for the representatives who are here for the negotiations," the first Ukrainian said. "Do you know if the German food is any good?"

Wilkins was finally shown into the small bleak room that the German delegation used as their office. The dapper and sophisticated Foreign Secretary, his black hair well-oiled and his black mustache neatly trimmed, did not bother to look up from his papers as Wilkins stood stiffly in his fine grey suit.

"Good afternoon, Baron," Wilkins said in the most formal German he could muster. "His Royal Highness the Crown Prince of Bavaria has sent me to attend these proceedings on his behalf and report to him my observations. It is of course his hope that my presence will meet with your approval."

"Yes, yes, of course," Kühlmann replied impatiently. "What is your name?"

"James Wilkins."

Kühlmann looked up. "That is not a German name."

"No, sir; I was born in England."

"'Wilkins', yes; of course you're no relation to Thomas Wilkins, are you?" Kühlmann asked with a mild chuckle.

"He is my father."

Kühlmann jumped to his feet in shock: "Good Lord! You are Lord Bartlett's son?" He asked.

"Yes, sir, and I am also the nephew of Crown Prince Rupprecht."

"Well, I'm damned if I know what to think of this, *Herr* Wilkins. The British government declined to send a delegation to these proceedings, you know."

"I do not represent Great Britain, sir; I am here solely as Crown Prince Rupprecht's personal representative, and I have brought this letter of introduction which explains everything." Wilkins passed over a letter from the Crown Prince. Kühlmann reviewed it thoroughly in silence.

"Very interesting," the Baron said at last. "I see you were in Petrograd last year. Undoubtedly, seeing the Tsar and his government swept away must have been quite shocking."

"It was, indeed," Wilkins replied. He wondered how much Kühlmann knew of Germany's own involvement in that episode, if anything.

"I have met your father, Lord Bartlett," Kühlmann said, "when I was stationed in London before the war – a very perceptive and honorable gentleman. May I assume that you share some of his quality, *Herr* Wilkins?"

"I hope so, sir, but I would tell you that I am here of my own accord; my father knows nothing of it."

"Undoubtedly; Lord Bartlett is not a man to send his own son into enemy territory, of that I am certain. Well, well, since you have given your parole to Crown Prince Rupprecht I am inclined to allow you to stay, *Herr* Wilkins, if only because I have no desire to obstruct the wishes of the Crown Prince of Bavaria. But I shall require you to behave yourself and to speak only with me, apart from your reports to the Crown Prince. Are you familiar with what has transpired here thus far?"

"I believe so, sir. As I understand it, you have agreed in principle to declare an end to the hostilities and to allow the Baltic regions of Latvia, Lithuania and Estonia to declare their independence from Russia based upon Germany's assurance that they will not be annexed without their consent. Of course, you made this assurance in the knowledge that these regions are currently occupied by the German armies and their interim governments were hand-selected by yourself, a detail that the Russians perhaps misunderstood at the time. They have since realized their error and have made the now far-more-credible claim that Germany's true aim in this war is to annex those Russian territories in all but name. In response to these scurrilous allegations, both the American President and British Prime Minister have attempted to embarrass you by declaring that these territories should become free and independent nations and permitted to elect their own governments. Meanwhile, the Turks want to annex the Caucasus territories, and General Hoffman wants you to demand Russia's immediate, unconditional surrender or else he will march his German armies all the way to Petrograd. You have been given no clear instructions, you are in possession of Slavic territories that you cannot govern but the Bolsheviks must not obtain, you have a Kaiser who demands conquest, a *Reichstag* that rejects annexation, and the Russian representatives sent to negotiate with you are madmen. Am I close to the mark?"

Kühlmann smiled. "Indeed, *Herr* Wilkins, very close. And what does Austria want?"

"Food," Wilkins replied.

Kühlmann nodded slowly. "I must ask, out of simple curiosity, Mister Wilkins, what an Englishman would have me do in such a situation." He gestured for Wilkins to sit.

Wilkins stepped to the chair beside the Foreign Secretary's table and sat down. "Well, as an Englishman, it seems to me that the controversy over who governs the Baltic States is one that can be postponed for a later date if Russia will at least acknowledge their independence now. I expect that Germany will eventually discover, as Austria has, that governing over non-Germanic nationalities is more trouble than it is worth and you will ultimately make these regions autonomous if not fully independent. However, I share the same concerns as you regarding the new Russian government. Germany and its allies must force Russia to surrender as much territory as possible. Before you get to that point, I believe it most important that you should slow down these discussions and engage the Russian negotiators in a wide-ranging discussion of more conceptual matters."

"What do you mean by 'conceptual'?"

"Let us presume that, in principle at least, the Baltic States shall be independent nations. How then shall they be governed? What form of government? What sort of economy? When shall they select their own governments? What preparations must be made? Who will be involved in those decisions? Will there be a national referendum or shall the decision be made by elected representatives or even by men selected by Germany? Who will be entitled to vote in those elections? These are all issues that would elicit wide-ranging discussion."

"Yes, I certainly suspect they would, but, why should we waste time discussing such matters with the Russians?"

"Do you know the old Russian proverb, sir: '*заставь дурака богу молиться, он и лоб расшибёт*'?" Wilkins asked. "It means roughly: 'Make a fool pray to the Lord, and he'll break his forehead'."

The next day the peace treaty negotiations resumed in the largest hall in the fortress, and even then the room was crowded with men who had arrived from across Eastern Europe, Russia, and Turkey. Baron von Kühlmann arrived with German General Max von Hoffman and Count Ottokar von Czernin, the Imperial Foreign Minister of Austria-Hungary. Hoffman, a pudgy, boyish-looking man with a *pince-nez*, was perhaps the finest General in the German military. He was known to be contemptuous of Hindenburg, for it was Hoffman's strategy that had won the pivotal Battle of Tannenberg against the Russians in 1914 and Hindenburg who had received all the credit. Count Czernin of Austria, a tall, gaunt man, was a career politician and diplomat who seemed overwhelmed by the tasks Emperor Charles had lain upon him: With the Hapsburg monarchy on the verge of collapse and their empire near starvation, Czernin was required to obtain peace at nearly any price.

The Russians, they now learned, had sent a new lead negotiator, a tall, thin man with a shock of rumpled black hair, a "goatee" and spectacles. Wilkins, seated in a back row near the corner of the hall, recognized the infamous Russian at once, and he was delighted. The Bolsheviks had sent perhaps the most stubborn and argumentative man in all of Russia, a man who could talk endlessly on any matter and would never concede a point without decrying that it as a setback for the worldwide proletariat revolution: Leon Trotsky.

Wilkins saw Baron von Kühlmann approach Trotsky to greet him. Trotsky, who held all imperialist nations in contempt, declined to even shake hands with the German Foreign Secretary. Kühlmann then turned to address the assembled representatives.

"Before we resume the discussions this morning," he announced gravely, in German, "I propose that we bow our heads and pray to our Lord that goodwill, the spirit of peace and the promise of security descend upon all those gathered here today."

Although Trotsky spoke German well, he insisted that the Baron's statement be translated into Russian, and then he replied, in German: "The Russian delegation rejects the German Foreign Secretary's proposal and denounces such superstitions. We demand to begin at once." Nearly everyone present was shocked. Trotsky, oblivious to the condemnation of the assembled representatives, walked away to take his seat at the table. Baron von Kühlmann turned about and looked over to Wilkins with a wry expression and winked.

For two weeks, Kühlmann argued with Trotsky over every topic even remotely relevant to the operation of government, from voting rights to the form of legislature to the authority of the judiciary to civil liberties and the rights of nations. The assembled representatives listened in horror as Trotsky extolled the worldwide worker's revolution and praised the dictatorship of the proletariat. He repeatedly demanded that Germany withdraw its troops from the Baltic States so that their independence and governance could be decided by popular referendum; General Hoffman, exasperated, was forced to remind the Russian delegates that the German armies had actually defeated the Russian armies. Newspaper reports of the proceedings transmitted Trotsky's words to the rest of the world, accompanied by editorials that denounced the Bolsheviks and their revolutionary ideology. The more Trotsky talked, the more he undermined his cause. Kühlmann patiently and good-naturedly allowed Trotsky to go on and on.

Nevertheless, there was great frustration among those present that the German Foreign Secretary did not bring the discussion back to the important matters that would need to be decided in order to reach a final peace accord, such as the location of the actual borders. At one point, Hoffman marched to the map, drew a line down the middle of Russia and announced that that would be the new border. After two weeks, however, Wilkins agreed that Trotsky had been allowed to go on long enough. He went to Kühlmann's office one freezing night to make a further suggestion.

"Have you been enjoying the show, Mister Wilkins?" Kühlmann asked.

"Immensely – Lenin could not have sent a better man for the job, from my point of view."

"Trotsky has no perspective on what he says. He may be a great revolutionary, but he is a very poor diplomat."

"I have another proposal for you to consider, sir," Wilkins said, "if you will hear it."

"I will listen, Mister Wilkins, and of course I will consider the source. I happen to know you have been diligent about complying with the conditions of your presence here, but you are still my nation's enemy."

"I have made every effort to avoid speaking with the other delegates, sir, but have found it difficult to avoid the three young men from Kiev. Do you know the ones I mean?"

"Yes, I do," Kühlmann said with disgust. "Those three are a disgrace – childish, drinking at all hours – and their self-proclaimed 'Ukrainian People's Republic' is a fantasy: It is only a matter of time before the Bolsheviks send the Red Army to Kiev to disperse the *Rada* and reassert control over Ukraine."

"Yes, Lenin may attempt to do so, but consider this: Germany and Austria have few troops in Ukraine now; it is not conquered territory. It is a Russian region that has, of its own accord, declared its independence from Petrograd. It is also a region rich with farmland, grain, food that is badly needed in neighboring Austria-Hungary."

"Yes."

"I suggest Germany and Austria formally recognize this new nation of Ukraine and get those three fellows in here to sign a treaty."

"Mister Wilkins, have you any notion ...," Kühlmann began angrily, then stopped himself. "Trotsky would go mad," he said.

"Trotsky has had his opportunity to speak. Give those Ukrainian fellows a chance to state their position tomorrow. It's merely a suggestion, but I am certain that Count Czernin would like to get his hands on the Ukrainian grain."

The next morning Wilkins was back in his seat in the corner of the large hall. After weeks of fruitless discussion, many of the representatives had drifted away as they tired of listening to Trotsky speak, but on this particular day they had all returned. Rumors were circulating that something was going to happen. The discussions that morning began as usual with an hour-long speech by Trotsky about the meaning of the term "self-determination", but when it came time for Baron von Kühlmann to give his response, he instead stood and simply said: "I yield to representative Lubynsjsky of the Ukrainian People's Republic," and returned to his seat. Trotsky was furious and whispered harshly to his colleagues. Then the "Foreign Minister" of the "People's Republic of Ukraine," a man no older than Wilkins himself, with fair light hair and a boyish appearance, stood to speak.

"It is with great humility that I address the prestigious delegates assembled here today," he began. "The People's Republic of Ukraine is a new nation, as yet unrecognized by any other, it is true. We have chosen to sever our bonds with Russia and its former government, a government that ceased to exist this past year when Tsar Nicholas abandoned his throne. But we are a nation formed by the duly elected representatives of the Ukrainian people and recognized by the people of Ukraine. We have heard from Minister Trotsky a great deal about the right to self-determination. Ukraine is the very embodiment of self-determination. It is Russia that is not.

"Russia is a country inhabited by many different peoples, peoples who have their individual political aspirations and who have grown under the most varying historical conditions. In 1917, Russia experienced a revolution, a revolution that is still in progress. It was a year that began under the reign of an Emperor and ended, after passing through several iterations of provisional government, with shootings in the streets of Petrograd. The current, Bolshevik government now proclaims the principle of 'self-determination", but it does so to more resolutely combat this principle in its practical application. The Bolsheviks' loud declarations about the civil liberty of the peoples of Russia are only coarse demagogic expedients. It is my duty to inform you all that the Bolshevik assurances that the right of self-determination will be respected in Latvia, Lithuania, Estonia and in the newly independent Finland are grossly exaggerated, just as they have been in Russia itself. It is only out of fear of a national insurrection that the Bolsheviks profess allegiance to this ideal, but the reality is far different.

"The Bolshevik government, whose electors received only a small percentage of the seats in Russia's recent elections, relied upon mercenaries and a private army to break up and arrest members of the Constitutional Assembly rather than heed the will of the Russian people. They rely upon their 'Red Army' to suppress newspapers and political speech, to break up political meetings, to arrest and murder politicians in the street. They depict the state of Russia in a false and biased manner for the sole purpose of preserving their own power to govern. The Bolsheviks are disseminating *propaganda* in the hope of spreading their revolution, but in truth they seek to extend their dominion over all of Europe. I tell you, the Petrograd government cannot abide self-determination because it has no respect for the will of the people, for whom it holds nothing but contempt. Our future, our history, our descendants, and the broad masses of working people on both sides of the front, in Russia and in Ukraine, will themselves decide which of us is right and which is guilty, which is Socialist and which counter-revolutionist, which creates and which destroys what has been created."

The speech went on and on, and Trotsky fumed at the insults hurled at the Russian revolutionaries. At the conclusion of the Ukrainian Minister's speech, Trotsky rose and left the room without saying a word.

Later that day, both Germany and Austria-Hungary recognized Ukraine as an independent nation and opened negotiations for a side peace agreement. More bad news for the Bolsheviks followed: Within days, the Russian territory of Bessarabia also declared its independence, followed by Latvia, Lithuania, Estonia, Belarus, and, in Transcaucasia, the regions of Georgia, Armenia and Azerbaijan. Russia had begun to fall apart, and the proceedings were suspended as Trotsky raced back to Petrograd to consult with Lenin and the Bolshevik's Central Committee. Germany and Austria-Hungary signed a peace agreement with Ukraine even as the Bolsheviks sent the Red Army to instigated civil war in Kiev and the new Ukrainian government fled the city.

The Bolsheviks had good cause to be anxious: Their revolution was in jeopardy, increasingly rejected by the Russian people, and it was essential in Lenin's opinion that the workers and soldiers of Germany rise up at once. The *propaganda* and radio transmissions coming from Russia took on a new, more urgent tone, calling for outright rebellion in Germany and for the assassination of Kaiser Wilhelm. The Kaiser and his Supreme Commanders, Hindenburg and Ludendorff, were outraged. As the proceedings in Brest-Litovsk were finally set to resume, Wilkins knew Baron von Kühlmann would have no choice but to address the issue, and undoubtedly, between the Kaiser, Hoffman, Hindenburg, and Ludendorff, a decision had been made to issue a final ultimatum to the Russian government.

That evening, Kühlmann sought out and found Wilkins in the musty and decrepit chapel of the fortress. The Baron appeared careworn and exhausted. He sat on the hard concrete pew beside Wilkins and came right to the point: "These actions by the Bolshevik government have made it impossible for me to delay any longer, Mister Wilkins," he said. "You must understand. My dear friend Matthias Erzberger was the driving force behind the *Reichstag*'s Peace Resolution: It is the official position of the Germany people to reject annexation of these Baltic regions, yet the Kaiser and the Supreme Command demand that Germany maintain control over them. With these new outrages by the Bolsheviks, I can delay no further. Under no circumstances may I agree to allow the new nations to hold popular referendums on the issue of independence or to form their own governments as Russia demands. Simply stated, the Bolshevik government must agree to our proposals now."

"Baron, I hope you will believe me when I say that it is in our interest as well as yours that you keep the Bolsheviks out of the new Baltic States even if that means Germany must commit a million soldiers to the task," Wilkins said. "Indeed, I would have your armies march all the way to Petrograd and put Lenin and Trotsky before a firing squad, if only because it would save Great Britain the trouble of doing so."

"But it would also prove to the world that Trotsky's accusations are correct, that Germany had no other aim in this war than to place the whole of Russia under her heel."

"Germany's aim? Germany? You speak of Germany as if your entire nation were at issue. I don't think so, Baron; I do not believe that Germany intends to annex these Russian territories. As you say, the *Reichstag* expressly denied any such intent, and such a declaration is not made lightly. But I do believe it is Kaiser Wilhelm's aim, and I will tell you bluntly that therein lays your problem, a problem that Germany must remedy. There will be no peace in Europe until you rid yourselves of Kaiser Wilhelm."

Kühlmann glared at Wilkins. "You speak far too lightly of such a serious matter."

"Go ahead and tender your ultimatum to Trotsky." Wilkins scoffed. "We are not all so naïve as to believe that Germany could ever annex such a wide swath of Russia." He abruptly rose and left the chapel.

The meetings resumed early the next morning. Wilkins saw Baron von Kühlmann enter the room haggard and gloomy. Entering behind him were

General Hoffman and Count Czernin, both jubilant. The final decision had clearly been made. Kühlmann would demand that Russia acknowledge the new independent states even though they were still occupied and administrated by German armies. As everyone took their seats, Trotsky entered the room. He had just arrived from Petrograd where he and Lenin had surely surmised that a German ultimatum was coming. The Russian government would have a terrible choice to make, either to continue the war or to surrender nearly a third of Russia's territory to Germany. Neither would be acceptable to the Russian proletariat they claimed to represent.

Trotsky clenched his papers in his fist. The first to speak, he approached the podium to address the expectant representatives.

"We have listened to the proposals of Germany, and we believe, after long discussion, that the moment has come to make a decision," Trotsky began. The room grew deathly still. "The people are awaiting with impatience the results of these peace negotiations. They are asking when this war, the self-extermination of mankind – a result of selfishness and the will for domination on the part of all governing classes of all countries – will finally come to an end. This war ceased long ago being a defensive war. When Germany occupies Serbia, Belgium, Poland, and Roumania, then that is not a defensive war. We are equally hostile to Imperialism on both sides, and we do not agree any longer to shed the blood of our soldiers to defend one Imperialist from the other.

"Today I must inform you that Russia is removing our armies and our people from the war. Our peasant soldiers must return to their land to cultivate the fields. Our workmen soldiers must return to their workshops and produce. Together, they must create a Socialist State. So we are going out of the war. We inform all peoples and their Governments of this fact. We are giving the order for a general demobilization of all our armies opposed to the troops of Germany, Austria-Hungary, Turkey and Bulgaria. We are waiting in the strong belief that other nations will soon follow our example. At the same time we declare that the conditions as submitted to us by the Governments of Germany and of Austria-Hungary are opposed to the interest of all peoples. These conditions are refused by the working masses of all countries. We cannot place the signature of the Russian Revolution under these conditions, conditions which bring with them oppression, misery and hate to millions of human beings. The Governments of Germany and Austria-Hungary are determined to possess lands and people by might. Let them do so openly. We will not approve it.

"We are going out of the war, but we feel ourselves compelled to refuse to sign the peace treaty. However, in refusing to sign a peace of annexation, Russia declares, for its part, the state of war with Germany, Austria-Hungary, Turkey and Bulgaria has ended."

The assembly murmured in shock and confusion as Trotsky marched stridently from the room. It was unheard of! Could Russia simply not wage war and still refuse to sign a peace treaty? What could it mean? Kühlmann, in a state of agitation, rushed to Wilkins and told him to come at once. They walked briskly to Kühlmann's office where Wilkins was surprised to find another gentleman waiting.

"May I introduce you to James Wilkins," Kühlmann announced as he went to his place behind the table. "Colonel Wilkins, this is *Herr* Friedrich Ebert."

"*Herr* Ebert, an honor to meet you," Wilkins said and nodded formally. Ebert was not well known to Wilkins. A portly gentleman with droopy eyes, curly black hair and a bushy mustache, Ebert was the leader of the majority Social Democrats in the *Reichstag*. For years he had encouraged the *Sozialdemokratische Partei Deutschlands*, the SPD, to support the German war effort; as a moderate, he had expected that the more radical members of his Social Democratic party would likely to be banned from office or even arrested by Ludendorff's secret police, so he had purged many outspoken members of his own party, a number that grew each month as opposition to the war increased. Some of those ejected from the SPD had gone on to form the "Independent" Social Democrats, a far more radical political party that was rumored to be in contact with the extreme, underground Marxist society known as the "Spartacus League" and perhaps also with the Bolsheviks in Russia However, Ebert was also a staunch opponent of annexation, the matter on which he had likely come to Brest-Litovsk. "I am at your service," Wilkins said. "What may I do for you, gentlemen?"

"You heard Minister Trotsky just now?" Kühlmann asked.

"Of course," Wilkins replied.

"You understand that Germany must now rescind the armistice."

"Naturally," Wilkins said without concern.

Ebert cleared his throat and turned to Wilkins. "How will London react?" He asked.

"On balance, *Herr* Ebert, London would prefer German soldiers to be fighting Bolsheviks in Russia than fighting Englishmen in France. Furthermore, I say with some confidence that the territorial issue is largely irrelevant: It will all be re-evaluated at the end of the war."

"You speak as if you know the war *will* end," Ebert replied, "and I notice you make no prediction as to who will be victorious."

"Well of course it will end," Wilkins insisted. "I won't pretend to say how or when, but anyone can see that there shall be no victors. Listen to me, gentlemen, I understand very well the position you have taken with regard to the issue of annexation, but the fact remains that a great many countries will no longer exist at the end of this war. Something must be done about that. I notice, Baron, you have assiduously declined to mention Poland or Roumania during these negotiations. The Turks have not mentioned what will happen to the Russian Caucasus regions that they now occupy. Austria is crumbling, yet, incredibly, Count Czernin has not mentioned Galicia, Hungary, or the Czech, Slovak, Bosnian or Serbian regions. Yet these are regions that border the very territories you are now discussing. Surely you are aware that the people in these regions are even now forming new governments-in-exile and making international alliances."

"There are always factions making such claims," Ebert scoffed.

"Then I suspect you are not aware of the negotiations taking place in Rome even as we speak. America, Great Britain, France, and Italy are all receptive to recognition of these new nations. But you fellows are positively oblivious. I tell you, even if Germany were to win the war, you are most assuredly losing the peace."

"I have discussed this with the Kaiser," Kühlmann objected.

Wilkins glared. "The Kaiser is an imbecile. As I told you before, there will be no peace until you have forced him out of Germany. When will you fellows wake up and discover that you are still playing the short game?"

Ebert smiled and placed one hand over his face to disguise his pleasure as Baron von Kühlmann shook his head. "That will do," Kühlmann said angrily.

Ebert came to Wilkins' defense: "Even if the Kaiser is disinterested in establishing communications with the representatives of these potential new nations, I might agree nonetheless that we have been somewhat negligent in keeping informed of the discussions and the diplomacy that relates to them," he said. "But if there is anything other than overthrowing our reigning monarch, that you would propose we do, *Herr* Wilkins, what is it?"

"In Great Britain, it has recently become our practice to name leaders of the opposition party to positions on a 'Shadow Cabinet'; they are the members of Parliament who are prepared to step into specific duties and form a new government should their party's fortunes suddenly rise. Perhaps you have a similar practice in the *Reichstag*, I cannot say. It seems to me, *Herr* Ebert, it would be prudent to make such arrangements and, having done so, at least establish informal communications with those who are very likely to be the leaders of these new nations as they will most certainly come into existence at the conclusion of this war. You might consider whether I, who can travel freely outside Germany, could be of some use to you in that regard, rather than keeping me as a prisoner of the Second *Reich*."

Kühlmann was shocked: "So you would not have us return you to your uncle at Stammheim. Instead, you would have us conspire with you to form a revolutionary government and then set you free. Perhaps you *should* be made a prisoner of war!"

"Oh, I don't believe he means that at all," Ebert argued. "Naturally, we must consider the possibility that Chancellor von Hertling will resign at some point; his cabinet might then be replaced."

"Replaced by Kaiser Wilhelm, if he so wishes," Kühlmann replied, "not by you."

"Of course, but it would be of potentially great benefit to the SPD to prepare those gentlemen that we would recommend to the Kaiser. Those we nominate for the Chancellor's cabinet are more likely to meet with Kaiser Wilhelm's approval if they are fully prepared to step into the shoes of the men they replace. There need be nothing covert or conspiratorial about it. Certainly, the SPD would wish for you to remain as Foreign Secretary, Baron."

"And you would be Chancellor, is that it, Ebert?"

"No, of course not. Some in your own Foreign Office have mentioned Prince Max as a possible replacement for Chancellor von Hertling, have they not?"

"Do you mean Prince Maximilian of Baden?" Wilkins inquired.

"Yes," Ebert replied. "Prince Max is a great advocate for democratic reform in Germany, and he has been a commendable intermediary on matters pertaining to prisoners of war for the past few years. He would make an excellent Chancellor, in my opinion."

"But Kaiser Wilhelm does not see the need for democratic reforms," Kühlmann said.

"He will 'ere long," Ebert said. "Win or lose, Ludendorff's dictatorship in Germany is unsustainable – we are positively driving our people into the hands of the Bolsheviks. Sooner or later, the Kaiser must see that certain democratic reforms are necessary."

"If I may say so, such reforms would also send a clear message to the West that Germany is prepared to negotiate a just end to the war," Wilkins added.

Kühlmann was agitated but sat silently. Ebert waited a moment but the Foreign Secretary had nothing left to say. "But this is all beyond the matters we are now addressing," Ebert said. "We were speaking of the proposed Balkan nations, and I agree that there might be a great benefit to establishing contact, quite informally, with the leaders of these potential new nations should, for example, Emperor Charles suddenly accede to the territorial demands of the Southern Slavs or the Croats or whomever."

"Perhaps," Kühlmann admitted, "although there could be no insinuation of our making an offer of any kind."

"No, of course there should not," Ebert agreed. "These contacts would be strictly unofficial in nature. But I am merely speculating. Perhaps *Herr* Wilkins should return with us to Berlin at the conclusion of the negotiations here in Brest-Litovsk so these questions can be addressed with more reflection; he can always be sent on to Stammheim later, if nothing comes of it."

"I am at your service," Wilkins replied.

Kühlmann sighed. "Alright, I will arrange it with Crown Prince Rupprecht," he said, "but he shall then be our responsibility, *Herr* Ebert. Let us be clear: Wilkins shall be *our* prisoner of war."

Once the peace treaty was rejected by Russia, Germany finally renounced the armistice and marched into Russia. Across most of the Eastern Front, the Russian trenches were utterly empty and German troops marched forward unopposed. In many places, the Russian troops simply surrendered. After one brief confrontation, six hundred Cossacks surrendered to a German Lieutenant and his six men. Within a fortnight, Germany had seized all of Estonia, Latvia, Lithuania, and Belarussia. Then a German naval fleet entered the Gulf of Finland

and approached Petrograd, prepared to bombard the city. The Central Powers sent its peace terms to Lenin and demanded that they be accepted within 48 hours. This time, Lenin secured the Central Committee's acceptance of the proposals at once. When the treaty was finally signed in early March, Russia was forced to renounce all claim to Finland, the Baltic States, Poland, Belarussia, Ukraine, and the Caucasus territories, nearly a quarter of Russia's population and industries, and to leave them in the custody of the German armies.

Belleau Woods

It was called the *Kaiserschlacht*, the Kaiser's Battle, but it was Ludendorff's plan. Imperial Germany would put forth a tremendous effort to finally smash the French and British armies on the Western Front and end the stalemate that had existed for nearly four years. The German commanders knew that it could well be their last remaining opportunity for victory before American soldiers and materiel filled the Allied lines making any further westward advance into France impossible. Ludendorff's plan relied upon Germany's temporary advantage in numbers, the nearly fifty divisions made available because of the treaty signed with Russia, and at Hindenburg's headquarters in the city of Spa, in German-occupied Belgium, Ludendorff told Kaiser Wilhelm that their armies would crush the British and force the French to plead for peace. Then Germany would become the peacemaker and grant peace on the condition that the British and American armies were withdrawn from Europe.

The first stage of the German offensive, codenamed *Operation Michael*, began at the Somme River, on the southern end of the British position. It was there, two years earlier during the five month Allied offensive, that the British and French had suffered more than 600,000 casualties. At 04.40 on Thursday, 21 March 1918, the German artillery bombardment began. In just five hours, over one million shells fell on a 43 mile wide section of the front lines occupied by the British Fifth and Third Armies. Seventy-four German Divisions, one million men under the command of the ambitious Crown Prince William, son of the Kaiser, and of Crown Prince Rupprecht, attacked the British troops behind a massive creeping barrage. Highly skilled, elite German infantry troops, *Stosstruppen* or Stormtroopers, men specially trained for infiltrating the British lines, exploited every gap. They surrounded and destroyed the weakest defenses even as 300 aircraft strafed the British positions. Heavy fog and the smoke and haze of the bombardment concealed their advance. Near Cambrai, and at Saint Quentin and Bullecourt, the Germans broke through at once and pushed the British Fifth Army back. There were over 50,000 British casualties on the first day of the offensive, and by the third day, having pushed the British back nearly ten miles, the British were in full retreat; tens of thousands had been taken prisoner. In the past, both the French commander General Philippe Pétain and the British commander Field Marshal Douglas Haig had been reluctant to send reinforcing troops to assist each other, but now General Pétain was forced to send several French Divisions to save the British from utter disaster (even as his own lines came under attack).

That same day, an enormous new German gun positioned some 74 miles from Paris began to lob 9.5 inch shells into the city, injuring or killing dozens of civilians and creating widespread panic.

British troops were transferred down from the Ypres salient to reinforce their positions on the northern flank of the German offensive near Arras. They gradually beat back the German onslaught, but Baupaume fell again after heavy fighting. The situation was critical and made even more difficult because the French, British, American, and now Portuguese armies were still under separate command. As the German armies threatened to split the British and French lines in their drive toward Paris, on 24 March, the Chief of the French General Staff, Ferdinand Foch, wired U.S. President Woodrow Wilson directly to plead that a coordinated response to the German offensive was urgently required. President Wilson, who had long insisted that the American Expeditionary Force remain solely under American command, relented and agreed that all of the Allied armies could be placed under one central commander. The Inter-Ally Supreme War Council elected Foch himself to fill that role. While the American troops would remain under General Pershing's direct command, Pershing, it seemed, would be at the service of the French *Généralissime*.

Yet even as the American 1st and 2nd Divisions moved up to reserve positions in the sectors north and east of Paris, the Germans' progress slowed. Ludendorff had overextended his supply and communications lines. By the time American troops reached the front, the *Michael* offensive had all but ended.

In the lull between battles, British commander Haig drew additional forces down from the north to defend Amiens, and Ludendorff's next plan of attack sought to take advantage of that adjustment. He decided to strike north toward Dunkirk and Calais so that the British would be forced to evacuate Belgium and northern France. However, by the time *Operation George* began on 7 April, the plan had been scaled down and the new target of the re-named *Operation Georgette* was simply to take Ypres, the Belgian city which the British had held since 1914. The German bombardment opened on the evening of 7 April upon the British and Portuguese lines between Armentières and Festubert. It continued for 36 hours. At 08.45 on 9 April, eight German Infantry Divisions at Estaires attacked the eleven mile front defended by the over-extended Portuguese. The Portuguese troops, who had already started to withdraw due to the bombardment, gave the Germans almost no opposition. Within a single hour, the front line was taken along with 6,000 Portuguese prisoners. The next day, the Germans struck at Messines, north of Armentières, and the British were forced to retreat a full four miles.

Fearful that the British forces in France were about to be overwhelmed, Haig issued a General Order to his men to stand firm:

There is no other course open to us but to fight it out! Every position must be held to the last man: there must be no retirement. With our backs to the wall and believing in the justice of our cause, each one of us must fight on to the end!

The British did fight. By mid-April, they had been forced to give up Passchendaele, but then the tide began to turn. Germany suffered terrible losses; tens of thousands of its elite Stormtroopers were captured or killed. It soon became clear that Ypres would not fall.

Yet, even as the British and French struggled to regroup, Ludendorff prepared for the massive and well-prepared third stage of his spring offensive. It was to be the *coup de grâce* that would bring victory to Germany at last. He would rend the French and British armies asunder, and the German armies would rush forward through the breach to capture Paris and, with it, the very heart of France.

It was a cold, overcast day in late April when David Gresham arrived on the French coast at the village of Étaples. He had been there once before, after he was wounded in 1915. What had once been a small commercial fishing port on the northern coast of France had become during the war a massive hospital for tens of thousands of British soldiers, most of them housed in the countless tan huts that had been raised throughout the city. The streets were crowded with men wounded at the Ypres salient, but also with many thousands more who were ill with influenza, an illness that was spreading rapidly among the soldiers. Its victims turned a frighteningly bluish hue, and a great many of them were dying from high fevers. Gresham had heard that the illness originated in Spain, but it seemed likely that the nations at war were censoring information about the number of people in their own countries stricken by the disease. Surely it was doing as much damage in Germany and Austria as it was in France, and there were rumors that the disease had also spread to Asia and the Americas.

Gresham had been asked by his new close friend and ally, the French intelligence chief Dupont, to attend an Allied briefing in Étaples on his behalf. Dupont had at last become rather amiable toward Gresham following the capture of Major von Trauth, and the French Intelligence commander had no desire to spend a day listening to representatives of the British Royal Navy describe their newest plan: A raid on the German submarine bases near Bruges. By April 1918 almost none of the food eaten in France was actually grown there and had to be imported; Great Britain was also suffering from raw material and food shortages, and the American armies crossing the Atlantic were in constant danger of submarine attack even as they arrived at port in France. Germany's "unrestricted" submarine warfare was taking a heavy toll on the Allies. Something had to be done.

Gresham, in his smartly tailored uniform, entered the Étaples city hall, an old white building with a red tile roof, shortly before the briefing was to begin. It seemed that only a handful of very high-ranking officers had been invited to attend, and Gresham took General Dupont's seat in the large, oak-paneled room immediately beside General Philippe Pétain, the Commander-in-Chief of the French Armies. Pétain, a tall, austere man with a large, white handlebar mustache, had commanded the French defense of Verdun in 1916 and had convinced the French soldiers to end their mutiny in 1917. He was, in Gresham's opinion, the finest commanding officer in France.

"You are in General Dupont's place," Pétain observed.

"Yes, I know," Gresham replied. "Dupont asked me to attend in his stead. We are colleagues."

"Ah, you are with British Intelligence, yes?"

"I am, Sir, although it would be closer to the mark to say I am freelancing."

"Oh, then you must be Colonel Gresham," Pétain said.

"Yes, Sir, indeed, I am," Gresham replied in astonishment.

"It is a pleasure to meet you, Colonel," Pétain said as he shook Gresham's hand. "I have heard about your meeting with Prime Minister Clemenceau; France is deeply indebted to you."

"On the contrary, Sir, it is to France that we all owe our gratitude."

Pétain nodded appreciatively. "You must know the American gentleman, yes?" He asked, looking across the room. Gresham followed his gaze and was surprised to see someone he did in fact know – the American intelligence man that Gresham had met outside of Passchendaele.

"Yes, I do," he replied. "That is Major Dennis Nolan from the A.E.F. General Pershing has had to create a new military intelligence service from the ground up – the Americans had nothing like it – and from what I hear Nolan has cobbled together a very fine organization."

"Well I am glad to hear they can do something well," Pétain said with undisguised disdain.

"How do you mean, Sir?"

"Have you not heard about the incident at Seicheprey?"

"No, I have not," Gresham said. "Where is that?"

"It is in a quiet sector of the St. Mihiel salient, near Toul," Pétain whispered. "This occurred just yesterday, you understand. An American infantry division was placed in the line, just to hold the position. There was nothing difficult about it, but the Germans decided to bloody their noses a bit. Mortars leveled the town and Stormtroops were sent in to finish the task. There were over 600 American casualties and 100 men taken prisoner. A great tragedy, no?"

"Dear God, you mean to say that the Americans cannot even fight?" Gresham asked rhetorically. "Tell me: Has Foch at least made headway with General Pershing on the issue of placing American troops in the lines?"

"Very little," Pétain replied grimly. "The Americans at Seicheprey were among the first Americans to come to France and they were considered the best trained. It seems that until Pershing allows Douglas Haig and I to train the Americans soldiers ourselves and to incorporate them into our own ranks, the Americans will remain useless."

"Forgive me for saying so, General, but since that will not happen, I pray we are wrong about the Americans' capabilities," Gresham replied.

Admiral Sir John Jellico of the Royal Navy then began his presentation: The raid he proposed would to take place upon the main U-boat port at Zeebrugge. It would involve a marine landing on the mole, the stone jetty that guarded the entrance to the Bruges canal. Two decommissioned submarines filled with explosives would blow up the viaduct connecting the mole to the shore. Once the batteries on the mole were seized, and the dredges that kept the canal from filling with sand destroyed, three decommissioned cruisers would sail into the entrance to the canal itself and be sunk. It was a daring plan, but everyone agreed that it was worth the risks. (Nevertheless, it seemed to Gresham that there was inadequate attention paid to the danger from the batteries on shore and the damage they could inflict if the planned smokescreen failed to obscure the approaching British ships. He hoped it would be a foggy night.)

After the briefing, Gresham bade farewell to General Pétain and prepared to return to Paris. He had just reached the door when Major Nolan approached him. Nolan was a tall, thin man with short, straight, fair hair and eyeglasses and no facial hair at all; Gresham thought he looked like a rather severe school master.

"Colonel Gresham, you recall we met at Ypres late last year," Nolan said.

"Yes, I do," Gresham replied as he shook Nolan's hand. "It seems you learned a great deal from your visits to the front lines, Major; the intelligence division you have created is widely admired."

"I'm grateful to hear it. Of course sometimes it's easier to start such an organization from scratch. Not that we didn't copy a great deal from your own regulations —aerial recon, radio intel, interrogation teams, propaganda, and so on. It's also helped that General Pershing has been personally involved. Yet the more I learn about British intelligence, the more I am perplexed about your particular role, Colonel, and who you work for. Cecil Cameron avoided answering the question when I asked."

"Well, Cameron and I are not on the best of terms," Gresham said.

"Counterintelligence, I suspect?"

"Is that a question?"

"I suppose it is," Nolan persisted.

"But you misunderstand: I am not with British military intelligence, Major. I am merely a soldier in the Border Regiment."

"A 'mere' soldier?" Nolan asked skeptically. "Is that why some people in Paris call you 'General Gresham'?"

"They are being humorous, I suspect. It is all in fun. Tell me, what do you think of Admiral Jellico's plan to shut down the submarine base at Zeebrugge?"

"Truthfully, I wish there were another way. A great many men are likely to be killed. But something must be done about the U-boats – the sinking of even a single United States troop ship could create insurmountable problems for President Wilson at home. Perhaps you've heard that we nearly lost the *U.S.S. Finland* last October? Thankfully she was able to make her way home for repairs."

"I am glad to hear it," Gresham said.

"Have you ever been to the United States, Colonel?" Nolan asked.

"To America? Good God, no. Until the war, I had never been outside of England."

"And your 'General' sobriquet, it has nothing to do with Roumania? Is that what you're saying?"

"Have you been investigating me, Major?" Gresham asked with concern.

"I am only trying to understand what we are missing."

"Missing?" Gresham snapped. "Missing! What about Seicheprey? Why don't you try to understand what you were missing there?"

Nolan grimaced. "Yes, a terrible loss of life, but we were at least able to recapture the village last night. I can assure you that we are already investigating our failure there. In fact, I am on my way now to our divisional headquarters at Mesnil-Saint-Firmin. Perhaps you would be kind enough to come along with me and review our preparations for yourself."

"That is well beyond my purview, Major," Gresham objected.

"Surely as a 'mere soldier' you might give us the benefit of your vast experience, and it seems to me, from what I've been told, that is, that the scope of your duties is broad enough to accommodate my request."

"Perhaps so," Gresham admitted. How many times had a little flattery enticed him to volunteer for some hazardous duty, he could not say, but this request seemed different. Nolan was all business; there was no guile in him, no blandishment, and furthermore Gresham was genuinely curious to see the American troops up close and judge for himself whether they would ever be of any use on the Western Front.

"You might also come to understand that a man in my position must ask certain questions even if the answers are not readily forthcoming," Nolan continued. "We are new to the game and, I admit, still have a great deal to learn."

"Perhaps, but you are learning much too quickly," Gresham replied. "Fine then, I will come with you."

Gresham and Nolan drove south to Mesnil-Saint-Firmin via Amiens. It was an uncomfortable journey. Nolan, a serious gentleman with little humor, studiously avoided asking Gresham any further questions about his past, but he told him a great detail about the new American intelligence operations. He would pause from time to time to see whether Gresham cared to make any observation or suggest any improvement. Gresham, driving, sat silently and listened carefully to what Nolan had to say about the massive new American intelligence operations. Everything the British and French had learned in four years – the interception of German military radio transmissions and decryption of enemy messages, for example – had been recreated by the Americans on a much grander scale and with far greater technical innovation. And it had all been accomplished in a matter of months. Then Nolan spoke at length about his "Enemy Order of Battle" operation, a section run by a Harvard University graduate, a "brilliant" young Major who gathered data from countless sources on the enemy's troop movements, their strength, composition, training, and supplies, to predict when and where the Germans would strike next. By the time Gresham and Nolan reached their destination, Gresham's head ached from the volume of information conveyed to him.

Mesnil-Saint-Firmin was in the heart of rich French farmland. The small village consisted of only two dozen small houses, yet everywhere Gresham looked there were soldiers of the American 1st Infantry Division. Although Gresham had seen a handful of Americans in Paris, here in their encampment what he saw was astonishing: The Americans were organized, disciplined, and extremely large. They ate an astonishing quantity of food, mostly hardtack and canned "Bully Beef" (which the Americans called "Monkey Meat"), and there seemed no lack of supplies as the men ate in a single sitting twice or thrice what their British counterparts would eat. The Americans seemed also taller and thicker. They were like a race of polite, cleanly shaved Nordic or Anglo-Saxon warriors. Even those that came from the foul, overcrowded American cities seemed immensely healthier and more physically developed than the British or French soldiers. The tan American uniforms, each emblazoned with a big red divisional "1" on the shoulder patch, were neat, crisp, and new, and no man lacked for proper equipment. The enlisted men were encamped in straight lines of neat canvass huts, and they drilled ceaselessly in the fields. They practiced throwing the new French F1 grenade (which looked rather like a small pineapple) and learned to lob them in an arc so that the fuse would have time to burn down and the enemy could not simply hurl them back. Others practiced their marksmanship with rifles and trench mortars. Still others practiced with the French-supplied "*Chauchat*" automatic rifles and the British-supplied "Lewis" machine guns. The officers, billeted in the village houses, were beloved by the few remaining French villagers even though not a single one of the Americans spoke a word of French. But more than all of this, Gresham was impressed by the Americans' attitude. These men had already visited the lines and knew what the war was like up close, but they had not lived through four years of war and hardship. They had not been worn down. They were still full of energy and excitement, eager to fight the "Huns", and smiled constantly. Thank God, Gresham thought, that Pershing had insisted on keeping the American soldiers as an independent fighting force. Had these men simply been thrown into the British and French ranks, they would have learned nothing but cynicism and despair.

As the sun began to set that evening, Nolan invited Gresham to join him for dinner in nearby Tartigny where the U.S. 1st Infantry was headquartered. The abandoned Sixteenth Century, yellowed-slate *château*, although in very poor condition, was bursting with American officers. There was a bustle of activity outdoors as motorcars quickly arrived and departed. Gresham and Nolan strolled up the pea stone walkway to the front door just as several other large, important-looking officers arrived. They nodded to Nolan without a word of greeting and gave Gresham a deeply inquiring look. The shutters on the windows of the *château* were kept shut due to the blackout regulations, but the house still exuded tremendous energy. Inside, the lights burned brightly, fires had been lit, and the French chefs had prepared what smelled like an excellent meal. Nolan led Gresham to the large, dining room where two dozen or more men already stood around the large table talking. Despite the water stains on the damaged plaster walls, the dry rot in the oak floorboards, and the rickety farmhouse furnishings, the room was warm and friendly. Heaping platters of red meat with brown gravy, roasted potatoes, sliced white bread, and fresh vegetables were already being placed on the table where each man could help himself. Gresham could not remember the last time he had seen so much food. The only thing about the meal that was French was the abundant wine.

Nolan brought Gresham to meet the 1st Infantry's commanding officer, Major General Robert Lee Bullard, a tall middle-aged man with very short, brown hair, clean shaven like all the Americans, who had a wide, inviting smile and twinkling brown eyes.

"Colonel, allow me to introduce you to General Bob Bullard, commander of the 1st Infantry Division," Nolan said. "General, this is Colonel David Gresham, from the British Border Regiment."

"Well it's a real pleasure to meet you, Colonel Gresham," Bullard said energetically, shaking Gresham's hand vigorously.

"And you," Gresham replied. "What an unusual accent you have, General. Were you raised in America or in another country?"

Bullard laughed heartily. "Born and raised in Alabama, Colonel. This is how we speak in the Old South."

"My apologies; I meant no offense," Gresham said.

"Oh, none taken," Bullard said with a warm grin.

"General Bullard is also a Colonel, officially," Nolan told Gresham. "He was raised to the rank of acting Major General when he was placed in command of the 1st Infantry; isn't that right, Bob?" He asked Bullard.

"Yes, it is," Bullard said.

"Colonel Gresham was similarly given the rank of acting Brigade General for a time in Roumania, I believe," Nolan said.

"Were you in command of a Division there, Colonel?" Bullard asked.

"Three Divisions, actually," Gresham admitted against his better judgment. He found it difficult to remain aloof in the company of these cheery Americans.

"Three? I don't think I'd be ready for that. Say, there are a couple of other fellows here I'd like you to meet," Bullard said as he took Gresham by the arm and led him and Nolan around the room. "The three of us were in Mexico together with Blackjack Pershing. This is Jim Harbord from Kansas; he's with the 4th Marine Brigade. And this is George Patton from California; he's got a particular interest in learning about these 'tanks' your boys are using over here, don't you George? And this here is Sam Hubbard, who works with Nolan in intelligence."

"A pleasure to meet you," said Hubbard. He was a thin, quiet, studious man unlike the other Americans Gresham had met. It was easy to understand why he had been assigned to intelligence work.

"Why don't we have a seat and dig in," Bullard said. "You don't mind if we talk a little business while we're eating, do you Colonel Gresham?"

"Not at all," he replied.

Gresham sat down with Nolan and found Sam Hubbard seated to his other side.

"Major Hubbard is in command of the 'Enemy Order of Battle' operations that I mentioned earlier," Nolan said. "He is currently attempting to determine where the Germans will attack next, is that right, Sam?"

"Yes, yes, but so far we have only suspicions," Hubbard said as he helped himself to an enormous serving of potatoes and brown gravy.

"Surely your French and British colleagues are working on this question as well," Gresham said.

"Yes, of course, I am certain they are," Hubbard replied hastily, "and if our results and their results match, then we may be doubly confident of our conclusion. Reproducibility is a fundamental axiom of the scientific method, Colonel. We must leave nothing to chance."

"And what are your suspicions? Will Germany strike again toward Arras in the north, or at the Somme, or perhaps south through the Argonne?" Gresham asked.

"Our data suggest that the next German offensive will take place near Soissons or possibly Reims, but that is only a preliminary analysis. We have data showing ammunition and medical supplies headed in that direction, although little of substance on troop movements yet," Hubbard replied.

"Soissons? Reims? That is not at all what I have heard. Have you discussed this with General Pershing?" Gresham asked Nolan.

"To some extent," Nolan replied. "As Sam said, this is only his preliminary analysis. In any case, you must be aware that Pershing is not prepared to commit additional American troops without further training, and I expect that is particularly true following the problems which surfaced at Seicheprey."

"That's why the 1st Infantry was sent to this sector to begin with," General Bullard said from across the table. "I was just telling Jim and George here that even though we are assigned to Fayolle's reserves, I'll at least have the chance to move four of my Regiments over to the French First Army for offensive training."

"General Debeney's army," Nolan clarified. "He intends to re-take Montdidier from the Germans," he told Gresham.

"That's right, Montdidier," Bullard said with obvious exasperation. "I'll tell you right out, I wouldn't mind doing it myself if Pershing would allow it. Harbord and I have gone blue in the face asking, but he keeps shooting us down. 'No,' he says, 'you'll just have to wait until next spring.' But we're just sitting on our keisters here, Colonel. You reviewed my troops today, Sir, so what do you think – aren't we ready for a go at the Germans?"

Gresham smiled. Although the reasons were still unclear, he had begun to understand at last why Nolan had invited him to review the American troops and to meet with General Bullard. Nolan wanted something, and he was betting that the mysterious but obviously-well-connected British Colonel Gresham would be able to assist him somehow. Gresham's first inclination was to be cautious, but when had he ever been cautious before? Furthermore, these Americans (apart, that is, from General Pershing and President Wilson) seemed anything but cautious. No, the Americans that Gresham had come to know were an eager, gangly people, gnashing at the bit, anxious to get into a fight. It was not at all what he had expected.

The room had grown silent, and every eye was focused on Gresham awaiting his answer. He could see the expectation in Bullard's face. It was unsettling.

"They'll do fine," Gresham said cautiously.

After dinner, Gresham and Nolan went to the *château*'s dimly-lit library to finish their wine. All the books had long since been removed, but they bent to look at the maps spread across the large rustic farm table. Nolan was carefully describing the German, French and American positions and noting the 1st Infantry's strength when Bullard entered the room with a bottle of liquor.

"I have to get you to try some of this," Bullard said. "It's Tennessee bourbon; I expect you'll enjoy it." He poured out the remainder of Gresham's wine onto the floor and filled the glass with bourbon. It was very good. "Well, Colonel Gresham, I have to admit I did not expect to get such an understated answer to my question," Bullard continued cheerily to Gresham.

"Why would you expect anything else?" Gresham replied innocently.

"Nolan here seems to think you've been around a bit," Bullard said.

"It is true that I have seen a great deal of this war, but I can't tell you anything you don't already know. Nor could you expect me to be more forthcoming when you and Nolan have not been honest with me. You have investigated me, and now you want something from me. Tell me what it is, and I will consider it. Otherwise, I have every reason to simply return to Paris tonight."

"It's not correct to say we have investigated you," Nolan said. "I have merely asked a few questions, nothing improper, but I have been met with a wall of silence. You must know that that, in itself, is significant. So, yes, I have my suspicions about you, and I believe you are a man worth knowing. For today's purposes, however, that is irrelevant. If we are not friends, we are at least colleagues. Tell us what you think of this business with Montdidier, and we will keep it between us. That is all I ask."

Gresham took a small sip of the whiskey. "You know as well as I that your men will do very well on the offensive. But why you should want to join in on the French attack is incomprehensible to me. To be of any real value in this war, the American Expeditionary Force must stand on its own. Your presence on the field must scare the hell out of the German soldiers, and give hope to the French and British. If you send a few regiments to join General Debeney's in his attack on Montdidier, it will only be another small French victory, and therefore useless. After the debacle at Seicheprey, it is more important than ever that you have your own victory; you must prove to us all, and damned soon, that the Americans can win. Choose your own target, something modest, this village here, perhaps," Gresham said as he placed his finger on the map, "Cantigny, or some other small village along this line. Call it an exercise or what have you, an offensive set piece. You will take it with no difficulty. But here is where my concern lies. Once you have taken this village, can you keep it? Will your men endure the hours, the days, the weeks of bombardment and counterattacks by the Germans? The German commanders will know the symbolic significance of your victory and will do everything they can to destroy you. The British and French have four years of experience in enduring the German counterattacks, while your men have none. So that is my question: You can take this village, but will you hold it?"

Bullard looked grave. "It is not the American style to just hold our ground, Colonel. Once we begin this thing, we will want to fight all the way to Berlin," he said.

"As do I," Gresham agreed. "But it will not happen. Hindenburg and Ludendorff cannot let it happen. This is a war of attrition, General. At times, you must simply hold your line and wait, even if it is only long enough to consolidate and reinforce your position."

Bullard stroked his chin thoughtfully as he stared at the map in silence. At last he turned to Nolan. "Do you think we can sell Pershing on an attack on this village, Cantigny, as some sort of set piece exercise?"

"Possibly," Nolan answered.

"Well, then, let's do it," Bullard said tersely. "I came to France to fight in this God-damned war. I'll admit, I don't know the answer to your question either, Colonel," he said to Gresham, "but it's about time we found out what it is."

Gresham returned to Paris the next day, but he suspected it would not be long before Nolan contacted him again. Indeed, little more than a week had passed before Nolan invited Gresham to return with him to Mesnil-Saint-Firmin. Pershing had agreed to a modest offensive exercise, a small test of the American offensive preparedness. There would be an American attack on the small German-occupied village of Cantigny, and Nolan and Bullard wanted to make sure their plans were complete. It was only four miles from Mesnil-Saint-Firmin to the front lines west of Cantigny, partly on new dirt roads through sparse woods, so Bullard, Gresham and Nolan drove out together to view the village from a slight rise in the battered fields.

"I've got the 75-mm artillery brigades preparing a creeping barrage for H-hour," Bullard said. "It'll start on the German wires and move back a hundred yards in two minutes and then a hundred yards in four minutes once the infantry begins its advance. Nolan has aerial recon that shows us the location of the main bunkers, some of the machine gun emplacements, and the artillery in the rear. We've asked the French to assist with the bombardment. I know that usually goes on a day or two at least."

Gresham could imagine the battle in his mind's eye, the men racing across the field, moving from cover to cover, the smoke, the smell. "Forget that," he said. "You don't want to level the village; you're going to need it. This will all be close-in work, rifles and bayonets. And if you really want to surprise the enemy, make your bombardment short, an hour at most. Then send your troops in behind the creeping barrage as close as your men can bear it."

Bullard nodded. "I get that, sure. George Patton is arranging for us to have a dozen tanks from the French," he added.

"Excellent," Gresham said. "You might have them spread out and cross the field into the village on a diagonal line," he added, swinging his arm to show the direction he meant. "Your infantry can use the tanks for cover as they advance – it's still a pretty fair distance for your men to cross. Keep them spread out and advance in three, maybe four waves. They should practice that with the tanks. Let the tanks take care of the German machine guns."

"With all the rubble we're seeing over there already, I doubt the tanks will be able to enter the village," Bullard said.

"No, but they'll still provide cover for your next waves. You'll have to clear out the village once your men are in. That'll all be hand-to-hand work. You might ask the French about using their flame throwers on the German bunkers over there. I wouldn't use explosives or gas – you'll want to use those bunkers yourself once the village is taken, and mustard gas residue tends to stick on surfaces for a few days," Gresham said. "Taking the village won't be difficult; the hard part will come after. As soon as the village is cleared, you'll need to send patrols out and set machine gun and automatic rifle posts to cover your consolidation. The second advance can work on the trenches and wires. You'll want the third wave to set up your strong points in preparation for the German counterattack. You've got to plan for the counterattack. Defend in depth. You can't just hold a single line – you'll need multiple lines of defense. Let the German troops come into your occupied zone, separate them, isolate them, and finish them. If you keep your heads down and your gas masks at the ready, you'll do fine."

Bullard had taken a strong liking to the British Colonel, and at his invitation Gresham spent another day at the *château* in Tartigny discussing the plan of attack and inspecting the efficient American artillery regiments that would take part in the "exercise" at Cantigny. Jim Harbord, the Marine Brigade commander from the American 2nd Division, came again for dinner since he was soon to be headquartered even further back from the front lines (although in a much more pleasant *château*). The next morning, Gresham accompanied General Harbord to review his Marine regiments, as well.

Harbord's Marines were, if anything, larger and even more formidable than the men of the American 1st Division. They were passionately disciplined soldiers who had taken advanced military training both in America and in France. Many of the men had been to university, and all of the officers had been promoted from the ranks – a far more democratic system than in any of the European armies. And although the Marines could disassemble and reassemble their Springfield rifles while blindfolded, Gresham was particularly impressed with their marksmanship: General Harbord was adamant that a good Marine should kill an enemy soldier with each and every shot he fired. It was a pleasant visit for Gresham, yet as Harbord lacked Bullard's ample tastes in food and liquor, Gresham returned to Paris that evening. He was more perplexed than ever that the well-trained and eager American soldiers had not yet been put in the front lines of battle. It seemed that the Allied commanders, Haig, Pétain and Foch, were all willfully ignorant or wrongfully dismissive of the Americans' usefulness, while Pershing and President Wilson were being foolishly cautious.

It had been a rainy spring, but the sun was shining as Gresham walked hand-in-hand with Princess Eleanor along the *Quai des Grands Augustins* beside the Seine. The river had swelled with the spring rains and was ruffled by a strong cool breeze. There were few boats on the water. The city was quiet and anxious.

The armies of France and Great Britain had been battered by the German offensives that spring and were still re-grouping, and the Spanish Influenza was spreading wildly both through their ranks and among civilians. The initiative remained strongly with the German armies, and it was already May. That meant Ludendorff would resume his spring offensive at any moment. No one knew when or where the next strike would come.

"Perhaps it would be best for you to leave Paris," Gresham said bravely, breaking the silence. He didn't want Eleanor to go, but the war now seemed far too close, only a short drive from Paris. The city was at risk. There was shelling. There could be further aerial bombardment at any time. There were casualties.

"I have been considering that; my parents have asked me to leave," Eleanor replied. "But I don't wish to go, David, and I certainly will not be returning to Bucharest."

"Is it the new treaty?" The treaty that Roumania had finally signed with the Central Powers ceded territory to Austria and Bulgaria, guaranteed exclusive rights to Roumania's oil for the next century, and allowed the country to be occupied by German forces for the foreseeable future.

"It is true that I could not stand the sight of German soldiers walking in the streets of Bucharest while you are still fighting here in France. I wish to stay," she said.

"I understand you don't want to return home, my darling, but you could still go somewhere far safer: To Barcelona or New York, perhaps?" He suggested weakly.

"No," Eleanor replied as she squeezed Gresham's hand tightly. "I must see my project through to the end."

"What project do you mean?"

"Why, I mean *you*, of course, David. I am not finished with *you* yet," she teased.

"Then you give me all the more reason to protect Paris," he said. "But I must warn you there are some things I mean to do that may create certain difficulties. As you know, I have already been arrested once, and I'm afraid that things are now going to get even more serious. Will you promise to trust me and trust that I know what I am doing?" He asked hopefully.

Eleanor smiled. She leaned in to whisper in Gresham's ear, and then he felt her soft lips on his neck. That was all he needed to know.

For many days Gresham had in fact been mulling in his mind what he had learned of the Americans, and he now believed he had discovered an opening, an opportunity, one that was likely to land him in a substantial amount of trouble, but that was perhaps part of the plan too.

After lunch with Eleanor on the banks of the Seine, Gresham sent a note to Nolan at the A.E.F. headquarters in the *Hôtel de Crillon* and asked to meet privately with him and Major Hubbard, the chief of the Enemy Order of Battle section. He suggested Napoleon's tomb in the nearby *Les Invalides*. Nolan replied that they could meet the next afternoon.

Gresham arrived early at the Dome Chapel within the *Hôtel National des Invalides*. The sarcophagus of the great emperor Napoleon I sat silently in the empty chapel surrounded by the tombs of his brothers and the statues that commemorated the Emperor's major victories across Europe. Napoleon was but one in a long line of conquerors who had sought to dominate the continent; Gresham wished he had been the last, but that was not to be the case, it seemed. It was Kaiser Wilhelm's turn now. Perhaps this war would finally make an end to such ambitions, but only if the Allies won. Nolan and Hubbard soon arrived together. Dennis Nolan, now a Colonel, was smartly dressed as always, clean shaven, his hair neatly oiled and combed, his eyeglasses resting firmly on his long nose. Hubbard, however, looked thinner and even more exhausted and rumpled than when Gresham first met him at Tartigny.

"Thank you for agreeing to meet here: It is quite private, as you can see," Gresham began. "Dennis, I would very much like to help you. By that, I mean, help you in the manner I am able and for the reasons I deem appropriate. We are all of us like pieces in a game of chess, are we not? All you need to know is that I mean for us to win. I will not say that again – you will trust me or not, and you may come to regret it either way."

"You must tell me what you want," Nolan said warily.

"Has Major Hubbard's analysis – that the Germans mean to attack between Soissons and Reims – become any more concrete?"

Hubbard looked to Nolan.

Nolan nodded his head slowly and considered Gresham's statement. Then he made his decision. Turning to Hubbard, he asked: "Have you become any more certain?"

"Yes, definitely," Hubbard told them. "Our analyses are highly consistent. Ludendorff means to have Crown Prince William's Army Group attack at the *Chemin des Dames*, the high ridge above the Aisne River between Soissons and Reims, in two weeks' time. That means he intends to take Paris. It is unmistakable."

"That is the sector assigned to the French Sixth Army under General Duchêne," Gresham said.

"Yes," Nolan agreed. "Do you know him?"

"By reputation – he is an ass," Gresham said. "Regardless, we must go to see him at once."

General Denis Auguste Duchêne was, in fact, notorious for his arrogance, temper and foul-mouth. He had once been described to Gresham as "un-tied", meaning he was quick to fits of extraordinary rage, as Gresham had once seen himself when Duchêne exploded at the chef at *Larue*. Although Duchêne was a career army officer who had served competently in the Battle of the Somme in 1916, he was widely disliked and a personal enemy of his new commander,

General Pétain, which is how Duchêne had come to be placed in command of the French Sixth Army at the front along the *Chemin des Dames*, a sector that was considered both secure and quiet. In fact, Pétain had specifically ordered Duchêne not to attempt to cross the Aisne River or make any move to attack their enemy.

Characteristically, Duchêne maintained his Sixth Army headquarters in Paris, more than 100 kilometres from his front lines. He agreed to meet Gresham, Nolan and Hubbard that very afternoon, but then kept them waiting outside his office until the early evening. When at last they were shown in, the General was already tired and edgy. Gresham had cautioned Nolan and Hubbard to say nothing until spoken to.

Duchêne was a short, solid man with a great brown mustache that strikingly contrasted with the white hair on his head; his face was red and his eyes were narrow and piercing. "It is already evening," he said, "and as you know, gentlemen, I have been quite f---ing busy today already. Perhaps you can make this brief, yes?"

"I quite agree," Gresham said casually. "My name is Colonel David Gresham and I am with the British intelligence office. These are Colonel Nolan and Major Hubbard from the American Expeditionary Force."

"Yes, yes," Duchêne said brusquely.

"In the course of my customary duties," Gresham went on, "these gentlemen brought to my attention certain information – their 'theory' you might say – regarding the location where *they* believe the German armies are likely to launch their next offensive. They claim it will take place at the *Chemin des Dames*, in your sector, and, quite frankly, it was my duty to find out whether you have any reason to believe they are correct."

"Of course I do not," Duchêne snapped. "There are several possibilities under investigation, but I know of nothing that supports this theory."

"And would you care to hear the information which Colonel Nolan and Major Hubbard have accumulated?" Gresham asked.

"If it can be told to me quickly," Duchêne said.

"Major Hubbard, in a nutshell, why do you believe that the Germans will attack at the *Chemin des Dames*," Gresham asked, "and please be very brief: We cannot waste the General's time."

Hubbard, exhausted and nervous, began to recite his data. Although an able analyst, he was clearly uncomfortable, and he rushed through the information. It was far from being a convincing presentation. Finally Duchêne stopped him.

"None of this changes my mind," the General replied. "Have you anything else?" He asked Gresham.

"No, Sir," Gresham replied, "but we thank you for your courtesy and attention. Gentlemen," he addressed Hubbard and Nolan, "would you mind stepping outside for a moment; I wish to have a word with the General privately." After they had left the office, Gresham turned back to Duchêne. "I want to apologize for having inconvenienced you, Sir," Gresham said. "They are Americans – they cannot possibly be correct – but it was my duty to confirm my own impression."

"Yes, yes, I understand," Duchêne replied impatiently.

"If I may make the suggestion, Sir, since you find yourself in a quiet sector of the front, perhaps these new American Divisions could be placed with your Reserves. It is merely a suggestion – I am not sure anyone knows what to do with them, and after their disgraceful performance at Seicheprey, well, in my opinion, they would learn a great deal under your able command. Of course, the added reserves would also lighten the burden on your own men."

General Duchêne nodded approvingly. "I will take that under consideration, Colonel Gresham; it is a very interesting suggestion, *merci*."

"Thank you again for your time, and a pleasant evening to you, Sir," Gresham said as he touched his cap respectfully and departed.

In the hallway, Nolan was extremely concerned and frustrated. "He did not believe a word of it," he said.

"I thought it went extremely well," Gresham said. "You know, I believe I will go up to Cantigny to watch your exercise. Bullard hasn't run out of bourbon, has he? Perhaps I can find him a case of single malt Scotch whiskey."

"But we must take Hubbard to see Pershing immediately," Nolan objected.

"No, Hubbard here, he needs a rest and must come along with me to Cantigny," Gresham said. "I insist."

Gresham and Hubbard were in Cantigny ten days later when, on 26 May, the rumor began to spread: Two German prisoners of war had revealed under intense interrogation that a massive German offensive in the *Chemin des Dames* region was imminent. In less than 48 hours, *Operation Blücher-Yorck* would begin and Crown Prince William's Army Group would attack the French Sixth Army, cross the Aisne River, then the Marne River, and then capture Paris. Hubbard, whom Gresham had kept quietly away from Paris, had been right all along, and the French and British had been wildly mistaken about Ludendorff's plan of attack.

From *Généralissime* Ferdinand Foch to Douglas Haig to Philippe Pétain to "Blackjack" Pershing, the Allied commanders were taken entirely by surprise. Orders were rushed to the Army commanders, but despite every conceivable effort, it was clearly impossible to shift enough troops into the area quickly enough to completely stop the German attack. A sense of panic descended on the streets of Paris; if the Germans captured the city, the war would be lost.

Pétain immediately contacted the commander of the French Sixth Army, General Duchêne, and ordered him to prepare to defend the *Chemin des Dames* "in depth." That meant multiple defensives lines that could absorb the brunt of the German assault. Significant ground would be lost, but the offensive might still be stopped. Duchêne, typically, decided to ignore Pétain's order. Duchêne believed only in taking the offensive and swore he would not lose an inch of ground; he would not even let the Germans cross the Aisne, he vowed. His troops, including six exhausted British divisions that had just been transferred down from Arras for rest, were rushed forward to the front trenches in the *Chemin des Dames* above the Aisne. His engineers prepared to detonate the few remaining bridges that crossed the river. Duchêne left very few men in the rear besides his newly-assigned American Reserve Divisions, the 2nd and 3rd, that were scattered between Epernay and Meaux near the Marne River.

On the morning of 27 May, the Germans began their bombardment of the Allied front lines. More than 4,000 artillery guns rained shrapnel and explosives and mustard gas down upon the British and French troops amassed in the front line along the *Chemin des Dames*. The number of casualties was enormous. Once the gas cleared, smoke shells were dropped and seventeen divisions of German Stormtroopers advanced. The bridges over the Aisne were seized before they could be detonated. The eight divisions in Duchêne's front line broke, and a 40 kilometer gap opened in the French defenses. The French Sixth Army was pushed back, retreating fifteen kilometres that first day.

Far to the north, on the morning of 28 May, the French began their bombardment of Cantigny. Standing with General Bullard on a rise overlooking the village, Gresham saw French artillery shells fall well behind the lines, falling in the area where the German guns were positioned. Shrapnel and mustard gas shells were dropped and the German artillery positions were quickly abandoned as the soldiers ran for cover. Then after a mere hour, the French barrage suddenly stopped and like a dark, heavy curtain the ground in front of Cantigny erupted into the air. Dirt and wire were thrown high in a straight, even line, and all sight of the village was lost. As the American curtain barrage continued, a dozen French tanks emerged from the *Bois de Cantigny* and rumbled across the fields toward the village. Behind them, troops of the American 28th Infantry Regiment, some 3,500 men, marched forward. Like clockwork, the curtain barrage began to creep steadily back toward the village. The Americans continued to advance behind it, smashing down the few remaining wires and posts until they disappeared into the haze and confusion of the village itself. Suddenly a wild boar bolted from the haze and fled toward the woods. The crack of gunfire and grenades and the flash of flame throwers lit up the hazy village. Then word came back: The Americans had captured Cantigny. It had taken less than 45 minutes. Bullard, beaming, shook Gresham's hand even as the 26th Infantry Regiment moved forward to help secure the village against the counterattacks yet to come.

The American 1st Division pushed the line forward another two kilometres before the German counterattacks began in earnest late that afternoon. The village was bombarded and gassed again and again, even as the furious German

General Oskar von Hutier threw his men against the defending Americans. After the Germans had failed in their fifth major counterattack upon the village the next afternoon, Gresham had seen enough: The Americans could fight and they could hold their ground. That was all he needed to know. He quickly said farewell to Bullard and sped south, anxious to locate the American 2nd Division.

General Duchêne's Sixth Army had been forced to retreat hour after hour as the Germans pushed west from the Aisne toward the Marne River. Thousands of French villagers crowded the roads and hurried toward the rear – old men, women and children exhausted with terror carried their few portable belongings, some leading their flocks of sheep or occasionally a cow. Among those in retreat were French and British troops who were wounded or exhausted, but, in the dark of night, those retreating included many who had simply lost hope. General Duchêne ordered his two best Brigade commanders to rush forward to defend Soissons, but they soon learned that the city had already fallen to the enemy. The American 3rd Division had not yet been allowed to cross the Marne to aid the retreating French and was deployed outside the village of Château-Thierry that sat astride the Marne River. The 2nd Division was initially deployed near Meaux, then moved to the right of the 3rd Division, then moved to its rear, then moved again to its left across the Marne between Montreil-aux-Lions and Château-Thierry. The American soldiers, carting their 60 pound packs, spent countless hours shuttling sleeplessly from one position to another in long convoys of fifty to seventy-five French *"camions"* that could barely pass through the heavily congested roads. Refuges would stare up at the American soldiers and plead for help. Orders were being cut again and again as the situation deteriorated. By 30 May, the Germans were approaching the Marne River, the last natural defense before Paris. *Généralissime* Foch ordered that the river be held at all costs, yet the defending British and French soldiers continued to be pushed back, to within 60 kilometres of Paris. The French had retreated all the way to Château-Thierry on the banks of the Marne.

On that day, the French reserves commander sent the American 7th Machine Gun Battalion, under Lieutenant John Bissell, into the town to cover the French retreat across the sole remaining bridge over the Marne River. As allied and enemy soldiers fought for control of the bridge, it was detonated prematurely, killing both French and German soldiers alike and stranding the Americans in Château-Thierry as the town was occupied by German troops. That night, the Americans escaped over a forgotten railway trestle bridge.

Gresham finally found Jim Harbord at the modest *Hôtel des Trois Rois* in Meaux with his 2nd Division commander, Major General Omar Bundy, and asked Harbord to come outdoors. The 4th Marine Brigade commander was an exceedingly tall and beefy gentleman in his fifties who walked in great, confident strides. Gresham had difficulty keeping up with him as they strolled down to the banks of the river. The town was completely dark and silent, but the sky was clear and the moonlight was quite bright. Harbord stopped at last and looked down at the smooth, slow-moving water for a moment, and then he turned sharply to Gresham.

"Nolan has told me everything," Harbord said with a hint of admonition. "I'm not sure what you are driving at, young man, but you have created one Hell of a mess. What do you intend to do about it?"

Gresham stood beside him and looked away. "It is perhaps worse than I expected," he admitted.

"I damn well hope it is," Harbord replied. "I hope you did not intend to let the Germans advance this deep into French territory."

"That is not important: The deeper the salient, the more vulnerable they will be on their flanks and the more stretched their supply and communication lines will become. Besides, Nolan does not know everything. Just tell me that your Marine Regiments are ready for battle. They are, General?"

"Hell, we've been ready since we first got to France a year ago, son," he replied.

"Then I must ask you come with me; we must speak to General Duchêne."

Harbord laughed. "Yes, you had better, and that's one conversation I certainly would not want to miss," he said.

Duchêne had finally come out from Paris to remain in close command of his battered Sixth Army. His headquarters were nearby in the magnificent, fully restored *château* in the village of Crécy-la-Chapelle, an enormous house situated among lush, well-manicured gardens. Gresham and Harbord arrived very late in the evening, and, at first, Duchêne was unwilling to leave his bedchamber. When General Harbord insisted, Duchêne at last stomped down the staircase in his nightshirt and robe in a furious temper to meet with the American General in the *château*'s magnificent oak-paneled library.

"What is so important that you require my immediate attention!?" He yelled at Harbord. Then Duchêne saw that Gresham was also in attendance, and suddenly he turned a bright hue of red. His eyes bulged: "You were wrong!" He screamed.

"Excuse me?" Gresham asked innocently, although with a malicious grin.

"You told me that the f---ing American intelligence was wrong! You see what has happened to my army?!"

"As I recall, General, you yourself found Major Hubbard's presentation quite unconvincing. You said that the Americans couldn't possibly be correct."

"I didn't say that! You did, you *petite conasse*!" Harbord had to step into the General's path as he began to rush at Gresham.

"Well, even if I did say it, you must admit that you are in command of an entire army, and I am no one. In fact, I do not even officially exist. Yet you, it seems, in your arrogance and stupidity, have allowed the Germans to march all the way to the Marne."

"*MERDE!*" Duchêne screamed. He picked up a vase and threw it against the wall where it smashed to pieces and fell to the parquet floor.

"You ignored the Americans' warning about the *Chemin des Dames*," Gresham said coldly, "and I am the only one who can take that blame away from you. I can tell your superiors that I specifically contradicted Hubbard's analysis, that I told you he was full of s—t."

"*C'est le bordel!*" Duchêne screamed. "Why? Why should you do so?"

"Give me your maps," Gresham said, "and I will show you."

Duchêne, puffing, stomped to his desk, grabbed a cache of papers, and threw them onto a low table beside General Harbord. The General had remained standing, unmoved, throughout the French General's tirade, but he bent now to search through the papers. He quickly found the map of Duchêne's sector and passed it to Gresham.

"Please, General Harbord, show us on this map where the French and American Divisions are now deployed," Gresham asked.

"Here on our right, Micheler's Fifth Army still holds Reims," Harbord said as he swept his hand across the map. "Maistre's Tenth Army and Humbert's Third Army on our left have lost ground but are holding. Here, in General Duchêne's sector, the Sixth Army has fallen all the way back to Château-Thierry at the Marne River. The U.S. 3rd Infantry and reserve regiments of the French Sixth Army are blocking any crossing of the Marne both in Château-Thierry and to the east. West and north of Château-Thierry, there is still fighting on the far side of the Marne. The Sixth Army is still retreating before the Germans, and the enemy is nearing the right bank of the river. There, on both sides of the Marne, to the west of Château-Thierry, is where the U.S. 2nd Infantry is deployed."

"Where are your Marine regiments?"

"The 5th and 6th Marine Regiments and the 6th Machine Gun Battalion are on the right bank of the Marne, deployed to the west of Château-Thierry between Vaux and Lucy-le-Bocage."

"Can the Germans flank you on your left?"

"No, the Ourcq River runs north from the Marne, here on our left," Harbord said.

"Well, then, it is all quite clear," Gresham said.

"Nothing is clear," Duchêne said dismissively.

"Our enemy cannot cross at Château-Thierry. They must move west to reach the Marne River, General," Gresham clarified. "They must control the entire right bank of the river between Château-Thierry and the Ourcq River to have any hope of crossing the Marne, so we cannot let them reach it. General Harbord, will you order your men to dig in?"

"We don't dig in, young man; the Marines hold where they stand," Harbord said proudly. "We've been fighting wars for 150 years and haven't lost ground yet."

"Indeed you must not now," Gresham said. "Here, then is the crux of the matter. General Duchêne, you will order your remaining French and British forces in the field to retreat west of Château-Thierry, to cross the Marne and to secure positions on the left bank of the River."

"Are you serious!?" Duchêne asked incredulously. "You would have me surrender the entire right bank of the Marne to the enemy?"

"No, Sir. That is not my intent. I believe it is time we asked the Americans to defend the front line. We will not win this war without them, but they must prove themselves. They must gain their own confidence and ours. They must show Foch and Petain and Haig that they will fight and hold this ground. They must show Pershing and Wilson, as well. But to do so, you must withdraw your men and leave the field to the Americans. So, I am instructing you: Order your men to retreat to positions behind the American 2nd Infantry, or else I will see that you are court martialed."

It took General Duchêne only a moment to realize his predicament. No one believed the Americans were ready to take on the Germany armies, but now he would be forced to let them do so or suffer the consequences of his arrogance and stupidity. As far as he was concerned, that was no decision at all: He picked up the telephone to send the order to his commanders immediately.

As the remaining French and British units began to withdraw the next morning, a handful of tenacious French commanders remained on the right bank of the Marne seeking to hold off the German offensive. All day long, German artillery peppered the American and French positions with shrapnel and mustard gas even as German infantry divisions took up positions in the villages of Belleau and Torcy-en-Valois nearby. One exhausted French commander being hotly pursued by the enemy passed through a Marine Regiment near Lucy-le-Bocage. He stopped to order American Captain Lloyd Williams to retreat. Unable to speak English, the Frenchman wrote down his instructions and passed them to the Captain. The American read the note, crumpled it up and threw it to the ground. "Retreat? Hell, we just got here!" Williams shouted back.

Throughout that day, General Duchêne's remaining French and British battalions crumbled. By that evening, the battered and disordered French and British had fully retreated over the river. The next morning, the only thing standing between the Germany Army and the Marne was the American Marines.

Between the Americans and the Germans lay meadows of wild flowers and fields of new wheat, and in their midst was the *Bois de Belleau*, a dense, privately-owned, mile-long wildlife preserve where the local French aristocracy had hunted before the war. Now the German 237th Division crept into the dense forest to take up positions opposite the defending Americans even as the 5th and 6th Marine Regiments used their bayonets to cut shallow firing positions into the dry French soil.

The defending line was stretched thin, and the German commanders were not impressed. They had also learned the effectiveness of the creeping artillery barrage, and when the German guns began firing on the clear cool afternoon of 3 June, the American soldiers huddled in fear as shells fell all around them. The barrage lasted an hour. Then dirt and stone flew into the sky and the shells moved back and passed over the American line to the rear. Through the smoke and haze, the defenders could just see the Germans in their grey-blue uniforms and pointed *Pickelhaube* helmets emerge from Belleau Woods in two long lines, steady as machines, irresistible. The Americans watched them come, down the slope in perfect lines, across a thousand yards of fields full of wild grass and scarlet poppies.

The Marine Sergeants ordered their men to hold and set their sights to 300 yards. The Germans came on slowly, and then suddenly a Marine Captain jumped up and yelled to his men: "Get the devils!" and the Americans instantly opened fire. Crack marksmen, the Marines decimated the first line of German infantrymen. Hundreds fell into the tall grass in seconds as the next line of German soldiers stopped in surprise and horror having expected little or no resistance from the inexperienced Americans.

The line was ordered to move forward, and it too was shot down, and then another, and another, and all that afternoon and evening until dark, and all the next day the Germans continued to attack, until in the days to come the truth became all too clear: The Americans had stood their ground and stopped the German advance. *Operation Blücher-Yorck* was over. The plan to split the British and French armies and capture Paris had failed. Germany had nearly exhausted its military supplies and had wasted its best soldiers on the futile spring offensive. And, by June 1918, over a million American soldiers were ready to fight in France. Now it would be the Allies' turn.

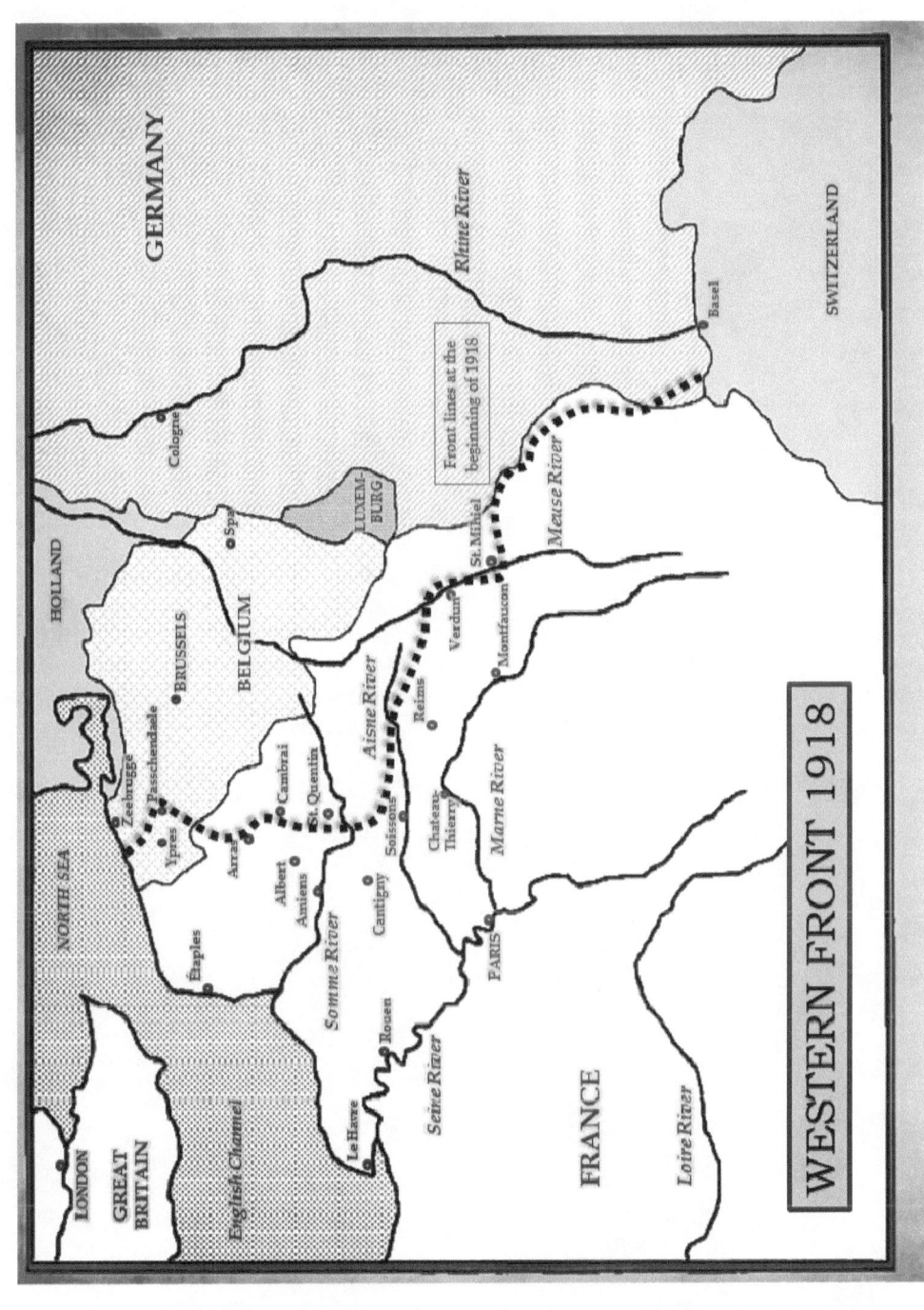

WESTERN FRONT 1918

Berlin

The small, gloomy room in the second-rate *Wilhelmshof* hotel on Leipziger-Strasse in Berlin, across the street from the massive new War Ministry building, was reasonably comfortable but for the armed *Oberleutnant* that stood patiently outside James Wilkins' door at all hours of the day and night, week after week. Outside the window, beyond the yellowed lace curtain, Wilkins could see the great bronze statue of Friedrich Wilhelm standing to one side of Leipziger-Platz. Across the street, throngs of German officers marched in and out of the War Ministry each day. The street was quiet at night, and few motorcars passed by.

Wilkins was not permitted outdoors in Berlin except for escorted walks about the Tiergarten. His bed, lamp, and chair were his sole companions. His meals were brought to his room, and, at any price, the food was appalling – there was a total lack of meat, milk or butter, very little bread, and many dishes made entirely of potatoes or legumes. His days passed slowly. He was a prisoner, and one who paid for his incarceration.

The inability to act, to move, or to speak soon weighed heavily on Wilkins' spirits, and he became increasingly despondent as it seemed he was simply to be forgotten. The notes he sent to Ebert and Kühlmann were met with silence; Crown Prince Rupprecht was occupied at the front. Wilkins was at least given a copy of the Berlin newspaper, *Vossische Zeitung*, so he could read the latest, censored, state-sanctioned news about the war each evening. He learned of the massive German offensive at the Somme that March, and his spirits sank even lower: Any major German victory would only strengthen the hand of the military commanders, Ludendorff and Hindenburg, and terminate Wilkins' diplomacies. To make matters worse, the Lys Offensive and Germany's drive toward Ypres in April threatened to knock the British out of France and Belgium altogether. But then, in the days that followed, the Belgian city miraculously did not fall. Germany's progress at the Somme was reportedly at a standstill. The great aviator Manfred von Richthofen, the "Red Baron" as he was known, was finally killed, shot down over France. There were references in the newspaper to a deadly "Spanish" influenza that was spreading throughout Germany. The Polish Legion leader Józef Piłsudski (the man that Wilkins had met in Warsaw) had refused to swear an oath of allegiance to the German Kaiser and had been thrown in prison with his officers. There was even brief mention of some defections in certain German army regiments, those far from the front lines that had been infiltrated by the "traitorous," Bolshevik-leaning Spartacus League.

There was even news of high-level civilian arrests by Ludendorff's secret police, of men who had been in contact with the government in Russia. Yet even these news articles seemed more like warnings than reports as the Supreme Command maintained its exacting control of the country.

Then, seven weeks after coming to Berlin, Wilkins' guard received orders to bring his prisoner to Friedrich Ebert's private offices near the *Reichstag*. After weeks of waiting, Wilkins was delivered to a small mahogany-paneled room in a grey stone building behind the Brandenburg Gate. There, he found Ebert, rotund with curly black hair and bushy black mustache, and with him several other men: The trim, dapper Foreign Secretary, Baron von Kühlmann; Matthias Erzberger, the leading Catholic Center politician and the principal architect of the *Reichstag*'s 1917 Peace Resolution, the resolution that had called for a negotiated end to the war with no territorial annexations; and a serious young man from the Foreign Office named Kurt Hahn.

"*Herr* Wilkins, we owe you an apology," Ebert began solemnly, once they were all seated around a large, round oak table. "You were kind enough to come to Berlin, and we did not mean to keep you waiting for so long. However, as you no doubt understand, timing is crucial in politics, and a great deal has happened in the past few weeks."

"Yes, I do understand," Wilkins said. Germany's initial successes during their Spring Offensive had forced the war's critics to hold their tongues for a time. Now that the fighting seemed no closer to its end, all the old objections had been renewed and perhaps become even more acute. The German people would bear little more of war. "No harm done, I suppose," he said.

"You are well?" Ebert asked.

"I have not been ill, if that is what you mean, and I see that you gentlemen have not contracted the influenza either." Ebert and Kühlmann looked at each other, surprised that Wilkins appeared to know how widely the disease had spread. "Am I correct that you have reached a decision about the matters we discussed in Brest-Litovsk?" Wilkins asked.

"There has been some progress, yes," Ebert replied. "That is why *Herr* Erzberger is here. He has been asked to, as you say, 'shadow' the Foreign Secretary and has come to this meeting simply to listen. *Herr* Hahn works for Baron Kühlmann in the Foreign Office."

"I would prefer it if you pretended I was not here," Erzberger said quietly. He was a large man with a very round face and spectacles who appeared decidedly ill-at-ease.

Ebert continued: "Beyond that, we are not prepared to say more. These are extremely delicate internal matters, and there is no need for you to know the details. You must understand that there is also a substantial degree of hesitance to make any requests at all of a British officer, and moreover a great deal of uncertainty as to whether you can be trusted, Colonel Wilkins."

"Certainly," Wilkins agreed. "I shall not ask for your trust. It has always been my intention that you and your colleagues should determine for yourselves whether there are matters of common interest between us and, if so, whether I might be of service to you in some regard. As for your trust, I intend to earn it."

"Agreed, but it has nevertheless taken us time to explore these issues with certain of our colleagues," Kühlmann said. "I must tell you there are many who believe you should be expelled from Germany and even some who would have you executed."

"But not to worry, *Herr* Colonel," Ebert interjected quickly. "There is no execution planned at the moment. You made to us a proposal in Brest-Litovsk. We understand your concern about the Bolshevik government; that is a concern we share, although there are those in the government who still support whatever actions will sow discord in Russia and frustrate our enemies. In my opinion, they are playing a dangerous game. We have decided to ask you to depart Germany with information that you may convey to those you deem appropriate. You have given your parole, and we will take you at your word as a man of honor that you will not take up arms against Germany again until you are released from that oath. You shall also be given authorization papers so that you may be escorted from the Swiss border back to this office with any reply. Nothing can be written down, however, and we must ask that you not send any telegrams to or from Berlin."

"Certainly, I agree," Wilkins said. "But from whom shall I to say this information was obtained?"

"It would be best if you do not use any names for now," Ebert replied, "for your safety as well as ours. You see the men assembled here. We represent a significant portion of the *Reichstag* and therefore of the German people, and we hold positions of high authority in Germany's government, its civilian government."

"Perhaps so, but will you gentlemen ever be in a position to implement your policies?" Wilkins asked skeptically.

Ebert shook his head. "That, I cannot say. Of course we hope to do so, and if we ever achieve such positions, then others will know which way the winds are blowing in Germany."

"And not just Germany. *Herr* Wilkins, have you heard of the letters that were published in France by Prime Minister Clemenceau?" Kühlmann asked suddenly.

"No, I have not. To what letters do you refer?" Wilkins asked.

"Peace proposals sent confidentially by Emperor Charles via the Empress' brother, Prince Sixtus, to President Poincaré," Kühlmann explained. "Clemenceau has published the letters, and they have become a tremendous embarrassment to the young Austrian Emperor. It has greatly unsettled his government and his people. Count Czernin has been forced to resign as Austria's Foreign Minister, for he apparently knew nothing of the letters before they were made public."

"Yes, I believe I know something about those letters," Wilkins said, suppressing his enjoyment at the mention of the correspondence he and Gresham had put into motion in Vienna some two years earlier.

"Moreover, you have seen the desperate situation in Austria-Hungary first hand,' Kühlmann continued. "In Russia, the Bolsheviks are waging civil war. There is fighting in Ukraine, and the Ukrainian food supplies for Germany and Austria have not materialized. Neither has Roumania yet become a viable source of foodstuffs; years of food stored there, not to mention petroleum, were ruthlessly destroyed or poisoned when the Roumanians retreated to Jassy. The situation for Emperor Charles is catastrophic, and it is worsening to the extent that we have grave doubts about the future of the Hapsburg monarchy.

"Of course, we are also aware of the aspirations of the Yugoslavs, Czechs and Slovenes," Kühlmann said. "We now believe it is probable that Emperor Charles will permit these new nations to be formed. We believe Germany must prepare for what we see as an inevitable development, even if Kaiser Wilhelm does not wish to discuss the possibility. We would consider these new nations our partners, not our adversaries."

"There is also the Baltic situation," Ebert said. "Latvia, Lithuania, and Estonia – it is our position that these new nations should be permitted to determine and elect their own governments without the threat of German army occupation."

"And what of Poland?" Wilkins asked. "There is Polish land in Galicia that is currently within the Hungarian border but most of their territory is now occupied by the German armies."

"That is more difficult because of the Prussian territory that overlaps somewhat with the Poles', but in theory, yes, Poland should become an independent nation as well," Ebert said. "It is merely a matter of where the borders shall be established."

"But the main issue is the Russians," Kühlmann insisted. "Russia is in chaos – it is a mad, destructive hurricane which at present is only a shadow of the power gathering behind it. Germany cannot permit the Bolsheviks to reach our doorstep or continue to agitate within our borders. Even Kaiser Wilhelm is adamant about that. We hear that the Russians have begun executing those who object to their revolutionary dictatorship. You must convey that we are shocked and appalled by these developments, and Germany will oppose the Bolsheviks with all our strength. We will support and defend any fair and independent government in these new nations that will work with us to oppose the Russians."

It was not difficult to discern the uneasiness and urgency in Kühlmann's voice or see the grave concern written on the faces of Ebert, Erzberger, and Hahn. Bolshevik propaganda had perhaps become a far more significant problem within Germany than these men cared to admit. They were desperate to place a buffer between Germany and the new Russian dictatorship.

"There is something else you should know," the young man named Hahn said. "We agree that democratic reforms in the German government are both necessary and would make a negotiated peace more palatable to our enemies. For several years, Colonel, I have served as the private secretary to Prince Maximillian of Baden. He has long advocated such reforms, and we intend to do everything we can to make him Chancellor of Germany. We believe that Kaiser Wilhelm will ultimately agree."

"These are our positions," Ebert explained. "It is our hope that you will convey this information to those involved in the negotiations in Rome and state plainly that these new nations *do* have support within the German government. We ask you to return to Berlin if there is any reply, or at the very least to tell us what is happening and by whom."

"I understand," Wilkins said.

"We realize that you would have to return to Germany as a matter of personal choice. Once you pass outside our borders, you will be entirely at your own discretion, and I must warn you that we cannot guarantee what will happen if you return, although for our part we would defend your presence in Germany."

"Yes," Wilkins said, "but this is precisely why I came to Germany, gentlemen, and why I asked Crown Prince Rupprecht to send me to Brest-Litovsk. I tell you unequivocally that Great Britain shares your aspirations for Eastern Europe and your abhorrence of the Bolsheviks. In that regard, you may consider me your ally and expect my return as long as I am able."

Wilkins was transported to the Swiss border and found his way first to Zurich. Although he was fairly certain he would be able to travel back to Berlin, he had no idea of the reception he would find in Italy. Not only had he abandoned his post in Rome, but he had resided in enemy territory for more than six months. It seemed likely that the Secret Intelligence Service would want to question him, or that another allied intelligence organization would be searching for him. So, at a pharmacy in Zurich, Wilkins purchased a solution of sulphate of copper and one of yellow cyanide which he mixed together into a dye that turned his hair black as tar, and he added pomade to slick his hair straight back. A lotion of olive oil and cocoa butter mixed with sodium borate made his face and hands ruddy, concealed the scar on his cheek, and gave him an olive hue. Then in a suit of cheap clothing, he secretly crossed Lake Geneva into Italy and traveled Third Class by train to Rome.

Wilkins's his first stop on the warm, cloudy evening he arrived in Rome was at the shop of his watchmaker, *Signore* Abato. The old shopkeeper, sitting on his stool at the counter crowded with clocks, failed to recognize the Italian-looking man who entered.

"*Serata piacevole, si?*" Abato asked casually.

"You do not know me, *Signore?*" Wilkins asked.

Abato looked closely at Wilkins, and then suddenly his eyes opened wide and a broad smile stretched across his face. "Why, hello, hello! It is *Colonnello* Wilkins, *sì*? How have you been, *Signore*? It has been so many months; I feared you had been lost in the war."

"I have been away but simply had to return, *Signore* Abato, for I never came to collect my luggage!" Wilkins replied. "I had to depart rather unexpectedly, you see, and I have long regretted that I did not return to collect the rest of the items I commissioned from you. You are my new Quartermaster, *Signore;* I shall call you *'Q'* for short."

"The other items, then, they have met with your approval?"

"Oh, yes indeed, they were marvelous, saved my life even," Wilkins replied. "The cigar case, that one was especially delightful. Tell me, what do you think of my disguise?"

"Well, to speak truthfully, it is not so good, *Signore*, for anyone who would make a close examination. Not to alarm you, but we had better get you something more concealing right away," he said.

"And why do I need a new disguise so quickly?" Wilkins asked with sudden concern.

"Because there have been many men asking after you, *Signore*. British, Italian, perhaps even German, it is difficult to recall, there were so many. You are a most wanted man."

"Then I shall accept your assistance gladly. In fact, I came also to see whether you might be able to create some identification papers for me. I must remain in Italy for a while, but I do not wish to have my presence here noticed."

"Yes, certainly, papers are not difficult at all. May I suggest that you take the name of the *Spagnolo*, a Spaniard? I have a perfect copy for that purpose, and no one notices what the Spanish do or where they go, at least here in Rome," Abato said.

"Good Heavens, I haven't spoken Spanish in years, *Signore*, but if you think it best."

"We had better begin right away. I will get my 'Brownie' – it is from America and takes very good photographs!"

Late that night, Wilkins (under the name "*Señor* Jaime Molina, envoy of King Alfonso XIII of Spain") registered at the *Hôtel Regina*. He had already confirmed that the Prince Regent of Serbia, Alexander, still maintained rooms there, and he left word that he wished to call upon His Majesty the next afternoon. Wilkins guessed that the Serbians and their colleagues would be eager to meet with a representative of the Spanish crown, and indeed "*Señor* Molina" received word in the morning that he should attend the Prince Regent in his suite at Noon.

With his improved cosmetics, Wilkins appeared convincingly Spanish but was still extremely nervous when he was finally admitted to the well-appointed Royal Suite to meet with Alexander. The Prince Regent was dressed in another expensive grey wool suit with *pince-nez* and his mustache neat and thin in the modern fashion. He was surrounded by Serbian officers and other civilians of various nationalities in their fine dark suits. Wilkins was relieved that the British representative, Wickham Steed, was not present, since Wilkins had met Steed the previous year and feared being recognized.

Alexander stepped forward at once to introduce himself to the "Spanish envoy": "*Señor* Molina, it is a great pleasure to make your acquaintance," he said shaking Wilkins' hand.

"Your Majesty, you are most gracious," Wilkins replied in Serbian with a thick Spanish accent.

"We are most grateful that King Alfonso has sent you to Rome, although somewhat surprised that he should do so."

"Yes; Spain still maintains her neutrality, and I must disappoint you, Sir, that this cannot to be considered an official state visit," Wilkins replied. "However, there are certain matters which I would like to discuss with you privately, if you will permit it. They are most urgent."

"Yes, of course, but you will allow me to retain my Aide, General Stepanovish," he replied tersely. Alexander then asked the other men to empty the room, and Wilkins was left alone with the Prince Regent and his "Aide," a tall, well-armed General and apparent bodyguard. "We may speak English if you wish, *Señor*, if that will assuage your concern: The General does not speak a word of English."

"Very well," Wilkins said in English, retaining his Spanish accent nonetheless. "First, sir, I must ask you not to reveal my name or make any motion of surprise at what I am about to tell you."

Prince Alexander stepped back and raised his eyebrows curiously.

Wilkins continued: "Some months ago you came to my flat near the Spanish Steps and asked me to conduct an investigation into the identity of the person who attempted to assassinate Mister Benesh, do you recall that meeting?"

Alexander stiffened and struggled to maintain an even expression. His eyes narrowed as he peered at Wilkins and looked carefully at his face. At last he stepped back and nodded. "Yes, I recall," he said at last, quite coldly. "It is quite a surprise to see you again. You were prudent to wear a disguise, for it is well known that you were the guest of Crown Prince Rupprecht at the negotiations in Brest-Litovsk and it is now widely assumed that you are working for Germany. You must tell me at once whether there is any truth to these rumors, or else I shall be forced to call for your immediate arrest."

"Well, just a moment, please," Wilkins complained. "That is a very complicated subject, and it is difficult to answer you. Yes, I was at Brest-Litovsk with the permission of Crown Prince Rupprecht, for, you see, he is a family relation of mine, but I was there only to observe the proceedings. I am here now at the request of certain worthy members of the German government. However, I assure you that I am not working for the Germans, nor am I in any way working against you or your allies. I come to you only as a friend."

"How can I take you at your word when you arrive in disguise and under a false name," Alexander objected.

"While it is true that I am no longer working for British intelligence, you must trust that I am doing what must be done for the good of Great Britain and for the good of many others, including you and your colleagues."

Alexander considered this statement a moment. "You must know that your countrymen are searching for you," he warned. "If you are captured, your life might be in danger."

"Perhaps, but I believe they would change their minds before the bitter end."

"At least tell me what you want, so I may consider your motives."

"Tell me: Are you any closer to achieving diplomatic recognition for your new nations from Great Britain, France, or Italy, or even the Americans?" Wilkins asked.

"Somewhat; yes, in principle at least," Alexander replied.

"Then I must tell you: There are powerful men in Germany, rising members of the *Reichstag* and members of Chancellor von Hertling's own cabinet, who believe that the Austro-Hungarian Empire is on the verge of collapse. They believe the rise of these new nations is now inevitable. They support the formation of Yugoslavia, as well as a Czecho-Slovak nation, and further independent states spanning Eastern Europe from the Baltic Sea to the Balkans. Why do they, you wonder? It is because they are mortally afraid of the new Russia. They are even now desperately combatting Bolshevism inside Germany. They want assurances that their future neighbors will be their allies in the fight against the Russians."

"How interesting," Alexander observed, "for the Western European nations and Americans are seeking the same guarantees."

"It is no wonder if you consider the state that Russia is in now. Have you given them your assurances?"

"Of course we have, we must, but they are patient and wait to learn more about us, especially my colleagues who purport to represent elements unknown to them. And, I tell you, it is not so clear from where we stand that Austria-Hungary shall fall, in which case the West is wise to be cautious."

"Yes, I see," Wilkins agreed. "Still, it may be to your advantage to disclose that you have been approached by a representative of the German government. It may worry the West to think that you have another option."

"Indeed," Alexander agreed. "That could be quite helpful."

"I tell you truthfully, Alexander, that to the extent I have cooperated with Germany at all it has only been with regard to the issue of Russia and the containment of Bolshevism. I am an Englishman through and through. I serve my country. Of course Germany is our enemy now, but I dare say it will soon be our ally against Russia. That is why I went to Brest-Litovsk."

Alexander nodded thoughtfully.

"I know you have no sympathy for the Bolsheviks," Wilkins continued. "I do not know the other diplomats with whom you are working. I would like to meet them, so that I may return to Germany and –"

"Good God! You mean to return?" Alexander asked in shock.

"Certainly," Wilkins replied firmly.

Alexander stood and walked to the window. As he gazed out thoughtfully, Wilkins waited patiently.

"I will speak to the others; I cannot make this decision alone," Alexander said at last.

Wilkins soon left the Prince Regent's suite.

Late that night, Alexander came alone to Wilkins' less-distinguished rooms to discuss the matter further over brandy and cigarettes. Many of the other diplomats, it seemed, were willing to meet with the Germans' unofficial representative "from Spain", if only because they knew that their nations would eventually be Germany's neighbors. Alexander explained the state of the negotiations to Wilkins in great detail. As usual, the main disputes related to where the borders would be drawn. Alexander, as Prince Regent of Serbia, and Ante Trumbic, a Croat, were attempting to form the nation of Yugoslavia out of territory in Serbia, Montenegro, and parts of Austria, Bulgaria and Albania. Edvard Benesh and Milan Shtefanik (who had served with the French Army), represented the Czechs and Slovaks who sought to form their new nation from parts of Hungary, Poland, and Austria. Mihaly Karolyi was there to discuss the independence of Hungary from the Hapsburg crown. And the Roumanian government had sent representatives who continued to seek territory from Hungary even after having signed a treaty with Germany that gave up land to Bulgaria and Austria.

"Unfortunately, there is one hurdle we cannot overcome. That is Poland," Alexander explained. "Roman Dmowski is the Polish National Congress representative who seeks alliances for an independent Poland, separate from both Russia and Germany. However, there is the dispute between Dmowski and the other potential leader of Poland, General Pilsudski, who now commands the Polish Legions for Germany. That presents the rest of us with a dilemma, as we do not know what Pilsudski will do. He is in Warsaw still, and without his agreement, Dmowski is essentially powerless," he said.

"I have met with Pilsudski," Wilkins said.

"You have?" Alexander asked in surprise.

"Yes, I went to see him in Warsaw," Wilkins said innocently. "Pilsudski has agreed to reconcile with Dmowski and has declined to make an alliance with Germany. Pilsudksi and his men refused to swear an oath of service to Kaiser Wilhelm and have recently been imprisoned."

"That is tremendous news, James! We must speak with Dmowski at once so you can tell him. But is Pilsudksi not at odds with Germany now? How does it serve your principals in Berlin if Dmowski and Pilsudski make an alliance with the West against Germany?"

"But you do not yet understand, Alexander," Wilkins assured him. "You are still thinking of Germany as it exists today. We are making plans for the nation that Germany has yet to become."

Roman Dmowski, Polish statesman and leader of the right-wing National Democracy party, was perhaps more pleased to hear that General Józef Piłsudski was in prison than that the Polish Socialist party leader now supported Dmowski's national aspirations for Poland. Regardless, word that Piłsudski backed the talks in Rome resolved a major difficulty, and soon the "Oppressed Nations" were united in their approach to the British, French, Italian and American governments. In addition, as a "Spanish" representative of members of the German government, and one who had attended the negotiations at Brest-Litovsk, "*Señor* Molina" was frequently asked for his thoughts about the future relations between Germany and its potential new neighbors. Thus, Wilkins remained in Rome for several weeks to meet with the representatives from each faction and to discuss privately the many potential difficulties of self-government in each new nation.

In early June, even as the latest German offensive in France came to crashing halt at Belleau Woods, the British, French and Italian governments finally issued declarations supporting the national aspirations of the Poles, Czecho-Slovaks, and Yugo-Slavs. Wilkins prepared for his return to Germany. Although his presence in Italy was still undetected by his former superiors in the Secret Intelligence Service, Wilkins had developed a sense that he was perhaps being watched, and he knew that many questions were being asked about him. It was time to leave Rome.

On his last night in the ancient capital, Wilkins sat alone in his small suite at the *Hôtel Regina* awaiting his supper in the room where he had privately dinned each evening since his arrival in Italy. The inlaid wood dining table had already been set for his meal as he relaxed in the leather high-back chair by the window with a glass of wine and the newspapers from France. There was a knock at his door, and Wilkins stood to admit the footman with his supper. But as he opened the door, Wilkins saw it was not the footman at all.

Standing in his doorway, he looked straight into the lovely blue, oval eyes of Derya Storch, also known by the name Josephina Hesketh, among others. Wearing a long silk dress that emphasized her lithesome frame, she smiled at Wilkins mischievously and laughed out loud.

"Really, James, you look nothing like a Spaniard," she said as she pushed past him and entered the suite.

"My dear, what a surprise to see you again," Wilkins replied as he shut the door. "I didn't expect to see you after Warsaw; I thought you had forgotten me. Am I forgiven, or are you here to finally kill me?" He asked.

She laughed again. "I rather like you with dark hair, James. It is very handsome. May I have some of your wine?" She marched to the chair and took the wine glass from the side table. As she sipped, Wilkins could see the deep red lipstick she left on the glass. It was marvelously erotic.

"How did you find me?" Wilkins asked.

"I know all the spies in Italy, James. After I learned that the new Spanish envoy had been to Warsaw, I knew straight away that it must be you."

'Of course," he conceded.

"So tell me," she asked, "now that you have been to see your sweet uncle Rupprecht, is there any hope left for Germany?"

"I would have said so, yes, but now that this latest offensive in France has petered out, I believe their chance for an outright victory is gone forever."

"I agree, and, furthermore, I do not see much of a future for Austria either. Did you know, James, I was born in Istanbul?"

"Truly?" He replied skeptically.

"I have no love at all for the Germans or the Austrians; they paid me very well, but they do not seem to want to pay anymore. And, for reasons I do not care to discuss, I cannot return to Turkey. Italy is rather nice, though; I think I would like to stay here after the war."

"Oh, I see," Wilkins said. *Madame* Storch had come to secure her own future. He went to the table and poured himself a second glass of wine. "Before you play the coquette, my dear, I doubt I am in a position to help you, and if you simply turn yourself in, I suspect the Italians would have you executed. Have you anything left to bargain with?"

"Indeed, I have something, something very big," she said with suppressed glee, "and you are so very good at playing the intermediary, James, that I hoped you would help me to make a deal." She glided up to Wilkins and pressed herself against him. "Did I say how very much I like your new hair?" She asked as she held his head in her hands, and then she kissed him.

For months, the German Supreme Command had insisted that Austria follow up on its great victory against the Italians at Caporetto, but through the winter Austria had suffered terribly. Many army units were badly undermanned and poorly supplied. Still, as part of Ludendorff's plans for 1918, he required Austria to undertake another offensive. The Austrians cobbled together the last of their reserves and the last of their provisions to launch one final attack across the Piave River to seize Venice or Padua or even Verona, if possible. The attack was to begin at 03.00 on 15 June. At 02.30 that morning, a half-hour before the attack was set to begin, the Italians opened fire on the Austrian front lines. The Italian government had received detailed forewarning of the attack from an unidentified source, and their artillery barrage killed thousands of Austrian soldiers assembled in the front lines for the assault.

In some places, the Austrians did succeed in crossing the river only to meet well-prepared resistance by the Italian armies. Unable to advance and under withering fire, the Austrian commander finally ordered his men to retreat but then discovered that the bridges over the Piave had been targeted and destroyed by Italian artillery. A sudden rain storm had also swelled the river, and the Austrians were trapped on open ground. They fought desperately, but cut off as they were from their supplies and reinforcements the Austrian soldiers became easy targets for the waiting Italians. Thousands of Austrians drowned attempting in desperation to swim back across the Piave River.

The Italians continued to press the Austrians in the Trentino as well. On the plateau north of Asiago, the Alpini drove back the elite Edelweiss Divisions of the Austrian army.

In only eight days, 175,000 Austrians were killed, wounded or captured. The Austrian army was utterly broken. It would never attack again. In the streets of Vienna, the starving Austrian populace rioted, and across the country factory workers went on strike. Austria-Hungary was on the brink of collapse.

Wilkins returned to Berlin just as news of the disaster reached the German ministries. Wilkins (with his hair still dyed coal black) was brought directly to meet with Kühlmann and Ebert:

"I pray you had nothing to do with this business at the Piave River, *Herr* Wilkins!" Kühlmann said sternly. "It is quite obvious that the Italians received advance warning of the offensive."

"How could I possibly have learned of the attack, gentlemen?" Wilkins asked evasively. "I was in Rome, not Austria, as you know. In any event, it is no more nor less than Austria deserves for acceding to Ludendorff's ridiculous demand: Austria should have known better than to attack when their armies are in such poor condition."

"Were you at least successful in meeting with your diplomatic contacts in Rome?" Ebert asked to change the topic of conversation.

"Indeed I was," Wilkins replied. "There can be no doubt that the Austro-Hungarian Empire has now been written out of all future plans for Eastern Europe. I believe it unlikely that Emperor Charles will even survive the coming winter. From Asia Minor to the Baltic Sea, you will have a host of new neighbors, but you shall be glad to hear that not one of them is sympathetic to the Bolsheviks and that all view the new Russia as their enemy. For the most part, I think you should be pleased, although the settlement of the precise borders still needs to be negotiated."

Wilkins went on to explain all he had done in Rome, the people he had met, and the platforms of their political parties. As he spoke, he could see the hopeful expressions on the faces of his colleagues: Ebert and Kühlmann were eager to imagine a world after war.

"So, if I may say so, gentlemen," Wilkins continued, "I believe it is finally time that we discussed how to bring this war to a conclusion."

Ebert and Kühlmann looked nervously at each other. "*Herr* Wilkins –" Ebert began.

"No!" Wilkins demanded. "I did not return to Berlin simply to give you this information, these names. Ludendorff sought to force the British from Belgium and France – he failed. He sought to split the French and British at Arras – he failed. Now there is news that his latest offensive at the *Chemin des Dames* has been stopped short of the Marne. You must face facts, gentlemen: Germany has had its last offensive on the Western Front. From here on, you will only be holding defensive positions, and I ask you: How long must that last? At what toll of life and property, I ask you? Will you weaken your country until you become prey to the Bolsheviks and their ruthless dictators? It cannot be allowed! You must end this war! You must build a democratic Germany now!"

Kühlmann sat silently gazing at the floor.

"It is not that we disagree with you, *Herr* Wilkins," Ebert admitted uncomfortably. "But it simply cannot be done – not with Kaiser Wilhelm still in command. This is no longer a war over colonial rights and free trade; Wilhelm now claims that we fight for the Germanic ideals of right, freedom, honor and morality against the 'corrupt' Anglo-Saxon worship of money and oppression of the weak. His son, Crown Prince William, is immensely popular, a war hero, although there are rumors that in this last offensive the Crown Prince was intended to assist Rupprecht to pin the British against the coast. It was his own ambition that drove William to attack only toward Paris. Ludendorff and Hindenburg still march in lock step beside the Kaiser and the ideal of empire. There have been a few defections among the lower ranks in the army, that is true, but not nearly enough to weaken the Supreme Command's hold over this nation, not yet."

"But for the Spartacus League, and the shop stewards, and the unions and workers' and soldiers councils, is that not so?" Wilkins asked. "Are the Bolsheviks' allies not agitating for revolution in Germany even now? Have you not suffered factory strikes and food shortages just as in Russia and Austria?"

"That is true, yes, and there can be no doubt there is a grave possibility of revolution," Ebert admitted.

"Then you must make it plain to Chancellor von Hertling that your nation is at risk. He must speak to the Kaiser about stepping aside."

"Chancellor von Hertling will not take that step," Kühlmann insisted. "He might speak in favor of certain democratic reforms if we were to place pressure upon him, but I tell you he is a true conservative and monarchist at heart. No, it will not happen. You speak of an end to the war. I am the Foreign Secretary. I must be the first to speak out."

Wilkins was uncertain, but it was a step. He decided to say nothing. Ebert too was uncertain: "We should continue our efforts to have Prince Max made Chancellor, first," he argued.

"No," Kühlmann said. "I am scheduled to appear in the *Reichstag* tomorrow. It is the perfect opportunity to introduce the possibility of peace negotiations, and then we shall see who stands up to support an end to the fighting now that we have once again reached a stalemate in France."

Wilkins waited patiently in the *Wilhelmshof* hotel all the next day to learn how the Foreign Secretary fared. The answer came that evening when the newspaper reported Kühlmann's speech: The Foreign Secretary had declared flatly that war could no longer result in victory and that a negotiated peace was the only means to preserve Germany. He had gone so far as to propose a free and independent Poland and suggested that the other former-Russian territories were also entitled to independence. In other respects, he had carefully intertwined themes more palatable to German conservatives: Russia was to blame for the conflict, he had said; Germany was aggrieved, and Germany was entitled to security; France, Great Britain and America had all extoled peace, he said, but they had abandoned their own proposals. Indeed, since American President Wilson had offered his "Fourteen Points", he claimed, America had essentially reneged on its own proposed peace terms.

The newspapers called Kühlmann a traitor, and the Foreign Secretary's attempt to begin a national dialogue to end the war met with swift retribution from the Supreme Command. Chancellor von Hertling was sent to the *Reichstag* the next day to "clarify" the Foreign Secretary's remarks, and, soon after, the Kaiser requested Baron von Kühlmann's resignation.

To Wilkins' dismay, one of his chief and only allies in Berlin had been dismissed. Ebert was also deeply concerned. He unexpectedly arrived at Wilkins' hotel near midnight to discuss the matter privately in the small, sparsely furnished guest-room:

"This is a disaster," he told Wilkins. "Kühlmann is to be replaced by Ambassador von Hintze, an able man and an advocate for democratic reform, but he is now likely to take a very conservative approach with the Kaiser."

"I agree with you there,' Wilkins said. "We now see that Kühlmann was wrong to believe that he, as Foreign Secretary, was the one to raise the subject of a negotiated peace. We should not have agreed to let him. The issue is still immature. To have a negotiated peace you must have reform; to have reform, you must eliminate the monarchy; to eliminate the monarchy, you must eliminate Ludendorff."

"Ludendorff alone? Not Hindenburg?" Ebert asked.

"Good God, of course not Hindenburg!" Wilkins replied adamantly. "You need Hindenburg. Consider what happened in Russia: The military became Kerensky's un-doing. It was General Korniloff's attempted *coup d'état* in Russia that forced Kerensky to make alliance with the Bolsheviks, with the workers' and soldiers' councils. Moreover, you must consider the military tradition in Germany, in Prussia especially. Whatever you wish to do, you will not be successful unless you have the agreement of Hindenburg. The soldiers will do whatever Hindenburg commands."

Ebert sat silently and considered his situation. At last he stood and went to the door. His hand on the doorknob, he turned at the last moment to tell Wilkins: "You must come with me tomorrow. Be ready at eight."

Wilkins and Ebert traveled by sedan all the next day. Ebert was silent; he seemed extremely nervous. They arrived in Cassel, halfway between Leipzig and Düsseldorf, at dusk and stopped at the old-fashioned *König von Preussen* hotel in

King Square. Ebert led Wilkins inside and marched directly to a small, private dining room in the back of the lobby.

A solitary figure awaited them there. He was a tall, thin man with a square jaw and short grey-brown hair who wore an elaborate German officer's uniform. Ebert and the officer spoke in whispers for several minutes. Finally, Ebert turned to Wilkins. "Colonel Wilkins, I would like to introduce you to *Herr Generalquartiermeister* Karl von Metzger," he said.

Metzger stepped forward and extended his hand.

"Perhaps you do not recall, but we have met once before, *Herr Generalquartiermeister*," Wilkins said.

"Is that so?" Metzger asked, taken aback.

"Perhaps I am incorrect. Have you not visited the 'Temple at Heaton Park'?" Wilkins asked.

Metzger's eyes opened wide and his hand fell to his side. He recognized at once the passphrase that the British Colonel had given him at Passchendaele, the phrase that David Gresham had said would identify himself and his accomplices in Germany, the phrase that Gresham had shared with Wilkins with only a moment to spare outside of Prime Minister Lloyd-George's railway carriage in France.

"Well, well, I believe you have," Wilkins said knowingly. "Now at last I believe we are getting somewhere."

Septsarges

Do you know this house, Colonel Gresham?"

Gresham sat upon a splintered wooden chair in an otherwise empty, windowless room in a small stone building. Since his arrest, he had been moved several times and had lost track of his precise location. He had sat, hands cuffed, smoking cigarettes and drinking weak tea in this particular room for more than ten hours. The arrest itself was of no great concern to him; he had expected that questions would be asked and his actions examined. He had deliberately misled a French General and then forced him to withdraw his forces from a desperate battle. However, Gresham felt it was his duty not to answer questions, and after several days he had begun to wonder how the matter would eventually be resolved. Most of all, he wanted to speak with Princess Eleanor and tell her that he had done nothing wrong, or at least that he had acted with the proper motives. It made him distinctly uneasy to think that she might misconstrue his actions.

But, now, *Généralissime* Ferdinand Foch himself stood before Gresham, the great commander, a short man with a wide grey mustache, deep, unwavering eyes, and no expression at all. His uniform was very grand, bright sky blue, his red cap and cape embroidered with gold filigree, and his arms crossed over his chest in an attitude of rigid skepticism.

"Do you know it, Colonel? No?" Foch asked again. "This is the Carriage House in Puiseux-le-Hauberger. It is very well-known. You see, during the Reign of Terror, at the height of the Revolution, noblemen fleeing Paris stopped here on their way to England. The irony, of course, is that your government now demands that I *send* you to England, in chains."

Gresham remained silent.

"*Bien sûr,* I have no misconceptions about *General* Duchêne's own culpability in this affair," Foch continued. "In many ways, he is the one more responsible. However, your actions cannot go un-remarked. It has been a great embarrassment for your government, particularly for Field Marshal Haig, and a great annoyance to me that you interfered so at the moment of crisis. Haig has insisted that you be court-martialed." Gresham had to agree that he had been enormously unfair to Douglas Haig; it had turned out that the Field Marshal had learned a great deal during the war and had become a remarkable commander of the British Expeditionary Force. Gresham had not meant to embarrass Haig or their government, but he had done so and there would necessarily be consequences, he knew. "For my part," Foch continued, "I cannot decide whether to award you the *Palme en Bronze* or to have you shot."

"Perhaps if you would allow me to choose…" Gresham said.

Foch smirked slightly. "I do appreciate your good humour, Colonel Gresham, I do. I took it upon myself to become more familiar with your record, or at least the small portion of it your government will allow me. Perhaps you are not aware that I myself commanded the French soldiers at the Battle at the Somme in 1916, so I heard a great deal of your raid at Foncquevillers: Quite a remarkable achievement, *oui*. I have also learned that you have served at Ypres, at Gallipoli, in Serbia, and even as a Brigade General in Roumania for a short time. I greatly respect your service to the war effort, Colonel. That is why you have not yet been executed. That is why I am all the more surprised that, for a soldier, you appear to have so little respect for the chain of command, am I not correct?"

"I must disagree with you there," Gresham said. "However, my duties have at times required me to disregard the chain of command."

"When *you* deem it proper," Foch said pointedly. "Tell me, do you consider yourself more the spy now than the soldier?"

Gresham had to think about the question a moment, and at last concluded: "No, I was given orders. I have only used the license I was given."

"Yet your government does not admit responsibility for your actions."

"My government in fact knew nothing of my actions."

"Your government claims that you acted outside your authority," Foch insisted. "Is that true?"

Gresham did not reply. He didn't know the answer. When he had been recruited by Compton Mackenzie, he had been told to do whatever he, Gresham, believed was necessary to serve his nation's interests. He had been told that Great Britain would deny responsibility for his actions. That had always been a part of the game. He thought it would be Germany or Austria that would finally condemn him, not his own country and its allies. How could he explain that he had been ordered to act outside the normal channels of command, especially when he had been forbidden to say anything at all.

"Well, it would be fair to say that you have played your last trump, Colonel," Foch said at last, "but I will not say that you have lost by any means, no, not at all. The German offensive is done, its objectives unrealized. In that, you and I have succeeded. But there is still a great deal of work to do, *n'est-ce pas?* We are preparing our own offensive for the autumn: The British will push on toward Damascus, the Italians will seek to take Trieste, the Serbians and Greeks will invade Serbia on the Salonika Front, and there will be three coordinated attacks on the Western Front: One by the French, one by the British, and one by the Americans. Germany cannot resist a coordinated offensive on multiple fronts simultaneously: Marshal von Hindenburg has neither the reserves nor the materiel remaining to him. There is much left to be done. It is a pity you will be in prison."

It was to be the Allies' endgame at long last; the end of the war was coming. Gresham felt a chill run down his spine, for there was one thing he truly feared

– that he would not be there to see the end. "You must allow me to stay in France." He pleaded quietly.

Foch could see Gresham's anxiousness. "I am a pragmatic man, Colonel Gresham. What do you propose?"

"I only wish to fight, please," he asked.

"You are no longer to be a spy, it seems. Are you prepared to conduct yourself henceforth as a soldier should and follow your orders?" Foch demanded.

Gresham could see the ruthless determination in the Frenchman's eyes. Foch believed he could win the war, and Gresham decided the time had come for him to believe in Foch. "Yes, as you wish, Sir," he agreed.

Foch regarded the British agent a moment longer. "I shall hold you to that, young man," he said and then turned and walked deliberately from the room.

There was a long, hushed conversation in the hallway, then footsteps approaching. Gresham looked up to find Dennis Nolan standing in the doorway. He held a wide, flat brown paper parcel.

"Hello, David," Nolan said in his usual, bland tone.

"Dennis, a pleasure to see you again," Gresham replied mutedly.

"I am glad to see you are well. General Pershing sent me to make you an offer." He tossed Gresham a set of keys to unlock his handcuffs. "You had better hear it before you take off those cuffs."

"All right."

"There's been a great deal of discussion about you during the past few days, as you might have surmised. I've finally come to understand that you work for a British intelligence agency, one we knew nothing about. Quite a very, very interesting business, the more I learn of it. In any case, you can continue to work for that organization if you chose, although frankly I think they are likely to require that you spend the rest of your days in jail. Alternatively, I have been authorized by General Pershing to make you an offer you, a commission in the American Expeditionary Force. Pershing wants you in our front lines, as a 'tactical advisor' or whatever you want to call it."

"I don't think that's really much of a choice, Dennis," Gresham objected.

"If you take the cuffs off, you must come with me; leave them on, and you're going to London and prison."

"When you put it that way – wait, I do have one question," Gresham said. "Yes?"

"Will you outrank me?"

Nolan chuckled. "Well, you will not have an actual rank until Pershing can arrange everything with President Wilson. But, in the meantime, you're to wear the uniform of a Brigadier General and you'll be assigned to the staff at General Headquarters."

"You're joking," Gresham said, dumbfounded.

"In the United States, David, when we want quality, we either build it or buy it. I have been sent to buy you. Do you really need to think it over?"

"Not at all, but I must get a new uniform tailored, you know."

Nolan held out the parcel he was holding. "Actually, in our army, we supply uniforms for our officers."

The muddy road was heavily congested with every sort of man, beast and vehicle, including endless miles of ponderous artillery guns drawn by motor and horse. Between them, the "Renault FT" tanks, far more compact than the ponderous British Mark V's, rolled forward with deafening noise and belching smoke. Lorries, wagons, carts, ambulances and staff motorcars forced their way through in both directions. Night began to spread as black as tar, and equally hot and wet. The American infantrymen, machine gunners and engineers who had been ordered to stay camouflaged in the forest throughout the day to remain unseen by the German reconnaissance aeroplanes joined next in the torrent of movement.

Gresham stood with a torch at the crossroads of the village of Cœuvres-et-Valsery directing soldiers through the narrow, stone-lined streets, just three kilometres from the American 1st Division's jumping off point the next morning. The American Doughboys had been ordered to advance silently along the sides of the road, but many struggled to keep from slipping down the damp and muddy banks. The night was so dark that they could not see each other, and contact was maintained by having each man place his hand on the back of the man in front of him. Suddenly there was a blinding flash of light and crash of thunder, and a deluge of rain began to fall, soaking the clothes and packs of the already-burdened men. They were weary enough from their days-long march. Gresham, wet through, ducked into the stone house at the corner of the village. He found there an assembly of American officers drying themselves silently, anxiously, by the hearth.

"Captain," he quietly addressed a tall, young officer, "the last of the 28th has just come through. I intend to join them on the line. Please go outside and make sure the French Divisions continue onto the correct road."

"Yes, Sir," the American Captain replied soberly. He saluted Gresham and went outdoors. Gresham looked longingly at the crackling fire and considered the men standing beside it. He was eager to learn more of these Americans, and it was to be expected that they would take advantage of whatever comforts came their way, but he also wanted to confirm that the American infantrymen were advancing to their proper stations before the early morning offensive began. Gresham turned without a word and went back out into the sheeting rain.

The German advance to the Marne River that spring had created a salient, a deep bulge, into French territory from the Aisne River and as far as Château Thierry. Foch was determined to eliminate the salient prior to his autumn offensive, and a plan was drawn up to attack the flanks of the German armies who occupied the salient under the command of Kaiser Wilhelm's ambitious son, Crown Prince William. The Allies would slice through the German-occupied territory, seize the Paris-Soissons road, and take the high ground at Berzy-le-Sec that commanded the road to Château Thierry. The German Divisions deep in the Marne Salient would then be cut off, and the French and Americans would be well-positioned to reclaim the city of Soissons from the German armies.

The 28th Infantry would be at the vanguard of the attack. It was part of the American First Division assigned to General Mangin's French Tenth Army. Mangin, known as "the Butcher" because of his aggressive style of attack, was known to have said that "whatever you do [attack or defend], you are going to lose a lot of men." He had assigned the 28th Infantry to the far left of the American position along the north and west of the Marne Salient, and everyone knew they were "going to lose a lot of men."

Gresham crossed the bridge out of Cœuvres-et-Valsery in the dark and blinding rain. His waxed overcoat streamed warm water down his neck and into his American-made boots. He marched along the muddy roadway and soon caught up to a trailing Company of the 28th. The men were talking quietly about their homes and where they came from. A Corporal summoned the courage to address the mysterious officer marching in the rain beside them: "Where are you from, Sir?"

"Manchester," Gresham replied.

"New Hampshire?"

"No, the one in England," he answered cautiously. He hadn't known that there *was* a city named Manchester in America, but then he wondered whether he might see it one day.

"Hey, you know what, Sir? I wasn't born in the United States neither," the Corporal said excitedly. "I was born in Düsseldorf, if you can believe that. Boy, it's sure strange to be back in Europe, don't ya think? I mean, my family moved to America to get away from this G--damned mess."

"Perhaps it is a mess," Gresham agreed, "and it will likely continue to be a mess for many years to come."

"Don't know why we care what happens over here, anyhow, to tell you the truth."

"We have not come to fight a war but to end one," Gresham replied. "The world is a far smaller place now, and we can't let a little thing like an ocean dissuade us from doing our duty."

The road led the Company into a dense forest. French soldiers came to lead the Americans to their positions at the jumping off point. They had to put on their gas masks as the path took them through a gas-infected marsh, and then they marched up the steep, wet slopes of the Cœuvres ravine. When they finally reached their positions outside the village of Cutry, the soldiers were exhausted and quiet. Gresham saw there were no trenches, merely muddy fox-holes that had been hastily dug on the edge of the forest, and he found one in which he sat alone in the midst of the sodden, silent field of wheat.

The rain tapered off at last, but the air remained thick and warm. Most of the men removed their gas masks to get a bit of fresh air, but they kept them close at hand. Gresham set off to visit a number of the fox-holes to remind the men to keep quiet and not to fire on any German sentries or patrols they might see, if it could be helped. The attack was to be a complete surprise. In one well-reinforced bunker, he found the 2nd Brigade's commander, Major General Beaumont Bonaparte Buck, a thin, serious Texan with a wide handle-bar mustache. Buck greeted Gresham warmly but then rushed away to find out why the 26th Infantry was late arriving at their positions further down the line.

Suddenly a red flare shot into the sky from the German lines and a terrific barrage fell on the American position. The men crouched down in their fox-holes and rode out the storm bravely. The barrage only lasted a few minutes, but Gresham was pleased that the men did not panic. Showing great discipline, not a single shot was fired by the Americans in reply. As silence fell once again upon the field, the men waited anxiously, checking the second hand on their watches for the moment when their attack would finally begin.

At 04.35, while it was still dark, there came a great roar from behind them and the clouds overhead glowed red. The French and American artillery erupted and their barrage fell just where it was expected, right in front of the American lines, even though the artillerymen had been barred from taking any preliminary adjustment shots. The barrage continued for only two minutes and then began to roll toward the Germans, one hundred meters every two minutes – there would be no extended barrage to soften up the German positions but instead a great and unexpected rush upon the enemy. The American Sergeants yelled at the men to get up and move forward. From a thousand small fox-holes, the 28th Infantry arose in the dark, blinded by their gas masks, and moved into the wheat field as close to their own rolling barrage as they dared. As soon as the barrage began, signal rockets went up in great numbers all along the enemy's line and his machine guns rang out. The French tanks rumbled out of the forest and quickly overtook the advancing Americans to attack the German gun nests in front of them. Gresham drew his Browning M1911 and stayed close beside one of the tanks.

The 28th Infantry's first objective was a road running north-east from Dommiers some two kilometres distant over solid, fairly even ground. There being no trenches, the German machine guns and field artillery were scattered throughout the fields making them difficult to locate. Gresham collected a small group of men to join him in flanking one enemy position after another, creeping up from both sides through the tall wheat, and using the new French grenades to great effect. Many of the German soldiers remained heroically at their posts, firing to the very end, and the number of their casualties rose rapidly. But the Germans were not alone in their suffering. They had built a stronghold at the Saint-Armand Farm nearby, and their flanking fire wounded or killed dozens of the advancing American soldiers. Although it was outside the 28th Infantry's sector, General Buck sent two companies to take the farme by direct assault.

After a final bloody firefight just outside the farmhouse, the first of many German prisoners surrendered that day. They were exhausted men, relieved to have survived the battle.

Having reached the first objective by 05.30, just as the sun began to rise and the wheat fields began to fog over, the creeping barrage continued on toward the village of Missy-aux-Bois, the 28th Infantry's second objective. With daylight, the French aviators joined the attack in their new SPAD two-seater bi-planes. They swooped down over the Germans just ahead of the barrage, targeting the field artillery with their front and rear machine guns. Gresham watched one of the aviators, flying low, struck by nothing more than a rifle bullet. It crashed into the field and burst into flame.

Suddenly there was a huge explosion just in front of Gresham – a German shell had burst and he felt his chest battered as he was thrown off his feet. He landed a dozen feet away, gasping for breath. He was afraid to look down. He raised a hand to his chest – it was wet, mushy – and several of the Americans nearby came rushing to his side. Fearing the worst, still unable to breathe, Gresham brought his hand to the front of his face as the soldiers ripped open his torn coat and shirt. He saw that his hand was coated with a dark brown sludge. "By God," he thought, "that's not blood - it's dirt!" The panicked soldiers tried to hold him down as Gresham struggled to sit up. He tore at his coat and. finally catching a small breath, croaked out: "Somebody find my bloody handgun!" The soldiers were relieved and elated and quickly helped Gresham to his feet. The shell had apparently done nothing more than throw a hundred pounds of mud against his chest. His gun was found, and bruised and battered he continued forward with the other soldiers.

A deep, wide, wooded ravine lay before the village. Formed around a marshy, brush-tangled stream, the 1,000 yard wide Missy Ravine was heavily defended by the Germans with artillery guns, machine gun nests and barbed wire that had all been brought in on corduroy roads. The French artillery barrage had failed to destroy the enemy emplacements located deep in the ravine because of the steepness of its western slope, and five French tanks were still burning on the western edge of the ravine, destroyed by enemy mortars as the Allies approached.

Gresham met with the assault commander, Major C.J. Huebner, and they decided to send two Companies of the 28th Infantry down into the ravine. From the first step, they were under heavy fire from the enemy on the eastern bank and their progress was slow. When they had progressed no more than a hundred yards down the edge of the ravine, artillery fire began to fall from the village of Breuil just to the north of the ravine. With tremendous losses, the two Companies were forced to withdraw.

Gresham saw at once that it would be impossible to take the ravine until the enemy fire at Breuil was managed. He found Major Huebner and received two support Companies of the regiment to join him in attacking the village. Gresham and his squad skirted the western edge of the ravine until they found a narrow, forgotten path that led through a dense wood to a bluff overlooking the village. Without being observed, and without having to attempt to enter the village (which was to be taken later by the French), Gresham was able to position his two Companies so as to fire down upon the heavy fortifications on the south end of the village. They kept the Germans there occupied as the assault on the Missy Ravine resumed. Two more Companies were now ordered into the ravine. The men swarmed down the banks and waded in mud and water up to their hips to reach the enemy positions, which were defended to the last man. Despite enormous losses on both sides, the ravine and its eastern edge were finally captured before dark that day, and the Americans re-took the village of Missy-aux-Bois.

The food carts eventually caught up with the Battalion that night with biscuits and cisterns full of water and hot broth, a meager meal, and the Germans continued their barrage on the Americans throughout the evening. Gresham, exhausted, fell asleep in a deep fox-hole amongst other weary men. He failed to realize that fresh Companies had been brought up that night until he was awakened before dawn by men he had never seen before. These replacements were delighted to find the unusual Brigadier General in his torn and filthy uniform sleeping soundly, snoring, in the middle of the front lines as artillery shells rained down around them. Gresham soon discovered that he would be accompanied everywhere by the admiring American Doughboys who now treated him as their battalion's mascot.

The rolling barrage began anew at dawn, and the 28th Infantry spent a blazingly hot day under the bluest sky pushing forward against the now deeply-entrenched German defenders, finally cutting across the Soissons-Paris road (their third objective) and even taking the village of Ploissy. Before them, however, lay the heavily defended town of Berzy-le-Sec.

Berzy-le-Sec stood atop a bluff that overlooked the Soissons-Château Thierry road and railway. The Germans understood that to lose the village would mean that their countrymen deeper out in the salient, as far as Château Thierry itself, would lose a vital route for supply and reinforcement. They spent the night moving in additional machine guns and were ordered to defend the town to the last man. Rather than commence with a ground assault, however, at dawn the next morning the Americans began a lengthy artillery barrage which lasted for nearly three hours. Having reduced the village to ashes, the 28th Infantry swept forward and captured the town by 09.15.

As the fighting continued for three more days, the Germans realized the increasing difficulty of their position. The losses on both sides were staggering, but the Marne Salient, the closest Germany had ever come to capturing Paris, could no longer be held. Crown Prince William ordered his men to withdraw to the Aisne River. Château Thierry was re-taken by French and American troops. The city of Soissons was re-taken two days later. By early August, Germany had been forced to give up almost all the territory it had seized during the Aisne Offensive that spring.

In the weeks that followed, Gresham worked closely with General Pershing's staff either at his headquarters in Chaumont or at the front, yet the Allies' guns were far from silent. At Amiens, where Gresham had served during the Battle of the Somme in 1916, the French and British Fourth Army launched an attack on 8 August with ten Allied divisions and more than 500 tanks. The scale of the attack shocked the German defenders: The British broke through the German lines and their tanks reached the German rear, creating outright panic. By the end of the first day, a 15-mile-wide opening had been created in the German lines; 17,000 German prisoners and 330 artillery guns were captured. The advance continued for two more days until the Germans finally withdrew from the salient that they had created that March.

Field Marshal Haig next launched an offensive by the British Third Army against the city of Albert on 21 August. The Germans were pushed back over a 34 mile front and Albert was re- captured. On 10 September, the French First Army attacked the German lines at St. Quentin, and the French Tenth Army attacked near Laon on 14 September. The remaining German-held salients were attacked on 12 September; General Pershing personally led the American forces and over 48,000 French soldiers to seize the St. Mihiel salient.

At Salonika, French General Franchet d'Esperey's enormous force of 29 Divisions, nearly 700,000 men from Great Britain, France, Serbia and Greece, were finally prepared to launch an offensive against the Bulgarians. The battle began on 14 September with a massive artillery barrage, and the Allies advanced into Serbia the next day. The city of Prilep, where Gresham and Wilkins had first met Serbian Prince Regent Alexander, was recaptured on 23 September. The Allies drove north as the Bulgarian armies retreated in good order, but the Bulgars could see that the war was lost: With the Turkish Ottoman Empire near collapse, the Austro-Hungarian government in chaos, and the German Army busy on the Western Front, the Bulgars were no longer willing to die for a lost cause. Five thousand Bulgarian troops mutinied and marched on their capital city of Sofia. The Bulgarian government requested an armistice, and their commander-in-chief, General Nikola Zhekov, traveled to Salonika to sign an armistice on 29 September, the first of the Central Powers to capitulate; four days later, Ferdinand I, the King of Bulgaria, renounced his throne.

With Bulgaria out of the war, a direct route for the Allies to invade Ottoman Turkey from the north was now open. However, on 19 September, General Edmund Allenby also launched a British offensive north from Palestine. The British had misled the Turkish Ottoman Army as to their intended target, and the Turks were taken by complete surprise when the British attacked and captured Megiddo. The Turks retreated in chaos as the British Royal Air Force continued to bomb the fleeing soldiers. General Allenby and Prince Feisal then selected their next target: The great city of Damascus. Two Allied columns marched north, the first composed mainly of Australian and Indian cavalry, and the other of Indian cavalry and the Arab militia led by T.E. Lawrence. Damascus was easily captured on 1 October. Then Beirut fell on 8 October. Allenby and Feisal next planned to march on Aleppo, the third largest city in the Turkish Ottoman Empire, and from there prepare to invade Turkish Anatolia from the south.

In France, Marshal Foch prepared to launch his "Grand Offensive", to push the entire front line forward at once. The main German defenses were on the Hindenburg Line, the vast array of defensive fortifications that stretched from the Aisne River to the city of Arras: Once that line was breeched, the Allies would be able to hound their enemy all the way to Germany. The first wave was scheduled to be launched by the American Expeditionary Forces at the front between the Meuse River and Argonne Forest, northwest of Verdun; their objective was to capture the indispensable railway hub in the Sedan-Ardennes region: Without it, Germany would no longer be able to maintain its armies in Belgium. Two days after the Meuse-Argonne offensive was planned to begin, an Army Group commanded by King Albert of Belgium would attack near Ypres, and then the central push on the Hindenburg Line would commence with the British Fourth Army attacking the St. Quentin Canal and the French First Army attacking the fortifications outside St. Quentin.

On 25 September, the eve of the Americans' Meuse-Argonne offensive, David Gresham was sent to the little village of Avocourt, twenty kilometres north-west of Verdun. The village was close to the front lines and had been shelled to rubble, but Pershing had asked Gresham to meet there with the commander of the American Fifth Corps, Major General George Cameron, to assess the corps' readiness: All along the front between the Meuse River and the Argonne Forest, the Americans were set to attack, but the Fifth Corps had the crucial objective of taking the heavily fortified crossroads town of Montfaucon, ten kilometres to the north, on the first day of the offensive.

Gresham found Cameron, a stodgy commander and rigid cavalryman with snow-white hair and a neat mustache, in the small, ruined chapel in Avocourt, meeting with his staff. Gresham took an immediate dislike to the man, particularly when the commander pointed at his papers and left Gresham to divine the General's plan of attack for himself. And the more Gresham read in the reports and maps, the more concerned he became. At last he approached Cameron to discuss the plan more fully.

"As I understand it," Gresham said, "you have placed the 37th and 79th Divisions in front of Montfaucon, yet the men in these divisions are novices who have never been in combat; hadn't you better place the 91st Division there?"

"I have inspected these Divisions myself, sir, and I deem them amply prepared," Cameron argued. "If there is any difficulty, the 91st can be directed to attack the enemy's right flank at Montfaucon."

"You assume they will not be occupied in their own right," Gresham said, "and, in any event, you cannot simply move them: it will leave your left flank exposed and an opening in our lines. There is also the problem of terrain: The Germans' right flank is a No-Man's-Land of abandoned trenches, wire, and flooded shell holes. I would expect land-mines. You should consider it impregnable. So I tell you, the 91st will be of no use at Montfaucon. In fact, the terrain on the German left flank, where the 79th is stationed, is even worse. At the very least, you must exchange the places of the 91st and 37th Divisions."

"I disagree," Cameron said as if to end the discussion. Several of his staff officers were now watching Gresham menacingly. "Pershing has no business telling me how to deploy my men, and I don't appreciate being told what to do by his errand boy. Now you must excuse us, but we are very busy," the General said dismissively.

Gresham was astonished, but he knew from long experience that there was no dealing with officers like Cameron. As he stepped outdoors, Gresham could see the front lines nearby. Some 500 meters beyond that lay the ruins of Haucourt, a ruined village held by the Germans in strength. Another half-kilometer beyond that was the village of Malancourt. Between them lay a maze of trench and wire courses, some occupied, others unoccupied, and beyond them the maps showed thick woods, rough steep slopes, and nearly impassable ravines. In the distance Montfaucon rose menacingly on the bluff, a commanding position so well fortified that the Germans called it "Little Gibraltar" and boasted it could never be taken. It was the most difficult objective on the whole Meuse-Argonne front, and General Cameron had given the task to the most inexperienced men under his command.

In the trenches, Gresham found the fresh young men of the 79th Division overwhelmed by the strangeness of their new surroundings. Having just arrived from tidy, well-organized training camps, the front was a nightmare for them. The battered, crumbling trenches, often just waist-deep, many full of black, fetid water, zig-zagged through a quagmire of shell holes. Unmistakable signs of death and destruction existed on every side: Scattered articles of French and German equipment, rusting helmets, broken rifles and bayonets, half-rotted bits of clothing, and here and there a bleached arm or leg bone protruded from the earth. Long stretches of revetted trenches, their bottoms lined with broken duck-boards and their sides covered with countless rusted strands of telephone wire showed the outcome of four years of continuous warfare. Gresham continued through the maze until he found the 79th Division's Chief of Staff, a young Colonel named Tenney Ross, in a bunker in the reserve line: Ross and his commanding officer, the trim, grey, older General Joseph Kuhn, were no more pleased than Gresham that the 79th had been tasked with taking Montfaucon. Together, Ross and Gresham returned to Avocourt, but General Cameron was unmovable. Gresham decided he must stay with the 79th himself.

At 23.30 that night, the offensive began: All along the Meuse-Argonne front, 2,700 American artillery guns bombarded the German positions. The barrage lasted nearly six hours. At 05.30, under a thick smoke screen, the 79th and eight more American divisions, 260,000 men across the entire front, went over the top. A rolling barrage preceded them, moving forward 100 meters every five minutes. The advancing 79th Division discovered that the Germans had already abandoned their forward positions in order to consolidate in the rear. The division quickly advanced three kilometres before running into strong resistance from well-entrenched German defenders. As the division slowed, the rolling barrage ran away from them, leaving the 79th exposed on open ground. Messages sent back to adjust the barrage produced no result. The smoke and a rising thick fog further complicated the division's advance, and it soon became apparent that whole battalions of the 79th were likely surrounded by enemy machine gun nests. A message came back from one such regiment's commander: "BEING FIRED AT POINT BLANK BY FIELD PIECES. FOR GOD'S SAKE GET ARTILLERY OR WE'LL BE ANNIHILATED." There was no possibility of reaching Montfaucon that day, although, even as night began to fall, an order was sent from General Cameron to press the attack.

Gresham met with Colonel Ross and General Kuhn that evening to reorganize the battalions of the 79th Division remaining in the field, and during the night burros were used to bring fresh supplies and food up to at least some of the men. However, by morning when the rolling barrage and the attack began again, the location of one battalion, the 443rd, 554 men in all, remained a total mystery. General Kuhn feared that they had been captured.

The attack continued all morning, but the American advance stalled on the outskirts of Montfaucon with heavy losses. Gresham was with General Kuhn in his headquarters near Esnes-en-Argonne when a communications officer suddenly ran in and passed to Colonel Ross a small, scrolled message, one taken off a carrier pigeon. He read it aloud: "WE ARE ALONG THE ROAD PARALELL 276.4. OUR ARTILLERY IS DROPPING A BARRAGE DIRECTLY ON US. FOR HEAVENS SAKE STOP IT. 443."

"Damn it!" General Kuhn swore. "For Heaven's sake, Ross, get the artillery off of them! Where is this damn road anyway?"

Reviewing the maps, he and Gresham discovered that the lost 443rd Battalion must have advanced the previous day according to plan but were unaware that the American 3rd Corps division on its right had been held up by strong German resistance; during the night, the Germans had moved into the gap to the rear of the battalion and cut them off. Now the battalion was trapped in the *Bois de Septsarges*, approximately five kilometres east of Montfaucon. Ross immediately left to give new orders to their artillery commanders.

"I'll have to send a reserve regiment up there to break out the 443rd," Kuhn told Gresham, "but I have no experienced men left to lead them."

"I'll take them up," Gresham offered immediately. "We have only to breach the enemy's line in order pull the trapped battalion out of those woods, but the sooner we do so the better. The Germans will be reinforcing that sector while your men are focused on Montfaucon, and when they are ready, the enemy will surely attack your right flank. We must rescue the battalion and secure the sector or else you will never reach Montfaucon. I'll take a single platoon right now, and you must send the rest of the reserve regiment after us."

"Thank you, Gresham, thank you," Kuhn said, quite moved by Gresham's offer. "Take whichever men you want, and I'll have two companies follow behind you as soon as they can be mustered out."

One reserve company was encamped nearby to Esnes-en-Argonne, and Gresham found that it was in the care of a tall, well-built Italian-American Sergeant with wavy black hair named Capizzi. "Sergeant," Gresham told him, "we need a dozen men or more who can be ready to depart in five minutes; they must bring as much ammunition and water as they can carry, but we must be able to move quickly. We have about eight miles to cover as soon as possible."

"Yes, Sir," the Sergeant said; he saluted and went off among the tan huts to call out his best men. The squad, four non-commissioned officers and thirteen privates, were ready in a few minutes, each carrying an extra canteen of water, ammunition and grenades. Gresham decided to bring a rifle along himself, as well as his sidearm, and he led them out of the village to infiltrate the enemy's lines and destroy the machine guns that pinned down the 443rd Battalion.

As his squad passed through the No Man's Land above Avocourt, Gresham was reminded of the destruction he had seen at Passchendaele – the ground had been churned by the rolling barrage and the long-dead rotting corpses of French and German soldiers littered the field. The young, inexperienced men in his squad became ill from the sight, and after one Private bent over to retch, Gresham stopped to talk to the squad. They took a knee and looked up at the Brigadier General from England hopefully.

"Listen, fellows," Gresham began, "it's damn bad, I know that. People have been fighting and dying over this land for a long time, thousands of years maybe, at least since the bloody Roman Empire. But right now you have to focus on what *you're* doing here: Your mates are trapped up in the woods outside Septsarges, and the Huns are going to keep attacking them until every single one of your mates is dead. But we're not going to let that happen, no, sir. We're going to rescue those men and kick Fritz's fat old arse all the way back to Germany." The men smiled; a few laughed out loud. "That's where you need to keep your focus now. The rest of this, it's all just ancient history. Now get up, boys, we have a long way to go yet."

Capizzi yelled the men into line and they marched off quickly through the sweltering heat under a hazy, overcast sky. Soon they left the road that led to Montfaucon, and Gresham led them east across the battered fields. By noon they reached the small battered village of Septsarges.

Their approach was well concealed by a small wooded glade that remained standing to the southwest of the village, the *Bois du Fayel* according to their maps. Gresham crept up beside an ancient, sprawling oak tree that lay on the edge of the glade and pulled out his field glasses. The quiet village was spread before him like a delicate model – a few dozen small houses and a handful of larger municipal buildings were mostly intact. "Sergeant Capizzi, tell me what you see," Gresham asked.

Capizzi lay down beside Gresham and shielded his eyes with his hand. "It's held by the Huns for sure," he said quietly, "There are two trucks over there by that white three-story building, the one next to the church."

Gresham located the small stone and brick church and focused on the building beside it: "Yes. That's their headquarters, I think," he said after a few moments. "There's a ridgeline along the north and east of the village, and beyond that is the forest. That's where the 443rd is entrapped. If we capture the German headquarters here, we can punch a hole through their encirclement and get our men out if we're quick."

There was a narrow but fairly deep stream that ran down from the glade, and Gresham could see where it entered a culvert on the edge of the village and became a narrow ditch than flowed through the center of town. He led his squad down into the stream. The men hunched over in water up to their chests and held their rifles high. The water was cool and refreshing, the banks were overgrown with hay, and the bottom of the stream was stone so the men made quick progress in their advance toward the village. As they neared the first outbuildings, Gresham ordered his squad to remain silent, and then they entered the dark culvert one by one.

As they passed out of the culvert and into the ditch, it became necessary for the men to advance in single file. Gresham went first and Sergeant Capizzi took up the rear. The ditch ran behind several buildings, and it soon became difficult to assess their proximity to the church. Gresham scrambled quietly out of the ditch and edged up beside a small white-washed house only to find they had slightly overshot their target. Capizzi led them back a few dozen yards to where the squad finally climbed out, dripping wet, to hide behind a low stone wall. On the other side of it, chickens were chattering and men were speaking in German.

Gresham followed along the low stone wall through the scrub brush to the back of a squat grey windowless building and peeked around its corner. He could see the front of the white three-story building, the "*Maison d'Ecole*" according to the letters embedded on the pediment. German officers were walking casually in and out of its pale blue front door. The church next door had been damaged by shelling, but for now everything was quiet.

Gresham signaled to Sergeant Capizzi to take three men, work their way around to the back of the building, and wait for his signal. As Capizzi and his men silently snuck through an alley, Gresham waited with the rest of his squad. His heart raced: It was risky to attack the German headquarters with so few men, and surprise was their only advantage. After a few minutes, he nodded to the men crouched beside him, shouldered his rifle, and drew his handgun, then pulled a whistle from his pocket and blew madly three times.

They leapt out from the side of the building and rushed across the narrow street toward the front door. Three of the Privates in his squad immediately knelt and began firing at the Germans in front of the building and at those who could be seen in the windows above. Gresham and the other men stormed through the front door and fired point blank at anyone that stood in their path. The German officers were shocked and began shouting, but very few returned fire. Some sought to escape through the back door and were shot down by Sergeant Capizzi and his men who lay there in waiting. It was all over in a few minutes. The remaining Germans trapped in the building raised their hands and surrendered without a fight.

There were 34 German prisoners, mostly officers, a large number for such a small squad to manage. The Germans had indeed been busy planning a flanking attack against the Americans fighting at Montfaucon, and Gresham sent two of his men off to find the 37th Division with the written plans and orders that he seized. His squad marched their prisoners outdoors, hands upon their heads, and had them sit on the steps of the church. He would have to leave at least four men to watch the prisoners while he and the rest of the squad took the narrow road north-east toward the *Bois de Septsarges* where the 443rd was trapped.

As Sergeant Capizzi and his squad approached Gresham with even more prisoners of war, shots suddenly rang out and the *rat-a-tat-tat-tat-tat-tat* of German machine guns targeted the area in front of the church. Amidst the rattling of the guns and swarm of bullets, the Americans and Germans alike dove for cover behind rocks and debris. Then the firing subsided. Wounded men, German and Americans both, lay in front of the church and upon its steps. Six of the soldiers in Gresham's squad had been killed. Another three were wounded including Sergeant Capizzi whose left knee had been shattered. The loss of so many men was a terrible blow.

Two German officers stood up and began shouting to their comrades on the ridge above the village.

"Bloody Hell, shut up!" Gresham yelled at them. One started to run away, and Gresham was forced to aim and shoot the prisoner in the leg before the man could make his escape. "*Ihr Menschen hinsetzen und ruhig sein!*" He yelled furiously at the remaining prisoners. They quieted instantly and sat. "The rest of you stay here and guard these prisoners," he commanded his men. "I'll try to find out how bad it is."

Situated behind the lines as they were, Gresham had no choice but to order his remaining men to stay under cover. He would have to work into a position where he could locate the German machine guns. There was no other way to reach the 443rd and no alternative but retreat. He dove into the dense brush and debris alongside the church and scrambled along its side and then ran to reach the low stone wall behind it. The uneven ground leading up to the ridge was pockmarked with dry shell holes and scrub brush. There was almost no good cover at all.

Gresham unshouldered his rifle and jumped over the low stone wall and rushed toward the nearest shell hole. The Germans saw him coming and their machine guns opened fired all at once, cutting down the undergrowth around him and sending shards of metal and stone flying in every direction. Gresham leapt into the open pit before him and slid down for cover. The German gunners yelled out to each other and targeted his position. Gresham carefully loaded his Enfield rifle and flipped the safety over. Wiping the sweat from his face, he rose and aimed carefully and found the sights on his rifle to be excellent. The Germans were so close upon the ridge overlooking the church that Gresham had no difficulty finding them in his sights. Each time a head popped up to locate him, Gresham fired. He soon realized that there were more than two dozen German machine guns scattered across the ridgeline. They fired continuously, and Gresham was forced to keep moving from one shell hole to the next, further and further from the church, in order to target one gunner after another, sharpshooting, moving to a new position, shooting again, and working slowly and methodically across the ridge, killing one man after another, as bullets and debris flew past his face.

After nearly a half-hour of trading fire, Gresham lay against the side of a bare dirt berm and could hear German soldiers whispering in the trench on the other side. Suddenly, six Germans rose out of the trench and charged at Gresham with fixed bayonets. He found his rifle was empty and had no time to re-load. He quickly drew his handgun, his Browning semi-automatic, and without hesitation shot down each of the six soldiers before they could reach him. He jumped out to seize one of the Germans' rifles and then moved again against the berm, continuing to fire on the machine guns above, putting one after another out of action.

Gresham charged over the berm and scrambled up out of the trench to the other side only to find himself on bare open ground without any cover at all. Just then an exasperated young German Lieutenant leapt up upon the ridgeline and stood overlooking the position where Gresham stood.

"*Verdammt! Keiner von euch Bastarde können ihn töten!*" The German screamed, and then he drew his pistol and fired.

Gresham stood frozen to his spot, his heart racing. The bullets whistled past his head and chest, barely missing him. The Lieutenant failed to hit him with every shot until at last his pistol was empty. Then, realizing that his losses were mounting and with little hope of it ending any time soon, the German Lieutenant threw his pistol aside and raised his hands. As Gresham found he had regained the ability to move and raised his rifle, the German shouted out: "*Wir übergeben, wenn Sie die Aufnahmen zu beenden!*" He had offered to surrender his entire unit to Gresham.

Gresham yelled back, his throat dry and caked with dust: "*Gehen Sie aus, halten Sie Ihre Hände auf die Köpfe! Stellen Sie sicher, jeder von Ihren Soldaten folgt Ihrer Aufträge! Niemand wird verletzt warden!*"

The Germans slowly came out of the trench unarmed, their hands placed on their heads, and walked under Gresham's watchful eye down from the ridge and along the path back to the village church. There were more than 100 additional prisoners. As the surviving members of Gresham's squad cheered him, Gresham sent one of the young enlisted men running off to the *Bois de Septsarges* to bring out the 443rd Battalion as he and the mass of German prisoners waited patiently at the church: The Germans were mostly overjoyed to have been captured. It meant they were out of the war and headed toward decent food and rest. They no longer had any fight left in them.

The remnants of the 443rd Battalion soon walked wearily into the village. Only 194 tired and dehydrated soldiers had survived the night. Gresham asked 100 of them to take over the German machine guns and to hold the village until the rest of the men sent by General Kuhn arrived. The remainder joined Gresham in escorting the crowd of German prisoners back to Esnes-en-Argonne.

To their west, a day late and with terrible casualties, Montfaucon was taken by the 79th Division at last.

By 5 October, the Allies had broken through the Hindenburg Line. By 8 October, the First and Third British armies had torn apart the crucial German defenses at Cambrai and begun pushing the Germans out of France. Near Roulers, the Belgian, British and French armies under the command of King Albert captured Bruges and Zeebrugge; they reached the Dutch border by 19 October.

On 24 October, the Italian Army broke through a gap in the Austrian lines near Vittorio Veneto and poured in reinforcements that crushed the Austrian defenses; more than 300,000 Austrian soldiers surrendered.

On 28 October, Aleppo was taken by the British, and on 30 October, Ottoman Turkey signed an armistice with the Allies, the second of the four Central Powers to surrender.

On 31 October, revolutions broke out in both Budapest and Vienna. Hungary declared its independence from Austria and renounced the dual monarchy. On 3 November, Austria too signed an armistice with the Allies, and Emperor Charles prepared to abandon his throne.

On 8 November, Brigadier General David Gresham was awarded the Distinguished Service Cross for rescuing the 443rd Battalion and for single-handedly capturing a German machine gun nest of 34 guns and taking more than 140 enemy prisoners. As he received his decoration from General Pershing at a quiet ceremony, he also learned that his commission in the American Expeditionary Forces had been confirmed by President Wilson.

Gresham was ordered to take a well-deserved rest in Paris, and as he sat in the back of Pershing's own motorcar and was driven to the French capital, the one-time British Lieutenant who had become a decorated American Brigadier General, "David Gresham", wondered what Princess Eleanor of Roumania would say when she saw his military decorations and in what manner she would tender her congratulations to him. It was a very pleasant thing to think about.

There was no doubt in his heart now that he had fallen in love with Eleanor. And although he knew she would one day be required to return to Roumania and marry another noble, Gresham believed he had at least grown into a man, a soldier and a gentleman, who half deserved her affection.

It was a long drive to Paris that evening due to the heavily congested roads. Gresham had reached the town of Meaux on the outskirts of Paris quite late when his driver was forced to come to a complete stop. Smudge pots burned by the side of the road and two black sedans were blocking their progress. American and French soldiers stood beside them. As Gresham waited patiently for the trouble to be resolved, he suddenly saw Dennis Nolan approaching his motorcar. Curious, Gresham opened his door and stepped out.

"By God, there you are, Gresham!" Nolan shouted; he was nervous, angry and exasperated all at once, his normally calm demeanor ripped away. "I have been looking for you all over France. By God, what have you done now?!"

Gresham was at a loss. "Why? What has happened?" He asked with genuine concern.

"There is a German delegation meeting with Marshal Foch right now near Compiègne. They say they have come to negotiate an armistice," Nolan said accusingly, spitting out the words, his face turning beet red, "but they have refused to discuss terms – they have refused to discuss anything at all – until you arrive: You, David Gresham; they have demanded you, by name. By God, I ask you again, *what have you done now?!*"

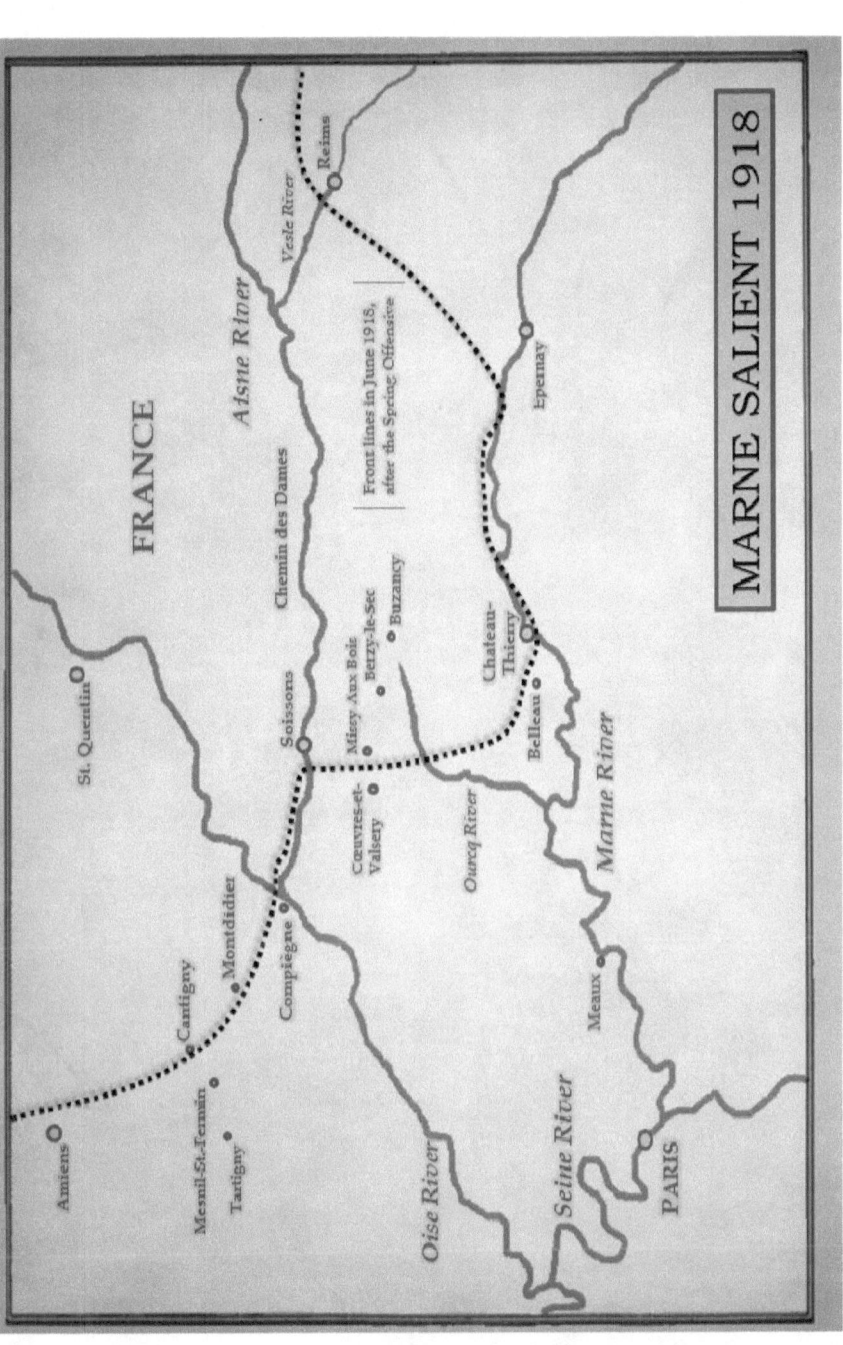

MARNE SALIENT 1918

FRANCE

Aisne River

Vesle River

Reims

Front lines in June 1918,
after the Spring Offensive

Épernay

Chemin des Dames

St. Quentin

Missy Aux Bois

Berzy-le-Sec

Buzancy

Soissons

Château-
Thierry

Belleau

Ourcq River

Cœuvres-et-
Valsery

Marne River

Cantigny

Montdidier

Compiègne

Meaux

Mesnil-St-Fermin

Tartigny

Amiens

Oise River

Seine River

PARIS

Spa

By early September when the Allies had recaptured the territory taken by the German armies during their Spring Offensive, even Deputy Chief of Staff Ludendorff understood that Germany could no longer conquer France, but by late September, when Marshal Foch's grand offensive was underway and the Hindenburg Line had all but collapsed, it was all too clear that Germany had lost the war. It was only a matter of ending it on the best possible terms, and while the Supreme Command and the Kaiser himself were dedicated to preserving the monarchy, Germany itself was on the verge of revolution. Turning to the man he believed could negotiate the best outcome for his battered empire, the Kaiser dismissed Chancellor von Hertling and appointed in his place Prince Maximillian of Baden.

Prince Max believed he had merely been appointed to reform the civilian government, and he was shocked to learn upon taking office that he had been appointed primarily to negotiate an armistice with Germany's foes. Although he was given some leeway by Ludendorff to institute democratic reforms that might soften the Allies' stance on post-war Germany, Max was not permitted under any circumstances to surrender the territories occupied by Germany along the former Eastern Front or to make any definite statement about the withdrawal of German troops from Belgium or Luxembourg. As a result, his peace overtures were summarily rejected by the Allies.

Even as Kaiser Wilhelm pleaded with his people for solidarity, as *Herr* Erzberger announced in the *Reichstag* that German militarism was at long last dead, as Prince Max announced his democratic reforms, and as the German constitution was amended to limit the Kaiser's power to declare war, mass demonstrations broke out across the country. Soldiers began to refuse their orders to go up to the front lines, and the *Reichstag* voted to accept the humiliating peace terms offered by the United States. All their protests were in vain: The Kaiser was unyielding, as were the Supreme Commanders Hindenburg and Ludendorff: The monarchy had to be preserved.

"Haven't you any further insights to offer?" Wilkins prodded General Metzger. He, Ebert and Wilkins met often in the little hotel in Cassel, but apart from their efforts (with the assistance of Kurt Hahn in the Foreign Office) to have Prince Max appointed Chancellor of Germany, they had met with little success. Metzger was particularly hesitant to reveal his true intentions to Field Marshal von Hindenburg, a staunch supporter of the Kaiser, out of fear of losing his position. So far, he had only managed to casually introduce Hindenburg to *Herr* Ebert.

"You do not comprehend the delicacy of my position, Colonel Wilkins," Metzger replied angrily. "It would only take a word from any of my superiors and you would never see nor hear from me again."

"But I have spoken to my uncle, Rupprecht, and he has assured me you are highly regarded within the *Oberste Heeresleitung*," Wilkins argued. "You are Ludendorff's right hand, especially now that the Kaiser and his son, Crown Prince William, have fallen out: The Crown Prince is even more adamant than his father that Imperial Germany and its monarchy should be preserved! We are no closer to peace and far from establishing a sustainable, moderate government in Germany. You can wait no longer."

"I must regrettably agree," Ebert said. "If we delay any further, it will greatly empower the revolutionaries. The *Reichstag* must make alliance with the Army now. You must stake your reputation on it."

"If the moment is not ripe I will not be able to convince Hindenburg that it is necessary," Metzger argued. "I must have an opportunity to show him that there is a genuine risk that Germany's soldiers will join the rebellion."

"Yet it is the very last thing we would want!" Ebert insisted. "If there is any indication that our armies are on the verge of joining a revolution, then the government could not possibly make an alliance with them or with Hindenburg."

"We must only convince Hindenburg that the risk truly exists," Metzger said. "That is a far cry from actually inciting rebellion in the armies' rank and file. By God, even the mutiny within the French armies last summer took months to quell. We can have none of that."

"You have put your finger on it, *Herr* General," Wilkins said excitedly. "Mutiny, indeed. You mentioned before that Admiral von Hipper and Admiral Scheer have proposed a desperate plan of attack. What more can you tell us of that?"

"Oh, it is an insane plan," Metzger replied dismissively. "They want to send the entire German Imperial fleet out to attack the British and American navies. It would be a suicide mission – our ships would be destroyed – but the Admirals believe that enough damage could be done to the British Royal Navy that Great Britain would be forced to negotiate an armistice on terms more favorable to Germany. As far as I can tell, the only thing likely to happen is that a great many people would be killed and the British and Americans will be very angry. Believe me, if the German sailors were ever to learn of the plan, I dare say *they* would mutiny!"

"But the plan has not yet been reviewed by the Kaiser? Could you see to it that he approves it?"

"Approves it? Why of course I could have some influence in that regard," Metzger admitted, "but why ever should I?"

"The *Reichstag* needs an alliance with the armies, and armies to maintain order in Germany, but it does not need an Imperial Navy. If the Admirals' plans were approved and if the sailors were to learn the truth of it, then, as you say, they are very likely to be provoked to mutiny. Wouldn't a mutiny in the German Imperial Navy convince Hindenburg that his armies are also at risk of imminent rebellion?"

"I dare say it would," Metzger agreed.

"It is a terrible gamble, Colonel," Ebert pointed out. "To incite mutiny in the Navy? It might spread."

"But ideally you, *Herr* Ebert, would have the assistance of Marshal von Hindenburg and his great armies to suppress the mutineers," Wilkins said. "I leave it to you gentlemen. Is it worth trying?"

Neither Ebert nor Metzger liked Wilkins' suggestion, but they agreed there was little else that could be done. The Kaiser was just foolish enough to approve the Admirals' plan of attack on his own, Metzger said.

Metzger returned to the Supreme Command's headquarters in the Belgian city of Spa late that afternoon. He spoke privately of his support for the Admirals' plan with Ludendorff and others but said nothing to Hindenburg. Within hours, the plan was approved. Metzger immediately sent a messenger to his "nephew" at the little hotel in Cassel with a package and a message that "our dinner will have to be postponed," one of the two passphrases they had agreed upon. Wilkins at once boarded a train for the coastal city of Kiel.

The last time he had been to the Baltic Sea coast, it had been with Sir Roger Casement, and Wilkins disliked the memory; he disliked that the Irish revolutionary had been executed. It was all a bloody bad business, he thought, as he walked quickly from the station to the docks. The streets bristled with anxious German sailors. These men had done little since the naval battle at Jutland and were sick of the war, but they had been given new orders that very day to prepare to go to sea. The entire navy was mobilizing, and it seemed that every ship in the harbor would be heading out to sea the next morning. For the sailors, it was their last chance to drink at the many cheap taverns near the docks. Wilkins chose a crowded one and went in. He ordered a beer and opened the package he has received from Metzger, a stack of papers, and placed them on the bar. "*Sehr Vertraulich*," they said: "Highly Confidential."

In no time at all, questions were asked, and Wilkins patiently answered. The papers were examined in detail by many of the sailors. Tempers rose. Within an hour, the entire fleet in Kiel was in an uproar. Sailors boarded two of the great German battleships and tore down the German imperial flag. By dawn, there were riots and not a single ship was prepared to leave the harbor. The entire plan of attack was hurriedly scuttled.

Hindenburg and Ludendorff arrived in Berlin that day to meet with Kaiser Wilhelm, Chancellor Maximillian, and the Secretaries of several government ministries to discuss the civil unrest. Pointing at the mutinies at Kiel, Ludendorff stated that the civilian government's democratic reforms had gone too far in undermining the Kaiser's authority and that the price of an armistice was too high. He argued that Germany should hold out and claimed that their armies could continue to defend the country through the coming winter. Chancellor

Maximillian replied that Ludendorff was insane, that Germany was on the edge of outright rebellion and its people already in a state of revolt. He warned of the great risk in providing such an opportunity to the Bolshevik-leaning revolutionaries who were awaiting just such a development. Ebert added that Ludendorff also risked turning the German armies against the Kaiser and their own government. Hindenburg sat silently and said nothing.

The next day, Kaiser Wilhelm asked for Ludendorff's resignation. On Hindenburg's personal recommendation, the Kaiser replaced Ludendorff with the highly-regarded *Generalquartiermeister* of Crown Prince Rupprecht's Northern Army Group: Karl von Metzger.

The mutinies in Kiel seemed to have been quashed when new demonstrations suddenly broke out at Wilhelmshaven on the North Sea coast. Then it became clear that the Kiel sailors had been traveling about the country to denounce the war, the Kaiser, and the Supreme Command. They called for revolution and found welcome ears amongst the shop stewards, factory workers and Spartacus League members. Revolutionary fever had seized all the large coastal cities, as well as Hanover, Brunswick, Frankfurt and Munich. In Munich, a "Workers' and Soldiers' Council" forced the last King of Bavaria, Crown Prince Rupprecht's father Ludwig III, to abdicate. For his safety, Kaiser Wilhelm left Berlin to join the Supreme Command at the *Hôtel Britannique* at Spa in Belgium. The situation in Germany was quickly getting out of hand, and *Generalquartiermeister* von Metzger gained the Kaiser's grudging approval to send a delegation to France, led by Matthias Erzberger, to discuss an immediate armistice.

Informed by Metzger, Ebert now made his move. A general strike was called in Berlin with the support of the Social Democratic Party and the mainstream unions; even the Spartacus League and shop steward guilds endorsed the demonstration. Citizens and soldiers marched raucously down the *Unter den Linden* to the Brandenburg Gate and then on to the *Reichstag*; they loudly demanded an end to the war and an end to the Kaiser. Workers' and soldiers' councils occupied government buildings; some were set ablaze. The city was tense, on the verge of violence. For Wilkins, it was just like Petrograd, far too much like Petrograd, and he told Ebert and Metzger that they must act decisively and at once.

Ebert and Wilkins called on Chancellor Maximillian in his grand offices on *Wilhelmstrasse*. Prince Max was a tall man, a genteel man, the aristocratic leader of the House of Baden, grandson of Grand Duke Leopold, and related to both Tsar Alexander II and Emperor Napoleon III. Yet he was clearly overwhelmed and confused by the demonstrations in Berlin. There was more: Nothing had gone as he had hoped during the past month; the war had destroyed Germany, his hands had been tied by Ludendorff, and his great nation now stood on the brink of revolution. He had stood by the Kaiser, and now he was a broken man.

"The time has come, Chancellor, to re-take control of our nation," Ebert asserted. "It is time to do what must be done in order to save Germany, in order to prevent the radicals from seizing control of our government. And if we do not make a reformed Germany strong again, we shall be the deserved targets of all those who have suffered during the past four years."

"I have no choice but to agree with you," Max said weakly.

"Chancellor, you will not remember me, I think," Wilkins said. "It has been many years since we met; I was merely a boy when I visited your home in Baden-Baden. My name is James Wilkins. I am an Englishman and third son of the Earl of Bartlett; Princess Elsa of Bavaria is my mother. I came into this war as a Captain, fresh from Eton College, but I have learned a great deal these past three years. I was in Petrograd during the revolution there, and I worked with Alexandre Kerensky to write a new constitution for Russia and to build a new nation after the Tsar abdicated. Although all my hopes there were frustrated, I persisted this past year to work with those rebuilding Eastern Europe, to help found the Baltic States, and to settle the disputes that have plagued the Balkans this past century. I came to Germany to meet *Herr* Ebert and have spoken with him on several occasions about what must now be done to save Germany. Do not be so surprised that I would desire it: Has David Lloyd-George not said again and again that Great Britain has no desire to destroy your nation? Of course we do not, because you know as well as I that Germany will remain a powerful nation after the war is done, a nation full of great potential and a great potential for harm, a nation that will dominate its neighbors or live with them in peace.

"You and I, Sir, we were born to aristocracy and have lived our lives by a moral code: We share a duty to care for those under our auspices. Indeed, that simple fact has guided all my actions and yours. Yet it has finally become clear, to me at least, that the world around us has radically changed. Our people will no longer have us care for them. They do not want us. Our duty now, such as it remains, is to merely establish the institutions through which our great peoples can govern themselves. I truly doubt they will make a very good job of it, but we must nevertheless let them try. They will surely fail, but by doing so they will eventually learn how to succeed."

"I understand you very well," Max replied.

"I must ask you: Will Kaiser Wilhelm abdicate his throne?" Wilkins asked.

"I have asked and asked, but still he resists," Prince Max said. "He is justly concerned for his country; he believes that his absence will cause our armies to mutiny and abandon our nation's defenses."

Wilkins shook his head. "It is predictable that Kaiser Wilhelm would consider himself indispensable to the bitter end. Listen to the Berliners in the street: They will no longer have him. Others must take up that responsibility, but you and I, Max, we can save Germany today if you will allow me to help you."

"What do you propose?" Max asked.

"You must announce the Kaiser's immediate abdication and, in your final act as Chancellor, name your successor: *Herr* Ebert. He leads the majority party and by all rights should be the man in charge of Germany's government. In the meantime, I will arrange for him to have the support of the German armies so that these civil disturbances can be quelled."

"But Wilhelm has not abdicated, as I told you," Max objected.

Wilkins smiled: "It is a *fait accompli*, Max," he said; "Wilhelm simply does not know it yet."

The Chancellor was a pragmatist with deep compassion for his people, but moreover he accepted that there was no other logical choice. At last he consented to Wilkins' requests. As Prince Max prepared his statement to announce the abdication of the Kaiser and the appointment of Friedrich Ebert to be the new Chancellor of Germany, Ebert prepared his own statement: He would peremptorily announce that Germany was now a republic and thereby cut off all potential discussion with the Bolshevik-leaning Spartacus League or the Independent Social Democrats about what form the new government of Germany would take.

Satisfied that his work in Berlin was done, Wilkins made a brief telephone call to the German Supreme Command headquarters in Spa, and then borrowed Ebert's motorcar to be driven there at once.

David Gresham returned the telephone to its cradle and turned to *Generalquartiermeister* von Metzger. "I have spoken to Wilkins. We must meet with Field Marshal von Hindenburg immediately."

The previous day Gresham had been taken to Compiègne, or more precisely to Marshal Foch's private carriage on a railway siding in the Forest of Compiègne, where the armistice talks were to take place. He had remained silent; he had not spoken a single word since he had been picked up by Dennis Nolan in Meaux. Foch fumed as Gresham was led into the private compartment where the German delegation was waiting. Gresham spoke privately with Germany's chief negotiator, Matthias Erzberger, for nearly an hour, and then he promptly boarded a motorcar with a German officer to speed to the German Supreme Command headquarters in Spa. Erzberger told Foch: "We are at last prepared to discuss the proposed armistice, and I pray our nations will finally cease this horrific struggle."

In Spa, Gresham was delivered to the *Hôtel Britannique* ostensibly as the Allies' representative should any issues arise during the armistice negotiations that needed to be resolved with the German commanders there. However, he was in truth sent to meet with Karl von Metzger, the Deputy Chief of Staff. The next afternoon Metzger and Gresham received a telephone call from James Wilkins. He had just completed his meeting in Berlin with Maximillian and Ebert.

It was at last time for Metzger and Gresham to speak to Hindenburg.

Metzger knocked and opened the door to Hindenburg's opulent suite one floor below the Kaiser's. "*Herr Generalfeldmarschall,* I must speak with you at once," Metzger said.

Hindenburg, a massive man with close cropped, bristling grey hair and a broad mustache, stood by the hearth, wearing his best dress uniform as always. "Yes, what is it?" He asked with concern in his deep bass voice.

"This is Brigadier General David Gresham of the American Expeditionary Force; he was sent from France by Matthias Erzberger. There is a matter of mutual concern we must discuss, if you would please be seated."

Hindenburg sat on a large leather chair. To Gresham he appeared extraordinarily weary. It was not clear what he had heard of the developments and demonstrations in Berlin, but surely he was aware that his nation stood on the edge of revolution.

"*Herr Generalfeldmarschall,* you are aware that, even as we speak, there is a rebellion beginning to take place within Germany," Gresham said. "It is most urgent that it be stopped and that your civilian officials take the lead in restoring peace and order and meeting the daily needs of your people. But it will not happen without your agreement and participation or without the assistance of your soldiers. You command the great German armies; they are battered but not beaten. Unlike your seamen, your soldiers are not in a state of rebellion, not yet at least. You must not allow them to rebel for they are needed urgently to aid in restoring order within Germany. They can only do so if they are not occupied in fighting this brutal war. Therefore, you must have an armistice. But how will you get it from your enemies? What is it that they have they demanded? What will satisfy the desire of your troops? And what will calm the heated spirit of the German people, a people who have suffered so much at the behest of *one man.* The solution is sadly obvious, as you must have realized. General Metzger and I have come to reassure you that the matter has already been resolved. Yes, the executioner's axe has already fallen. Even as we speak, Chancellor Maximillian is transferring his post to Friedrich Ebert and announcing the abdication of Kaiser Wilhelm II."

"That is outrageous!" Hindenburg huffed. He struggled to get his huge, weary body out of the deep, leather chair.

"Yes, perhaps it is, but it is already done," Metzger said with brutal coldness.

"It is interesting that the resolution of the war should all come down to you, *Herr* Field Marshal. You see, you are now in a situation not unlike that in which General Korniloff in Russia found himself one year ago," Gresham continued. "You command great armies, unbeaten armies, and you are therefore perhaps the most powerful man in Germany today, but you have been betrayed by others. They have changed the rug from right under your feet. There can also be no dispute that the Bolshevik-leaning revolutionaries in Germany must be put down immediately; you have no choice but to fight them. But what shall you ask of your men, your glorious German soldiers; what shall you ask them to fight for? To establish you as dictator or possibly even to restore the despised Kaiser to his throne, or instead to preserve the newly-proclaimed German republic? It is no choice at all. I know you are a great General, *Herr* Field Marshal, and like all great Generals, you will do what is best for your men and for your nation."

Hindenburg had never made it out of his seat and now, to Gresham's surprise, the Field Marshal, his face red and swollen, began sobbing.

"I am sorry we have been so blunt," Metzger said. "I know *Herr* Ebert well, and he is a man who will lead our nation with courage and honor. I intend to tell him in your name that the new government shall have the full and unconditional support of the Supreme Command and to order troops to return to Berlin and our other major cities immediately to maintain order."

Hindenburg wiped his red, watery eyes with one hand and gently nodded. Metzger and Gresham rose to leave.

"I will tell the Kaiser myself," Hindenburg said softly.

"Of course," Metzger replied.

Late that evening, a motorcar quietly departed Spa for the Netherlands. It contained Wilhelm II, the Kaiser of the once and former *Deutsches Kaiserreich*.

Hindenburg and Chancellor Ebert wired Erzberger together that an armistice must be signed immediately at any price. An agreement was reached at Compiègne early on the morning of 11 November, to come into effect in six hours' time. Wires were sent immediately to every corner of the globe, and the news was broadcast by radio across Europe from the Eiffel Tower.

The fighting continued to the very last minute. But then suddenly the guns went silent. The dust began to settle. The survivors raised their eyes to see who and what remained. The war was finally over.

"Good heavens! What are you wearing!?" Wilkins exclaimed. He arrived after midnight in Spa and found Gresham sitting alone in the lobby of the *Hôtel Britannique* only moments after the Kaiser had departed. They shook hands and embraced each other with tears in their eyes.

"I am very happy to see you made it, James," Gresham said. "Metzger is quite busy with Hindenburg now, but you must speak with him in the morning."

"Of course, but how is it I find you wearing the uniform of a bloody American, and a General at that? Have you gone rogue? I assumed you would have the more tedious mission in Paris, but it appears you have made some new friends."

"It would be more accurate to say that they made me. And was Rome so terrible? Is it true that you were actually forced to run off? *Control* very nearly sent me to find you, you know, but I told him that you must have had some trouble with a woman. I hear the women in Rome are irresistible."

"They are lovely, indeed, but with claws," Wilkins replied ominously. "And the women in Paris? I hope there is *something* decent you can tell me of your time there; you must have met someone by now."

"I'm afraid that's rather complicated, James, and I fear you're not going to like it," Gresham replied, grinning.

They retired into the lounge to eat and drink and spent the night sharing their stories. Although Gresham had been the one in the thick of battle, he wondered at his friend's subdued demeanor: Wilkins seemed exhausted and sad, despite all that they had achieved together. It seemed difficult to believe that it was over.

In the morning, after the armistice came into effect, Gresham and Wilkins went to meet with Metzger and Hindenburg in the Operations Room. They had just placed a call to Ebert to discuss sending troops to the larger cities in Germany when a huge commotion broke out in the hallway. Suddenly, Crown Prince William, the Kaiser's son and heir, a staunch German nationalist, a regal, fair-haired man with piercing blue eyes, swept into the Operations Room like a bolt of lightning. He was furious that he had not been consulted about the armistice:

"*Generalfeldmarschall* Hindenburg, you will explain to me at once what has happened and who it was that agreed to this cowardly armistice!" the Crown Prince shouted angrily. "I know for certain that it was not my father; nor would he ever agree to abandon his throne! Never!"

Hindenburg pulled himself up to his full height like an angry bear. "The Kaiser has already departed for Holland, Your Highness. The matter is settled. You, as the Crown Prince of Prussia – "

"No!" William shouted. "You have made a very grave error," he said threateningly, "for if my father has abdicated his throne and left Germany, then I am now the rightful Emperor of Germany and King of Prussia. I did not authorize this armistice and I, only I, have the power to do so. I tell you I do not authorize it. Germany will continue to fight until a just and proper peace can be secured."

The room was in shocked silence as the Crown Prince strode menacingly to Hindenburg: "*Herr* Hindenburg, I hereby relieve you of your command. I intend to issue new orders immediately for our armies to continue the war. You there," he said pointing at Wilkins. "Bring me a pen and paper at once!"

Wilkins took a sheet of paper from the table and retrieved his gold Montegrappa fountain pen from his jacket. "Here is the paper, Your Highness," he said as he passed the sheet to William. He then unscrewed the top from his pen, the pen Gresham had given him for Christmas in 1915 and modified by *Signore* Abato in Rome, and twisted a tiny lever. The gold nib receded to expose the needle of a hidden syringe. "And here is the bloody pen," Wilkins said as he quickly jammed the syringe into the neck of Germany's Crown Prince. Wilkins pressed the rubber bulb and, in a flash, the monarch collapsed to the ground in a profound stupor.

Crown Prince William awoke two days later and discovered that he lay upon a soft bed in a small, plain bedroom. Through a small square window he could see the sky was overcast and he could smell the sea. He threw off his blankets and strode barefoot, in his underclothes, out into the dark narrow hallway. Finding the staircase, he stumbled down to the front room of the little house where he found David Gresham and James Wilkins playing cards.

"Have you then no desire to return to England, James?" Gresham asked his friend with deep concern: Wilkins had been distracted by his own dark thoughts ever since they had left Germany and had just admitted he did not wish to return to England.

"I don't think I do," Wilkins said sadly. "Whatever I thought we would return to at home, it isn't there anymore, at least not for me. All I truly feel right now is a great sense of loss."

Gresham smiled gently. "You are not an innocent as you once were, that is true," he said, "but we all must live with what has happened, and you and I must both learn to live with what we have done."

"We have only done what was necessary, more or less, and I accept that, but I have no idea what to do with myself next," Wilkins replied. They heard a noise in the hallway and turned suddenly to find Crown Prince William standing shakily at the bottom of the staircase. "You're awake, thank God!" Wilkins said. "I feared I had given you too much of the sedative."

"Come sit down and I'll get you some tea," Gresham said. He rose and went to the kitchen.

Crown Prince William came into the front room and sat at the table. "Where have you brought me?" He asked quietly in his weakened state.

"We are in the Netherlands," Wilkins said, "on a little island called Wieringen; I doubt you've heard of it: There is nothing here except for a few fisherman and sheep."

"But why did you bring me here?"

"It was the Dutch government's choice. They instructed us to bring you here; they have arranged for you to have this fine house."

"Why?"

"Why? For you to live in, obviously. This is where you are to live now. I can't tell you for how long: It is not a prison precisely, but you are not permitted to leave."

"The village is actually very pleasant," Gresham said as he brought William a cup of strong tea. "There's a wonderful pub."

The Crown Prince looked around at the inexpensive furnishings and bare wood floors and plaster walls. Out the cracked front window, there was a short iron fence in need of paint and a dirt road. Beyond that, there was only grass.

"Come then, it's not as bad as all that," Gresham said.

"Here then, I shall make you a proposal, Your Highness," Wilkins said sympathetically. "There's nowhere for me to go, and it's a rather pleasant house on a pleasant little island. What do you say you and me stay here awhile and seeing how it fits us, all right?"

Gresham had never been to London before, but the city was enchanting at Christmastide. His suite at the *Savoy* was among the finest in the world. The glorious holiday passed joyfully and Londoners celebrated as they had not done for five bitter years. They flocked to church to thank God that the war was finally over and to sing and pray for their lost loved ones. The next day, the entire city came out to see and celebrate the man who they believed had saved them all: The United States President, Woodrow Wilson.

Wilson arrived at Charing Cross Station that morning from France and was to be paraded to Buckingham Palace. Tens of thousands of Londoners flocked to the narrow two miles of street to see him pass. The stony façade of London was disguised beneath a brilliant mask of countless American flags; there had not been such a show of colour in the city or such genuine light-heartedness in the crowd since the Coronation of King George in 1911. All the joy and gaiety pent up through the war were released in a great, raucous outburst of cheering and waving and crying. Twenty thousand soldiers with brightly shining bayonets stoically lined the route, and a jingling cavalry escort preceded the royal carriage in which President Wilson and King George V sat side by side, the President in a black suit and top hat with his dour smile and spectacles and the King in military regalia waving enthusiastically to the crowd. As the procession passed by St. Martin's Church, the bells rang out joyously. In the clear sky overhead, a flight of aeroplanes flew in arrowhead formation.

Gresham had come to Trafalgar Square to watch the joyous procession. He stood at the base of the Nelson Column and turned to the beautiful woman standing beside him. "Are you quite sure, my darling," he asked, "that you want to have this sour old fellow as our President?"

Princess Eleanor smiled and squeezed Gresham's hand. "I believe we'll get to pick a new one every four years, dear. Are you unsettled about our move to America?"

"No, not at all; it will be a great adventure," Gresham assured her. "Nolan has been very generous to secure the opportunity for me to set up an intelligence office for the War Department, but I could never be happy in Washington if you were not pleased, my dear."

"I shall be very happy once we are finally married, David." She paused before continuing: "I have been meaning to ask you about Colonel Wilkins: Will he be able to attend our wedding, do you think?" She asked with sympathy.

Gresham frowned. "I fear he will not come," he said sadly. "He is still staying over in Wieringen. He was even asked to become the new Ambassador to Poland, but he has turned the King down. I think it has all taken quite a lot out of him, and it will take time before James finds his feet again. I am not certain that he is entirely comfortable with everything he has done – attacking the Crown Prince, for example, after he had given his parole. He is old-fashioned that way. And James knows better than anyone how much the world has changed these past few years."

"I suppose it has, hasn't it? It shall come as a great shock to many people."

"Like your father and mother? Do you really believe they will finally come to accept our marriage?"

"Oh, have no concern there, my dear. I am to marry a decorated and wealthy American General – they are very surprised, certainly, but they seem delighted nonetheless. Just look around you, David: Five years ago, no one gave the Americans a second thought, but now the whole world believes that America is their savior!"

"Perhaps. But you are mine, my darling," Gresham said as he hugged Eleanor tightly to his chest and kissed her.

Epilogue

In October 1922, thirty thousand "Blackshirts" led by Benito Mussolini, the former British-sponsored propagandist, marched on Rome to demand the appointment of a new Fascist government in Italy. That same year, the Soviet Union was officially founded, and Crown Prince William, still residing in his small house on the island of Wieringen in the Netherlands, published his *Memoirs* and decried to his countrymen the terrible fate Germany had suffered:

> Fettered by the chains which the impossible and criminal Treaty of Versailles has forced upon our powerlessness, Germany has lain prostrate and helpless for three years. She is helpless because she squanders her strength in internal feuds, because a large proportion of her people continue to the "Pied-Piper" melodies of those rogues and madmen who sing them the alluring lay of universal brotherhood in a paradise of internationalism. How long is it to last, how long? Open your eyes and look around you; and you will see that this world by which you are encompassed is one homogenous proof that nowhere is a hand held out to help you and that only he who helps himself finds recognition. Above all, be Germans, and take your stand firmly on the ground of practical politics in this so eminently practical world, reserving your romanticism for better days in which it will be less fatal to the whole fabric.

> Believe me, a German people which buries its party quarrels, which liberates itself from the miserable materialism of these recent years and which, united in its love for our impoverished and yet so gloriously beautiful Fatherland, struggles for freedom with an indomitable will, such a German people can shake off its shackles and burst its manacles.

> But you must display sternness, and you must wrestle with that fervor which knows only the one ardent longing and cries: "I will not let thee go, except thou bless me."

> I do not summon to revenge or to arms or to violence. I call upon the spirit of Germany; let that be strengthened; for the mind makes the deed and destiny, and *senseless is the tool without the master.*

Possibly this saying is the key to that destiny through which we have been passing for a generation, and also to that which lies ahead and into which we may enter as victors over all our opponents if we do but bind together all the best of our energies into a potent whole.

POST-WAR EUROPE

Afterword

The difficulty of historical fiction is that it is both history and fiction. Although this novel is a work of fiction and includes fictional events and characters, it was inspired by and incorporates real historical persons and events. It was my hope that by first publishing this novel during the Centenary of the Great War, non-historians could learn something of one of the bloodiest periods of human history, get a sense of the major events and remarkable persons involved in the conflict, and be inspired to learn more. True historians, both professional and amateur, will hopefully understand and appreciate how I have attempted to weave those persons and events together into the narrative, despite the artistic license, and to do justice to their sacrifice.

Gavrilo Princip's role in sparking the Great War is often underappreciated today: To many, it is almost ridiculous that the shooting of an aristocrat in Sarajevo could have set off the chain of events that resulted in such a devastating global conflict (especially when one considers that the assassination might only have been possible because the Archduke's driver made a wrong turn). Indeed, many factors likely made war inevitable. Yet Archduke Franz Ferdinand was more than just an Austrian aristocrat. With Franz Joseph's health deteriorating, Ferdinand was about to become ruler of the largest nation and one of the oldest empires and most important dynasties in Europe. His death was not only a threat to those specifically but was also symbolic of the threat to the established monarchical power structures in Europe as a whole.

The Mediterranean Expeditionary Force's landing at Suvla Bay was intended to break the deadlock at Gallipoli and failed in large measure because the surprise attack was suspended for several days by commanding General Stopford. During the delay, the Turkish army was able to draw up reinforcements, rendering the initial plan to encircle the Turkish forces impossible. Among those reinforcements was a brilliant young officer who later became the founder of the Republic of Turkey, Mustafa Kemal Atatürk. The Tenth Manchester Regiment made tremendous progress advancing up the Kiretch Tepe ridge during the first day of the Suvla Bay landing, only to be held back there by their commanders.

The story of the Fifth Norfolk Battalion is the stuff of myth. The battalion crossed the Anafarta plain and turned in the direction of the small village, passing into the mist or smoke, and that was the last anyone ever saw of them. Stories of the "Lost Sandringhams" have been quite overblown as it appears in the end that the members of the battalion were killed not far from the village; their remains were not located until some years after the war. I have tried to treat the experiences of these men with respect, although some of the details of these engagements were obviously adjusted or invented for the sake of the story.

Eventually, the attack at Suvla Bay ground down into another entrenched stalemate, and it became immediately clear to most that the allies would never force their way through the Turkish lines and gain Constantinople. General Sir Ian Hamilton was replaced by General Monro for the sole purpose of evacuating the peninsula. The evacuation began in December 1915, only eight months after the first landings at Gallipoli. The last British troops were taken off on January 9, 1916 and the Gallipoli campaign concluded.

An enemy officer from Damascus named Muhammed Sharif al-Faruqi crossed the lines at Gallipoli to provide the British with information about a secret society of Arab officers in Damascus. The society, called *al-Ahd*, favored Arab independence from the Ottoman Turkish Empire. Some historians have given al-Faruqi credit for inspiring, or at least nurturing, Great Britain's support for the Arab Revolt of 1916-1918, including the efforts of T.E. Lawrence, known to most as "Lawrence of Arabia."

While Enver Pasha is given the discredit of having been one of the chief instigators of the Armenian Genocide, it is purely speculative to assert that the massacre of Armenian civilians motivated the Arabs to rebel. The total number of Armenians killed in the Ottoman Turkish Empire during World War I is a matter of dispute, but a December, 15, 1915 article in the *New York Times* claimed that, as of that date, over one million Armenians had been either deported or executed by the Turkish government.

It is unlikely that a British intelligence agent played any role getting al-Faruqi safely across the lines at Gallipoli. However, there were British intelligence officers on the island of Imbros nearby, including a recent volunteer, Compton Mackenzie, who before the war was a popular author residing at Oxford. Mackenzie eventually became the chief of the Aegean branch of Great Britain's fledgling Secret Intelligence Service (now popularly referred to as "MI-6"), which was established in 1909 under the direction of Mansfield Smith-Cumming. The S.I.S. at the time of the Great War was still a fairly new organization and its structure and its place in the government were still evolving. In the early years, it appears that most S.I.S. agents (there were many women in the Service as well as men) were primarily information collectors, although in many instances at the risk of their lives. By World War II, the S.I.S. had agents who were more proactive on the government's behalf. Mansfield Smith-Cumming signed his correspondence with a "C" for "Cumming", but it was interpreted by his subordinates as "C" for "Control" and to this date the MI-6 chief signs his or her correspondence with a "C". The novel speculates that "M" of James Bond fame originated from Compton Mackenzie's name.

After the Great War, Mackenzie ended up in Athens. He was an ardent "Venizelist," that is, a proponent of the democratic reforms in Greece advocated by Prime Minister Eleftherios Venizelos. The political crisis in Greece in September and October 1915, brought about by the impending Bulgarian invasion of Serbia, was a key initiator of the "National Schism" that eventually resulted in King Constantine's departure from the throne in 1917 and chaos in Greece for decades.

The British and French landings at Salonika, the city now known as Thessaloniki, were indeed too little and too late to stop the occupation of Serbia by Austro-Hungarian, German and Bulgarian military forces. One intrepid British Nurse, Flora Sandes, made her way to Serbia and served the Serbian Red Cross at Prilep. She joined in the great retreat over the mountains into Albania and, for her own protection, enlisted in the Serbian army where she reached the rank of Sergeant Major (after the war she was promoted to the rank of Captain). The retreat through Albania to Corfu itself was planned by Premier Nikola Pashitch, Marshal Putnik, King Peter, and Prince Regent Alexander at a conference at Petch in November 1915. Massive numbers of Serbian civilians and soldiers died during the winter retreat, but the Serbian army was saved and returned in 1916 to fight for Serbian independence until the end of the war.

Archduke Charles, who became Emperor of the Austro-Hungarian Empire when Franz Joseph died in November 1916, was ill-prepared to take over as leader of the House of Hapsburg. He had not had the same opportunities as Archduke Ferdinand to learn the role or duties of Emperor nor to gain the insights of a grand statesman nor to form the political alliances needed to rule such a complex multi-ethnic nation. Soon after ascending the throne, he secretly proposed peace terms to end the war by sending personal letters through his brother-in-law, Prince Sixtus of Bourbon-Parma, to political leaders in France, Great Britain, Italy and perhaps other nations. Two of the letters were made public by French Prime Minister Clemenceau, and the "Sixtus Affair" became an embarrassment that disgraced the new Hapsburg ruler. Soon after publication of the letter, Charles' Imperial Foreign Minister resigned and a political party was formed in Austria that was dedicated to the removal of Emperor Charles from the throne. In addition, the peace initiative seriously undermined Germany's support for the Austro-Hungarian Empire, whom the Kaiser thereafter regarded as an unreliable ally. Emperor Charles relinquished the throne at the end of the war and died at Madeira in 1922. In 1949, the Catholic Archdiocese of Vienna began a campaign to canonize Charles as a Saint in the Roman Catholic Church, citing his efforts to find a peaceful resolution to the Great War. In 2004, he was beatified by Pope John Paul II, and his canonization is still under consideration by the Vatican.

Plans for the proposed German offensive at Verdun were reportedly sent to Emperor Franz Joseph at Christmas in 1915. French commander Joffre learned of the planned offensive sometime in advance (perhaps because the build-up of German troops and materials was simply too massive to obscure). Joffre was busy planning his own summer offensive at the Somme and basically ignored Minister of War Gallieni's alarm. Gallieni was able to direct some French troops and supplies to Verdun and, providentially, the attack was delayed by bad weather for nine days. Even then, the huge German offensive received very little public notice for several days, and it was not until three days into the battle that Joffre assigned General Philippe Pétain (who later in life would lead the French Vichy government during World War II) to command the French forces at Verdun. Pétain's demands for more men and materials eventually caused Joffre to replace him as well.

The Battle of Verdun in 1916 was one of the largest and costliest battles of the war and went on for nearly ten months with virtually no change in the two armies' final positions. The crushing blow envision by Erich von Falkenhayn, who later claimed that the offensive was only intended to wear down the French army, ended up exacting an almost unbearable toll upon Germany itself. Over two million men fought in the great battle, and approximately 700,000 men were wounded, of which over 300,000 died (some authorities claim that as many as 700,000 men died, but that figure may include all the battles along the Western Front during that time period), with almost as many German casualties as French. The Douaumont Ossuary, built near the city of Verdun to memorialize the men who fell in the battle, contains the skeletal remains of 130,000 soldiers, and another 16,000 graves line the hill in front of the memorial.

In this, the second part of the novel, *The Korniloff Affair*, certain historical events were more fictionalized in order to integrate Gresham and Wilkins more deeply into those events. An obvious example is Gresham's ploy to bring the United States into the war. Although German State Secretary Zimmerman did send his pivotal telegram to the German ambassador in Mexico, there is no reason to suspect that Great Britain staged or provoked that incident. The text of the telegram set forth in the novel was the actual text sent by Zimmerman (translated from German), and it was instrumental (along with Germany's declaration of unlimited submarine warfare) in convincing the United States to enter the Great War at last, and only a few months after Wilson was re-elected President on a pledge to keep the United States neutral.

The chapter beginning in Munich deals with the return of Sir Roger Casement to Ireland in April 1916. Although the story depicts the Easter Uprising as futile and perhaps even a foolish endeavor, and portrays something of Casement's failure and hospitalization in Germany, there is no intent to denigrate Casement or any others who pursued Irish independence. However, the Easter Uprising was a non-starter and the nominal support offered by Germany (the arms shipment via the *AUD*) never arrived: That ship was captured by the British Royal Navy and scuttled by its crew off the coast of Ireland. Casement was captured at Banna Strand, and after his personal diaries came to light he was executed on August 3, 1916.

The German/Boer agent "Dunn" in this novel is fictional, but inspired by real German spy Fritz Joubert Duquesne. It is unlikely that he ever met Herbert Kitchener, the 1st Earl Kitchener, who died when the HMS *Hampshire* exploded and sank at Scapa Floe on its way to Russia. Duquesne later claimed that he had posed as Russian Duke Boris Zakrevsky on board HMS *Hampshire* and had signaled a German U-boat to torpedo the ship. However, the evidence indicates that *Hampshire* actually struck a German mine and that Duquesne was in the United States at the time. Duquesne went on to run a German spy ring in the United States during World War II, and that is where he was finally arrested.

The "Fräulein Doktor" is based on "urban legends" of a German spy in Belgium during the war, and these myths eventually became the subject of several melodramatic films after the war. The real "Fräulein Doktor" was probably a German woman named Elsbeth Schragmüller who held a doctorate in political science and became a German intelligence officer in Belgium during the war. She was a member of Germany's secret police force, the *Abteilung IIIb*, which was the predecessor of the *Geheime Staatspolizei* – the Gestapo.

The Battle of the Somme (and many other events of the war) certainly deserves more attention than the one chapter afforded to it in this novel. The Battle of the Somme was a catastrophic loss for the British and Germans both and after two years of war astonishing in its poor strategic conception. Even two years into the war, adherence to antiquated tactics made military advances on the fronts unimaginably costly in human lives. It is the futility of such engagements that is hopefully displayed in the scenes at the Somme and in Italy. Gresham's and Wilkin's raid at Foncquevillers in this novel is entirely fictional but hopefully demonstrates a few of the tactics (some innovated by General Brusilov in Russia, such as the creeping artillery barrage) that were gradually being adopted on the Western Front by Germany, France and Great Britain in 1917 and 1918 with greater effectiveness.

On the first day of the Battle of the Somme, among the most successful units was the Queen's Westminster Rifles in their assault on the village of Gommecourt. Contrary to orders to "walk" across No Man's Land, the soldiers there dropped their packs and charged the enemy lines as soon as the artillery barrage stopped.

The character of "Emma Wolczak" is fictional but was inspired by real life American Agnes von Kurowsky, the nurse with whom author Ernest Hemingway allegedly fell in love during his service as an ambulance driver in Italy during the war and who was also the inspiration for the character "Catherine Barkley" in his *A Farewell to Arms.*

Romania's entry into the war was particularly unfortunate. Although it is unlikely that Great Britain, France or Russia lied intentionally to the Romanian government, undoubtedly there were miscommunications and promises made that went unfulfilled. It is also true that Romania was primarily interested in recovering the territories of Transylvania and Bessarabia, and a look at the map of Romania today shows that Romania did make substantial territorial gains after the war as a result of their alliance with Great Britain, France and Russia. Would Germany have not invaded Romania but for Romania's incursion into Transylvania? Possibly, and one is forced to wonder whether Romania might have indeed fared better by invading only Bulgaria, and what might have happened had a single catastrophic rainstorm not ended Averescu's offensive over the River Danube. The events of the autumn of 1916 in Romania, as they did play out, were nevertheless a travesty for the Romanian people and demonstrated how efficient and well-coordinated the German military had become, especially once Germany became, in effect, a military dictatorship under Hindenburg and Ludendorff.

"Oliver Locke" is a fictional character inspired by several British spies including Oliver Locker-Lampson (who is alleged to have been involved in both the assassination of Rasputin and the attempted military coup by General Kornilov), Sidney Reilly (known as the "Ace of Spies"), and Sir Robert Bruce Lockhart (who was alleged to have plotted the assassination of Lenin). The city of Petrograd was renamed from "St. Petersburg" in 1914 because it was thought to be too German-sounding; it was later renamed Leningrad and eventually became St. Petersburg again after the collapse of the Soviet Union.

The novel sets forth a very small part of the story of the Russian Revolution, and even then it comprises a large portion of *The Korniloff Affair*. One might argue that the revolution was unrelated to the war, yet it seems quite clear that a crucial factor in the events in Russia was the disaffection of the soldiers and their willingness to stop fighting against Germany regardless of the cost. Perhaps the single most persuasive promise made by the Bolsheviks was that there would be an end to the war. Kerensky, who did not wish to cut off relations with the Allied nations, was hesitant to simply end the war. What is certainly clear is that after centuries of struggling under a virtually medieval, autocratic government that allowed the wealthy to exploit the majority of Russians, the people had simply had enough. Many of the events of the Russian Revolution depicted in the novel are true. In particular, the Bolsheviks did receive assistance from Germany, although the extent of that assistance is unknown. The authenticity of the bank records later published as the "Sisson Documents" which purported to prove German funding of the Bolsheviks are disputed by some, but it is widely acknowledged that the German government assisted Lenin to travel through Germany to Finland so that he could then return to Russia for the revolution. The story also takes the position that Kerensky would have declared a constitutional republic in Russia and would have created a more moderate (albeit Socialist) state had it not been for the attempted *coup d'état* by General Kornilov and Kerensky's need to arm the Red Guard. The attempted coup, if that was Kornilov's true intent, changed everything. As the novel depicts, Vladimir Lvov played a crucial role in creating the crisis, and it is unclear still on whose behalf he was communicating with Kornilov and Kerensky. The teletext "conversation" between Kornilov and Kerensky, presented almost verbatim in the novel, was somewhat ambiguous about Kornilov's true intentions. The effect, however, was that the Bolsheviks were released from prison and given arms to protect Petrograd.

The Wieringen Proposal begins during the July Crisis and envisions the conversation that took place on 5 July 1914 between Kaiser Wilhelm and Austro-Hungarian Ambassador László Szőgyény-Marich in Potsdam. The main result of this meeting was the Kaiser's unequivocal statement of support for Austrian military action against Serbia. It is also implicit that Germany's military commanders, if not the Kaiser himself, would have understood not only the ramifications of such a decision upon the scope of any potential war, but also the necessity to begin mobilization of German forces to prepare for such a conflict. Since Germany's battle plan, the legendary "Schlieffen Plan," contemplated the conquest of France as its initial step, it is probable that German forces began quietly moving toward the Belgian and French borders in July, thus we learn of fictional Colonel von Metzger's worrying transfer to Aachen.

Von Metzger reappears three years later, a General Quartermaster of the North Army Group, at the Battle of Passchendaele. Just as Verdun became an iconic battle for the French, as the Somme became for the English, as Gallipoli became for Australians and New Zealanders, so Passchendaele became a pivotal moment for Canada. The long, horrifying lead up to the final assault on the village is the real story, for as the novel depicts, the final attack was relatively quick, successful partly because the anticipated German counterattacks did not immediately follow. One explanation offered for this failure by the Germans was that the commanding German General Quartermaster was allegedly captured in Passchendaele and was therefore unable to order the counterattack. Whether that is an accurate explanation or not, that anecdote became the inspiration for the meeting between Metzger and Gresham. Later in the novel, Metzger also takes the place in history of General Quartermaster Wilhelm Groener, the man who actually replaced Ludendorff on 29 October 1918 and who reached an agreement with the new German Chancellor, Friedrich Ebert (known as the "Ebert–Groener Pact"), to support a new German republic without a Kaiser.

The character of Private Roberts was inspired by James Peter Robertson who earned the Victoria Cross during the final assault on Passchendaele on 6 November 1917. Robertson's platoon was pinned down by a German machine gun. One of five who volunteered to rush the enemy position, Robertson found an opening on the flank and rushed the gun. He killed four of the German crew, and then turned the enemy's own machine gun on the rest. When his platoon continued forward, he held the captured machine gun in his hands and fired it at the enemy. Later that day, while attempting to carry two wounded men out from an area of heavy gun fire, Robertson was killed by an artillery shell. Robertson is buried at Tyne Cot Cemetery in Passchendaele, Belgium.

Gresham's speech to David Lloyd-George was inspired by (and quotes) the Prime Minister's own statement issued on 5 January 1918 and his subsequent Trade Union speech where he set forth Great Britain's war aims, and Wilkins was inspired by General Smuts' May 1917 speech, one made at a banquet in his honor given by members of Parliament wherein Smuts envisioned a new British "Commonwealth of Nations." That speech, which was subsequently printed in pamphlet form, was widely distributed among British "colonials" fighting in France and Belgium, and spread the idea that Great Britain should become a commonwealth of equals rather than an empire run exclusively from London.

In Rome and Paris, Wilkins' and Gresham's stories include some of the legendary espionage tales of the First World War: The "Gerlach Affair" within the Vatican; the alleged conspiracy to scuttle the Italian Dreadnought *Leonardo Da Vinci*; the French newspaper conspiracy involving Senator Humbert and Paul "Pasha" Bolo; the German agents Irma Staub, Despina Storch (who inspired the character "Derya Storch"), and Mata Hari were members of the spy network run by "*Herr* Koertiger" (whose actual name was Koeniger) and Major von Trauth.

In Paris, Gresham receives the assistance of Roumanian Princess Eleanor, a character that is fictional. She takes him to meet newly-appointed French Prime Minister Clemenceau whose reaction to the Pasha Bolo scandal, including the arrest of Senator Humbert and former French Prime Minister Joseph Caillaux, provoked a Motion of No Confidence in the National Assembly. Clemenceau's response to that motion, a speech made to the Delegates that is liberally translated in the novel, set the tone for France to keep fighting for the duration of the war. Meanwhile, in Cologne, Wilkins receives assistance from his uncle, Crown Prince Rupprecht of Bavaria. Unfortunately, Rupprecht never had a sister named Elsa nor one who married a British Earl.

While the fighting continued on the Western Front, events on the Eastern Front and in the Balkans continued to plague the Central Powers for years to come. The negotiations in Brest-Litovsk (including the recognition of Ukraine) foreshadowed both the Cold War and even the Ukraine crisis beginning in 2014. The negotiations culminated in Trotsky's remarkable announcement that Russia would no longer fight but would not sign a treaty. His speech is set forth almost verbatim in the novel.

Returning to France, by the spring of 1918 the Americans had still not joined the fighting on the Western Front. President Wilson had insisted that the American soldiers remain under American command, and Pershing felt further training was necessary. French and British commanders agreed, believing that the Americans were unprepared to wage a modern war. Indeed, the European powers had worked hard and suffered much from four years of brutal experience to refine both their tactics and their weapons. By 1918, Haig and Pétain had become excellent commanders who, along with Foch's administrative oversight, were quite capable of holding back the onslaught of Ludendorff's Spring Offensive. That is not to say that all the Allied commanders were so competent. American predictions that the third phase of attack would come at the *Chemin des Dames* were disregarded by the French and British on the assumption that the Americans could not possibly know something they themselves did not. General Duchêne was a particularly headstrong commander who disobeyed a direct order from Pétain to defend the *Chemin des Dames* "in depth." Although Duchêne did not expressly order his Sixth Army to retreat behind the Marne, his army did retreat and left the field to the newly-arrived American Marines who courageously held their ground at Belleau Woods. In reality, Foch, knowing that the German army could not be allowed to reach the banks of the Marne, had pleaded with Pershing to send his men forward and Pershing had at last relented.

Although it was the American 1st Division, the "Big Red One", that showed their mettle at Cantigny, it was Harbord's 4th U.S. Marine Brigade, attached to the U.S. 2nd Division, that stood their ground at Belleau Woods and showed that the Americans were prepared to fight Germany.

In Rome that spring, the "Congress of Oppressed Nations" met to reach an agreement on the disposition of the rapidly crumbling Austro-Hungarian Empire. After the public disclosure of Emperor Charles' confidential peace proposals, his government was in turmoil. Austria's disastrous defeat at the Piave River sealed the empire's fate. In August, Emperor Charles (Karl) traveled to Germany to say that Austria-Hungary could not survive the coming winter. Germany was experiencing its own difficulties as Bolshevik-leaning agitators were turning the German people against the war. In this novel, the characters and events that led to the German Revolution (1918-1919) have been simplified in order to avoid introducing a host of new characters and events. For example, Friedrich Ebert also takes on the role of his colleague Philipp Scheidemann, the elder statement of the SPD at that time.

Internal difficulties were only one reason for Germany's collapse. Allied advances on the Western Front, the collapse of Austria (Emperor Charles abandoned his throne on 12 November 1918), the surrender of Bulgaria on the Salonika Front, the crumbling of Ottoman Turkey, the Allies' blockade of Germany, and the need to maintain a million troops on the tumultuous Eastern Front even after the signing of the Brest-Litovsk treaty, were all factors that doomed Imperial Germany.

Gresham's participation in the Second Battle of the Marne beside the American 28th Infantry Regiment is based on that regiment's actual experience in the battle. His participation in Meuse-Argonne Offensive, however, was inspired by several events: First, the actual experiences of the 79th Division as recorded in the division's own memoir and in the Combat Studies Institute's "Battlebook" regarding the Battle of Montfaucon (incidentally, General Cameron was replaced in early October 1918 due to his poor planning of the assault); the experiences of the "Lost Battalion", nine companies of the United States 77th Division, roughly 554 men, who were isolated by German forces in the Argonne Forest; and, most importantly, the truly heroic actions of American Sergeant Alvin York. York, from Tennessee, was a member of a squad sent behind the lines to destroy an enemy machine gun nest as part of an operation related to the rescue of the Lost Battalion. After a number of his squad members were killed, then-Corporal York took command. "Fearlessly leading 7 men, he charged with great daring a machine gun nest which was pouring deadly and incessant fire upon his platoon. In this heroic feat the machine gun nest was taken, together with 4 officers and 128 men and several guns," according to the Medal of Honor citation which he later received.

Although Crown Prince William (Wilhelm) did end up a virtual prisoner on the island of Wieringen, his renunciation of the throne was actually announced by Chancellor Maximillian at the same time as the Kaiser's (apparently without either's prior consent) and William went to the Netherlands of his own accord. Soon after the Armistice was signed, Ebert and Hindenburg entered into a series of agreements with the major German industrialists and unions to back the new German republic. Sporadic fighting with the German Communists continued for several months, and so the German Revolution did not officially end until the Weimar Constitution was adopted on 11 August 1919. Unfortunately, many Germans at that time believed that the new government was wrong to have capitulated to the Allies, and so the Weimar Republic was detested from the beginning by both left-leaning and right-leaning Germans.

The Paris Peace Conference, which Woodrow Wilson spent months attending, stretched on into 1919. Among the most difficult issues to be addressed were the demands of France and (to a lesser extent) Great Britain for reparations and that Germany acknowledge responsibility for the war. In the end, Germany had no choice but to agree, even though Wilson and many others believed those terms would eventually force Germany into another war. The Treaty of Versailles was signed on 28 June 1919.

Of all the historical figures that do not make a "cameo" appearance in these novels, there is an especially notable absence. Adolf Hitler, born in Austria, enlisted in the German army in Munich and served much of the war as a lance-corporal on the Western Front, an experience he described as "the greatest of all experiences." He fought at both the Battle of the Somme in 1916 and the Battle of Passchendaele in 1917. In October 1918, Hitler was injured in a mustard gas attack and was in hospital when the Armistice was signed on 11 November.

After the war, Hitler returned to Munich where he joined the German Worker's Party, attracted by the party's anti-Semitic, ultranationalist, anti-capitalist, and anti-Marxist ideals. Many members of that political party were also members of the Thule Society, the new name for the Munich branch of the German Order *Walvater* of the Holy Grail. Hitler was also soon asked to join the Thule Society, and the German Worker's Party soon changed its name to the *Nationalsozialistische Deutsche Arbeiterpartei*, the National Socialist German Workers Party, known now as the "Nazis". It became a magnet for anti-Weimar government nationalists determined to crush Marxism and undermine the new republic. As the government weakened over the next decade, Hitler's Nazi party became more powerful until, in 1933 and unable to form a majority party in the Reichstag, then-President Paul von Hindenburg, Kaiser Wilhelm's former Chief of Staff, appointed Adolf Hitler to be Chancellor of Germany.

Finally, a note regarding names and spelling: Throughout these novels I have attempted to use British spelling of certain words and to use the names and spelling of names contemporary to the events in the story. Thus, for examples, General Kornilov's name is spelled in the more antiquated form "Korniloff", and "Romania" becomes "Roumania". Most of the time, these spelling "errors" are intentional, but as always I beg your forgiveness for my own poor grammar and wordcraft.

About the Author

Edward Parr is a retired attorney now living in New Orleans. His previous works of historical fiction include the award-winning *Kingdoms Fall* series, available as e-books and paperbacks from Amazon. His new novel, *Tamanrasset – Crossroads of the Nomad* will be released in 2025.

Other Novels by Edward Parr

Kingdom's Fall – The Laxenburg Message

Kingdom's Fall – The Korniloff Affair

Kingdom's Fall – The Wieringen Proposal

Tamanrasset – Crossroads of the Nomad (coming soon)

www.ingramcontent.com/pod-product-compliance
Lightning Source LLC
Chambersburg PA
CBHW032253020726
47495CB00001B/93